Martina Reilly, forme a number of bestsellin
Something Borrowed. She teenage books. Martin
Evening Herald and doe
In her spare time she a

For more information, please visit www.martinareilly.info

Praise for Martina Reily

'Like Marian Keyes, Reilly takes a cracking story and adds sharp dialogue and buckets of originality'   *Scottish Daily Record*

'Has all the elements of an excellent read: mystery, drama and romance'   *Woman*

'A top holiday read'   *Closer*

'Martina has the wonderful knack of combining sensitivity for a serious subject with a big dose of humour'   *Irish Independent*

'Martina Reilly's characlers are so well observed . . . a substantial read'   *She*

'Hard to put down, laugh-out-loud funny . . . perfect holiday reading'   *Woman's Way*

'Reilly is a star of the future'   *Befast Telegraph*

'[Will] have the most hard-hearted reader wiping tears – and not just of laughter – from their eyes'   *Irish Evening Herald*

'Good, solid entertainment'   *Irish Examiner*

'Reilly has a wonderful comic touch, both in the way she draws her characters and in her dialogue . . . a brilliant read'   *U Magazine*

'Brilliant'   *Liffey Champion*

MARTINA REILLY OMNIBUS

The Summer of Secrets
Second Chances

MARTINA REILLY
Formerly writing as Tina Reilly

SPHERE

This omnibus edition first published in Great Britain in 2010 by Sphere

A CIP catalogue record for this book
is available from the British Library.

ISBN: 978 0 7515 4471 8

Printed and bound in Great Britain by
Clays Ltd, St Ives plc

Sphere
An imprint of
Little, Brown Book Group
100 Victoria Embankment
London EC4Y 0DY

An Hachette UK Company
www.hachette.co.uk

www.littlebrown.co.uk

THE SUMMER
OF SECRETS

For Ali Gunn and Joanne Dickinson –
this is their book as much as it is mine.

Thanks to:

Gerry Kenneally, cognitive behavioural therapist, for all his help on PTSD. This book couldn't have been written without his input.

Thanks also to the staff of Irish Ferries for providing me with the times of ferries and plotting journeys from England to Ireland.

To all at Sphere – Jo Dickinson, brilliant editor, Louise Davies, Emma Stonex and Kirsteen Astor for making being a writer such a lovely experience.

To Dingle – the inspiration for the location of this book.

And finally to Colm, the ever patient, and Caoimhe and Conor, the best family in the world.

1

'A DAM?' I WHISPER.

'Yeah?'

'I got the sack.'

'Bloody hell, Hope. Not again.'

His voice rises and someone behind tells him to 'shh'.

I giggle and Adam grins before remembering what I've just said and mouths 'You got the sack?'

I nod and turn my attention back to the stage. I've been trying to break the news to him and Julie all evening, but Julie is now ensconced behind the stage and Adam and I are unfortunately ensconced in front of it. We're surrounded by proud parents and school governors. I've taken advantage of the fact that the Wicked Witch of the West has once again forgotten her lines to break the news to Adam, my landlord and friend. The Wicked Witch has by now started shuffling from foot to foot and twiddling her broom in embarrassment.

'I'll kill you, Dorothy,' Julie's prompt comes loudly from somewhere backstage.

Dorothy, who has been glaring ferociously at the Wicked Witch, takes umbrage. 'Why kill me?' she says, marching towards the wings. 'I ain't the one that's forgot me lines!'

A titter ripples through the audience.

'Oh,' the Wicked Witch says delightedly, 'that's me line.' She assumes an aggressive pose. 'Yeah, I'll kill you, Dorothy!'

And the play starts to move on again.

'I thought you liked that job,' Adam mutters a few minutes later as Dorothy breaks into an out of tune song, accompanied by a miserable scarecrow, who looks more in need of dancing lessons than a brain.

'I did like it. But that web client, Michael Doyle, rejected my web text again.'

'Again? The tosser!' Adam is suitably aggrieved.

'Yeah, that's what I thought.'

'You didn't say that to him?'

I shrug. 'Well, what I –'

'Shh!'

Adam winces. 'Sorry!' he nods an apology to the woman behind. Then he mouths at me, 'Tell me later?'

'I'll have forgotten what happened by the time this play is over.'

Adam snorts with laughter then tries to turn it into a cough.

I wink at him and look demurely innocent.

Later is ninety minutes later, after the Wizard forgot all his lines and Julie had to shout them out while he opened and closed his mouth.

It was the funniest scene of the play.

Adam and I are in the half-empty school hall waiting for Julie to emerge. The only people left now are the organisers and assistants. Adam and I helped pick up the litter and are now hanging about like two spares. Adam hasn't asked me any more about my job, or lack thereof. I know he's waiting for Julie, so I can tell them both together. Julie works as a teacher in this school; it's a tough job but she loves it. Doing *The Wizard of Oz* with the children had been her idea, and she'd directed it too.

'Here she is,' Adam starts to clap as she comes towards us. Julie beams at us. 'Well?' she asks.

'Brilliant,' Adam pronounces. 'Best Wizard I've ever seen.'

'Totally.' I nod in agreement.

'Would you have noticed that anyone forgot their lines?' Julie looks from me to Adam.

'Hope lost her job again.' Adam deftly changes the subject, saving us some lies that we're bound to get caught out on.

'No!' Julie gawks at me. 'Hope!'

'No hope is right,' I joke.

She smiles briefly, before saying, 'But you liked that job!'

'The tosser rejected her web text again,' Adam says. 'How many times did you do it for him, Hope?'

'Twenty-five times in three weeks.'

'Tosser,' Julie agrees.

'So what happened?' Adam asks. He's leading the way towards the car park. There's still a queue of cars to get out. I don't answer until the three of us are sitting in Adam's monster car – a perk of his job as regional manager for a load of building supply companies. Out of the three of us, Adam is the rich one; he owns the house Julie and I live in, and two more besides. He works all the time and takes life very seriously, which is why Julie and I like to make him laugh. Before we came along, I wouldn't say Adam had much of a life. 'So?' Adam turns to me as I climb into the back seat, 'are you going to tell us what happened?'

'I know what happened,' Julie pronounces. 'You sent the muppet a really crappy draft, didn't you? Something along the lines of –' she thinks for a second – 'At Doyle Computers,

3

we specialise in screwing up your computer system. We give your system viruses, bugs and, even better, we won't be able to repair the damage.'

Adam laughs.

'Damn!' I grin, 'That's what I should have done!'

'So what did you do?'

'I e-mailed the tosser my first draft again.'

'You didn't!' Julie laughs lightly. 'And he noticed? Is that why you got fired?'

I shake my head and say casually, 'Actually, he accepted it.'

'He accepted it? Your very first draft?'

'Yep.'

'But that was good.'

'Well, it would have been if I hadn't decided to take a taxi over to his office and ask him why he thought it was fun to waste my time.'

'Oh Hope, you didn't!' Adam looks at me in amused exasperation.

'I did.'

Julie begins to giggle.

'And naturally he was furious with me, but I just hopped back into the taxi and when I reached work, the taxi driver says –' I put on a terrible cockney accent – 'That'll be one 'undred pounds.'

'One hundred pounds,' Adam winces. 'Did you go via Mars?'

'That's what I asked and he got really stroppy and followed me upstairs into my office where my boss was waiting for me.'

Now they both start to laugh.

'And my boss is screaming at me that I'm fired and the taxi driver is looking for his hundred pounds, which I did not have so I turn to my boss and I ask him for my pay in advance.'

'Bloody hell, Hope!' Adam snorts.

'So then my boss starts yelling.'

'And what happened?' Julie giggles.

'I put up my hands, told the taxi driver that I would get the money out of the bank if he'd be good enough to trust me. And he says, how could he trust me when he's just seen me get fired. So I told him to take it or leave it. So he followed me to the bank and when he got back to his car it was clamped.'

They're laughing so hard now, I join in.

'Worst day of my life,' I pronounce.

'Aw, never mind,' Julie says and pats my arms, 'you'll get another job, you always do. Did you count to ten before you went over there?'

'I counted to fifty.'

Adam chortles.

'Anyway,' I continue, suddenly becoming serious, so they'll *know* I'm serious, 'I've enough money to cover the rent on my room for this month, Adam. And then, well,' I pause, before taking a deep breath and blurting out, 'you can rent out my room to someone else.'

Adam gawks at me in disbelief. 'Don't be stupid. You'll get another job.' He cracks a smile. 'I've never known anyone to get as many jobs as you.'

'Ha ha.' I poke his arm. 'No, I'm serious, Adam. I'm leaving.'

'Leaving?' the two say together.

'Well, just for a bit,' I clarify when I see their looks of dismay. 'I've decided, after all the excitement, to take a break and go away for a while. On a holiday.'

5

'A holiday?' Adam looks aghast. 'Hope, you've just lost your job!'

'Yeah and the shock of it makes me need a holiday far away.'

I'm gratified to see them smile.

'How long will you be gone?' Julie asks quietly, sounding slightly shocked.

I shrug. 'I don't know.'

'A month, two months, how long?' Her voice is a bit tearful now.

'Ju, don't.' I place my hand on her arm. 'I'll come back.' They're looking at me as if I'm bonkers. I try to explain the reasoning behind my decision, though I'm not sure I fully understand myself. 'Look,' I bite my lip, 'it's not normal to lose jobs all the time, is it?'

'You just haven't found the right job,' Julie says. 'That's all.'

'Ju,' I say, 'if I keep going, I'll have tried out every job in Britain by next year.'

She doesn't even smile.

'I just think that if I see a bit of the world, it might, you know, settle me down and I might be happy in a job.' So far, in London, I've lost about sixteen jobs in eight years. I truly don't know what's wrong with me. Most jobs I get, I quite enjoy. Give me a computer screen and some text and I'm happy. But unfortunately, for some reason, I also manage to get myself fired with alarming regularity. I've thought about why this might be and my problem it seems is that I don't like to be bossed around. I can be getting along great with everyone and then a boss will order me to do something and it's like another person inside me takes over. I FLIP. And that is meant to be capitalised. I get on great with all my co-workers and they're

6

always sad to see me leave, but the bosses are another matter.

'I'll pay your share of the rent,' Julie breaks into my thoughts. 'You can pay me back when you get a job.'

'That's not the issue, Ju.'

'Hope,' Adam says earnestly, 'you know I'd let you stay for free.'

I swallow hard at his kindness. 'I know.' I pause, touched. 'But you have to pay a mortgage, Adam and I'm a liability.'

'No!'

'Yeah,' I grin. 'I'm a disaster. You know it, I know it. I just think if I can get away and maybe get some perspective on it, things might make sense.'

'So go to Ireland,' Adam says. 'Go back to Dunport – you're always saying how much you love it. That's bound to be cheaper than going around the world. Bloody hell, Hope, just don't blow all your cash on a holiday.'

The mention of Dunport makes me flinch. I try out a smile. 'Yeah. Good idea. I'll check it out on the internet. Can I use your laptop when we get back?'

'Course.'

There is a silence. Neither of them knows what to say.

I feel a little guilty because I don't want to have spoiled Julie's night. I search for something to get us back on track. 'How many more nights is your show on for, Ju?'

And she's off. Haltingly at first, because she's shocked that I'm leaving, but it's not long before she's in full flow.

And as I listen to her, watching her face glow as she talks about her pupils, I realise, with a pang, that she has found what I so desperately crave.

2

I SPEND THE next few days on the internet looking for cheap flights. I have a bit of money saved, but I still need to be careful. I decide, mainly because I can afford it, that Boston will be destination number one. I book my flight and a motel and leave it at that. To be honest, I'm not exactly sure where to go from there.

But it's a start.

Julie and Adam are not so convinced. I think they reckon that I'm having a minor breakdown.

'Do you have enough money in case you might move on?' Julie asks.

'Yes.'

'And have you got your visa and passport and map?' That's Adam.

'Yes.'

'And have you changed your money to dollars?'

'Yes.'

'And have you checked your transport from the airport to your hotel?' Adam again.

'It's a motel and yes.'

After I satisfied them with these answers, they finally decided to leave me alone and accept the inevitable. And now, unbelievably, it's a week since I lost my job and our last day together before I go. Julie has pulled a sickie from work and brought me out for lunch and shopping. Later on, we're meeting Adam at his workplace, for a surprise night out. Neither of them will say where they are taking me.

It's going to be awful leaving them in the morning. So far, I've tried not to think about it.

'Here.' Lunch over, Julie places a small parcel on the table between us. 'Just a little good luck present.'

'Aw Ju, you've done enough.'

'Open it, will you!'

I smile and, forgoing all restraint, rip the paper off. 'A cap, cool.' It's pink and girly and the word *Tourist* is emblazoned across it in fake diamonds. I laugh and place it on top of my bouncy hair.

'Pink suits you,' Julie nods approvingly. 'And it's such a cute cap.'

'Yeah, isn't it? I'm going to wear this for the rest of the day!'

Julie gulps hard. 'Oh, Hope, I'm really going to miss you.'

'And I'll miss you too.'

We look at each other.

I turn away first.

We're in Topshop. Julie is busy examining the tops while I stand idly by. I can't afford anything new at the moment. And anyway, I hate buying clothes.

'White or off-white?' Julie puts both shades to her face.

'White,' I pronounce.

She frowns. I know she'll go for the off-white. She doesn't trust my judgement at all.

'Oh, I dunno. I think –' she stops mid-sentence and her eyes shift from me to a girl browsing a rack of expensive jeans. 'Oh shit!'

'What?' I lower my voice because she has lowered hers.

'See that girl over there?'

My head swivels around abruptly.

'Don't look,' she hisses, pulling me back.

'How can I see her if I don't look?'

'Don't make it so obvious.' Julie is still hissing. 'Turn around slowly, that's it. See the girl in the white top?'

'Yeah.'

'That's Angela.'

'Angela, your sister?'

Julie nods.

I've never met Angela, though I feel as if I know her from hearing Julie talk about her. They don't get on too well. According to Julie, Angela is the brainy one, the golden girl of the family. Julie, while not quite the black sheep, caused untold disappointment to her parents by becoming a teacher. Julie's parents sound a bit mad, to be honest. If I'd become a teacher, I'd imagine my mother would have been proud. Well, if she'd managed to forget her own life for a bit and thought about me, she would have been proud. As it was, it was maybe just as well she didn't know what I was up to. From this distance, Angela looks just like I thought she would.

'I suppose I'd better say hi,' Julie mutters.

'You don't have to. There's no law says you have to say hello to your sister when you meet her.'

'No.' Julie wrinkles up her pert nose and sighs. 'If I don't and she sees me, she'll think I'm jealous of her promotion. You'll come with me, will you?'

'Sure.'

I trail behind Julie as she walks towards the girl. Angela is even better dressed than Julie if that's possible. She's wearing a floaty white top that looks very feminine and a

10

pair of wide trousers. A light loose cardigan hangs from her shoulders. Her hair is pinned back in a messy bun and little escaped ringlets, that look carefully positioned, trail along the back of her neck and on to her shoulders.

'Hi Ang,' Julie says, startling me with the false brightness in her voice. 'How's things?'

Angela freezes, her hand on a pair of dark navy denims. Then her shoulders relax and she turns to face us. She's like an older version of Julie, only I think Julie is prettier. She looks from Julie to me and back again. 'Julie, hi,' she stammers. 'Day off?'

Julie flushes. 'Eh, yeah,' she lies. 'School is shut today. Are you off too?'

Angela gawks from one to the other of us like a rabbit in headlights. She flushes too and pulls her cardigan around her in a defensive gesture. 'Yes!' It's very abrupt and sharp and makes me jump. 'Day's leave,' she shrugs. She tugs at a ringlet and winces. 'Eh . . .' she says haltingly, 'Mum was saying you were doing a show in your school?'

Julie sniffs. 'Was she?' she says. 'Surprised she remembered. Neither she nor Dad came to see it.'

'Well, they're busy people, I suppose.'

Julie rolls her eyes and makes a scoffing sound.

Angela flinches. 'Well, I hope the show went well.'

'Do you?' Julie gulps hard. 'You never came to see it either.'

Angela rubs her hand across her face. I can't figure out if she is annoyed or upset. But, I think, she could at least invent some excuse as to why she didn't bother going to Julie's show. Instead, to my disbelief, she says, 'I'm actually in a bit of a hurry Julie, so eh, bye now.'

It's like she can't get away fast enough. In silence, Julie

and I watch her disappear through a crowd of shoppers. I can't look at Julie, I feel so hurt for her.

'It's her loss,' I say eventually. 'She missed a bloody good show.'

'Yeah,' Julie lifts her chin, 'what do I care if she goes or not? I am finished with her. I even rang her to tell her about the show. She hardly ever rings me. In fact, I haven't heard from her in months. I'm never ringing her again.'

I don't like to hear that. I've done that and it hasn't made me feel any better. 'Don't be too hasty, Ju.'

'I'm not being hasty, this has gone on for long enough. Jesus, I could kill my family sometimes.' Then she flushes. 'Oh sorry, Hope, I didn't mean – well, I'm sure it's better than having no family.'

'Yeah, I'd imagine it is.' They think I've got no one, you see.

'So now,' Julie tries to get things back on track by smiling brightly. 'Let's go meet Adam and have a brilliant night.'

'Yeah, let's.' I don't care what they have planned for me, as long as it cheers her up.

An hour later, Julie and I are outside Adam's office. Well, I suppose it's not technically his office. Whichever store he happens to be regionally managing, that's where his office is. He's working out of south London today. We have to meet him at six.

By ten past six, he still hasn't arrived and the two of us are getting weird looks from builder-type men who are going in and out of the place.

'Hey girls,' an ugly leery fella quips, 'Would ya like anything laid, ey?'

'Yeah, you out on a mortuary slab,' I say back.

12

His builder friends laugh.

'How about a drink, gorgeous?' That's directed at Julie.

'No,' she says smartly, 'I might start seeing double and that wouldn't be nice.'

They clap at that and then wander off, but not before telling me that they love my hat.

'Did Adam say to meet him inside or outside the shop?' I ask Julie.

'I thought it was outside,' she says, stamping her feet up and down. 'Ohh, I'm freezing.'

'Let's just go in and get him, ten minutes' drinking time has been wasted with us just standing here.'

'Good thinking,' she says, falling in behind me.

We enter a huge warehouse cum shop. The ceilings are about a hundred feet high and the place is crammed with wood and tiles and flooring. And it's freezing. I don't know how people can work in it all day. The whole place has a frantic, tense air as staff rush here and there helping out customers or just for the sake of rushing about, it seems to me. Julie and I gaze around, not sure where to find Adam. This place is huge.

'Over there,' Julie points to a big sign saying INFORMA-TION DESK.

We cross the building towards the sign and are asked about a million times if we want assistance. Talk about a hard sell.

A cute-looking fella is behind the counter. Julie and I get into the queue and wait our chance to ask about Adam. Eventually the guy turns to us and bestows a gorgeous smile upon Julie. 'Ladies, what can I do you for?'

'Hi,' Julie bats her eyelashes. She looks at his blue shirt on which a name tag is pinned: 'Ben,' she says.

13

'Hi yourself,' he says back.

'We're looking for Adam Williams?'

'Adam Williams,' he repeats, frowning slightly. 'OK. Is he expecting you?'

'Yes. So he hasn't left the building yet?'

Ben looks as if Julie has just asked the most obvious question ever. 'Eh no, duh.' He waves his arm towards the heaving shop floor. 'Can't you guess?'

Julie and I look at each other. 'Guess?' Julie says. 'Is he on the floor? I can't see him.'

Ben frowns slightly. 'Eh – is this business?'

'No, we're his friends,' Julie says.

Ben glances from Julie to me and back again. The smile slides from his face and he sits back down in his chair. 'His friends?' he says. 'Oh, OK. I'll just give him a call.' He picks up the phone and dials a number. Then he tries another number. Finally he puts the phone down and says, 'I can't get through, do you mind waiting?'

'We'll go up to him,' I say. 'Just tell us where he is.'

Ben looks uncomfortable. 'Oh, I don't know – Adam, eh, Mr Williams, likes us to phone ahead with any visitors.'

'It's just us,' I say. 'He won't mind, honest.' I smile at Ben. Julie says my smile is my best feature. 'Please, Ben?'

Ben shifts uncomfortably.

'He's expecting us,' I say then more firmly.

'Right, well,' Ben licks his lips and points to his left. 'See those stairs over there. Go up to the top and Adam is in the office at the very end. A blue door, you can't miss it.'

'Great. Thanks.'

'Bye now.' Julie gives a flirty wave but Ben merely nods.

'Flirt,' I tease.

'Well, you smiled,' she jokes back.

14

Together we climb the stairs, Julie tucking her skirt in as all anyone would have to do from the ground floor is look upwards and they'd get a view they hadn't bargained for. When we reach the top, we hear voices. They seem to be coming from the office at the end. The nearer we get, the louder the voices become.

'Is that Adam shouting?' Julie asks.

'Nah,' I scoff. 'Adam never shouts.' Though I have to admit, it does sound like him. Outside the door we pause and look at each other. There is definitely a row of some sort going on inside. 'Will I knock?' Julie whispers.

I just rap hard on the door. If someone is shouting at Adam, well then they'll have Julie and me to contend with.

'What?' comes irritably from inside.

'We're looking for Adam Williams,' I say loudly. And a bit threateningly.

Silence.

Adam opens the door: he's red-faced but trying not to look it. 'Hi,' he smiles uncomfortably, 'who let you up?'

'The man on the information desk, we told him you were expecting us.' Julie tries to look over Adam's shoulder, but he's too tall. Then she points to her watch. 'It's after six,' she whispers.

'Yeah, I know, Ju. Just give me a second, all right?'

'Is this a bad time?' I ask.

'Nah,' Adam looks back into the office and then at us. 'Just give me a second.' He closes the door. This time there is no shouting. A few seconds later he comes out, pulling on his jacket. His face is still red. 'First thing Monday, OK?' he says over his shoulder to a man standing in the middle of the room.

'It means I'll have to come in on a Sunday,' the man says belligerently.

15

Adam pulls the zipper up on his jacket. 'Yeah,' he says, quite assertively, I think. I want to clap him. 'That's right.' Smiling at Julie and me, he pulls us from the office.

'What was going on there?' I ask as I climb into the back of Adam's car. 'Was there a row?'

'You could say that.' Adam fires the engine and then, pulling on his seatbelt, drives out of the car park. 'He hadn't half the invoices sorted and he thinks that was going to cut the ice with me. No bloody way, that's what I told him.'

His face is set in a hard grimace and Julie shoots me a look. Neither of us has ever seen Adam like this before. The guy must have really got to him. I hate that someone has upset him like this. 'Good for you,' I say and reach out from the back to pat his shoulder.

'Yeah, forget about it now,' Julie squeezes his arm. 'It's Hope's last night and we're going to have a blast.'

'Too right we are,' Adam is back to himself. It's like a light going on behind his eyes. 'We're going to give Hope the best night so she won't go away and leave us.'

'I'm not leaving you in spirit,' I say back. 'Just in body and mind.'

'Yeah, but we love your body and mind,' Julie pouts. 'It's your spirit that's the trouble. If it wasn't for that you might actually keep a job.'

'Ha bloody ha,' I sneer at her. Then I notice where we're headed. 'Hey, are we going back to the house for something?'

Neither of them answers me.

'Are we going back to the house for something?' I ask again.

There is a silence.

'We are, aren't we?'

16

'Aw, just for a party,' Julie says casually. 'You know, your surprise party for going away. The one that your friends have been arranging all day.'

'No way!' The shriek I give almost makes Adam crash his car.

The party is seriously wild. People I don't even know come. One of the bands from our local pub has set up in the sitting room and is playing tunelessly to anyone who will listen. Some of my old work colleagues arrive, and believe me there are quite a few of those. I'm good at keeping in contact with people. Well, most people. Adam spends his time drinking lots of beer and drunkenly chatting up the women while Julie does the same with the men. Neither of them scores.

I dance drunkenly to some of the band's tunes, around and around and around. Some time, in the early morning, Julie, Adam and I find ourselves together again. We're sitting on the sofa as the party winds down around us. People are asleep on the floor and others have gone home. I'm drunk and tearful.

'Thanks for this great surprise,' I mumble, my arms around the two of them. 'You are the bestest, brilliantest people I have ever met.'

'We are nice, aren't we,' Julie agrees. She is smashed. 'I really like myself.'

I laugh.

'I really like you too,' Adam says.

'I wish *he* liked me,' Julie points to a guy who is fast asleep on the other side of the room. 'He never even noticed me. He reminds me of the first man I ever slept with.'

'Why? Did he not notice you either?' I joke.

'Ha ha.' Julie sighs drunkenly. 'He did. Then I dumped him but then I wished I hadn't. He made loads of money afterwards.'

'So did the first guy I slept with,' I say to console her. 'He slept with me, told me he loved me and then dumped me. And then made a fortune running a hotel or something.' I sigh and say glumly, 'Stupid bastard.'

'You sound so over him,' Adam says drolly.

'I tell ya, I wish I'd never got over him.'

The two of them laugh loudly.

'Did your first girlfriend make loads of money?' Julie turns to Adam.

He flushes a little and coughs a bit and eventually mumbles, 'No, but she had a great time.'

We call him a liar and he tells us that if we want we can try him out for ourselves.

Julie rolls her eyes. 'Sleeping with you would be like sleeping with my brother or something.'

'Why? Is he a sexual magician too?' Adam asks.

They continue to banter, Julie replying that Adam probably was a sexual magician in that he could make all his girlfriends disappear, then she asks him how many girlfriends he ever had. He taps his nose and tells her to mind her own business. I take a sneaky glance at my watch.

It's after three. I really don't know how I'll get up in the morning but it's been worth it.

3

JULIE AND ADAM come to the airport to see me off despite the fact that they must be feeling horrendous. Adam is sporting a pair of dark glasses and he's been quite sick all morning. I don't think he can even remember the latter half of the party. He insists that he never got up and sang with the band. But he did, because Julie and I remember it. He made them sound even worse.

Julie looks quite fragile too.

I'm not too bad but it's only because I drank my pint of water before going to sleep. Still, I've a bit of a headache that won't shift.

We look an odd trio standing together at the departures gates. Adam, tall, skinny with over-long blond hair that he keeps pushing behind his ear, Julie, model thin, in skinny jeans and her new 'off-white' blouse, her thick blond hair shining under the artificial lights and me, average height, curly haired with a figure a basketball would be proud of. Anyway, I digress. Julie is making me promise to text her when I arrive. 'And you've definitely got your dollars and map and car booked from the airport to where you're going, have you?' she asks anxiously. Again.

'I've got the map,' I pat my shoulder bag.

'And you've got your phone and your bank book?'

'Yes, Mammy.'

She flaps her hand at me and adds defensively, 'Well, who knows how long you'll be gone?' She pauses, before enfolding me in a bear hug. 'Oh, Hope, we'll miss you.' Julie is an affectionate person. I think that's why I like her so much. I'm not really touchy feely. I wish I was. I'm never quite sure how hard to hug or how long to hold on for. Julie eventually lets me go.

Adam stands by awkwardly, looking at the pair of us. He's like me. He never hugs. He towers over everyone in the queue. 'Take care,' he says, patting me on the back. 'I'll keep your room free over the summer, just in case you decide to come back.'

I appreciate the gesture for the friendship that it is. Sometimes, like now, I feel almost guilty about how good they are to me. Sometimes, I think that if they really knew me, they wouldn't like me. The thought brings unexpected tears to my eyes.

'Aw,' Julie says, sniffing. 'Stop. Don't get me started.'

I try to smile. 'I'll keep you updated,' I tell them. 'Promise.'

'And I'll cut out all the jobs available in the newspapers,' Adam announces, 'and I'll send your CV in to them and if you get an interview, I'll let you know and you might come back.'

'Only jobs with no bosses,' I grin.

'No problem.' He smiles back. Adam really has a cute smile. 'There are loads of those about.' He pats me on the back again. 'Well, Hope-less, you'd better go.'

'Yeah.' And still I stand there, like an eejit.

'Yeah,' he says.

'Oh, for God's sake, give her a hug,' Julie mutters in exasperation. 'It's not that difficult.'

He flushes and I flush. Then he holds out his arms in an awkward way and I hold out mine and we embrace briefly. 'Now,' he says, his duty done. 'Off you go.'

'Off I go.' I hold up my small bag of hand luggage. 'Bye, you two. Take care of each other.'

'Bye!' they call out and I see that Julie is sniffing. She's buried her head in Adam's chest and he stands stiffly upright, rubbing her shoulder. His face has gone a weird colour and I think he's going to be sick again.

We wave and wave and wave.

Then they're out of sight and I'm left facing a long tunnel that'll take me into my holiday.

And something else, though I'm not sure what I want that something else to be.

The plane is a huge jumbo, all quite modern with cool green and beige décor. I find my seat beside a window, put my bag in the overhead locker and settle down to have a read of a magazine I've bought. There are a few articles in it on anger management. Well, I presume the one entitled 'Show your boss who's boss' is aimed at people like me.

A man plonks down beside me, breathing heavily.

'Nice cap,' he grins.

'Ta.' I turn back to my magazine.

'I nearly didn't make the flight,' he says in an unmistakably Dublin accent. 'I got up late.'

I smile at him politely. He's young and quite scrummy though very dishevelled. His hair is sticking out all over the place and his grey shirt looks as though he slept in it. 'Well, it wasn't that I got up late,' he continues, as he opens a packet of cheese and onion. 'It was more the fact that I never got to bed.'

21

Oh God, I think. I don't need some guy sitting beside me for hours droning on about his cool drunken sex-fuelled lifestyle. 'Really,' I say drily. 'Good for you.'

'Naw, it wasn't,' he says. 'I couldn't remember the name of the hotel I was staying in so I spent all night in a taxi while the driver helped me to look for it.'

'You're joking.'

'I wish I was. Feckin' taxi cost me a fortune. The wife is going to kill me when I get home.'

'Yeah, she probably will,' I smile. 'What was the hotel?'

'The Savoy.'

I start to laugh. 'How could you forget that?'

He shrugs, all wide-eyed bewilderment. 'I've never been in London before. I just went for business and even if the company was paying for everything, I could hardly charge an eight-hour taxi journey to every hotel in London to my expense account, sure I couldn't.' He offers me a crisp.

I take one and munch slowly as I say, 'Well, you could. Did your company actually forbid you from riding around in a taxi for eight hours?'

'Well, no but –'

'There you go so.'

He grins. I'd say he's a lovely husband. 'Right. Fine. So I'll charge them for the taxi and just lose my job, ey?'

'It's not a big deal – I lose jobs all the time.' What had been mortifying comes out as quite flippant as I talk to this stranger. It's a big act, of course – he doesn't know me and my very bad job reputation and so I can make a joke about it. Well, I suppose it would be funny, if it was someone else.

'Really.' He raises his eyebrows. He has lovely brown eyes, sort of twinkling. 'How many jobs exactly?'

'I've lost count.'

22

This makes him laugh. I used to laugh about it too, in the beginning before it became a habit I couldn't seem to break. Sort of the difference between biting my nails and biting my nails down to the quick. 'Maybe about sixteen.'

He whistles. 'How come?'

He has angled himself towards me now and I fold up my magazine, suddenly glad to be able to talk to someone for the duration of the flight. I don't like flying at the best of times. 'Well, I have a problem with authority figures,' I say with aplomb. 'At least that's what I think. I get on well in jobs until someone actually starts telling me what to do.'

'That would be a problem,' he acknowledges in mock seriousness. 'So what happens?'

'Various things.' I'm turning my life into a joke which I'm good at doing. I've been doing it for years. 'Sometimes I'll just not turn up for a few weeks and leave them in the lurch. Other times I've typed up letters with really offensive sentences in them.'

'Yeah?'

'Uh-huh. Things like . . .' I screw up my face: 'Dear sir, we regret to inform you that your application for a house has been turned down because we found you to be a wanker.'

The guy explodes with laughter. 'No way.'

'Yeah. Well, the boss didn't read the letters and he was supposed to. And my defence was that I'd meant to type banker. Which the man was. Still got fired, though. And just a week ago, I got fired for getting into an argument with a client of the firm I worked for.' And, as the plane taxis to the runway, I tell him that story.

'You were dead right,' he nods. 'He was power-tripping you.'

'I know.' I look at him. 'So what do you do?'

23

'I'm in marketing. I've been in London working on an angle to market this ironing board that's just been invented.'

'An ironing board? Was that not invented years ago?'

'Funny.' He crumples up his crisp bag and stuffs it in his equally dishevelled jacket. 'This is a special ironing board. It works with a special iron and irons both sides of a garment at once.'

'Fascinating,' I say drolly, as if he'd just explained the intricacies of algebra.

'It really is.' He's trying not to grin.

'Well, that sounds great.'

'Yeah. And it's my job to sort out the various campaigns. I was in London yesterday and now it's Boston and New York.'

'Great life.'

'Nah,' he shakes his head. 'I'm only married a year and it's hard on my wife. I'd prefer something where I didn't have to travel. But we need the cash.'

'Yeah?'

'My wife is expecting our first baby in a few months.'

'Congratulations.' He looks way too young to be a dad. He's got quite a boyish look about him, sort of like Adam only not as awkward.

'Ta. It's a bit of a surprise for us, though.' He rummages about in his plastic bag. 'I bought this for the baby.'

It's the most enormous rattle I've ever seen. Scary looking too. The child would want to be Hulk Hogan to hold it up, much less rattle it. 'Lovely.'

'Yeah, I thought so too. And it's not too boyish or girlish, so it's not?'

'Nope.'

As the plane takes off, he bends down and carefully puts the rattle away.

I hate the build-up to take-off. The trundling down the runway, the picking up of speed and finally the way the plane lifts up into the air. It doesn't seem to bother the guy beside me at all. 'Joe Ryan,' he introduces himself, just as we get airborne.

'Hope Gardner,' I say back.

'You're Irish, yeah?'

'Yeah.'

'Let me guess.' He screws up his face and says, 'Cork?'

'No.'

'Waterford?'

'Jesus, no.'

He then names about every county in Ireland, before I say, 'I'm from Kerry. And you're from Dublin.'

'Yeah. Well done.' He sounds impressed, obviously not aware that he has the thickest Dublin accent ever.

Just then the seatbelt sign, which had gone out, flicks back on again.

'Oh,' Joe rubs his hands together. 'Turbulence, I love a bit of turbulence.'

'Will passengers please return to their seats, we are experiencing some difficulties and may have to go back to Heathrow.'

Joe is still going on about turbulence, telling me of a trip he took once where the plane dropped hundreds of feet in seconds because it hit an air pocket.

'Did the captain say we're turning back?' I ask.

'Nah,' Joe shrugs. 'Why would he say that?'

I want to believe him but I'm sure that's what I heard. I take a quick glance up the aircraft and see the air hostesses belting themselves in. Is it my imagination or do they look a little freaked out?

'Sorry –' the woman who is on the other side of Joe

leans towards us. 'Are we turning back? Is that what he said?'

'That's what I thought.' I can barely get the words out. My mouth has gone dry. 'I hope everything is OK.'

'I was on a plane once where a lot of birds flew into the engine on take-off.' The woman nods. 'Apparently that's dangerous. Oh, my.' She grabs her seat as the plane banks sharply. It is turning back, and at speed. The overhead luggage slides about.

The murmuring from the other passengers grows louder. Someone at the back actually laughs.

'All passengers remain in your seats. Keep your seatbelts on. We are experiencing difficulties and are turning back to Heathrow.'

'Oh great.' Joe rolls his eyes and settles back in his seat. 'We'll be held up for hours now.'

His nonchalance reassures me. The noise level in the plane has decreased again. People are nervously glancing out their windows and whispering to each other.

'I don't mind telling you –' the woman leans over Joe to talk to me again – 'I always felt I'd die in a plane crash.'

Joe gives a guffaw of laughter and I manage a smile. 'You'll be fine,' I tell her. 'The pilot wants to get home to his wife and kids too.'

'It's probably a woman pilot,' Joe says. 'Panicking over nothing.'

The woman and I laugh a little but stop abruptly as the plane drops. It just falls straight down as if a huge weight has landed on top of it. Oxygen masks tumble and appear in front of us. People scream and a little girl behind starts to cry. Then just as suddenly the plane levels out again.

26

'Turbulence,' Joe says, though his voice is a little strained. 'That's all. That happened to me before.'

'Please fit on oxygen masks,' the Tannoy advises. 'Emergency strip lighting will now come on. We are experiencing some difficulties and for your own safety please keep your seatbelts on.'

Jesus. Jesus. Jesus. I feel sick. I fumble with my mask and Joe, his own in place, helps me with it. I am doing my best to stay calm.

POP!

POP!

POP!

Each bang is louder than the last.

'Oh God!' someone shrieks. 'Look!'

Smoke is pouring out of the wing on my side of the plane. I can only stare at it. I can't even scream or shout, just gawk at it in horrible fascination. It's as if I'm out of myself, just not quite able to believe this is happening.

POP-POP-POP.

More smoke.

The woman beside Joe starts saying prayers. She has her eyes closed and her hands are white on the grip of the seats. Silence in the cabin. Not one person is screaming and, save for the little girl behind, no one is crying. It's as if a weird fatalistic mood has overtaken people.

The plane lurches suddenly, left to right. The smoke is billowing out now but blessedly, I can see land. The smoke seems to stream back into the air at an incredible speed and I realise just how fast we are going.

'They've cleared a runway for us,' Joe says, in what I suppose is a reassuring voice. 'See, out there?'

I can't answer him. I wish I'd looked at what the air

27

hostess had done when she'd given her demonstration at the beginning of the flight. I fumble under the seat and pull out my life jacket.

'Are we going to die?' a little girl sobs.

'No,' her mother says, in a remarkably calm voice: 'the pilot knows what he's doing.'

Joe has his life jacket on and he turns to me and helps me on with mine.

'Thanks.'

POP-POP-POP.

The sound is louder.

The lights go off and the plane plummets. It's dark inside and bright outside. Overhead baggage starts to smash and thump. Some of it falls out. The plane is lurching about wildly.

Joe turns to me. His brown eyes are scared. I can only imagine what mine must look like. 'It was nice to meet you,' he says.

'You too.' I think I might cry. 'Will you hold my hand?'

'Sure.' He grasps my hand in his and I notice that he's holding the other lady's hand too. She's still praying.

'If you survive,' he says then, 'will you find my wife and tell her I'm sorry – Mary Ryan in Baltimore, West Cork – will you do that?'

'Tell her that you're sorry?'

'Yeah. She'll know what I mean.' He has to shout as the plane is screeching now. The poor child behind is bawling her eyes out in terror. 'Will you do it?'

'I will.' The noise is unbelievable. I clasp his hand tighter. 'And will you find my mother and tell her I'm sorry – Helen Gardner, Dunport, Kerry?'

'Will do.'

We hold each other as the plane careers downwards.

And I wonder if I'll see my life flash before my eyes.

4

I SEE BLACK shoes and I hear crying. I see a small girl jumping up and down, only wanting a little attention. I see her climbing into bed in her clothes and crying too.

I hear someone shouting. I feel a weight being lifted from me. Then I'm moving. Fast. The wailing of an ambulance.

Bright blue sky stretching on for ever. Bright blue sky and bright yellow sun. Down below I see a dark-haired girl, she must be nine or ten, climbing sulkily from a car, pulling a stumbling boy in her wake. She puts her arms about the boy, holding him to her and glaring defiantly up at a tall, lanky man in a grey suit. The little boy is crying. He doesn't like change, I know that.

I hear someone saying my name. Hope Gardner, the person is saying. Her name is Hope. Then the same voice says that I'm from Kerry and I've no next of kin. No next of kin? I think I do, though. Hope lives in London, the voice says. London? Am I not in Dunport?

I see a girl with black hair talking to a small boy. I see her handing the small boy a doll and he takes it and studies it and pushes it away. I see the small girl forcing it into his hand so hard that he pushes her

29

off and tells her to 'go away'. I see the small girl dance and clap and laugh. I see an older woman smile a little.

The small boy smiles a bit too.

Two voices. A man's. He's saying that he should never have let me go. Jack? It doesn't sound like Jack. A woman's voice then. She's clasping my hand. She's begging me to open my eyes. But my eyes are open . . .

I see a dark-haired girl with a big black eye, smiling hugely. The small boy is bigger now and he's cheering. A girl, Amanda, is crying, because the dark-haired girl broke her nose. The dark-haired girl lets no one call her brother an idiot.

'Her eyes are open!'

Someone else says that's a normal thing. Coma patients sometimes do that.

The woman says in a whisper, into my ear, because I can feel it, 'I know you can hear me. I know you can, Hope. Please wake up. Please.'

The dark-haired girl and the small boy are cleaning. Cleaning so that things sparkle and shine.

The man is back. He's holding my hand now. He's saying that if I get better he'll take me on holiday. He doesn't care about work any more, he hates work, he says. Him and Julie will mind me, he says.

There is a telephone. Big and red and huge. It grows bigger and bigger and the little girl wants it and is afraid of it. She picks it up but it's too late now.

'She moved!' the man calls out. 'She moved and she squeezed my hand.'

I need to get away. It's too hard.

I see the dark-haired girl lose her smile and her sparkle and I see her run. Sometimes things leave her, sometimes they catch her up and when they catch her up, she runs some more. But she's tired now and needs to rest.

I see white and black and colours around the edges. I hear beeping and popping and voices. I hear someone say, 'Is she moving?' I hear someone else say, 'I dunno. Maybe.' I hear the first voice say, 'I think she is, look!' The second voice says nothing. I feel pressure on my hand. I turn my head and suddenly there is lots of noise.

Very slowly, I open my eyes. Two figures stand gawping at me. Blurs. Then a white blur taps my face gently. 'Hope? Hope? Can you hear me?'

My voice seems to come from somewhere very far away. 'Yes. Yes, I can.'

And somewhere someone laughs.

I like that sound.

5

I DON'T REMEMBER anything about the crash. Where once there must have been an experience, it's now a blank. Well, I do remember getting on to the plane, I remember sitting down with my magazine, but after that, everything is blurry. I can see the air hostesses looking anxiously at each other, but they would have done that so I don't know if it's an invented memory or not. And anyway, when I do start to think about it or ask questions, I shake and feel sick, so I just leave it alone. Like the way you would a wound, if touching it hurt. Apparently, the plane made it back to the airport but careered all over the place and smashed up and only seventeen people survived. Seventeen. I feel sick when I hear that. Seventeen people out of what must have been at least a hundred.

I was found hours into the search. I was unconscious and bleeding but I was alive. It has taken me almost two weeks to wake up.

Julie, who has spent those weeks mostly at my bedside, tells me of how she waited for news, of how, when they found my body, she and Adam thought I was dead.

'Take more than that to kill me,' I croak out. My voice is not my own. It's weak and it trembles and I hate it. My body is bruised and my head is encased in a bandage.

Apparently, I hit my head and my brain swelled and they had to operate on it to relieve pressure. I don't understand all the details but according to Julie, I am so lucky to be alive.

I suppose I am lucky, though my ribs are sore and my leg is lacerated and, hey, I have no hair. I don't know what my face is like, but Julie tells me that the bruising should clear up. I reach out and awkwardly pat Julie's hand. 'Thanks, Julie,' I mutter. 'Thanks for being here. I really appreciate it.'

'Yeah, I know you do.' Unexpectedly, tears glisten in her eyes. 'Oh, God, Hope, we were so worried. And all Adam kept saying was that he knew we shouldn't have let you go on your own and that he'd never forgive himself if you died.'

I roll my eyes a little and God, it hurts. My whole face feels like a swollen sore balloon. 'That's silly. It wasn't Adam's fault. I wanted to go.'

'Yeah, but even when you'd left to board the plane, Adam said he had a bad feeling about it.'

'Has he thought of going into the psychic business?' I kid gently. 'I believe there's a fortune going if you're any good.'

'Don't make a joke of it. He was serious.'

'Sorry.'

She squeezes my hand.

I find my thoughts drifting to everyone who must have died. I wonder why I'm alive and others are dead. What loss would I have been to the human race? The funny thing is, I can't even remember anyone on the plane.

The two of us sit for a few minutes in silence. I'm still clasping Julie's hand and she's rubbing my hand with her free one. No one has done that for me since I was tiny.

'Adam and I made a decision last night,' she says, unexpectedly breaking the silence.

'Yeah?'

'We're going to take you on your holiday!'

My heart lurches. I'm going to laugh. It's a nervous re-action. 'Julie, there is no way I'm getting on a plane again in a hurry.'

She giggles and then looks guilty about laughing. 'No. Sorry, I should have explained. We're taking you somewhere you'd like to go and yet you won't have to fly.'

'Where?'

'Dunport!'

She announces this triumphantly, as if it is the best surprise ever. I suppose, if I wanted to go back to where I'm from it would be a lovely surprise, but I don't. The thought of it makes my head reel.

'You're always saying how lovely it is and now me and Adam are taking you home.'

'No.'

She mistakes my 'no' for delighted disbelief. 'Yes!' She grasps my hands. 'Oh, Hope, it's a great idea. I mean, you so wanted to go on holiday and now . . . now, well,' she pauses delicately, 'well, you couldn't possibly look after yourself, or drive there or anything, so Adam and I decided that we'd take you.'

I stare at her. I can't speak. My throbbing head begins to throb some more. 'I, eh, can't let you do that,' I gulp out. 'That'd be too much.'

'Well, we already have. We've booked a cottage about two miles outside Dunport and paid for it in full.' She pauses and with shining eyes announces, 'for three whole months. That's how long the doctors said a complete recovery would take and it'd be so much better for you to recuperate in nice surroundings than in dirty old London.'

I always knew, that at some stage my lies would come

34

back to bite me. I just never thought it would be like this. I stare at Julie and feel as if I might cry. I don't want to lose my friend but I will. Oh God . . .

'Julie,' I say, and I can't look at her. 'I can't go back there.'

'Why?' She looks into my face. 'We're taking the ferry, we won't fly.'

'It's not that,' I whisper. 'It's just that, well, I can't go because . . .' I take a deep breath and say softly, 'my mother is still there.'

Julie doesn't move. The silence in the room is broken only by the monitors I'm wired to. Eventually she does speak, 'Your mother? But I thought –'

'I never said she was dead, Julie, I just, well, I just never talked about her.' My eyes meet hers.

'But you let me and Adam *think* she was dead.'

'I know.' I bite my lip, shame coursing through my body. I can't look at her. 'I know I did and I'm sorry.' I know she thinks I'm a freak. Well, wouldn't anyone? How many people go about pretending their mother is dead?

'And your father and brother, are they alive too?'

'No, they *are* dead.'

Her hand is still in mine, but she's not saying anything.

'We're not close,' I say at last. It's the first time in years I've spoken about her and it's like drawing back a rusty bolt. I don't know how to start or where to start. And like something that hasn't been unlocked in a long time, my words are stiff and creaky. 'It's my fault, I suppose. And hers too. She, well, she wasn't a great mother.'

'Why? Did she beat you?'

'No, nothing like that.'

'Did she keep comparing you to your sister the way my mother did?'

35

'I didn't have a sister, but no, she never did that.'

'So what then?' She is struggling to grasp it. 'Why should you pretend she was dead?'

'She, well, she was depressed a lot – OK?' Saying it makes me sound selfish and I know I am. I hate myself for it. But sometimes to survive you have to be selfish. 'I left Dunport when I was eighteen and I did keep in touch with her in the beginning, but Julie, you have no idea what it's like. Every time I rang her, it was like being dragged down a black hole, listening to her. And once I put the phone down I had to climb back out of the hole. So, after a while, I just stopped ringing. It was too hard. I was going mad myself.'

She doesn't say anything for a bit, then, softly, 'You could have told us.'

'I couldn't.' I shake my head, wondering how she can sound so calm about me deceiving her like that. 'I felt so bad about it. And, well,' I gulp, knowing I'll sound pathetic, 'I wanted you and Adam to like me.'

'Oh Hope,' she says and squeezes my hand. 'You're such a muppet. We would have liked you anyway.'

She looks at me as if I'm an idiot. Maybe I am. Slowly, hardly daring to believe it, I mouth, 'Would you?'

'Yes!' She laughs a little. 'And, anyway, I would have understood,' she goes on, surprising me once more. 'That's the way I feel when I talk to Angela or my parents on the phone. I ring them, feeling good cause I got a child maybe to understand and appreciate a poem or I got them to act on the stage and all I hear about is how Angela's inventing some huge world-famous thing or how they're too busy to go and see other people's kids on stage. It steals the good out of your life: it's hard to bounce back, I know.'

Her words seep into me, like medicine for my guilty feelings. 'You know?' is all I can manage.

'Yeah.' Her arm is about my shoulder and she says, softly joking, 'Only thing is, I don't go about pretending my sister and mother are dead.'

I manage a weak smile. 'I never said she was dead. I just omitted the fact she was alive.'

'Oh my God!' she shrieks, making me jump.

My head jars.

'I told the police you had no next of kin. I'm sure your mother would have wanted to know about your accident.'

'No, forget it. It'd only stress her out. It's better this way.'

Julie nods and gets up from the bed and walks to the window. My room overlooks the car park, which is not the best view for recuperation. I watch as she fiddles with the blinds and feigns interest in the comings and goings of various cars. 'You nearly died, Hope,' she says eventually.

'Nearly,' I nod. 'Isn't that a nice word?'

'The best word in the world,' she agrees. 'So wouldn't you like to make it up with your mother? Maybe this is your chance.'

I must admit, I'd been thinking about that in the last few days. Thinking about how unexpected life was and how you couldn't control it and that maybe it was best to be at peace with everyone. But the idea of seeing my mother now scared me, quite frankly. 'I don't know,' I stammer out. 'In theory yeah, I'd love to be able to talk to her, but Julie . . .' I can't continue. It means talking about stuff that I have shut away so firmly that to take it out now would be like releasing an emotional atom bomb. 'I just don't know if I can.'

Julie, I think, senses that there are things I'm not telling her but she doesn't push it and I'm grateful for that. 'You could come on holiday still,' she says, 'and make up your mind. You're fragile now, but in a couple of months you'll be a different person. I mean,' she presses on, sensing my weakening stance, 'I've already arranged for special leave and Adam is taking leave from his job for three months, so it's no problem. Plus we've paid for it.'

'Adam?' Now I am surprised. 'Three months?'

'Yeah,' Julie nods. 'He asked them yesterday and apparently it's cool.'

'I thought he was an important person in work.'

Julie giggles. 'He is. According to him, they let him go because they don't want to piss him off. But get this – he's still bringing his laptop and printer as he might need to work.'

'Oh yeah, that sounds like Adam – honestly, he's the only guy on the planet who could get leave and still have to work.'

'I know,' Julie smiles fondly. 'He's terrible, isn't he?'

'He's too soft,' I answer. Then I ask, 'Julie, have you seen Dunport?'

'No, but you make it sound gorgeous.'

'It is gorgeous.' It makes me smile a little, thinking about it. 'But there's no major night-life. It doesn't have a cinema and it's not like Ibiza or anything.'

'So? I'll be fine.'

'You'll go bonkers. And so will Adam.'

'This is for you. For you to get better.'

'I'll get better in London.'

'But it's paid for!'

'I'll pay you back.'

'No – you know you love the place, come on, it's two miles from Dunport anyway, so you don't even have to go into it if you don't want.'

'Two miles away? Is it up the mountains?'

'I think so, yeah. Adam booked it.'

The mountains. I'd like that. Once upon a time, I knew those mountains like the back of my hand. I'd climbed them, all over them. I knew the views from every angle. I could maybe climb them again – just once more. I could –

'How's the patient?' Adam bounds into the room. He's carrying the most enormous bunch of grapes I have ever seen and some magazines. Turning to Julie, he asks, 'Have you told her yet?' He actually sounds excited.

'Her mother is not dead. She's alive.'

'Bloody hell,' Adam drops the grapes on to the bed, his mouth agape. 'When did you find that out, Hope?'

Julie and I start to laugh. We're laughing so much, I can't even get the words out to explain.

I never thought I'd laugh about it.

In the end, I let them persuade me. Two miles outside Dunport isn't Dunport. I can avoid the town if I want. And if I do decide to see my mother, I can do that too.

And I need their help as I can't exactly walk very far or do too much and besides, they've paid for the place and can't get their money back. It was the only place left for the summer, apparently.

I find that, despite everything, I'm a little excited to be going back.

Later that week, a doctor comes in and offers me counselling. It's for the trauma I suffered during the crash, he says. I tell him that I can't remember the crash. I tell him that I don't think I need counselling. He gets a little stroppy about it, to be honest. 'I'll be fine,' I tell him in as firm a voice as I can muster. 'I survived the crash, I'll survive the life I've been given back.'

'So you haven't suffered from nightmares since?' he asks.

'No.'

'Or flashbacks?'

'No. I'm fine, honestly.'

'If you're sure . . .' He rises from the chair and his voice is laden with so much doubt, I could practically eat it.

'I'm sure,' I say.

'Well, I'm going to forward your files to the nearest hospital in Kerry and you can go there to have your leg cast removed and things like that. If you feel any need for counselling, or experience any strange sensations, just contact the hospital and they'll arrange it.' He leaves some papers beside my bed. 'They're just some notes on Post Traumatic Stress Disorder,' he says. 'People experience it to different degrees after a trauma like yours. If you have nightmares about the crash or feel in any way –' he pauses – 'different about things, please get counselling. Read the leaflets and try to recognise if any of it applies to you.'

'OK.'

I watch him walk out of the room and when he's out of sight, I glance through the leaflets. Then I bin them. Talking about the crash is not what I want to do. All I want is to get out of here and get better and go back to my life with my friends.

If I've learned anything from what happened, it's that life is short and you have to make the most of it.

I hold on to that as I drift into sleep.

6

THE DAY I get out of the hospital is the day we go on holiday. Adam picks me up. He's wearing, rather self-consciously, a pair of faded denims and a loose shirt. Despite their cool appearance, Adam still manages to give them an air of uptightness. I think it's his highly polished black shoes or something. I suppress a smile as he crosses towards me.

'All set?'

'Uh-huh.'

'Let's get you out of here then.' He picks up the small black bag that holds my hospital stuff. 'Julie's in the car and we're all packed. We decided that rather than take you back to the house, we'd drive straight to the ferry.'

'Oh, thanks.' I'm touched that they knew that returning to that house would be like taking a step back for me. I'd left it with the intention of going on a long holiday and that's what was going to happen. The hospital was merely a diversion on the road. If you can call a broken leg, swollen face and skull operation a diversion.

I hadn't realised how weak I was until I begin to walk alongside Adam. Being so tall, he strides ahead of me without even noticing. I'm too proud to tell him to slow down, and at the back of my mind I'm worried in case the nurses think I'm not fit enough to leave. They hadn't been too impressed

41

when they'd heard I was going to recuperate out of the country.

'Bye. Good luck,' a nurse calls as I hobble by.

Another one holds up an enormous box of chocolates. 'There was no need,' she smiles.

'Yes there was,' Adam jokes back. 'Putting up with Hopeless is no mean feat.' They laugh and Adam blushes furiously. I belt him with my crutch and they laugh harder.

As we stand, waiting for the elevator, Adam gently lifts the hood of my sweatshirt up over my head. 'There are a couple of photographers out front, Hope. You might feel better with this up.'

'What?' Jesus, my one moment of fame and I'm going to look like a Hallowe'en reject. 'Oh God. Is there another way out of here?'

'I told them on the way in that you'd pose for one photo and to leave you alone after that. They seemed happy enough.'

'But, but, I've no make-up on.'

He looks surprised. 'You never wear make-up.'

'Yeah, and I never normally have the complete set of colours from the red spectrum on my face either.'

'Hope, you were in a plane crash – they want to see the bruises, it'll help them sell newspapers.'

'Well, thank you for your sensitive analysis of the situation.' I don't know if I should laugh or be annoyed with him.

'Look – you have bruises – big bloody deal. Your hair is gone – it'll grow back. You broke your leg – they were never much to look at anyway.'

That makes me laugh.

He grins. 'That's the Hopeless I know.' Then he awkwardly pats my back. 'You're alive – that's what matters.'

It takes a lot for him to say that; he starts to cough like mad and it's his excuse to turn away from me.

'Thanks, Adam,' I say and it takes a lot for me to say that.

As we get out of the lift and make our way to the front door, he puts his arm about my shoulders and says, 'Stand with me in the picture, that way you'll look good.'

'Can't argue with that!'

'Bitch.'

The photographers are as good as their word. They actually applaud me as I come through the door, which makes me feel like a complete fraud. I did nothing special. I just survived, which was pure luck. It was hardly a heroic act. I manage a weird sort of grimace as a smile for them and thank my lucky stars that I'll be out of the country when the photos are printed.

Adam ushers me towards his fancy car where Julie is waiting. She's munching crisps and turns to smile at me as I get in. 'Want one?'

I reach out to take one when suddenly I feel an overwhelming panic. I can't let them see it, so I lie back on the rear seat and close my eyes. 'No. Ta.' Something hard and pointy is pushing into my back and Adam pulls it from under me. 'Bloody car is crammed – Ju, did you bring everything you own?'

'It's three months, Adam,' Julie says, munching again. 'And I'm not planning on doing a whole load of washing.'

'Bloody hell.' Adam throws her little vanity case on to the floor and there is an immediate tinkling sound. Julie doesn't seem to notice as she's crunching like mad on her cheese

43

and onion but Adam winces and I try out a smile. My panic is slowing, receding and I don't know what caused it.

'Julie packed for you too,' Adam says.

'Packed what? I brought most of my good stuff away the first time.'

'Mmm,' Julie agrees. 'I just bought you some new track-suits, you can't wear much else with that cast.'

'Thanks. I owe you.'

Adam starts up the car and we're off.

Julie turns to smile at me. 'Oh, isn't it great,' she announces delightedly, 'the three of us going away together?'

'Brilliant,' Adam agrees as he eases his monster of a car into the traffic. 'I've always wanted to go away with a couple of good-lookers for a few months.'

'Pity we can't say the same,' Julie snorts and Adam pinches her hard in the arm.

The sun is gone from the sky by the time we reach Kerry. The ferry crossing was OK but the drive from Rosslare to west Kerry has taken a while and Julie is now snoring loudly in the front seat of Adam's car.

Just the sight of the sign saying that we have crossed from Cork into Kerry makes my heart beat a little faster. Every stone on the road seems almost familiar. Not loved exactly, just familiar.

And then, another while later, the sign WELCOME TO DUNPORT appears.

'So, this is where you're from.' Adam peers out the window as he drives. It's grown dark and there really is not a lot to see. 'Do you want to call in on anyone?' The question is deliberately careless.

'No, it's fine.' I make my voice light. 'My mother is not

44

one for surprises. And anyway, like I said, we haven't talked in a while.'

'Well, maybe another time,' he says.

'In another life,' I joke and he doesn't smile. So I add, 'Maybe.'

Adam peers out the windscreen. 'Bloody hell, are there no directions?'

'Where's the cottage?'

'About two miles outside Dunport, on the Dingle road.'

'Straight on through the town,' I say. I know these roads like I know my name.

'Right.' Adam nods and doesn't say much more. After a bit, he begins to whistle tunelessly. We're on the main street now, if you could call Dunport's main street such a thing. There's a small shop that sells probably everything ever invented. It's run by an old Dunport family and has been there for generations. McCoys. Beside that is one of Dunport's three pubs. The biggest one and the one that normally has the entertainment – The Poitín Jar. It's run by the parents of a boy I went to school with. Then there is the massive church, way too big for the local population and freezing cold in winter. Then another pub and then a small shopping centre. The shopping centre is new, it must have bought over the old butcher shop. The entrance to the ruins of the Dunport castle I and some friends used to play in as kids, is bordered off. A big sign says, ACQUIRED AS HOTEL FOR THE GLEESON HOTEL GROUP. That's a step up – Dunport with its own hotel. And then, on the way out of the town there is a small garage selling overpriced petrol, the road to the small harbour that gets crowded in high season and another pub cum restaurant. They serve the best fish in west Kerry. Or so the sign says. The main street would be attractive in

45

daylight, I think, as I notice the big urns of flowers on the grass verges. It's a little deserted now and a little depressing. Growing up, I lived outside the town and as Adam passes the roadway leading to my old house, I involuntarily glance up as if maybe I could see a winking light from one of the windows, but of course it'd be impossible, what with the sharp bends in the road.

'Now keep going and you're on the Dingle road,' I tell him.

He does and the car begins to climb. Up and up and up. The road grows ever narrower. 'Bloody hell,' Adam mutters, half to himself.

'Look out the passenger window,' I say and smile.

It's dark but he gasps anyway. We're right on the edge of a mountain, with what looks like a shaky stone wall to keep us plunging to our death. Below us is sheer mountain rock and heaving black ocean.

'Is this safe?' he gulps.

'Are you worried about your car or us?' I joke. Then add, 'Of course it's not safe, that's why you have to drive carefully.' I point to a luminous sign. 'See.'

'Ha ha.' But he sounds ever so slightly nervous. 'Now,' he says, 'according to the directions given by the landlord, our house should be around here somewhere. It's just after a signpost that says "Dingle four kilometres". The cottage will be on the right.'

'OK.'

We both gawk intently out the window, before I make Adam jump by shouting out, 'There it is, there it is!'

Julie jerks awake. 'What? What?'

'We're nearly there.' I feel ridiculously excited. I can't wait to see the place. 'There's the signpost!'

'And here's the cottage,' Adam announces as he points

upwards to a small, run-down place with an unkempt piece of land and a broken stone wall about it.

The three of us stare at it, not quite in horror, but with something akin to it. Adam drops a gear to drive up the sheer driveway.

A man is standing in the lighted open doorway looking up and down. He's as grubby and as run-down as his property. He smiles slightly as Adam pulls the car into what is meant to be a driveway.

'*Fáilte*,' he calls, coming over to us. 'I thought you'd lost yerselves on the road.'

'No.' Adam gets out and slams his door. Julie does the same and both of them forget about me as they stare in dismay at their holiday home.

'Here,' I call from the back seat, trying to clamber out. 'Can I get out?'

Julie hands me my crutch as Adam asks the man, 'Are you Maurice?'

'Maurice Murphy, that's me.' He jangles his keys. 'Come and I'll show ye around. It's not that big but the three of you should fit.' He pats the top of his head for some reason and it's then I notice the oversized hairpiece. It's jet black and looks even more false than Jordan's boobs. In fact, it looks more like a rat than hair. Julie has noticed it too and she elbows me hard in the ribs as I join her at the door.

Ouch, it hurt.

'Oh,' Maurice spots me, and his jaw drops. 'What happened you, *a stór*?'

'Accident,' I say.

'Poor thing.' He shakes his head. 'Well, you couldn't be in a better place to recover.'

He turns his back and walks into the house. We follow

him into a small square room. A battered sofa and two chairs take up most of the space. The floor is stone and surprisingly clean. A fireplace with a fire laid. A huge window dominates the room. 'Wait until morning comes,' he points at the window. 'Lovely views.' There's also a small table and four chairs. He then leads us into a kitchen. Well, he leads Adam; Julie and I can't fit in. It's basic. There's a long wooden press holding cups and plates, an old gas cooker with an old-fashioned kettle sitting on top of it. 'As you can see, it's all gas,' Maurice points out. 'If you need a new cylinder, you can buy it in Dingle or Dunport. Which way did ye come?'

'Dunport,' I answer.

'Well, the local shop sells gas. The new shopping centre there is hopeless. They sell nothing but fancy wines and coleslaws.' Then he looks at Adam. 'Though maybe your sort are into all that.'

'I like a nice wine,' Adam answers pleasantly, unaware that he's just been insulted. The Kerry people have a funny way of insulting you. With their accent you never quite realise it's an insult until the last minute. But Adam is even slower than that. He goes on, 'I hope they do Australian wines, there's nothing like a good red from Australia to put me in good humour.'

Maurice looks him up and down. And again. Up and down. Then he nods. 'Right. I can believe that.' He gives a sort of grimace and pushes past him. 'Now here's the stairs to the bedrooms.' He indicates a set of steep wooden steps that lead from the living room. 'There's only two rooms, and whatever way you organise it is yer own business. Go on up and have a look if ye like.'

Getting up a set of steep stairs, almost narrower than

oneself, on a crutch, is no easy feat. I hold everyone up. When I eventually reach the top, I find myself on a landing, about two feet square. To my left is a door, and another to my right. I open the one to my right and am in a small bedroom with quirky sloping ceilings. A single bed is pushed over to the window. Besides that there is a small chair and a chest of drawers. The other room is the same.

'That chair folds down into a small bed,' Maurice informs us in the second bedroom.

'So you could sleep two in here.'

'Right.'

'There's no toilet in this house,' Julie says. Her face has fallen with everything she's seen. I reckon, if she lives to be a hundred, she'll never let Adam book a holiday for her ever again.

'It's outside,' Maurice explains. 'Sure when this place was built, toilets were a luxury. This house must be –' he screws up his face – 'oh, about one hundred years old. My grand-mother died in the room here.'

'No!' Julie sounds as if she's just seen the decayed remains for herself. 'She didn't.'

'She did.' Maurice mistakes her tone for amazement. 'She died roaring. That's what my mother told me. I never knew her. Some contagious disease she had that was rampant in those days. Oh, screaming and yelling, she was.'

'And she died here?' Julie repeats faintly.

'Right where you're standing.'

'Oh.' She turns anguished eyes on me and I have to look away or I'll laugh.

Maurice, undeterred, pushes past us and walks back down-stairs. I go last and hobble behind them all out into the pitch black of the night. The toilet is enclosed in a little shed about ten feet from the house. Maurice opens the door and, to our relief, it's modern and clean. It even has a power shower. 'So that's it,' he smiles around at us in the dark and we can really only see the gleam of his teeth. 'I'll leave the keys with ye and my number is on the fridge in the kitchen if you want to contact me. I'm in Dingle so I'm not too far away. Now, there's a few cottages around here, not too close, so you're fine really. The only one you'll have to be careful with is the one about a mile from here.' He points behind him, to his right. 'Now, the man moved in about a year ago and according to himself, he's an artist. A con artist, if you ask me. He doesn't talk that much and can be very grumpy. Mental, that's the only word for him. I've never seen him so much as draw a blade of grass never mind anything else.' He nods to us, pops the keys into Adam's hand and saunters confidently off in the dark.

The three of us lurch and stagger towards the house, tripping on bits of wood and tufts of grass that we can't see. In the distance, I hear a strange droning sound.

'Hope?' Julie says as I stop dead and start looking around. 'That noise, what is it?'

'What noise?'

'That!' I'm almost shouting. 'That noise, can't you hear it?'

They stop now too and listen. It's faint but growing louder. I can't move. I'm standing in the garden and my legs won't move. I mean, I'm trying to walk but I can't. I know what the noise is now, it's a plane, somewhere high above. I can feel a weird sort of panic taking me over, I don't want to be here when a plane goes by.

'Come on in,' Adam takes me gently by the arm and with him holding me, I stagger inside. 'You've gone pale,' he says as Julie shuts the door. 'Are you OK? It was just a plane or a helicopter or something.'

50

The noise is gone, blocked out by the shut door. I can breathe again. I shake my head and mumble, 'I'm fine. Thanks, Adam. It's just been a long day.'

I think the two of them are swapping glances, but they don't say anything. 'It has,' Julie agrees. 'A long day with an outside toilet at the end of it. Oh my God!'

'And a death in the bedroom,' I contribute, trying to smile.

'Yeah,' Julie agrees. 'How could you book this, Adam? Oh my God.'

Adam shrugs. 'Well, it was the only one left that wasn't booked.'

'And are you surprised?' Julie groans. 'Didn't you for one moment think, oh, I wonder why this cottage isn't booked?'

'I thought it wasn't booked because no one had booked it,' Adam says calmly, unfazed by Julie's hysterics.

'Did you know there was an outside toilet?'

'I didn't ask.'

'Imagine traipsing out there in the middle of the night – oh, God.'

'Buy a bucket for your room,' Adam suggests, jokingly. 'You can slop out in the morning.'

'Ha ha.' Julie glares at him. 'Well, just so you both know, I'm having the room that the grandmother didn't die in. Contagious disease,' she shudders. 'God knows what we can catch living here.'

'I'd imagine Maurice thought that it was a nice little piece of history he was imparting to you,' Adam grins. He turns to me. 'So, Hope, I'll be the gentleman, where would you like to sleep?'

I shrug. 'Down here. I'll take the chair bed from the bedroom,' I say. 'I can't make the climb up the stairs anyway.'

If I'm being perfectly honest, I don't particularly want a dead grandmother's bedroom either.

'Are you sure? I can help you up the stairs,' Adam says.

'Nope, I'm really sure,' I say and I've never, in my life, been more sure of anything.

'OK then,' Adam nods. 'Now, who's for a cuppa?'

Without waiting for an answer, he marches into the kitchen and begins washing out the kettle before filling it up. Julie and I plonk down on the sofa which groans under our combined weight. In the kitchen we hear Adam trying to turn on the gas. It finally gets going with an enormous bang.

'Almost blew my hand off.' Adam pokes his head out the kitchen door. 'But I've got the hang of it now.'

'Great,' Julie mutters. She's sitting very straight on the sofa, almost as if she's afraid of being contaminated by it. I don't blame her really, it's quite stained. But, to show my faith in our holiday, I lie back on it. It's not as if I have any hair that could be in contact with the dirty fabric. There is silence. The only sound is the bubbling of the kettle. It's a lovely silence, the kind you can only get in the heart of the country.

Julie shifts about uncomfortably.

'We'll make the best of it,' I say haltingly.

Julie sniffs and then flicks a glance at me. Her gaze softens slightly. 'Yeah. We will. And after all it's your holiday, Hope. And we're only here to help you.'

'So it's my fault, is it?' I nudge her.

'No, it's bloody his fault,' she hisses in an undertone. 'Honestly, why on earth did I ever let him book this? Sure, he's never been on a holiday in his life before, I bet.'

'Aw stop, he did his best.'

Julie rolls her eyes. 'Where's the tea?' she calls out, trying to inject some happiness into her voice.

'Only coffee.' Adam arrives in carrying three mugs of coffee. 'The tea was a little bit suspect.'

Jesus, why did he have to say that?

'Yeah?'

'A spider must have crawled in some time ago and rotted there.'

Both Julie and I look at him, our mouths open. Julie can't even reach to take the coffee from him.

'Joke?' Adam grins cheerfully. 'There was no tea!'

'Tosser!' Julie shrieks, belting him and he gives a huge guffaw of laughter, slopping coffee out on to the floor.

'Gotcha,' he says as we take our mugs. He raises his in the air. 'Cheers.'

'Cheers.'

'Cheers.'

7

IT's DARK. OPPRESSIVELY dark. It's as if the dark is sitting on my lungs and pouring itself into my mouth. I try to fight it, to keep my mouth closed but it's fighting back and it's winning and it's –

'Hope, Hope.' Someone is calling out my name. And again, 'Hope. Hope. Wake up.'

Wake up?

I'm cold. I'm shivering. I try to open my eyes but I can't.

'Hope. Bloody hell, wake up!'

Now someone has their hands on my face. I can feel their touch through the cold. I know I'm dreaming now, but I can't wake up. In the dream, someone is holding me. Their hand is holding mine. Squeezing tight.

And my eyes shoot open and I'm gasping for air, almost as if I've been doing a David Blaine and holding my breath. I don't notice Adam at first, I'm so shaken, but as I calm down, I feel his breath on my face and I turn towards him. He's crouched down beside me. He's wearing these awful check pyjamas and he looks a little scared. 'Are you OK?' His voice is shaking.

I try to breathe normally. In. Out. In. Out. My forehead is beaded with sweat. 'Fine now.' Bits of my dream are floating away from me. 'Was I dreaming or something?'

'A nightmare more like,' Adam says. 'You were shouting and calling for help and saying that you promise to do it. And I couldn't wake you.'

'Really?' I wince. Nightmares? Wasn't that one of the symptoms –

'Really,' he nods.

I hoist myself up to a sitting position. 'Thanks for waking me.'

'No problem.' He still looks concerned. 'D'you want a glass of water or something?'

'Yeah.'

I rub my hand over my face and try to recall the dream and yet I'm afraid to.

Adam comes back in with two glasses of water and hands me one of them.

'What time is it?' I ask.

'Around five.'

'It's hot in here, isn't it?'

He doesn't answer. Maybe he doesn't think it's hot.

'I'll just get up and go outside and cool off.'

He helps me stand and hands me the crutch and I hobble out the back door. He follows me. Outside, it's still quite dark though the sky is streaked with crimson. The silence and stillness is so refreshing. A cool breeze is blowing very gently and it caresses my face. The sound of the ocean in the background calms me. When I moved away from here, it was that sound I missed the most. Hearing it now makes me feel quite emotional, the first real emotion I've felt since the accident, which is weird. Since coming out of the coma, I've been trying to get back to the Hope I was, I feel sort of detached somehow as if I can't quite connect with things. I mean, I joke and laugh, but it doesn't come as easy as before, it's as if I'm performing. I suppose it's normal; I mean, trivial things don't mean as much when you've almost died.

'Here,' Adam pats the back step for me to sit beside him. It's nice, just the two of us. It's like we're the only people awake in the whole world. We don't say anything for a bit and it occurs to me that I'm comfortable with that. I'm usually no good at silences, feeling as if I have to fill them. Eventually, I give in to old habits as I ask uncomfortably, 'Was I shouting very loudly?'

Adam shrugs. 'Yes, quite loudly. I woke up after hearing something – first I thought it was Julie snoring, but it wasn't. Anyway, it was you I heard. You were shouting and yelling for help.'

I don't know what to say to that, so I stare into my half-finished glass.

'Were you dreaming about the accident?' Adam asks it quietly, almost as if he's afraid of offending me.

I swirl the water about, clench the glass tighter in my hand. 'I dunno. I think maybe I was.'

'Do you want to talk about it?'

'It was only a dream.'

'A scary dream, though.'

I shrug, embarrassed.

'Hope,' he swallows nervously. 'Why didn't you get counselling after the accident?'

'I didn't think I would need it,' I say. 'They wanted me to talk about it. I didn't want to. I can't remember it anyway.'

'Well,' Adam seems to be choosing his words rather carefully, 'they mentioned to me and Julie that if you had flashbacks or nightmares you should see a doctor immediately.'

'One nightmare?' I make a face. 'I'm fine, Adam.'

'But maybe you need to remember, Hope. Maybe that's what the dreams are telling you.'

I don't reply. I wonder if maybe he's right. There was another time, years ago when I had nightmares and they eventually went but this nightmare was so real . . . I point to the sky which is lighting up a brilliant red and yellow. 'Look at that. Isn't it great?'

'Yes.' Adam says without interest as he takes a slug of water. 'Counselling works, Hope,' he says, then, 'It helps you deal with stuff.'

I wrap my arms about my legs, beginning to feel the chill in the early morning air. 'It helps only if you can talk about it,' I say. 'I don't think I can, Adam, I feel sick when I think of what happened. I can't even hear a plane in the sky any more without tensing up.'

'I noticed,' he says softly. 'You really should get help, Hope.'

I just stare at the dawn coming up.

'I got counselling when I was about sixteen, you know,' Adam says.

At first I don't believe I've heard correctly, so I turn to him and he flushes and looks quickly away. I put my hand on his arm. 'Why?' I ask quietly. 'Were you in an accident?'

'My whole life was an accident,' he says ruefully. He doesn't look at me as he says it; instead he stares at the brightening skyline. 'I've never really told anyone that before.' He laughs slightly.

I don't know if I should ask what for. After all, I haven't told him any of my secrets. I haven't told him that I've a fear of counselling. I'm afraid I'll be like my mother who never seemed to get cured no matter where she went. But at the same time, I don't want Adam to think that his telling me something so private is a thing to be dismissed. 'You're not a mess now,' I say and, without thinking, I link my arm through his. 'You're great.'

'I wish.' He gives another sad sort of smile. Then his blue eyes crinkling up, he says, 'You're great too, you know, and if you need to go to a counsellor, don't be ashamed.'

'It's not that,' I shrug, looking away from his steady gaze. 'I just, well, I don't want to end up like my mother, you know.'

'She was depressed,' Adam says. 'You're not.' He pauses. 'And it worked for me. I mean, I didn't think I needed it. But my mother made me go. She told me I was going to the doctor and instead I end up in a counsellor's office. I was furious; I didn't talk to her for months.'

He pauses and I wonder if he wants me to ask what he was there for. Instead, I surprise myself by saying wistfully, 'She cared about you. That was nice.'

'I'm sure your mother cared about you too.'

I shrug.

'Are you going to see your mother while we're here?'

'Perhaps.' The out-loud admission scares me slightly. Am I going to see her? And if I do, what will I say to her? 'Maybe,' I say.

'You should.' He sounds so confident. 'It's good to confront bad things.'

I think he knows what he's talking about. So I ask him. 'Why, did you?'

'I did.' Now he's looking at me. 'You'd never guess it, but in school I was the swotty one. The one with brains.'

I suppress a smile. How wouldn't I have guessed?

'I went to an all boys school and believe me, Hope, girls have nothing on blokes when they get their knife into you.'

'You were bullied?' I look at him and am not surprised.

Adam is kind and gentle and charmingly funny. He's also got a bewildered vibe about him and doesn't have the loud raucous sense of humour some guys have. The sense of humour guys tend to adopt when all together. He's probably too honourable for that.

'Yep.' He shrugs and winces. 'I hated sports. I was a good runner, quite fast, so I think that saved me at first. I pretended that I wanted to be on the sprint team and acted all macho for a while, but a macho guy that is into English and poetry and studies hard is soon found out.'

'I'll bet.'

'Anyway, I think you can always tell when someone isn't themselves and those blokes were like top-class sniffer dogs the way they hounded me down.'

His analogy makes me smile a little.

'They started off with name-calling and pushing and shoving and after a year or two, they started the physical stuff. I wasn't a complete wuss, mind, I did try to fight back and I could outrun them but my life was awful. In the end, I wouldn't get out of bed or go to school or do anything. My mother was in bits.'

'Yeah, I'd say so.' I snuggle into him. 'Poor you.'

'Poor me.' Cautiously he wraps his arm about my shoulder. It's nice. 'Apparently I was depressed and had no self-esteem and apparently I was also really angry. Anyway, it's true what they say – what doesn't kill you makes you stronger. I recovered, aced my A levels and now have a really good job. More than the rest of them have.'

His tone, slightly bitter, surprises me a little. Then, when I think about it, I'm not surprised. He should be bitter. 'Good for you.'

'And it'll be good for you too,' he says. He looks away

59

and says, in a practised casual tone, 'They gave Julie and me a list of counsellors over here, in case you decided to see one. And also the name of a doctor or two.'

'They gave or you asked?'

'Both.' His gaze meets mine. 'Anyway, you know they're there if you want.'

'Yeah. Thanks.'

'And there's something else, Hope –' He stops. 'No, no, forget it.'

'What?'

He studies me carefully and seems reluctant to go on. When he does, he speaks cautiously. 'It's about the accident, something you should know.'

'About the accident?'

'Yeah.'

He doesn't go on. I think he's waiting for me to give him permission; the only thing is, I can't even think about the accident, much less talk about it. 'Well?' My voice is quivering.

'You were buried underneath a lot of stuff when they found you.'

'I know.'

'A man was on top of you. They reckon he saved your life.'

'What?' I stare dumbly at him.

'They think that man saved your life.'

I turn away from Adam and stare at my hands. What can I say? I don't remember. I feel numb. 'Oh,' is all I can manage. I don't want to think about it.

We sit there for another while, saying nothing and watching the sun come up.

Later that day, after not thinking it through, but just going on instinct, I decide to go with the counselling. I suppose I made the decision because I don't want to have any more nightmares or feel sick whenever I see a packet of crisps. It was the crisps that had panicked me in the car, I realise now. Also, I suppose I'd like to know if my life was saved by a man I've never met and of course, I want Adam to think that his telling me about his bullying wasn't a complete waste of his time. I feel like killing those bullies for him. I was bullied too when I was a kid. Only bullied wouldn't be the right word, because I was a right vicious little thug myself. Our neighbour, Amanda Coonan, whose family ran the auctioneer business in Dingle, used to slag off my brother and me because we weren't as clean as she was. She poked fun at our house and our mother and everything. Most especially, however, she picked on Jamie, my little brother, because he wasn't able to defend himself as well as I could. Our mother kept telling us to ignore her, in the weary voice she used because she was depressed. But one day, I couldn't ignore Amanda any more. It started because she told Jamie he smelt. I remember throwing down my schoolbag, rolling up my sleeves and bursting into her cocoon of friends and demanding that she take her comment back. Of course she didn't, so I got into a fight with her. It was a real girly fight, pulling hair and scratching, until I gave her an enormous push. She ended up breaking her nose and it couldn't be reset. She left us alone after that. Even now when I think of her and of how she treated Jamie, my heart rate increases.

'Now Hope, soon to be cured person, this is your surprise!'

Julie has ordered Adam to drive to Dingle and now she's enquiring in an office about the three of us going out on a boat to see Fungi. Fungi is a dolphin that has lived in Dingle harbour for the last twenty years and Julie, ever since reading about him on the net, has been dying to see him. She, however,

61

is trying to make out that she's doing it for me as a celebration of the fact that I'll soon be back to the Hope I was. Once I told her and Adam that I'd go for counselling, the floodgates had opened.

'Thank God,' Julie said. 'You really need it.'

'What?' I almost laughed at her bluntness.

'Well,' she shifted uncomfortably, 'you're not the person you were, you know. You snap a lot and are very jumpy. You were never like that before.'

Of course, I'd snapped and demanded to know what she meant, and she and Adam had exchanged wary but amused looks. Julie had just shrugged in a 'point proven' kind of way.

And according to them I also flinch a lot and don't laugh like I used to. So, today I'm making a conscious effort to be more like I was. If I can remember how I was.

Julie comes back out to Adam and me and tells us that if Fungi fails to show, we won't have to pay. I grin. The dolphin always shows up. We're directed to a waiting area at the harbour and the three of us sit down outside in the weak sunshine. If I had known we were going on a boat, I'd have worn something a lot warmer. Julie is dressed in light white trousers and a T-shirt.

'Julie, will you not be cold out on the boat?'

She looks down at herself. 'I don't think so, it's a nice day.'

I decide not to say any more.

'And I don't feel the cold anyway,' she states, before giving a delicious shiver. 'Oh, I can't wait to see the dolphin. Have you ever seen him, Hope?'

'No.'

'I've eaten dolphin, though,' Adam says.

62

His comment is met by a gasp from a few tourists. I laugh and Adam announces loudly that it was a joke.

'It's not funny,' Julie says piously. 'Dolphins are very nice animals.'

'Mammals,' Adam corrects her. 'Dolphins are mammals.'

Julie glares at him. I swear, the two of them seem to be constantly bickering; they're like some old married couple. Just then Julie's phone rings with an unusual *Jaws* ring tone.

Adam sniggers at its significance.

Julie glances at it before obviously flinching and rejecting the call. 'I hate people who use their mobiles when they're talking to others,' she says cheerfully. As if on cue, Adam's phone rings. His is playing some classical music. He looks at it, then looks desperately at Julie, then looks at it again. 'Work,' he winces. 'Sorry.' He flicks it open and goes, 'Hello?'

'So rude,' Julie says loudly, folding her arms.

'What?' Adam says sharply, causing people to look at him. 'You have got to be joking!'

'No I'm not,' Julie says.

'He's talking into the phone,' I tell her.

Adam walks away from us and then Julie's phone rings again. Once again she rejects the call.

'You can answer it if you want,' I say. 'I don't mind.'

'No, it's fine.' She doesn't sound as if it's fine. It starts to ring for a third time.

'It might be important,' I say. 'Obviously someone wants to speak to you.'

'Sorry about that,' Adam rejoins us, tucking his phone into his pocket. 'Bloody head office is going mental because one of the branches is down fifty grand. Some stupid mix-up or other. I said I'd sort it.'

'Sort it? How?' Julie almost laughs. 'Can you bi-locate? Anyway, you're on leave.'

Adam pauses. 'Eh, actually,' he begins, 'I'm not.'

'What?' both of us say together.

'I'm not on holiday, they refused me leave in work, so I just went anyway.'

'No!' Julie gawks at him, sounding a little impressed. 'Are you mad? You'll be fired.'

'Nah.' Adam shakes his head. 'I can work just as well from here anyway. It's no big deal. They'd never fire me. I'm too –' he pauses, seemingly arrested by what he was about to say – 'good,' he finishes off slowly.

'But –'

'Don't look so shocked,' he says and grins at us. 'You know me, I play things safe.'

That at least is true. He'd never risk his job.

'And as for bi-locating,' he continues, 'I don't need to, I have a computer. I can send horrible e-mails to the staff in the shop telling them to get their fingers out.'

'Oh yeah, I'd really worry getting an e-mail from you.' Julie rolls her eyes. 'What do you do, write them in capital letters so they know you're cross?'

'Hey,' Adam says, and I don't know if he's mocking her or serious, 'good idea. I'll do that.'

Just then, the few tourists who are waiting on the marina surge forward and we notice that the boat has arrived to take us to see Fungi. We climb aboard, everyone jostling for the seats at the edge, and within minutes we're bouncing about heading for just outside the harbour. Julie's phone continues to ring until it's out of coverage and I can't help noticing that something akin to panic crosses her face every time it buzzes. We soon forget about the phone as

Fungi makes his appearance. Adam, who has his state of the art camera with him, attempts to take a photograph but is thwarted by the fact that Fungi keeps appearing and disappearing and it's impossible to tell where he'll be next.

'It's like the KitKat ad,' he moans, as yet again he takes a picture of the heaving waves. 'You know the one where the bears do all their tricks when the people turn their back.'

'J-J-Just look at the dolphin and enjoy it,' Julie says, through chattering teeth. 'You'll miss him completely if you insist on taking a photo and what's t-t-t point in that. Y-y-you have to grab what's on offer.'

'G-g-good point,' Adam mimics her, as he flicks his camera off. 'V-v-very profound.'

Julie ignores him. 'I wish someone had told me it was going to be this cold,' she says. 'I can't feel my fingers. H-h-how much longer?'

'It's about an hour,' I tell her. 'So, another twenty minutes.'

'U-u-ugh.'

Adam, in a gallant gesture, wraps his jacket about her shoulders.

She smiles at him and he smiles back at her. They look nice, I suddenly think.

At last we disembark after what has been a brilliant hour. Julie's phone begins to ring again.

'Who is it?' Adam asks, as we make our way back to the car.

'My mother,' Julie winces. She's still shivering. 'I don't want to talk to her.'

'And why don't you want to talk to your mother?'

'Because if I talk to her she'll know I'm not in class. She'll know I've taken unpaid leave.'

'So?'

'She'll go bananas.'

'So do what I do,' Adam says. 'Just pretend you are in work.'

'How? Being here doesn't exactly sound like a playground, does it? No, I'll ring her tonight, find out what she wants.'

'It might be important,' I say. 'I mean, she really is trying hard to contact you.'

And her phone rings again.

'Go on,' I press, 'just in case something's happened.'

I swear, Julie pales as she flicks it open. Adam gives her the thumbs-up and she sticks her tongue out at him. 'Hello? Mother? Hi.' Her voice couldn't be any more nervous if she tried. 'What's up?'

Her mother says something.

'In school,' Julie says and I wince. She sounds as if she's lying. Then she says, 'Yes, I am in school.'

'Miss Adcock, can you come in a minute,' Adam says, in what is meant to be a schoolteacher's voice.

Julie glares at him to shut up.

'Well, yes,' she snaps suddenly, 'OK, Mother, I am on holiday. Are you satisfied?' Pause. 'No, I didn't feel I had to tell you. You're not interested. You didn't even come to my show. Anyway, my friend –' she stops and holds the phone away from her ear. Her mother is screaming at her now. 'Mother, you are not listening to me. My friend –'

Adam and I don't know what to do. Julie is shaking violently, though whether it's from the cold or her mother's ear-bashing, we don't know.

'Ju,' Adam begins, 'Are you –'

'That is Adam,' Julie says. She sounds really upset. 'No,

I have not gone away with a man. I am with two friends, one who almost died and another one who, well, who is my other friend who didn't almost die. Thank you.' Julie slams the phone closed and blinks rapidly.

'Maybe you shouldn't have answered it,' I say meekly. 'Sorry about that.'

I think Julie might cry. 'She rang me at work and found out I wasn't there. So when she heard I was on leave she just lost it.' She sounds as if she's just run a marathon. I can't imagine being that scared of a parent. Surely that's not the way it should be? 'Do you know what she said? Do you?'

Both of us shake our heads. We're blocking up the narrow street as we stand there in a small triangle, but people move on to the road to get by us.

'She told me that taking leave is not a good option if I want to get promoted. Can you imagine?' Her voice comes out on a small sob. 'Nothing I do is ever good enough for her.'

'Hey,' I put my arm about her. 'Don't cry. Come on. She's probably just angry you never told her you were coming over here.'

'I think –' Julie takes a sleeve of Adam's jacket and wipes her eyes. 'I think she wants me to become some famous revolutionary teacher – you know teaching kids by telepathic transference and, and, winning loads of awards.'

'And can you not do that?' I deadpan.

She chokes back a laugh and sniffs, 'I'll say Dad will be on now. She always gets him to call to back her up.'

'Well, definitely don't answer the phone any more.'

'I won't!'

After shopping for a few bits and pieces, including the local rag, we go back to the cottage, where Julie has the longest shower on record to try to get warm again and then later Adam offers to bring us out clubbing. 'We'll find somewhere, what do you say?' he says to us.

He really is so good. Julie loves dancing and she's still quite upset about the phone call from her mother. I don't think her father has rung yet.

She agrees and they turn to me.

'Sorry, guys, I'm tired.' And I am. I'm tired pretending to be myself and laughing and joking with the two of them when all I really want to do is – well, I don't even know.

So they bid me goodbye and I wave them off.

It's nice to be on my own, where I don't have to talk. I sit down, my leg sore from all the hobbling about, and something in the local paper, thrown across the sofa, catches my eye. It's in a column titled, DUNPORT'S SUCCESSES. A picture of a handsome man smiles out at me. My heart thumps so hard, I feel sick.

Jack.

Jack Dunleavy.

The Jack Dunleavy that I'd fallen for way back when I was eighteen. The Jack that had bunked off school with me, the Jack I'd told all my secrets to, the Jack I'd lost my virginity to and finally the Jack that had done brilliantly in his exams and gone to college and who I'd never heard from again. I pick up the paper and read:

Local man, Jack Dunleavy, is the managing director of the Gleeson Hotel Group. The newest hotel in the chain will be opened in Dunport in August. 'I'm very excited to be coming back and giving employment to the local area,' Jack said when interviewed. 'Dunport is a beautiful place and more people should get to know about it.' Jack will be in town in July for the official opening of the Hotel and promises us a famous mystery guest to do the honours. Well done, Jack, we're proud of you.

I stare at the picture some more, then very deliberately turn over the page. That is one man I do not want to see again. And yet . . .

8

THE DAY OF my counselling session, I wake up early. I know that some time in the night I had another nightmare because I woke up suddenly, sweat pouring off my body and I had to hobble up and change my pyjamas. I found it hard to go back to sleep. Finally, at around six, I haul myself out of my sleeping bag and to my surprise find it's really warm in the cottage. Bright light is seeping in under the curtains and I pull them apart. Sunlight dances through the window, pouring over the tattered furniture and giving the room a beauty I didn't know it possessed. It is going to be a glorious day. I stand for a few seconds, just drinking in the view. It's by far the clearest day we've had so far. God, I think I had forgotten how beautiful the landscape is. Blue sky meeting sun-drenched aquamarine sea. Blue mountains in the distance. Green trees, yellow gorse. It is a riot of fabulous splendour and in complete contrast to the duller days of the past two weeks.

I head into the kitchen and put on the kettle and while I'm waiting for it to boil, I butter a couple of slices of bread.

A few minutes later, I carry my mug of tea and my bread outside to the front of the house. It's not as easy as it sounds and it takes me a couple of trips due to the crutch. The sun is already warm on my face and I sit awkwardly down on the grass, one leg tucked under me, one leg splayed out, eating my breakfast and staring at the panoramic view. It's so peaceful. The only sound is the swish of the sea from far away and the occasional car going by on the road outside and someone shouting 'fuck' very loudly.

Fuck? Very loudly?

I turn and stare about. Striding along across the field, wearing faded, tattered jeans and a black T-shirt, is a man. He's about thirty with long tangled dark hair and dark stubble. As he gets closer, I can see his eyes are an angry flashing blue and his face is incredibly handsome except for the extraordinarily cross expression he seems to have adopted. 'I'm trying to sketch,' he says, standing about five feet away from me, legs apart, hands splayed in an exasperated manner.

'Excuse me?' I quirk an eyebrow, resenting his tone.

'I said –' he crosses towards me, hopping over the fence that separates his field from ours – 'that I am trying to paint.'

'And?' I stand up, scrabbling for my crutch and wondering if the tea I have is hot enough to throw at him if he's some kind of looney. 'What has that to do with me?'

'Nothing,' he states, snorting. 'Nothing at all. Thank you.' He continues to glare at me.

'Well then.' My hackles rise, my new bristliness coming in handy for dealing with this obnoxious man: 'don't confront me in that manner again. I am quietly having my breakfast and you decide to shout at me.'

'Yes,' he nods emphatically. 'You are in the way of my view.'

'It's not your view,' I state. 'Are you mad?' The question pops out without me thinking about it. As it does, it occurs to me what a stupid thing it is to ask someone who is obviously unhinged.

71

'Yes, I'm bloody mad,' he snaps. 'You are in my view.'

'Sorry, I don't know what you're on about.' I decide that it might be safer to go into the house than stay outside with this guy. 'I'm going in.'

'Good,' he says. 'Hurray!'

The nerve! 'Actually, I won't. I'm staying here.' I sit back down again.

He looks at me as if he can't quite believe what I've just done. 'You mean,' he splutters, 'you're just going to stay there and ruin my picture?'

'What picture?'

'The one I'm bloody trying to sketch.' He jabs in the direction he has come from and in the distance I see an artist's easel all set up. 'I'm sketching and you are blotting out the yellow gorse.'

The gorse stretches for miles. 'I'm not that big,' I say sarcastically. 'And if you'd come over and asked me politely to move, then maybe I would have. But seeing as you didn't, tough luck.' I give him a pleasant smile, only it's meant to annoy him. He stares at me for a few seconds, his blue eyes a combination of anger and confusion. Then he takes a few deep breaths and says in a strangled sort of way, 'Will you please move so that I can get on with painting my picture?'

'Move where?'

I think he thinks I'm being difficult. 'Any bloody where,' he snaps.

His snapping makes me cross again. I move two inches to my right. 'Here?'

'Oh, don't be ridiculous.' He glares at me. 'You're a very thorny person, aren't you?'

'Have you ever heard something along the lines of pot,

72

kettle and black?' I enquire. This guy has ceased to bother me. I think of him rather as I would an unpleasant boss.

'Have you ever heard something along the lines of silk purse and sow's ear?'

'What?'

'You are ruining my picture!'

'So move your easel.'

'Move your big round bulk!'

Oh. That hurt. 'No chance.'

More glares. He's moving his mouth but no words are coming out. Daintily I eat my bread, knowing I'm infuriating him. And glad that I can vent my anger on someone other than my best friends.

'Please,' he eventually spits out. 'Please will you move your, your, yourself?'

'All you had to do was ask,' I say sweetly as I hoist myself up, balancing on my crutch. 'Now, please can you tell me where I have permission to sit in my own garden?'

He's working inwardly. 'Maybe over there,' he answers evenly. 'Beside the wall.'

'That's in the shade.'

'Well, perhaps you can sit over there.' He points to the corner of the house.

'Fine.' I slowly stand up. 'I will sit there.'

'Thanks.'

I watch him as he turns his back and stomps off. He's got quite a nice bum and good broad shoulders. Pity about his personality. Still, I quite like the fact that despite my being on a crutch, with a bald head and a slowly healing face, he offered me no sympathy whatsoever. It's seems so long since I've been treated like a normal person.

* * *

73

At three o'clock precisely, I'm sitting in the counsellor's office. Apparently I have to be assessed to see if there is anything wrong with me. Julie and Adam have told me that they'll pick me up in an hour's time. They've spent the whole trip annoying each other. Adam chatted up a girl called Corina in a club the night before and Corina gave him her number. Julie keeps asking if he's going to ring her.

'Why? You jealous?'

'No,' Julie looked incredulously at him. 'Just curious.'

'Well, the answer is no,' Adam said. 'I am not going to ring her. I am here for a holiday. I'm not here to spend money on some girl I'll never see when it's over.'

'You tight-arse,' Julie snapped.

'Nothing wrong with having a tight arse,' Adam sniggered back at her.

And even though I'm terrified to be spending a whole hour in a doctor's office, it's better than listening to the two of them. I'm alone now, just sitting on the edge of a chair, waiting for the counsellor to come back in. His office is like any office anywhere. There are no fancy gadgets or machines bleeping away, unless you count a rather tatty ancient Dictaphone sitting on the desk.

'Hope, how's it going?'

I glance at the door where a man, surprisingly young, has just entered. He's tall, rangy and is wearing faded jeans and a white T-shirt. There's a tattoo of an angel on his wrist and on his finger he sports a bright and shiny wedding ring. His brown hair is long and he wears it in a ponytail. He really isn't what I was expecting and I feel a bit more relaxed. Just from looking at him, he gives off a vibe of living with a hippie girlfriend who spends her time cooking organic meals and wearing shoes spun out of hemp.

74

'Tim,' he says, holding out his hand.

'Hi.' I manage a smile.

'Well now,' Tim says, in a voice that conjures up lazy summer days, 'I was reading your file, Hope. Pretty bad experience for you?' He sits himself down in a chair opposite me, ignoring the chair behind his desk.

'Yeah.' I can't look at him now. Please don't make me talk about it, I silently pray.

'Well,' Tim says, 'First, I'm going to ask you some questions –'

'Not about the accident,' I blurt out. 'I can't remember it.'

Tim pauses and seems to be studying me. 'No,' he says softly, 'not about the accident. What I have to do first is get a picture of how you're coping since the accident. This will tell me how severe your symptoms are. It will also tell me if you do or don't have PTSD. Working on what I find, we can begin helping you – is that OK?'

'Yeah. I suppose.'

'Now, I've a form here,' he reaches behind him and retrieves a form from his desk, 'and I'd like you to answer these questions. Your answers can vary from none, which means no symptoms to a lot, which means –'

'A lot of symptoms.'

'Yeah.' Tim nods, grinning. 'OK?'

'OK.'

'Cool.' Now he begins to search for a pen. He finds one, bitten to bits and sticks it in his mouth. 'Right, let's start. Number one, do you have upsetting memories about what happened?'

'I try not to think about it.'

'But if you did think about it?' he presses.

I shrug. 'I suppose a lot,' I admit.

75

He ticks that answer off. 'How about nightmares?'

'A few but getting more frequent.'

'I'll put that down as moderate.' Another little tick. 'Flashbacks?'

'None.'

'Anything make you anxious that didn't before?'

'Planes,' I admit with a smile and he smiles too.

'Understandable. Anything else?'

'Crisps. Sudden noises.'

He ticks a box. I don't know what one. 'Have you lost interest in work or any other activity?'

'I don't like going out as much.'

'How about your relationship with other people? Has that changed?'

'I suppose a little. I find it hard to be interested in them. But,' I hesitate and decide to go on, 'well, mainly it's me. I feel I've lost myself. It's like I'm numb and all I can feel is anger now and again.'

'OK. Good.' He nods a little. 'That was my next question. How about imagining the future, do you have any thoughts on that? Is it hard to imagine?'

'Well, I kind of think there's no point really. I can't control it, can I? I mean, I could work my butt off and still die.'

'Did you always feel that way or is it just since the accident?'

I don't answer. Instead I swallow hard.

'Well,' he presses.

'I've felt like that, well, since,' I pause. I can remember the exact moment only I don't want to. 'Since I was about sixteen, I guess.'

'Sixteen, eh? Did something happen then?'

I shrug, aiming for casual but failing quite badly as my voice trembles. 'My brother died.'

'I see.' He pauses, writes a note down. 'Sleep? Is that hard?'

'Yeah.'

'Do you get angry more often? More irritable?'

'I suppose. I feel edgy or something, I can't explain it. It's like I don't feel safe.'

Tim relaxes into his seat and puts the form back on his desk. 'OK, Hope, well done. That wasn't so bad was it?'

'Nope.'

'OK,' he says again and nods. 'So now, you mentioned that your brother died?'

'Yeah.' I sound cautious.

'Can I ask you, Hope, if you've ever had any other trauma in your life? I feel that his death was a trauma, am I right?'

I blink and the silence seems to go on for ever.

'Trauma,' I eventually stammer out.

'Yes,' he smiles slightly and nods in an encouraging way. 'Trauma can mean different things to different folks. Basically, I'm asking if you've ever had anything unpleasant happen to you that changed the way you viewed things or that made you feel that the world was an unsafe place to be? Anything at all?'

'Everything?' I gulp out. 'Like all the bad stuff?'

Now it's his turn to blink. 'Has there been a lot?'

'Well, it was all a long time ago. I mean, stuff happened a long time ago. I'm over it all now.'

'Well, if you're over it, you should be able to talk about it. Tell me and we'll see.'

I start at the beginning. I can't quite make my voice work the way I want it to. It's as if it doesn't want to come out. I wonder if talking will oil it a bit. 'Well, my daddy died when I was six.'

'That would be scary for a little kid. That would make them rethink things.'

I hardly acknowledge that. I feel as if I'm talking about someone else. A stranger's life. 'Well, I wasn't there. He died in work from a sudden heart attack. I didn't understand at the time, not fully. I remember his funeral and me and my little brother playing among the black coats in the hall. And my mother crying all the time. That was scarier. I mean, you don't expect to see your parents cry, do you?'

Tim shakes his head.

'I remember thinking he was going to come back and make my mother happy again. But he didn't and that was awful. I couldn't understand that. I was angry at him then. And I thought, well, if he's gone, then other things can go too. Do you know?'

'Yes.'

'I became a bit of a worrier after that.'

'And did your mother not explain and reassure you?'

The question is like a well-aimed missile at my defences. The numb feeling I have when discussing it begins to crumble slightly. 'Well, you know, she did her best. Things sort of changed then.'

'How?'

I try to speak and can't. My mouth sort of opens up and some strangled word comes out. Tim holds up his hand. 'Don't, it's OK.'

I shake my head. Bloody hell. 'My mother just got sadder,' I state as matter-of-factly as I can.

'Sadder? As in depressed?'

'Yeah. Only I was six and didn't know it. Maybe I should have. I mean, she used to be so happy and all. She cried a lot at first and then she stopped. But after she stopped, she didn't get up or clean or cook or do anything. And we didn't go to school, we just played all day – me and my brother. And we never got washed or anything.' And that's when I really dry up. Well, my voice dries up but my forehead is coated in sweat.

Tim passes me a tissue and nods. 'That's OK, Hope,' he says gently. 'We don't have to go into it all now, anyway. We've loads of time. The whole summer.'

'I don't know if I can anyway.' I pat my forehead with the tissue. 'It was a long time ago, I never think of it. Never talk about it.'

He says nothing but I think I've just said too much.

'I'll book you in for next Friday morning,' Tim says. 'That's a week away. Does that suit you?'

I nod. There is no way I'm saying any more.

'I want you to fill in these forms over the next week.' He passes me three forms, which I take and feign interest in. I'm really sweating now. And breathing hard.

'Now Hope,' he says, 'between now and next week, you have a bit of work to do. I want you to fill that form out every time you find yourself in a situation that evokes traumatic memories. That's the trigger. Like the crisps you mentioned or the planes. Then I want you to write how it affects you. Then I want to know if you deliberately avoid the trigger. And finally, I want you to record your anxiety level from one to ten. Ten is the worst – OK?'

I study the form. There are boxes and things to be filled in but it all seems easy enough. 'OK.'

'I'll see you back here next Friday then. And we'll talk about treatment and diagnosis.'

'Right.' I pocket the form and turn to go, before turning back to add 'Thanks.'

'No problem. See you next week.'

I don't know why, but I come out of the office feeling a little brighter than when I went in. I think it's the fact that with the forms in my hands, I feel a little in control. I haven't felt in control of my life for years.

9

'HEY,' JULIE IS peering out the window. 'There's a strange man in our garden.'

I'm struggling to fit into a pair of jeans. It's the first time I've worn them and they are not easy to get on, especially as I have to make them fit over the plaster on my leg. We're going out to a pub in Dunport and already I feel sick in case I meet someone I know. But I don't want Adam and Julie to think that I've gone all weird and hermit-like by refusing to go out. I want to try and get back to the pub girl I used to be.

'A strange man as in you don't know him or strange as in odd,' I ask, cutting my finger a little on the zip as I suck my stomach in as hard as it will go.

'Both,' Julie mutters.

'Here, let's have a look.' Zip still open, I peer out the curtains with her. When I see the easel going up, I realise who it is.

'That's the guy from the cottage across the way,' I say. 'He's horrible.'

We get a glimpse of profile.

'Mmm, not that horrible,' Julie nudges me. 'How'd you know him?'

'I met him yesterday morning. Trust me, he's horrible.'

I suck myself in, squeeze my eyes shut tight and hoist up the zip.

'What is he doing?' Julie is still staring out at him, albeit in a discreet way.

'Painting, apparently. But he really shouldn't be in the garden.'

'Maybe he'll knock and ask permission.'

From what I'd seen of him, I think this is highly unlikely.

And so it turns out. He sets up, adjusts his chair, sits down and begins to do whatever artists do.

'Jesus, he has a nerve,' I mutter. 'I'm going out to say it to him.'

'Maybe Adam should go out to him.' Julie attempts to pull me back as I make my slow way to the front door.

'Adam is busy sorting out his work problems,' I explain. 'And that guy shouldn't be in our garden. Besides,' I wave my crutch menacingly, 'I have this.'

Julie looks askance at me. 'Oh, Hope, I don't want a fight. Fighting with my mother is enough for me at the moment.'

'So stay here.'

She hops about from foot to foot, her fingers to her mouth. 'Ohhh, no, I'll go with you. I'll stand behind you, but I'll just tell Adam. Just hang on until I get Adam.' She flies up the stairs and I watch her go.

I don't need Adam. I hop towards the front door, fling it open and bellow, 'What are you doing?'

'Fuck. Shit!' He stands up and I note that he's somehow drawn a big brown line right through his picture. He glares at me. 'Do you know what you've just done?'

'No.' I hop towards him. 'Do you know you're spoiling our view?'

'You have just made me make a major mistake with this

82

painting. You've probably knocked me a month off schedule.' He approaches me. Shit, I think, he's tall and menacing. He walks like a tiger, all loose-limbed and nonchalant. Though he's not very nonchalant at the moment. 'Have you any idea what this means?'

I stand my ground. 'Do you know that it's polite to knock and ask permission before you go setting yourself up in someone's garden?'

He glances about at the overgrown grass. 'It's hardly a garden.'

'Don't get personal.'

'It's not personal. It's not your garden.'

'At the moment it is and you have no permission to be here.'

That seems to throw him. 'I need to be here.'

'Hope,' Adam says, striding across the grass. 'All right?' Julie is tottering along on her high heels behind him.

'I'm just telling this guy that he shouldn't be in our garden.'

'Adam,' Adam holds out his hand. 'And you are?'

Ice blue eyes regard Adam angrily. 'Logan.'

Despite my annoyance, I explode in a laugh. 'Logan? Nobody is called Logan. What's your real name?'

He looks offended. 'Logan,' he says again.

'Oh. Sorry.' I bite my lip so I won't giggle.

He gives a 'hmph'.

'Well, Logan,' Adam says in a very reasonable tone of voice, 'are you planning on staying here long?'

Logan swallows hard. It's obvious he's not used to being reasonable. 'As long as it takes.' He glares at me. 'And it'll take longer now because she –' he says 'she' in an outraged tone – 'she has set me back about a month. Look,' he jabs at his strange-looking picture with his brush. 'I'll have to get rid of that line. See, look what she made me do.'

I roll my eyes. I feel a tiny bit guilty but not enough to apologise. Anyway, he shouldn't be here.

'And don't roll your eyes. It's obvious you have no idea of the finer things in life.'

'Well, I know what manners are,' I snort and fold my arms.

Julie giggles nervously and tries to make out she's coughing.

'Right, well,' Adam attempts to right the situation with a smile. 'It would have been nice if you'd asked to use the garden.'

No answer.

Adam cocks his head to one side. 'Otherwise, we'll have to inform the landlord that we have a trespasser.'

'Maurice won't do anything.'

'Oh he might,' Adam says casually, turning away. 'When we ask for our money back and he's left with an empty cottage until September.'

'It's only a garden,' Logan snaps.

'Exactly,' Adam nods. 'Our garden.'

'Ha ha.' I do a passable impression of Nelson from *The Simpsons*. I want to cheer and clap Adam on the back.

'You are getting on my nerves.' Logan jabs his brush at me now. Then he swallows hard and with major effort says, 'Can I use your garden to paint?'

'Yes.' Adam nods. 'Well, that's if the girls agree as well.'

'Oh,' Julie gives a bright, charming smile up into his sullen face. 'I don't mind. I'd love to see you paint. I love paintings.'

'I work alone,' he says. 'I need silence.'

'Oh.'

'Hope?' Adam asks.

I think he's got off too easily. I want to say no but Adam

would kill me. 'He has to move when I want to see the view,' I say instead.

Logan's eyes widen incredulously. 'Are you completely mad?'

'That's a yes.' Adam glares at me. 'So, we'll leave you to it.' He looks at me and Julie. 'Are you ready?'

'Yes we are,' Julie says.

The last I see of Logan, as we drive off is him staring at me in a way that I can't quite figure out. So I stick out my tongue and he gives me the two fingers and a scowl.

Charming.

Dunport is hopping. Any pretty fishing village on a sunny evening in June in one of the most beautiful places on earth is bound to be busy. The little harbour is all lit up with white twinkly lights that reflect on the black water. The slap and plash of water against the fibreglass boats is so rhythmic, you could fall asleep to it. The smell of chips and sea is a heady one, and always reminds me of home. And of summer. I begin to wonder why it's taken me so long to come home. But even as I'm wondering, I know it'll only be for a fleeting moment. And if I think harder, I'll wonder why on earth I've bothered to come. Julie and Adam had suggested Dingle as an alternative but I know they really wanted to try out Dunport.

It's a warm night and people have gathered along the harbour wall and outside the pubs and are drinking and laughing and chatting to each other. Mingling with the outside noise is the music from inside the pubs. A sign on a road leading from the harbour reads *Site for new Gleeson Hotel. Opening August.* I can just about see, in the half-light, the hulk of a new building in the distance.

'So, Hope,' Adam intrudes on my thoughts, looking expectantly at me, 'where to? Which pub is best?'

I turn from the sign. 'I don't know now,' I answer. 'Lynch's used to be.' I point to the Poitín Jar. 'It's also called Lynch's,' I explain. 'It was the only pub with entertainment but I suppose that's all changed.'

'Lynch's it is,' Julie links her arm in mine. 'Come on – let's go.'

Lynch's is the biggest pub in the town. We push past a crowd of people gathered about the front door and enter. It has changed but not too much. It's cleaner and airier but it doesn't have the modern minimalist décor that so many pubs are going for. It's still quite cosy and even though it's June, there is a turf fire burning merrily up at the back. Musicians are setting up and to Adam's delight it's a traditional Irish band. He plonks down on a seat almost in front of them. 'Come on, sit down.' He pats the seats beside him. Julie does as she's bid but I hesitate. I do not want to draw attention to myself and Adam certainly will if he insists on clapping and cheering along to the songs. 'Hope,' Adam says. 'Sit, before our seats are taken.'

I have no choice. I sit beside Adam, my jeans screaming in protest about my hips.

'So, my round.' Adam digs his hand into his pocket and asks what we want.

'Southern Comfort and red,' I say.

'Red?' Adam raises his eyebrow.

'Just ask,' I grin.

I've missed my southies and reds in London. There is no such thing as red lemonade over there. It's the first time I've had red in ages.

'Julie?'

86

'I'll have . . .' Julie screws up her face. She likes to try out different drinks all the time. She maintains that you can't have a favourite drink unless you've tried everything. 'I'll have the same as Hope,' she declares. 'I never had red before.'

'OK.' Adam saunters off, and is soon swallowed up by the crowd at the bar.

I focus my eyes on the wood grain on the table. I pretend to study the beer mats and my nails and anything really to avoid looking up and perhaps making eye contact with someone I knew. Though to be honest, it's unlikely. All my peers have probably left long ago. The opportunity for employment in Dunport wouldn't exactly be great, but I'm sure some of the older people would know me. Julie however is looking about. 'There aren't many great-looking fellas here, are there?'

'Most of the younger guys will probably have left for Dublin,' I answer. 'Or else they're sitting outside. No one with any cred is going to be listening to this band. It's only the auld wans in here.'

'Oh really.' Her eyes widen with disappointment. 'Maybe we should sit outside then.'

'And deprive Adam of the Shamrocks?' That's the name of the band.

'Well,' Julie lowers her voice and says, 'I think he's gay. That's probably why he likes hairy men.'

'Julie!' I don't find it funny. 'That's not nice. Adam is not gay and even if he was, so what?'

'Well then, why didn't he contact that girl he met the other night? She was mad into him.'

'Maybe he wasn't mad into her!'

'Have you ever known him to have a girlfriend?'

'That doesn't mean anything.'

87

'A guy like him should be straight,' Julie pouts. 'He's kind and considerate and knows how to treat a girl.'

Her phone starts to ring. She glances at it and turns it off. 'Your mother again?'

Julie nods glumly. 'Every time I turn it on, there's about six million messages from her. Dad hasn't rung at all, which is weird. She's obviously keeping him in reserve, like a machine-gun in a war.'

'And have you talked to her since?'

'No. She'll just have to let it go. When I became a teacher she was like this too, but she stopped eventually.'

Before we can say any more, Adam arrives back with the drinks in his hand. He's just bought orange for himself. 'I'll drink when we get home,' he says. 'I'm not leaving my car overnight.'

'Ohh,' Julie takes her drink from him. 'It'll be no fun being sober when Hope and I'll be drunk.'

'Well,' Adam says glumly, 'I need a clear head for tomorrow. That shop is sending me all their accounts for the last few months. I need to locate that missing fifty grand.'

'Oh, have they still not found it?' I'd forgotten about that.

'There's something they're not telling me,' Adam says grimly. 'So I've ordered all their files to be e-mailed to me. They're arriving in my mailbox as we speak.'

'Do you think they're on the fiddle?'

'I don't know,' Adam stares into his orange. 'But I have a week to sort it before my boss totally flips.'

'Poor Adam.' Julie pats his arm.

'But we all have tonight,' I say, then raise my glass. I take a gulp of my drink and savour the sweetness of the whiskey and red. Julie, on the other side of me, winces as she tastes hers. 'It's like lollipops.' Another cautious sip. 'Melted lollipops.'

Adam then has a try and he likes it. So he decides that as Julie doesn't want it, he'll drink it, then he says, aw bloody hell, he might as well get drunk with us. Drown his sorrows.

The Shamrocks have just begun playing and Adam is listening with rapt attention to the noise they're making as they sing about emigration and other general horror in an upbeat, bodhrán-beating way. The lead singer, if that's what he is, is doing some sort of an Irish jig about the stage, his heels clicking just ever so slightly out of rhythm with the music. His fuzzy grey hair is bouncing all over the place and he's yelling 'yahoo' in a very cowboyish way as he kicks his heels up as high as they will go. It's complete shite but Adam is lapping it up. He's not the only one. Some Americans behind us are clapping along and reading deep and sombre meanings into the man's performance and declaring loudly that the entertainment is 'so Irrrrrish'. I roll my eyes and think that Dermot Lynch, the guy that owns the pub, is a genius. And so are the Shamrocks. I wonder how much they get paid.

Eventually, it's my round. I dread going to the bar. So far, however, I haven't seen anyone I know. Mostly it's tourists. As Julie drains the dregs of her pint, I stand up. I hope that she or Adam will offer to go to the bar for me and I do a little stumble on my crutch, but Julie is attempting to make eye contact with some big bulky, bodybuilder fella she's spotted. She is such a flirt. Adam is so caught up in the music that he hardly registers I've stood up. And so, hopping slightly, I get out of my chair and make my way through the crowd. The good thing about being on a crutch is that people do let me through. I flirt with the idea of using it every time I walk into a pub. It's like the Red Sea parting before Moses. In no time, I'm tapping my fingers expectantly on the long polished wooden counter. The two barmen are flying about in a frenzy as if it's the last time anyone in the world will get a drink ever. That certainly has changed. Slow was the buzz word for a long time behind Lynch's bar. Unfortunately because I've no hair and my face is still slightly swollen, I don't exactly feel attractive enough to catch the barman's eye. I wait for a while. Beside me is a man sitting on a bar stool nursing a pint and he seems familiar. He's quite drunk and I spend the time trying to figure out who he is.

'Now, Mr D,' the barman says to him, ignoring me for the millionth time, 'what's it to be?'

Of course! It's Jack Dunleavy's dad. He has a look of Jack about him, though a much older, beer-bellied Jack. He mumbles out something and the barman goes to get it. When he comes back, the barman places a pint in front of Mr Dunleavy and ignores me again. 'Oy!' I finally shout. 'How long are you going to keep me waiting?'

One of the barmen turns to me. Looks at me and I look at him. And all I can think is, Oh shit. Oh balls. Or whatever curse word best describes attracting attention to yourself and then wishing you hadn't. It's Declan Lynch's son. The one who would have been a year behind me in school. To my absolute horror he crosses towards me, a hesitant grin on his face. I can only assume it's because he knows who I am. Normally people don't smile at others who have been complaining. 'Hey, *cé bhfuil tú?*' he says.

I feign a blank look at his Irish. He's asking how I am. A lot of people in Dunport would have Irish as their first language.

'Isn't it yourself?' he asks over the noise. His accent is as strong as mine used to be.

I decide there and then to draw on my meagre acting experience, which involved playing a tree in a primary school production of *Hansel and Gretel*. 'What sort of a question is that?' I ask archly, putting on an American accent. Well, it's a cross between a Kerry accent and an American accent.

'Hope?' the fella says. I can't remember his name. 'Are you Hope Gardner from beyond the cross?'

'I'll tell you who I am,' I say, 'I'm a customer and I want a drink.'

I notice uncertainty in his eyes. 'Are you not from around here?'

'Does every customer get a quiz before they order a drink?' I snap. I feel a bit mean as the semi-smile dies on his face. Another man behind me yells that he wants some service and he wants it now. He's a big loud Texan or something.

'I'm sorry,' the barman says. 'I thought you were a neighbour of ours come back. You look a lot like a girl that used to live around here.' Then he studies me, oblivious to the American, who's getting more annoyed. 'Or maybe you don't,' he says. 'The girl I knew had more hair for starters.'

I don't know if I should be offended.

'So what would you like?' he asks.

'Two Southern Comforts and red and a pint of Guinness.'

He looks again at me and too late I remember my accent. 'Pronto,' I Americanise.

'OK.'

The drinks arrive after a while. The Guinness takes ages to settle. As he brings them over, I notice him point me out to the other barman. I now see that he's the other brother, Greg, the one who had been in my class in school. He glances curiously in my direction. I dip my head so he can't see me properly. As the younger lad approaches with the drinks and takes my money, he says, 'My brother thinks

91

you're the image of Hope too. Are you sure you're not a cousin or something?'

'I think I know who I am,' I scoff as I take two of the drinks. I'll send Adam up for the Guinness. 'Can you keep an eye on that pint until I come back and get it? I'm on a crutch see?'

'I'll bring it down for you if you like?'

'No, you're very busy, it's OK.'

I take the drinks and head down to the table.

'Adam,' I hiss, 'go up and get your Guinness, would you? The barman recognised me and I don't want him to.'

He and Julie look at me. 'My mother doesn't know I'm back yet,' I explain. 'It wouldn't be fair for her to hear it from someone else.'

Adam jumps up and heads to the bar.

'We could have gone somewhere else,' Julie says gently.

'I know.' I stare into my drink. 'Perhaps we should have.' I can't explain it. I think I came tonight because I needed to see the town from an observer's point of view before I go getting tangled up in it again. 'But I wanted to come tonight. To see if it's like I remembered.'

'And is it?' Julie asks.

'Yes and no,' I answer.

She looks at me a second more before I shrug and say again, 'Yes and no.' I lift my glass into the air. 'Cheers.'

'Cheers.'

I mean 'yes' because it's the same as I remember – the pubs, the *craic*, the noise. But I mean 'no' because it's not the same – the pubs are different, the *craic* is different and the noise is different. But it's down to interpretation, I think. As I look at Adam who is now carrying his pint down, being careful not to spill it, and Julie happily chatting up that bronzed, bodybuilder type, who is telling her that he's a self-employed businessman, which is impressing Julie a lot, I realise that Dunport is lovely, was always lovely, but when you're miserable and unhappy, nowhere ever seems good or safe and I'd blamed it on my home town.

I look at the Lynch boys behind the bar – well, glimpses of them, trading banter with the customers and laughing loudly at jokes – and I realise that I'd always felt threatened by their good humour, felt it was directed at me, instead of enjoying it as I might have done.

I find myself thinking of my mother. And that's when the lightness begins to leave me. How could I think of her differently? Maybe in order to do that, I'll have to see her. But in seeing her, I'll be looking back on myself. And that might just be too painful.

It's a strange night. We all drink too much. Through the haze, I see Julie writing her mobile number down on Mr Bodybuilder's arm. Then he kisses her briefly on the cheek and leaves with a load of mates. They all look like Action Man clones. They're shouting and laughing and back-slapping each other. Adam looks a bit miffed at the fella writing his number on Julie's arm but he soon forgets about it as he's invited up on stage by the Shamrocks to bang a bodhrán as accompaniment to some song. He dedicates his playing to his friends. He doesn't say our names. Julie, I and the Americans behind us all cheer loudly at him as he plays terribly but with passion.

And then the pub closes and we're all turfed out.

Night over.

10

THINGS WITH ADAM'S job must be in a very bad way because two days later he hands Julie the keys of his car and tells her to drive it into Dunport and get the shopping.

'But, Adam, your car,' Julie stammers as she stares at the car keys with disbelief, 'it's expensive and not for the faint hearted.'

That's what Adam always says about his car.

'It won't be my car for much longer if I don't sort this mess out,' Adam says without taking his eyes from the print-outs lying scattered over his tiny box room. 'So go on, knock yourself out.'

'D'you want a hand?' Julie asks. 'I'm good with figures.'

'And I'm good with words,' I offer.

They both shoot weird looks at me and don't comment.

'Buy me a nice Australian red,' Adam says, 'the one we had last week – that would help.'

'OK.' Julie jangles the keys: 'just don't blame me if I crash your car.'

The fact that he doesn't reply is a bit worrying.

Julie and I get the grocery shopping in Tralee and then divert to Dunport, to the gorgeous deli and wine shop, to buy Adam his Australian red. I hobble out of the car behind Julie and she holds the door of the shop open for me.

'Now, Australian wines,' she says as we enter. 'Where are they again?'

'Right at the –' my voice trails off.

Julie, oblivious, keeps going while I stand, completely frozen, my stomach somersaulting crazily as I look towards the deli counter. My mother. It has to be her. In fact, I know it's her because she's probably the only fifty-year-old woman in the whole of Kerry that still dresses like a hippie. Her grey hair is tied back with a patterned handkerchief and she's wearing long dangly earrings that touch the top of her shoulders. She has a grey, washed-out coat with tassels that reach to just below her calves and her feet are clad in brown leather sandals.

It is her.

I feel sick.

My mother is chatting to the woman on the deli, a Pole, and the words Warsaw and Pope John Paul the Second float across to me. She always liked talking to people from other countries, I remember suddenly.

I want to run, only I can't because I'm drinking in this first view of her in ten years. Maybe drinking is the wrong word. It's like I'm the scope of a gun, and I zeroed in on her and everything else is just background. Noises just seem to vanish. Julie has turned the corner and is now out of sight as I stand inside the door of the shop. Then, slowly, slowly, as if underwater, my mother turns towards me. I notice that she's still small and, despite the weird clothes, still beautiful. She's gazing at her coleslaw and she's smiling at it, for some reason, then she puts it into her basket where she already has a litre of milk and some rolls. Everything I see in the most amazing detail. And she looks younger than her years: maybe it's her clothes or the way she insists on bouncing along. She never bounced along when we were kids. Well, not that I can remember. And then, perhaps she's wondering why this practically bald woman is staring at her, but she looks in my direction and the smile freezes on her face for just the tiniest instant. Then it slides very slowly down it and her mouth opens a little. Almost protectively, she puts a hand on her coleslaw and now, now she's walking quickly towards me, a puzzled look on her face. I want to run away but I can't because my legs won't work.

'Hope?' My mother's voice breaks the spell I seem to have been under.

I flinch at her saying my name.

'Is it you?'

I don't know what to say. I try out a smile. 'Hi.' My voice is cracked.

She doesn't smile back. 'Oh my God.' Now her hand moves to her neck. Her mouth opens, then closes, then opens again. Her gaze travels the entire length of my body. 'Why . . . how . . . what?'

I'd forgotten what I must look like to her.

'Your hair.' She is staring, horrified, at me. 'And your leg?' She attempts to touch me, but I pull away. I don't know why. Her shoulders droop. 'What happened?' she asks softly.

'I was in an accident.' It hurts me to talk to her.

'What sort of an accident?'

I really don't want to discuss this, at least not here. 'Just an accident,' I say. 'I'm fine.'

'But your hair?'

'It'll grow back.'

'But, but . . .' she shakes her head and says with such hurt in her voice that I feel my stomach somersault all over again, 'you never told me.' Then she stops and says half tearfully, 'I'm OK now, Hope.'

I rub my face hard with my hand. 'Mammy, please . . .' It sounds like a plea. A woman going by stares at me.

'But I am. I can cope now.'

'Good. Good.' I can't seem to say anything else. And as the silence builds between us, I add in another 'good'.

'Just so you know,' she says. 'You can tell me what happened. You can tell me anything now and –' It's as if she realises that she's gabbling. She stops suddenly and shrugs. 'Sorry,' she mutters.

'No need.' My reply is terse. Please stop, I want to say. It's the first time since the accident that I've really felt anything and I wish I wasn't feeling it.

'Hope?' Julie's voice, anxious, is raised. 'Hope, where are you?' It's as if she's looking for a kid. 'Hope?' Julie slides to a halt beside me. 'What –?' She takes in the situation. 'Right. OK. I'm just . . .' she flaps her arm uselessly about and backs off. Then, from the corner of my eye, I see her taking out her mobile and phoning someone, probably Adam.

'Your friend?' my mother says.

I nod.

'Are you just, you know, passing through?' She tries to make it sound casual, but fails.

'I'm on holiday,' I answer.

'Oh.'

'I was going to call in,' I say. I wonder if it's a lie. 'Explain about –' I indicate my face and body – 'this. The accident.'

Is it my imagination or does her face brighten? 'Really?' It's as if she can't believe it. She moves her basket to her other hand. 'That'd be nice.' She pauses before saying fervently, 'I'd really like to see you, Hope.'

I wait for her to fix a date or something, but she doesn't. So I do. I feel I'm putting my hand close to a flame, one I'd told myself I'd never go near again. 'Maybe later this week?' I suggest.

'Any day is fine,' she nods. 'Any day at all. I have a mobile, you know.' Now, with a new purpose, she sets her basket on the floor and pulls out some paper from her pocket. 'Have you a pen?'

'No. Sorry.'

'Oh.' Disappointed, she slowly puts the paper back in her pocket. 'Right. Well, never mind, I'm in every day next week. I shop for things on a Monday,' she holds up her basket, 'but other than that . . .'

'OK.'

Neither of us moves. The distance between us is only a couple of feet but it might as well be miles. 'Where are you staying?'

'A cottage up the Dunport pass.'

She smiles at that. I remember suddenly how she used to smile years ago and I wonder how it all went so wrong.

'You always liked it up there. Is it Maurice's cottage?'

'Yeah.'

'I know his wife, she goes to flower arranging.'

'Oh.' I latch on to that. 'So you do flower arranging now, do you?'

'I teach it.' She's like a kid, boasting to a parent. 'Lots of people come to it.'

It knocks me sideways. My mother teaching? 'Wow,' I say. I feel, irrationally, a little angry. How dare she get better, I think, and here I am, a complete mess. And I know that sounds horrible and petty but in the second I think it, I take it back. I'm glad for her. 'That's good.'

Her lip trembles. 'I'm trying so hard, Hope. I really am. It'll never happen again, I swear.'

Oh God. I don't need this. Not in the middle of a tiny supermarket. I wish Julie would come back and rescue me. I think I might cry but not in front of her. Never in front of her. 'Better go.' I indicate Julie, who is being really good about not looking over, now that her phone call is finished.

'OK. Right.' Again she shifts her basket. 'Later in the week, so. Any day. I'll be there.'

'Right.'

And we step away from each other in a sort of dance, not wanting to draw closer than necessary.

It hurts.

Julie doesn't ask me anything as we get into the car. Instead, she squeezes my arm in a nice gesture of support.

'That's my mother,' I say unnecessarily.

'I guessed,' she says. She still hasn't started the car. 'She looks nice, Hope. Much nicer than my mother.'

I ignore that. 'I said I'd call in to her this week some time. Would you say Adam would mind driving me there?'

'No. Adam loves driving this horrible monster.' She hits the steering wheel with her hand. Julie hadn't liked driving it at all. It was too powerful and too big to park comfortably.

'I'll probably go Friday, after the counselling session.'

'Right.' Then she touches my arm again. 'Are you OK, Hope?'

'Yeah.' But my voice wobbles. I gulp hard to get it under control. I don't like the way this has made me feel. 'I'm fine, I'm fine.'

Julie doesn't seem to know what to do. If I was the old Hope, she'd cuddle me or crack some silly joke, but with this new brittle version, she doesn't know how I'll react. And I don't know either. So she just says, 'I remember once I ran into my sister Angela after she'd just got this gigantic promotion in work.' She smiles a little ruefully as she talks: 'and being the horrible sister I was, I was avoiding contacting her so I wouldn't have to congratulate her.'

'That is horrible,' I tease gently. 'Your own sister.'

'Yes, I know, thank you.' Julie sounds as if she couldn't care less. 'Anyway, I ran into her in Marks and Spencer's one Saturday and there she was and there I was and she says,' Julie puts on a very posh voice, 'Oh, Ju, did you hear about my promotion?' And I said, 'Yeah, congratulations.'

I look at her blankly.

'I found out I didn't care,' Julie beams at me. 'I was actually glad for her. I had my job, she had hers and that was it.'

'And that helps me – how, exactly?' I grin slightly. But I do know what she's trying to say. She's saying that maybe if you meet up with what you dread it won't be as bad as what you dread.

I hope she's right.

11

JULIE AND I are sitting in the front garden and it's truly summer. The ground is baking. Even the grass seems to have turned ever so slightly brown with the scorching heat. Julie has thrown caution to the wind and has donned her bikini top and tiny shorts and lathered herself with baby oil.

'You'll fry,' I say, horrified. 'Haven't you ever heard of skin cancer?'

'And haven't you ever heard of a tan? Besides, I have factor 50 on my face.'

I had factor 50 everywhere. I burn like a piece of dry paper. I go all red, then I peel and my tan never appears. I'm wearing a pair of rolled-up jeans; well, rolled up on one leg, the other is still in plaster. And I have a navy T-shirt. I think it's one of Adam's, I just took it off the line and put it on.

I lie back on the quilt Julie has taken off her bed and enjoy the feel of the sun caressing my body. We're supposed to be heading to the beach but Adam is beavering away on his laptop. He still hasn't figured out where the errant fifty thousand pounds has disappeared to. It's put him in foul humour and Julie and I have allowed him an hour before we give up on him coming with us.

'All we need now to ruin the day completely is for artist asshole to plonk down in front of us and start painting.'

'Oh,' Julie flaps at me lazily, 'he's not so bad once you talk to him. He smiled at me yesterday.'

'Every fella smiles at you.'

'Well, maybe if you smiled at him, he might smile back.'

'No chance.'

Logan has been coming all week to paint from our garden. He glowers at me every time I emerge from the house. And he stops painting and gets all guarded. I deliberately go out to annoy him, just to let him know he's there on my good will. Again, I know I'm being unreasonable but it helps me cope. It keeps me in touch with some sort of feeling.

Julie rolls over and looks down on me. 'Well, I hope my date tonight makes up for the lack of action in you and Adam. Honestly, I've never met two more boring people.'

Bodybuilder Boy rang her on Monday night and they arranged a date for tonight. The tragedy is she can't even remember his name.

'I like being boring.' I close my eyes and sigh contentedly. 'I'm going to stay here all night, slob out, drinking wine and eating chocolate, and you'll have to shower and dress and put on make-up and try hard to impress some guy you don't even know.'

'It's not like that.' I sense Julie rolling away from me and lying down now too. 'It's fun getting to know a new person, especially one like him.'

'Like him?'

'Yeah, well, he must be dynamic, mustn't he if he's got his own business. He runs a gym, I think.'

'I know, you told me.'

'People like that are always exciting.'

'Well, once you've convinced yourself, that's all that matters.'

'Piss off!'

We lie there for another while, listening to Adam curse every now and then from inside. He's sending e-mails all over the place and seems to be talking them through as he types. His bad mood is getting worse. I don't know if I fancy being with him on my own tonight. After a bit, it goes quiet again; the only sounds are of Julie shifting about beside me and insects humming and buzzing in the grass.

'*Julie!*'

Both of us jump. It's Adam: he's leaning out his window and beckoning Julie to come inside. 'Would you come in and have a look at this?' Then he glances at me. 'You too, Hope, if you like. I could do with a third opinion.' He's flushed, as if he's been out in the sun himself and got rather too much. 'Come on,' he says, disappearing from the window. 'Hurry.'

'Wonder what's got him so fired up?' Julie stands up and dusts herself down. 'I haven't seen him so excited since he was watching the paint dry in the house in London.'

'Stop!'

She grins.

Poor Adam, she's always on at him for being too boring.

Adam is pacing up and down his tiny room when we enter. As before, reams and reams of paper are strewn about the place. 'I'm in shit,' is all he says.

'What?' Julie sits on the bed, moving some of the paper out of the way. 'Have you found your fifty thousand?'

'Not exactly.' Adam sits down beside her. He picks up a sheaf of paper that looks like some kind of stock control sheet. 'But I know what happened to it. Just have a look yourself.' He pats the other side for me to sit.

With Julie and me sitting either side of him, he starts to explain. His voice is breathless, rushed and pathetically bewildered as he begins. 'A few months ago,' he says, 'I issued all the shops with a warning about fake bank drafts.'

'Right,' Julie nods.

'Anyway, in one week, this shop took in two bank drafts. One for ten thousand and the other for forty.' He shows us where they were lodged. 'They then give out stock to this company worth fifty grand. Only thing is, the bank drafts were fake.'

'But that was months ago,' Julie says.

Adam nods and half groans. 'Yeah. And ever since, they've been trying desperately to recover the money before I found out. So what they've been doing is this –' he points to another row of figures. 'See that bank draft, it was lodged in February, but they offset it against stock for January. They've basically used other people's money to cover the fifty grand originally swindled, leaving themselves fifty grand in debt going into the following month.'

'Clever,' I say, quite impressed.

Adam shoots me a look. 'Yeah. Until the boss decided to do a spot check and they hadn't finished up the accounts.' He groans. 'I should have noticed, but once the figures balanced, I didn't bother to check things.'

Julie picks up the statements and things and Adam shows her where the fiddling went on. After about half an hour, she nods. 'Yep, that's your money, all right. But what's the problem, isn't it insured?'

'Not if the bank warned us in advance and I issued letters to all the branches.'

'Are you in trouble, Adam?' I ask.

He sighs heavily and pushes himself up from the bed to

look out the window. 'I don't know,' he says, sinking his hands into the pockets of his jeans. He refuses to wear shorts. 'I suppose I am. If I'd been over there, I might have picked up on it, but I don't think so. Bastards,' he says bitterly. 'I'll kill them all.'

Julie joins him at the window and wraps her arm about his waist. 'Don't,' she says, 'don't be like that, Adam. It doesn't suit you. It'll be fine, you'll see.'

He rests his head on top of hers and snakes his arm about her waist. 'Hope so,' he says, sounding very despondent. 'I bloody well hope so.'

They look surprisingly nice together like that. I suddenly feel like an intruder, which is weird. I hop up off the bed and announce that I'm going to make a cuppa and does anyone want one.

Adam opts for wine and so we all join him.

Bodybuilder Boy arrives on time. He's way bigger than I remember from the pub. He pulls up to the cottage in a nifty sports car and after gazing at it lovingly for a few minutes turns towards the cottage, adjusts his cool denim jacket, which barely fits across his shoulders and, strutting in a cool sort of way, he arrives at the front door and hammers on it with his huge fist.

I open it as Julie has told me to pretend that she isn't ready – though of course she's been ready for ages. It's not a 'play-hard' tactic either, it's to see if there is any way I can find out his name.

'Hi,' BBB drawls, his thumbs resting in the loops on his jeans as he leans nonchalantly in the doorway. 'I'm here to pick up Julie.' His voice has a contrived American twang. God, he's such a stereotype.

'Oh,' I quip, 'I thought you'd done that already.'

It's lost on him. He winces, his coolness deserting him to be replaced by a Dublin accent, 'Eh, I haven't been here before, have I?'

'That's too philosophical a question for me at this time of the day.'

My witty repartee only succeeds in confusing him further. 'Is Julie here or not?' he asks.

'Yes. Come in,' I hold the door open a little wider. 'She's not quite ready yet. Who will I say is here?'

'Nelson,' he says as if it's obvious. Then his eyes narrow suspiciously. 'Why, is she seeing anyone else tonight?'

'No,' I give a passable laugh. 'Nelson? That's your name, right?'

'Eh – yes.'

I can't quite believe it. What a horrendous name. 'Nelson as in Mandela?'

'Pardon?' He's glancing about the room now. I know he's thinking how ugly it is and he's probably wondering if I'm unhinged.

'Like, is your name Nelson as in Battle of Trafalgar?'

He gawps. 'Huh?'

'Nelson as in *The Simpsons*?'

'Yes. My name is Nelson,' I notice that he's turned to the window and seems to be staring at his reflection in it. 'Now,' he spikes his hair and asks over his shoulder at me, 'is Julie here or not?'

'I'll just go get her.' I hobble to the end of the stairs. 'Julie!' I shout, though in reality she is sitting half-way down, 'Nelson is here! Are you ready?'

'Thank you.' Julie grins gratefully. Putting on her kilowatt smile, she stands up, marches on the spot for a few steps, to make like she's coming downstairs, before finally beginning to walk.

Nelson, who has been examining the manky sofa, gives a low whistle when he sees her. 'Wow, I thought you looked good the other night, but I was drunk then.' Julie's smile freezes ever so slightly. 'I was drunk too,' she says sweetly. 'Shall we go?'

'Yes, Julie, let's go.' He holds out an arm to her in an old-fashioned kind of way and she takes it. Only problem is, they won't both fit through the door together and so she has to let him go while he squeezes out in front of her.

I watch, like a mother hen, as he strides towards the car and with a fist the size of a rugby ball wrenches open the door for her. Julie is impressed by the car, I can tell. She slides into the front seat with a grace that belies her limited experience of bucket seats. He marches around the other side, eases his huge body into the driver's seat and the car roars into life, then stalls. He looks mortified and I try not to laugh. The car roars again and jumps about the place before taking off down the driveway.

And Julie is gone.

I feel a little lonely. Adam has promised to take me out tonight but he probably won't now, what with his work problems and everything. He hasn't been downstairs all day, except to grab a coffee now and again. I think he's composing a damage limitation e-mail to work. I'm good with putting stuff like that together, I suddenly think. I'm also good at telling lies that could be the truth, so I wonder if he'd like my help. It'd beat sitting on my own all evening. Plus, sorting out his problems will keep mine from skittering about in my head and popping up at the weirdest times. The form I'd got from the counsellor is pretty full at this stage. He's going to think I'm a basket case when I visit him in two days' time.

I hobble up the stairs and knock gently on Adam's door. 'Yes?'

I poke my head in. He's lying across his bed, a morose look on his face. His hair is dishevelled and his T-shirt is creased. He looks quite sexy, in fact, in a prim sort of way.

'You OK?'

He hauls himself up to sitting and shoves his feet into his bright trainers. 'Nope. Has Julie gone out with that ridiculous-looking man?'

'Yes. His name is Nelson.'

'Figures.' He glares at his shoes.

'Need a drink?'

'Aw, Jesus, Hope,' he says and rubs his hands over his face. 'I think I'm going to have to fly back for a week or so to sort this mess out.'

'D'you want me to help you compose an e-mail?'

'No. Thanks anyway. There are no words to describe the cock-up. It's a bloody mess,' he groans. 'I'll fire the lot of them.'

'You won't.' Adam firing people, what a laugh.

'And what do you suggest I do?' He looks crossly at me. 'I'm responsible for that branch. In fact, I'm responsible for all the branches in south England. If I let one guy off with losing me fifty thousand, what does that say to the rest of them?'

He's actually serious. I can't quite believe it. For the first time it dawns on me that Adam is a boss. He's in charge of others. He's a member of a club I seem to despise for whatever reason. If I worked for him, I'd probably have been fired long ago. 'He made a mistake,' I mutter. 'He hardly set out to lose you fifty grand.'

'But he bloody well did!' Adam glares at me. 'And now my head is on the chopping block.'

'They can't fire you.'

'Really?' He raises his eyebrows. 'And how would you know?'

'Because you told us you were too important for them to fire you!'

'Yeah.' He rolls his eyes. 'Lesson, Hopeless: don't believe everything people tell you.'

I don't like his tone. 'Don't talk to me like that.' I sound cross myself now. 'I only came up to see if you were OK and obviously you're not, so I'll leave you!'

'Thanks.'

Ooooh. I slam the door really hard and give it the two fingers. And again.

I hop back downstairs, wishing heartily that I hadn't made the effort to climb up in the first place. Marching into the kitchen, I take a bottle of white wine from the fridge, uncork it and pour myself a large glass.

Then, just as I've begun to calm down – two glasses of wine in the garden would do that – Painter Boy comes along, complete with easel, paints and a scowl. Without saying a word, he begins moving about the garden, looking for the best place to set up, I suppose.

I stare at him, trying to make him uncomfortable. Trying to show him that really now is not a good time to be plodding about making a nuisance of himself. He ignores me. It's like I'm invisible. Each time it seems that he might have to look at me, he does so, but it's as if he can see right through me. Eventually, after consuming another half-glass of the most delicious wine, I say, 'A "hello" would be nice.'

His dark eyes flick across to me. 'Yes, it would,' he agrees.

'I meant from you,' I mutter darkly.

'Oh, right.'

He turns his back to me and continues. His easel is set up, he's doing something with his paints now. Mixing up colours, I think.

I can't bear his superior attitude; he treats me as if I'm dirt or something he trod on. Who does he think he is, I wonder? How dare he ignore me! What I should do is make a dignified exit. I should tell him calmly that he's the most ignorant man I've ever met and that I feel sorry for him. That's what Julie would do. But I don't. Of course I don't. Even as I know I'm losing it, I lose it. Part of it's at Adam but most of it is at him. 'One can only hope,' I say smartly, 'that your manners are in indirect proportion to your talent. I reckon you'd be the best painter in the world if it were true.'

He turns slowly about to face me. His eyes are narrowed and his lip curls dangerously. 'Firstly,' he says, taking a step towards me and brandishing a paintbrush, 'I'm not a painter, I'm an artist. Secondly, unlike your charmingless self, at least I have a talent.'

I'm gobsmacked. He's good. 'There is no such word as charmingless,' I retaliate weakly.

'There is in your case.'

The calm way he says it infuriates me. I think he's even smiling a little. I think he's enjoying himself. I think he wanted a row with someone and that's why he chose to come here, to row with me.

'If I were you,' I breathe heavily, 'I'd rather kill myself than have your kind of attitude.'

He eyes me up and down. Up and down. A small smile definitely curls about his lips. 'Looks like you already tried,' he says.

110

His aim is true. I blink once. Twice. Open my mouth and can't think of a thing to say. In fact, I think if I say anything, it'll be drowned in a sob. So I look like shit. So I've no hair. So I limp when I walk. My lip trembles. 'Thanks,' I gulp out before turning and legging it back inside. Well, as much as I can with a crutch.

'Hey –' he calls out after me. 'Hey!'

I slam the door and pull the curtain so he can't see how upset I am.

I try to be quiet. I drink and cry as quietly as I can but Adam obviously hears. Or maybe he was coming downstairs anyway, I don't know.

'Hey, why is it so dark in here?' he asks.

'I like it dark,' I snap.

'Hey, what's wrong?' He crosses towards me. 'Are you crying?' He sounds surprised. I suppose it's because he's never seen me cry before. I don't know if *I've* ever seen me cry before. This is a hiccuping sort of thing. Reluctant and sporadic. 'You are,' Adam says, 'Aw, don't cry. Come on. You know how useless I am with all that.' He sits opposite me and attempts to look up into my face. 'I'm sorry about earlier, Hope, I really am. I just had a gigantic shock.' He attempts a smile. 'Once I fire a few people I'll be OK.'

'I'm not crying over you. So, don't flatter yourself.'

'Oh.' He takes the bottle of wine from my hand. 'That's OK then.' He finds a glass and pours himself the remaining dregs. 'So what's up?'

It'd be too humiliating to tell him. So I just say, 'I had a fight with the painter guy.' Then I stop. 'Oh, sorry, artist.' I drawl out the word.

'Not again.' He sounds amused.

111

'It's not funny. He said dreadful things.'

Adam surveys me over his glass of wine. 'He's like you, Hope. Even Julie says it.'

'Says what?' Honestly, is Adam going all out to get at me tonight?

'He's kind of, I don't know, unhappy like you.'

'I'm not unhappy!' We both know it's a lie.

'Well, sorry, but you know what I mean. He seems to be, I don't know, a bit . . .' he pauses, then settles for 'unhappy' again. 'So give the guy a break, eh?'

'You can't be serious.' I stand up. 'Give him a break? He insulted me.'

'Hey,' Adam's eyes widen. 'You stood up without using your crutch.'

'Yes. I can do that now.'

A big stupid smile breaks out on his face. 'Well, good for you! That's great!'

And I suppose it is. Eight weeks ago, I'd been crippled. I look down at my leg. 'Isn't it?' I feel it should be but I don't know if I really care. Still, I manage a smile.

'Soon, you'll have your hair back and you'll be yourself again.'

I wish it was that easy but I nod anyway. 'Yeah.' It takes a second before I remember what we'd been talking about. 'But I'm not like that painter fella. And I won't be.'

Adam, his fifty grand momentarily forgotten, decides to open another bottle of wine in celebration.

12

ADAM TAKES US sightseeing the next afternoon. He'd spent the morning in his room, booking flights. He reckons he'll be away for at least a couple of days. His boss has been on the phone already, demanding to see him, having obviously found out that Adam's been running things from his laptop in Kerry.

Julie is quite impressed now by Adam's rebellious streak.

Anyway, Adam decided that he might as well get out and enjoy himself before the shit hits the fan. 'So,' he asks, as Julie, still sleepy from her late date, climbs into the front seat. 'How'd the date with Action Man go?'

'I'm more interested in how your meeting with your boss will go,' she says, lathering on the lipstick in the passenger mirror and fluffing up her hair.

'It'll be shit.' Adam winces as he puts the car in gear.

I close my eyes and clench my fists hard. Adam and Julie don't remark on me doing this every time he has to reverse the car down the driveway and out on to the road. I can't help it. It terrifies me.

'Maybe it'll be fine,' Julie says when the car is safely reversed.

'Nah, he's really mad. Technically, I'm supposed to visit all the branches at least once a month and give them pep talks and frighten them into working harder. And, in this case, warn them of bank draft forgeries. This branch is saying that they never got the bank draft e-mail I sent – well, that's their defence. So, it's all my fault.' He takes the Dingle road. I've recommended the Conor Pass as a scenic drive. It's the highest mountain drive in Ireland. 'I'm seeing the boss first thing Friday morning.'

Adam is flying out tonight. It's costing him a fortune at such short notice. He has no suits to wear, so he has to visit his house first.

'You'll be fine,' Julie says and pats his hand. 'You're able to talk complete shit so you'll wrangle your way out of it.'

'I'll need to talk a lot of shit to get out of this.'

We're silent for a bit as I direct Adam where to go. Once we're in Dingle, all he has to do is follow the road signs.

'So – Action Man – how'd it go?' Adam goes back to his previous question. 'I liked the car.'

'Yeah,' Julie nods. 'Car was nice.'

'So, where'd you go?'

'He took me for dinner and he knocked over a table on the way in. He's quite a bulky sort of a bloke.'

'I thought he looked very –' I try to think of a nice way of describing him – 'big.'

Julie is not impressed. 'He's not big,' she exclaims, 'he's *muscular*. He showed me his biceps last night. He rolled up his T-shirt and it was like he had a football bursting out of his arm.'

'Wow.' God, what a disgusting image.

'Apparently he co-owns a gym.'

'Oh, right.' That would make sense, the guy is way too muscled out for my liking.

'I thought he was self-employed,' Adam says. 'Co-owning something is not the same as being totally self-employed.'

'Yeah right,' Julie brushes his comment off with a wave of her hand. 'Anyway, he's picking me up tomorrow again.'

'Why not tonight?' Adam asks.

'Because my dear, you are leaving tonight,' Julie smiles at him. 'I have to be here to wave you on your way.'

Adam flushes. 'Oh. Thanks.' He smiles delightedly.

'And to make sure you're suitably dressed for your boss. If you project a Mr Cool image, you'll feel cool. What suit are you wearing for your meeting?'

Adam shrugs. 'A clean one, anyway.'

'We could buy you a new one today,' Julie says. 'Let's face it, Adam, your other suits scream "boring bastard". We could get you a dynamic one. A brighter one than your black ones.'

From the back, I see Adam's shoulders tense. 'I dunno. I think "boring bastard" is the image they want of me. Boring bastards don't take off to Kerry without telling anyone, do they?'

'Boring bastards can be replaced,' Julie says determinedly. 'Dynamic Dans can't.'

'I'm not a Dynamic Dan.'

'You are.' Julie is annoyed. 'Or at least you could be. You're quite good-looking, Adam, well, if you'd invest in a haircut. Your hair is altogether too long and floppy and girlish.'

'My hair is not girlish.' He flicks it off his face.

'And you need to be more assertive and powerful.'

'I am in my job.' Adam does sound a bit assertive now. 'They hate me in my job. Men quake when they hear I'm coming.'

'Yeah!' Julie and I laugh at the same time.

'Yeah.' Adam nods. 'This is what I do.' He coughs slightly before shouting out 'You!'

Julie and I jump.

'Show me last month's invoices!' Pause. 'Has this been paid? Why the bloody hell not? Are you a moron? Can't you read a date? Well, obviously you can't as it's not paid. Get that money by tomorrow. Well, I don't care how you get it, just do it. Got that?' And then he changes back to Adam again. 'See?'

'Oh, Adam, you're very sexy when you do that,' Julie teases. 'Who would have thought?'

He doesn't smile back.

The Conor Pass is a disaster. Julie freaks out because the roads are so narrow and we're going so high. I probably would too only I know the roads so well. She spends the entire journey with her eyes closed. That's when she isn't nagging Adam to get a haircut. In the end, to shut her up, I think, he agrees. Poor Adam, I reckon he was lying about what he's like in the job as he really can't stand up to Julie at all. Or maybe he doesn't want to stand up to her.

'I think quite short would suit you,' she muses.

'Do you?' Adam actually sounds interested. 'Do you go for guys with short hair?'

'Oh yeah,' Julie nods. 'I love that military look. It's really sexy.'

'Oh right,' Adam says. 'Maybe I'll get it chopped short.'

'Spiky would be nice,' Julie suggests and Adam nods. 'Let's go back to the cottage and get some money.'

Adam then freaks her out completely by attempting to turn the car on the narrow road.

I'm sitting in the car, waiting for the two of them to emerge from the cottage with cash when I see Painter Boy in the next field. He seems to be debating whether to come into our garden or not. One minute he hops over the wall and the next he's back on his own side again. He doesn't have an easel but there is something in his hand. I watch, amused at his indecision and he must sense me, for his gaze flicks towards the car and he spots me.

'Great,' I mutter.

He starts to make his way towards me. He clothes are covered in splashes of red paint. He could do with a haircut himself, I think, as he comes closer.

'Hi,' he says hesitantly, bending down to look at me in the passenger seat.

I glare at him, remembering how he made me feel yesterday. 'Yes?'

He takes a deep breath. Then he stares at his feet and then up in the air.

'Is there something you want?' I ask. 'Besides unlimited use of our garden?'

'Oh, I see you've not sustained any lasting damage then,' he says back, 'after our verbal combating yesterday?'

He's good. Really good. Way better than Julie's guy yesterday. I narrow my eyes and glare at him. 'It'd take more than a few ill-chosen words to upset me,' I say with spirit. I toss my head, forgetting for a second that I have no hair. I'd look so much better if I had all my lovely curly hair swishing about my face.

'OK. Good,' Painter Boy says and I think he actually means it.

I notice for the first time that he has his hands behind his back. I also notice that he's hopping from foot to foot. His trainers are in a state. Old and falling apart. A bit like mine, actually.

'I thought,' he starts up, hunkering down suddenly, so he's at my eye level, 'Well, I thought, I just thought . . .'

He's like a car that can't quite go.

'Most people think,' I say. 'It's not something I'd go bragging about.'

'You're good,' he says.

His comment catches me by surprise and silences me.

'I just thought that I upset you yesterday,' he mutters then, really quickly. 'And well, I'm, I'm a bit sorry.'

'A bit sorry?' I hope he doesn't think that's an apology.

'And here,' he thrusts out his hand. In it is a small unframed picture. 'For you. To say that I'm a, well, a bit sorry.'

I'm amazed. I mean completely speechless. Totally stunned. Ashamed. Annoyed that he's made me feel ashamed. Slowly I take the picture from him. It's a picture of the sea. A stormy, black, blue, grey and white sea. Very powerful, quite abstract and quite disturbing. It's a weird picture to give someone to say sorry. 'Thanks,' I mutter. I want to add, 'I think' but I don't.

'Thought you might like it,' he says then.

'It's, eh, great.' I don't actually think I do like it. Imagine staring at that when feeling depressed or cold. It'd hardly cheer me up.

'Right. So, well – I'll, eh, go.' He stands back up again and thumbs in the direction of his cottage. He keeps staring at me, though.

'Hope,' Julie calls loudly, coming from the house, Adam in her wake. 'We're ready.' She smiles at Painter Boy. 'Oh, hi Logan.'

'Yeah, eh, hi.'

'We're going to Killarney. Adam is getting a haircut.'

'Thanks for telling everyone,' Adam says. 'Hey, Hope, what's that you have?'

118

'Picture.' I show it to them. 'Eh . . .' I can't say his name, 'eh, he gave it to me.' I point to Logan, who looks mortified.

'I was really horrible to her yesterday,' he says proudly, by way of explanation.

'Hey, cool,' Julie admires it. 'Wow, Logan, did you paint that?'

'Yep. It's an old one. No one wanted it.'

'Gee, thanks.' I sneer at him.

He ignores me. 'Are you going to Killarney, did you say?'

'Yep.' Adam jangles his car keys. 'Need a lift?'

'Well, yeah, if there's room. I need to get some paints and things. I normally book a taxi . . .'

To my dismay, my two friends insist that it's no problem, that there is loads of room and I find myself sitting as far apart as I can from him, in the back seat as Adam drives at his usual breakneck speed through the narrow country roads.

'So Logan,' Julie tosses him one of her flirtiest smiles, 'what is it you do?'

He looks a bit stunned at her question. 'I'm an artist,' he states as if talking to a moron.

'No,' Julie giggles a little. 'Like, is that your house, that little cottage or are you renting it like us?'

'Well, I rent it but I live there. It's a long-term rent thing.'

'Oh.' Julie nods politely. 'Must be lonely.'

Is it my imagination or does he flinch slightly? 'Well, it can be,' he acknowledges, 'but I have my sculptures and paintings.'

She snorts a little with laughter. 'Yes, but they can hardly talk, can they? You can't break open a bottle of wine with them, can you?'

119

'Well, at least I don't have to share the wine or listen to them moaning about the weather and the lack of job opportunities the way my ex did.'

No one quite knows what to say to that.

'Sorry,' Logan says after an uncomfortable silence has descended. 'Scratch that. My ex is a bit of a thorny subject. Yes, Julie, it's lonely.'

Julie and Adam manage a laugh as Logan, to make amends, offers, 'I'm working on a commission at the moment, so the loneliness is good for me.'

'A commission for what?' Julie asks.

'For the new hotel in Dunport.'

'The Gleeson Hotel?' I'm interested, despite myself. 'A guy I know – used to know –' I clarify, 'is in charge of that.'

'Yeah?' He's doing his best to sound interested, but the surprise in his voice at my civil tone is obvious.

'Jack Dunleavy?' My voice rises at just saying his name.

'Oh him,' he nods briefly. 'Yeah, I've talked to him. I don't think he's into my work that much. Anyway, I've to do a series of landscapes for the foyer and the main ballroom.'

'Great,' Adam says.

'It's money,' Logan clarifies. 'I'd prefer to be working on my own stuff. I'm not mad about doing what other people tell me to do, but it's money.'

'Hope hates doing what people tell her to do too,' Adam announces. 'You two have a lot in common.'

I bristle. I'll kill him for that. Logan looks as if he's bristling too. We move even further away from each other.

We all meet back at the car at four. I'm the first back and Logan is second. He's carrying enormous amounts of stuff and it's all large stuff. Big folders and bits of wood and huge boxes of paint. I'm carrying a big bag of toffees. I offer it to him and he attempts to take one but all his stuff falls on the ground.

'Shit!'

I'm tempted to leave him scrabbling about trying to rescue all his things, but that'd be horrible. I pick some art materials up and in silence load them into his arms.

'Thanks.' It's gruff.

'No problem.' I'm equally gruff.

Adam and Julie arrive back. They look as gruff with each other as Logan and I. Adam's hair has been butchered. That's the only way I can describe it. It's certainly short but instead of looking cool, he looks like a thug.

'I didn't mean that short,' Julie grouches as she gets into the car and pulls her seatbelt on. 'You know I didn't. You heard me tell the girl.'

'Well,' Adam starts up the car without looking in her direction. 'At least if I lose my job, I can enrol in the National Front.'

'It'll certainly frighten your employees,' I say, half jokingly. 'You won't have to do your tough act with them.'

'It's not an act,' Adam says shortly.

'Well,' Julie has the last word before we all lapse into silence, 'it's better than the girly cut.'

Adam takes a taxi to the airport that night with promises to ring us about the meeting. Julie hugs him hard as he leaves and, surprisingly, he hugs her back. 'Next time, I'll get to work on your hair,' he tells her. Then he turns to me. 'And you'll have met your mother when I get back and have your cast off. Sorry I won't be here. But you and Ju feel free to use the car, OK?'

'Yeah. Thanks.' God, I feel sorry for him heading over to a horrible meeting.

'Hug her, for God's sake,' Julie urges.

We do our awkward hugging thing that embarrasses everyone.

And then we watch as he drives off in a trail of dust.

13

JULIE DRIVES ME to the counsellor on Friday morning.
She managed to infuriate everyone on the road as she
refused to drive Adam's car faster than forty miles an hour.
I swear, from the amount of abuse and horn-blaring we
encountered, we both need counselling after it. As we pull
up outside Tim's office, Julie's phone starts to ring. 'I'll just
park here and answer my phone and when you come out,
I'll be waiting,' she promises.

I climb out, holding my filled-in pages firmly in my hand.

'Good luck,' she calls.

I wave back in return.

Tim is sitting at his desk as I enter. He gives me a cheery smile
and congratulates me on how diligently I've filled in the forms.
He reads them and then looks at the notes he made last Friday.
Then he ticks boxes and writes more notes and finally he clasps
his hands together in front of him. 'Well, Hope,' he says, and
he sounds less casual than he has done, 'at this point, from
the information you've given me, I feel that a diagnosis of Post
Traumatic Stress Disorder is probably the right one.'

'OK.' My mouth is dry, my mind reeling, but I manage
somehow to sound calm and composed. 'Is that, you know,
is it a big deal?'

Tim takes his time answering and when he does, I feel that every word he says is carefully chosen. 'Firstly, let me tell you that PTSD is a very understandable response to a traumatic event.' He pauses, to let that sink in. 'Are you following me, Hope?'

I nod. So what I have is understandable. The fury, the panic, the isolation.

'Basically, what happens is that you got on that plane with a certain belief system. You believed that planes were safe, that very little could happen; that there was a better chance of winning Miss World than being hurt on a plane.'

'Yeah, I always reckoned I had a good shot at the Miss World title.'

Tim laughs briefly before continuing. 'And then what? Those beliefs, the feeling that you had a certain amount of control over your life were shattered by what happened. Would this be about right?'

'I suppose, yeah.'

'So then, your poor old brain has to assimilate the experience into your life. It does this by trying to remind you of it, but your waking self can't comprehend the enormity of the change, it has no way of understanding the new belief system so it avoids thinking about it, because it's too scary to relive the trauma. As a result, the mind tries to assimilate your experience through nightmares, flashbacks and panic attacks. So you might avoid going to sleep or you avoid going out in case a panic attack happens. You can see, Hope, how it would lead to all sorts of problems.'

I nod.

'In some cases, like yours, you start numbing yourself to various emotions. You don't want to feel scared or threatened, so you avoid situations that would let you feel this way, you don't think about the accident, you don't put yourself in other scary situations, but it's impossible to cut just one emotion out; eventually it leads to the cutting out of others so that in the end you can't feel much of anything. And finally, a dissociation from other people can occur.' He paused and finished, 'That's what might happen if the PTSD was left untreated.'

That's what was happening.

'And does it make you angry too?' I ask. 'I feel edgy all the time.'

'Yes. When you're in a situation where you feel out of control, you react by getting angry. Because your experience has led you to believe that life itself is out of control and you don't like to feel that way. It's a vicious circle.'

'Oh.' I bite my lip. It's good to have a reason why I feel so bad. Almost a relief.

'And can I get cured? Can I feel like I used to?'

Tim pauses, which frightens me a bit. In fact, he seems hesitant to commit himself.

'Hope, I'll be honest with you. From talking to you the other day, it's obvious to me that this plane crash wasn't the only awful thing to happen in your life.'

'Yes but I never felt like this before.'

'Sometimes, when we have earlier trauma or repeated traumas, our view of the world changes anyway and then the latest trauma only strengthens this. It takes longer with someone like you. I can't cure you. You cure yourself. It means you'll have to work hard.'

Again, as before, my mind begins a slow internal spin. 'But will I be OK?' I ask. 'If I work hard.'

Tim nods. 'Yes. If you work at it. That's all I'm saying.'

'I will work. I promise.'

It seems to be the answer he's looking for. 'Good.' He nods. 'Now, let me explain what we'll be doing, so you'll be prepared for it. Basically, what I do is to tackle three things. First, I'll teach you how to cope with the feelings and tension that come with the memories you get: relaxation techniques, basically. The second thing I'm going to do is help you face the memories. Because you've had more than one trauma, we'll tackle the earlier ones first, the ones about your mother's depression. And from there we'll move on to the plane crash. This is called exposure. The more you talk, the less hold the memories have over you, does that make sense?'

No, it didn't, actually. How could I talk when I couldn't even let myself think?

'It's like, for instance . . . say someone is blackmailing you. They say to you if you don't do what I say, I will tell your great big secret. So you live in fear. You are basically in that person's control. But, say one day you turn around and tell that blackmailer to get lost. You say to him, do your worst, I don't care, I'll survive it. He immediately loses his control over you. You take back control.'

'Oh?'

'It's like that with the nightmares or the panic attacks. Just let them run their course. When you wake up at night, imagine a good ending to the nightmare. Write it down. It works. The same with the panic attacks. Just be aware that you can't die from them, they can actually do you no harm. Take back control.'

'Oh, I see.' It couldn't be as easy as that.

'Obviously, it's not as easy as that,' Tim says, 'but it's easier than you think. And thirdly,' he goes on, 'I'll be helping you change the way you think. For instance, you might say you can't control things so what's the point, and I might say

126

in return, well, name me something you do have control over and how important is that or I might say list the advantages and disadvantages of that belief. You'll find that the advantages are not as compelling as the disadvantages. Things like that.'

'OK.'

'Is there anything you want to ask me?'

I'm sure there is but my mind is blank. There is so much stuff to understand.

'If you can't think of anything,' Tim smiles, 'you have my number, you can ring me any time.'

'OK.'

'So Hope, I'm going to ask you a question. What is it you expect to get out of this? What are your aims?'

'Normality.'

Tim allows himself a grin. His teeth are quite crooked, I notice.

'To feel that things aren't normal *is* normal, Hope, believe it or not. Just have a think during the next few days and decide what it is you want from this therapy. And we'll work at that.'

I don't need a few days to think about what I want. 'I want the nightmares to stop,' I say haltingly. 'I want to be able to relax. I want to hold down a job and not over-react. I want to see a plane in the sky and wave at it the way I did when I was a kid.' That last bit sounds stupid but it had just come out. Me and Jamie loved doing that. I used to pretend I could see into the plane and would drive him mad by telling him that all the passengers were waving at me and not him. 'Just those things for the moment,' I mutter.

Tim nods. 'Cool, yeah. Well, for next week, Hope, I want you to keep filling out the forms. Keep monitoring your triggers. Most importantly, I need you to stay off the drink. And when you see a plane in the sky, look up for maybe a second and wave. Just a second. Just remember, it can't do you any harm.'

If it fell out of the sky, it would do me a lot of harm, I think. Then immediately I have the thought: how likely is that?

'And if you manage to hold it for one second, the next time you see a plane, hold it for two seconds and wave. Just keep building on it and let me know by next –' he consults his diary – 'Friday how you get on. And let your friends know what you're doing, they might help you.'

'OK. I'll try.' I take the fresh forms he's proffering me.

'And have a think about next Friday, Hope,' he says, just as I've opened the door. 'We're going to talk a little about your mother – OK?'

I nod. Little does he know I'm on my way to see her. Maybe by my next session, my slant on my mother will be very different.

'. . . and I have to start looking at planes in the sky and wave at them,' I say finally to Julie, who has asked how my session went.

She doesn't respond. It dawns on me suddenly that she hasn't responded to a thing I've said. In fact, she hasn't even looked at me since I started to speak.

'And he told me that what I had was incurable.'

'Really?' Julie turns to me and I nod. 'Oh, Hope, that's fantastic.'

Her eyes look a bit red, but it's hard to be sure because she seems to have plastered on fresh make-up. 'Julie, have you been crying or something?'

'No.' She doesn't look at me; instead she fires the engine.

'So you think it's good that I'm dying?'

'You're dying?' Now her eyes widen in horror. The car splutters to a standstill. 'Dying?'

'No, no I'm not,' I say hastily as her eyes fill up. 'It's just when I said I was, you told me it was fantastic.' I attempt a smile.

'Did I?' She still sounds weepy. 'Sorry about that.'

'That's OK.' I study her. She definitely was crying. 'What's wrong, Ju?' What could have happened in the last hour? 'Has Nelson cancelled or something?'

She flaps a hand in my direction. 'Nothing.' She sniffs. 'You don't need my problems. You've got to see your mother now.' She makes another attempt to start the car.

'She isn't expecting me at a particular time.'

The car judders and jumps and eventually stalls. 'Damn!' Julie says in frustration. 'Damn! Damn!'

'Come on.' I take the car keys from her and give her a gentle shove, 'Tell me. I'll probably make it a whole lot worse for you, but I'm listening.'

She rewards me with a half-hearted smile.

'Well?'

She sighs and looks at me despondently. 'That phone call, just before you went, remember?'

I nod.

'Well, it was Dad.'

'Oh, so he rang at last, did he?'

'Yeah,' she nods. 'They have this bad cop, good cop routine going. He's generally the good cop. He told me how terribly disappointed he was at the way I'd treated my mother.'

'What?!'

'I reckon if I'd murdered someone, they'd forgive me easier.'

'Julie, you took early leave to go on holiday, it's no big deal. People do it all the time.'

'Not the Adcocks,' she says in a tart voice. 'The Adcocks value their careers.'

Poor Julie, I'm thinking. But the scary thing is I'm not feeling it. I can't let her see that. 'Well, you're an adult now. You can do what you like. You're an adult Adcock.' And for some reason, that sets us giggling.

Then just as I think Julie has cheered up, she says, 'He told me how terrible it was that I had upset my mother so much. She's devastated that I took off without telling her, she felt like a fool when she rang my school and I wasn't there, and if that was all the appreciation I could show them for the years of sacrifice they had made for me, I was no daughter of theirs.' Her voice cracks a little. 'Imagine.'

'Bloody hell,' I borrow Adam's favourite phrase.

'Well, he didn't say it in an angry way,' Julie said, 'he was all mournful and disappointed, which is worse than anything. I think he expected me to apologise.'

'I hope you didn't!'

'I'm not that pathetic,' she says with some spirit and I give a little cheer.

'Then he goes on about how upset she is that I'm not taking her calls any more and then he started on about how Angela never takes holidays and that's why she's advanced so much in her career and that maybe I should think about it.'

'Saint Angela.'

'Exactly. And then,' Julie gulps, 'worst of all, he got to saying how he'd be in Ireland on business next weekend and that we should meet up. Oh God, Hope, what will I do?'

'He's coming to the cottage?'

She shakes her head. 'No, he wouldn't find that. He'll be in Killarney, he said and he'd love to see me.'

'Well, that's understandable.'

'No, I know he's going to give me a parent heart to heart. If I refuse to see him, it'll cause war. If I see him . . .' She doesn't finish; instead she says, 'Hope, why can't they let go?'

I think of my mother who let me go a long time ago, probably not deliberately, but it had happened, and I don't know which is worse. 'He just maybe loves you too much?' I suggest.

'No,' Julie says bitterly, 'he loves what he thinks I am too much.'

'So see him,' I say. 'If you want, maybe Adam and I will go too. That'll wrongfoot him.'

She gives a horrified giggle. 'Yeah, it would, wouldn't it?'

'Yeah, we'll hang about with the two of you all day and he won't get a word in.'

'Brill!' She smiles.

And I'm glad I've made her smile so I make myself smile too.

14

THE JOURNEY FROM Tim's office to the cottage on the outskirts of Dunport only seems to take seconds. One minute I'm looking at streets and shops, the next we're driving by the sea with shops and pubs to our right.

'This turn,' I say to Julie and she dutifully indicates left and begins the short drive up the road to my mother's house. I get her to stop just a stroll away from it. I don't need my mother quizzing me on Julie. I'm not ready to tell her things yet. And I'm not ready for Julie to see where I grew up. I was always half ashamed of our house – my mother never cut the grass or washed the windows like other people's mothers. She never painted the door or swept the footpath. Our net curtains were a dirty white and were never changed. Once, when she was feeling well, she did take them down and wash them, but she never hung them back up. I did that, months later, when I eventually located them. She liked growing things, though, and we had a passable garden, but that was it. Most of the time, our house looked unloved and reeked of decay. It was in direct contrast to Amanda Coonan's house which was a little down the road from ours. They had landscaped gardens and waterfalls and rockeries. They were the first people in Dunport to have venetian blinds and their brass doorknob was always sparkling.

'Good luck,' Julie calls, her good mood restored by the massive ice-creams and large cappuccinos we'd had before leaving the vicinity of the office.

I hold up my mobile. 'I'll ring you when I want you to come, OK. I shouldn't be more than twenty minutes.'

'Yeah, I'll go for a walk along the beach.' Julie does a three point turn, which takes ten attempts, and heads off back in the direction of the main road. I watch until the car is out of sight and then, taking deep breaths, I begin to walk towards home.

The Coonans' is immaculate as always and I scurry past it, not wanting them to see me. I don't know how I'll feel about Amanda Coonan now; I'll probably still hate her. I get safely by and in the distance I see the white gable wall of my mother's house. My step slows and I almost stop and flee but something inside makes me go on. Step by step by step I advance towards the house until soon I'm standing at the end of the short driveway. The garden is still unkempt but amazingly in a nice sort of way. Summer flowers sprout from unexpected places. Poppies and daisies flutter alongside the cultivated ones. The windows are clean and she has bought roller blinds. I take all this in as I walk towards the front door. There is no handle. It must have fallen off, but there is a bell. I stare at it a while before reaching up to press it. A dull buzzing sounds inside the house.

No one comes.

I press it again.

And still no one comes.

I can't believe this. Surely she has to be there. Surely she wouldn't leave when she knows that there is a chance I'm going to call? And so I press it a third time.

Inside, I hear footsteps coming up the hallway. My breath quickens as the door is slowly pulled open. And she stands in front of me, smaller than me, her tiny-boned hand holding the door ajar.

'Hello,' I say, rather formally. 'It's eh, me.'

'Hope,' she says back, pulling the door wider to allow me in. She gives me a smile which I half-heartedly return. 'Come on in.'

Her voice is as soft as ever and her eyes follow me as I walk by her into the hall. It has been transformed. Wooden floors and painted doors. Pictures on the walls. One of me, I notice, smiling out of the frame and holding a little boy. I was probably about five in the picture. And Jamie would have been only one or so. He's struggling to get out of my arms. I had a habit, when he was a baby, of picking him up and cuddling him really hard. There is another one of the four of us. My mother and father, arms around each other, gazing at me and Jamie with pride. Jamie's slightly slanted eyes glitter with mischief. And yet a third, of me and Jamie when we were older. At my twelfth birthday party. Jamie has his arms around me and is hugging me tight. I can't look at that one. In fact, I don't realise I'm looking at all until she says, 'They're my favourite pictures and one of the local lads framed them for me.'

'Lovely,' I croak out.

'Would you like a coffee? Or a tea?' She sounds anxious.

'Tea, please.' I don't really want one but I think it will be better to be holding something or sipping something when I can't think of things to say.

My mother moves towards the kitchen and, as I enter, I notice again, how much improved it is on what I remember. Clean. Bright. For some reason, there are flower arrangements everywhere. Half-finished ones and ones only begun. My mother waves her hands at them as she picks up the kettle. 'I'm always working out what arrangements to do at the evening class, I like to keep things different.'

I go around examining the flowers as she pulls out biscuits and sugar from the press. 'They look great,' I say. I point to a pretty spray of white orchids. 'This is like something you'd see at a wedding.'

'Yes, I'm doing a wedding in a few months.'

'Really?' I'm impressed. 'A wedding. Is that not a big job?'

She turns to face me and her steady gaze unnerves me a little. 'I can cope with big jobs like that,' she says and her tone is faintly chastising.

'Oh.' I flush. 'I didn't mean . . .' my voice trails off, but of course, I had meant it and we both know it. I leave the flowers and sit at the table.

'I've been working hard to keep it together,' she tells me in a gentle voice. 'It was difficult at first but it's getting easier.' She sits opposite me at the table. 'I know I let you and Jamie down, Hope.' Her voice falters and her eyes water and I turn away. I'm not able to cope with her emotion. 'I can't say anything to make it better. But at the time, I couldn't help the way I was.'

Yes she could have, I feel like saying. How come she works hard at it now and she couldn't when Jamie and I were there? I want to say it, to shout it at her, to demand an answer. Instead, I find I'm staring at the table, unable to meet her gaze and unable to take her apology. I think I'm afraid to row, I'm afraid of the emotion and I'm afraid that it will set her back in her own recovery. I learned early never to argue with my mother, it only left me feeling guilty when she cried for days. And angry that I had to bottle it all up.

135

So, looking at the table, I notice that it's new and scrubbed and clean. Not like the brown stained thing we grew up with. In fact, its cleanness seems to mock me. Did we not matter enough for her to pull herself together for us?

The kettle clicks off and she stands up to make the tea.

I just want to go now. I feel more hurt than I ever thought I could. But I sit there and watch as she stirs the teapot and pours the tea into two bright yellow mugs. I even mutter 'thanks' as she places mine before me.

'So, what happened to you?' she asks. I get the impression that that's all she's wanted to know since I came in.

'I was in an —' I gulp slightly as I find I'm unable to speak about the accident without choking up — 'well, it was an accident. In a plane.'

'In a plane?'

'Yes. It crashed. Lots of people died.' I give what I hope is a laconic smile. 'I didn't.'

Her face pales. It's ages before she speaks. 'Oh God.' Then something clicks, 'Was that the London plane last May?'

'Yeah.'

Her expression swings between bewilderment and hurt. 'And how come no one contacted me?'

I can't tell her that my friends thought she was dead. 'A mix-up, I suppose. Anyway, I'm telling you now and I'm fine so —'

'But you might not have been!'

'But I am.' I say it firmly. Let's not go that route, is what I mean. I half expect her to keep going. To ask if maybe I didn't want her there or for her to say how upset she feels that she wasn't there.

But to my surprise, she says instead, 'They shaved your head.'

'Yeah.' I explain about the operation and the fact that my hair will grow back and that I'm getting the cast off my leg in the next week. That cheers her up. 'Good.' She nods. 'That's good.' Then she asks a little about my life in London and I tell her and she asks if I'm working and I lie and say that I am. I don't tell her about all my job losses and my PTSD. I guess I'm doing what I always did, filtering out the bad bits of information to protect her.

Just then the front-door bell rings. My mother motions for me to stay sitting. 'It's probably just Amanda to look at an arrangement I've done, I'll tell her to call back later.'

She hops up from the table and closes the kitchen door behind her. As she opens the front door, I hear an unmistakable nasal voice and my heart tightens. My mother laughs at something this Amanda says and then the Amanda says goodbye and that she'll call later and my mother closes the door and comes back into the kitchen. She sits back down, oblivious to my shock.

'Who was that?' I dip a finger into my cold tea.

'Just Amanda, I'm doing her wedding for her. She's marrying –'

'Amanda? Amanda Coonan?'

'Yes. Why, would you have liked to meet her?'

I flinch from the insensitivity of the question. 'No!' My voice cracks. 'No I would not!'

She knows something is wrong but to my disbelief she doesn't know what. 'Oh,' she says.

'Amanda Coonan?' I say in disbelief, again. '*The* Amanda Coonan?'

She winces at my change in temper. I can see it but I can't control it. I'm an onlooker to my own anger. But, I think, even if I hadn't had the PTSD, I'd have been fuming.

My mother nods and then says in an unfamiliarly steely voice, 'Yes. Amanda.'

'Amanda that used to call me a dirt bag and say we were all descended from rats? Amanda that picked on . . . Jamie?' My voice catches as I say his name and I notice the way my mother balks. 'That Amanda?'

My mother swallows hard. 'Yes, Hope,' she says evenly. 'That Amanda. The girl you punched so hard she had to stay overnight in hospital. And whose parents very nicely made her apologise for what she'd said to make you hit her. The Amanda that for the past few years always offers to get my shopping when I can't make it to the shops. Or when I'm feeling down.'

'Oh, good for her!' Now I'm fighting. I've never fought with my mother before. 'Good for her.' I stand up. 'Well, maybe she should be here drinking tea with you instead of me.'

'No.' My mother sounds distressed. 'No. I'm glad it's you. I'm so glad it's you, Hope.'

I can't answer. I can't say anything or it'll sound petty and mean, but I so desperately want to lash out. To tell her how I felt all those years ago. To tell her how I still feel, I suppose. But instead, I do what Julie advises and count to ten. At the end of the count I stand up and say, 'Well, anyway, I have to go now. I have some shopping and stuff to do.'

'Hope?'

I hold up my hands to fend her off.

'Hope, please –'

I shake my head.

We stare at each other. I can't go until she lets me. But I can't stay either.

'OK,' she says and if she's disappointed, she doesn't let it show. 'Will you call again?'

'I don't know.' I start to back out of the kitchen. 'I might have to go back. I don't know.'

She crosses towards me and I pull back. I can't have her touch me. I don't know what I'll do.

'OK,' she says. Her shoulders sag. 'Well, I'm glad we met, Hope.'

I can only nod.

'And please keep in touch with me. Let me know how you're getting on.' A pause. 'And I'm sorry about Amanda. I'm glad you're fine. You are fine, aren't you?'

'Yes, Mammy, I'm fine,' I say firmly. I'm right back to my childhood when she'd awaken, half crazy in the afternoon and ask me if things were fine. And assuming my teacher's voice or whoever else impressed me back then, I'd lie and say things were fine. Me and Jamie were fine, the house was fine, and school was fine. Lies, lies, lies until I was sick of them. 'I'm fine now. And I have to go now.'

'But you'll be back?' Her eyes look pleadingly at me. 'Won't you?'

I'm not going to lie to her. Instead I shrug.

'Oh.'

We look at each other for a few long seconds. Finally, she says, 'All I can say is sorry, Hope. If I could turn back time, you know I would.'

I would too, I want to say. If I could turn back time, I might just have done things differently. 'Bye, Mammy.'

'Bye, alannah.'

That term of endearment spears me. I don't say anything, just walk as quickly as I can away from the place.

15

IT'S THREE DAYS later. I'm sitting with Julie in the hospital, awaiting the doctor who will, at last, take my cast off. It's over four days since Adam left for London and we still haven't heard from him. He should have had his meeting by now and Julie and I are beginning to get very worried. Julie has just tried to ring him again and all she has got is Adam's voicemail.

'Say he's done something stupid,' she says, redialling. 'I mean, he really liked his job and say he's lost it.'

'Did he really like his job?' I must say, I'd never noticed that about him.

'Well, if you had a job that enabled you to buy three houses and boss people about, wouldn't you like it?' Julie asks as if it's a no-brainer. 'He loved that job.'

There is something flawed in her logic but I don't bother pointing it out. I can't wait to get the cast off as my leg is so itchy. I just want to scratch and scratch it. The hospital in London has sent my file over and apparently after getting my cast off, I've to go and get my head examined. Julie thinks that's funny.

'Oh, I do hope he's OK.' Julie flicks off her mobile and stares at me with big anxious blue eyes. 'Would you say he's OK, Hope?'

'Well, he's not the sort to do something stupid,' I answer. I'd thought about this a lot in the last couple of days and didn't quite know how to say it delicately. 'Like that's kind of a spontaneous thing to do, isn't it, and he's not like that.'

Julie gives a horrified laugh. 'Oh, when you put it that way . . .'

'Hope Gardner?' someone calls, interrupting us. 'You can see the doctor now.'

'So, he'll be OK,' I say over my shoulder to Julie as I pick up my crutch and hobble down the corridor into the doctor's office. I reckon I could have taken the cast off myself but Julie had shrieked at the idea. The doctor is a youngish man, probably a trainee or whatever you call them. He has my cast off in no time and he asks me to do various things with my leg and then asks me if I feel any pain.

'None. It's just a little weak,' I say. It's also pale and hairy, which horrifies me. The minute I get back, it's out with the razor.

'Gentle exercise will soon have you as right as rain,' he says. 'You're a lucky girl.'

'Isn't she?' Julie beams at me like a proud mother. 'She was in a plane crash, you know.'

'And how is that lucky exactly?' I deadpan.

The doctor smiles. 'Well the best of luck with the rest of your life, Hope,' he says, as I stand up and automatically reach for the crutch. 'You don't need it any more,' he says and grins.

And I don't. Suddenly I have two free hands. It's weird, but I hardly know what to do with them as I leave the office. I settle for swinging them back and forward and gazing in admiration at my leg.

My head is healing well too and I'm congratulated on

the fact that my hair has grown an inch. 'You're a survivor,' the surgeon tells me. 'And whoever operated on you did a wonderful job.'

Aren't doctors great? Whoever invented medicine was a genius.

Nelson arrives to take Julie out that evening. It's the last night of his holiday and he's going back to Dublin the next day. However, he has promised to keep in touch with her and to call down every weekend until she goes back.

When Nelson pulls up in his little car, Julie and I watch amused as he huffs and puffs and pulls and tugs and eventually emerges from it and plants his enormous feet on the ground.

'Hi, Nelson.' Julie hammers on the window and he waves a big shovel of a hand in greeting.

She beckons him to come on in.

He enters and nods hello at me before turning to Julie. I reckon that first-night conversation with me frightened him off. He has hardly said two words to me since and apparently asked Julie if the accident affected me mentally.

'Hope got her cast off today,' Julie says to him. She's busy applying a deep red lipstick to her rosebud lips.

'Oh yeah,' Nelson nods, eyeing me. He has dropped his twang, but still stands like some extra from a cowboy movie. 'Nice one. So you can walk proper and all now, can you?'

'I can.'

'Great.'

'And her hair is growing back,' Julie announces.

'Fantastic,' Nelson nods. 'Women always look nicer with a bit of hair.'

I smile. It's impossible to feel offended. The poor guy hasn't a clue what to say to me.

'Indeed. Have a good night now.'

'Will you be OK on your own?' Julie turns to me. 'I thought Adam would be back by now and I don't like leaving you. Do you want to come with us?'

Nelson shoots her a panicked look but fair play, he refrains from refusing outright. Instead, he says, in a phoney, regretful voice, 'I've only booked a table for two.'

'Sure cancel it and we'll go to a pub,' Julie says.

He looks hurt. 'It's the best table in the restaurant.'

'I'll be fine,' I say. 'Go on, enjoy yourself. I'll probably go for a walk or something.'

'You can't go for a walk on your own,' Julie exclaims. 'It's so lonely around here – anything could happen.'

'I should be so lucky!'

'Promise me you won't go for a walk.'

'Promise me you won't snog Nelson!'

'That's hardly fair.'

'Bye now.' And before she can say any more, I close the door on both of them.

Of course I'm going for a walk. I know this area like the back of my hand. Still, with my leg only just out of plaster, I don't think I'll go too far. Maybe just to Painter Boy's house and back. I'll go across country as well, rather than sticking to the main road. It'll be nice to stroll through the warm early evening air and maybe sit down and just drink in the view. Julie and Adam are great company but neither of them is that interested in walking. They're pub and club people. When I was in London, I was like that too. I think I'd let myself forget the way I used to be.

Before I leave, I check my phone for messages. None.

Adam still hasn't rung. I shove my mobile into my pocket, pull on a raincoat and gingerly push my feet into my trainers. It's weird wearing shoes again. My leg feels weak and heavy at the same time. I close all the windows, though it's highly unlikely we'd have a break-in, take the key and lock the front door. Shoving my hands into my pockets, I begin to walk.

It takes a lot longer than I anticipate to get to Logan's cottage. I approach it from the side and when I get there, I'm exhausted. I sit on his wall and admire the lovely bunch of wild flowers I have picked and then I find my eyes drawn to his house. To my surprise, it's in good nick. The white-washed walls gleam brightly, the dying sunlight making them look a sort of rosy red. And the windows are cleaner than ours at the cottage. His garden is a bit untamed though, but in a nice way. Wild flowers – poppies, buttercups, daisies, dandelions and some blue ones that I don't know the name of – are in bloom and sway about in the light breeze. I lean over the wall and take a few of the blue ones to add to my posy. A big fat ginger cat sits in the shade of the porch, eyeing me malevolently. I like cats but this one seems a bit too much like its owner for comfort. It stares at me, before getting to its feet and arching its back. Then it hisses a little at me, making me jump.

'Piss off,' I hiss back.

The cat hisses a little more.

I hiss back and give it the two fingers.

'Have you permission to be here?' a voice behind asks, making me fall off the wall. It's him. With a stupid grin on his face and his hands in his pockets.

'Your cat is a danger.' I scramble to my feet, mortified to be caught hissing back at his stupid cat.

'Here, Ginger,' Logan says, calling the cat, his hand outstretched. 'Here, Ginger.'

Ginger. What an inspired name.

The cat eyes me, then eyes Logan and finally comes towards us, its tail in the air. With a nimble leap, it hops on to the wall and from there on to Logan's shoulder.

'Ginger, meet Hope. Hope, this is Ginger.'

The cat and I grimace at each other.

'She's very unfriendly and aggressive, but you'll get used to her.'

I'm about to say that I have no intention of getting used to his cat, when it strikes me that he's talking about me to his cat.

'I could say the same about you,' I retort. I brush myself down. 'Now, sorry for trespassing, but I knew you'd understand, being a superior trespasser yourself. I'll go now.'

When I turn to leave he exclaims, 'Hey, you've no crutch.'

'No.' I feel shy at his look of delight. 'I, eh, got my plaster off today.'

'Brill. I broke my leg once, the itch nearly killed me.'

'Me too.' I smile briefly before turning away again.

'So how'd you break it – fall from some high moral ground, did ya?'

I'll show him and his very smart comments. 'Actually, I was in an aeroplane accident.'

My heart lurches at the words. I wonder will I ever get used to saying it.

'Ha ha.'

'It's true.'

Doubt clouds his black eyes. 'Really? When?'

'May.'

'That London plane – the one that crashed on landing?'

'The very one.'

That silences him. He looks at me with something akin to awe. 'Wow.'

His look silences me. In fact, I very nearly feel tears in the back of my eyes. I don't know why, I can't explain it. Anyway, I blink them back hard and again attempt to leave.

'I know when I broke my leg, it hurt like hell when I walked any distance on it.'

I smirk slightly, unable to resist. 'Well, that's not surprising; it was probably hard for it, having to support your inflated ego.'

He laughs. 'Good one. Still, your leg must be sore now. D'you fancy –' he shrugs, pets his cat, which has curled itself about his shoulders and is rubbing the side of his face with its nose – 'well, d'you fancy a cuppa or a can of beer to help you on your way home?' His eyes slide away from his cat and meet mine.

I suppose it's a kind of peace gesture. Like the way his stormy painting was. I'm not sure if I need another peace gesture, though. There is something about this guy that sends prickles of irritation up my skin. It's the way he won't let me win, I think.

'Well?' he asks.

'I suppose I could spare a moment to keep you company,' I answer airily. 'Do you not have many friends then?'

He flinches a bit but rallies. 'Well, most people with a life probably are doing something tonight. I just thought, seeing as you weren't . . .' He gives a cocky grin, puts the cat down and strides into the cottage.

I allow myself a smile now before following him inside.

The first thing that strikes me is that it's so cool. Not cool as in trendy, cool as in it could be freezing in winter.

It's surprisingly bright too. The big window at the front floods the front room with light. He uses this as a studio: large canvases are stacked against the wall, smaller ones beside them. Some paintings are hung, to help them dry, I suppose. The stench of oil paint is everywhere. I remember the smell from art class at school. I don't get much of a chance to stare at them; all I get is the impression of lots of green and blue and red before Logan calls me from the kitchen.

His kitchen is bigger than ours and there is a small room leading off it – a sort of den where I notice a TV and DVD recorder.

'Tea? Coffee? Beer?'

I opt for the coffee. He gets a beer for himself from the fridge then puts on the kettle and leans against a counter top as we wait for it to boil. I don't know what to say now I'm standing in front of him on his own territory. He's taller than I realised and leaner and better looking. In a mean, rangy sort of way. His hair is mussed up, standing in spikes all over his head and he needs a shave. His eyes are an intense blue and he has the sort of mouth that seems to wear a permanent sardonic grin. Or at least it does whenever I see him. He's grinning at me now.

'So you don't drink beer,' he says, breaking the silence.

'Nope. I don't drink.' A complete lie and I have no idea why I'm saying it. 'I hate drink.'

'I love it. Cheers.' He raises his can and takes a big long slug. 'Ahhhh,' he says then. 'That's good.'

'Your cottage is bigger than ours.' It comes out like an accusation.

'Yep. Nice, isn't it? I hope to buy it from the landlord one day – I only have the money to rent it at the moment. When

I get the cash from the hotel commission, I might be able to make a deposit on it.'

'Oh. Good.' I study my ragged nails. I really would like to sit down, I think. My leg is aching. 'How's that coming along?'

'Well, aside from a mishap here and there –' he grins a little – 'pretty good.'

'Good.'

More silence.

He breaks it again. He coughs a bit and says awkwardly, 'Look, Hope, I know we got off to a bad start. To be frank, you really pissed me off when you sat in the middle of my sketch, but I was having a bad day overall, anyway.' The kettle clicks off and he turns to fill my cup. 'Sorry about that.'

It's a nice apology, I think. 'It's fine. I can barely remember it.'

'Yeah. Right.' He rolls his eyes and hands me the cup.

'Thanks.'

'Come on,' he indicates the sitting room. 'Let's sit down.'

The room is small and cosy. I make for a battered but comfy orange chair and sink into it with relief.

Logan sits opposite.

'So, can we start over?' he asks, hunching forward towards me.

There's a surprise. I half smile at him. 'OK,' I shrug, 'why not?'

'I mean,' he goes on, smiling back at me, 'it's important to quit when you're ahead.'

'You're not ahead,' I say. 'You surrendered.'

'Yeah, I suppose, you're better at it than I am.'

'Thank you.'

'You must have had a hard and bitter childhood to get so good.'

Bastard. If it wasn't so true, I'd admire him for that one. 'You mustn't have had a childhood at all to act so childishly when I met you,' I say sweetly.

He grins slightly. I realise that I too am smiling. That's a bit of a shocker. We smile at each other for a few seconds until we both realise that we're doing it and avert our eyes.

'I'm Logan,' he says after a bit, standing over me. 'Logan Jones. I'm from Dublin. I'm twenty-eight and I sculpt. At the moment, I'm stuck doing a bloody commission for a new hotel as last year I won a prize for my work. I earn fuck all, love this part of the world and have a mean temper when someone ruins a picture on me. I don't get to talk to many people and I like it that way. You?'

He's got a nice voice when he talks conversationally. It's warm and sweet and friendly. Despite my reservations, I'm warming to him. I don't know if I want to.

'I'm Hope Gardner,' I begin. 'I'm from Dunport. My mother still lives here. I'm twenty-seven and at the moment I'm between jobs, having been fired from my sixteenth job a couple of months ago, don't even go there. I, too, as you can guess, am earning fuck all. I live in London and share a house with Adam and Julie. And I have a mean temper when people shout at me.'

'And why did you lose your sixteenth job?'

'Piss off.' I take a gulp of coffee. It's not so hot now and tastes great.

'How'd you ever swap here for London?'

I smile at him. 'London is great. Mad night-life. Good fun.'

'Yeah, but you love it here, I know you do. I saw you that

149

day when you were in the garden, you just drank in the view. Just like I do.'

'What do you sculpt?' Not that I'm interested, but I don't want to think about how I love this place.

'Mainly wood.' He regards me for a bit before asking, almost shyly, 'D'you want to see some stuff I've done this summer?'

'Sure, yeah.'

'Come this way.' He pulls open his back door and strides ahead of me into the field. He has a small shed behind his house, which he unlocks. Flicking on a light, I am amazed to see a workshop with various kinds of wood all lying about the place. The smell of the shaved wood is gorgeous too. Logan picks his way through the mess and, beckoning me over, he holds up a beautiful bird, in full flight, all carved in meticulous detail. Its feathers actually seem real. The whole thing gleams from the inside out, almost as if it had a spirit. 'I finished this last night. What d'you think?'

Reverently, I touch it. It's warm. 'You did that?'

'Yep.' He gently puts it down. 'It just appeared out of the wood. You like it?'

'Yeah.' It touches me somehow, that bird. The freedom of it. Of course I don't say this. 'It's really good. Beautiful.'

'I like birds,' he says. Then grinning a little, he adds, 'The human variety especially.'

'How original,' I say drily. 'You should stick to the sculpting. Or carving or whatever you call it.'

'I figured that out myself a long time ago,' he says back. 'Nothing but heartbreak otherwise.'

'You said it.'

'So, d'you want another coffee?'

It's getting quite dusky out. It'll be dark if I stay any longer. 'I'd better head off.'

'Don't be a stranger now – call over again, eh?'

I don't really think I will. Still, it hasn't been as bad as I thought and he actually does seem nice. 'Thanks for the coffee,' I say.

'No problem. Safe home.'

We nod to each other, then he turns to his workbench and I make my exit.

It takes me what feels like hours to walk home. I have definitely overdone the whole leg bit. By the time I reach the front door, I'm feeling so sorry for myself that I barely register Adam sitting on the doorstep.

'Hey!' He startles me out of my reverie and I jump about ten feet in the air. 'Sorry, Hope.'

'Nah, it's fine. God, it's good to see you.' He looks totally dishevelled, despite the fact that he has a suit and tie on. His tie is pulled loose and his shirt is hanging out over his trousers. 'Where have you been?' Without giving him time to answer, I unlock the front door, saying, 'Julie and I were so worried. We left about a hundred messages on your phone. In fact, I wouldn't be surprised if Julie is ringing you even now and ruining her date.'

'Oh,' Adam plonks wearily down on to the sofa and pinches the bridge of his nose with two fingers. 'So she's still seeing Gym Boy.'

'Yep.'

He heaves a great big sigh, closes his eyes and leans his head back. Something is wrong. Something awful. 'Hey,' I sit down beside him and catch his arm. 'Was it really bad?'

He doesn't answer for a second. Then, he gulps and says, 'Yep. Any wine?'

I jump up, grab a bottle of red and uncork it. All the time, he sits, staring at his hands and his feet until, after I hand him an enormous glass of red, his eyes meet mine. His hand is shaking as he lifts the glass to his lips and takes a huge gulp of the drink. I wish I could join him. 'So?' I probe gently.

'I'm, eh, suspended,' he mutters, looking into his glass.

'Suspended?'

'Surprisingly, they didn't like the fact that I took off to Kerry and never told them,' he tries to make a joke about it. 'Nor did they like the fact that the fifty grand was missing for months.'

'But that bit wasn't your fault!'

'I'm in charge. And anyway, the guys in the stores said they never got the memo.'

'But you sent it!' Oh, I'm full of indignation for him. 'And did you tell them that your friend was at death's door and that's why you came to Kerry!'

'Nope.' He grins a little now. 'With all due respect, Hope, whether you live or die is of no importance to them.'

'Huh – that's bloody businessmen for you.'

'Yeah.' He nods in agreement but I don't think he really means it.

'So, how long are you suspended for?'

He winces. Swirls his drink about in his glass. 'Until September, then they'll review the situation.'

I think that's great, though I don't say it. He's got all summer with me and Julie now. He won't have to go upstairs to his laptop any more. We can have a blast together and then he can resume work when we all go back to London.

'That long?' I say, trying to sound sympathetic. 'How'll you manage for money?'

'I do have savings,' he says as if it's obvious. 'And if the worst comes to the worst, I can always sell the houses. In fact, I'll probably have to sell one of them as the mortgage is huge on it. And I won't be getting paid.'

'Oh no!'

'Oh yeah.' He takes another gulp of wine and clears his glass. He really is turning into a bit of an alco. I pour him half a glass and he raises his eyebrows so I fill it. 'So, where were you tonight?'

I welcome the change of subject. To be honest, it's a bit rich me sympathising with him over his job. I'd never stand to be suspended. I'd probably tell them that if they didn't trust me they could shove their stupid job. In fact that's what Adam should have done. I flirt with telling him this but he asks again where I've been. For some reason, I don't want to mention Logan so I just stick out my plasterless leg and say airily, 'Oh, just exercising my completely healed leg.'

He doesn't say anything for a bit, just smiles at me affectionately. Then he nods. 'I'm so proud of you. You're such a fighter.'

'Yeah, going into battle with all my bosses over the years has stood me well, eh?'

He laughs. It's good to see him laugh. 'So, did you go far?'

'About two miles in all.'

'Isn't that a bit far?'

'Yeah. I know that *now*.'

Another laugh, and then he asks, 'And Julie, how's she getting on with Gym Boy?'

'OK, I think.'

'Does she like him a lot?'

He asks the question in a casual manner but by the way he looks at me, I think he really wants to know. Jesus, I wonder if he fancies her. I hope not, I don't want our friendship to be ruined by him liking her and her turning him down. I shrug and decide to opt for a casual tone. 'I don't know. I think he likes *her* a lot. He's a bit phoney, to be honest. It's like he's trying to be something he's not.'

He doesn't say much to that, just drinks another large mouthful. 'And your mother?'

And so I spend the next forty minutes or so telling him about the meeting with my mother. 'So it didn't go well?' he asks at last.

'Not brilliantly,' I admit. 'If only Amanda hadn't called, it might have been better.'

'Yeah, but Hope, how can you let her have this hold over you? So she picked on you, maybe you should just let it go. Move on. Try and rebuild.' He's slurring his words now, he's quite drunk I think. I wonder if he's been drinking at the airport.

'She bullied me,' I say.

Adam laughs at that. 'Hope, she didn't bully you, believe me, you don't know how bad real bullying can get.' He laughs again, half to himself, and pours the dregs of the bottle into his glass. 'And Julie? What's the story with her folks, have they rung yet?'

I tell him about that and about my counselling until at last I dry up. It's just as well, because he seems to be falling asleep.

'Maybe you should go to bed?' I suggest gently.

'Yep.' He puts his glass on the table and, swaying quite a bit, stands up. 'Night.'

I swallow hard and almost lose my nerve, but just as he turns to the stairs, I say in a rush, 'Sorry for being partly responsible for you being suspended.'

He freezes and turns back to me. To my relief, he looks incredulous. 'It's not your fault,' he says and shakes his head in amazement. 'I chose to come. I wanted to be with you both. I wanted a holiday. You having that accident opened my eyes, you know? You can't think like that, Hope.' He says all this in a drunken way, but he means it. He crosses towards me. 'You getting better is worth losing my job for.'

'Losing?'

'Yeah.' He nods vigorously, his face red. 'You know, if I did lose it.'

'You won't lose it.'

'Come here.' He attempts to enfold me in a hug but ends up missing me and walloping his hip off the side of the table.

'Bloody hell, that hurts.'

I'm so glad he's back.

16

JULIE GIVES ADAM a huge hug when she sees him the next day. He and I are up early and munching on some stale bread. He looks tired and hungover, as if he hasn't slept and I probably look the same. I awoke at some weird hour in the morning after having the most horrendous dream about the crash. This time, I was being shoved away and pushed hard and things were hurtling towards me and falling down on top of me. I woke up, sweating, right down at the bottom of the sleeping bag. I'd been a bit afraid to go back to sleep after it.

So, I'd done what Tim suggested. I'd got up, found a stray piece of paper and a pen and written down an alternative ending to the dream. Even recalling the dream had left me quite shaken, but I had. Then, I'd changed it. In my imaginary dream, the things falling on top of me were soft and gentle and weren't hurting me. They were pillows, things that would give me a good night's sleep.

Adam manages a pretty convincing smile when Julie waltzes downstairs. She's tired looking too and her hair is messed up. 'Hey,' he grins. 'Good night?'

'Adam!' She flings her arms about him and then, holding him away from her, she scolds, 'Why didn't you return any of my calls?'

'I had a lot on, sorry.'

'That's not good enough.' She sounds quite cross. 'Hope and I, we thought you'd done something stupid.'

'Yeah, I took off to Kerry and didn't tell my boss.'

'No. You know what I mean. We were so worried.' She sits down beside him and stares up at him. 'Only for the fact that I'm so glad to see you, I'd ignore you for the rest of the holiday.'

'Sounds tempting.'

I excuse myself as Adam starts to tell Julie what he'd told me last night.

I'm just emerging from the shower when I see him. Logan is tramping across our garden and to my horror I see he has a bunch of wild flowers in his hand. *My* wild flowers. I'd forgotten all about them and now he's going to present me with them and Julie and Adam will know that I've been in his house.

Then I think, so what? What's wrong with me being in his house?

The answer of course is nothing, but if there was nothing wrong with it, then why didn't I mention it? That's what they'll ask. Why didn't you tell us, Hope? Why did you forget to tell us that you'd been in Logan's house? I thought you hated him.

Oh God! I watch hopelessly as he gets nearer and nearer the back door. I want to call out but as I'm standing in nothing but my tracksuit trousers and bra, I can't. My clean T-shirt is blowing about on the line and I never brought it in with me. It had still been damp and I thought that maybe another ten minutes in the sun would dry it.

Fool, I curse myself.

Frantically, I scrabble about for my pyjama top and can't find the stupid thing. I poke my head out again and he's about three feet from the door.

Shit! Shit! Shit!

'Logan!' I yell. 'Over here!'

He stops and turns towards my voice.

'Over here,' I call. I still can't find my top. How far can it go in a bathroom?

Logan begins to walk towards me and I hastily slam the bathroom door closed.

'Hello?' he says hesitantly.

'Out in a minute.' I force the panic from my voice.

And there it is, drowning in a pool of water. I pick it up, squeeze it out and pull it over my head. Yeuch.

'Hi,' I say breezily, opening the door and running my fingers through my hair. It's a bit embarrassing, emerging from a bathroom to talk to a guy you hardly know. I'm a bit anally retentive like that, so I say, 'I was just having a shower.'

'Yeah . . .' his upper lip rises in a smirk: 'with your clothes on and everything.' And then he looks at my clothes and he grins a bit more. 'Wow, is that true then?' He nods at the slogan on my pyjamas.

Honestly, why do pyjama manufacturers do that? Why do they think it's cute or funny to have messages scrawled over pyjama tops? Mine says, *I think this is hot*, with the 'hot' written in big tall letters. There is a picture of a chilli beside it. And I'd bought the pyjamas in the mistaken belief that it was an innocent message about chillis. But Julie, ever the wise one and always looking for the unsaid in the English language, pointed out to me that the chilli was in fact a very phallic symbol and that it also rhymed with *that* particular part of the male anatomy. I'd been a little shocked but mostly disbelieving and had continued to wear my suggestive attire. Logan's mind obviously worked on the same one track as Julie's.

'Have you never tasted a chilli then?' I ask innocently, looking at Logan.

'Nope.' His grin has broadened out. 'But I did hear that women prefer the bigger ones.'

I'm left with my mouth open. I can't think of a reply. Logan reaches out his free hand and gently puts his finger under my chin and before I'm aware of it, he's closing my mouth! 'Your flowers from yesterday.' He holds them out to me with an exaggerated gallantry.

'You didn't have to.' But I take them from him all the same. My face is flaming red, I'm sure of it.

'Oh I did,' Logan nods in an infuriatingly smug way. 'I also heard that when a woman leaves something behind her, it's a signal that she wants it brought back as an excuse to see the person again.'

'You're listening to the wrong people,' I scoff as I attempt to march by him.

'I added a few flowers of my own to the bouquet,' he calls after me. 'Yours was a bit pathetic – the colours were all wrong.'

'I was wondering what the pansies were doing in it all right,' I retaliate. 'Now I know.'

'They're not pansies,' he says patronisingly. 'They're –'

'Who's out there?' Julie pokes her head out the kitchen door. 'Oh, hi Logan,' she beams. 'Come to paint?'

'No he hasn't.' I attempt to go by her and close the door on him.

'Just came to bring Hope back the flowers she left at my place yesterday.'

159

Now Julie's mouth is open. She gawps at me as I stalk in past her.

'She was in your place yesterday,' she says. 'When?'

'I wasn't actually *in* it,' I attempt to explain before he can make matters worse. 'I more or less had to go in as I was tired from my walk.'

'That's it,' Logan spreads his arms wide. 'She was tired and so she had a cup of coffee and a chat, and what an entertaining companion she is. Full of put-downs and *joie de vivre*.'

Julie giggles and then at my expression stops and starts up again. 'She's great really,' she says, flustered.

'Yeah, I thought that too,' Logan nods. 'I'm a bit upset as I only gave her a cup of coffee. I would have given her a chilli if I'd known she liked them,' he goes on in a mock-regretful voice.

Julie guffaws loudly.

'It depends on whose chilli it is,' I say, grinning. 'Yours would probably be too small.'

Julie laughs again.

'I can work on growing it bigger.'

'Oh,' I say, feigning disgust as I move from the door. Julie thinks he's hilarious altogether and I leave her to talk to him while I busy myself looking for a mug to put the flowers in. They do look nice with the extra ones he has added and when I put them on the windowsill they add a lovely splash of much-needed colour to the kitchen.

A couple of hours later, after Julie and Adam had become completely juvenile about my visit to Logan's, we head to the beach at Inch.

It's one of the nicest beaches in the area. You'd swear a

kid got a box of crayons and painted the sky bright blue, the sand pure gold and the cliffs bright green.

'I wonder if Logan's chilli is an Inch,' Julie says airily, as she spreads the rug from Adam's car on the sand.

I ignore her and plonk down, an edition of the *Dunport News* in my hand. Adam and Julie change into swimming gear and while Adam heads off down the beach to the water, Julie plasters herself in factor 2 and lies down. I put on sunglasses and start to read the paper. There's a big piece about the progress of the new hotel and of how Jack Dunleavy has commissioned lots of Irish companies to supply things for it. Suddenly, a drone in the distance causes me to freeze. It's an aeroplane. It's coming in across the sea and I see it without even looking for it. The sun glints on the steel and immediately, behind my sunglasses, I close my eyes. I can't help but think of all those people up there, staring down at me. I want to run but there is nowhere I can go. I'm out in the open. I shove my hands into my ears but Julie must have heard the plane too.

'Hope, it's a plane,' she says.

Since the session with Tim, I haven't actually seen any planes. This is the first one. But I wrote about my nightmare, I tell myself. I can't be expected to do everything all at once.

'I have to get out of here,' I breathe heavily. My eyes are still closed. 'Please Julie, let's go.'

'But Hope, you –'

'Julie!'

'Look up, Hope,' Adam says. He must have come back up from the sea. 'Look up and I'll count one second and you can look down.'

'I can't.' I stare fiercely downwards.

161

'Yes you can.' He takes off my sunglasses. 'Come on.'

'No.' I try to push past him.

I'm sure people are looking at the three of us. I don't care.

He grabs me by both arms. 'One second. Pretend it's something else you're looking at.'

'I can't.' The drone is getting louder; the plane is more or less overhead now. I'm sweating. 'Let me go!'

'I'll buy the wine for tomorrow night?'

'I can't drink. Please let me –'

'We'll stop teasing you about Logan?' Julie offers.

I don't think even that will tempt me.

'If you don't look you'll think, why didn't I do it? It was only one second. Come on, Hope.'

Adam sounds as if he thinks I can do it. And he's right, I will regret it. Steeling myself, I ask him to count. Slowly I drag my gaze away from the rug, up to Adam's legs, up to his blue swimming shorts and his encouraging gaze. Up past his butchered hair and on to the blue sky and the wispy clouds.

'There,' Adam points to the plane as it trails smoke in its wake. 'See it.'

I glance up, he counts to one and my gaze shoots down. I am wrecked.

'Well done!' It's as if I've won the lotto. 'Good girl!' He cheers a little and says, 'Next time two seconds.'

Julie claps her hands.

I have to take deep breaths. But I force myself to listen to its drone until I can't hear it any more. And I feel proud of myself. Probably for the first time ever.

Two more planes fly over that day and with Adam and Julie by my side, I steel my nerve and look at them. The third time, I don't feel as apprehensive. In fact, I manage to gaze at it for three seconds as Adam waves away at it like a loon, making me laugh. 'You're such a kid,' I joke.

'Don't remind me,' he smiles back, then says, 'I'll have you waving by the end of the holiday.'

In fact what happens is that when the fourth plane goes over, some kids beside us think it's a game and they join in waving. Then the little girl says to her brother, 'They're waving at me, not at you!'

And I laugh out loud.

17

ANOTHER WEEK, ANOTHER counselling session. Adam drives me this time and he's under instructions from Julie to buy some nice wine as she has decided to cook dinner for us on our return. Neither Adam nor I is too excited at that prospect.

I stand outside Tim's office, half afraid to go in. He seems to be shouting at someone. I knock and he yells out something; I think it's a 'come in', so I open the door. He's got his back to me and is on the phone. 'You are such a stubborn cow,' he hisses before turning to me and reddening. 'Eh, have to go, talk later.' He slams the phone down on a shrieking voice.

'I hope that's not the last person you treated,' I joke feebly.

He gives an equally feeble laugh and doesn't answer. Instead, he sits down and beckons me to do the same. Then he begins by asking me how I've got on in the past week. I find myself telling him that despite all my hard work, I have continued to wake up screaming at nights. I can't recall the dreams, I only remember the feeling of utter terror that I'm being suffocated.

'Did you try and change the ending of the dream?'

'Yes.'

'OK, well, keep reviewing your ending over and over

before you go to sleep, visualise it, tell yourself that you don't care if you have the nightmare, that you will deal with it. Get your mind into that sort of mode.' He flashes me a quick smile. 'It's like brainwashing yourself.'

I nod, then tell him about the work I've done listening to the planes. He's very pleased with that. 'OK,' Tim nods. 'You've done well, Hope. You can listen to a plane without running inside. I know it's still scary, but can't you see how well you're getting on?'

'Yeah.'

'What I want you to do for next week then is to work on the crisps. Try and see if you can just look at a packet without getting panicky. Then maybe get someone to rustle them. Then open them. Then smell them. Do it in small stages. If the anxiety for one step goes away, go on to the next step. If you find that you get very agitated, slow it down, come and talk to me about it, OK?'

'OK.'

'Now what I'm going to do with you this week –'

He is interrupted by the phone ringing. 'Sorry about this.' He picks it up and immediately I hear an angry voice yelling at him. Tim doesn't reply. He listens until the voice has run out of energy then says as pleasantly as he can, 'Thank you for your call. Your comments have been noted.' With that, he hangs up the phone.

Offering me no explanation, he re-starts his sentence but, as before, the phone rings. Tim flushes, then says, 'I'm just going to disconnect this, Hope, if you don't mind.' He pulls the lead out of the phone and looks very satisfied with himself. Then he continues as if nothing out of the ordinary has happened. 'As I was saying, what we're going to do this week is to work on relaxation exercises. I'm going to give you techniques you can use whenever you feel panicky or agitated. You can use these during your homework exercises and also during the exposure therapy I will carry out here.'

'OK.'

Tim looks like he could do with some relaxation himself, I think.

'Now you have to practise these exercises,' he continues, somewhat sternly.

'I will.'

He then proceeds to show me different ways of relaxing both my body and mind. 'You'll use these the next time you come,' he tells me. 'What I'm going to do in the next session is to create your first exposure tape. It'll be you describing your early memories of your mother's depression and as you talk about it, you will get anxious. If your anxiety reaches a level of ten, we'll stop and try to get you relaxed before beginning again. Does that make sense?'

'Yes.' I'm tempted now to cancel the next session but I know Julie and Adam won't let me. And I suppose, if push came to shove, I wouldn't let myself either. It's strange, but being able to conquer my fear of the aeroplanes has brought me back in touch just a little. By facing the fear, I know I can face other things.

Tim goes over and over the relaxation techniques with me and then makes out a step by step chart of how I should deal with the 'crisp' issue. God, it sounds so trivial but it's not. Everywhere I go, people munch on cheese and onion. I can't stop going out just because of the smell of them, can I?

The hour ends very quickly and as I leave, Tim tells me that the next time we will have an hour and a half. 'This day next week,' he says.

I see him reconnect the phone and immediately it rings. He looks furious as he answers it.

Julie has invited Logan to dinner. 'He was passing and he looked hungry,' she says.

And, as dinner progresses, I realise that he is hungry. Starving, in fact. Any man that can ingest meat that looks like the remains of an abattoir fire has got to be ravenous.

'Nice one,' Logan says, polishing off his last potato. 'God, it's ages since I had a decent meal.'

'And after today, it'll be even longer,' Adam chortles as he cracks open more wine. Julie throws a spoon at him from across the table.

Adam pours wine for everyone as I get up to fill my glass with water.

'So you really don't drink,' Logan calls after me. 'I thought you were fooling me that day in my house.'

'No challenge in fooling a fool,' I say back as the water splashes into my glass. The water up here is lovely.

'Hope drinks all right,' Julie says. 'She just can't at the moment.'

I freeze. Water runs over the top of the glass and on to my hand. What did she have to say that for?

'Why not at the moment?'

A pause before Julie babbles, 'Oh, well, eh . . .' Her voice dies out to be replaced by an awkward silence.

'Did I just put my foot in it?' I hear Logan ask.

'No,' I call from the kitchen, turning off the tap. I steel myself and come back into the room. All three look at me. 'I can't drink because I'm having counselling about the accident.'

'Yeah?'

'Yeah. I'm still a bit freaked out by certain things, so the counsellor told me that it was best not to drink.'

'That's rough,' Logan nods sympathetically and for once there is no joke behind his remarks.

'Yeah,' I stare at my hands. 'But it'll get better.'

'Of course it will,' Julie gushes. 'No doubt about it!' I think she's trying to make up for her lack of discretion. 'Hope is a fighter! Isn't she, Adam?'

Adam nods silently.

'So, what things freak you out?' Logan asks.

God, I hadn't banked on him being quite so frank. 'Mainly guys shouting at me first thing in the morning,' I joke.

Logan smiles, tipping me a half-salute, '*Touché!*'

'You don't have to be in counselling for things to freak you out,' Julie says, over-compensating again for her remarks. 'It's normal, Hope, to be freaked out by certain things. Adam,' she pounces on him, 'what would freak you out?'

'Dunno.'

'Well, who would freak you out?'

Adam is pretty well on. Again. He thinks deeply before saying, 'Well, when I was sixteen, I had a breakdown.'

'Where?' Julie says. 'On the motorway or something?'

'A mental breakdown,' Adam says without a trace of his usual discomfiture. He's going to die in the morning, I think. And it won't be from a hangover. 'I had a breakdown and my mother took me to counselling. And I told that guy everything. I'd hate to meet him again. It'd be so embarrassing.'

Julie looks gobsmacked. I don't think she was expecting that. 'Right – OK – Logan?'

'I'm not finished,' Adam says grumpily. 'I'd also hate to meet his secretary, I had a crush on his secretary and made a fool of myself. I'd also hate to meet the blokes in the store

168

who said I didn't send on that e-mail and I'd also hate to meet –'

'That's a lot of people,' Julie says uneasily.

'Mmm.' Adam nods and nods and fills up his glass again. He's been in a strange mood since he got back from London.

'Logan?' Julie asks.

Logan is not so drunk as the other two but he's getting there. He's got no respect for wine, tossing it back as if it's water. 'My ex,' he grins a little but it doesn't quite meet his eyes.

'Why?' Julie asks.

'Well, because she's my ex,' Logan shrugs. 'Not a nice business meeting your ex.'

'Oh I dunno,' Julie says airily. 'I always like to meet my exes when I'm done up and show them what they missed out on. I quite like that, actually.'

'Well, my ex only missed out on a rented bungalow in the middle of nowhere.'

'Ah, but what a nowhere,' I say. 'Best nowhere view in the world.'

'True,' Logan agrees. 'But unlike your good and intelligent self, Hope, my ex thought it was the dingiest, most horrible place she'd ever been. We owned a house in Dublin and she wanted to move back but I didn't. She missed her beauty salons and her shops.' He's smiling but he sounds incredibly hurt.

'So you split up?'

'Yep. Acrimoniously.'

'That's awful,' Julie remarks.

'It was. But life goes on.' He doesn't sound as if he believes it.

'And now, me,' Julie says. 'Who would I hate to meet?' Another frown. Then a shrug. 'I can't think of anyone. God,' she smiles, 'I like everyone.'

'What about your dad?' Adam drawls.

Julie's face clouds over. 'Oh yeah.'

'And your mother?'

'Yes.' Julie sounds uncomfortable now.

'And your sister?'

'Yes, Adam, thank you. I think Logan has got the picture.'

I don't think Logan was even listening. He's swirling his wine about in his glass with a sad look on his face.

Later that evening, Julie whispers to me, 'Adam isn't gay after all.'

'Yeah? How do you know?'

'Well, he said he fancied his shrink's secretary, didn't he?'

'You can have a male secretary,' I answer. 'You're very sexist.'

'Oh yeah.' Her face falls. 'Never thought of that. Damn.'

18

'THERE,' JULIE POINTS him out to us. 'See that man by the gift shop, with the briefcase, that's him.'

Adam and I gape at this first glimpse of Julie's dad. He's tall, thin and grey haired. That's all we can see, for he has his back to us. He is peering into the gift shop window, oblivious to the three of us staring at him. He's carrying a brown leather briefcase which he is swinging from side to side.

'Oh God,' Julie starts to chew on a nail. 'Oh God, I feel sick.'

I slap Julie's hand away from her mouth. I know she can't bear ragged nails mainly because mine are in bits and she gives me awful grief over them. 'He looks fine,' I say, cocking my head to one side, 'and he seems quite calm.'

'It's always calm before a storm.' Julie hops from foot to foot. 'Oooh, I think I'll ring him and say I'm sick.'

'Come on.' Adam grasps a reluctant Julie by the elbow and steers her towards her dad. When we get close, he drops her arm and hoists himself up to his skinny six foot two. Julie's father looks suddenly shorter.

'Hi, Dad,' Julie says to his back, a fake smile failing to illuminate her face. 'I see you found the shop.'

He turns to face us. He doesn't look so bad, I think. He's quite a handsome man in an older person type of way.

Tanned, rugged features, bit of a beaky nose, but with Julie's sparkling slate grey eyes.

'Hello Juliet.' His smile is curt and efficient, his voice brisk and to the point. It's as if he's talking to a business partner. It makes me recoil slightly. His gaze flicks to me and Adam.

'My friends.' Julie indicates me. 'This is Hope. She was injured in the plane crash, the London to Boston one – remember?'

'Yes,' he nods at me. 'You're a lucky girl. Nice to meet you.'

His handshake is reassuring. Nice and firm.

'And this is Adam,' Julie says. 'He's another friend.'

'Hello, Adam,' Mr Adcock says. 'Are you the man with all the houses?'

'Mortgaged to the hilt, you mean,' Adam says pleasantly.

'No matter. Initiative, I like that. Don't I like that, Juliet?'

'Yes,' Julie says wearily. 'Initiative equals success.'

'Initiative equals success,' Mr Adcock repeats as he rocks back and forward on his heels. 'Well, it was nice to meet you two. I hope you don't mind if I take Juliet off you for lunch.'

We'd rehearsed this. Unfortunately acting isn't my strong point.

'Lunch?' Adam says. He sounds so natural. I'm impressed. 'We haven't had lunch either. D'you fancy lunch, Hope?'

'Yes I do,' I say. I sound like a five-year-old repeating a poem she has learned. 'I – am – starving.'

'Maybe we can join you?' Adam says. 'I bet Julie is taking you to the Store, because if she is, that's our favourite place to go too.'

Mr Adcock visibly balks. 'Well,' he tries to say pleasantly, 'I had hoped to have my daughter to myself. I haven't seen her in a while.'

'Aw, that's great,' Adam ignores Mr Adcock's last comment and grins. 'Let's go.'

He strides ahead of the man and I scamper to catch up with him.

'Shit, he made it clear he doesn't want us there. Julie assured us that that wouldn't happen,' Adam hisses at me from the side of his mouth.

'And you made it clear that we're going anyway,' I say back out of the side of my mouth. 'Well done.'

He doesn't look so sure.

The Store is madly expensive. It's OK for Julie, her dad is paying for her, but for Adam and me, it's a different story. I think I can just about afford a lettuce leaf, while Adam's funds stretch to a sandwich.

'I thought you said you were both starving.' Mr Adcock looks sourly at our meagre plates.

'I am.' Adam rubs his stomach and says with a forced joviality, 'My favourite food is sandwiches.'

I'd laugh only Mr Adcock is making me nervous. No wonder Julie is scared of him.

'And Hope can only eat small portions at a time,' Julie chimes in, obviously not trusting me to come up with my own lie. 'Because of the operation.'

'What operation?' Julie's dad asks me.

'On my head,' I say.

Julie rolls her eyes. It's obviously the wrong answer.

'How would an operation on your head stop you from eating?' He seems genuinely interested. 'I've never heard of that before.'

'Oh,' I stare at my minuscule lunch. 'I can't remember all the details. It's all a bit fuzzy.'

'Mmm.' Mr Adcock stares at me for a moment, making me even more uncomfortable. Then he turns his attention to his dinner and attacks it with relish. Julie barely touches hers; she keeps giving him sideways glances and she can't seem to sit still.

The minutes tick past and no one says a word. Adam finishes his sandwich and I finish my tiny salad. Mr Adcock clears his plate and Julie plays with her food. More minutes pass and eventually the four of us are staring at each other and no one is saying anything. Mr Adcock has begun to look at Adam and me expectantly, as if he'd like us to leave, which I'm sure he would. Only Julie is almost imperceptibly shaking her head at us.

'So, eh, Mr Adcock, what are you doing over here?' My voice is a squeak. I fiddle with my fork.

'Attempting to have lunch with my daughter,' he says back. Quite rudely, I think.

'Oh,' I flush. 'I meant, work wise. Julie said you were over on business.'

'Medical conference,' he says abruptly.

'Dad is a surgeon,' Julie offers. 'Very well known. Very successful.'

'Oh, good for you,' I say lamely.

Mr Adcock acknowledges the compliment.

More silence.

Adam shuffles a bit. For all his brave talk, he doesn't seem to know what to say now. I cough and tell myself that I will not be the first to break. I will not be the first to break. I will not be the first to break.

'Oh Dad, just tell me why you're here!'

Adam and I jump.

Julie is staring desperately at her father. 'Go on, tell me.'

'To see you,' her father says evenly. 'To talk to you.'

'Well, talk then,' she says and I think she has decided to dive right in, for which I am secretly relieved. We could have been sitting there all afternoon otherwise. 'You can say what you want in front of Adam and Hope,' Julie continues. 'They're my friends.'

Mr Adcock shifts uncomfortably in his seat and fixes Julie with a steely glare. 'I don't think I want to discuss this in front of them.'

'Really?' Julie raises her eyebrows. 'Were you planning on discussing how I threw my career away?'

'If you want to put it like that, yes!' Her father nods, his gaze sweeping the table. 'Yes, I was.'

'Newsflash: I didn't throw anything away.' I have to admire Julie. Her voice shakes only slightly and she's maintaining the semblance of a smile as she speaks. 'I am a teacher, Dad. I teach children. I will always teach children because it's what I want to do.' She pauses and her voice rises a little. 'I do not want to be Angela.'

'Will you keep your voice down,' he snaps. 'No one is asking you to be Angela. And why didn't you tell your mother you were going away if you thought there was nothing wrong with it?'

'Because of this!' Julie spreads her hands wide. 'You. Your reaction.'

'I have done nothing bar have lunch with you and your friends.'

'Oh come on,' Julie's voice rises some more. 'You're only here because Mum sent you.'

'I am here because I am on business,' her dad matches her. 'But yes, your mother is upset. She feels that she has sacrificed herself to give you and your sister the best education she could, and how do you repay her? You take off without telling her.'

'And what about what I sacrificed for you,' Julie says and throws her knife down on the table where it bounces a little before landing in front of me. I don't know where to look and neither does Adam. Everyone else does: they are all staring over at us. From the corner of my eye I see a little man bustling across the room. 'I sacrificed my friends so I could study and be what you both wanted. I sacrificed my childhood to be a bloody swot and for what? For nothing.'

'Excuse me,' the manager tries to intervene. 'You can't really argue in here. We are trying to create a special ambience –'

'It's nothing because you didn't go for it,' her dad says back. He doesn't look so handsome now. A big cross line has appeared between his eyebrows. 'You could have been anything and you chose teaching so don't blame us for your nothing.'

'An ambience of calm, an oasis of –'

'The nothing is the fact that I have nothing from you. No childhood memories, no holidays unless they were to educational places, no funny times, no joy.'

'Folks,' Adam stands up.

'– peace. And we ask all our customers to –'

'I'm not sitting here taking this from you!' Mr Adcock bellows furiously, all composure gone now. 'How dare you speak to me like that!'

'Dad, I'm not scared of you or Mum any more. Another reason I never told her I was gone was because I was scared. I was scared of your reaction. Well, now I've had it, it's not so scary.'

'– respect that. So please –'

'Oh shut up,' Mr Adcock snarls at the manager. He throws a pile of notes down on the table and then jabbing his finger at Julie, says, 'We never scared you, don't try and put that on us.' He starts to leave the table.

'Oh yes you did! Do you know when you couldn't figure out how your car had the big scratch on it? Well, Dad, it was me. I accidentally scraped it with my bike, but I couldn't tell you because I was so bloody scared. Do you remember the time when –'

But he has gone.

Julie stands there for a second before swaying and bursting into tears.

'If I'd known your dad was going to pay, I'd have had a bigger dinner,' Adam says a little later, as we sit in a dark, old-man's pub. 'I'm so hungry, I could even eat something that you've cooked, Ju.'

Julie slaps him absently and picks up a beer mat. She begins tearing it to pieces. 'I'm sorry about the scene,' her voice wobbles. 'I didn't know that was going to happen. I thought, I don't know, that he'd,' she crumbles the card-board between her fingers, 'well, I don't know what I thought.'

Adam looks at me over her head.

'You did the right thing, Ju,' I say. 'Only thing is, what happens now?'

Julie shrugs. 'Well, I'm not apologising. I did nothing wrong.'

'Just, you know, don't lose contact.'

'Are you joking?' Adam says playfully. 'If that was my dad, I'd run very fast in the opposite direction.'

Julie's giggles turn into sniffs and soon she's crying again.

177

'He's not so bad,' she says tearfully. 'But I just, well I just can't put up with it any more. Their rules, their expectations. I just can't.'

'Aw, come on, Ju.' I watch, in a sort of detached way that scares me, as Adam takes her face between his hands and wipes her tears away with his thumb. Then he lays her head against his chest and runs his long hands up and down her hair while making drinking signals with his free arm.

I head up to the bar, glad to be able to do something to help. Adam is a lot better at the touchy-feely stuff now for some reason, while I, who was never fantastic but who would have been able to hug a friend, am floundering.

As I look at him murmuring gently to her and her smiling back at him, I vow that I will get back to the land of the living if it kills me. For no matter how bad Julie is feeling, it's a hell of a lot better than not feeling anything at all.

I bring the drinks down to the table. Three oranges. Julie is still snuggled up in Adam's arms and they look nice together, in a friendly sort of way. 'D'you know something, Ju, your dad can give out all he wants about you, but he really can't afford to. He's not exactly a hot-shot doctor himself, is he?'

'Isn't he? Why?'

'Well,' I sit down and take a sip of my orange, 'he'd never heard of the "eat-less-head-operation", had he? I mean, come on, who hasn't heard of that?'

Her laughter is definitely my best medicine.

19

T IM IS NOT pleased with me at all. 'So you haven't
exposed yourself to crisps?' he says.

I'm not in the habit of exposing myself to packets of
crisps, I could say, but I haven't the nerve. He really isn't
impressed with me and I feel a little ashamed of myself too.
'It's just that some friends of mine have been upset recently
and I kind of forgot about it.'

Tim raises his eyebrows. 'Now look, Hope –'

'I'm sorry, OK. I'll try it for the next week.'

Tim nods. 'Make sure you do. I really can't work with
you if you're not going to put in the effort, Hope.'

'I've practised all the relaxation.' I attempt to gain some
Brownie points. 'I'm ready to talk or whatever today.'
Actually, I've been terrified of it, but now I'm afraid to admit
that.

This at least elicits a small smile. 'Good.' Tim turns to
his Dictaphone. 'Now Hope, I'll ask you questions as you
talk. If you feel anxious, stop and relax. Let me know the
quality of anxiety you are experiencing on a scale of one
to ten, all right?'

I can only nod. Tim talks me through some relaxation so
that by the time he switches on the recorder, I'm feeling
very chilled.

'Right, Hope,' Tim talks slowly, 'you told me that when your father died your mother began to get depressed. What age were you?'

'Six, almost seven. My brother was about three.'

'And you also said,' he consults his notes, 'that you never got washed or went to school or anything. What was your mother doing?'

'Just lying in bed all day. She didn't sleep, I don't think, and she hardly ate.'

'And did anyone notice?'

'Eventually, yeah. I don't know how long later. It could have been days or weeks. I was only a kid, time meant nothing to us. I think it was because I wasn't turning up in school so they sent someone to the house. No one really called in on us after the first few weeks after the funeral so none of the neighbours knew, or maybe they did and they sent the woman who came, I never really found out.'

'And what happened then?'

I stop and take deep breaths. What happened then is vague, an impression mainly of people's reactions to me and Jamie.

'Take your time,' Tim says, 'you're doing really well. Are you feeling anxious?'

'A little.' I concentrate on my breath, listening to it go in and out. 'Sorry,' I mutter. 'It's not so much what happened, it's the way I remember it. It was so confusing, so weird and no one explained anything to us. And I don't know how Jamie felt, he was only three.'

'Take your time.'

'OK.' I let a long slow breath out and continue: 'People came and talked to us. They took my mother away, they brought me and Jamie to a centre somewhere, they weighed

180

us, washed us, talked about us. Next thing we know, we're in a new house with a new family.'

'And did no one explain that it was temporary or tell you what was happening?'

I shrug. 'They probably did, but all I could focus on was that they'd taken Mammy away. And Jamie . . .' My eyes fill up, I blink my tears away. I try to breathe again. 'Well, Jamie, he cried a lot and wouldn't talk. It went on for weeks, so one day I kept pretending to think he was a girl and giving him a doll to play with and he eventually got really mad and told me to go away or something. It was the happiest day of my life.'

'That must have been awful.'

I shrug.

'And did you see your mother during this time?'

'After a while, they let us visit her. I don't know if it was a good idea. Jamie cried for hours when he had to go back to the foster home. I was the only one who could comfort him.'

'Big responsibility?'

'I didn't mind.' My voice is sharp. 'He was a good boy. I didn't mind at all.'

'You're doing well, Hope. So what happened then? Did your mother come home?'

'Yeah.' Suddenly I feel really numb. 'My mother was cured then and we went home and my brother was thrilled.'

'And you?'

'I, well,' I run my tongue around my lips, he's going to think I'm awful now. Here it comes. 'I was happy but not happy.'

'Can you tell me why?'

'Do I have to?'

'If you think it'll help.'

I scrunch up my eyes and try to explain it better. 'I was angry at her for making me ashamed, for not being like other mothers and I was furious and jealous too. Jealous of the way my brother loved her. I'd been the one who minded him.' I bite my lip. 'Though it wasn't her fault, I suppose. She couldn't help it.'

'Neither could you.'

'I could have been happier. I don't think I talked to her for a week.'

'You couldn't help the way you felt and it's healthier to express it. Look what's happening now when you're trying to avoid feeling.'

I'd never thought of it like that before. It's a kind of relief. 'I suppose so.'

'So your relationship with your mother changed, did it?'

'Yeah. I couldn't trust her not to leave us again. My whole childhood was spent trying to keep her from feeling sad. To keep her with us. I tried to control everything. I thought if I kept her happy, we'd all be happy and I was stupid enough to think it would work.' The bitterness in my voice surprises me.

'You were a child. That's the way children think. It's too scary for them otherwise.'

'Well,' I glare at Tim, though I don't know why I'm doing it. 'When she got sick again, I ignored it for ages.'

'She got depressed again?'

Jesus, I think. My life sounds awful. He must think I'm a real sad case.

'After a good few years. Like, we were OK for ages.'

'And what happened then?'

I swallow hard. Without even realising I'm doing it, I start

182

rubbing my hand really hard across my face. 'She got sick,' is all I can manage.

'Is this upsetting you?' he asks gently.

I can't even talk or react. I'm sweating now. And breathing hard. 'I'll be fine in a minute.'

'It's OK. You can leave it for now. Relax, OK. Take deep breaths. It's fine.'

He waits for a little while and I feel myself return to normal. I don't know what happened there, I was doing great, telling him about my life. Relaxing. I manage a grin of sorts.

'What's the anxiety like now?' he probes.

'It's bad, at least an eleven.'

Tim allows himself a small smile. 'OK, we'll leave it there for today. Now Hope,' he says as he ejects the tape from the recorder, 'I want you to listen to this over the weekend as many times as you can. The idea is that you become almost immune to it, that instead of it upsetting you so much, it just becomes a memory. A sad memory, but just a memory. I think you'll be fine with it: despite your anxiety, you've coped well. I want you to come back to me on Monday, we'll gauge how you're getting on and maybe take it a bit further, if that's OK? And I want you, in your mind, to replay the next part of your story, even the beginning of it, just to help you get a handle on telling it. We can take as long as you want over it. Just remember, it's a memory, it can do you no harm. Yes, it seems to have upset you but you have survived.'

Surviving is a lot more than just being alive, I feel like saying.

'Of course, surviving is a lot more than existing,' he says. 'We all get damaged as we go through life, our perception changes. Yours unfortunately changed radically at a very young age, we have to address that.'

'OK.' I take the tape from the desk and put it in the pocket of my jacket.

'And here?' Tim pulls out another recorder from a drawer in his desk. 'I don't suppose you packed a Dictaphone when you decided to come on holiday.'

I grin. 'No, and I forgot I'd need one to listen to the tape.'

'Very disturbed thinking,' Tim teases gently. He checks that the Dictaphone is working and shows me how to operate it. 'Now, see you Monday and I want to hear some progress on the crisps.'

'I promise,' I say.

Julie is determined to help me with the whole crisp issue. I think she needs a diversion; she's been so miserable since she met her father. Nelson is only visiting at weekends, so she doesn't even have him to escape with and Adam and I are just a reminder of what happened that day. I think it's awful that her parents haven't been in touch since, but then again, she hasn't rung them either.

'So I just show you a packet of crisps, is that it?' she asks.

'Basically yes. That's the first step.' I feel good. Calm.

Adam bids us goodbye as he trots upstairs to his laptop. Julie has taken to christening it his lapdog because she says that Adam is pathetic to be working still for a company that has suspended him. Adam never bothers to defend himself, but I think she hurts him.

'One packet of crisps.' Julie duly waves a packet of Tayto Cheese and Onion in front of me.

I feel surprisingly OK. A slight increase in heart rate but

184

that's only nerves. 'Now shake them, make them make a noise,' I say, consulting the steps Tim has drawn up for me. Julie shakes them, scrunches the packet between her hands. 'All right?'

'Yeah.' My heart is hammering now. I don't want her to see it. If I can only get over this, I think, I'll definitely get better. 'Now,' my voice trembles as I look at the list, 'open the crisps.'

It's like looking at a soon to be car crash. Even if I wanted to I couldn't tear my eyes away. As Julie pulls open the crisps I see every little tear along the opening slowly revealing what's inside the packet. Deep breaths, I tell myself, deep breaths. They're only bloody crisps, for God's sake. But it's no use. I can't stand it. I think I'm going to die. In. Out. In. Out. My breath is coming too fast.

'Hope?' Julie's voice comes from far away. 'Hope?'

I bolt for the door, wrench it open and run right into the centre of the front garden, Julie following behind. 'Are you OK? Hope?'

The terror is receding now. The urge to run seems ridiculous when looked at logically. 'I'll be fine.' I sit down on the grass. It's warm. 'Sorry.' I rub my hands through my hair, pulling it, feeling the pain of it. It helps bring me back. 'Sorry.'

Julie sits beside me. 'No need to be sorry. We just did too much too soon, I reckon.' Breathe. In. Out. In. Out.

'Like, imagine you were scared of water, would you go from the shallow end to the deep in under three minutes?'

Her perception pulls me right back. 'No, I guess not.'

'Well then,' she nudges me. 'We'll start over. Take out the crisps for about two days and when you feel you can really cope with that, we'll move on – how about it?'

She's so good. There she is with massive family problems and she still cares about me. What did I ever do right to deserve her?

'Sounds good to me.'

20

I T'S SATURDAY NIGHT, early July, and the three of us are getting ready to go out. We're only going to Lynch's in Dunport. I haven't been there since I pretended to be an American, but tonight, whatever happens, I'm determined to be Hope Gardner.

To be honest, I don't really want to go out, but Adam has persuaded me to come along as he doesn't want to be on his own with just Julie and Nelson and all Nelson's friends that he's bringing down from Dublin. I tell him that Logan is going, but he says he still needs me there. I think it's a ploy to get me out; the two are afraid to leave me on my own. Julie was more freaked out by my panic attack than she let on.

She comes into the front room now and surveys me in my casual attire of jeans and a T-shirt. 'Are you putting any make-up on, Hope?' she asks almost accusingly. She looks amazing. Yes, she is wearing jeans and a shirt too, but on Julie the clothes look like they're celebrating. And her make-up is cool. She's lathering on lip gloss now and the result is fabulous shiny pouty lips.

'D'you want some?' She sees me gawking and holds the lipstick out to me. 'Go on, you've nice lips, they're kind of like Angelina Jolie's.'

I take the gloss from her and copy what she has done. It's hard, as she's hogging the hand mirror.

Julie looks at me with narrowed eyes. Gently she takes the gloss from me and studies my face. 'Eye shadow,' she pronounces, 'you need brown eye shadow – let me do it, would you?'

'Aw no, I'm not wearing make-up, I just wanted to try it out.' I go to wipe my lips clean but she squeals and grabs at my hand.

'Don't rub it off, it's made a huge difference to you,' she chastises. 'No, come on, a bit of eye shadow won't hurt.'

I suppose it won't and anyway, I don't want to be the only girl not wearing make-up. If Nelson is anything to go by, the whole lot of his friends, men and women, will be image conscious. Plus Julie is discreetly plastered in the stuff. 'Right.' I sit down on the sofa and Julie gives a little cheer that makes me smile. She scrabbles about in her well worn make-up bag and with the air of a pro scrutinises millions of shades of eye shadow. She chooses a smoky brown and a grey.

'You seem in better form,' I remark as I close my eyes.

'A little.' She smudges some colour on my lids. 'It's awful what happened, but I'm free now to an extent. And I've got you and my other friends in London. What is it they say? Friends are the family you'd choose for yourself?'

I like that. It's true. Me, Julie and Adam are a family of sorts.

Julie begins to mix the colours on my lids.

'I don't think your mam and dad would like me much.'

'Are you joking?' Julie says a little bitterly. 'They'd love you!'

'Yeah?'

'Yeah! Against you I look great. You're unemployed. They'd encourage our friendship, that's for certain.' She stands back and surveys me. 'Some eyeliner now,' she says, searching her bag again. 'When my parents tried to make me into this showpiece daughter, they were damn lucky I didn't go in completely the opposite direction and learn nothing.'

'Why didn't you?' I had learned nothing in school but that was because my mother took no interest in me. I thought maybe I'd get her attention that way. And there was Julie with an abundance of attention and she hated it.

'Because I knew what I wanted to do, that's why. And I wasn't going to let them with all their pretence and snobbery put me off. Now, eyes up.'

I look upward and feel her pencilling my eyelids. It's a horrible sensation.

'You should think about what you want, Hope. I haven't heard you talk about your mother since, but you should really keep up the contact now it's been re-established.'

I shrug and Julie squeals as her pencil veers off course.

'Sorry.' I wait while she fixes up my eyes before saying, 'I probably will. I mean, I don't know if I'll visit her again but I'll call and write. I need time. It's funny, I find it hard to see her as, you know, *capable*. It's like she's a different person.'

'Yeah well, she probably is. A better, stronger person. You should give her another chance. It's important to make the best of things, for you.'

'Did you practise that speech?' I tease, feeling a little touched.

'Look.' She holds up the mirror for me to look at myself and I have to say, it is a bit of a transformation. My eyes look huge in my round face. In fact they look so big, my face actually looks smaller. And my lips are fab.

'Use whatever you have to make the best of things,' Julie says, patting her make-up bag. 'You know what I'm saying.'

Then she turns towards the stairs and yells for Adam to come down.

How did she ever become so bloody wise and clever?

The Shamrocks are playing really loudly as we enter. Nelson and his friends have taken over a corner of the pub and have a major amount of drink lined up in front of them. As we enter a huge cheer goes up and Julie waves back at them.

'Oh, everyone is looking at us!' she laughs.

I keep my head down as the bar staff look over. Still, with the crowd jammed into the pub it'd be hard for them to spot me. I manoeuvre myself in between Logan, who has come with us in the taxi, and Adam so that they block me from view.

'Hiya babe.' Nelson pats the seat beside him for Julie to sit down.

Babe? Oh God. The man gets worse.

'Hiya.' Julie plants a kiss on his lips and he ruffles her hair. I don't know what she sees in Nelson really – he's kind of false looking with his massive arms and his huge bulk. He's not that friendly to Adam and me either, though, I think, surveying the crowd around the table, he must have something going for him to have so many friends of his own. There are at least five men, none of whom look as beefy as Nelson. Some are passably good-looking, and all seem quite friendly. There's a few women too, as done up as they can possibly be, and I see one or two of them eye up Adam as

190

he sits down. Or maybe it's Logan, I can't be sure. Nelson introduces us and they all shout out a hello before turning back to their drinks and the music. I sit in beside Julie and Logan sits beside me. Adam sits opposite us. Then a girl, quite pretty, joins the table, having bought some drinks at the bar. She hands them around before searching for a place to sit. I think we must have taken her seat. She ends up squeezing beside Adam. 'Hi, we haven't met,' she says, holding out her hand. 'I'm Kate.'

'Great,' Adam shakes her hand.

'And you are?' Kate looks at him with amused eyes.

'Oh, yes, sorry. Adam. I'm Adam.'

'Oh, I love that accent,' Kate says pleasantly. 'All sort of posh. Are you posh?'

'Eh,' Adam actually ponders this. 'I suppose if you call growing up in Kensington posh, then I could be considered such, yes. But I don't feel posh.'

'No, that's David Beckham's job,' the girl jokes.

Adam doesn't get it. I cringe for the poor girl as her laughter splutters out like a dying car engine.

'Good joke,' I offer feebly.

She smiles at me and stares into her glass. Adam looks away from her, seeming very uneasy. Kate asks him something else and he makes a tepid reply. I can't bear to look, so I turn to Logan, who's watching the exchange with amusement.

'He could be in there,' Logan whispers to me. 'What's wrong with him?'

'He's not himself in the last while,' I defend him. I remember suddenly what Julie said all those weeks ago, about Adam being gay. Maybe he is. He's dying a death in front of that poor girl. He just can't seem to be his funny, charming

191

self and I can't even think of a way to intervene and save him. But aren't gay men good with women? Nah, I dismiss that as a pathetic stereotype.

'Is that Nelson, the guy Julie was on about on the way here?' Logan's breath is warm on my ear.

'Yes,' I say back. 'Quite a specimen, eh?'

'Christ!'

'He'd like to think so,' I joke and Logan laughs, showing me his even white teeth.

'Hey, Hope, Nelson is buying,' Julie calls. 'What are you having?'

'An orange, thanks, Nelson.'

'Logan?' Julie asks.

'Carlsberg.'

'And Adam?'

Adam jumps and wipes a hand over his face. 'Sorry, what?'

'If we can tear you away from Kate,' Julie smiles, 'what are you having?'

'Kate hopes he's having her, isn't that right, Kate?' Nelson booms out heartily.

'Oh shut up, Nelson,' Kate snaps. 'I'm only being friendly.' She gets up and finds a spot among her other friends.

'I'll eh, have a Guinness,' Adam says, sounding despondent.

Nelson glares at Kate as he stands up. Almost upending the table, he squeezes his way past us to the bar.

'So, that's the famous Nelson,' Logan says to Julie.

'No, that's not him,' I say. 'He was killed years ago. That's Julie's Nelson.'

'Ha! Ha!' Julie makes a face at me. 'Yes Logan,' she clarifies, 'that's him.'

'Big bloke.'

Julie nods. 'That's because he owns a gym, he does a lot of weights.'

'What gym?' Logan asks. 'My sister has worked in loads of gyms in Dublin – she's a fitness instructor.'

Julie shrugs, 'I don't know, he showed me photos of it, but he didn't tell me the name.' She turns to his friends, 'Hey, what's the name of Nelson's gym?'

There follows a bit of a debate, which is odd, you'd imagine they'd know the name of their friend's business. But then again, maybe they're his football buddies or something. Eventually they settle on 'Northsiders Gym'.

'Ring a bell?'

Logan shrugs. 'Nah. But maybe he knows her. Debbie Jones.'

Just then, the Shamrocks begin to play again, drowning out all conversation.

'Adam, you love this song,' I say and kick him under the table.

'Yeah.'

Nelson bangs my orange down in front of me.

'Thanks, Nelson.'

'No problem.' He gives out the rest of the drinks and then goes and sits beside Julie again.

'Did a Debbie Jones ever work at your gym?' Julie asks Nelson. 'She's Logan's sister.'

'A fitness instructor?' Logan offers.

Nelson shakes his head and I miss his reply because abruptly Adam stands up from the table, taking his drink with him, and disappears into the crowd.

'Where's he gone?' I ask.

No one bothers to reply. I wonder if I should go after him, but maybe he's just gone to get a better view of the woeful Shamrocks. That's the sort of anorak thing Adam would do.

After about twenty minutes, Adam still hasn't come back. I'm a little worried about him now, which is stupid, I suppose, he's a grown man, but he really hasn't been himself since he got suspended from his job. In order to have a look for him without being too obvious about it, I offer to go to the bar for drinks.

'Anyone want a drink?'

No one answers, they're all too busy chatting so I say it a bit louder and I'm met with a series of 'no's'.

'Right, excuse me.'

Logan has started to chat to one of Nelson's mates. They follow the same football team or something ridiculous like that. Anyway, they're bonding really well. Both of them are wearing the exact same T-shirts, red and white. That's how they found out, apparently.

I wish I followed something that I could bond with someone over but no one really chats about designing text for a website, do they? And even if they did, it would only mean that they're about as exciting as I am, which might not be a good thing. Thinking these saddo thoughts, I push my way to the bar, only to remember that I don't want either of the barmen brothers to see me. There are three barmen on tonight and I only hope the third one serves me. Every time Davey or Greg Lynch goes by, I dip my head. But of course, Greg eventually asks me what I want. I flirt with doing the whole American thing again and eventually chicken out.

'Orange,' I say as casually as I can.

'Hope Gardner,' he says, grinning widely in recognition

as he rests his hands on the bar top. 'I heard you were back – how you doing?'

'Fine.' Please don't ask about the last time I was in here, I silently pray. Please don't. 'Are you going to pretend to be an American tonight?' he asks. 'I can play along if you want me to.'

'No, no it's fine,' I laugh a little over the raucous roar of the Shamrocks, trying to pretend that disguising my voice and acting as if I'm someone else is perfectly normal. 'I only did it because I hadn't seen my mother and I didn't want her to hear I was about before I'd called in to her.'

'You could have just told Davey to keep it to himself,' Greg says, smiling.

'Yeah well,' I shrug, 'that wouldn't have been any fun, would it?'

'True,' he grins. I know he thinks I'm a total freak-head but sure so what? Nothing will have changed. 'So what are you having again?'

'An orange juice.'

'Wow. We'll make our fortune out of you,' he jokes as he gets a glass.

'Yep.'

'D'you want anything else?'

'No thanks.'

'You're not in on your own, are you?'

'No, I'm with a crowd.' I indicate the corner we're in.

'Oh. Right. It's great to see you again. I've a break coming up in a few minutes, can we catch up?'

Catch up? On what? What had I done except be in a plane crash? Still, Greg was a decent enough guy. 'OK. That'd be fun.'

I hand him the money for the drink but he waves it away. 'On the house!'

'Thanks.' I smile at him and just as I turn to leave, I spot Adam sitting on his own on a bar stool. He's gazing into his pint and looking as if he's just been told that he has PTSD or something.

'Hi, handsome.' I sidle up to him.

It's like I've electrocuted him. He jumps about a mile out of his seat. 'Oh you,' he mutters. 'Hi.'

The guy is smashed.

'How much have you drunk?'

'Not as much as I'm going to drink.' He grins wickedly and lifts his pint to his lips.

'And what are you doing here, why aren't you sitting with us?'

'Too many people there. That Nelson fella is like . . .' he frowns and thinks for a while, 'he's like King of the Friends.'

'What?'

Adam waves a hand at me and says a bit narkily, 'Go on, go away back to the table. I'll join you when we're going home.'

'What the hell is wrong with you?'

He lifts his face about an inch sideways and says with slurred deliberation, 'Go down to the table, see you later.'

'Fine.' I take my orange and leave. At least I know where he is. That's a relief of sorts.

Fifteen minutes later Greg comes down to the table. I stand up to let him in. 'Sit in, do,' I say and he sits in between Logan and me. Logan glances curiously at him, before ignoring him completely and resuming his boring chat about 'what's the greatest goal you've ever seen?'

'This is Greg,' I tell Julie and Nelson, who are the only inquisitive ones, it seems, 'he was in school with me.'

'When she bothered to come into school!' Greg jokes and I manage a laugh.

'Just cause you were a big swot,' I joke back.

'Well you were too up until about fifth year,' Greg says. He thumbs to me. 'I'm telling ye, this girl was the best one for English ever. You did everyone's English homework, d'you remember?'

'Yeah,' I nod. 'Two quid a shot.'

'You charged?' Julie sounds impressed. 'I would never have figured you for a businesswoman, Hope.'

'I'm good at English,' Nelson says. 'I speak it all the time.'

There's a bit of a silence as no one knows if Nelson is joking or not.

'Joke?' he quirks his eyebrow and then we laugh. In relief more than anything.

'This one here,' Greg nods at me. 'She went down in school folklore, didn't you?'

'Did I?' God, I hope he's not going to tell about the time I got thrown out of class for arguing with the history teacher. That was in sixth year, I'd been a bit mental that time.

'Yeah!' Greg says it as if I should know what he's talking about. 'The charity Countdown gig?'

God, I'd forgotten that.

'What happened?' Julie asks.

Greg looks at me and I shrug, 'You tell them.'

'You may not know it,' Greg says, as if he's building up to some big climactic story, 'but Hope is brilliant with words, right. I mean, totally freakily brilliant.'

I flush, embarrassed. 'Don't mind him.'

'Anyway, one year, they had this charity Countdown

197

competition in school based on the *Countdown* show on TV. Anyone could enter, it was mostly sixth-years and teachers. No one could believe it when Hope entered. What age were you?'

'I dunno. About fifteen, I think.'

'The idea was that everyone had to place a bet on who they thought would win before the competition started. Of course, everyone was betting on the teachers. So Hope told our class to bet on her, didn't you, Hope?'

I wince. This isn't exactly my proudest moment in life. 'I told my class to bet on me and if I won, they were to give me 50 per cent of their winnings and if they lost, I'd pay them back their initial bet.'

'We couldn't lose,' Greg grins at me. 'So we bet all we had on her. And she stormed into the final, didn't you?'

I shrug.

'And she was up against some geek from sixth year and she just blew him out of the water, she got two nine letter words, *two*, and because we'd all bet a pile of money on her, we cleaned out the bookies.'

I giggle in embarrassment at the memory. 'Fifty to one was the odds on me.'

Greg laughs. 'They had to use the charity money to pay us and Hope made a fortune.'

'And the charity?' Julie asks.

'Made nothing,' I flush, ashamed.

'Aw, God, Hope!' Julie doesn't know whether to laugh or be shocked.

'I didn't know that would happen,' I defend myself. 'I mean, the greedy little feckers put loads of money on me.'

'I had ten on her,' Greg nods. 'And I won five hundred.'

I don't tell them, but guilt had made me give back some

of the money I won. 'Two hundred and fifty of which you had to give to me,' I say sweetly to Greg. 'All in all I made over a grand.'

'You must have been really good,' Julie looks at me with admiration.

'Genius,' Greg confirms. 'I mean, give the girl a nine-letter word all jumbled up and she can guess it like that!' He clicks his fingers.

'Any number of letters,' I tell him, trying to sound modest.

'When did you discover you could do that?' the girl, Kate, asks.

'When I used to watch *Countdown* as a kid. I kept beating the contestants.'

'You must be very clever.'

'No, I was as thick as that,' I hammer the table. 'But I was big into Scrabble as a kid. In fact –' a memory pops into my head, a lovely happy image that makes me smile – 'My dad and mam played it a lot and I'd watch them. I could read really early too. I was just good like that.'

'Hey, hey,' Julie claps her hands. 'Anyone got a pen and paper?'

'Oh yeah,' Logan looks over from his riveting conversation, 'I always bring a pen and paper to the pub.'

Everyone laughs.

'Naw, serious,' Logan pulls a pen and paper from his pocket. 'I bring them everywhere.'

'Nerd' and 'anorak' are flung at him but he just grins good-naturedly.

Julie, much to my embarrassment, passes the pen and paper around and asks everyone to write down the longest word they can think of. 'I'm going to jumble up the letters and see if you can guess them,' she announces. As an afterthought, she says, 'And it's two euro a word which Hope can win. Anyone who catches her out, gets the kitty.'

'Aw, Julie,' I groan. 'I want to talk to Greg here.'

'I don't mind,' Greg says amicably. 'Let's see if you're as good as you were.'

'She's good at something?' Logan asks jokingly, suddenly giving us his attention. I notice that his conversation partner has left the table. 'And what would that be?' his eyes sparkle, 'besides colonic irrigation.'

'Ha ha,' I sneer, knowing what he's going to say.

'Colonic irrigation?' Julie asks. 'Are you, Hope?'

'Yeah,' Logan nods. 'You know, she can annoy the shit out of just about everyone.'

More laughter. Logan grins cockily at me. I have to smile.

'So what is it you're good at?' he asks again.

Julie tells him and he smirks. 'OK,' he says, putting a two euro coin on the table in front of me, 'I got one.'

I realise I'm the centre of attention. Everyone is looking at me. I try not to squirm.

'You want to take it?' Logan asks.

'Go on,' I say coolly. 'But it better be good and hard.'

'That's a bit personal, isn't it?'

'Ha ha.'

'Garden-sou.'

The letters rearrange themselves in my head. I make a face and say in an anguished voice, 'Oh God, it's so difficult.' I see him smile a bit before I quash it by adding, 'and DANGEROUS!'

Now he looks a little impressed. Someone claps. I smile triumphantly at him and take his two euros up from the table, waving the coin tantalisingly before his eyes. 'Ha ha,' I half sing. 'Up yours.'

He gives me a devastating grin. I say devastating because it is. It knocks me for six, it's so wide and sunny and friendly. It's the nicest smile I've ever seen, quite frankly. My own smile transforms itself into a jaw-drop.

'Here you are, Lo,' Logan's new best friend arrives back at the table with a drink for each of them and he forgets about me again.

I can't believe that he had that effect on me. I'd blame the drink if I was drinking.

'OK,' Julie breaks into my thoughts. 'How about C-I-I-O-U-E-S-L-D?'

'I need to see it written down.'

She passes me the paper on which the letters are written.

Unlike Logan, Julie doesn't realise that the hardest way for me to spot the words is by putting the letters into some kind of logical arrangement. 'Delicious?'

Nelson cheers. It had been his word.

After a few more futile attempts to catch me out, everyone makes admiring noises and conversation starts back up again.

Greg asks me what I'm doing these days. I give him a sanitised version of events and tell him briefly about the plane crash and then quickly steer the conversation on to him. He's been working in the bar since he left school and now he's officially the manager.

'And do you mind being tied to the business here?' I ask.

He shrugs. 'I used to but now I don't.'

'How come?'

'Well, it was expected that I'd work here. It's not so bad, though. But I still think that you were lucky you could get away.'

I shrug and admit, 'Sure I sort of had to get away, the way things were.'

Greg smiles sympathetically at me. Everyone in Dunport knows the story of my life. It had been splashed all over the *Dunport News* at the time. 'Yeah, it must have been tough on you.'

'Horrible.' I look at my hands. I really don't want the conversation to go down this road.

Greg senses it I think. 'Well, things always work out. They did for me. I'm happy now. I'm marrying Amanda Coonan in September, she works in Dingle, so we're both here for life. D'you remember Amanda?'

Amanda. I can't believe a nice guy like Greg would marry her. It seems that she's going to haunt me for the duration of my stay here. I force myself to smile. 'Oh yeah, I remember her. Congratulations.'

'Thanks.' He looks at me. 'So, are you seeing anyone?'

'I'm single,' I answer lightly. I don't admit that I've never really been serious about anyone since Jack.

'You won't stay that way for too long,' Greg, ever the gentleman says. 'Anyway,' he stands up, 'I better get back. Nice seeing you again, Hope. Sure no doubt you'll be in again.'

'No doubt at all,' I say, smiling up at him. 'Great to see you too.'

'Oh yeah, and do you know who's coming back to Dunport next month?' Without waiting for my reply, he says, 'Jack Dunleavy.'

Jack's name makes my heart flutter. 'I heard,' I try to say with as much nonchalance as I can.

'You and him had a thing going in sixth year, didn't you? We used to wonder what ye got up to on your days off.' Greg laughs at his humour.

'Believe me, it wasn't very exciting.'

Greg laughs again. Then with a general goodbye to the table he's off.

'He's lovely,' Julie says. Then, as if it's just occurred to her, she asks, 'Where is Adam? I don't think I've seen him all night.'

'He's up at the bar, completely smashed.'

'Why?' Julie looks in concern at me.

'I have no idea. He just got up and left the table.'

So then Julie gets up to see if Adam is OK. She arrives back with a face like thunder. 'Bastard,' she sniffs and she looks like she might cry. 'Well, there is no way I'm looking after him.'

Great!

21

IT'S THE END of the night and Logan and I are on each side of a completely hammered Adam. The guy can barely walk and he staggers between us as we make our way towards a taxi.

'Eh, I hope now he won't be sick in here,' the taxi driver says with justifiable concern. 'I'm telling ye now, I won't be the one cleaning it out.'

'He'll be fine,' I bluster. 'He's not as drunk as he looks.'

Logan gets in and I push Adam in after him, like a delicate parcel. 'Now to find Julie,' I say.

'Is she not going off with Nelson?' Logan asks.

'I don't know, I'll just find out, I don't want to leave her behind.'

I walk back through the throng of people milling about outside the pub. Julie sees me and waves. 'Hey, hiya Hope.'

'Are you coming with us or what?' I drag her to one side.

Julie smiles a little uneasily. 'Well, would it be OK if I brought Nelson back?'

'What?'

'Well, he's in a B&B and he's sharing with someone, it's hardly ideal.' Julie looks pleadingly at me. 'Please.'

'Julie, you don't really know this guy, and besides, I sleep downstairs and I don't want him tripping over me and everything. Come on, it's hardly fair.'

'Well where are we supposed to go then?' she says grumpily.

I feel like telling her that if Nelson wanted to advance things further, he should have taken out a room for himself in the B&B. Why should we have to accommodate them?

'I'll ask Adam, see if it's OK with him,' I mutter, hoping that she'll blame Adam instead of me. 'Come on.'

'But Adam is so drunk, he won't know what he's saying,' Julie pouts. 'He told me, when I went to see him at the bar, that he didn't want to sit at the same table as Nelson. I mean, what has Nelson done to him? Nothing, that's what. And you think he's going to be happy that Nelson is staying over.'

'Let's just see,' I try to say reasonably. I'm not used to being the sensible one in our relationship. 'Come on.'

Julie stomps behind me towards the car, Nelson calling after her.

'Hey, Adam,' I say brightly, 'have you any objection to Nelson staying over?'

Adam opens bleary eyes. 'Nelson?' he drawls. 'I hate Nelson. Why didn't someone kill him at Waterloo?'

'Because he wasn't bloody at Waterloo, that's why!' Julie folds her arms and glares at us, though why she's glaring at me, I don't know. 'Well, Nelson and I are getting a taxi back to the cottage. I have paid for my room and I can bring anyone back I want. So I will and I am.'

'Fine,' I say narkily. 'You do that.' I hop into the taxi and close the door on her.

'Ouch,' Logan says in amusement.

'You might not want to,' Logan says, as we near the cottage, 'but there's a spare bed in my place.' He looks from me to

205

Adam. 'The sofa converts, if you like. And one of you can take the floor.'

'I paid for my room, I'm using my room,' Adam says stubbornly. 'I'm using my room as I paid for my room.'

'Hope?' Logan looks at me. 'What about you? Did you pay for the floor downstairs?'

'Eh, no, as it happens.' I smile. 'Adam and Julie paid for the cottage. I buy the food as much as I can.'

'Anyway, you know the offer is there,' Logan says. He smiles that smile again.

'I hope,' Adam says, 'that she snores and he can't get to sleep.'

'Hate to break it to you, mate,' Logan winks at me, 'but I don't think Nelson is planning on getting any sleep.'

'Shit. Yeah.' Adam nods.

That's it. What with Adam being completely drunk and probably in a bad temper and Julie and Nelson not getting any sleep, I decide that I want out. 'Logan, d'you know what, I think I will join you in your cottage.'

'Fine.' Another smile. 'I would have done the same.'

We arrive at the cottage before Julie and Nelson and although Logan and I try to get Adam upstairs, he refuses to go. 'I'm going to sit here,' he says, plonking himself down at the table. 'Sit here and wait.'

'And I'm going to sit in the taxi and wait,' Logan says, giving up.

'Yeah, see you in five,' I say to him.

When he goes, I grab my toothbrush, pyjamas, under-wear and some fresh clothes. Just before I turn to go, I try to talk to Adam again.

'What on earth is wrong with you tonight, Adam?'

206

'I'm drunk,' he says. 'I'm a failure as a human being, I'm terribly terribly cross.' He lays his head on his hands and declares, 'Oh God, the world is spinning and I forgot to get on the roundabout.'

There's no point in talking when he's like this. I don't even know if I should leave him. He really is acting very weird.

'Go,' he waves me away, his head still buried in his arms, like a kid falling asleep in school. 'Go!'

Maybe I'll talk to him tomorrow, when he's back to himself. 'Well, try and get some sleep,' is the last thing I say as I close the door.

The five-minute drive to Logan's is done in silence. It's a bit weird actually to be spending the night under the roof of a guy I hardly know. I imagine he feels the same way. The driver lets us out at the cottage and Logan's horrible cat springs out from somewhere to greet us. It's quite taken aback to see me there and hisses at me for a bit as Logan laughs.

'He's the jealous type,' he grins as he scoops the cat up in his arms. Unlocking the door of the cottage, he tells me to come on in. He flicks on the lights in his studio and saunters on into the kitchen where he grabs some cat food from a press, opens it and puts it into a bowl for the cat. It's soon purring loudly. Logan opens the door to the small sitting room and, pulling on the orange sofa, changes it into a bed.

'Now.' He surveys it for a second. 'I have a quilt, I think, and a sheet or two. Is that OK?'

'Great. Yeah.' I put my overnight bag on the floor. Well, it's a plastic shopping bag, really. I don't possess anything like an overnight bag, hardly ever having done this sort of thing.

Logan goes out of the room and I'm left standing like a spare in the middle of it. I can't sit down as I'll be sitting on my bed, which would be a bit weird. But of course, there's another chair in the room, so I perch on the edge of that. From somewhere in the small house, I hear Logan pulling at stuff and he soon comes back in with a duvet and one sheet. 'Now, I'll just put this on for you and that'll be you all set up.'

'Thanks for this.'

'No probs.' He makes up the bed with the air of someone who has never made a bed before. 'I'd offer you my bed only the cat normally sleeps on it. He'd probably attack you.'

'No, this is fine.'

He gives up trying to get the sheet straight and just dumps the duvet over it. Then he stands back to survey his work. 'There.'

'Great.'

Neither of us knows what to do next.

'I have an opened bottle of wine in the fridge, d'you want to help me finish it off before we call it a night?'

'I, eh, can't drink,' I say.

'Oh right, well d'you want some tea?'

'Yeah. That sounds good.'

It isn't good, though. Logan, I think, would win a prize for the worst tea in the universe. It's so black, even when milk is added, that I fancy he actually burnt it.

Logan wisely has the bottle of wine for himself. He looks around for somewhere to sit and realises that the only place available is the newly made up bed. I feel like laughing with the awkwardness of it all. It's like the sofa bed had suddenly become enormous in the room.

He smiles sheepishly and indicates the bed. 'D'you mind?'

I shrug, feeling in control. 'Why should I? It's really only a chair.'

'That's right.' Logan sits on it. Right at the edge. He takes a mouthful of wine and swallows.

We look at each other.

'So,' I swirl my tea about, trying not to look at him sitting on my soon to be bed, 'did you enjoy yourself tonight?'

'Aw yeah.' He nods. 'It's nice to go out with a crowd, it's ages since I've done that.'

'So you don't get out much?'

'Naw,' he shrugs. 'Maria, my ex, she was the social one.' He looks a little wistful as he talks about her. 'If there was a party anywhere, she'd be at it.'

'She sounds like fun?' My voice is a bit strangled. I wish he didn't look so sad, as if he missed her.

'Yeah, she was.'

'And did she like art?' I can't help it now, I have to nose.

'Yeah. She especially liked my art.'

'Really?'

'Yeah, when it sold for a lot of money.' He laughs at his own joke. 'Naw, Hope, she wasn't into stuff like that, which was why I liked her and why I guess she drove me nuts, too. She was into movies and rock music and shopping and clothes and hair.'

'Oh. Right.'

Logan's smile fades slightly. 'Nope,' he says, half to himself, 'it was all wrong.' He pours himself more wine and nods at my teacup. 'D'you want some more?'

'Eh – no, thanks.'

We sit a while in silence, sipping our drinks and gazing at everything bar each other. I can't look at him because he's obviously forgotten he's on a bed and he is now lying on it, with his head against the wall. Long lean denim-clad legs with bare feet, his red and white T-shirt creased. He looks quite desirable if you like your men dark and sombre. I normally prefer blond hair myself. Anyway, eventually he finishes his drink and hauls himself off my bed, the duvet creased from where he has been lying on it. 'Bathroom is at the top of the stairs,' he says, sounding a little embarrassed. 'I'll leave you now.'

'OK. Thanks.' I can't look at him.

And he's gone.

Once I'm sure he's safely upstairs, I dump my tea down the kitchen sink.

There is someone shaking me. I grab an arm, gasping, and wallop – snap awake. Logan is standing over me. 'What the hell –?'

Oh God. Oh God. I let him go abruptly. 'Bad dream,' I say. My pyjama top is soaked with sweat. I shake it slightly. 'Sorry if I woke you.' I can't look at him.

'That was some dream.' He sits down beside me. 'D'you want a glass of water or tea or anything?'

'No, honest, I'll be fine.'

He looks doubtful. 'Does it happen often, dreams like that?'

'Logan, just stop. I'm fine. OK?' It's typical, my dreams have been easing off and then I have to have a horrendous one in a strange house with a strange man living in it. 'Just leave me,' I say again, 'I'm fine.'

Usually that stroppy tone would have people running for cover. Not him.

'You are not fine,' he says back equally stroppily. 'That

wasn't an ordinary dream. Jesus. You scared the hell out of me for one. I couldn't wake you.'

'I said I was sorry!'

He sounds taken aback. 'I don't want apologies, Hope. Dreaming like that is not a sign of someone that's fine.'

'Yes it is. I've always had vivid dreams.'

'Was it about the plane crash?'

He's not going to go away, I realise. Logan is not like Adam, he's oblivious to the rules of normal society. 'Yes, it was,' I admit reluctantly. 'I mean, if you nearly died, wouldn't you dream of it too?'

'I guess so.'

'See?'

He sits down beside me on the bed and asks, 'Is this the sort of stuff you're getting counselling for?'

'Yes.' I sound abrupt, but it's only because I am completely mortified. I lie back down and turn my back to him. 'Logan, just let me go back to sleep.'

'OK. Once you're all right.'

'It's only a dream.'

Despite the fact that I have my back to him, I sense that he has not left the room. 'Only a dream to you,' he says, and I think he sounds a little cross and upset, 'but Jesus, I thought you were being attacked.'

I turn towards him. For the first time I notice how pale he is. I've been so caught up in how I feel that his feelings didn't really register. He must have got a horrible shock. I'm ashamed of being so selfish. When did I become like this? I sit up in the bed and, wrapping my arms about my knees, I give what I hope is an apologetic smile.

'I never thought of that, Logan,' I admit softly. 'I'm sorry for scaring you.'

He looks at me and I become aware that I'm wearing my chilli pyjamas.

'I'll treasure that apology.' He half smiles. Then, standing up, he says, 'And I'm sorry if I embarrassed you about the counselling.'

I stare at the quilt he's thrown on my bed. It's a kids' one, showing Superman saving Lois Lane from a burning building. Jamie had loved Superman. 'My mother was depressed a lot of her life,' I say. I don't know why I'm telling him this. It's easier than talking about me, I suppose. My finger traces the outline of Superman's face. 'And I'm, you know, scared that I might have something like that. Or some branch of it.' I look up at him. 'Counselling is scary for me, I react accordingly.'

A small silence, before he says cautiously, 'Depressed people don't have brilliant comebacks like you do.' A pause. 'And I don't think if you were depressed that I'd enjoy your company as much.'

That's a nice thing for him to say. 'You enjoy my company?'

'Well, I've always had a thing for thorny objects.'

'Ha-ha.'

We look at each other. 'Thanks, Logan.'

'You OK, then?'

'Better than I was, thanks.'

'Good.'

He switches off the light and the last thing I see is his lovely smile.

22

I'M AWOKEN THE next day by the sounds of Logan pottering around outside. He's talking to his cat. I lie for a while and listen to him, grinning a little. I suppose being alone on a hill in the middle of nowhere would make anyone a bit mad. Well, I smile until I remember the night before. It's all like a bad dream now – ha ha. Eventually, I swallow my embarrassment and get up, pulling on my jeans and sweatshirt, before running a brush through my hair. Then it's out to the kitchen to locate some strong coffee.

'Hey,' Logan spots me and comes into the kitchen. 'How are you today?' He looks good.

'Fine. Sorry again about last night.'

He ignores that, for which I'm grateful; instead he reaches up into the press, pulls out the coffee and tea and bread. 'Here, you look like you could do with a bit of a feed.'

Is he telling me I look awful? Or maybe he's telling me I look skinny, which would be a first. 'Thanks.'

'OK.' He holds up the bread. 'Toast? Bread?'

'Toast. Two please.'

He switches on a gas grill and puts the bread underneath. 'You're welcome to stay as long as you like. Only thing is, you'll have to walk back to your place unless you want me to call you a taxi.'

'I'll walk.'

'Thought you might.' Pointing to various presses, he says, 'Butter in there, Coco Pops in that press and marmalade beside it.'

'Marmalade?' I half giggle. I can't help it. 'I thought only old people ate marmalade.'

'I'll have you know, Dunport marmalade is the best you can buy. Full of whiskey.'

'Right,' I make a face. 'I'll stick to the butter.'

'You don't know what you're missing.'

'Yeah, I do.'

He holds my gaze and I hold his and then flush a little. To break the moment, I gabble, 'Well, you go on, I'll find my way about. Thanks for letting me stay the night.'

'No problem. Now, when you leave, just pull the door behind you. I'll have the key.'

'Why, are you going somewhere today?'

'Yeah. I'm spending the day walking the mountains to try and find the best place to sketch from. I want a spectacular sea view, or rather, that's what bloody Jack Dunleavy wants for the foyer of his hotel.'

'A sea view?' I pull the grill pan out and flip over the bread. 'Have you gone up by Kinsella's waterfall?'

'Kinsella's waterfall?' He frowns. 'I've been here a year, I've never seen a waterfall.'

'Ah, but I grew up here. I know all the best places.'

'So where is it? Are you having me on?'

'As if.' I'm indignant that he would think I'd sabotage his work. 'It's . . .' I try to describe how he could get there and then I think, damn it, I haven't been up there in such a long time, it'd be nice to go. 'If you want, I'll show you. I'd enjoy the walk.'

214

'And it really is a good sea view?' Logan sounds doubtful. 'I was hoping to head away towards Dingle, to the highest place there.'

'Amateur,' I scoff. I pull the bread from the grill, I like my toast, like my tea, very un-brown. 'Let me eat this and I'll give you a visual experience you will never forget.'

Too late, I realise how it sounds. Logan opens his mouth to make a quip and I hold my finger up. 'Ah, ah.'

So, without any smart comments, he sits beside me and joins me in a coffee.

We leave about twenty minutes later. I've told him it'll take about an hour to reach the waterfall. Logan looks at my footwear. 'D'you want some boots or anything?' he says. He opens a press in the corner of the kitchen that I hadn't noticed and some wellies fall out.

'Maria left these behind when she left,' he says, holding up a fancy pair of pink ones with a picture of a pig on the front. Maria, I think, might have loved clothes, but these wellies were a bit on the pathetic side. Still, it'll save my trainers. I slip my feet into the boots, which are a perfect fit. Logan hands me my trainers in a plastic bag. 'You could leave your clothes here,' he says, 'pick them up on the way back. It'd save you carrying them.'

'Naw, I'll head back once we get there,' I tell him. 'I need to see how Adam is.'

Logan packs a sketch pad and some charcoal and pencils into a small rucksack and hoists it over his shoulder. 'OK, lead on, this had better be good.'

It's so long since I've really walked the hills that I'm sure I bore Logan by pointing stuff out to him. Still, give him his due, he doesn't seem bored. And even if he was, I wouldn't be able to stop myself.

'Wow, David Attenborough has nothing on you,' Logan grins as I identify some birds by their calls. He's staring at me in a way I can't quite fathom. 'You really love it around here, don't you?'

'I used to,' I admit. 'Now, it's like seeing a friend that I haven't met for ages.'

'Well, obviously that friend hasn't changed too much,' he says back.

I shrug. 'Some things you just don't forget,' I mutter.

But my friend *has* changed, I find out, or else my memory has altered drastically. The climb gets suddenly steeper. I'd forgotten that. It comes rushing back to me how, when I was a teenager, I could scamper up this hill. I was used to it, I suppose. Now, not having climbed it in a decade, the backs of my legs start to ache and the boots, the ones I thought were a perfect fit, have begun to chafe my heels. Still, I've told Logan where we're going and go there we will.

'Wow,' he pants, behind me, 'this is some climb.'

'It's worth it,' I pant back, wondering indeed if it is worth having a major heart attack for. Or even worse, sweaty stinky clothes for. Thank God I have very little hair, as it would be in bits at this stage.

The climb seems endless. In fact, gazing upwards, I begin to feel that it will be endless. How could I have thought it only took an hour?

'Are you sure we're going in the right direction?' Logan asks a few minutes later. 'We've been climbing now for the last forty minutes. I thought you said it was only an hour away.'

'Slight mistake about the time,' I admit sheepishly, 'but no mistake about the direction.'

'Well, Hope, I'm going to have to sit down, I'm totally wrecked.'

'Weakling,' I tease, but half-heartedly. Wrecked doesn't even describe how I feel. I think if I sit down, I'll never get up again. But I sink to the ground beside Logan and gratefully take a chocolate bar from him.

'Drink?' He pulls a bottle of water from his haversack. 'I bought one each. Just as well, eh?'

I take it and try to act like I'm only a little thirsty. I wish I'd brought sunscreen as the day is beginning to heat up and my face is burning, though whether it's from exhaustion or the sun, I'm not quite sure.

After about ten minutes, Logan stands up and stretches. 'Right,' he looks up at the hill, 'onwards and upwards. Up you get.'

My legs are stiff. My broken one is on the verge of rebellion, I think, as I try and fail to get up.

'Here.' Logan thrusts a hand out. 'Come on, my Kerry guide.'

The touch of his hand in mine as he yanks me to a stand makes my insides feel as if I've just done a loop the loop on a particularly dangerous rollercoaster. His grip is so strong and firm that he seems to have a problem letting go.

'Thanks,' I mutter, as he releases me. 'My bad leg is having a bad day.'

'And what about your good leg?'

'That's having a bad day too,' I admit reluctantly. 'It's trying to make up for the bad leg.'

'Oh dear.' Logan eyes me up and down with a speculative

217

grin. 'Well, my legs, though tired, are having a pretty good day overall.'

'Show-off.' I give a brisk, dismissive smile as he laughs. 'Let's get on.'

He gives a mock-salute and falls in behind me.

Ten minutes of excruciating pain later, Logan stops, cocks his head to one side and asks, 'What is that noise?'

'That,' I grin triumphantly, 'is the waterfall. Not long now.'

Pushing past trees and climbing rocks and squelching through damp earth, we emerge, at last on a plateau above the waterfall. The sound of it is fantastic in itself, just the roar of the water.

'Now look,' I say as I beckon Logan forward.

We have ascended the hill on the less steep side. The waterfall is to our right and a little further right is a sheer drop down to the ocean.

Logan stands beside me, totally speechless.

'Well?' I know I sound smug, but I can't help it.

'I'd never have found this myself,' he admits delightedly. 'Hope, it's brilliant. Just what I need. Thanks.'

'No problem.' I have to sit down or else I'll collapse. 'I'll just forward you on the doctor's bills.'

'I'd pay them a hundred times over for what you've given me,' he says seriously. He rummages about in his rucksack and finds some chocolate. 'Here, eat this.' Then he pulls out his sketch pad.

I wonder if he wants me to leave. After all, he seems to get very narky when he's working. But the truth is, I can't start walking again, even if it is downhill. My legs are too sore.

'Logan,' I say as I break off a square of chocolate. 'Like, it's not that I love your company or anything, but I'm staying here for a while. I'm too knackered to move. I'll try not to disturb you.'

'No worries,' he nods. 'You eat that and I'll work. These pictures are going to be great.' So saying, he begins sketching.

I find a shady tree and, legs outstretched, I munch on the chocolate while watching him. Head bent in concentration, his hand flies over the pages. There's something incredibly sexy about a man absorbed in his work. The more I look at him, the more turned on I feel. It's just because he's working, nothing to do with *him*. Every so often he turns and grins at me, almost as if he's making sure I'm still there. So, to avoid his gaze, I close my eyes.

I wake up, I don't know how long later, and Logan is still sketching away. The sun has begun to dip in the sky but it's stayed warm, and even at this height insects are buzzing about. I shift a bit and immediately groan.

Logan flinches.

Oops, I think I've just messed up another piece of art.

'Sorry,' I call out, feeling a lot more sorry for myself than him.

He puts down the sketch pad and shrugs. 'Naw, it's fine, I was just doing a few extra ones and letting you sleep. How are you?'

'Great,' I lie. I attempt to get up but the pain in my legs is unreal. 'Oh my God.'

'Sore, huh?'

'You could put it like that or,' I gaze heavenwards, 'you could say that someone has shoved hot pokers into my leg joints.'

'Not guilty,' he grins, 'much as I was tempted.'

'God, Logan, you should be in stand-up.'

'Well, I'd do better than you, that's for sure: you can't even stand, for starters.'

'I can,' I say, rising to the bait and with a superhuman effort I clutch the tree and, trembling, haul myself up.

'So, will we go?' he asks.

If someone had offered me a stretcher, I would have gladly climbed on to it. 'We can try,' I answer. I'm a bit sorry that the day is ending for us now. It's been surprisingly enjoyable and it's nice to share my favourite places with someone who genuinely appreciates them. 'Jack won't believe you found the waterfall,' I remark as I gingerly put one foot in front of the other. 'Not a lot of people know how to get to it. It's a well-kept local secret.'

'You knew Jack well, huh?'

'Yep.' I answer. Then add on with a laugh, 'my first love.'

'Well, at least you learned some sense. He's a pain in the arse to work for. I think he regrets employing me, he doesn't much like my pictures.'

'Jack never had much taste.'

'So that's why he went out with you, was it?'

'That's not nice.' I belt him one but before the blow can land, he catches my arm.

'Neither is that,' he says, grinning. 'If you do it again, I'll be forced to hold your hand all the way down to protect myself.' He lets me go.

I'm tempted to hit him though why I'm not quite sure. I don't want to find out.

'And you should, in all fairness, apologise for trying to hit me. I was only wondering about Jack's bad taste.'

'My arse, I'll apologise.'

'Well, you do generally tend to speak out of it, so off you go.'

'Oh feck off!'

His laughter scares all the birds away, but it makes me smile.

It doesn't take as long to get down. I think I confused the time it took to climb up with the time it took to climb down.

'Well,' I say, once we reach the road, 'I'll go on.' His place is to the left, mine to the right.

'OK.' He seems at a loss for what to say. 'See you.'

'Yeah.' I stand, unable to move.

'Thanks for today. One of the best days I've had here.'

'Me too.'

'Maybe,' he shrugs and says in an offhand manner, 'maybe you'd like to show me some more places I should see?'

I nod in an equally casual way. 'Sure, just let me know. You bring the chocolate and I'll bring the intelligence.'

'Great. It's a date then.'

I roll my eyes. 'A date to me, Logan is fine wine, fancy food and a decent companion, not sore legs, midge bites and severe sunburn.'

He laughs, lifts his hand in a wave and walks off.

I walk on quite painfully, though for the first time in ages I feel as if I'm actually alive. Maybe it is the jolting pain in my legs that keeps me focused on the world, or maybe it's the breeze in my face, or the sun on my back or the colours of the grass. And the freedom of the open space and knowing that I can go anywhere and do anything I want. And yes, Logan too, who made me laugh and shared his chocolate with me. To be able to enjoy the company of someone other than Julie and Adam and let them enjoy my company. I'm in touch with a small part of myself that I thought might be gone and it's the most wonderful feeling, as if I'm coming home, back to myself after a terrible separation. I am, I realise with a jolt, content. Content just being here, in this tiny moment of time. Awareness of that makes me feel even better. And then my bad leg stumbles on something and I almost fall. And boom! I realise that being happy never really lasts. I could have slipped and banged my head on a rock and died. Or someone close to me could die. Which has happened twice already. Or someone connected to me could have a car accident. Or get on a plane. Or be run over by a drunk driver. The whole uncertainty of life hits me like a bowling ball smashing into a skittle and my happy thoughts shatter into the ether and this whole void of black emptiness opens up before me. Sucking me in and pulling me down. I think that if I don't run, if I don't get away, I too will shatter and break up and fall away. But my legs are sore and my breath becomes all uneven and my heart speeds up and my head swirls and I really do feel as if I'm going to die. I'm afraid to sit down as I can't think of where exactly I am. My breath is ragged. I try to control it. Tim's voice comes into my head and he's telling me that this won't kill me. It's a panic attack. So I don't run. I stand and breathe in and out instead. In and out. Breathe in and out slowly. Focus on it. I do this and it takes a while and I feel I'm swimming through black until, at last, I can see the end and the shimmering world waiting for me when I finally crash through the surface. I feel the edges of the panic ebbing away as the world comes back to me. I'm shivering, but OK. I hear the sound of the birds and the sea. I'm feeling the breeze on my face. But I find I can't enjoy it now. Being unguarded like I was lets the other

222

thoughts in too. And I can't let that happen. I have to control myself.

But I've beaten it. I've got through it, another part of me says. In a way, haven't I been controlling myself all my life? And trying to control others? I've never been spontaneous. Except for the times when I lost my jobs. But even that was a sort of control, because I didn't want anyone controlling me by telling me what to do.

Maybe it had been my only way of breaking out, but it had only imprisoned me all the more.

Maybe – I let the positive thought through – maybe I'm finally beginning to understand something.

I'm fairly OK when I get back to the cottage about forty minutes later.

'Hi,' I call, wondering how last night had gone. It strikes me that I haven't thought about my friends all day and I find that kind of amazing.

Julie and Nelson don't seem to be around and a very sick looking Adam is sitting at the table, pretending to read the newspaper. I know he's pretending because it's open at the gossip pages and Adam never reads those.

'How's the head?' I ask.

He looks up at me shamefaced. 'Yeah, sorry about last night. I wasn't exactly good company, was I?'

'Well, it would have been hard for you to be, seeing as you spent all night up at the bar and we were at a table.'

'Yeah. Sorry.'

He doesn't seem inclined to say any more. In fact he doesn't even ask me where I've been all day, which is unlike him. 'Where's Julie?'

'I don't know. We had a row.'

'Oh, Adam.'

'Apparently, I ruined her night,' he says. 'I kept getting sick and I ruined her night.'

'Yes,' I agree, 'that would ruin anyone's night.'

He gives a bitter sort of a scoff before turning back to the paper.

'D'you want a cuppa?' I ask as I cross into the kitchen. 'I'm making one for myself.'

'Yeah. Go on.'

I take my time making the tea, wondering if I should ask him what the matter is. I carry his tea in to him and sit beside him at the table. 'Adam,' I ask carefully, 'can you please tell me what the problem is?'

'I don't have a problem.'

'You were in quite good form until we went out last night and then, for some reason, you left the table and got completely smashed and fought with Julie.'

There is a long silence. Adam stares into his tea morosely.

'Did that girl Kate say something to you?' It's the only thing I can think of; he left right after she talked to him. 'Did she hurt you or anything?'

'Hope, stop, OK?' He buries his head in his hands. 'Just leave me.'

'But I can't. Look, you helped me feel a lot better after the accident, now for God's sake let me help you.' I'm a little worried about him. It's awful but fabulously brilliant. 'I'm worried about you, Adam.'

More morose tea-staring.

'Is it,' I bite my lip, the thought I had last night flitting through my head, 'well, you're not gay, are you?'

I've got his attention now. 'What?' He stares at me incredulously. 'What?'

'You know, it's OK if you are. Me and Julie won't mind.'

'You think I'm gay?' He looks at me, shell-shocked. 'I'm like your –' he makes quote signs with his fingers as he says savagely, making me flinch – 'gay friend?'

'No!' God, this was all wrong. I was only trying to help him if he was. 'No. I don't see you like that.'

'Good.' He shakes his head. 'Jesus!'

'Sorry, Adam.'

He shrugs, then mutters something.

'What?'

'I said,' he raises his bloodshot eyes to meet mine, 'I said, that I can't blame you for thinking it.'

I don't know what he means by that, so I say nothing.

'After all,' he says bitterly, 'I'm hardly a Don Juan, am I?'

'Don Juan was a cad, you're not like that.'

Another scoff. 'No, I'm just a saddo who can't even talk to a woman without practically vomiting.'

'What? That's not true. Julie and I are women.'

He laughs a little, though it's not a nice sounding laugh. 'Is there something wrong with that?'

'You and Julie,' Adam says, deliberately slowly, 'are women who rent a house from me. It's easy to feel good about the two of you.'

I think I should be annoyed. But I'm too stunned to reply. And hurt. He can hardly mean it. He's our *friend*, for God's sake.

'Shit! Sorry!' Adam says in frustration. I think he's still a bit drunk. 'In the beginning, Hope, it was like that.'

'Oh, thanks.' I want to belt him. Stupid tears threaten to spill over.

'I'm sorry, but it was.' Adam looks at me. 'It's not like that now.' He manages to take my hands in his. 'But Hope,

225

being your landlord gave me confidence with you and Julie.' He bites his lip. 'I'm such a total fucking loser.'

'What? You're saying that unless you feel superior to a girl you get terrified of her.'

'Basically, in a nutshell, that would be about right.' He can't look at me and his flippant tone belies the desolation on his face.

'So, what are you telling me, that you've only had relationships with girls you considered beneath you?'

He looks at me for a long time. Then he turns away. 'Hope,' he says softly, 'when you have zero confidence, there's not a lot of people below your level.'

'What?' I try not to sound taken aback. 'You've never had a girlfriend?'

He shrugs.

'Never?'

'Nothing serious.' He bites his lip. 'One could almost say my relationships were a joke.'

I don't know how to respond.

He shakes his head. 'When that girl Kate talked to me last night, I started to tremble, for fuck sake. I broke out in a sweat.'

'So that's why you left the table.'

'Yep.' He manages a sad sort of grin. 'There am I, looking over at Nelson, the weirdest bloke you ever saw and he's got Julie. How? I could never pull a bird like her in a million years. It just hit me, sitting at that table, looking around, how totally screwed up my life is.'

I don't answer. Instead, I do what comes totally unnaturally to me, I reach out and ruffle his hair and rest my head on his shoulder. 'I don't know why,' I whisper. 'You're not a bad-looking bloke for an Englishman.'

He laughs a little miserably. 'Ta.'

'But I've seen you talk to girls in London, in the pub and stuff?'

'No one else our age goes into Joe's pub in London. And when we go out, I'm usually drunk.'

That's true, actually only I'd never noticed it before.

'D'you remember a few weeks ago, Ju and I went out?' I nod.

'Well, I got totally smashed and talked to this girl. A lovely-looking girl. She even gave me her number. I couldn't ring her, though. I tried for days afterwards to dial her but I kept hanging up at the last minute. I panic around women the way you panic around crisps.'

'Well then,' I say, nudging close to him. 'We'll do exposure therapy on you. The first thing we'll do is to –' I think hard – 'we'll get you to go up to a girl and ask her the time. Easy peasy. But you have to be sober and presentable.'

'Aw no, I don't think so.'

'It'll work, Adam. Give it a try.' God, I feel desperately sorry for him. 'We'll take it step by step, Julie will help.'

'Julie won't help,' Adam groans. 'She hates me.'

'Julie doesn't hate you.'

He allows himself a dejected smile. 'Oh, yes she does,' he nods. 'Truly.'

'Look,' I say forcefully, 'just let go this holiday. Chat up a few girls while sober, I'll help you out. You'll see it's not so bad.' I study him. 'You should have told us this before, Adam. We never knew you had so little confidence.'

To my surprise, he looks more miserable than ever. 'There is a lot you don't know about me, Hope. I'm a terrible person.'

'No you're not.'

He doesn't look like he believes me but he manages a smile of sorts.

Who on earth, I think, would have thought that a guy with three houses and a big job would be so insecure? But then again, the smart part of my brain tells me, maybe that's why he has the three houses and the big job. Which means that I must be supremely confident. Which is crap.

Julie of course spoils any good I might have done Adam by completely ignoring him when she comes back. She waltzes into the house, humming some irritating tune and talking over to me as I sit on the couch trying to find a comfortable position for my aching joints.

'Hi, Ju,' Adam says, trying to be friendly. 'How's Nelson?'

Julie makes a face at me that he can't see. 'As if you care,' she sneers. 'Do you know what that idiot sitting over there did last night, Hope? Do you?'

'Let's just let it go,' I say. 'You're sorry, aren't you, Adam?'

He makes a face at me that she can't see. 'Sort of,' he concedes.

'Sort of?' Julie whirls on him. 'Sort of? You bloody well sat up in here last night until we came back, then you told Nelson that you were mystified as to how any woman went out with him, then you came over to me and asked if my taste was up my arse.'

Adam winces. 'Did I?'

'You know you did.' Julie folds her arms and stalks over to the table where he is still sitting, nursing what must be a massive hangover. 'Then you told Nelson to watch out for my plays. My plays are crap, you said. *The Wizard of Oz* was more the Wizened of Odd, you said.'

Adam opens his mouth to say something but Julie snaps,

228

'Just because you were a total loser with Kate last night, don't try and wreck my relationships! Kate said you were a weirdo!'

Oh Christ!

Adam shoves his tea away and stands up. He's gone quite pale. He shrugs and says in a remarkably composed voice, 'Fact, Julie: Nelson is the weirdo. Fact: you shouldn't have brought him back last night. Fact: if I behaved appallingly and said stuff, I'm sorry.'

'If?!'

'Julie, he's apologised.'

'Fact,' Adam turns around: 'you can do better than Nelson.' Then he stumbles towards the stairs. At the top, he slams his bedroom door really hard.

'Oh Ju,' I whisper, quite horrified, 'you shouldn't have said that.'

I'm about to tell her about Adam when she snaps, 'So my play was crap, was it?'

'That's not really that important now,' I say. 'If you'll just –'

'And were you and him,' she stabs a finger towards Adam's room, 'laughing over it? Was he sniggering away?' She turns her face to the ceiling and bellows at full volume, 'Toerag!'

'Julie, will you just let me explain –'

'Don't bloody bother.'

And she stomps upstairs and slams her door.

'Will you both cop on!' I shout.

Neither of them answers.

The whole night alone stretches before me. I take out my tape, put it in my ears and continue at least trying to make myself better.

23

JULIE DIDN'T GET up this morning at all. Despite the fact that Adam and I made a lot of noise shouting at each other, she didn't come down.

Yes, I rowed with Adam today.

I asked him why did he think it was necessary to inflame an already bad situation by not apologising to Julie. He told me that though he regretted ruining her night, he was not going to say sorry for stuff that he'd said that was true. Mainly the things about Nelson. I told him that he'd want to cop on and apologise or the rest of the holiday would be ruined.

He said his holiday was ruined anyway.

I asked him why so.

He clammed up on me and snapped, 'Do you want a lift or not?'

So we travelled to Tim's office in silence.

Just before I climbed out of the car he did mutter 'Good luck.'

Unfortunately I told him to get lost.

And now I'm sweating as Tim sets up the recorder again so that I can relate to him details of my miserable existence. He's quizzed me on my exposure therapy and I spoofed a little about the crisps. Since Julie scared me stupid, we haven't attempted it again. But I tell him with pride about my panic attack and how I handled it and he's pleased with that.

'So, you see, Hope,' he grins. 'By accepting that sometimes we have no control, that gives us a certain amount of control. And I'm sure you found out that there were things you could control – for instance your response to the panic attack.'

I nod. 'Yeah.'

Tim then asks me for the tape and I hand it to him. 'Now you've been listening to this over the weekend – how did it go?'

'OK, I think.'

As he replays it for me, I have my eyes closed and I have to visualise the situation as far as I can remember it. At various points he asks me how I feel. Because I've listened to it a few times now, I don't feel too anxious at all.

'How does not feeling anxious make you feel?' Tim asks.

I want to tell him that it makes me feel great, but instead I blurt out, 'Guilty.'

'OK,' he nods. 'Can you tell me why?'

'Because it was a horrible time and it got worse and if I let it go, does that mean that I don't care about what happened any more?' I have to swallow hard after saying that.

'If you care, you care,' Tim says. 'Carrying a big stone of guilt around with you doesn't make you care any more or less, does it?'

I shrug. I don't know.

'Well?' Tim presses, 'does it?'

'Maybe not.'

'Maybe not,' he repeats in a more positive tone than I had used. 'Now, Hope, seeing as you've done so well this week, we'll move on with the next part of the story. I'll slot this tape back in.' He pops the tape in and begins to speak. 'OK, so you were saying about your mother getting sick again, Hope. Take your time with this. Relax as you talk. Now close your eyes and visualise it.'

I was about fourteen. Jamie was ten. And it wasn't noticeable at first. She just stopped checking our homework. Instead, she'd sit in at the television and look at it but not look at it. Then maybe a couple of months later, I noticed that nothing was being done in the house when we were in school. I'd come home and wash up the breakfast dishes and put a wash on and tell Jamie to take a bath and make some dinner for us. She wouldn't eat.

'And did she talk to you at all?' Tim asks. 'What would she say?'

I shrug. 'She was always polite. She'd ask us about our day in school but she wouldn't listen. I don't know if Jamie noticed anything. It was all so gradual. But I worried.'

'Can you tell me how you used to feel?'

'I'd go to school in the morning and I'd spend my time praying that when I got home she'd have done some little something in the house to give me hope that she was all right. But she never did. I'd walk up towards the house after school, with my stomach clenched and a sick feeling right at the back of my throat. And I could never invite friends over and as a result I could never go to friends' houses either. There was so much to do at home.'

'OK,' Tim says, 'what happened then?'

She stopped talking. She stopped getting out of bed and she stopped eating. I used to go in to her and make up lies to try and jolt her back to us. I told her all sorts of crazy stuff. I made up one day that some boys had tried to attack me on the way home from school. That got her sitting up but then she just looked at me and shook her head and said I was a liar. I told her about exciting things like funfairs and stuff that was happening in school. I remember once winning piles of money in a school charity thing, a Countdown competition, and she didn't even say 'well done'.

'And how did that make you feel?'

'Hurt. Angry. Scared. I didn't know what to do.'

'Did you think of ringing a doctor?'

I feel a small tear trickle down my cheek. 'I wish I had now,' is all I manage. 'Everything that happened was my fault.'

'How are you feeling, what's the anxiety level like?'

'About an eight.'

'OK,' Tim says, 'I'm going to switch the tape off and you're going to start over. Then we'll see if you can continue.'

I start from my mother getting sick the second time. This time I remember more detail. How the curtains were always closed. How I was afraid the neighbours would notice. How I pulled open all the curtains before I left for school as I knew my mother wouldn't bother getting up to close hers again. How I bought the shopping in different places every week so people wouldn't notice; how I lodged money that came for her in the bank and how I forged her signature on withdrawal forms. Lots of little deceptions that I couldn't break. That became a comforting habit. That eventually led me into fooling Julie and Adam into thinking that my mother was dead.

Tim nods. 'OK, we've a half-hour left, do you think you can continue?'

233

The worst part is coming, I want to tell him, but I can only nod.

I wanted to call the doctor. It was the day when she hardly moved at all. The only thing to tell she was alive was that she was breathing. She didn't talk to us or look at us. I told Jamie I was going to have to ring the doctor and he started to cry. Jamie was all I had left. He was my most precious thing. I couldn't bear to see him cry. He didn't want to go and live in a stranger's house, he said. Imagine, he still remembered how he'd hated it. All he wanted was for us to be together. If I rang the doctor, they'd take Mammy away and put us in a new family and maybe a new school for a bit and he didn't want that. He didn't want Mammy to go. And so I fooled myself into thinking we'd cope.

Tim stops me. Gets me to relax and hands me a tissue. He tells me that it's good I'm upset. Some people can't even get in touch with their long-ago feelings, he says. But he doesn't want me to get too upset.

I tell him I want to go on.

He nods and presses the record button.

We did OK for a few months. I even thought at one stage that my mother was improving because she started to eat a little more though she was so thin. It was like some weird self-preservation thing kicked in, as if she wanted to disappear but not to die.

But then, the horrible thing happened, Jamie –

Tim holds up his hand.

I'm hyperventilating.

'Let's leave it there, Hope. Just listen.' He presses the tape and I hear myself talking about that time. And then he does it again. Each time, my anxiety levels rise.

But the third time, I can visualise and listen and I feel a slight shift.

'Good.' Tim takes out the tape and hands it to me. 'Listen to this for at least forty-five minutes a day between now and next week, Monday, OK?'

I slip the tape into my pocket.

Then he gets me to close my eyes and he relaxes me. When I get up to go, twenty minutes later, I'm calm and relaxed again.

'Good girl.' Tim smiles at me. 'You're doing great, you really are.'

His smile gives me confidence. 'Thanks.' But he still hasn't heard the worst part. I haven't talked about that yet.

'See you next Monday, Hope.'

I'm just at the door when I pause. I wonder if I dare. I probably shouldn't but he can only say no. 'Tim, can I ask your advice?'

'Shoot.' He's tidying up his desk, putting all my files away.

'Well, it's not about me, it's about a friend I have.'

'Go on.' He allows himself an amused smile.

'No, it really *is* about a friend of mine,' I stress. 'The thing is, he panics around women. Is there anything I could get him to do to make him more confident?'

To my surprise, Tim guffaws. 'Hope, if the guy has any sense he'll stay well away.'

'What?'

Tim makes a small gesture of surrender as he says, 'Sorry, I shouldn't have joked like that.' He frowns a little. 'Your friend needs what you're doing, exposure therapy. Just get him to relax and then approach a woman and ask her something, it might be the time or it might be for a match or whatever. That's step one. The next step would be to get him

235

to prepare a sort of chat-up line. You know, a "hello" followed by a "do I know you from somewhere". Things like that.'

'That's what I told him!' I'm chuffed.

'Aw, you'll put me out of business, so you will. Go on.' He flaps his hand at me to leave.

As I close the door, I suddenly remember that I'm fighting with Adam.

Great.

To my surprise, Adam smiles at me as I climb into his car.

'Oh, hi,' is all I can manage.

'I was going to get lost,' he says, jangling his car keys, 'but I was afraid you wouldn't be able to get your big mouth into a normal size car.'

I take this for the peace gesture it is and smile.

'I'm sorry, Hope,' he says as he eases the car into traffic. 'I've been a complete jerk, especially to you. You were great to me yesterday.'

'Yeah, I was,' I smile back. 'You big fool.'

'And I'll apologise to Julie when I get back, OK? I should never have gone on about her snoring.'

'Yeah, but she should never have said you were a weirdo.' As he opens his mouth to agree, I hold up my hand. 'But you started it. You should never have ruined her and Nelson's night.'

'She's too good for him.' He glares straight ahead as he manoeuvres the car into the right lane.

'That's not your business. He seems OK and he must be pretty successful, running a gym.'

'I'm successful but she doesn't make a fool of herself over me, does she? No. What has he got that I haven't? I've got a cool car.'

'You've got a big car, Adam. There is a difference.'

'Ha.'

I look curiously at him. 'Adam, is there something you want to tell me? Do you fancy her for yourself?' It would certainly fit; his behaviour was pretty bad.

'As if!' Adam snorts.

I don't know if I believe that but I let it drop. 'So,' I say, 'we'll all say sorry to each other and then we'll all go out for lunch. And maybe head to the beach.'

'Yeah. Good idea.'

It's just what I need after the morning I've had.

There's no need to apologise to Julie when we get back because she has gone. There is a note on the table saying that she taken a taxi to the train station and that she's spending the rest of the week in Dublin with Nelson. She'll be back on Monday and there's no 'goodbye' or 'take care'.

'Ouch,' Adam says. He sounds ever so slightly devastated. Tossing the note into the bin, he snaps, 'Well, let's hope she'll have calmed down by Monday.' He looks at me. 'So, disturbed cognitive therapy patient, what do you want to do? Grab a towel and head to the beach?'

And that's what we do.

There's a girl on the beach, looking in Adam's direction. He doesn't look half bad in swimming shorts actually. For one thing, he doesn't seem to have an awful lot of body hair and his skin is surprisingly smooth and tanned.

'Adam,' I kick him gently, 'see that girl over there, the one with the blue togs.'

Adam hoists himself up on to an elbow. 'Yeah?'

'Walk over to her and ask her the time.'

He pales. 'No. Not on a beach.' He attempts to lie back down again.

'Where is more ideal?' I kick him again. 'I don't see any massive clocks hanging about in the sky, do you?'

He ignores this.

'Look, do you remember when you got me to look at the aeroplane and I was terrified and you told me I'd regret it if I didn't? Well that's exactly how scared I was. Just go for it.'

I don't think he's going to bother, but then he sighs and hoists himself up. 'OK. I'll just ask her the time.'

'Yes and say please and thank you and just make believe it's me or Julie.'

I pretend not to notice the sheen of sweat that breaks out on his forehead. He lopes self-consciously towards the girl and I lie back down and watch him through half-closed eyes. Please don't chicken out, please don't chicken out, I pray. I can't hear the exchange but he arrives back a minute or so later, flops down beside me and says, 'Well, that was embarrassing.'

'How so?'

He holds out his wrist on which his big expensive watch resides.

'Oh shit!'

'Yeah.' He lies down beside me and says casually, 'So I told her it wasn't working and she believed me.'

He's breathing heavily but he sounds thrilled with himself. 'Good man!'

His hand catches mine. 'Thanks, Hope.'

'Now you have to keep doing that until you're not so anxious about it. Then we'll work on harder stuff.'

'Yeah. Yeah. Fine.'

We both lie there and fall asleep.

24

TUESDAY MORNING. AGAIN, the sun is warming the room through the curtains; outside, I can hear birds singing and the faint drone of a car on the road. I'm a bit burnt from the sun yesterday and I groan as I climb out of the sleeping bag.

Adam and I had stayed on the beach for hours, not having had anything else to do, and while he read an important-looking literary book, and asked two more women for the time, I lay back on my beach towel and fell asleep. Luckily I wasn't wearing a bikini or togs or I would have been fried. Instead, my arms are a purplish colour, as are my shins. I'm half afraid to look in the mirror at my face but as I wash myself, I take a quick glance.

'Oh no!'

I look as if I'm about to have a major heart attack. If post traumatic stress doesn't get me, skin cancer will. I've never been one to get a tan and I've always used sun cream before but yesterday I'd only put it on once before falling asleep. And I'd slept for six hours.

I lather on some aftersun, but it dissolves on contact, making my face gleam.

I wonder if I have sunstroke.

I wander glumly back inside and meet Adam in the kitchen.

'I think I have sunstroke,' I say, leaning against the counter as he fills the kettle.

'Well, you look as if you're going to have a stroke OK,' he chortles, dodging a belt from me. He dumps two teabags into two mugs and shoves some bread under the grill.

'Any plans for today?' I ask.

'I might drive into Killarney and buy some trinkets to take home; you know, souvenirs for my mum. I might even ask a few more women what the time is, I'm getting good at that.'

'Brilliant.' I'm glad he's in better form. The morose, badtempered Adam of the last couple of days was not someone I'd like to meet again. 'But before that,' he continues, 'I'm just going to do some work on the net.'

'Adam, you're mad. You're suspended.'

He pours out the tea. 'So if you want to tag along to Killarney you're welcome,' he says. Then, with a mug in his hand and a slice of toast between his teeth he wanders back upstairs.

I sit outside in the shade of the house, my cup of tea balanced on the overgrown path. Taking my mobile phone from the pocket of my jeans, I dial Julie's number. It goes straight to voicemail. 'Hi Ju,' I whisper, not wanting Adam to hear, 'hope Dublin is going well. When you come back, we'll all talk. Just so you know, Adam confessed to me that he's afraid of women. I think seeing you and Nelson and other couples together just got to him that night. Please ring me back.' I hang up. It's a little weird she didn't answer, I muse. Surely she'd want to gloat about what a brilliant time she was having, if nothing else. Or maybe she is still really mad at both of us. I sigh and settle back against the hard wall of the house. Really, I think, Maurice should have supplied the cottage with some patio furniture. And a clean sofa. And some new chairs. But the state of the place had lost its importance. It was all surface.

'Hey, knew you'd be waiting for me!'

It's Logan, striding across the field, haversack on his back and a smartarse grin on his face. He's wearing his football T-shirt and a pair of tracksuit bottoms that frankly have seen better days. In fact, all of Logan's clothes have seen better days.

'Would you be totally devastated if I said I wasn't waiting for you?'

'Absolutely, yep.'

'Well, then, I wasn't waiting for you.'

'Aw, you can lie, but your eyes tell me a different story.'

'Really? You can see "feck off" written in my eyes?'

He laughs and plonks down beside me. 'Any plans for today?'

'You are the second man to ask me that,' I say. 'I'm flattered. And the answer is no, no plans as yet. Adam is going into Killarney to buy some ridiculously expensive touristy rubbish and I'm not sure if I want to accompany him.'

'So accompany me.' Logan is so close, I can smell the minty smell from his breath. 'I'm heading cross country to Dingle. I was wondering if you could show me a good place, midway up, for getting the whole landscape?'

My legs are still quite stiff, but I don't tell him that. 'Midway up,' I say, thinking of all the nicest places along the mountainside. 'Yeah, I reckon I can manage that.'

'You might want to bring some sunscreen,' Logan nods at my face. 'It's meant to be a scorcher today. And here –' he hands me a plastic bag. Maria's wellies are inside. 'A gift to you from me. I don't use them at all.'

'Wow, your generosity knows no bounds! A pair of your ex's second-hand wellies, fab!' I pull off my trainers, but before slipping on the boots I say, 'Back in a sec, I'll just let Adam know.'

'No rush.'

I go back inside, run up the stairs in my stockinged feet and burst into Adam's room. As he said, he's on the computer, but he's in a Job search page.

'Job search?'

'Yeah,' he smiles sheepishly. 'Well, if those idiots at my place think I'm going back with my tail between my legs after the summer, they can think again. I mightn't go back at all.'

'Good for you!'

'I might even resign.'

'Oh no, I wouldn't do that, not until you have another job.'

Adam flushes and nods. 'Yeah. Maybe. So?'

I tell him that I'm heading off with Logan to show him a few scenic spots to paint from. Adam grins. 'Wow, very friendly, aren't you?'

'Don't be stupid. Look, if a blow-in is going to be painting my county, I want him to do a good job, right?'

'Oh yeah,' Adam sniggers, 'that's very important. And I'm sure Logan, who has been living here a year, wouldn't have a clue where to paint from.'

'As a matter of fact, he doesn't.'

I ignore Adam's juvenile laughter as I go back downstairs.

'Right,' I say in a very businesslike tone to Logan, 'come on then.'

'Hadn't you better put on your wellies first?'

'Your ex's wellies.'

'No, I gifted them to you.' He smiles munificently. 'They are now yours.'

'Sorry, how could I have forgotten?' I pull them on and, with Logan running to catch up, stride away from the house.

We walk for most of the day. It's not so tough this time as we're not going too far up the mountain. Logan has, as promised, brought along some chocolate. And a bottle of Club Orange. The man seems to live on sweet things. 'Don't you ever eat anything that's fresh?' I ask.

He looks puzzled. 'Why? Is that chocolate out of date?'

'I mean fresh fruit and vegetables?'

'Boring!' He rolls his eyes. 'You sound like Maria. She was a big one for organic things. She spent a fortune on organic bananas one time. Organic bananas!' He says it with the wonder of someone who has just seen a spaceship landing. 'I told her if she grew some stuff in the garden, that'd be better. I told her that the amount of greenhouse gases emitted by the plane that carried those bananas to Ireland probably deleted any organic benefits of them.'

'Fresh fruit is good for you.'

'Do I look like I'm suffering?' He holds his arms wide away from his body and grins.

He looks pretty damn good, I have to admit, faded tracksuit and all.

'More chocolate?' his eyes sparkle.

'Go on so.'

We trudge another while in silence. The only sounds are the birds and the grasshoppers.

'She'd never have come walking with me like this,' Logan says out of the blue. 'Not in a million years.'

'Who?'

243

'Maria.'

'Oh.'

He spends a lot of his time thinking about Maria, I think. And his voice is quite bitter when he mentions her name. Things must have ended very badly.

'How's the counselling going?' he asks.

I have to admit, I'm a bit taken aback by that. 'Eh, OK,' I mutter.

'Sorry, should I not have asked?'

I shrug.

'It's just that I don't want you to think I don't care. Or that I wouldn't ask.'

He sounds uncomfortable but not as uncomfortable as I'm feeling.

'Tell you what, if you want to tell me, you just tell me, I won't ask again. Deal?'

'Counselling is going well. It's slow but OK.'

'Oh.' He shifts his haversack to his other shoulder. 'Do you have to talk a lot about the crash?'

'We haven't even got to that yet,' I say.

'Really?' His jaw drops. 'So what else is there? Like, is that not why you went in the first place?'

And so I explain to him about my reaction to the crash being so much worse because of other stuff that happened before. Wisely, he doesn't go there. Instead he just nods and smiles and says that his first impression of me was obviously right and that I did need help.

'Not as much help as you'll need if you say something like that again.'

'Point taken.'

We smile at each other and it dawns on me that I'm falling for this guy. I'm falling for him because he's funny in the

244

same sarcastic way that I am. I'm falling for him because he loves living here, which I did once upon a time. I'm falling for him because he doesn't treat me as a victim. And I'm falling for him because he's so bloody gorgeous.

But I wonder if he's falling for me.

I take him to a midway point above Dingle and he hums and haws and doesn't seem all that impressed with it. 'It's just that the view to the sea is blocked by all the heather,' he says.

'Can you not just paint in the sea,' I grouch. I'd been looking forward to a sit-down. 'Just pretend that it's there.'

He looks faintly shocked. 'Eh, no.'

'Right, come on.' I start marching again. 'You're a hard man to please.'

'Would you prefer if I lied?' He runs in front of me. 'Would you prefer if I said, Oh yeah, Hope, that's a fantastic view of the ocean there. Hang on now while I paint the sea.'

'Yes, I would, actually. I would prefer if you lied.'

'No you wouldn't. If I lied about that, how could you trust me again?'

'I don't trust you anyway.'

'Liar,' he jokes cheerfully.

At last we get to a place that he likes. I sit down, as before in the shade, and plaster my face with sun cream. It's quite sore but not as sore as my legs have got. Being with Logan is pretty torturous on my poor body.

'Hey, stay like that,' Logan instructs.

'What, like this?' My hand is putting cream on my neck.

'Yeah, I love the curve of a woman's neck.' Logan begins a quick sketch.

'You can't draw me!' Immediately I take my hand away and he groans.

'Aw come on, Hope. You're totally gorgeous.'

That comment floors the both of us.

'In that pose,' Logan clarifies. He looks appealingly at me. 'Please?'

And so, semi-flattered and with my heart beating fit to burst, I sit like that for another twenty minutes until he's satisfied.

'Can I see?'

'Nope.' He holds the sketches to his chest. 'One day I'll show you, OK?'

'I have a right to look.'

'No you don't.' He turns away from me then and begins sketching the surrounding countryside.

I don't pursue it. I think maybe it's that I don't want to see how he perceives me. I want to hold on to the 'totally gorgeous' comment. If he's drawn me in some weird way or in some pose that I consider unflattering, I'll be disappointed. I've never let any man close enough to me since Jack told me I was gorgeous. I've gone out with some nice guys since, but only about once or twice. I just didn't want to get left again, I suppose.

Logan finishes up pretty quickly. He puts all his stuff away and turns to where I'm sitting on the grass. 'We must be near enough to Dingle now,' he says.

'Yeah, about a mile.'

'What say we walk into it and grab something to eat? My treat.'

I'd been thinking along the same lines myself. Logan's chocolate isn't doing it for me, I want something a bit more substantial. 'Yeah, why not, but I'll pay my way.'

'No, I insist.' Logan crosses towards me: 'you've been great today, so it's like a payment.'

I don't bother to argue. My funds are depleting rapidly, what with all the food the three of us eat. 'OK,' I smile. 'Thanks.'

We arrive in Dingle about half an hour later. The two of us are quite scruffy compared to all the fresh-looking tourists milling about the place. There's a big queue for Fungi, the dolphin. Logan asks me if I've ever seen him.

'Yeah, Julie, Adam and I came last month.'

'Me and Maria went one day. It was right before our relationship broke up and Fungi never appeared and she blamed me.'

I laugh.

He laughs too. 'So, where would you like to go?'

I shrug. 'Don't mind.'

We go into a small restaurant. Logan orders beef with vegetables and I order a big plate of seafood pasta. Then we find seats outside in the sunshine.

'Well,' Logan says, biting his lip, 'it's not fancy food, it's not a fancy place and I'm probably not your ideal companion, but hey, I'm not complaining.'

He's smiling but there is an anxious look on his face.

'Neither am I,' I say back.

'Good,' he nods.

'Well –' a plate of dinner is put down before each of us – 'I hope ye'll think your dinner is good.'

We both laugh, but as we begin to eat I become aware that the moment has been lost. I wonder where that conversation might have led.

* * *

We catch a taxi back to Dunport and the silence stretches between us. I desperately want to ask him what he meant by saying that he wasn't complaining. Maybe he likes me? But chances are that that's all he does – like me. What a bloody fool I'd feel then.

Logan chit-chats about various things with the taxi driver and as we reach my place first, I have to go.

'Thanks again for today,' Logan says. 'I'll be in touch.'

'Yeah. OK.' Just before I close the door, I screw up the courage to say, 'And I enjoyed dinner.'

'Great.'

There is nothing else I can say. He won't let me pay for the taxi either and I don't want to add to his bill, so I slam the door and wave them off.

25

IT'S EIGHT O'CLOCK. Adam is showing me what he bought in Killarney and it is just as I feared. Horrendous leprechauns with big bright gaudy pots of gold and Irish dancing dolls with flaming red hair and freckles.

'Adam, how much did you pay for all this?' I ask, but before he can answer, I hold up my hand. 'No, please, don't tell me. It's best if you don't.' As he puts them back in the bag, I ask, 'And how did you get on with the girls of Killarney? Did they have the *time* for you?'

He grins at my pathetic pun. 'Yep, no problems there. That was an easy step.' He dumps his bags on the floor. 'So, what comes next? I'm up for it.'

'Let me have a think and I'll let you know.'

He's about to say something else when we hear the crunch of tyres on the gravel outside as a car pulls up.

'That's a bit odd,' Adam remarks. He glances out the window. 'It's a taxi, hey, it's Julie. What's she doing back?'

We get to the front door in time to see the driver pop the boot and hand Julie a large case. She takes it and pays him and turns to see us standing silent in the doorway. She looks at us and we look at her. She doesn't look happy.

'Ju?' Adam breaks the silence as he asks uncertainly, 'Are you OK?'

At his voice she glares at us, though her eyes are watery. 'Oh, you'll be gloating now, the two of you,' she sniffs, pushing past us and running inside.

'Julie!' I run after her but she's only gone as far as the sitting room. She plonks down on the sofa and scrubs her eyes with the sleeve of her gorgeous white jacket. She must have been crying in the taxi, I think, as her face is a mess, full of splodgy make-up and streaked lipstick.

'Julie?' I ask gently, 'What happened?' I sit beside her.

Adam comes in carrying her case. Depositing it on the floor, he shuts the door and looks down at us. Then he sits on the other side of her. 'Ju?' he says tentatively. 'What's wrong? Come on, I rang you and apologised.'

'You rang her?' I look at him. 'So did I.'

Then we both look at Julie. 'I turned my phone off because I didn't want any messages from *him*.'

'Who? Nelson?'

At the mention of his name, her eyes fill up with more tears but she blinks rapidly to stem their flow. Hesitantly, I put my arm about her shoulder.

Neither of us says anything.

Her eyes fill up again. A tear plops on to her hand. 'He's a liar, that's what happened,' she sniffs. 'He's a big, fat, testosteroned, bulky liar and I hate him. And you were right, Adam, my taste was up my arse.'

'I was horribly drunk when I said that,' Adam mutters.

'You were still right.'

'What did he do?' I ask. I'm not surprised, really. There was something suspicious about him. I can spot a liar because I was one myself.

Julie sniffs again but sits up straight in a state of righteous indignation. 'Well, firstly, he doesn't own any gyms.

250

None. Oh God, I feel so stuuuupid.' She bites her lip. 'I stood, like a, like a stupid prat, inside the gym he said he owns. I asked to see him. The owner, I said to the girl behind the desk, Nelson Curry, I'd like to see him. They said that he wasn't the owner but they recognised his name as one of their members. I thought there must be a mistake. So I ring him. I tell him I'm in Dublin, outside his gym. I don't tell him what the receptionist said on the desk. And he tells me to wait outside, that he'll meet me.' She pauses for a bit. 'Anyway, he comes in a taxi to meet me. He pulls me into the taxi and starts chatting away about stuff. Stupid stuff, like what's in the papers and what he heard on the radio and then he tells the taxi driver to stop and out we get. Then he asks how you and Adam are and then I know he doesn't own the gym.'

'How?' The story is a bit meandering but I'm getting the gist of it.

'Well, I knew he didn't like Adam much after the other night, so why should he care about how he is?'

'Good point,' Adam says wryly.

'And suddenly, I hate that he doesn't like Adam, even though I was finding it hard to like him myself. So I say, why didn't you introduce me to your staff. And he says, oh they're all very busy and they don't like all that sort of thing. And I say, you don't own a gym, do you, and he says no. And I say, what else don't you own. And he says, I'm a milkman and I own a milk float.'

'What?' Jesus, I think, Nelson a milkman.

'Bloody hell,' Adam says.

'Yeah. Now, I've nothing against milkmen. But I do have a grudge against lying tossers who make a fool out of me and get their friends to do the same. So I told him that and

251

I left him shouting after me, telling me that he was self-employed, that he hadn't lied about that. Anyway, I booked into a hotel and ignored all his calls and then I came back here.'

'Wanker,' I say.

Adam doesn't say anything.

'Isn't he a complete wanker, Adam?'

He shrugs. 'Stupid, maybe.' He shifts uncomfortably. 'But, you know, understandable.'

'What?'

'What?!' That's Julie and she is not happy. 'Do you have some kind of an anti-Julie agenda?' she says, half crying. 'I tell you that this guy has made a complete fool out of me and you say it's understandable. Thanks!'

'Adam?' I hold out my hands in a for-fuck's-sake-what-are-you-playing-at-here gesture.

'No, Ju,' Adam says, in a hopeless kind of way, 'I'm not trying to get at you, but what was the guy meant to do?'

'Eh,' I make a face, 'maybe, oh, I dunno, tell the truth?'

Adam gulps hard. He starts to chew his lower lip. 'Look,' he says, as if talking to two morons. 'Nelson sees Julie. He thinks she's hot. She tells him she's a teacher. So a hot babe who's obviously clever, what is he meant to do? Say, "hey, I'm Nelson the milkman"?'

'Yes.' Julie can't believe she's hearing this and neither can I. 'What's wrong with that?'

'Nothing, except he thinks he mightn't stand a chance with you.'

'That's ridiculous!'

'And maybe,' Adam says over her, 'when he told the lie, he just wanted a bit of a one-night stand. Like, what's sexier – a guy who owns a gym or a milkman?'

252

'So it's OK to lie to get someone into bed, is it?' Julie asks tearfully.

'No!' Adam shakes his head. 'It's not about getting someone into bed,' he explains desperately, 'it's about, I suppose, trying to be better than you really are to impress someone you think is better than yourself.'

'Crap,' Julie pronounces. 'It's a sicko who'd do that.'

'I've done it,' Adam says softly.

What is Adam playing at tonight? We both glare at him.

'I did it to impress you two,' Adam says. He stands up and shoves his hands into his pockets. He fixes his gaze firmly on his grey socks. One of his toes is poking out.

'What, do you not have a big fancy job then?' Julie asks hotly. 'Did you steal your big fancy car and your three houses?'

'No,' Adam shakes his head. 'No, I had all that.' He takes a deep breath. 'I don't have it now, though.'

'Adam?'

'They let me go in my old job, OK? They fired me.'

'No!' That's Julie. 'Oh Adam, that's awful!'

'Suppose it is,' he agrees.

'But that's not the same as Nelson,' I point out. 'You never told us because you didn't want to ruin the summer.'

Adam gives that strange laugh, the one he'd given the day after he'd got really drunk. It's a horrible sound. As if he almost hates himself. 'I never told you because,' he pauses, and raises his gaze to our eye level, 'because you would have hated me.'

'Don't be stupid!' Julie stands up beside him, her own drama momentarily forgotten. 'How could we hate you?'

He smiles bleakly. 'Because –' he looks at Julie – 'because you'd find out what a bastard I was at work.'

We look blankly at him.

'The blokes hated me,' Adam goes on, startling us. 'They informed management that I was away. Yes, the fifty thousand was a mistake but it might have been OK if they hadn't hated me enough to squeal on me.'

'Why did they hate you?'

Adam pales and gulps hard. It's obvious he's finding it difficult to admit why. Taking a deep breath, he says quietly, 'I bullied them.'

Julie and I recoil.

Julie recovers first. 'You?' she gawps at him. 'You?'

'Yes.' Adam nods, looking ashamed. 'I spent my life being picked on,' he says bitterly. 'I was this scrawny, girly-looking boy and great fodder for abuse. So when I got working, I just said to myself, there is no bloody way these blokes are going to get one over on me. So I stamped over everyone to get to the top. I didn't let anyone away with anything. I quizzed them about their sick days, their days off. Blokes resigned because of me. Had breakdowns because of me.' He pauses and looks at both of us, then says slowly, 'And it suddenly hit me, when I was fired, I'd turned into the one thing I despised. I guess I was ashamed. I couldn't tell you – not then. That's why I never rang in the day or so afterwards.'

There is silence after this speech. Adam won't meet our gaze; instead he focuses on his socks.

'So why now?' I ask, breaking the silence.

'Because . . . I don't know . . . because we'll be going back and I'm tired of lying.' He pauses. 'I've been lying for so long now, I barely know who I am any more.'

'I, eh, can't imagine anyone being afraid of you,' Julie ventures.

'Me neither.'

Adam shakes his head. 'You and Hope were the only ones that kept the nice part of me alive.'

More silence.

'Look,' Julie says, her fingertips brushing his arm, 'this is your chance to start over, Adam.' She links her arm in his. 'To be the nice guy you know you are. You are not like Nelson.'

Adam pulls his arm from her grasp and walks away from her. 'I'm not a nice guy,' he says almost savagely.

'You are, isn't he, Hope?'

'A very nice guy,' I confirm.

He turns to face us. Bows his head and says nothing.

'Come here.' Julie crosses to him and enfolds him in a hug.

He wraps his arms about her. His eyes are suspiciously shiny.

'Ta,' he mumbles.

26

THE WHOLE HOUSE is awoken by the squeal of tyres on gravel the next day. In fact, a spray of stones clatters against the dining-room window, waking me up quite suddenly. The dream I'd been having slides away. It had been horrible, I know that much, for my forehead is filmed with sweat. Of course that could be a result of the sunburn too.

A furious banging starts up at the front door and peering out, I see Nelson, with yet another fancy car, standing in front of the house and hollering up at Julie's window. 'Julie,' he's saying. 'I'm sorry! Please, listen to me!'

Julie doesn't seem to be reacting at all. I don't know whether to let him in or not. I stand, in all my glory, in a pair of cotton pyjamas with teddy bears printed all over them.

'Julie, I've been a fool. I know I have. Please, just give me a chance to explain.'

I take a step towards the door.

'If you let me explain, I'll give you free milk for life!'

'What on earth —' Adam has come downstairs without me hearing him. He looks wretched, as if he hasn't slept.

'Nelson,' I say.

'Let him in,' Adam says.

'But Julie —'

'Will have to sort it out herself.' He strides determinedly towards the door.

'Is she here?' Nelson steps inside and looks wildly around. 'Did she tell you?'

Both of us look at the ground.

Nelson sighs. 'I've been a twit,' he mutters. 'I don't know how I thought I'd get away with it. And I wouldn't mind, but coming down here every weekend has lost me a few customers. They don't like getting all their milk on a Thursday. I gave them up for Julie.' He plonks down on the sofa, which shakes violently.

'Pity about you,' Julie's voice, ice cold, comes from the stairway.

Nelson stands up again. 'Just let me explain?'

'Don't you dare upset her,' Adam says quietly. 'Just say your piece and leave her.'

'Eh, I was talking to Julie,' Nelson says a bit snottily.

'Yeah, and I was talking to you,' Adam says. 'Now Ju –' He walks back to her and his hand caresses her shoulder – 'me and Hope will get out of your way, the place is all yours.'

I pull some stuff from the jumble of clothes on the floor. 'I'll just get changed and I'll be gone.' I shoot a look of solidarity at Julie but she's glaring at Nelson. I don't know how he can stand there and face her, I'd be terrified.

'You were so hot,' is the last thing I hear as I leave the room.

Adam and I stroll through the streets of Dingle, licking some rapidly melting ice-cream cones.

'I hope she doesn't take him back,' I mutter.

'Me too,' Adam says. 'She's better than that.'

'Yeah.'

'Had any luck on the job front?' I ask.

He flushes. 'Thanks for being so decent last night.'

'Only because you are,' I smile. 'So go on, any luck?'

'I've sent my CV out to a few places all right,' he admits. 'I'm hoping to hear back soon. I've sent yours out too.' He pauses. 'Are you coming back to London with us?'

'Of course I am.'

'Oh, it's just that I thought with your mother and everything –'

'I haven't seen her since that day in her house,' I admit. I dump my ice-cream into a bin. It's dripping all over my fingers. 'I mean, I think I'd like to, you know, because it's the normal thing to do, but for me, I, well, I think my life would be easier without her in it. Does that sound horrible?'

'Nothing is horrible if the reasons are right,' Adam says. He dumps his ice-cream too and begins licking his fingers, one by one. 'It's just a question, I suppose, of understanding the reasons. And you, Hope Gardner, are not horrible.'

'Thanks.'

'Just like I'm not horrible.' He grins suddenly. 'Isn't that right?'

'Yeah.'

We pass a small shop selling pictures. One in the window catches my attention. It's the colours. Bright and vibrant. Then I notice that it's by Logan. Wow. He does have talent.

'Let's go in here.' I take Adam by the arm and guide him into the shop. 'I want to see what else Logan has done.'

His pictures dominate the shop. Oh, there are others, but

258

his are so loud that I'm drawn to them. Adam follows me about exclaiming over them too.

Two girls come in some minutes later. They look nice, I decide.

'Now Adam,' I whisper, 'this is your chance. Walk up there and tell those two women that you know the artist.'

'What?'

He says it loudly and the two girls look over at the commotion and then turn away again.

'Are you mad,' he hisses, looking in desperation at me. 'I can't do that.'

'Why not? You're sober, you do know the artist and there are two girls there who look like a bit of a laugh – go up and talk to them.'

'No.'

'Adam, think of me –'

'With the planes, yadda, yadda. I'm sick of you and the bloody planes.'

'Go on,' I laugh and give him a gentle shove in the back. 'Pretend that you're thinking of buying the picture, ask them what they think of it.'

'What if they think I'm weird?'

'So, they think you're weird. Big deal.'

He considers this. 'OK, Right. OK.' He starts to psych himself up. I wish he'd worn nicer clothes than his cords and cream T-shirt. Not exactly babe magnet stuff. Still, as he makes a slow walk towards them, I think that his one saving grace is his ass. He has a class A ass.

I see him study the picture the girls are looking at, then, as casual as anything, he turns to them and says, 'I'm thinking of buying you, think of the picture, yes?'

They look at him.

He flushes and I want to die for him.

Then one of the girls laughs. 'Pardon?' she giggles. 'What was that?'

'Yes,' Adam nods, trying to grin, 'I probably should rephrase that.'

That makes them both smile.

And he begins to chat to them, talking about the picture he's going to buy. I can see his shoulders hunch up and he starts that nervous thing with his hand through his hair, but the girls don't seem to notice. In fact, they agree that his choice is a good one.

And then, after about five minutes he excuses himself and comes back to me. 'I'm going to have to buy it now,' he says. 'Thanks.' But he's grinning.

Two hours later and two hundred quid down, Adam and I make our way back to the cottage. Adam has the number of one of the girls; they'd joined us for a coffee at my instigation. He has promised to call her, but I don't think he will. He's not ready to go there just yet, I don't think.

'Hey,' he says as we drive up, 'Nelson is gone.'

'Well, we have been away for hours,' I answer.

The back door is open and we shove it in. Though neither of us will admit it, we're both a bit nervous.

'Hello?'

I wonder if Julie has gone out. I'm just putting the kettle on for coffee when she comes into the kitchen. 'Hi,' she says quietly. She looks pale and sort of shocked. Even though she's dry eyed, she still manages to look ten times more upset than she had been.

'How did it go with Nelson?' I ask.

'What did he say?' Adam says.

Her lip quivers and she looks like a five-year-old. Leaning against the back door, she says as she wraps her arms about herself, 'I'm so shallow, I really am.'

'You? Shallow? Never?!' I make my voice sort of jokey. Of course she's shallow, everyone is shallow sometimes.

'I know you're joking, Hope, but it's true.' She shakes her head and says, 'I'm shallower than . . .' she tries to think of a comparison, 'shallower than a baby's paddling pool.'

'Did that muppet Nelson say you were shallow?' Adam sounds furious. 'Did he?'

'No.' Julie heaves a great big sigh. 'But he made me see that I was. Thanks.' I hand her a mug of coffee and, wrapping her hands around it, she takes a noisy slurp. 'When Nelson was here today, I realised that I'm a whole lot shallower than I even thought.'

'How come?'

'Well, when he stood here, telling me how he thought I was "hot". God, I hate that word, well, when he stood here today, I looked at him. I mean, really looked at him.' She stresses the 'really looked at him'.

'And?'

'Well, I realised that,' she swallows hard, 'that yes, I was only going out with him because I thought he owned a gym.'

God, I think, that is shallow, but I don't say it.

Adam does, though. 'That is a bit shallow all right.'

'Adam!' I nudge him furiously.

'He's right,' Julie says without any anger. 'I mean, without the gym, Nelson is just a ridiculous-looking man, isn't he? All horrible muscle and massive thighs. D'you know, Hope, his thigh is as big as your head.'

'Too much information.' I wave my free hand about.

She smiles briefly. 'Sorry. Anyhow, I looked at him today

and realised that I actually didn't like him. I didn't like him at all.' She sounds as if she can't believe that she went out with him. 'I didn't like the way he was always giving off about Adam. I think he was jealous of you, Adam. Imagine.' She rolls her eyes.

'Yeah, imagine,' Adam repeats, though he doesn't sound as convinced.

'We had a row once about you, Adam. And I didn't like the way he loved himself, I didn't like his pathetic lies. I wonder why I bothered with him.' She bites her lower lip. 'I mean, how could I have been so stupid?'

I don't know, myself.

'I don't know,' Adam says.

'And it was his gyms.' She pauses. 'But it wasn't only that.'

'No? What else?' I ask.

'You'll both think I'm pathetic. I know you will.' She points at herself, '*I* think I'm pathetic.'

Neither of us says anything.

'I went out with him because he owned those gyms and I thought –' for the first time her composure cracks slightly, her voice wobbles as she goes on – 'well, I thought, it'd impress my parents, didn't I? And I thought that it'd make Angela half crazy with jealousy. I mean, her boyfriend is only a professor of something or other.' She swallows hard. 'Isn't that awful of me?'

I borrow Adam's line of the night before. 'Awful but understandable.'

'Yes, understandable because I'm so superficial.'

'No.' I put my coffee down and try to choose my words. It's strange, me counselling Julie; it's normally the other way around. And it's nice that she's upset, it sort of makes me feel more connected to the world. 'It's understandable because no matter what, everyone cares about what their parents think.' Even me, funnily enough. 'I mean, I rebelled because I wanted my mother's attention. You conformed because you wanted to please them. It's all down to them, in the end.'

Julie is silent for a bit, then she says, in a surprisingly surprised voice, 'That's really good, Hope.'

'So,' I pat her hand, 'you can blame your folks. I blame my mother for everything.'

She grins. Then says, 'But I thought I'd outgrown all that. I did what I wanted by going into teaching. I gave my dad what for when we went for lunch that day. It's such a shock to realise that I still want their approval.'

'Yeah well . . .' I shrug. 'It's nice to have your folks' approval.'

'And I was trying to get one over on Angela. I'm pathetic, aren't I?'

'No, Nelson was pathetic.'

'We suited each other.'

'No. Never.'

'Never.' Adam nods vigorously. 'I told you you could do better, remember?'

'Yeah, Adam, I remember.'

The two of them smile at each other.

'You can do so much better,' he says intensely. 'And,' hesitantly he holds out his new purchase, 'if Logan can give a picture to Hope to say sorry, then I can give one to you. Sorry for all the stuff I said, about your play and everything. It was a brilliant play.'

I'm stunned. What an apology. The picture cost a fortune.

Julie looks at the picture and then at Adam. 'Thanks,' she says, taking it from him. 'But I knew you didn't mean it.'

Adam flicks me an amused glance but I keep my face straight.

27

T HE DAY I'VE put off thinking about for the past week arrives. I've begun to dread the thought of the weekly counselling session, mainly because I'm knackered for about two days afterwards and today will be the worst day so far. Today will be the day I have to talk about Jamie. Really talk about Jamie. Talk about the day Jamie died. I think it's the day I died too, in a way.

'Hiya,' Tim beckons me in.

'See you eleven-thirty,' Adam and Julie say simultaneously.

It's all a bit embarrassing, everyone knowing I have to go to therapy.

Tim's office doesn't look as neat as before. It's messy with files everywhere. Something like Tim, actually. He looks a bit rough too.

'Sorry.' Tim scoops up some files and dumps them into an open cabinet. 'I'm hopeless at keeping the place clean.' To my surprise, he lifts a sleeping bag off the floor and, opening the messiest filing cabinet I have ever seen, shoves it inside and slams the drawer shut. 'Now,' he surveys his office, scratches his hair and pulls at his ponytail. 'Now, where is the recorder?'

'On the desk.'

'Sure. Of course.' He flashes me a smile and busies himself

looking for batteries for it. 'You're doing well, Hope,' he mutters from under the table where he is rummaging about in a box. 'Someone with your background can be very difficult to work with.' When he pops his head back up, I glimpse two new batteries in his hand.

'Really?' I don't know whether to feel proud or not.

'So now . . .' he assumes his position in the chair, inserts the batteries into the recorder, and looks at me. 'How have you got on with the other tape?'

'Good.' I think about how to say what I want to say. 'I mean, I can listen to it and it isn't as horrible each time but it makes me feel, I dunno,' I gulp hard, 'well, really sad, I suppose.' I sound defensive.

'Well, you told me your brother died,' Tim says gently. 'Of course you should be sad. Maybe at the time you weren't sad enough.'

'Maybe.'

He takes me through some relaxation and finally asks if I'm ready to talk. 'Just stop if the anxiety gets too much.'

'OK,' I gulp hard and decide to jump straight in. 'One day, Jamie didn't feel too good.'

I stop.

'Hope?' Tim looks at me quizzically.

'I, I can't.'

'How anxious are you now?'

'Ten.'

Tim switches off the recorder. 'OK. Now here's what I want you to do.' He talks me through another relaxation technique that he has made me practise. It takes a while but eventually I calm down.

'Now, I want you to imagine what happened when Jamie felt sick. Just think about it.'

I do. I feel sick.

'And again. Think about it again. What happened when Jamie felt sick.'

I do. I still feel sick. But Tim gets me to keep at it. When my anxiety level is at an eight, he asks me to go on.

I close my eyes. I'd talked about this only once before. With another counsellor. I can still see that day. In all its horror. The horror of a child who is powerless. And the horror of unforgiving time. I would have sold my soul to turn back time that day. To take back the choices I made.

I've been making the wrong choices ever since, I think.

He felt sick, he said, and he was pale. A funny blotchy pale. But he got out of bed and said that he would go to school, otherwise I'd have to forge a note for him and he knew I hated doing that in case we got caught. So he climbed out of bed and stood swaying for a second before getting sick all over the place. I made him climb back in. He felt hot. I cleaned up his sick and said that I'd take the day off school too. I could say we both had a tummy bug. Jamie nodded and closed his eyes. They were sore, he said. Turn off the light.

I did what I was told and tiptoed out of the room.

I spent the morning trying to get Mammy to eat some toast and doing the washing. About two hours later, I checked on Jamie. He had a headache. He was delirious. For the first time I felt uneasy. 'Will I get a doctor?' I asked him.

I made out a 'no'. Or at least I thought I did.

I thought he said 'no'.

'Hope, relax,' Tim says. 'Just relax. It's a memory. A bad memory but you can't change it now. You have to live with it. Relax.'

I breathe deeply. Oh God, how I wish I didn't have to

live with it. All the lies I'd told came back to haunt me that day.

'So,' Tim says when he sees I'm relaxed, 'what happened then?'

I told Mammy that Jamie seemed to be very sick. But she told me to stop lying and to leave her alone. I kept insisting. Crying and insisting and asking what could I do? I told her I was going to call the doctor. I don't think she answered.

I sat for the next hour with Jamie, holding his hand, trying to talk to him. He didn't respond, I watched him sleep, only he wasn't sleeping, not really.

Then I noticed the rash.

I'm crying. Tim switches off the tape. 'Let's leave it there, OK?' His voice is soft and caring. 'OK, Hope? Take a little break.'

I can only nod.

But the memories are sweeping in now that the door has been opened a crack.

The blue of the sky that day. The red quilt on Jamie's bed. The way my mother looked like a skeleton, though I hadn't noticed at the time. The dirt in the house, the washing piled high. The way I shook constantly.

The red-purple rash on Jamie's hand.

If only I'd made other choices.

Tim plays the tape for me. I listen to it and I cry my eyes out. I haven't even got to the worst part. And Tim plays it again. And again. And again. And again. I don't think I'll ever stop crying. There's a hole in my belly that's heaving with all the tears I want to cry. But amazingly, after a while, I don't know how long, they dry up. I listen to the tape for what must be about the tenth time and I hear the sadness in my voice and I feel like crying for me instead.

Tim waits a second or two before asking me if I want to continue. 'We can stop now if you like.'

But I'll have to face it again next week and I'm not sure if I can do that. I might chicken out. There's a very high percentage of that. 'I'll go on,' I say. 'There's not a lot more to tell.'

'OK, in your own time.'

I saw the rash. Purple. Spreading as I looked.

'Mammy!' I screamed. 'Mammy!'

Jamie hardly stirred.

In my mother's room, I heard a low moan. I ran in, screaming and crying and telling her what the matter was. Screaming as loud as I could. Screaming so that everyone would hear. I shook her so hard, her bones seemed to rattle under her skin. I shook her so that maybe something could happen to change things. In the end, when she'd pulled herself up in the bed, I didn't even wait for her to say anything, instead I half fell, half tripped down the stairs to the red telephone. For seconds I stared at it, knowing that the world was now going to come crashing into our lives. Knowing that Jamie didn't want that but having no choice. I rang an ambulance.

Jamie died in his bed with his mother cradling him and me sobbing in the doorway.

I sob again as I tell the story. Cry as if my heart is breaking. It seems so long since I've cried. It *is* so long since I've cried like this. I'm not good at it. I heave and almost retch. 'All he needed to be happy was his family and we let him down.'

269

Tim lets me cry. I cry for ages. Eventually he passes me a suspect-looking handkerchief which I try to look as if I'm using.

'Are you ready to go on?'

He was buried. Meningitis, they said. My mother was let out of the hospital for the funeral but was brought back in again and she stayed for a long time. I was sent to a foster home in the area but kept at the same school. Everyone knew and nobody talked about it. When they tried to get me to counselling, I went missing. What was the point? I'd told so many lies to so many people that I hardly knew what the truth was any more. And facing the truth would be hard. And Jamie would still be dead at the end of it.

'What's the worst thing about that story for you, Hope?'

'That my brother died.'

'Did you feel guilty? How did you think? How do you think now?'

His questions come at me like bullets. He probably isn't talking so fast, but to me, it seems overwhelming.

'Of course I felt guilty. I still live with the "if-onlys".' I clench the handkerchief hard in my hand and lean towards Tim. 'If I'd only rung earlier, if only I hadn't let my mother get into such a state, if only I'd told someone. But we didn't want to be sent away. And Jamie trusted me. And depended on me.'

'You did the best you could at the time, didn't you?'

'I was a kid. I had no power. I just tried to keep all the people with power out of our lives. And by doing that, I killed Jamie.'

'You did the best you could at the time, didn't you?' he repeats. 'You made him happy in the months before that.

270

He might still have got sick and died and you'd still blame yourself – wouldn't you?'

Those words halt the other words I'm about to say. I think about what Tim has said. I think about me and Jamie with a foster mother and him getting sick. Yes, I realise, I would have blamed myself. I'd have thought it was something he picked up at the foster mother's or something.

'No matter what happened, you would have blamed yourself. Hope, you did your best.'

I did my best. I blink.

'You did what you felt had to be done. OK, it ended sadly, but if you could turn back time, would you really have done it differently?'

I think back. I feel the fear creeping over me of being sent to a stranger's house. Even now, I can never sleep when I go somewhere new. I feel the pity for my mother and for Jamie and I think that maybe I would do the exact same thing again. Maybe.

'Thanks,' is all I can whisper. And it's the most heartfelt thanks I have ever uttered.

Tim plays the tape for me. I listen to my halting words. That girl on the tape is me, I think. The real, hurt me. Not the smartass woman I present to the world. Not the kid that lied her way from childhood to adulthood. For a long time, I despised the child in me that had messed up so badly. Now, I just feel glad that I was once her and that I once felt so deeply and cared so deeply. The new me and the London me too, I realise, just gets angry when stuff doesn't go her way. It's the easiest thing to do. I can't bear to feel powerless so I give myself power. I walk out of jobs when someone makes me feel less than valuable. I walk out of jobs rather than accept my lack of power.

I listen to that tape and suddenly I understand myself a little better. I make sense to myself.

'Hey, what happened in there?' Julie asks when I emerge. 'You've been crying.'

'Yeah.' I wipe a hasty fist across my eye. 'It's been a bit of a rollercoaster.'

'Is it working?'

'I think it is.'

'Have you remembered the accident yet?'

'We haven't even gone there yet.'

She looks surprised. 'But, you've been going for weeks now.'

I stare at her. My best friend. Oh, I have other mates, but none like Julie. I wonder how I let her get so close. Maybe because she was so different to me, I just never figured that I would get to like her so much. And they've been so good, bringing me to therapy and never pressing for information. Adam is behind her, smiling at me in his lovely gentle way. I imagine him living his lie of a working life and I feel that I have to explain to them. To let them see the real me.

'Can we go for a coffee?'

They've never yet refused that invitation.

It's Adam's idea. He suggests it and I probably would never have thought of it myself, but once he says it, I know it's the right thing to do. So we hop into his car and twenty minutes later I find myself outside a graveyard that I haven't visited in a decade. I've bought a bunch of roses at the entrance and Julie and Adam have bought some flowers too, which is lovely of them, I think.

I lead the way to the grave. The direction is burnt into my memory the way a farmer brands an animal, hot and painful and always there. To the right, straight on and finally we stop at a surprisingly well tended grave marked with a simple white headstone.

In loving memory of Frank Gardner, loving husband, sadly missed by his wife Helen and children Hope and Jamie and also our precious little boy, Jamie, who died age 12. Missed by his loving mother and sister.
Rest in Peace.

A picture of Jamie sits on top of the grave and Julie picks it up. Her face softens and I think she might cry. 'Oh Hope, was he –?'

'Yes, he was.'

I take the picture and study my little brother. He's about eight in it. Dressed in shorts and a T-shirt with a big banana-shaped smile. His happiness in the picture is palpable. Jamie was a very happy kid. 'Hi Jamie,' I whisper. 'It's Hope.'

Adam and Julie lay their flowers beside some others that have been left on the grave, then, squeezing me on the shoulder, they move off.

I sit down on the grass and place my flowers alongside my friends'. 'Just came to say hi,' I mutter and then I don't say anything else, just sit there, feeling peaceful and sad all at the one time. Every so often I hear Julie exclaim aloud over what she's reading on the various headstones. Things along the lines of, 'Oh God, three brothers in this one, isn't that terrible?' And another time, 'Wow, imagine being that old!'

The two of them arrive back, Julie red-eyed and Adam

looking at her in faint amusement. 'Well,' he half grins, 'there's nothing like a graveyard for a bit of fun.'

'Stop!' Julie thumps him. 'It just makes you realise, when you read all those headstones, how lucky you are.'

And she's right, it really does.

28

I TAKE THE Dictaphone around the back of the house. It's the eighth time I've listened to the tape since it was recorded. It's a cool enough day, with more cloud in the sky than in the last month. It looks like the heat wave is nearing an end. The thought depresses me slightly. I sit down in my usual spot, my back against the wall of the cottage, plug in the earphones and listen to a voice that I barely recognise as mine, talking about an event that shattered whatever hope I'd ever had.

To my amazement, it doesn't hurt as much listening now. I mean, my heart speeds up and I break out in a sweat, but instead of it consuming me whole, I can half recognise the real emotion underneath the terror. And when I recognise the emotion, I feel more terror. It's like a huge black grief-ridden hole inside me. I think that if I get too near, I'll fall in and never come out. But each day the terror of the event diminishes is a day I get nearer the grief. Which is scary enough. Each time I listen, I remember things in a little more detail. This time I recall Jamie saying, 'I just want us all to be together, Hope.' He didn't speak really well, Jamie, but I could understand him. And I could understand why he'd say that.

Going to his grave has taken the edge off the grief too. It helps, knowing that it's neat and tidy and remembered.

'Hey.' Adam, smiling, comes out into the garden about ten minutes later, just as I'm pressing the rewind button to listen again. 'I got some good news at last.'

'What?'

'He's got a job interview,' Julie answers, following behind him. 'What's it for again, Adam?'

'Manager of a small hardware store.'

'Oh, yeah, great,' I try to sound enthusiastic. 'Good for you.'

'Yes,' Adam reads my mind, 'it is a bit of a comedown.' He doesn't sound too unhappy about it, though. 'But I have to start somewhere. I have to think positive.'

'But what will you say when they ask why you're interested in that job when you've had a bigger and better job?'

Adam shrugs, unperturbed. 'I don't know. I'll cross that bridge when I come to it.'

'Well, if it's a half-decent hardware store, you'll probably build the bridge too,' Julie says, giggling.

'Awful joke.' Adam makes an anguished face.

'So when is the interview?'

'Two days' time. I have a suit in London, so I'll fly over tomorrow night and pick that up. I should be back the next day then. I'll just go up to the computer and book my flights.'

He bounds inside, full of enthusiastic energy.

Julie looks at me, her eyebrows raised questioningly. 'What if he doesn't get it?' she whispers. 'Like a piddling little job like that – what if they turn him down? It'll dent his confidence horribly.'

'Hopefully they'll see how good he is,' I say. 'Let's just wait and see.' I wrap the earplugs around the Dictaphone and lay it on the ground beside me. Julie is just about to sit down too when a shout makes us both look up.

It's Logan. I don't know how we didn't spot him before this. I wonder if he wants me to go walking with him again. I haven't seen him in a good few days and just looking at him now, I realise that I've missed the unpredictable creature. One-handed, Logan jumps over the low stone wall dividing our garden from the field next door and strides towards us.

'Cor,' Julie whispers in an undertone to me. 'Get a load of that. A bit of all right or what?'

Logan has had his hair cut. It's now very short and very shiny. It shows off his fine arched eyebrows and wide-set blue eyes. But his clothes are still on the manky side. 'Hi, girls,' he greets us with a big sunny smile. 'Enjoying the clouds?' He indicates the sky, which is getting more sullen looking by the minute.

'Fabulous,' I smirk. 'I come here for the clouds every year.'

'I like the hair,' Julie says admiringly.

'Lack of hair, you mean,' Logan says, running a paint-splattered hand through it. 'Got it done yesterday.'

'Suits you,' Julie nods. 'Doesn't he look much nicer, Hope?'

I can feel myself flushing. 'Yeah,' I mutter, reluctant to say any more.

'Go easy on the praise now, Hope, don't go overboard or anything.'

'I wish someone would throw you overboard,' I retaliate, grinning.

Logan laughs. 'Anyhow, witty and all as you are, Hope, I was looking for Adam. I need a favour.'

'In his room,' Julie says. 'Go on up.'

Logan disappears into the house. 'Wonder what he wants?' Julie muses.

I shrug, pretending not to care. I'm disappointed that he hadn't wanted me because I would have liked to go on a walk. Adam and Julie hate walking. They can't see the point of having a car if you're going to walk. The environment doesn't stand a chance with the two of them. From Adam's room, I can hear murmured voices. Adam arrives down a few seconds later, with Logan in tow.

'Just heading to Logan's to help him move some furniture and stuff,' Adam announces. 'Back in a while.'

They jump into Adam's car and are gone.

For some reason, I feel a weird sense of foreboding.

About three hours later they arrive back. Adam is in bits. He's obviously not used to any sort of major physical work. 'Just going to have a quick shower,' he says as he lopes by us. He grabs some fresh clothes from the line and disappears into the shower room.

Logan has obviously showered at home. He's also changed into a gorgeous sparkling white T-shirt and a cool pair of denims. All in all, the effect is sexual heaven.

'New clothes?' Julie asks.

'Was I that bad before?' Logan grins. Without waiting for an answer, he says, 'I've just ordered some food from the Chinese in Dunport, do you eat Chinese?'

The three of us are Chinese addicts.

'Yummy.' Julie immediately begins setting the table. She pulls out a bottle of wine and uncorks it. 'Hope, get some forks, would you?'

I do as I'm bid as Logan stands there, his hands in his pockets, watching us.

'Adam was a great help today,' Logan says, 'so I decided that I'd better treat you. And what with Hope doing her guided tours for free too, I really owe you one.' He winks over at me.

I'm not exactly happy with my help being in the same class as Adam's.

'You don't owe me anything,' I say, shyly. 'I like the walks, I told you that.'

'Aw well, I've finished the commission now. Tell ya one thing, I'd never work for that fecker Jack again.'

Finished? Is he telling me he won't need me to walk with him any more? To show him new places and new sights? Did he really only want my help with his art or did he want my company too? I don't know, and the disappointment of not knowing comes as a big surprise. I feel that if we'd even had one more day together, things might have got off the ground a bit more. That instead of him telling me he liked me, he might have kissed me. Oh, the thought of him kissing me sends shivers right through my body.

'Are you cold, Hope?' Julie asks.

I jump. 'No. Why?' My face has flushed again.

'You shivered and now you've gone all red. I hope you're not coming down with something. Do you feel poorly?'

'I feel fine.'

The fact that I'm in counselling, I think, might be a factor against going out with someone. But how would I feel if someone else moved in on him while I was faffing about? Then again, I'm going home in a few weeks, so a relationship is definitely out. No, I decide, I won't make a move on him, it wouldn't be fair. If he, however, made a move on me . . .

'Move up there, Hope,' Adam says, reappearing, his hair damp from the shower, but looking a lot less wrecked. 'Make some space at the table.'

The bell rings, announcing the arrival of our dinner. Logan answers the door and arrives back in, his arms laden with boxes and packets. That's the great thing about Chinese, there are so many *bits* to it. Little dips and different types of rice.

'Hope ya can eat all this,' Logan says as he dumps the food on the table. 'I'm totally starving. I haven't eaten dinner for about a week, trying to get myself organised.'

'Organised for what?' I ask, helping myself to some fried rice.

'The pictures had to be ready for the Gleeson Hotel opening by tomorrow, so I've been working flat out.'

'And his ex is coming down as well,' Adam says, heaping his plate high with chow mein, 'so he had to do a bit of a clean-up.'

Logan chortles. 'Yeah, that's why I got the new clothes and the haircut, she's a hard girl to impress, so she is.'

His ex? I glance up at him. He smiles back at me. His ex is coming and he's trying to impress her. His ex is coming. But he'd told *me* I was gorgeous.

'Your ex?' Julie is agog. She loves relationship stuff. 'But if she's your ex, why is she coming? I thought the word ex meant you never saw them again.'

'She's coming to sort things out,' Logan says with a big smile. 'At last she sees sense.'

They're going to sort things out. I bite my lip and I don't think I can eat anything else. I feel ill. I think of what might have happened if I'd told him I liked him. Thank God I didn't. But he made me vulnerable. He *almost* made a fool out of me. He reminds me of Jack suddenly, of how I fell for Jack and he left me. And thinking like that makes me angry. I haven't felt the white searing anger since I started counselling, but I can feel it now.

'But she's not coming till tomorrow evening,' Logan

continues, oblivious to my mounting anger. 'As I'm away tomorrow afternoon.'

'So where are you off to tomorrow?' Julie asks.

'Probably getting a facial done to impress his ex,' I say, with only a hint of anger in my voice.

Logan laughs. 'God,' he mock-groans, 'I should have thought of that when I was buying the new clothes.'

I feel sadder than ever.

'Naw, no facial, Hope,' he grins that grin at me and I feel the loss of him so keenly it hurts. 'I've to bring the pictures down to the hotel and tell them how I want them hung. There's a van coming tomorrow to load them up. I'll probably be there until tea time.'

'How you want your pictures hung?' I say. My nasty tone is stronger now. I wish I could stop it, I know I should stop it, but it's either that or cry. 'Does it really matter? They're only pictures.'

He doesn't seem to take offence. 'Yeah, course it matters. You can't have a big picture on a small wall unless you want it to cover the wall. You need light to show off some pictures to their best. It all matters. Some pictures have to be hung in sequence. All that kind of thing.'

'Most people wouldn't notice.'

'You'd be surprised.' He grins at me.

'Yeah, I would, actually.'

He stares at me, not sure how exactly I mean that comment. I think he's a little thrown. 'Maybe you wouldn't notice,' he concedes, 'but if they were hung wrongly, you wouldn't think the pictures were as good.'

'I suppose with the way you paint, you need all the help you can get.'

'Hope!' Julie exclaims.

'Joke.' I raise my eyebrows and don't smile.

Logan looks at me, confused, I think. When I still don't smile, he spears a piece of chicken. 'Well,' he says, chewing carefully, 'I think your jokes are about as crappy as you obviously think my painting is.'

And with that comment, the evening is ruined. It's his sour voice and his morose expression combined with my sneering tone and my morose expression. Never before have I deliberately hurt him. But he has hurt me too. Or at the very least, he led me on. And he did lead me on. It wasn't my imagination. Still, I do feel like a heel. But to apologise would be like saying to him, Oh yeah, it's OK to hurt me, go right ahead. And I can't do that.

He doesn't stay long after that. And when he goes, Adam and Julie turn on me. I'm stacking the plates, pretending that things are fine, but Julie surprises me by grabbing them off me and slamming them down on the table. 'What the hell did you have to go and ruin the night for?' she demands. 'I thought you liked Logan.'

I bite my lip. 'I just don't like his paintings.' It comes out sounding defensive.

'So, you decide to tell him that? You think that's nice after he's just spent ages painting stuff for the local hotel?'

'Can we just clean the kitchen?'

'No, Hope, we can't. How would you feel if I told you what I don't like about you?'

'Fire ahead.'

Of course, she doesn't. Instead she looks at me, all concerned, 'Hope, why did you do it? It just came out of nowhere.'

I can't tell her. I just can't, the humiliation would be too much to bear.

Adam surveys me from his position on the sofa. 'I don't know,' he says cagily, 'I thought there was a nice little fling blooming there for a while. Him calling for you with little picnics, bringing you for coffee, you showing him around.'

'I was just helping him out. And anyway, he and his ex are sorting things out: why would you think we'd have a fling?'

'Because the guy liked you, Hope. It was as obvious as the nose on your face.'

'Well, if he liked me so much, why is he going back to his ex?'

Silence.

'Rewind,' Adam says quietly. 'Logan is going back to his ex, is that what you said?'

'No, it's what he said. Sorting things out, he said.'

'Yeah,' Adam glares at me, but he's smiling, albeit in an incredulous way, 'they owned a house in Dublin, she sold it, she wouldn't pay him his half and now she's coming to sort things out.'

Oh shit!

'But he got his hair done and moved furniture and –'

'To show her he was doing fine without her.'

I am the world's biggest mouth. Biggest idiot. Biggest bitch. I can't even react.

'Julie,' I turn to her for some support, 'didn't you think he was getting back with his ex?'

'No,' Julie shakes her head. 'I got the impression that she hurt him too much for that.'

I look from one to the other of them and suddenly want to get out. I don't want to discuss what I just did, how I ruined what could have been a lovely friendship by my stupid insecurities. Blindly, I push past Julie.

'Hope, come back.'

But I leave.

I arrive back at about three in the morning. I spent the time sitting and looking at the ocean, until it became too cold for me. I think about what I did. How I felt out of control again and how I lashed out. Have I learned nothing from all my previous experiences? Before, though, it was bosses who got the brunt of it. Now it was someone I'd come to care about. Why hadn't I clarified things?

I owe him a huge apology.

I sneak back in and all is quiet. Though I do hear Julie moving about upstairs. I think she's been waiting up for me. As silently as I can, I pull out my sleeping bag and without undressing or washing, I crawl inside.

I will do the right thing, this time, I swear to myself.

29

'WELL,' JULIE SHAKES me awake the next day, 'did you go and apologise to him last night?'

I groan, pretending not to be fully awake and crawl further down in the sleeping bag. Last night uncoils itself from my memory like a rattlesnake.

'Hope! Did you apologise or not!' Julie almost deafens me; her mouth is so close to the side of my face.

'Ouch!' I sit up and rub my ear. 'Do you mind, I was asleep!' Then at her unrelenting stare, I shake my head and mutter 'No'.

'So where did you get to?' she asks, sitting back on her hunkers. 'I thought you'd jumped into the sea or something, I was about to call out rescue services. It was Adam's idea that maybe you'd gone over to Logan's.'

I probably should have, I realise then. That would have been a good idea. 'Well I didn't,' I say back. I pull the sleeping bag up to my chin, like a comfort blanket. 'Sorry if I worried you, I just went for a walk and had a bit of a think. It's not easy to hang around when you've just made a big fool out of yourself.'

'You fancy him, don't you?' It's a statement.

I squirm under her gaze and mutter, 'I'm not sure.'

'Oh, Hope, come on, be honest with yourself. You light up

when the bloke walks into the room. And you had a big hissy fit last night because you thought he was getting back with his ex. That must mean you at least want him for yourself.'

I think about this. I know one thing: I don't want anyone else to have him. 'Well, yes, I do like him,' I admit.

'Fancy him,' Julie interjects.

I ignore that. 'But I don't know if he likes me, and after last night I'm sure he'll never want to talk to me again.'

'Well, regardless of whether he does or not, you still owe him an apology.' Julie surveys me. 'And I hope you're going to give him one.'

'I could make a rude comment just there.' I crack a smile.

'Don't joke your way out of it, Hope.'

'I know,' I heave a big sigh. 'You're right. I'll call over this morning.'

'He's busy this morning, moving all his pictures. You'll have to leave it until tomorrow.'

That's right. Shit! And then his ex is coming and who knows what might happen there. I just hope he remembers all that he said was wrong with her. 'First thing tomorrow morning, I'll be outside his place.'

'Good.' Julie nods approvingly. 'Only thing is, you'll have to walk over because Adam will have the car and won't be able to drive you.'

'Yeah, I don't mind walking.' It'll help build up my courage.

'I'll go with you if you like.'

'No thanks, Ju.'

'Are you sure, because you know you might die of shock having to apologise.'

'Ha bloody ha.' I reach out from my sleeping bag and grab the sofa cushion which is lying on the floor. Julie hates that cushion as it's so manky. Aiming it, I fire it at her retreating body. Laughing a little, I lie back down. It dawns on me, slowly, that I was upset last night. I actually felt upset. OK, I was angry but I was upset too. I almost wanted to cry when I heard Logan going on about his ex. And it's scary having to apologise for being so horrible to him, but I feel scared, and I feel regret and I feel guilt and now, Julie has made me smile.

It dawns on me slowly that I can *feel* again.

Some part of the old Hope is back.

At last.

Later that day, Adam drives off, but not before he gives me a lecture on how badly I behaved last night and how I really should apologise. I agree with everything he says and promise him faithfully that I will. He tells me that he thinks Logan really likes me and that if I liked him I'd be mad to blow it over a stupid misunderstanding. 'I'd just like to see you with someone nice,' he says.

I get a lump in my throat at his concern. 'And I'd like to see you with someone nice too,' I tell him. 'So, after the interview, I want you to go into a coffee shop and buy a coffee for a girl on her own, OK.'

'Yeah. OK.'

We hug each other without any awkwardness. 'Give 'em hell at the interview!'

'Will do.' He turns to Julie. 'Bye.'

'Yeah. See you. And don't buy coffee for a really good-looking girl,' she says. 'They're always the bitches.'

'You must get a lot of coffee bought for you then, eh?' Adam jokes.

'Oh, go get lost.' Julie pushes him into the car. 'Go on, safe driving!'

With a beep of his horn, he's gone.

Julie and I run out into the road after him and wave until he's out of sight.

We're in Dunport, having walked there from the cottage. Julie is in bits, she's never walked as far in her life. And no one has ever walked as far in high-heeled sandals either.

'It's my mother's birthday next week,' she says as she sits down on the small harbour wall to examine her feet. 'I don't know if I should ring her.'

'You should ring her,' I say. I sit down beside her and wince at the massive blister on the ball of her foot, 'but what you really want to know is, do you want to ring her?'

'Yep. That's it exactly. She'll probably rip my head off.'

'So? Just do it, at least you won't regret it.'

'Mmm.' Her blond hair falls across her face as she gazes at her foot. 'Is there a chemist here at all?'

'McCoys will probably do a plaster.' I stand up. 'You wait here.' And then I spot him. Striding along the main street, bigger and more mature than I remember, but still with the ability to make me weak at the sight of him. My heart lurches and I sit back down on the wall, hoping like hell he won't spot me. The last time I'd seen this guy was when I was eighteen.

'Oh God.'

I feel suddenly ill.

'What? What?' Julie looks up at me.

'That guy, coming towards us, I know him.' I gulp hard. 'Julie, how do I look? Quick, tell me how I look?'

'Just normal.' She looks at me, puzzled and then at Jack, who is getting closer and who seems to be heading in our direction.

288

'Ohhh.' I wish I'd worn my nice jeans instead of my tracksuit this morning, but it's too late now. I want to get up and race across the street, but that'll only draw attention to us. I just have to sit tight and hope he walks on by.

'Julie,' I hiss, 'that's Jack!'

Julie is looking in bewilderment from me to the man. 'Jack who?' she hisses back.

'Jack, the, the, fecking guy I used to go out with. The one who owns the hotels now.'

'Oh God!' She looks me up and down. 'You don't want to look like that when you meet an ex.'

'I know,' I groan.

He's getting nearer.

'Quick, put your head down,' I say to Julie.

I pretend to be looking at her foot. She pretends she wants me looking at her foot.

'Hey, Hope? Hope Gardner?'

He's stopped and is standing over us.

I take a deep breath. Fuck it, I suddenly think. What the hell does it matter what this guy thinks? Why should I have to look good in front of him? So what if he thinks I'm a slob. So. Bloody. What. At least my hair is OK. There's not much of it to be in a mess.

'Hello?' Slowly I look up. I try out a puzzled look as if I don't know who it is.

Jack stands, hands in his pockets, trying, I think, to look relaxed and casual. 'Hiya, Hope.' He smiles a tad nervously. 'I thought it was you. It's me. Jack. D'you remember?'

How could I fucking forget, I want to snap. But I don't. I'm very proud of myself as I smile and nod and say, admittedly through gritted teeth, 'Hey, Jack. Yes I remember you. How's things?' If only I could have been so calm with Logan yesterday, I would have been better off. But better late than never. I stand up so I'm on his level.

'Things are good.' Jack nods, trying out a smile. 'I heard you were back. Greg Lynch told me, so when I saw you walking along, I thought I'd catch up and say hi. I was going to call in to see you in Maurice's cottage tomorrow.'

'Oh, were you?' Jack looks, well, without exaggeration, totally great. Nice faded denims, expensive ones. Expensive trainers and a white grandfather shirt with the crocodile label. 'Oh, by the way, this is Julie. She's a friend of mine.' I indicate Julie who has been looking at us anxiously, unsure what to do.

'Hi, Julie,' Jack proffers a clean hand, his nails shaped and in better condition than mine. 'I'm an old friend of Hope's from school.' He winces as he catches a glimpse of her foot, 'Ouch, that looks nasty.'

'We walked a long way,' Julie smiles, taking his hand in hers.

Jack smiles back. 'That's Hope for you. D'you need a plaster?'

'I'm getting her one,' I say, thinking how ridiculous this whole conversation is.

'Good,' Jack grins. Then he says, 'I was going to call on you tomorrow, Hope, to ask you if you'd like to come to the hotel opening Saturday week.'

I'm stunned. Behind me I can hear Julie suck in her breath. Anything remotely glamorous and she's up for it.

'Hotel opening?' I can't resist pretending that I don't know what he's talking about. 'What hotel opening?'

Julie hops up and pokes me in the back.

'Oh,' Jack flushes. 'Well,' he tries to say modestly, 'I don't know if you know, but I'm in charge of the big new hotel

290

there,' he points to the entrance gate, 'and we're having an opening night on the twenty-eighth of July for friends and business people and anyone associated with the hotel. And when I heard you were about, I just wanted to invite you.' He pauses. 'It'd be nice if you could come. It should be a good night and it'd be great to catch up.'

He sounds as if he means it. A small part of me thinks he wants to show off to me, which is a little flattering.

'Oh right,' I nod. 'That sounds good.'

'So the opening is Saturday week. And everyone who comes gets to stay over in the hotel too. It'll be fun.'

'I'm sure it will,' I say, and my voice has grown steadier and more pleasant as I go on. 'But I might be doing something, I'll have to check and get back to you.'

He looks slightly taken aback. 'Well, yeah, of course. Sure, I tell you what, I'll reserve the room anyway, how about that?'

'OK,' I nod. 'But I actually have two friends staying here so –'

He doesn't let me finish. 'You can all come.' He looks beyond me to Julie, who is barely able to contain her delight, there is this massive smile on her face about to break out. 'Would you like to?'

Julie shoots a look at me before nodding and going 'mmm' in a really high-pitched way.

'That would be great, thanks for thinking of us, Jack.'

'No probs.' He smiles again and seems about to say something else but then nods and indicates the street. 'Anyway, I'll go. Nice to see you, Hope.'

We watch as he saunters off.

Julie turns to me and squeals. 'Yes! Yes! Yes!'

'Well, I'm glad you're happy,' I say to her, amused.

'I'm more happy for you,' she says, her hands grabbing my arms. 'You were magnificent! Oh, I'm so proud of you! God, I thought you were going to chew him up and spit him out, I really did! And you didn't. You were great!'

'Was I?' I know I was, but I want her to say it again.

'You. Were. Fab.' Julie shakes her head. 'I think I could learn a thing or two from you, you were so, so . . .' she scrunches up her cute face as she tries to find the right word, 'so mature,' she finishes.

'I just didn't want another Logan scene,' I admit. 'It was totally the wrong thing to do last night.'

Julie nods. 'He'll be all over you when you apologise,' she says. 'I think he's mad about you.'

'He's mad at me, more like.'

She ignores that. 'And wow! Oh, Hope, we're going to the big opening, how cool is that?' She does a one-legged dance and her excitement makes me laugh. Then she frowns. 'But we've nothing to wear. We're going to have to go shopping!'

Shit! I hadn't thought of that.

30

I'M UP EARLY the next morning. The apology to Logan is hanging over me like a swarm of midges. Just when the worry has disappeared, a little part of my memory gets stung again and I quake at the thought of what I should say. Over and over in my head I've played out various scenarios. 'Sorry about the other night, I got the wrong end of the stick.' Of course, then he'll want to know what the wrong end of the stick was and I'll be forced to admit that yes, I was jealous and annoyed because I thought he was going back to his ex. That would be embarrassing. I'm not an up-front girl that can just grab a man. For one thing, I don't feel attractive enough to do that, especially now with only an inch of hair on my head. It's typical: if only my waistline was as slow growing, I'd be thrilled. So no, I cannot confess that I like him. It's OK for Julie to tell me she thinks he's mad about me, but so far, apart from him saying he *likes* me, which is not in the same league at all, I have no proof of that.

Some time in the early hours, I had the, quite frankly heinous, thought of blaming my outburst on my unstable mind. 'It's the counselling, Logan, I can't help it.' Yes, it's a cop-out but I don't care.

Later on, I decide to plumb for a wait and see what

happens tactic: going in totally unprepared and just letting the dialogue take its course. That way I don't have time to be nervous. Maybe a simple 'sorry' will suffice.

At seven, before Julie even turns over for her second sleep, I am washed and dressed and ready to leave the cottage. Logan is generally up early and I just want to get the apology over with and be able to enjoy the rest of the day. As the morning is damp and misty, I pull on the horrible pink pig boots over my jeans and stride off across the field.

There is a car outside his house.

A blue car with teddies strewn all over the back seat. It can only be *hers*! She must have stayed the night. I feel sick. For some reason I thought she'd be staying in a B&B somewhere.

I think about leaving. Yes, I still owe him an apology, but I never banked on his ex being there to witness it. I stare at the car for a few minutes and decide to turn back. I'll talk to him another day, when she has gone, assuming she *is* going to leave.

The cat crawls out from under the car and glares at me with malevolent green eyes. It starts to hiss so I hiss back. It arches its back and spits. 'Go away, you mangy thing,' I say, making big whooshing motions with my hands. 'Go away.'

The cat is not intimidated. Hissing and spitting, it crouches down, back legs ready to leap into the air and attack me. I let out a scream. And another one.

Logan comes running from his workshop and stops, hands on hips, and snaps, 'Ginger!'

Immediately the cat does a complete schizophrenic. It's as if it smiles, then it starts to purr and rub itself along Logan's legs, all the while glaring balefully at me.

'I'll thank you not to frighten my cat,' Logan says.

Shit! His voice is as cold as the ocean that provides the backdrop to our exchange.

'You should keep your cat under better control,' I retort, trying not to sound confrontational. 'It was going to attack me.'

'Yeah, well . . .' he shrugs.

My heart plummets. Now that he's in front of me I will apologise, but his icy manner tells me that this apology will probably not be easy.

'He just doesn't like you,' Logan continues as he scoops the cat up into his arms and they both glare at me. 'I wonder why?'

He doesn't say it in the joking way of before. I feel as hurt as he must have done the other night.

'I didn't come here to talk about your cat,' I stammer.

'No?' He widens his very cold blue eyes at me. 'Come to give me some more of your expert opinions on art?'

'Logan, stop.'

He does and we both stand there like combatants.

'I'm sorry, OK.' My voice trembles.

'OK.' He shrugs.

'I really mean it.'

'Just like you meant all that stuff you said the other night?'

'I didn't mean that. I was being . . . well,' my face flushes. I can't tell him how I feel, not like this, not with his ex in residence. 'I was nasty.'

'You got that right.' He nods and says, 'Fine. Thanks. Good.' Then he walks away from me, still cradling the cat in his arms.

At first I can't believe it. Then I feel dreadfully hurt. OK, it wasn't exactly the apology of the century. But I did apologise. Before I know what I'm doing, I call, 'Logan?'

He turns.

'Is that it?' I say. 'Is that all you're going to say?'

'What else is there?'

He is being deliberately horrible. I blink. In my scenarios, it had all ended really well. I'd never envisioned this. 'Well, you could mean it when you say it's fine.' A touch of belligerence has crept into my voice.

'I do mean it. It's fine. Thanks for the apology. You should get back now, I've work to do.'

'Well, don't walk away from me. Did I walk away when you apologised to me before, did I? No, I was very nice to you.' I sound like a four-year-old.

'I gave you a picture.' He sounds like a three-year-old. It gives me a bit of comfort.

'Yeah, well unlike you, I don't have to bring a gift to say sorry to someone. I hope I sound sincere.'

'I accepted your apology.'

'So that's it,' I say. 'You accept my apology and we never speak again.'

'Why would you want to speak to me?' he asks. The cat is squirming in his arms now. I think it's feeling a little uncomfortable with his master's palpable annoyance. 'You obviously can't stand me. You know, I thought we were getting along OK. I sort of liked being with you. I liked our bickering. I didn't mean half of it.'

'Neither did I. You'd better watch that cat.'

'Oh yeah.' He drops it to the ground and it takes off. He looks at me. 'So why? Why were you so horrible to me then, the other night?'

The insanity excuse would be a lie. I'm not going to tell lies, I've told lies my whole life. But can I tell the truth? The only truth I know at this moment is that I can't tell him how I feel. Maybe he's back with Maria. I'm scared to have this cold man reject me even more than he has my apology. 'I . . . I, I don't know.' I stare at Logan's feet. He has new trainers on. He must really have tried to impress the ex.

Logan stays completely still, not saying anything.

'I'm just sorry.' My voice is contrite. 'Really sorry. I do like your paintings. I have no idea why I was such a cow.' I chance a quick peek up at him. There is a funny look on his face. Sad or tender or what, I don't quite know. 'Logan,' I blurt out, 'I really thought we had something.'

It's exactly the wrong thing to say. His face shuts down and he nods. 'Yeah,' he says, slowly, and every word is like a knife, 'so did I.'

And then, just as the humiliation is working its humiliating way from my feet up through the rest of my body, a woman pokes her head out the back door. Long and lean, dark haired and dark eyed, tanned, smooth skin, her very being everything mine isn't. 'Logan,' she says, and her voice is pure golden honey, 'where do you keep the shower gel?'

She's dressed in one of his T-shirts. It barely covers her.

'In the shower,' Logan says and I'm comforted that he doesn't glance in her direction.

'Fine,' she says a little snottily. Then she turns to me and is about to ask me my name or something, when she notices my footwear. 'Are they my boots you're wearing?'

Double humiliation.

Every single humble bone in my body evaporates at her accusatory tone. OK, I still want to cry at the fact that Logan is obviously no longer my friend but there is no way his ex-girlfriend is going to look down on me. 'Well,' I say, my voice wobbling at what I'm about to do, 'fair exchange is no robbery.'

'Pardon?' She arches her already arched eyebrows at me.

'You slept in my bed, I wore your boots.'

And I turn my back on the two of them.

'Logan!' I hear her screech as I walk off. 'Who is that woman?'

'She slept in the spare bed,' I hear Logan tell her and I think he's laughing.

I hope Maria slept there too.

Julie laughs too when I tell her, though she can't believe Logan was so horrible to me. 'Well,' she says supportively, 'the least he could have done was accept your apology.'

'He did.'

We're sitting in the beer garden in Lynch's, waiting for Adam. He's meeting us there on his way back from the airport.

'No,' Julie shakes her head, 'he didn't. Not really. If he had, he would have been friendlier. I think he has a nerve. You accepted his when he gave you the painting.'

'I told him that.'

'Good for you!'

We clink glasses and drink. Despite my cheery demeanour, I'm gutted. I'm trying not to think about it. I'm trying not to get too upset over it. I let Logan in and that's why it hurts. It's part of life, Tim would say, and he's right. At least it showed I cared. I haven't cared for a man in ages. So it's a horrible sort of progress, I suppose.

'I wonder did he sleep with her?' Julie asks. 'Do you think he did?'

'I don't know.' I don't want to think about that either.

'Are you going to ring your mother?' I ask instead, changing the subject.

'Boo!' I jump as Adam squeezes my shoulders.

'Fecker!' I belt him and he laughs. 'You gave me a fright!'

He's dressed in a suit and carries a bag. 'Sorry,' he grins.

'Hey,' Julie asks. 'How'd it go?'

Adam plops down into a seat beside us and rolls his eyes, 'Bloody awful,' he smirks triumphantly.

'It can't have been that bad,' I murmur.

'No, everyone always thinks that,' Julie agrees.

'Oh believe me, it was bad.' Adam is still smirking. 'In fact, can I just say that that interview was the low point of my professional life.'

Julie and I exchange a look. She asks the obvious question, 'So why are you so happy?'

I think she thinks he's having a kind of a breakdown. It must be great to have a breakdown and feel happy about it.

'I am happy because,' Adam says easily, 'for the first time in my professional life, I was myself.'

'What?' Julie is baffled. 'Adam, are you OK?' She touches him on the sleeve. 'Are you OK, really?' she asks.

Adam kisses her hand extravagantly. Then he sighs deeply and contentedly, while still keeping hold of her hand. 'Hope, run up to the bar and get a Guinness for me, would you?'

'Get it yourself, you lazy git,' I chastise him but I go, and return a few minutes later with a pint for him. Greg has given it to me on the house.

'So, go on.' I place it in front of him. 'Tell us.'

Adam lets Julie's hand go, lifts his pint and drinks deeply. 'Oh, they know how to pull a pint here,' he says approvingly.

'Adam!' Julie belts him. 'Spill.'

Adam nods. 'Right.' He shifts about in his seat and begins, 'When I went over, I was determined, in my mind, to tell the truth, no matter what, at this interview, wasn't I?'

'God,' Julie looks at him, 'is this going where I think it's going?'

Adam ignores her. 'So, I went into the room, and there were three blokes there, all dressed in suits and ties, the works, and they're all really impressed by my CV and my experience. And it's all going really well and I'm telling them ideas to help their store improve and they're all nodding away, really impressed. Then the middle one asks me why I left my old job.' He gives the two of us a wide grin. 'So I said that I hadn't left, I'd been sacked.'

'No!' That's me.

'You bloody idiot!' That's Julie.

'Uh-huh.' Adam smiles at the memory. 'So as you can imagine, that sort of threw them. One of them asked why I'd been fired so I told him that the staff hated me and that I'd gone absent without leave and apparently I was being blamed for losing the company fifty thousand which, for the record, was not my fault.'

Julie and I are speechless. I don't know whether to hit him or hug him.

He nudges me. 'You know the way your lot are so fond of telling your sins to a vicar?'

'Priest,' I nudge him back. 'Our lot call them priests.'

'Priest, sorry,' he says. 'Well, I can kind of understand it. It was liberating, just telling all my failures to a group of people. I told them about my childhood and my counselling and then I told them that I was telling them all this because

300

I was going to be myself from now on and that if they didn't like it they could ask me to leave.' He grinned. 'So they asked me to leave.'

'And that's good?' Julie whispers.

'That's great,' Adam beams. 'Don't you think so?'

'I think so,' I say, much to Julie's chagrin. 'I mean, who else can you be?'

'Exactly.' Adam slams his fist on the table. 'Good one, Hope.' He looks at Julie's concerned face and concedes, 'Unfortunately, though, Ju, I do realise that I have to earn some money so I might have to gloss over the exact truth in my next interview.'

'Good,' Julie nods vigorously. She screws up her eyes. 'You could say that the staff in your previous job resented your work ethic. Which is true.'

'And you could say,' I add excitedly, 'that the workers took the fifty thousand and blamed it on you.'

'Eh – there might be a legal issue with that,' Adam laughs. 'You know, false accusations and stuff.'

'Well, you were accused falsely,' Julie says.

'If I were you, I'd have them sued for false dismissal,' I chime in.

'If you were me, Hope,' Adam said, 'you'd know that losing that poxy job was the best thing that ever happened. In fact, and I hate to say it, you being in that plane crash made me see what was important and I realised what a shit I was.' He stands up and, holding his pint aloft, says, in a posh English accent, 'May all those who are shits suddenly wake up and smell the roses.'

'And what a lot of roses grow in a shit-pile,' Julie giggles, standing up and clinking his glass.

She's right. My shit-pile of lost jobs and aeroplane accident have shown me who my mates are. And given me a chance to be normal again.

Such a lot of roses.

As Tim might say, you can't have the roses without the thorns!

31

M Y NEXT COUNSELLING session consists mainly of Tim
asking me how I am and how I feel and how the
last week has gone and me telling him about every little
farty thought I had during that week. It's quite exhausting,
analysing everything. He comments that I seem a little down.
For someone who has made such amazing progress, he says,
you seem a little down.

'I lost my cool with a friend,' I tell him. 'I said some awful
stuff. And when I apologised, he accepted it but he didn't
really. He hasn't called me since.'

'And why do you think that is?' Tim asks.

'Because he didn't forgive me, not really,' I say. 'I hurt
him too much, maybe.'

Tim nods. 'Maybe you did but you apologised. He should
have met you half-way.' He stops. Nods. Pulls at his hair. 'It
really is important to do that,' he says again. 'Really important.'

'So you don't think I should call over again?'

'Do you feel you did your best with the first apology?'

'Yes.' I shift about on the chair. I suppose I hadn't told
Logan the *exact* truth but it probably wouldn't have made
any difference.

'And do you understand why you rowed with him?'

'Unfortunately, yes. I didn't think in the way you taught me to think and I blew it.'

Tim nods. 'Well then, give him some time.' He smiles a little sadly. 'Sometimes it just takes a little time. I need lots of time after someone apologises to me,' he says. 'Your friend is probably the same. Is that the same friend who had the trouble with the women?'

'Oh God, no. It's a different friend.'

'Oh. And how's he getting on?'

I tell him about Adam. 'He's kind of stuck, he's buying drinks for girls and he says he's going to be broke.'

'So let him take it a bit further next time,' Tim says. 'He should get a number, ring a girl. Just a casual date, maybe for an hour. See how that works.'

'I'll let him know that.' I laugh. 'You should set yourself up as a relationship adviser, Tim.'

'Believe me, Hope, I could possibly be the worst person on the planet to do that.' He sounds a little down himself now. He glances at the clock on the wall. 'Anyway, you've done great this week. I think the next time we meet, we'll start tackling the accident, are you happy with that?'

My heart lurches but I nod. 'Fine. Thanks, Tim.'

'See you –' he consults his diary – 'in two weeks' time – is that OK? I've to go to a conference next week. If you want me, just ring.'

Two weeks' time, it's like a reprieve. I actually smile. 'Great. No problem.'

Julie and Adam are waiting for me when I get out. Julie has declared that today will be the day that we get some clothes for the hotel opening. Adam has wriggled out of buying anything, saying that his interview suit will do the job. Julie has called him a cheapskate and he's a little upset at this. Unfortunately the fact that she can't dress Adam means that all her attention is focused on me.

'We will make you into a real babe,' she declares. 'Wait until Logan sees you, he'll be so sorry for the way he's behaved.'

'The only way he'll be sorry is if I deck him one,' I mutter darkly.

'He'll get over it,' Adam says. 'If a girl told me she hated my life's work, I'd say I'd be a bit annoyed too.'

'Thanks for that, Adam,' I deadpan. 'That makes me feel a whole lot better.'

We arrive in Killarney, and the place is buzzing with tourists. Julie drags me into a designer shop where she immediately spots this gorgeous beaded aquamarine three-quarter-length dress. It looks great on her. Four hundred euro lighter, we leave the shop, her dress wrapped in tissue paper and resting in a bag. 'Now for you, Hope,' she sighs happily. 'Have you any idea what you'd like to wear?'

I shrug. 'No. I can't remember the last time I wore a dress, Ju.'

'So what's your favourite colour? You wear a lot of yellow, would you like a yellow dress?'

'If I wore a yellow dress, I'd look like Big Bird from *Sesame Street*.'

Adam and Julie laugh, much to my alarm. They could at least have disagreed.

'Well, let's go in here,' she says and takes my arm. 'This looks like a nice shop.'

It is a nice shop. If you're into shops like this. It's the sort of place that invites people to whisper and where the assistants look like they earn a lot more than their customers.

'Now have a look and pick something out,' Julie orders in a whisper.

Adam gives a snort of laughter as I gawp uselessly at the rails of dresses. 'See you outside,' he says merrily, winking at me and exiting.

I turn to Julie. 'I don't know if a dress is me.'

'But you have to wear a dress.' Her voice has a touch of panic in it. 'Like, what else can you wear?'

Oh God. 'Maybe I just won't go.'

'Hope, you have to go. You're the one that got invited.'

She sounds annoyed now so I grab the first dress I see. It's blue and long and has spaghetti straps.

'There you go,' Julie smiles. 'Now try it on.'

Feeling extremely self-conscious, knowing her eyes are on me, I make my way to the dressing room. 'And if you can't pay for it,' Julie shouts after me, causing just about everyone in the shop to look, 'I'll lend you the money.'

'Great,' I say weakly. 'Thanks.'

The dress is horrible on. Even Julie says it is. Spaghetti straps do nothing for my big fleshy shoulders. Scooped necks do nothing for my huge cleavage. Julie informs me that I need a dress with wide straps and a V-neck and an Empire waistline.

The shop assistant, a woman with long talons of fingers and a deep voice agrees and the two of them spend hours handing me in dresses. My confidence is on the floor when I realise how long it's actually taking them to find something I look good in. Finally Julie hands me in the ugliest dress I've ever seen. It's red and shimmery. Wide straps and a plunging V. In fact the V plunges to the waist. 'Julie, it's pornographic,' I hiss at her. 'I can't put it on.'

'Try it,' Julie hisses back.

And so I do.

The dress is like liquid the way it falls down over my body. It flows and sparkles over every curve, from my breasts to my hips, and from there it drops down to the floor in a sort of asymmetrical way.

I stare at my reflection, awestruck. Never have I looked so good. So feminine. Even with my hair shorn, I look like a proper woman, not the round basketball person I'm so used to.

'Let me see,' Julie commands.

I walk out, faintly awkward.

'Wow!' Julie walks around me, looking me up and down. I feel the heat of embarrassment breaking out all over me. I've never liked being scrutinised. I suppose I've always wanted to be invisible on account of all the lies I told as a kid, and anyone paying too much attention to me makes me acutely uncomfortable. The sudden flash of insight doesn't help alleviate my uneasiness, however. Julie says 'wow' a few more times before declaring the dress a success.

'It's fab,' she tells me. 'And I don't want you saying it's too tight – you've lovely curves, Hope, you should make the most of them.'

'You think?' I try to sound modest.

'Lovely.' The woman in the shop has come over, no doubt hoping for a sale. 'Well chosen,' she says to Julie. 'You've a good eye.'

'I know,' Julie nods. No false modesty about her.

They stand back to admire some more and I cringe.

'Well, Hope, what do you think?' Julie asks.

'It's . . . it's nice,' I say.

'Look at yourself, will you?' Julie laughs and pulls me to a mirror and once again I stare at my reflection. 'You are hot, Hope. Hot. Hot. Hot.'

And I think I actually am. A little.

That night, Julie screws up her courage and rings her mother. She'd put it off all day, which was why I reckoned she focused so much on buying clothes for us. 'OK,' she whispers as she takes out her phone and begins to dial.

I have to admit, my heart is hammering. She's a lot braver than me, I still haven't contacted my mother, much as I'd like to. I guess I'm too afraid of it all falling apart again.

'Mum,' Julie says, as Adam and I hold our breath, 'It's, eh, Julie.'

Her mother says something back.

'Nothing. Just to wish you a happy birthday.'

I give her the thumbs-up.

And then Julie is holding the phone away from her ear and a tinny voice at the other end is yammering away. Julie looks hopelessly at us.

'Hang up,' Adam says calmly, taking the phone away from her and pressing it off. 'You don't need that,' he says as he tosses the phone aside.

Julie doesn't move. 'It'd be a happy birthday for her if I did my best at work,' she says, sounding eerily calm. She shakes her head, her voice wobbles. 'Bitch!'

'Bitch!' I say too, putting my arm around her and sitting her down.

'You don't ring her again,' Adam sounds quietly furious. 'Don't let them boss you, Ju.'

'I won't,' she says. There are no tears in her voice now.

In fact, she even manages a smile, 'So, come on, who's for Scrabble?'

Adam looks at me and I look at him.

Scrabble it is.

32

EIGHT O'CLOCK. SATURDAY night. I'm standing in my silver shoes and red dress, my hair looking exactly the same, despite the blow-dry. Julie has done my make-up and I feel as if someone has caked a mask to my face. My eyes are heavy with mascara, my lips dry from the lipstick. But my two friends think I look great, which makes me feel great. Adam is being an eejit and pretending he doesn't recognise me.

'Who is this?' he keeps saying. 'Where has Hope gone? Has she been kidnapped?'

'Ha ha.' I make a face.

'And you are?'

'Adam, stop, would ya.'

He contents himself with a grin, only to say two minutes later, 'They've kidnapped Hope, you know.'

Julie, fabulous in her blue dress, leaves the room and comes back with a package. 'Here,' she thrusts it at me. 'You look lovely and I'm proud of you and this is for you. From me and Adam.'

'What is it?' I open it excitedly, I love presents. And then I stop, finding that I'm unable to take her gift out of the bag. Instead, I turn my gaze on her. 'Julie,' I whisper. Something in me breaks a little at the kindness.

She smiles and wraps her arm about my shoulder. 'That's for you,' she says softly, 'to say we're proud of you and all you've been through and that tonight, you look lovely. Now take it out, for God's sake and let me see it. I was hoping you'd go for silver shoes and you did!'

It's a beaded silver bag with a red fringe. It must have cost a fortune. Reverently, I take it out and I love it. I can't believe it's mine. I've never treated myself to beautiful bags before. 'I don't deserve this,' I mutter, touching it and running my fingertips over it.

'Of course you deserve it.' Julie gives me a playful punch. 'Everyone deserves to have something lovely.'

'Yeah, but she's got us,' Adam says, 'so technically she's had her quota.'

I stare down at myself. Prettified. Girly. Almost beautiful. And to my horror, a big fat tear rolls down my face. And then another. And another. And before I know it, I'm scrubbing my face with a tissue and I just can't stop.

Julie isn't happy. My eyes are red and swollen and my make-up had to be redone. She's kicking herself for giving me the bag. I keep telling her that I don't care what I look like, I look better than I ever have before, and she really can't argue with that.

At around eight-thirty, the taxi we've ordered pulls up. Adam hurries out to put our overnight bags into the boot and when he has finished, we all hop in; Adam in front, with Julie and me in the back.

It takes about ten minutes to get into town and then our taxi joins the line of taxis slowly crawling up the enormous curved driveway of the new hotel. It's an impressive structure. When I was a kid, we'd climb the old crumbling walls

311

and play hide-and-seek behind enormous trees and pillars in the grounds. Now, it's transformed. It's been restored to the stately house it once was with two new wings added on to each side. As is the way with many hotels in Ireland now, it's also got its own golf course and the grounds sweep away behind it in various shades of green. Lights twinkle from the trees and lanterns light the way as the taxi pulls up in front of the wide steps which lead up to the front door. Julie hops out first and I pull myself out behind her. My leg is still quite stiff and not as nimble as it was in doing things like that. I'd never have been able to hop in and out of the cars Nelson hired, yes HIRED, when he visited Julie. Adam drags the bags from the boot.

'Do ye want help with all those bags?' the taxi driver asks as he observes Adam struggling up the steps. Julie has brought a suitcase with her. A full to the brim suitcase.

'Please.'

The taxi driver takes Julie's case, wincing at the weight. Adam carries my bag and his own. The doors to the opulent reception area are open. It's breathtaking. Huge floors, wide and expansive, in white and black marble. Up above us an enormous chandelier hangs from the vaulted ceiling. The smell of fresh, polished wood dominates.

'Dunport has arrived,' the taxi man says loudly as he dumps the case down beside the desk and peers around. 'No doubt about that.'

Oblivious to the tooting of horns outside, he has a good look around the foyer before leaving. We hear him telling the other drivers to 'chill'.

Adam checks us in. The receptionist tells us that our bags will be brought up to our rooms if we'd like to go on into the reception.

'Come on then,' Julie is breathless with excitement. 'Let's go meet the Kerry elite.'

It's packed. Chatter and noise and hum. Clinking of glasses and the tinkle of polite laughter. A big window dominates the massive room and everything seems very civilised and posh. I glance quickly about and recognise a few faces I really don't want to recognise. Neighbours and business people from the town. Jack's parents – his mother looking as snobby as ever, dressed to perfection and his father, dishevelled, trailing in her wake. Adam asks me if I want a drink and before I'm aware of it, I tell him that I want a nice large glass of white wine. It'll help me cope, I think, meeting all the people from the past.

'You're not meant to be drinking,' Julie, ever the spoilsport, intones. 'Get her some water, Adam.'

'I'll have a wine.'

Adam looks from one to the other of us in confusion. 'Eh, Hope, I think –'

'She wants water,' Julie says.

I roll my eyes. 'Right, water it is.' I'll sneak in a wine at some stage, when she's not looking. She's bound to start flirting with someone here sooner or later.

Adam grins. 'I wouldn't have got you wine anyway.'

Before I have a chance to say anything, he's gone. Bloody typical. A free bar and I can't even sample its delights.

'Hey.' The simple greeting makes me catch my breath. I'd forgotten Logan would be here. He has come up behind Julie and tapped her on the shoulder. 'What you all doing here?'

Julie shoots a look at me. We haven't heard from Logan since my apology, whether it's deliberate or not, I don't know.

Adam has met him, I think. He hasn't exactly talked about it and I haven't asked. As far as I know, he gave him a lift into Dunport a couple of times to get some shopping.

'Hiya, Logan.' Julie shoots a look at me and smiles up at him while I try to gaze into the distance beyond his shoulder. 'We're here because Hope knows Jack Dunleavy.'

'Oh, that's right.' Logan nods in my direction. 'Well, you both look great – almost didn't recognise you.'

'Thank you,' Julie smiles again.

'Yeah, thanks,' I say in an offhand manner. I still can't bring myself to look at him.

Silence descends.

'Well,' Julie says brightly, 'I'm just going to find Adam.' I gawk in disbelief at her. 'He's taking ages with the drinks. Excuse me.' Pushing past me, she has the nerve to wink and suddenly it's just me and Logan on our own. Well, I think, I'm not going to start a conversation. No way. If he thinks for one moment –

'Your bed is missing you,' he says, shoving his hands deep into the pockets of what I notice must be an incredibly expensive suit. 'Every night it asks, where has Hope gone. I liked her sleeping on me. Even if it was only once.'

'If I got you into trouble with your ex, well . . .' I pause; I had been about to apologise, then I think, why should I? I apologised enough. 'Well, I'm delighted,' I finish off.

He laughs.

Oh God, he is gorgeous, my traitorous mind says. If Logan looked good in jeans, he's about a million times handsomer in a suit. 'You couldn't get me in trouble with that woman,' he chortles, 'it's an ongoing thing. She hates me.'

His words reassure me. He doesn't sound at all put out about it, which makes me smile a little.

Another silence descends.

'About your apology –'

'About that day –'

He nods. 'You first.'

'No, you.'

'OK.' He pauses. 'Well, I'm just going to say that I'm –'

'Hey, Hope!' A tap on the back and Greg appears at my shoulder. 'I didn't know who you were at first. You look great!'

Talk about bad timing. I feel like someone who has just got five numbers instead of six in the national lottery. 'Hi, Greg.' I try to smile but it lacks enthusiasm. 'How's things?'

I hear Logan give an impatient sigh and much as I like Greg, I want to kill him for interrupting.

'Totally great,' Greg says, oblivious. 'Hey, hey, Mandy, come over here and see who it is!'

Mandy?

A tall blond woman turns to look in Greg's direction and when she sees me, the smile slides from her face. I'm sure my own face mirrors hers. Amanda Coonan. Taunter supreme.

'Come on!' Greg gestures for her to come over. God love him, he hasn't a clue about vibes and undercurrents and all that.

Amanda, wearing a very clipped smile, totters towards us on impossibly high heels. She looks as snotty and as snobby as I can remember from school. She's wearing a midnight blue silk dress that makes her look even skinnier than she is. Her highlighted hair falls softly over her shoulders and half-way down her back. I have such an urge to pull it. The biggest diamond I have ever seen sparkles on her ring finger.

Greg puts his arm around Amanda, pulling her towards

us. 'This is Mandy, my fiancée. D'you remember Hope, Mandy?'

'Yes.' Amanda gives me a stiff smile.

I give her one back. Then I realise how stupid I'm being. People change, I think. OK, I haven't, not yet, but that's just sad old me. So I hold out my hand. 'Nice to see you again, Amanda.' The lie almost chokes me.

Her handshake has all the aplomb of a flat sponge cake. 'Really?' she says, arching her eyebrows. 'Thanks.' Her voice is as clipped as her smile. She lets my hand go quickly and stares about the room. 'Come on, Greg and let's see if we can find Jack. I'm dying to talk to him after all this time.'

'Well, you haven't seen Hope in a long time either,' Greg says, a little embarrassed.

'Yes, and we've talked to her. Come on.' She starts tugging his sleeve.

Logan quirks his eyes at me, wondering, I suppose, why she's so horrible.

Adam and Julie come back then with a glass of wine each and a big pint of water for me. Adam hands it to me over my shoulder. 'Hi,' he says easily, recognising Greg. 'You're the barman, aren't you?'

Greg is thrilled that he's been remembered. 'And you're the Shamrock lover.'

'That's me!'

'This is Mandy, my fiancée.'

'Hello.' Adam proffers a hand, which she shakes. 'I'm Adam. How do you do?'

She responds to his warm tone. 'Great, thanks. Enjoying the night, are you?'

'Free drink, beautiful women, who wouldn't?'

My, but Adam has improved his line in chat, I think, feeling slightly amused.

Greg takes heart from Amanda's change in humour. 'And this is Julie.'

Julie smiles and shakes her hand too.

'And this is Logan, Mandy – he did the artwork in the hotel, didn't you?'

Logan nods. 'Uh-huh.'

'Wow!' Amanda is seriously impressed now. She touches Logan lightly and points to a massive picture which I hadn't noticed until then. 'Did you do that fantastic one opposite the window?'

'Yeah,' Logan nods. 'That was the biggest one.'

The picture is massive, measuring about ten by ten. It hangs opposite the bay window but is a picture of the view outside the bay window, minus the hotel and driveway. It really is very clever, showing how the landscape should look without a hotel in the middle of it. It's quite subversive and it makes me smile.

'It's brilliant,' Amanda says. 'Did that take you long?'

'Yeah, too long,' Logan says, mock-groaning.

'I must go and look at the other ones,' Amanda says, smiling up at him. 'Will you tell me about them?'

'Sure, be glad to,' Logan says easily, and chatting together they walk out of the room, Greg following them.

I glare at Amanda's retreating back. She was always one for the fellas. I turn back to see Julie and Adam looking expectantly at me. 'What?'

'Well,' Julie's eyes are gleaming, 'what did he say?'

'Logan? Nothing. Why?'

'It was obvious he wanted to talk to you.'

'Was it?'

317

'He stood there, shuffling from foot to foot and staring at you and if you'd bothered to look at him, you would have noticed that.' She pauses. 'So what did he say?'

'Nothing. Greg came along.'

The two of them groan loudly, which makes me laugh. Oh God, I hope he comes back.

But for the next couple of hours, as Julie and Adam get slowly sloshed and I remain sober, Logan stays firmly surrounded by what seem like adoring fans. I notice with some disquiet that they are mostly women and that they all seem to find him hilarious.

I try not to glance at him but my gaze is drawn time and again to his handsome profile and his laughing face. I can't seem to concentrate on what Julie and Adam are saying at all, I just want to talk to him, assure myself that we're friends again. That he likes me again.

In fact, I'm so preoccupied by Logan that I fail to notice Jack at all, until he breaks into our group and tells me I look great. I get such a shock that my water slops out all over my dress. So much for being calm and composed. 'Eh, hiya,' I stammer out. 'Thanks.'

'These must be your friends?' He's totally confident, totally in control of the conversation.

'Yes,' I try to match his tone. 'Julie you've met already and this guy here is Adam.'

'Hi, Adam.'

'Hi, Jack,' Adam nods. 'Great party.'

'Thanks. It's great to be finally back in Dunport.' His gaze sweeps me from top to toe. A pause, before he says slowly, 'I loved it here.' There is a whole other meaning in his tone, which I can't ignore.

Adam has no problem ignoring it. 'Yeah, we love it too. We're having a great time, aren't we, Hope?'

'Well you are,' I smile. 'Free booze and free parties and crappy traditional music.'

'Exactly,' Adam raises his glass. 'Nice wine, by the way.'

'Thanks.' Jack touches my arm. 'Great to see you,' he says again. He looks uncomfortable suddenly. 'D'you fancy meeting up for a chat some day? To catch up?'

Funnily enough, seeing him is not at all like I imagined it would be. This was the man I'd invested so much in when I was seventeen, the boy I'd lost my virginity to, the one I'd told things to, the one who'd discovered where my tickles were when I thought I didn't have any. But he was also the boy who had gone to college and never contacted me once. I'd written and written and he'd never replied. Meeting him again after ten years, I suddenly realise that none of that matters any more. I have moved on, I think with some surprise. Just as the world turns and you can't feel it and if it wasn't for the sun rising in the morning and setting at night, you wouldn't know that you'd just revolved three hundred and sixty degrees. Well my life had turned too without me noticing and if I hadn't met Jack again, I'd never have known I was over his rejection of me. Yeah, I'd been angry seeing him at first, but now, what did it matter?

'Well?' he asks and there is such a funny look in his eyes that it almost makes me sad for him.

'Catch up?' I say.

'Yeah.'

'There is no need,' I reply. 'I've caught up.' And I smile at him.

I don't think he understands. He looks at Julie and Adam and then at me. 'Just for a chat, some time?'

'Well, I'm going back to London so . . .'

'Maybe I could talk to you now, for a second?' He stops. 'In private?'

'OK.' I find his urgency to talk to me a bit unnerving. 'Why?'

In answer, he pulls me gently away from my curious friends, who make no attempt to follow. He leads me out into the foyer, where the first thing I notice, besides the hush, is Logan's fabulous painting of the waterfall. Jack turns to me. He takes a deep gulp of air, runs his fingers through his hair and says, half defensively, 'I'm sorry, Hope. OK. I'm sorry.'

I don't say anything. In all honesty, I can't quite believe it.

'I've felt guilty about the way I treated you for ages,' he says. 'I got your letters when I was in college and knew you'd phoned me and everything, but Jesus, Hope, I was only eighteen.'

'Yeah. I know that.'

'And you were so needy,' he goes on, 'it was like you wanted me to save you from your life and I couldn't do that. I felt like I was drowning in quicksand.'

Is this an apology?

'You were suffocating me and I just thought that the best thing to do was to not write.'

It's not like any apology I've ever had before. Now I'm the one feeling guilty.

'Eh, Jack,' I hold up my hand. 'Enough said. There's no need to do this. It doesn't matter any more, honestly.'

He doesn't seem to get that bit. 'And also,' he looks at his highly polished, highly expensive shoes, 'I had to get away too. It wasn't just you I ran away from, just in case you think it was.'

I don't say anything, not fully understanding.

'My dad,' he gulps out. 'He can be very difficult to live with. I just wanted to get away, make a clean break.'

As if he senses that he's being talked about, Jack's dad comes staggering out into the foyer, being supported by some of the waiting staff.

'Put him upstairs in his room,' Jack says wearily, before turning back to me.

My world tilts slightly. I think back to those lazy, weird, teenage days. How I'd sit on the grass on the mountain top with Jack and tell him everything, but never, I realise, ever, ask him about himself. I'd been as selfish then as he had been later. I'd been so absorbed in my awfulness that I hadn't thought about anyone else.

'Jack,' I say softly, 'it's your big night. You don't need to apologise to me. I shouldn't have expected you to look after me. I know that.'

He nods slightly.

'Now you've opened a hotel in Dunport, will you just let go and enjoy it.' I rub his arm briefly. 'I know I will.'

The sound of his dad falling up the stairs reverberates around the lobby.

He catches my hand. 'Thanks, Hope. That means a lot. It's the one thing I'm really ashamed of.'

'No need to be.' I pause, thinking of my own mother. 'Sometimes we need to be selfish just to survive. I understand that.'

He squeezes my hand and just walks away.

I watch him go and wonder if I'll ever stop being selfish. If I'll ever see my mother and not feel that I'm suffocating.

Dinner is served at around ten. Adam, Julie and I sit together. Three other people join us. Jack had obviously thought that

321

I'd like to sit with people from school, so, much to my dismay, Greg and Amanda are there and so also is a guy I barely remember from school. Dylan. He'd joined in sixth year and, as that had been a very patchy year for me, I didn't really know him. It turns out he and Jack had gone to college together and done the same course. He's chatty and funny and he sits beside me. Greg and Amanda are over the other side, beside Adam. I notice that Amanda seems to be charming Adam the way she charmed everyone in school. The teachers had loved her.

Dylan notices me looking over at her. 'I had a big crush on her in sixth year,' he says. 'I even asked her to the debs.'

'Yeah? And did she go with you?'

'Are you joking? I was skinny, spotty and scrawny. She told me she'd let me know and then she goes with him.' He nods towards Greg.

'Wow, they've been together a long time.'

'Who did you go with?' he asks. 'Or did you even go?' He laughs. 'All I can remember of you that year is your grumpy face on the days when you did turn up.'

I laugh too. 'I didn't go.'

'We all thought you'd go with Jack. You were seeing him, weren't you?'

I nod. 'Yeah. But it was over by then.'

'He liked you a lot, I think.'

I suppose he had, in his way. But for Dylan's benefit, I just snort scornfully, and then change the subject. From the corner of my eye, I see that Logan is the centre of atten-tion at his table. He really has changed from the dour man I'd first met a few months ago. He seems to be taking a lot of business cards from people and tucking them into his pocket. I look at him and he must sense it, because at one

322

point he stares in my direction and gives a hesitant smile. I give him one back. Then he gives me a big huge one and the feeling of happiness that washes over me makes me almost feel like crying.

I will talk to him after dinner, I decide. I'll just walk up to him and talk to him and explain what happened with the whole ex-girlfriend thing.

A gong signalling the speeches shatters that train of thought.

'And now . . .' Jack stands up at the podium, his confident manner back in place, his resonant voice filling the room. 'I hope you've all had a lovely dinner and are looking forward to our mystery guest. Ladies and gentlemen, the hotel will now be officially opened by –' he pauses for dramatic effect – 'David Dunne.'

The film star! No way! Dunport had definitely arrived!

A huge gasp, mainly it has to be said from the women, goes up and Julie, who has drunk way more than is good for her, stands up and cheers loudly, much to Adam's obvious mortification. People nearby laugh and Julie is then joined in her cheering by a few others.

David Dunne is gorgeous. Ten times nicer in the flesh than on film. He shakes Jack's hand and turning to the microphone gives his trademark wink and people whoop and whistle. All I can think is that it's not half as sexy as Logan's. I look towards him but he's laughing at Julie's antics. He has a lovely smile too. And a nice easy way of going on, when he's not glowering over something. I wish, in that moment, that he was mine.

David makes a speech but I barely hear a word of it, so busy am I telling myself sternly to be sensible. I live in London, he lives here. It'd never work. Plus there is the small matter of my cruel words.

After David's speech, all the uncool people rush up to him for his autograph. Julie is first in line, a napkin and a pen lent to her by Adam clutched firmly in her hand.

I decide to go and retouch my lipstick – lent to me by Julie – so that when I see Logan next, I'll look as good as I can look.

On the way to the bathroom, some photographer from the *Dunport News* asks me to pose for a photo. I meet Maurice, our landlord, who I wouldn't know only for the hideous hairpiece on his head. He's with a woman, presumably his wife, who's doing a feature on the opening for her paper. 'I hope to get front page,' she confides to me. Maurice stands proudly beside her and tells me that she's a top-class journalist; that she broke the Dunport story of the killer chips. 'Well, not that they'd actually kill you,' he says, 'it was just that they were reheated ones from the night before.'

I manage to look suitably impressed, while at the same time amused by the idea that that was the most dramatic thing to happen in Dunport in recent times. What a lovely place to live if that's the main problem.

Some other locals I can't avoid bumping into say hello and ask how I am after the crash. It's not as bad as I'd feared.

After what seems ages, I make it to the Ladies, which is just as fancy as the rest of the place. I stand in front of the full-length mirror and see myself in my entirety for the first time. I do look nice. Very nice, even. The dress slims me down, as do the shoes. The only odd thing is my really short hair, but there isn't a lot I could do about that. As I'm applying my lipstick, someone flushes a toilet in one of the giant cubicles and to my dismay, Amanda comes out. She flicks this disdainful glance in my direction and then ignores me. IGNORES ME. The nerve. I feel the old anger rise in me. The anger that I felt for her years ago. Unfortunately, I haven't outgrown what she did, probably because most of her bile was directed at Jamie and not at me. I begin to stare hard at her as she flicks her hair this way and that and pouts her lips and uses a big brush to sweep powder over her face.

'It's only polite to say hello,' I say witheringly, knowing I should just ignore her too.

She turns to face me. She's about three inches taller than I am. 'I don't want to say hello to you,' she says back in this ultra-polite voice.

For a second, I'm speechless. 'Really,' I reply. 'I guess that's because you're just as big a bitch as you always were.'

Oh my God, I sound like a five-year-old.

I watch in slight alarm as she slams down her make-up bag and crosses towards me. 'Where you're concerned, I guess I am.'

We are less than a foot apart. I look up at her. 'I did nothing to you. You always picked on me and Jamie. You called us names.'

For a split second, at the mention of Jamie, she looks a little ashamed, but then her arrogance reasserts itself. 'I know,' she nods. 'And you used to throw muck at me, and get Jamie to do the same. You pushed me and I ended up in hospital. But, you know, I can forget that even if you can't.'

'Oh, you can forget it by not saying hello, is that it?'

'Why would I want to say hello to someone who treats their mother the way you treat yours?'

It's as if she's slapped me. I open and close my mouth before finally spluttering out, 'I beg your pardon?'

'You should be begging your mother's pardon, not mine.'

She does a big sniff sort of thing and makes to turn away. Huh, she's not getting away that easily.

I catch her arm and squeeze it. 'My relationship with my mother is no concern of yours.'

She shakes me off. 'Oh yes it is. I visit your mother every day, did you know that? She's such a nice woman. She told me you were calling and she was so happy. I don't know what happened between you but you haven't called since and I know she's hurt over it. And I think you're being so selfish. The whole of Dunport knows you're back and you haven't called in.'

'You said it, Amanda, you don't know what happened, so keep your big nose out.' God, she is tall. I find my gaze level with her neck, so I have to stretch my head back as I say, 'And unlike you, I've never cared what the neighbours thought.'

She ignores that. Instead she snaps, 'So why did you come back? Was it to torment your mother, make a show of her? Because if it was, you're doing a wonderful job. She was sick last week, did you know that?'

I open my mouth to answer but nothing comes out.

'So don't say hello to me. Don't come near me, actually. Your mother is a great woman and you make me sick swanning about the place with your friends. Do you know how hard she has struggled to keep going after you left?'

I gawp at her.

'No, you don't, how could you, you left. But I was here and so was my family and we saw how hard she had it. She was an ill woman. She'd lost her son and been deserted by her daughter. She crawled back to life, Hope. That's what she did. And now you come breezing back into town as if nothing has happened.'

'Lots happened,' I blurt out. 'Lots.'

She pauses and says softly, 'I know lots happened, Hope. I know what happened when we were kids was wrong, I know what happened to Jamie was terrible, but staying away is not going to make things any better, for anyone.'

'You stay away from my mother,' I say stupidly, my voice shaking.

'Like you do.' She arches her eyebrows. 'No chance.' She holds my narrow-eyed gaze for a second or two before turning on her heel, grabbing her brush and bag and slamming the door of the Ladies behind her.

I stand there for ages, not able to move.

Of course, I have to go back out. But I can't face anyone now. I'm sure Amanda will tell Greg what happened and it'll get around the room, the way gossip does in a small town and everyone will be staring at me. I wonder if they all think I'm selfish. I'd lied to Amanda: of course I cared what people thought. I'd cared so much, I couldn't stay in Dunport. I place my hands against the flat of the tiles, letting their coldness shock me into clear thinking. I just have to get out. Get away. I take a deep breath and, head down, I walk from the Ladies, up the corridor and instead of going into the ballroom, go through reception and outside to the garden.

No one is about. It's a warm evening, so I totter on my heels into the shadows of some trees and sit down on the grass, not caring that my dress might get stained. I ease off my expensive shoes and rub my feet, observing the twinkling lights and the shadows of happy people in the ballroom. I just want to stay here, away from everyone so that I can't be judged, so that I can't make mistakes, so that I can just breathe. And so I stay there.

And I think about what Amanda has said, about what

327

happened with Jack, and it hurts a lot because if I look at myself from the outside, I see me as a big selfish bitch. But inside, I know I'm not. Inside, I'm just about coping. Inside, I want to ring my mother but it's too scary. Way too scary to make that initial contact and see it fall apart and both of us hurt all over again. It's way too awful. Inside I'm scrabbling about like a moth in the dark trying to find some light. And I can't seem to find the switch to turn things on.

People come out during the evening, some for a smoke, some for a snog. I watch it all from my trees. Julie and Adam come out at some stage. I think they're looking for me but I can't join them. They look well together, I think absently, from my vantage point. Both blond, both tall. Julie is very drunk. Adam holds her up. Then he puts his arm about her shoulder and begins to pull her back inside, his head resting tentatively on the top of her head.

I wait until they are out of sight, then creep from my hiding place and scurry up the stairs to my bedroom.

I spend the night lying on top of the bed, looking at the stars out of the window and trying not to think.

33

I FALL INTO a fitful sleep which is shattered by a frantic tapping on my door. Glancing at the television, which has a digital clock on it, I see that it's after ten. The sun is up and streaming through the window. I've probably missed breakfast but last night's dinner is sitting in my stomach like cement, so I wouldn't have eaten too much anyway.

'Hope! Hope!' It's Julie. 'Hope, are you in there?'

'Yeah,' I call out, then heave myself up from the bed and walk barefoot to the door.

Julie bustles in and shuts the door firmly behind her. She's about to say something when she notices what I'm wearing. 'You're still in the dress from last night,' she says. 'Have you only got back now?'

'No.' I know she's wondering if I was with anyone. 'I just fell asleep in it.'

'Oh,' she pauses. 'So, where did you get to last night? We were looking for you.'

I shrug. 'Nowhere, really. Amanda and I had a few words and I just wanted to get away for a bit. Have a think.'

'Words? Horrible words?' She looks concerned. 'What did she say?'

I sit back down on the bed. 'Nothing that wasn't true, unfortunately,' I admit. 'It was hard to hear.' Oh God, I don't want to think about it. I've thought about nothing else. 'And you,' I ask, 'did you have a good night?'

Her silence tells me more than any words. So does her rueful expression. 'What happened?' I feel momentarily fearful. I don't like the unexpected.

'Oh shit, Hope, I've done something stupid!' She presses her hands to her face and looks at me with anguished eyes. 'Really stupid.' And she sits down beside me on the bed, then winces. 'Oh, my head,' she moans, clutching it.

My heart sinks. 'What?'

'Now,' Julie looks fearfully at me. 'Promise you won't be shocked.'

'That means I will be shocked.' I gaze at her, dreading what she might say. 'What happened?'

'Oh Hope, I am so thick, I've gone and ruined everything.'

'How can you ruin everything?' I half smile at her dramatics. 'Have you killed someone or something?'

'No!' Julie says. 'It feels worse than that.' She closes her eyes and mutters, 'I kissed Adam.'

'Kissed?' For a second I am lost. 'Adam kissed you?'

'No!' Julie shakes her head, '*I* kissed *him*!'

'You kissed him?' I repeat, just so I understand properly. 'Like as in snogged?'

'Yeah.' She nods. 'Kissed, snogged. Whatever you want to call it.'

'Why?' Jesus, I am shocked. If he'd kissed her, it might make some sort of sense, but for Julie to kiss Adam, well, she must have been really drunk.

'I don't know,' she groans. 'I know I was drunk but Hope, he was up at the bar, buying some girl a drink and all I could think of was that he was going to get her number

330

and call her and so I went up and dragged him outside to look for you and then I threw myself at him.'

'You threw yourself at him.'

'Yeah.'

'Why? D'you fancy him?'

'Hope, this is *Adam* we're talking about. He's our friend.'

'I think he fancies you,' I say slowly. 'I've sort of thought it for ages now.'

In answer, Julie turns over on the bed and buries her head in the duvet. She mutters something that I can't make out.

'What?'

'I said,' she says, turning back, 'that he told me that it wasn't a good idea and that maybe I should go to bed.'

'Well, in fairness –'

'And I said, oh God –' Julie stops as if she's only just remembered, 'I said only if he came too. Oh God. Can you believe I said that!'

'I can't, actually.'

'What am I going to do?'

'Do you fancy him, Julie?'

'You asked me that already.'

'Do you fancy him?'

She shrugs. 'I don't know. D'you know the way you have hair?'

I point to my pretty bare scalp.

Julie manages a panic-stricken giggle. 'Well, I don't mean just *you*, I mean everyone.' She touches her own blond mane. 'You know the way people have hair and they get it cut and they think it's only OK?'

'Yep.'

'And then a few weeks later the hair grows and they suddenly realise that they like it. Well, that's the way I feel

331

about Adam. First off he was just there, he was my friend and I liked him, but this holiday, well, I think he's grown on me. I was pissed off at him last night for chatting that girl up.'

'So you do fancy him.'

'A bit, I suppose.'

'So tell him.'

'After he told me to get to bed? Are you joking? I never want to see him again.'

'That's going to be difficult, seeing as we all live together.' And even worse for me, I want to add and don't. 'Maybe, Julie, he was just being a gentleman if he stopped you from going any further last night. It shows he cares about you.'

'No,' Julie shakes her head. 'No, he didn't want me.'

Bang!

Bang!

Bang!

More knocking. This time it's Adam. 'Hope, Hope, are you in there?'

'Shit!' Julie looks at me, 'don't answer. Pretend you're not here.'

'Hope!'

'Adam, hi,' I call out. There is no way I'm taking sides in this. 'Hang on a sec.'

'I have to hide,' Julie says. 'How could you do this?' She runs madly about the room like something from a comic strip as I open the door on a very dishevelled Adam.

'Ju kissed me,' he announces, before catching sight of her and going red. 'Shit!'

He coughs slightly, 'Hi, Ju.'

'Adam, hi,' Julie stops mid-run. 'I, eh, was just explaining the situation to Hope. Like, it was all a big mistake and I

332

apologise for being so drunk and, well, embarrassing both of us. I know I made a complete idiot out of myself.'

Adam looks as if she's just hit him full force with a cannon. His eyes linger on her for a second before meeting mine. 'Yeah,' he half laughs, 'right. OK. Good, then. As long as we're all friends, that's all that matters.'

'So you do think I made an idiot of myself?' Julie says, a little crossly. 'Is that what you really think?'

'Well, like I only —'

'Thanks.' Julie sounds hurt. 'That's great.'

'Hang on here,' I attempt to intervene. 'Let's just try to find out what we all feel.'

'Hope, there is no need for that counselling stuff.' Julie moves over to stand right in front of a bewildered-looking Adam. 'We all know how we feel. He thinks I'm an idiot.'

'I never said that,' Adam defends himself. 'You said that.'

'You led me on. You kept telling me I looked beautiful.'

Adam looks for help from me. I shrug. What am I meant to do?

'Yeah, well, you did,' Adam says clumsily. 'And you know, I liked you being an idiot, it was the best feeling I ever had.'

The words fall into dumbfounded silence.

'So why did you tell me to go to bed?' Julie asks, and her voice is not quite as cross. 'I was prepared to snog you and you told me to sober up.'

I wish I could leave but Adam is blocking the doorway. Instead, I cross over to the window and watch the two of them from that vantage point, though I don't think they're even aware I'm there any more.

Adam is running his hands up and down the leg of his jeans and audibly gulping. I know he's about to take the biggest risk of his life. 'Because,' he says, and his voice, though awkward, is so sincere and honest that I wish he was saying it to me, 'I got scared and also because I want to be with you when we're both sober and know what we're doing.' A pause while he rubs his hands together hard. 'It's all I've wanted for ages, Ju. It's not every woman I'd let take me to the hairdresser's and get my hair butchered.'

'It wasn't butchered, it was lovely.'

'As long as you thought so.'

They stare at each other as if they've never quite seen each other before.

'So, you like me?' Julie looks up at him. 'You fancy me?'

'Totally.' He laughs a little. He's embarrassed, I think.

'I'm sober now,' Julie says.

Adam looks thunderstruck. 'What?'

'I said I'm sober now. Are you?'

I wish I had her nerve.

'Well, yeah, yeah, I guess.'

'Come on then.' Julie tugs his arm. 'Show me what all the girls have been missing these long years.'

I don't know how I feel as they leave the room. It's great for them, but sad for me.

I hate it when things change.

34

J ULIE AND ADAM are most definitely together in the next few days. I catch them touching and smiling at each other and despite their best efforts to be discreet, I do feel like the prize-winning gooseberry in the village fair. Adam has made a major leap in the therapy stakes. From buying women drinks to full sex is quite an achievement, and I'm glad for him. He's got a whole new air about him that is surprisingly sexy, a complete ease with who he is. A Logan air, I call it in my head. I know that when I go back to London I'm going to have to find somewhere to live on my own. It's a bleak thought. But I guess I can't go depending on the two of them for moral support for ever. There comes a moment when we all have to be self-sufficient, and mine has come.

Unfortunately Logan hasn't come. I really thought that he'd be around the day after the hotel ball but we haven't seen him at all. Still, it's probably for the best: with Julie and Adam being all lovey-dovey, just being friends with Logan would be quite difficult and yet I know there's no point in being much else if I have to leave for London.

Adam drives me to my counselling session the next week. Tim isn't in his office when I arrive and I see that for once the place is clean and organised. His desk even seems to have been polished. Adam offers to hang on until Tim arrives but I wave him off. I know he wants to get back to Julie so they can have some time together while I'm out.

'Ring me,' Adam taps his mobile, 'and I'll collect you.'

'Sure. Thanks.'

Adam leaves and five minutes later Tim arrives. 'Sorry about that.' He grins and holds up a paper. 'I just nipped out to buy this and look who I see on the front!!'

Oh God, it's me.

'You look great,' he says.

The headline screams, *Babes at the Ball*.

'The babes were pretty thin on the ground,' I shrug jokingly, 'so they used me instead.'

'Don't be so modest,' Tim grins, putting the paper away in his drawer. It's then I notice that his ponytail has gone.

'You've chopped your hair,' I say, surprised.

'Well, actually, I paid someone to do it,' Tim says wryly. 'They mustn't have done a great job if you think I chopped it myself.'

I laugh. 'That's what I meant. You got your hair chopped.'

'Yeah.' He shrugs. 'My wife made me do it. She's been at me for ages – she hates long hair.'

'Oh. Right.' So much for the hippie chick wife I thought he had.

I wonder what people think when they see me? Do they think I don't care about things when in fact, I do? Better not to try than to try and fail, that's always been my motto. I'd tried to keep a family together and failed. I hate the feeling of powerlessness that failure brings.

'Is your wife really fashion conscious?' I ask.

'No,' he shrugs. 'She just always hated my hair. But as she cleverly pointed out at the weekend, I was just letting it grow to hold on to my own identity in the relationship.' He smirked. 'She's reading too many of my books.'

I wonder if that is why he had his sleeping bag with him at the office one night. I don't have time to think about it though as his tone becomes serious. 'Now Hope, you know that today might be a tough one. We're going to talk about the accident. I know you can't remember much, but once you open your mind you'll begin to remember other things. It's a case of preparing yourself and when you're ready, you will remember. OK?'

'Yeah.'

Tim asks me again about the previous two weeks – my thoughts, actions and exposure therapy.

'Good,' I answer. Then, haltingly, 'But, well, I feel I'm letting go of a lot of things when I listen to the tapes.'

'Like?'

'Jamie. And I'm not sure I want to let go of him.'

'He's already gone,' Tim says softly. 'He's been gone a long time. What you have to let go of is the feeling that any of it was your fault. That maybe his illness was something you could control. We have to see that we can't control everything, Hope. And we have to accept it. That's the hard part.'

He is right. But thinking like that is scary. It means that feeling powerless is something I might have to get used to. Feeling that it's normal that life can change in an instant. But what other way is there to live? I can't go on as I am – rigidly controlling myself. Losing control to have control. At least now, after listening to the tapes, I can think of what happened. I can examine it as you would a rare object, by holding it up to the light and trying to be objective. Things about that time keep popping into my head. Things that soften the image I've held on to for so long. The way my mother had told me that it wasn't my fault. The way she had held me at the funeral and said over and over again that it wasn't me. That it was her. That I mustn't feel I let Jamie down. I'd stood, frozen, unable to react as they'd buried my little brother. I blocked it all out. Held on to the anger because it had kept me going – kept me in some sort of powerful position. If just once I'd allowed myself to feel the full extent of the grief I might never have got up again. And now here I was, talking about it, listening to myself talk about it every day and remembering. And grieving. But remembering how my mother had shouldered the blame herself. Little by little the truth is getting through.

'So now,' Tim says, 'let's get cracking.'

I really don't want to do this. I know I've improved a lot since seeing Tim first. I sleep a little better at night but for months I've resisted this. 'Tim, if I didn't do this, would it be a big deal?'

He seems taken aback. 'What do you think?'

Julie and Adam come with me to the airport. I'm happy to be leaving. I'm feeling a little depressed at myself. I don't want them to know, so we joke and laugh. I don't know myself why I'm leaving unless it's to get perspective.

'Do you know now?'

I nod. 'I think I just wanted to escape more than anything. To be another person. It's what I did when I came to London first. It wouldn't have worked, I know that now.'

Tim nods. 'OK. Go on.'

I get on to the plane. It's a small one. Beige seats, I think. A child behind me. A man sits in beside me.

Then I wake up in hospital.
Adam said some man saved my life, but I don't remember.

'That's all,' I say. I sound a little defiant. 'That's it.'

'The man? The one that sat beside you, what was he like?'

'Young, I think. Friendly.'

He's not letting me away so easily. I watch as he takes a newspaper from a drawer.

'I have a paper here,' he says. 'Maybe you can recognise him?'

I hadn't known there were pictures of us in the paper. I suppose I hadn't wanted to know.

'Oh, I don't think so.' I don't hold out my hand to take it from him.

'Try.' His voice is sterner than ever before. He passes the paper across his messy desk.

Without touching it, I reluctantly study the pictures. The victims. Was the person who sat beside me a victim, then? I feel a chill as I look at it. Little did they know when these pictures were taken that one day soon they'd be used in an article about their deaths.

I scan the photos and stop at the fifth picture. Scan them again. I point at the man identified as Joe Ryan. He's handsome and looks good-humoured. 'He looks, I dunno, familiar.'

Tom nods, pleased. 'That's him, all right,' he says.

'How do you know?'

He leans across the desk. 'Haven't you read anything about the accident since? Or even at the time?'

I shrug. 'I was in a coma at first,' I say. 'And then, I suppose people tried to get me to talk about it, but I didn't want to. Then, I went on holiday and Adam talked about it once, just briefly. He told me that someone had saved my life. But I feel sick when I think about it, so we just don't mention it.'

He nods.

'So how do you know he was sitting beside me? We could sit where we liked on the plane.'

'Well,' Tim nods at the paper. 'Maybe you should read it, see if anything jogs your memory.'

My hand trembles slightly as I lift the paper from the desk. There's stuff about the flight. How it was a nice, cloudless day. How everything had been fine on take-off. Then some sort of a problem with the engine. A noise. I remember the noise now. Pop. Pop. Pop. 'A popping noise,' I say. 'I remember that. I looked out and saw smoke coming out of one of the engines.' I gulp. 'And, oh God, we started to go down and the pilot tried to turn the plane back.'

'Stop if you get too stressed,' Tim advises. 'I just want to try to kick-start the memory.'

According to the report, we'd made it back to the runway. The plane had then skidded, turning round and round at a high speed. Luggage was strewn inside and outside the craft. And people had died, including Joe Ryan. 'How do you know he was sitting beside me?' I ask.

Tim points to a small paragraph, inset into the main body of the piece.

The latest survivor is an Irish citizen identified by friends as Hope Gardner. Her survival is being described as 'miraculous' by rescue workers. It is thought that a fellow passenger shielded her from the worst of the accident by covering her body with his.

340

He has been identified as Joe Ryan originally from Dublin. He is survived by his wife who is currently expecting their first child.

I read this paragraph again and again. And again. This man made the ultimate sacrifice and I can't even remember. I jab at the photograph. 'This was the man – he saved my life?'

'Supposedly.'

It's a blank. A black hole. I feel guilty. 'I can't remember.'

Tim looks at me. 'But I bet now you want to,' he says.

And he's right. I owe it to this man to remember. To myself to remember.

'Now close your eyes,' Tim says. 'I want you to talk it through again only this time, I'm going to try to get you to remember colours, smells, sensations, OK?'

Julie and Adam come with me to the airport. I'm wearing tracksuit bottoms. As usual. Julie is dressed up and Adam looks tall and lanky and awkward. They wave to me as I go to Departures. Julie is crying, Adam is comforting her. I get on the plane with the beige seats, definitely green and beige, and I sit beside a window. I like window seats, it makes me feel more in control. I know I sat there because later, I looked out the window and saw the black smoke coming out of the engine. A man sits beside me. Young. I think about Joe Ryan's face. Joe Ryan. Nothing. But I can remember crisps suddenly. I think he was eating crisps. Cheese and onion crisps. I think he offered me one. Then the popping sound. Yes, I remember that. I heard it before anyone else. Then it got louder and suddenly I see smoke coming out of the engine. Then the pilot said they were turning back. Then I am in hospital.

By the time I've finished, my heart is pounding. I've reached a ten on the stress scale. Tim holds up his hand, rewinds the tape and plays it back to me. I listen to my voice talking about the accident. I feel sick at every sentence. My stress is still a ten. Tim plays the tape again. And again. By the end of the session, I can bear it. My stress has gone down to an eight. Tim tells me that if I listen to it over the next two days it'll lessen even more. I believe him. I don't believe that I'll remember anything much more, though. It's like trying to blow a feather through a brick wall.

'We'll find the crack in the wall,' Tim says. 'Memory walls have unsteady foundations, you'll see.'

'Can I have that?' I indicate the paper.

'I was hoping you'd take it,' he grins.

'Thanks.' I fold it up, looking once again at the man who allegedly saved my life. How can I not remember?

35

A DAM PICKS ME up as promised and he's in great form. 'Got another interview next week,' he tells me. 'And this time it's as a supervisor in two stores for a rival chain.'

I laugh. 'How will your ex-bosses feel about that?'

'D'you know, Hope,' he grins at me, 'I don't care.'

'Well, I hope you get it.' I pat his arm. 'Serve them right. D'you have to fly over again?'

'Yeah, this job-seeking is costing me a fortune in air fares but if I get this one, it'll be worth it. At least,' he says, suddenly serious, 'it'll give me a chance to prove that I can actually be a half-decent boss.'

'Of course you will.'

He smiles and flicks on the CD player. Adam has invested in some of the Shamrocks' CDs and they are woeful. But he enjoys them, tapping his fingers to the beat on the steering wheel.

'Adam,' I ask without thinking I'm going to, 'what happened the day of the accident?'

He shoots a look at me.

'Yes,' I confirm, '*that* day. Can you tell me anything? I know I haven't wanted to talk about it but I think I have to if I'm going to remember.' I pause. 'I couldn't remember anything in counselling today.'

Adam indicates and eases the car on to a grass verge, just off the road. Then he gazes quizzically at me. 'Are you sure you need to know just now? You looked pretty upset coming out of Tim's office.'

'I'm sure.' Actually I'm not but I don't know if I'd ever get up the nerve to ask him about it again.

'D'you want to go back to the house and talk or go for a coffee?'

'Here is fine.'

'In the car?' He looks incredulously at me.

'Yeah, if that's OK.'

I know Adam will give me a better version of things than Julie. Her story would be too emotional and too descriptive and I'm definitely not ready for that.

'Well, OK,' Adam smiles a little at me. 'If you're sure.' He waits a second, then begins, 'Well, after you left, Ju and I went for something to eat. Ju was pretty upset so she didn't eat much and we didn't stay long. Then we hopped into the car to head back to the house. I was working later that day and I wanted to go over some files. Ju was going shopping to cheer herself up.' He smiles at the mention of her name.

'Anyway, we were driving along, about four miles out of the airport, when a newsflash comes on the radio about a plane crash-landing in Heathrow. I don't know, Hope, but somehow we both knew it was your plane. And Julie got completely hysterical and started ordering me to go back but we're on the wrong side of the bloody road and I think she thought I'd somehow, by some miracle, get the car to molecularly move to the other side. We had a huge row about it, but it was only because we couldn't face the fact that maybe something had happened to you. So anyway, I drive and drive and find a turn and get back on the road to the airport but it's jammed. The airport is blocked off and the tailback goes for miles so we're sitting in the car, Ju is hysterical, I'm trying to drive and make calls and then the news comes on that yeah, it was the Heathrow to Boston plane and that a lot of people seem to be dead.'

I shiver and the guilt of a survivor washes over me.

'So Ju gets out, slams the car door and announces that she's walking to the airport. I drive the car to the grass verge in the middle of the road and that's what we do.'

'You walk?'

'Yeah. It takes ages. When we get there, we can't get in. We can't get any information. We're told to go to the hospital or go home. It was a nightmare, Hope. A bloody nightmare.' He looks at me and I'm stunned to see tears in his eyes. 'We thought you were dead.'

'Hard to kill a bad thing.'

'So we go home. There's nothing else to do. And we sit and watch the telly all day and feel useless and get pissed off with each other. And all the time the news is on and nothing about you. It's wall to wall, this accident. I think they thought it was terrorism at first but it was an engine fault. And then they announced that they've recovered another two bodies from the site, a young woman and a young man. And then we get a call to say that it was you and that you were alive.'

'And the man?'

'He was the guy that saved your life, or so they said.'

'Joe Ryan?'

'Yeah, that was his name.'

'I don't remember him, Adam. I feel so guilty because I can't remember anything.'

'He was young, about twenty-six or something. I think they said he was a salesman.'

Salesman? Salesman? It's blank. 'Maybe I didn't talk to him.'

Adam shrugs. 'Maybe,' he says. 'Anyway, Hope, that's all I can tell you. That's all that happened.' He pauses. 'I wish I could help you more.'

'No, that's great. Thanks.'

'No probs.' He fires the engine and gets the car going before looking at me again. 'It was the most horrible day of my life,' he says quietly.

My answer is to touch his hand and he squeezes mine back.

Julie is a lucky girl.

Julie certainly doesn't feel lucky when we arrive back. She runs out to meet us, her mobile phone held aloft as if it's about to explode. 'Where were you?' she says, her voice quite panicky. 'Oh God, since you left, Adam, I've had about ten calls.'

'So?' Adam asks, amused. 'I haven't banned you from answering your mobile phone, wench.'

'My mother and father!' Julie hisses as the phone begins its *Jaws* theme tune. 'They've been ringing all morning.'

Since the row with her mother, Julie's phone had gone silent. Julie has pretended to be cool with it, but her reaction now proves what I'd suspected. She's still not fully over it.

'Would you not answer it?' I say. 'You can always hang up. And at least they're ringing you.'

Julie stares at the phone which has gone silent but then starts up again. 'They've probably thought up some new strategy.'

'Here, give it here.' Adam holds out his hand. When Julie gives him the phone, he presses the button to switch it off. 'Now.'

'You can't do that.' Julie presses it on again. 'Say it's an emergency?'

'Then answer the bloody thing,' Adam tousles her hair. 'The sooner you know, the sooner you can get on with things.'

'Oh God,' Julie dithers as it starts to ring again. This time it's her dad. I know because the ring tone is different. I think it's from *The Omen*. *The Omen* ceases after about ten seconds to be replaced by *Jaws*.

'I'll answer it,' I say, 'and if it sounds important I'll pass it to you, OK?'

'OK. Good idea.' Julie hands me her phone. 'Good, good, Hope.'

I take it. My own heart is pounding now. Just witnessing Julie's mother and father in action has made me scared of them. 'Hello?' I say cautiously into the receiver.

'Hello? Juliet?' God, the woman sounds frantic. 'Is that you, Juliet?'

'Eh, no, it's her friend, Hope.'

Julie gives me the thumbs-up.

'Is Juliet there?' Her voice breaks a little. 'Please put her on, it's important.'

'I'll just check,' I say, feeling awful. The woman is obviously upset. I turn to Julie, point at the phone and make a tearful face while mouthing silently, 'Crying.'

Julie flips her hand at me.

'Eh, I can't seem to see her. Can I give her a message? She should be in soon.'

'Oh, well,' her mother gulps at the other end. 'I don't like you having to tell her. It should be either her father or me.'

That sounds bad. 'Oh,' I say. 'Hang on, here she is now!'

I thrust the phone into Julie's hands but she resists. 'Julie, your mother has some news for you.'

Julie takes it from me slowly and stares at it before putting it to her ear.

Adam raises his eyes at me behind Julie's back but I just shrug in reply.

'Mum,' Julie says in this false bright sarcastic voice, 'what's the occasion?'

Then her face registers shock, she pales and sways and if it wasn't for Adam behind her she'd have fallen, I think. 'No!' she says, as if she's about to cry. 'When did you find out?'

Her mother answers.

'And no one knew?'

Another reply from down the line.

'But I only saw her a while ago and she said nothing.' Then Julie does a lot of uh-huhing and nodding before hanging up with promises to keep in touch.

'What happened?' I ask.

Julie turns to me and Adam with blank eyes. 'I can't believe it.'

'Ju?' Adam gently takes the phone from her and leads her inside. 'What is it?'

'Angela's just had a baby!' she whispers. 'And my mother only just found out now.'

'Angela, your sister?'

'Yeah.' She sounds dazed. 'I can't believe it. God, you think she'd tell us! In the end, her partner rang. Apparently her baby was born this morning, he's a month early, he's very small and sick.' Julie starts to cry. 'Oh the poor baby!' She looks in bewilderment at us. 'Imagine not letting us know.'

'Maybe she thought your mother would go mad.'

'She is going mad!' Julie shakes her head. 'She's hurt and upset and angry too.'

I say nothing.

'I'll have to ring her,' Julie says and picks up the phone. Then puts it down again. 'Oh, I don't know what to say, we haven't talked in months. And she's got so much to worry about now.'

'Well, maybe Angela will want to hear from you now,' Adam says, holding out the phone.

'We're not close. Maybe if our parents had been different we might have got on better.'

'Just deal with what is, Ju,' he says. 'Ring her – would you like her to ring you if things were the other way round?'

Slowly she takes the phone from him, 'Yeah. Yeah, if it was me, I'd like my family there.' She calls but hangs up as it starts to ring at the other end. 'Oh God, I was horrible to her when we met the last time.'

'That wasn't just your fault,' I remind her. 'You made the effort. Go on, ring her.' I bite my lip. 'Don't be like me.'

They both stare at me, but it galvanises Julie. She dials again. This time she allows it to be answered. 'Hi,' she says, 'this is Julie. Is Angela there?'

The person at the other end says something and Julie winces. Another deep breath. 'Angela, it's Julie. How are you? I believe you had, had a little baby? How is he?'

Angela seems to be talking back, so Adam and I leave the room and head out the door, not wanting to earwig on the conversation.

We're sitting in the long grass at the back of the house, enjoying the air skimming over our faces. We're trying to make conversation but both of us are keenly aware that Julie's phone call has ended and she still hasn't come out.

'I'll just go in and check on her,' Adam says, standing up. 'Make sure –'

'Hi.' Julie arrives out at that moment. We scan her face for news, but she looks surprisingly OK. 'Well, that was hard.'

'How'd it go?' Adam pats the grass between us and Julie sits down.

'OK.' She looks a little guilty. 'The baby is small but they reckon he'll be fine after a while.'

'Good.' I smile. 'You're an auntie.'

'Some auntie! I feel awful for not contacting her before now. D'you remember, Hope, when she met us in the shop that time?'

'Yeah.'

'And I said I was never going to talk to her again. Well, I wish I had now.'

'Hindsight is a great thing,' Adam mutters.

'The reason she reacted like that, she said, was that she'd only found out she was pregnant and was totally shocked. She said she kept putting off going to the doctor's because she was terrified of what would happen if Mum and Dad found out.'

'Jesus.'

'I just assumed it was me, you know. I assumed that she didn't want to talk to me. If I'd only rung her to find out why she was so distant. But I assumed it was me.'

'What else were you supposed to think?'

'I should have made the effort and then at least I could have a clear conscience now.'

I decide not to pursue it. She'll have to come to terms with that herself. Instead, I ask how Angela is.

'Worried about the baby more than anything. She says

she doesn't care what Mum and Dad think any more, that the baby is what matters.'

'Too right,' I nod.

'Plus,' Adam pinches her cheek affectionately, 'you messed up a lot more than she did, so she won't get into too much trouble.'

'Thank you!' Julie slaps his hand away, but she's smiling. 'Angela said she thought it was brilliant the way I stood up to Dad. She said Dad was going mad. She said how could she tell him she was pregnant after that bombshell.'

Adam and I smile at her.

'But everything is fine otherwise.'

I marvel at how they're both so scared of what their mother thinks. I'd never been scared of my mother. Maybe a bit of fear would have been a good thing, I don't know.

'I'd never have thought that she'd be afraid of them,' Julie muses, half to herself. 'She was the golden girl.'

'She was probably more afraid than you were, which is why she was the golden girl,' Adam says.

Julie and I look in surprise at him. 'Wow!' Julie teases, 'I'd never have put you down as a psychological whiz-kid, Williams!'

'I have many talents,' Adam says. 'As you know.'

'Oh God,' I stand up. 'The big green gooseberry is getting out of here.'

'Stop!' Julie, laughing, pulls me back down. 'You are not a gooseberry and you never will be.' She taps her phone. 'Anyway, I've promised to ring her every day to get a progress report.'

'You should.'

'And,' she looks at me a bit guiltily, 'I'm going to fly over next week to see my new nephew, which means both Adam

351

and I will be gone, is that OK? Will you be all right on your own?'

'I'll be perfect on my own,' I tell her. And at her doubtful look, I say, 'I can look after myself you know.'

'Of course you can,' she says, sounding as if she doesn't believe it for a minute. 'And you can always call on Logan, our friendly gorgeous neighbour if you need anything.'

'The way he's called in on us?'

'He's away this week, didn't you know?' Julie says. 'He got so much work offered to him the night of the hotel do that he's talking to people this week. Did you not know?'

'No, when did you find that out?' It's hard to disguise the delight I feel at the fact that he hasn't been avoiding me. THANK YOU, GOD!! And that's capitalised because that's how I feel.

'Oh yeah, you weren't there much after dinner on Saturday – we were talking to him then. He said he'd have to disappear for the week to sort all his new work out. He was looking for you actually, wasn't he, Adam?'

'Uh-huh.'

Now she tells me. 'Oh.'

'I said you probably went to bed or for a walk. But anyway, he's coming back next week, so he's there if you need him.'

'Right,' I try to say nonchalantly. 'But I'll probably be fine.'

36

OVER THE NEXT two days, I try to remember more about the accident. Adam and Julie try to help me by describing what I wore on the day. Well, Julie remembered that, Adam hadn't a clue. I'd worn a 'horrible pair of tracksuit bottoms and an old faded T-shirt'. Nothing they say jolts any memory at all and so I listen to the tape and listen to the tape and still nothing happens. I'm in the garden, listening to it for what must be the five-hundredth time when Julie taps me on the shoulder. I jump about a foot in the air and she starts to apologise. It's a legacy of the accident, one I'm sure that will go in time. I jump at anything at all unexpected. Anyway, Julie is grinning like a cat.

'Visitor for you,' she says.

'Where?'

'Out at the front door, he's being very polite, I must say.'

'Logan?'

'Yep.' She looks gleefully at me. 'He fancies you, he fancies you,' she sings in a low chant. She sounds about fourteen.

'Don't be silly.' I try not to sound too thrilled. Approaching from the back, I see Logan before he sees me. He's leaning against the porch, his hands shoved into the back pockets of his jeans. Julie hasn't followed me, for which I am grateful.

'Hi,' I say, my hands shielding my eyes from the sun. 'Were you looking for me?'

He turns and, hands still in his pockets, surveys me. 'Yes,' he answers, coming towards me, 'I was.'

'Why?'

He stands about two feet away and cracks a sort of smile. It's that of a cheeky kid who knows he's in the wrong but is hoping he won't get into trouble. 'I came,' he says, dragging out the 'came', 'to apologise for the appalling way I acted when you apologised to me. I was a total wanker.'

'Well, you won't find any argument here,' I say lightly. 'But, yes, unlike you, I will behave with dignity.' I make a big production of bowing my head. 'I accept your apology.'

He smiles a little. 'Don't make me feel honoured that you've done so or anything.'

'Oh,' I smile back, 'do you not feel honoured? I must do it again.' I bow my head. 'I said, scum, that I accept your apology.' He laughs a little. 'And,' I continue, 'I also want to say that I love your paintings and I especially love the one just behind the desk in the foyer.'

A small silence before he says, 'I was wondering if you'd notice it.' His voice has gone all quiet and sends delicious shivers up and down my spine.

'Of course I did.' My own voice quivers slightly. It's the one he sketched the day we went to the waterfall. 'You did it justice.'

He seems to be closer to me now. 'Thanks.'

We stare at each other. I desperately want him to come closer and I don't know what he wants. The moment seems to go on and on, zinging with possibility. He steps even closer to me and I catch my breath. I can smell him, a mix of earth and oils and soap. I want to touch him. To feel the roughness of his jacket and the softness of his skin. The silence stretches until I ache for him to touch me too. I can feel his breath on my face, I can see the faint hint of stubble on his upper lip. I close my eyes.

'It was Maria's fault.' The tension snaps like a bit of elastic band. I don't know if I imagined it.

'Was it?' I stammer out. My mind takes time to adjust. Had he been going to kiss me or not?

'Yeah.' He shrugs, flushes, turns slightly away from me. 'She was meant to come down to sort things and she was a complete cow. Maybe I was in bad form too, I don't know, but it was a disaster. And when you came along, I took it out on you. Well, if I'm honest, I thought there wasn't much to choose between you and Maria.'

'What?'

Logan shakes his head. 'Don't get me wrong. You're much nicer than her, it's just that the way you went on at me that night was the way she used to go on at me, only her horribleness was all the time: Get a job, Logan. Your pictures are crap, Logan. Let's move back to Dublin, Logan.'

I don't know what to say. Being much nicer than his much-hated ex is not exactly a compliment.

'Anyway, sorry again.'

'Like I said, no problem.'

He looks at me and I look at him but it's gone. The time was there and he ran from it. Maybe I would have done the same. So, I manage a smile and ask him if he'd like a coffee. He's about to say no but I can't bear him to leave so I walk on by him and beckon him inside.

Julie is going shopping for her new nephew. Adam has no choice but to drive her. I'm tempted to refuse to go. I can't think of anything more boring than shopping for a baby, but I do want to buy the baby something myself, so I agree. I haven't got a lot of money left in my bank account, but there's enough for a couple of nice babygros or something. Logan says he could do with some art stuff, so we go to his house first, he grabs some money and we head off. 'I don't know what I'll do when you go back,' Logan says, clipping his seat-belt. 'You've saved me a fortune in taxi fares this summer.'

'Don't you drive?' Julie asks.

'Can't afford to,' he says. 'I think now, with all the extra work, plus the exhibitions I've been promised, I'll be able to get a car.'

'Brilliant!' Julie grins.

'It'll take time to save,' Logan says. 'But I'll get there. I just have to be patient.'

'That'll be hard for you,' I joke.

'Yeah, it'll be as hard for me to be patient as it'll be for you to be nice.'

'Folks, folks,' Adam says mildly. 'Let's try to be civil to each other.'

'Leave them alone,' Julie belts him. 'They love it.'

I can't look at Logan. Instead, I stare out the window. I think he does the same on his side.

The city isn't as busy as normal. The summer is drawing to a close. The really hot weather has changed and it is now cooler and breezier. Ten more days and it's all over. Ten more days and I have to go back to London. I don't know if I want to. I don't know what I want to do. This summer hasn't been at all like I'd imagined. It's been better in that I've finally come to some sort of peace with myself and worse because it wasn't done by meeting my mother.

'Now,' Julie is all business. 'I'm going to go to all the shops with baby things. I'm an auntie,' she says to Logan.

'Congratulations.' He sounds amused.

'Do you want to come with me, Hope?'

'Yeah.' I know she's dying to ask my advice on bibs and bottles and dummies and all sorts of stuff I haven't a clue about.

'Goody.' She hugs herself, like a little kid would. 'Let's go. Meet you boys back at the car in three hours.'

'Three?' Adam is shocked. 'But what will I do for three hours?'

'And me?' Logan says. 'I only want to get a few canvases.'

'I dunno,' Julie shrugs. 'Think of something.'

And, her arm through mine, she waltzes me away.

I'm bored. It was great at first, admiring all the tiny trousers and shoes and cute little things but after about two hours they all run into each other. Julie seems determined to buy this baby everything. I think in a way she's trying to make it up with her sister too. We're in a baby toy shop at the moment and she's rummaging through every conceivable rattle ever invented. Winnie-the-Pooh ones, Mickey Mouse ones, Dora the Explorer ones. I'm looking at a little electronic keyboard for babies of three months. Three months, I mean, come on . . .

'Hey, what about this?' Julie holds a giant rattle under my nose and gives it a shake.

My first thought is that the child would want to be Hulk Hogan . . .

And I'm back there. It's the most enormous rattle I've ever seen. Scary looking too. The child would want to be Hulk Hogan to rattle it. 'Lovely.'

357

'Yeah, I thought so too. And it's not too boyish or girlish, so it's not?'

'Nope.'

As the plane takes off, he bends down and carefully puts the rattle away.

Just then the seatbelt sign, which had gone out, flicks back on again.

'Oh,' Joe rubs his hands together. 'Turbulence, I love a bit of turbulence.'

'Will passengers please return to their seats, we are experiencing some difficulties and may have to go back to Heathrow.'

Joe is still going on about turbulence, telling me of a trip he took once where the plane dropped hundreds of feet in seconds because it hit an air pocket.

'Did the captain say we're turning back?' I ask.

'Nah,' Joe shrugs. 'Why would he say that?'

I want to believe him but I'm sure that's what I heard. I take a quick glance up the aircraft and see the air hostesses belting themselves in. Is it my imagination or do they look a little freaked out?

'All passengers remain in your seats. Keep your seatbelts on. We are experiencing difficulties and are turning back to Heathrow.'

POP!

POP!

POP!

Each bang is louder than the last.

'Oh God!' someone shrieks. 'Look!'

Smoke is pouring out of the wing on my side of the plane. I can only stare at it. I can't even scream or shout, just gawk at it in horrible fascination. It's as if I'm out of myself, just not quite able to believe this is happening.

POP-POP-POP.

More smoke.

POP-POP-POP.

The sound is louder.

The lights go off and the plane plummets. It's dark inside and bright outside. Overhead baggage starts to smash and thump. Some of it falls out. The plane is lurching about wildly.

Joe turns to me. His brown eyes are scared. I can only imagine what mine must look like. 'It was nice to meet you,' he says.

'You too.' I think I might cry. 'Will you hold my hand?'

'Sure.' He grasps my hand in his and I notice that he's holding the other lady's hand too. She's still praying.

'If you survive,' he says then, 'will you find my wife and tell her I'm sorry – Mary Ryan in Baltimore, West Cork – will you do that?'

'Tell her that you're sorry?'

'Yeah. She'll know what I mean.' He has to shout as the plane is screeching now. The poor child behind is bawling her eyes out in terror. 'Will you do it?'

'I will.' The noise is unbelievable. I clasp his hand tighter. 'And will you find my mother and tell her I'm sorry – Helen Gardner, Dunport, Kerry?'

'Will do.'

We hold each other as the plane careers downwards.

And I wonder if I'll see my life flash before my eyes.

The plane screams and lands with a bounce on the runway. We're going too fast. Joe pulls me down and makes me put my head between my legs. He makes the woman on the other side do the same. The poor little girl behind is screaming as her mother tries to get her to keep still. Everywhere, luggage is still tumbling from lockers all around us. The screech of brakes outside rips through the plane. Smashing. Banging. Thumping. And then the plane starts to spin and spin, round and round and round. So fast, it's like being on a giant chairoplane. Weirdly, the world slows down. I see everything in super-slow motion. I see everything that happens.

Thump. Thump, thump goes the luggage.

Something large hits me on the head. I can't even feel the pain. Something else hits me. Joe yells out and pushes me over. Taking off his seatbelt, he covers me with his body.

I'm suffocating. He's telling me it'll be OK.

The spinning and screaming and sound of falling things seems to last an eternity. I can't breathe. Things are still falling on top of us.

Then there is silence.

There is a crowd around me. Julie is pale-faced, crying. 'Hope. Hope, are you OK?'

I sit up shakily. In the distance I hear the siren of an ambulance. I feel sick and weak and very scared.

'I think I had a flashback,' I say. My voice trembles, but I'm smiling a little too. I catch Julie's hand. 'Ju, I remember now. I remember everything.'

37

TIM VISITS ME in hospital the next day. I'm sitting up
in bed, impatient to go back to the cottage. I'm not
ill. In fact, I feel quite good. I remember now and somehow,
the memory is not half as scary as not knowing.

Tim tapes me telling my story and gives it to me to listen
to. All I want to do, however, is contact Mary Ryan and talk
to her. 'I promised him I would,' I say urgently, 'and I can't
let him down.'

'I understand that,' Tim nods, 'but you've got to be able
to cope with the accident yourself before you go explaining
it to someone else. Someone who has been horribly affected
by it.'

And of course, that makes sense, so I spend the whole
day in hospital, listening to the tape. It stresses me out, but
not as much as I'd expected. Not as much as talking about
Jamie. In fact, what amazes me is that I also remember
that I'd wanted him to say sorry to my mother for me. I
don't quite know how I feel about that. What had I been
thinking of?

Tim tells me that he'll see me in four days, and that if
I'm up to it, he'll give me permission to talk to Mary Ryan.
He'll go through what I should say. I'm not out of the woods
yet, he says sternly. I've a long way to go. But I think I'm

coping a lot better. Don't get me wrong, I'll probably never go on a plane again, but I can talk about being on one and almost dying. I think I can do that.

Adam and Julie take me home later on.

'I'll need post-traumatic stress counselling with what you've put me through,' Julie jokes as I climb into the car. 'God, all I did was shake a rattle and you freaked out.'

'Too much information.' I hold up my hands to ward her words off. That's another thing I'll never do – go into that shop again. Apparently I'd frightened everyone. People had run out in panic, others had frozen to the spot. Oh God, the embarrassment.

'So what now,' Adam asks. 'Are you finished with counsellors and stuff?'

'No, I have to go to someone when I get back to London. Tim's recommending a few people to me.'

'I'd love to go to counselling,' Julie announces. 'I think it must be great to understand yourself.'

'Julie, if they don't understand the whole three persons in one God concept, they're hardly likely to understand you,' Adam snorts.

I laugh at her indignant expression. Three months ago, Adam would probably not have said that to her. But if things can change in the blink of an eye, things can certainly change in three months.

It's three days later. Less than a week before we go home. I'm sitting on my own, looking out at the blue sea. The sun is setting and a blood red path has cut it right through the middle. Adam is inside, getting ready to fly out the next day for his interview. He's quietly hopeful, he says. Julie is on the same flight, only she's decided that she's leaving for good. Her sister and new nephew are expecting her. She's a bit nervous about meeting Angela but they've talked at length on the phone, discussing how they both feel about their parents and I think it'll be fine. Anyway, Julie's adoration of the baby and her piles of presents will more than make up for any awkwardness.

Adam is coming back to bring me and his car home on the ferry but I'll be on my own for six days in the cottage. I don't know if I'll like it. As I'm sitting there, I sense someone looking at me. I see Logan, standing a field away, and when I look he raises his hand in greeting and begins to stride towards me. I smile at him as he sits down.

'How's things?'

'Good.'

'Good.'

There's silence for a moment.

'If you need someone to stay with you when they're away, just ask,' he says. A week ago, I would have read all sorts of signs into that, but now, after what happened in the garden, I know Logan is not interested in a relationship.

'Thanks.'

'I mean that, OK?' He nudges me gently with his elbow.

'I know,' I smile. Then, 'I've to go to my counsellor tomorrow to see if he thinks I'll be OK to visit this Mary Ryan in Baltimore. I'll need help tracing her and, well, I'll need someone to go with me to see her.'

'Mary Ryan?'

'Yeah.' I stare at the ground. 'She's the wife of the man that saved my life on the plane and I have a message for her from him. Will you bring me? Adam's car will be there.'

Tim hasn't exactly given me the all-clear, but I think he

will. And if he tells me it's fine, then I'm going to have to find out where the woman lives. I'm not leaving it until Adam gets back. I've left it too long already.

'Consider it done.' Logan isn't looking at me. He's staring at the sea too. 'Will you miss this place when you go?' he asks.

'I won't know till I go,' I answer.

'If you miss it will you come back?'

I glance at him. He's still not looking at me.

'If someone misses something, they always come back,' I say.

He nods. 'I suppose so.'

We leave it at that.

38

'WELL, HOPE,' TIM sits back in his chair and regards me. 'You certainly don't seem as anxious as you were before when you talked about the accident.'

I had just described the whole thing to him in the most amazing detail and I only had to stop once because my anxiety level had risen to an eight. I know that if I listen to the tape in the next couple of days I'll be fine about it. Of course, I'd still be upset, but not so bad that I want to block out the whole thing or be unable to talk. It's contacting Mary Ryan that's important to me now. It's a small way to make up for the man who saved my life.

'So?' I lean across the desk. 'Can I try and find Mary now?'

He nods slowly. 'Listen to the tape, Hope. Listen to it well over the next couple of days and I'd say by Thursday, you'll be ready.'

'I will,' I promise. 'Thanks, Tim.'

'Don't thank me,' he says. 'You did all the work.'

I hop up out of my seat. Now that I've been given permission to talk to Mary, I want to get on with the job of finding out who she is. 'Can I go now?'

'Go on.' He flaps me away with a grin.

'Oh, by the way,' I fumble in the pocket of my jacket and pull out a gift. 'It's only small, but I thought you might like it.' I hand it over to him. 'It's a thank-you for giving me my life back.'

Tim has blushed, I'm delighted to see. 'Oh,' he seems genuinely touched. 'Thank you, Hope. But I didn't give you your life back, I'm not that great. You did the work yourself, I only pointed you in the right direction.'

'Oh spare me the cliché,' I groan, 'I'm sick of them.'

He laughs and pulls at the wrapping paper. Then he laughs some more. I've given him a brand new Dictaphone and some spare batteries. 'I think I wore your other one out,' I explain. 'And here.' I hand him a card and a box of chocolates. 'Enjoy.'

'I did enjoy you, Hope,' he smiles at me. 'Now good luck with the rest of your life.'

We shake hands and I know he's one person I really will miss.

Adam drives me back to the cottage armed with the Cork telephone directory. There hadn't been one in the house and so we'd asked Greg in the pub for a lend of his. I'd already been on to the airline but, unless I requested it in writing, there was no way they'd release Joe's home address to me. And that, in my opinion would take far too long.

So, telephone book at the ready, I'm going to do some detective work. Unfortunately Adam and Julie have to leave this afternoon, so they can't help me, but Logan has promised to come down and lend a hand.

The minute we pull up outside the cottage, Julie runs to meet the car. 'Well?' she asks as I get out.

'Yeah, I'm allowed to talk to her.'

'Great! I knew you would be. Oh, I wish I could still be here.'

'No you don't.' I punch her lightly on the arm. 'You're only dying to see that little nephew of yours.'

'Aw yeah, I am too.' She whips out her mobile and shoves it in front of my face. 'That's him, isn't he gorgeous?'

I can just about make out a very blurry picture of a tiny blue bundle. I take it from her and peer at it before handing it back. 'He is the cutest baby ever!'

'Andrew, that's what they're calling him. It's after my dad. I think it's to sweeten him up.'

'And has it?'

Julie giggles, 'I think so. They're buying him his pram.' Then she stops and looks serious. 'Aw Hope, they're devastated. I almost feel sorry for them. They just can't believe Angela never told them. They can't believe how scared she was.'

'That's no harm though, is it?'

'No.' She shakes her head. 'Might do them good.'

The taxi to take Julie and Adam to the airport pulls into the driveway and stops any more conversation.

Adam goes inside to get the cases, which he then hefts into the boot of the taxi.

'All ready,' Adam calls. 'Come on Ju, let's go.'

Julie turns to me. 'Time to go,' she says, a little breathlessly.

I can't believe it. Our holiday is drawing to an end. Julie won't be back at all. The next time I see her will be in London. 'I'll miss you,' I say. 'Give that baby a kiss for me.'

'Oh, I will.' She enfolds me in a hug. 'Take care. And make sure Logan minds you, especially when you go to see Mary.'

'I have to find her first.'

'Oh, you will.'

We hug for ages. It doesn't feel at all awkward. Eventually I let her go and we regard each other. 'It's been a blast,' she says. 'Every little thing, even horrible Nelson.'

'It has,' I nod. 'I'm so glad I wasn't in Boston on my own.'

The three of us gaze at each other, all of us thinking the same thing, I hope. That it was a much better holiday, the three of us together.

'Oh Adam, just let's go or I will cry.' Julie blinks hard and hops into the car.

'See ya, Hopeless,' Adam says. 'Back in five days, OK?'

'See you then and good luck with the job.'

We hug then too.

Both of us have come such a long way.

Logan is as good as his word. He arrives about thirty minutes later and can't believe that they've already left. 'I never got a chance to say goodbye to Julie,' he moans as he sits down opposite me at the kitchen table. I've the phone book open at the 'Ryan' page and all the Joe and Mary Ryans marked out.

'You'll see her again,' I say absently, wondering who to call first.

'How?' Logan peers at me. 'Unless you're all coming back next year?'

And it hits me suddenly, we might never see Logan again. Despite my guilty feelings, I haven't rung my mother. I wonder if I ever will. Phoning her is all I might do, so I might never venture here again. It seems too hard to grasp that this man opposite with his dark, sullen but incredibly sexy manner and cute grin, might be out of my life in a few short days. An episode in my life. My heart keeps thinking that he should be so much more but my head is saying no.

'Well,' Logan says and he sounds hopeful, 'are you coming back?'

'I don't know,' I laugh it off. 'So,' I take the book and push it towards him, 'what do you suggest we do?'

Logan studies it. 'Well, I suppose the best thing is to ring all the Joe Ryans and ask for Mary and if we get one, we'll just hang up.'

'Hang up?'

'Well, what else do you suggest?'

He has a point. At least if we had an address, we could go there. There was no easy way of saying over the phone who we were. No way at all, in fact.

'OK,' I said. 'There are five Joe Ryans. Will I go first?'

'I can ring them if you want,' Logan says. 'Don't sweat it. You just take it easy.'

I want to hug him for that. 'Thanks, Logan.'

He winks at me and gastric gymnastics start in my belly.

He takes out his mobile and dials. A few seconds later a tinny voice somewhere in west Cork answers. 'Hey,' Logan says, 'how's it going? I'm looking to speak to Mary Ryan?'

The person at the other end mumbles something and Logan says, 'Sorry about that.' He hangs up and shakes his head. 'One down.'

The next call proves fruitless, as does the third. The fourth, to our delight, results in a Mary Ryan and he gives me the thumbs-up. I write down the address. 'I'll ring the last one,' he says, 'just to be sure.' He dials. It's answered almost immediately. 'Hey, can I speak to Mary Ryan please?'

And he hangs up.

'Two Mary Ryans.' He looks at me, half in amusement,

half in exasperation. 'Why couldn't your rescuer have a more unusual name?'

I groan as I realise I have no idea what to do now. 'How do we find out which one it is?'

Logan shrugs. 'I don't know. We can hardly ask to speak to Joe, can we, that'd be a bit upsetting.'

'Yeah.'

We sit and stare at each other in silence; my hands are cupped about my chin, elbows on the table while Logan lies sprawled back on his chair, tapping his foot as he tries to think.

'We could pretend we're from the hospital and ask about the baby,' I suggest. 'You know, how is your baby feeding or something?'

'And what if something has happened to the baby?'

'Shit!'

More thinking. More silence. 'What would an ace detective do?' Logan asks speculatively.

'Probably spy on both of them,' I mutter. 'See who's a more likely candidate.'

'Yeah!' He grins at me. 'Genius! That's what we'll do. We'll drive down to Cork, park a little away from their houses and see who looks more like the Mary Ryan we want.'

'Oh, that's a good idea. And you wouldn't mind?'

'No, Hope,' he says, earnestly, 'I wouldn't mind.'

With that decided, Logan takes out a map and plots out our journey while I make us some sandwiches. I put a plate in front of him and without looking up, he pats the seat beside him and I sit down. 'See –' his long finger traces a path from Kerry to the outskirts of Cork, 'this looks like the shortest way. What do you think?'

'I think I haven't a clue,' I admit, taking a bite out of my sandwich. I push the plate nearer him. 'Here, eat up, you must be starving.'

We munch contentedly, enjoying the silence. We seem to be able to sit with each other and not talk. He folds up the map and shoves it into his jacket pocket. 'You eat really weird,' he remarks, 'you sort of chew a lot.'

'Thanks!'

'My sister does that.'

It's only the second time he's volunteered any information about his family. 'You have a sister,' I slag, 'and she hasn't killed you!'

He smirks. 'I'll have you know I have four sisters and they all love me. I'm the youngest.'

'Oh God, I should have known. No wonder you have a superiority complex.'

'It's not a complex, it's actually very simple. I am superior.'

'Ha di ha.'

'And you?'

'I had a brother. Younger. He died.' I find I can tell him without choking up the way I used to.

'Oh, that's hard.'

'Yep.' I chew a bit more, then become conscious of my chewing. 'He was twelve,' I add. And before I know it, I'm telling Logan everything. I don't mean I'm doing it in a needy way or a self-absorbed way, I'm just telling him and it all seems so simple and I wonder why I never told anyone before this summer.

'Christ,' Logan says when I finish. 'That was rough.' He's cross-legged on the floor; how we ended up sitting on the floor I have no idea. 'I thought it was bad when my folks died.'

'Your parents are dead?'

'Well, my mother died first, she was sick for ages. And then, about six months later, my dad just didn't feel well and went to bed.' He pauses. 'I found him the next day, he just died some time in the night.'

'Oh, that's terrible.'

Logan shrugs. 'Yeah, it was. But he was so broke up after my mother died, I reckon he would have just faded away without her anyway. It was better the way it happened.'

I nod. I can understand that. 'Yeah, I think that's what happened to my mother, she never got over Dad.' A sudden image of the four of us pops into my head. We're on a beach. Me, Jamie and Dad are splashing about in the water and my mother is telling us sternly not to splash her, that she's going to immerse herself in the water in her own time. 'Own time me arse,' Dad laughs and with one lunge, he has picked her up and ducked her under the freezing water. Jamie and I laughed and laughed . . .

'It was after that happened that I started seeing Maria,' Logan says, interrupting my train of thought. 'I think I just wanted someone to be with.' He gives a self-deprecating laugh. 'Didn't realise I'd just chosen the bride of Frankenstein.'

'Stop!' His expression makes me giggle.

'Naw, I was as bad. We were about as happy together as two cows in an abattoir.'

'Stop!'

He laughs. 'Never thought I'd joke about it,' he says and takes another sandwich. 'You have a good effect on me, Hope.'

'That's not what you said three months ago.'

'I was a fool three months ago.'

'An arrogant fool.'

'Uh-huh,' he agrees good-naturedly. 'Tell you what, though, the whole Maria experience has frightened me big time.'

'Aw, poor you.'

'I will not be going there again for a while.'

I try to keep the smile on my face. 'Probably a wise decision.'

'Well, not unless the girl is very special and loves me as much as my sisters do.'

'Logan,' I shove him gently, 'you will remain alone for the rest of your natural days.'

His answer is one of his gorgeous smiles.

I am really going to miss him too.

39

LOGAN SITS UNEASILY behind the wheel of Adam's car. He spends some time checking what all the buttons and switches do. Then, taking a deep breath, he turns the key in the ignition and the engine roars into life. The car jerks forward then cuts out.

'Way to go,' I joke.

Logan quirks his eyebrow and dangles the keys in front of my face. 'Would you like to drive? Would you?'

'Sorry,' I shrug, grinning.

'Then button that –' he points to his mouth, turns from me and tries again. This time the car surges away. And cuts out. After about five more attempts he gets the hang of it and soon we're winding our way towards the village. I feel a little sick. Tim had offered to come with me, which was pretty decent, but I'd told him I'd be fine. Now that I'm actually on my way, I'm not so sure.

'So, what's the story with your work now?' I ask Logan, once we're well clear of Dunport. 'The hotel opening obviously got you noticed.'

'Yep.' Logan nods. He doesn't talk much while driving. In fact, I don't think he's a very good driver: the car keeps surging forward one minute and stalling and juddering the next. He's staring out the windscreen now with the fierce concentration one might use when dissecting a brain. 'A lot of gallery owners seemed to be there. Your Jack Dunleavy is very well connected.'

'He's not my Jack.'

'Whatever. Oh shit!' He slams the brakes, puts on the hazard lights and attempts a U-turn. 'Wrong bloody way.'

I wince as a chorus of horn-blowing begins.

'Fuck off,' Logan mutters under his breath.

'Just keep going,' I tell him, as calmly as I can. 'We'll find a turn and go back.'

'Yeah, maybe that would be best.' He jams the gears and the car screeches but it gets into the flow of traffic again. Logan waves an apology at the driver behind, who looks like he can't believe what he just saw.

'Anyway,' Logan continues, as if nothing major had occurred, 'I've been offered three galleries, two in Dublin and one down here. They'll take the sculptures too, which is good. And I've two more commissions.'

'Brilliant.'

'Yep, I'm pleased.'

'I thought you didn't like commissions?'

He thinks for a second and says, 'Put it like this: do you mind earning money?'

'Nope.'

'Neither do I.' We come to a roundabout and after some careful negotiation, we're back on the right road. 'I used to be a bit sniffy about commissions all right –' he flicks a glance at me. 'But hell, I can't bloody rent all my life and the money from the sale of the house in Dublin plus what I earn on commissions should get me a place here. I hope to buy the cottage I'm in at the moment.'

'That'd be a great place to live, right on the mountain like that.'

'Yeah, I think so.'

It must be nice, I think, to know exactly where you want to belong.

We arrive in Baltimore a good while later. The minute I see the road sign advertising the fact that we've arrived, I want to tell Logan to turn back. But of course, I can't. I close my eyes and take deep breaths, trying to calm myself down.

'Now . . .' Logan pulls in and consults his map. It's in bits from him constantly looking at it and checking our way. He has a hopeless sense of direction too, I've discovered. 'The first Mary lives –' he peers at it for ages – 'there somewhere.' He jabs his finger at the name of the road we found in the phone book. 'So, let's go.'

It takes about thirty minutes longer than it should because Logan goes up a one-way street and blocks all the traffic for ages. Eventually he has to reverse and I know Adam would have a heart attack if he'd seen how close Logan came to scratching his highly polished car.

'I hate driving,' Logan admits as everyone on the road gawks at us. 'Especially when I haven't a clue about a place.' He acknowledges the horn-blowing and rude hand gestures from his fellow drivers with an apologetic wave.

I wisely remain silent.

We find ourselves in a cul-de-sac of eight houses arranged in a horseshoe around a tiny green. Iron gates lead up small concrete paths to houses of thick walls with net curtains hanging in the windows. Some inner instinct tells me that this is not the place but nevertheless, I have to check it out.

'I don't think this will be the right Mary,' Logan surprises me by saying. 'These houses just seem too old for the guy you described. Like I'd imagine anyone who lived here would have to be hitting ninety.'

As if we've been overheard, an old man emerges from the house two doors away from the one we're interested in and begins walking up the road towards us.

'Hang on a sec,' Logan says and he bounds out of the car and up to the old man.

After a lot of nodding and pointing and shrugging between the two Logan hops back into the car again and with a bip of his horn takes off, waving to the man as he does so.

'Bingo!' he says, smiling at me. 'That old guy knew every single person in the place. The Mary Ryan that lives in this estate is eighty, she hasn't had a baby in about forty years, her husband is still alive but he's bedridden. Our Mary Ryan, however,' he pauses for dramatic effect and my heart wallops in my chest and I suddenly feel very sick indeed, 'lives two miles from here and just had a baby boy a month ago.'

I can't even speak. The reality of meeting this woman is beginning to dawn on me. Once again, I have nothing prepared, beyond a certain point.

'You OK?' Logan looks at me in concern.

'Yeah. I'll be fine.' I smile briefly. 'You've been great. How did you find out? Did you just come straight out with it?'

'More or less. I just asked him if Mary Ryan lived around. Her husband was killed in a plane crash, I said, and you know yourself, if people didn't know her before, they'd certainly know her now. He gave me directions, I hope I can remember them.'

* * *

He does remember and ten minutes later, we arrive outside a bungalow, set deep into the hillside above the fishing village. It needs the grass cut and a lick of paint but otherwise it's like a small piece of heaven. We drive up the short driveway and Logan pulls the car to a stop outside the front door. He switches the engine off and turns to me. 'You OK from here?'

'Will you come in with me?' I'm terrified. I don't know why. I want him with me. I can't imagine doing it without him.

'Sure.' He looks reassuringly at me before getting out. Together we walk to the blue-painted door. Putting his hand on my shoulder, his eyes meet mine. 'You'll be fine. I couldn't think of a better person to turn up on my doorstep.'

I grin shakily, take a deep breath, fling a silent desperate prayer to Joe, wherever he is, and press the bell.

It takes a couple of minutes before we hear movement inside. The door is opened by a woman, older than I'd been expecting. She's dressed quite smartly in blue trousers and a cream T-shirt. Her hair is a mixture of grey and black and cut quite short. She peers at us; I reckon she normally wears glasses. 'Yes?' Her accent is very thick.

'Eh, Mary?' I ask, taken aback, wondering if we've got the wrong address again.

'No, I'm Rosemary. Mary's inside with the baby.'

'Well, would it be possible for us to see her?'

The woman shuffles from foot to foot. 'She's not really up to having visitors at the moment. She's had a very bad few months and she's just had a baby.'

'I, eh . . .' I lick my lips and turn to Logan, who nods encouragingly. 'Well, I know about her husband,' I stammer out.

The woman nods. 'Then you'll understand why –'

'I was with Joe on the plane.'

The woman reels back a little to look at me. Her face pales. 'Joe?' Her voice softens as her eyes fill with tears. 'My Joe?'

'Joe Ryan.'

'He was my son. Mary's husband.' She pulls the door wider. 'You'd better come in, so. Mary!'

We're ushered into a big kitchen where a woman in a dressing gown is sitting beside a Kosangas heater. Her hair straggles down in front of her face and she's clutching a big mug of tea in both hands. A baby is sleeping in a Moses basket at her feet.

'Oh, what a lovely baby,' I automatically say.

Mary takes a sip of her tea and regards us. 'Who are you?' I know her dead voice. I know that blank expression. I feel horribly sorry for the tiny baby in the basket. And for the woman sitting beside it.

'This girl says she was on the plane with Joe,' Rosemary says gently. She pulls a few papers from a sofa and nods for us to sit down. Logan sits beside me. I reach for his hand and he holds mine tight.

'Hi, Mary,' I manage weakly.

Mary lifts her head up slowly. She's so pretty, I think. And so young. 'You saw Joe?' Her voice is a whisper.

'He sat beside me,' I answer. I think I might cry and I don't want to. 'We talked.'

'That was Joe,' Mary says, nodding, almost to herself. 'He talked to everyone.'

I'm about to tell her that he saved my life, when she asks, 'What did you talk about?'

'Oh,' I try to remember, 'we talked about his job and I

379

told him I hadn't got a job. He laughed at that.' I bite my lip. 'Eh, we talked about his ironing boards.'

To my surprise, both women chuckle gently. 'He loved those ironing boards,' his mother says. 'They iron on both sides. They were his baby, weren't they, Mary?'

'Yes.' She looks at me, a small smile hovering about her lips. 'Joe was determined they were going to be the next big thing.' A small lull before she says quietly, though bitterly, 'He had so many plans, so many ideas for our life.'

'Hey, hey.' Rosemary bends down to wrap her arms about her. 'Stop now. Come on. He had a great life.' She looks at us. 'That was the only thing that kept us going, that *has* kept us going – that Joe lived life. I mean, he really lived. He'd travelled, he was successful, he did everything he wanted to do, didn't he?'

Mary just nods. A solitary tear drips down her face and plops into her tea.

'He saved my life,' I blurt out, not at all in the way I was intending. 'When the plane was going down, he threw his body over mine and saved my life.'

Both women are silent, regarding me. Mary's hands grow white on the mug.

'I'm sorry he died because of me,' I say on a sob, 'I really am.'

'Hey,' Logan wraps his arm about my shoulder. 'Hey, Hope, come on now.' He gently kisses my cheek and wipes a tear away with his thumb. 'Don't,' he says, looking right at me. 'Don't.'

'So you're Hope,' Mary says quietly. 'I read about you in the paper. I wondered who you were.'

'Well, now you know,' I respond softly.

'Don't be sorry,' Mary says. 'It wasn't your fault.'

'I know but –'

'If he saved your life, just value it.' She is quiet but firm. In the Moses basket, her little baby stirs.

'I value it, every day.'

She nods, her eyes never leaving mine. 'That's good then.'

'I've been in Kerry, recovering,' I explain, after a small silence. I swallow hard. 'And, well, I've something else to say and I'm sorry that it's only now I'm saying it, but I had trouble remembering the accident until recently.' Logan takes his arm from around me, but keeps hold of my hand. I can feel his steady gaze on me and it helps.

'What else?' Rosemary asks, almost fearfully.

'As the plane was going down, he asked me to tell you something, Mary.'

'He did?' She hunches forward in her chair and I'm afraid she'll crush her mug between her two hands. 'What?'

Rosemary lays a hand on her shoulder.

'He said –' I take a deep breath. This is the hardest thing I've ever done – 'he said "tell Mary I'm sorry". He said you'd understand.'

Her eyes widen for a second and then her face crumples up and she stifles a sob. 'He said that?' She leans further forward. 'He really did?'

'He did.'

'Oh God. Oh God.' And she starts to cry. Huge, heaving sobs that shake her body. Her tea slops out but she hardly notices.

Gently Rosemary takes the mug from her and places it on the table. In the basket the baby starts to cry.

I look at Logan. Jesus, what have I done? He looks at me as if to say that there was nothing else I could have done.

His hand tightens around mine. 'Sorry if I've upset you,' I stammer out.

'No,' Mary shakes her head. 'No, it's good. I'm glad.' She wipes her hand across her face, ridding it of tears. 'Joe had our lives all planned out,' she says shakily. 'Hush, hush,' she bends over and picks up her baby. Holding him close, she says again, 'He had our lives all planned out.'

'Mary, you don't have to explain. Joe just told me to give you that message.'

'You've come all this way,' she says, 'you deserve to know. And besides, I want you to know. He saved your life.'

'Yes, he did.'

She smiles at me and continues softly as she rocks her baby, 'Joe had big dreams for us, big dreams for his ironing board, his house, our lives. He had such energy and fun and he made me laugh a lot.' She pauses and strokes the tiny head of her son, looking at him now, instead of me. 'But he never figured on kids,' she sniffs. 'Not until we were on our feet. But this little guy,' a gentle kiss on his forehead, 'well, he didn't want to fit in with any plans, sure you didn't? When I got pregnant I didn't tell Joe for about four months.'

Rosemary silently pours the water into the teapot and swirls it about.

'And, so, when eventually I told him, he went off the deep end. Said we couldn't afford it – we had a big row the day he left on that plane.' She bites her lip. 'Just as he left to go to Departures, he said goodbye and, well, I didn't answer him. I mean, he rang me when he was in London, but it was all so strained. And I never saw him again.'

Her voice breaks.

'We all do those things,' Rosemary murmurs as she hands us each a mug of tea. 'It's just human nature.'

'He was excited about the baby when I met him,' I say. 'He, well, he'd even bought it a present.'

'He had?'

I cross over to her and hand her the baby bag I'd brought in with me. 'This is the same rattle as the one he'd bought.'

She balances the baby in one arm and peers into the bag. 'He bought a rattle?' She smiles as I take the rattle out of the bag and hand it to her. 'Oh Rosemary, look. Isn't it just like Joe to buy the biggest rattle he can find?'

Rosemary laughs, takes the rattle and shakes it. It produces a very weird sound.

'I guess he was expecting Hulk Hogan for a son.' I smile too.

'See what your daddy bought,' Mary whispers to her son, pointing at Rosemary as she rattles it in front of him.

'I told you he'd come around,' Rosemary says.

They both peer at the baby, Rosemary rattling and both of them making soft cooing sounds. Then Mary looks up. 'Did Joe say anything else?'

I tell her about him not being able to find his hotel and driving around for ages in a taxi looking for it.

'That was Joe,' she laughs. The word 'was' seems to catch her and she swallows. 'I don't know how I'll survive without him. Babies are hard work and I miss him every day.'

Rosemary looks at me hopelessly over her head. 'You'll cope,' she says. 'I know you will.'

'My dad died when I was six,' I say. 'He died and left my mother on her own.'

'Really?' Mary looks at me with a sudden hope in her face.

'Yeah. I was six and my baby brother was two and he was mentally disabled. Like, there was a lot you had to do for him and he was a lot of work for my mother.'

'And how did she manage?'

I gulp hard and go for what I know now is the truth. 'She did the best she could.'

'That's all anyone can do.' Rosemary nods, kneeling down in front of Mary and giving the rattle another shake. What a lovely mother-in-law, I think.

'It wasn't perfect,' I continue, 'but she did her best. And I'm here now. And I survived.'

'Yeah.' Mary stares at her unblinking, solemn-looking baby, its little fists curled up and cute blue eyes staring back at his mother. 'I named him Joe,' she says to me. 'After his daddy.'

I smile and touch the baby's face. 'Hello, Joe. Your mammy is going to be great.'

Mary smiles gratefully up at me.

I'm so glad I've come and I send silent thanks to Joe, wherever he is. Without realising it, he's just saved my life for the second time.

40

'ARE YOU SURE you want to?' Logan asks.

We're in a small coffee shop, about an hour from Dunport. Logan is starving and despite the fact that I'm in a hurry to do what I know I should have done a long time ago, I couldn't deny the poor guy something to eat. He is half-way through a fry and chips and has just ordered dessert.

'I'm sure.' All I have in front of me is a cup of coffee and a cake and I can't even eat the cake, though it's my favourite, a cream doughnut.

'You've had quite a stressful day already,' he says, forking about three chips into his mouth. 'I'll bring you tomorrow, if you'd prefer.'

'Logan, today was the best day I've had since the accident.'

He looks incredulously at me. I know my eyes are red and puffy, I know I'm so tired from meeting Mary, and yet, today has been such a relief.

'Honest.' I reach across the table and touch his hand. 'Thanks.'

He entwines my fingers with his and both of us look at where his long fingers cross over with mine. I am suddenly incredibly turned on, Jesus, this guy presses all my buttons. I lift my eyes to his face, but he's still staring at our joined

385

hands. Slowly his inscrutable eyes look up. 'OK,' he nods slowly. 'Anything.'

And he lets my hand go and continues eating as if nothing just happened.

We arrive outside my mother's house and all is as it was before. The house looks clean enough, the garden is still overgrown but with a lot of brown grass due to the hot weather. The brass bell on the front door is gleaming, which is a surprise.

'So,' Logan glances at the house and then at me, 'this is where you're from.'

'This is it.'

'Nice place.'

'It's OK. Not as nice as living up the mountain, though.' I stare at my mother's house through the car window.

'And this – you want to do it on your own?'

'This – I have to do on my own.'

'OK.' He taps the steering wheel, 'I'll be back in an hour. If you're not here, waiting outside, I'll hang on for you.'

'Logan, I don't know how to thank you.'

'Oh, I'll think of something, don't worry.' He winks at me. 'Go on.'

'OK, see you.' I climb out and slam the door closed behind me.

Logan rolls down the window. 'And for what it's worth, Hope, you're doing the right thing. I'd give anything to have my mother again.' With those words, which bring tears to my eyes, he's gone.

I turn to face the house, feeling differently towards it than I had a couple of months ago. The tension inside me has gone, replaced by a sort of acceptance. I can't control events, I know that now. But I can control my response to them and what I had done to my mother, though it had seemed right at the time, was wrong.

It starts to rain as I make my way up the path. I feel a little sick and nervous, but hopeful too. I want to see her, I want to explain stuff to her, I want to have a mother again, even one that isn't perfect. And maybe she might want a less than perfect daughter again too.

I reach the front door and my hand is poised over the doorbell when I hear voices coming up the hallway from inside. Oh God, it's bloody Amanda Coonan. I don't want her to see me here. I don't need her judging me. The words she'd said to me the night of the hotel ball still have the ability to sting me with their truth. I look around for somewhere to hide. The only place is behind the big tree in the centre of the garden. I'll have to hope I'm thin enough to be hidden by the trunk. I make a dash for it and only get there as the door opens.

'See you, Mrs Gardner,' Amanda says cheerily.

Mrs Gardner? How babyish. Still, I'd probably call her mother Mrs Coonan.

'I'll order in those flowers for you,' my mother says. She doesn't sound like my mother, I think wonderingly. She sounds confident and in control. 'You'll have the nicest flowers of any bride.'

Amanda laughs. Then stops and I have the uneasy feeling she's spotted me. 'Hello?' she calls out, confirming my suspicions. 'Who's behind that tree?'

I stay very still.

'Behind the tree?' My mother sounds puzzled. 'I can't see anyone.'

'There is definitely someone there,' Amanda says. 'Look, you can see the front of their trainers. Come out, whoever you are.'

Wow, she's brave, I think with a grudging admiration.

'Out!' she shouts again. 'Are you some kind of pervert?'

Shit, she's coming closer. I close my eyes, hoping somehow that it'll make me invisible. Then realise it won't. 'It's me,' I stand out and glare at her. 'I was just looking at the tree.'

To say they look stunned would be a gross understatement.

'Do you like trees?' Amanda asks. She tries to make it sound as if hiding behind a tree in my mother's garden is perfectly normal. I suppose that's nice of her. She looks so good, all dressed to perfection, and she makes me painfully aware of my poorly co-ordinated outfit. Still, I bet I'm a lot more comfortable than she is.

'Yes, as a matter of fact I do.' I sound defensive and want to kick myself.

'Hope always had a thing for trees,' my mother says quickly. 'Didn't you?'

She's on my side. Unexpected tears spring to my eyes. Even after all this time and all that's happened, she's on my side and telling lies for me. I take a second to absorb this and to steady myself. I focus my attention on her and she nods slightly, as if encouraging me to go along with her. 'I'm here because I came to talk to you,' I say, gulping a little as I go for the truth. 'And when I heard you both coming out, I got cold feet and hid. I wasn't looking at the tree.'

'Oh,' Amanda smiles at me and I see the kindness in her eyes. And the fact that it's not her fault she looks so snooty. 'Well, I was just leaving, so I'll say goodbye, Mrs Gardner.'

'Yes, goodbye Amanda,' my mother says absently. 'Talk to you in a couple of days.'

Amanda leaves without looking back and my mother and I face each other across a swath of dried-up grass with the rain falling lightly on our faces.

The silence seems to last for ever.

'Will you come in, Hope,' my mother says at last, sounding unsure.

'Yes. I'd like that.'

She smiles at me shyly before turning around and leading the way. I follow her across the grass, wiping my feet on the doormat as I go into the hall, and from there we move into the kitchen. Everything is clean and tidy and in its place. This is the home of a woman in control of her life. When she reaches the centre of the kitchen, she turns and faces me. Her earrings jangle and flash in the light coming from the window. I'm about three feet from her. 'I'm so glad to see you,' she says earnestly.

How can she be glad when I was so horrible to her?

'I'm so glad to see you too.'

I don't know how it happens, but suddenly we're in each other's arms and for the first time in years, I feel a sense of home, of belonging, of being safe. I never want to let go. She smells of flowers and earth and grass.

'I'm sorry, Mammy,' I gulp out, not having been aware of what I was going to say until right that minute. 'Sorry for leaving you, sorry for not writing, sorry for not understanding how hard you had it and for being so difficult.'

She relaxes her grip and pulls herself back to look at me. Her hands are still on my shoulders. 'Sorry?' she says and she sounds shell-shocked. 'You're sorry?' She shakes her head and asks wonderingly, 'What on earth have you to be sorry for?'

389

'For –'

'You were the best little girl anyone could have had.' Her fingers tighten their grip. 'The best little girl,' she stresses 'the best' and furiously blinks back tears. 'I didn't deserve you. If you hadn't been so good, we'd all have gone under. You minded Jamie, you cooked and cleaned. I'm the one who's sorry. I let you both down. Jamie might still be alive –'

Her voice cracks.

'You were sick, Mammy. You couldn't help it.'

'I was your mother,' she says definitely. She gives my shoulders a little shake. 'Your. Mother. I was meant to protect you both. I let you down. For a long time, I found it hard to live with that failure.'

'It wasn't your fault,' I say. 'I know now that you did the best you could.'

'Oh, Hope,' she says, letting me go and walking to the window. She places her hands on the sink and looks into it, her shoulders drooping. 'I struggled badly after your daddy died. I did try but . . .' she pauses and continues, 'You have no idea how sorry I was about what happened, but nothing I could do or say could give you your childhood back, your brother back or your daddy back.'

I can't answer her. I'd wished it all back too many times.

'And the fact that I knew that made me even more depressed and more bitter and I know that's why you left.' She turns around. 'And I don't blame you.'

'I just found it hard to cope, Mammy.'

'You shouldn't have had to cope.'

I bow my head.

'Even though you left, you still rang,' she goes on, crossing towards me. 'And even then, I managed to drive you away with my sadness. Hope, I knew I was doing it but I couldn't help it.'

'I shouldn't have stopped calling. I was selfish.'

'No.' She shakes her head. 'You were right. You couldn't make me better.'

'Really?'

'Really,' she confirms and my guilt at the way I've treated her dissolves like salt in hot water.

'I was glad when you stopped,' she continues, 'because you needed to get away from me. You would have gone mad otherwise. And I needed to let you go because I had to accept that there was nothing I could do to make it up to you. The only thing I had left to show you how much I cared, was to give you your freedom. That's why I didn't ring you.' She pauses and gives a hesitant smile. 'I always hoped you'd come back.'

'Well, I have.' It's a whisper.

'Thank you.'

And she hugs me again.

I remember the other times she's hugged me. The other times I've been happy in this house, the times I blanked out because to remember was so painful. I remember them the way I'd suddenly remembered them when the plane was going down. I remember that that's why I'd told Joe Ryan to apologise on my behalf. But I was lucky enough to be able to do it myself. And I know that this time the memories will stay with me for ever.

I've come home.

We talk about Daddy's death. I tell her that I can't really remember him and she finds a massive photograph album and as we turn the pages together, she tells me stories.

'When he died,' she says, as she stops at a picture of him on our very last holiday together as a family of four, 'it was such a shock. My head couldn't accept it. Every day I kept wondering where he was, why wasn't he coming home. The doctor told me that I got depressed so that I wouldn't have to face life without him.' She runs her finger up and down the picture of a man that looks like me. I've got his big build, his round face and basketball shape. 'He was such a lovely man.'

And at that, I think of Logan. Oh shit! Startling my mother, I jump up from the sofa and peer out the window. Sure enough, there he is, in Adam's car, waiting patiently for me to come out. 'Oh no!'

'What?' My mother looks alarmed. The photo album falls from her lap.

'Sorry, Mammy.' I glance at my watch. Jesus, the poor guy is out there at least two hours now. 'A friend said he'd pick me up ages ago and I forgot and he's still sitting out there.'

'Well, ask him in,' my mother says as she picks up the album. 'I'll make you both something to eat.'

'Really? That would be OK?'

'That would be fine.' She smiles at me and indicates the album. 'We've the rest of our lives to talk, haven't we?'

'Yeah.'

We smile at each other.

As I go to rescue Logan from the car, it dawns on me that this is one of the few times I've ever had a friend home.

And it feels so good.

41

IT'S TIME TO go. The summer has ended and the rain is bucketing down as Adam and Maurice put the cases into the boot of Adam's car. I'm sitting in the front of the car watching them, wondering if Logan will come to wave us off. But of course he won't, it's way too wet. The last time I'd seen him was when he'd driven me back to the cottage to get some nightwear so I could stay at my mother's. My mother had been charmed by him. Well, he had been on his best behaviour, smiling and joking and nodding. She'd asked him about his sculptures so he'd been charmed by her. The night before last, he'd picked me up to bring me back to the cottage so I could pack. He'd given me a chaste hug and told me he'd be in touch. A phone call last night to wish us a safe trip home had been all he'd done.

I don't know what I'd expected; after all, he was just a friend. That's all he wanted to be, he'd made that quite clear in subtle ways.

My mother and I had reached a peace. All my life, I realise, I'd been looking for that peace and I'd been looking in all the wrong places. I'd hoped to escape my past and fill the hole in me, but you can't fill a crack in a foundation with superglue or cotton wool. You need to try to rebuild from scratch, go back to the source and repair it in that way.

Now I am ready to begin over, though I reckon I'll still bristle if I feel I'm being taken for a ride, only now I'll be able to distinguish who is actually taking advantage of me instead of feeling permanently persecuted.

'There now.' Maurice throws a final case on the back seat. 'That's everything. Sure we'll probably be seeing you again, Hope. You'll be visiting your mother, no doubt?'

'I will.'

Adam grins at me.

'I'm glad ye are both talking again, a lovely woman your mother is,' Maurice nods approvingly.

Dunport. The home of everyone's business. 'Thanks for that, Maurice. I'm so glad to have made you happy.'

Adam splutters out a laugh.

'Oh you have,' he nods. 'Sure, no matter what happened between ye, there comes a time to let go.'

'Yeah.' I look at the house. At the view of Dunport. 'Time to let go.'

'And you?' Maurice looks at Adam. 'Will you be back?'

'Maybe.'

'Well, give me a call if you come back next summer. The cottage will still be here.'

'Will do,' Adam grins.

'OK, so.' Maurice slams the car door and as we pull away, he waves furiously after us.

'Shall we call in to Logan to say goodbye?' Adam asks. 'We've plenty of time.'

I was hoping he'd say that. I just want to see him once more.

'Yeah, why not?' I make my voice deliberately casual. 'That'd be nice.'

'Yeah, nice,' Adam scoffs as he turns the car towards Logan's house. Ten minutes later we're pulling up outside. It's quite a depressing sight in the bad weather, the whole place looks sort of run-down. Adam and I make a dash for the front door and hammer on it.

Nothing.

'Logan!' I call. 'Logan!'

It's hard to make ourselves heard above the wind, which is picking up nicely. It's going to be a horrible day for a ferry crossing. 'He could be in his studio,' I shout. So we make a dash for it. He's there all right, chipping away at some wood. His horrible cat is lying curled up at his feet. When I rap on the window, his chisel, or whatever he's using slips and seems to cut him because he jumps up and hops about the place, holding his hand.

'Oh shit,' I wince. 'I think I've just done him an injury.'

He isn't mad when he opens the door, despite the blood seeping from his wound. 'Hey,' he gives me a big bright smile and flicks his glance to Adam. 'All set for going?'

'Yes,' Adam nods. 'We just thought we'd say goodbye in person.' He holds out his hand and Logan grips it in his firm one. 'So long.'

'Yeah, safe trip.'

They nod and Adam indicates his car. 'Well, I'll leave you to it, Hope.' He saunters off and leaves me and Logan on our own in the studio.

We stare at each other for a bit. 'So,' Logan eventually says, 'you're leaving.'

'You'd better get something for that hand,' I say uneasily as blood drips on to the floor.

'What? Oh yeah.' He holds it up and, finding a piece of

dirty-looking rag, he wraps his hand in it. 'I'll shove a plaster on it in a bit.'

'What? When it gets gangrene?'

He smiles.

A pause.

'Thanks, Logan,' I stammer. 'I know I've said it before but these last few days you've been so good to me. I'd never have managed without you.'

'It was my pleasure.'

'And mine.' My voice shakes. 'I . . . I liked being with you.'

'And I with you.'

God, he's so beautiful. And it's not just his face. It's him. I love everything about him. His smile, the way he glowers when he's cross, his nonchalant way of walking, his sloppy dress sense that mirrors my own, his hair that has begun to lengthen despite its recent cut. His sallow tan that I'm sure is there all year around. I love the way he loves my mountain. My sky and sea.

I realise suddenly that neither of us has said anything for the past minute or so. He seems to be looking at me the way I'm looking at him. He crosses the space between us and my body liquefies as he wraps his arms about me and hugs me to him hard.

'My pleasure,' he says again.

I entwine my arms through his and feel the broadness of his back under his green T-shirt. His chin is resting on my head and I can smell him. All clean and gorgeous. I rest my head on his chest and press his body to me. Very slowly he begins to rub my back and my senses spin into erotic heaven. His face lowers itself to mine and oh my God, he kisses me. Right on the lips. I feel as if I can't quite breathe. I respond and my heartbeat goes off the Richter scale. His lips are hungry, insistent and I can hear his ragged breathing. His hand caresses the back of my head as he presses my mouth to his.

And then, he pulls away.

'Shit!' he says, rubbing his hand over his face and looking at me in exasperation. 'Sorry, Hope.'

My poor body doesn't know what hit it. 'Sorry?' I mouth. 'For what?'

'I shouldn't have.' He shakes his head. 'That was stupid of me.'

'I liked it.' I don't care now. He likes me, I like him. 'I really did, Logan.'

'So did I,' he says almost angrily, 'but does that mean you're going to stay around?'

I shrug. 'Well,' I indicate the door. 'No. But so?'

'So?' he says. He pulls the cloth tighter on his hand. 'I had a girlfriend once who didn't want to live here, I'm not going to have another.'

Point taken. I'm not as important to him as his art. As this place. 'I see what you mean,' I say, more calmly than I feel. My heart, which had been singing, drops in my chest like a stone in a pond. Only the ripples remain to remind me what has just happened. 'But couldn't we –'

'Call in when you visit your mother, won't you?'

His interruption is to stop me making a complete fool of myself.

'Won't you?' he asks again gently.

'Yeah.' I don't know if I will. I don't know how I could bear to hear about his life if I'm not in it.

He smiles, lovely white teeth. 'Good. I'll look forward to that.' Pause. 'Well,' he says slowly, as if he doesn't want the words to come out, 'So long, Hope.'

'Yeah, so long.'

He doesn't attempt to shake hands. Neither do I. Instead he turns briefly away to look for something for his hand. The rag is pretty soaked. I wish he'd say something to me. I wish he'd go for a long distance relationship, just for a bit. Just to see how it'll pan out. But he doesn't. Instead, he finds another equally vile rag, then we look at each other again. The silence seems to zing with what I find I can't say.

'Bye, so,' I mutter and my voice is small.

His answer is to chew his lower lip and wave his hand.

It's not much fun being on the ferry with Adam. I'm morose and grumpy. I thought we'd have a laugh going home but I find I can't get Logan out of my head.

Eventually Adam asks, 'What's the matter?'

I stare into my orange. 'Nothing.'

'Oh, come on. You've been more miserable than this weather since you left Logan this morning.'

I sigh, dip my finger in my drink and suck it for a bit before answering, 'He kissed me. Then he told me he didn't want me.'

'What?' Adam gawks at me, his mouth open. 'He kissed you?'

I shrug.

'Then he said he didn't want you?'

I shrug again. It hurts too much to say it twice.

'Well, that's bollix,' Adam pronounces, to the horror of some older women sitting nearby. They cough loudly and look in our direction. 'Bollix,' Adam says again, unintimidated. 'The guy – and take this from me, Hope – is crazy about you.'

I laugh. 'Adam, no offence, but you're hardly an expert on relationships.'

'Offence taken,' Adam says back good-naturedly. 'Look, the time you had that row, you know the row where you were very mean to him and then you went to apologise and he was very mean back to you, d'you remember that?'

'Eh, yeah.' It's not something I could forget in a hurry. I don't think I've ever been as nasty to anyone, ever.

'Well, I gave him a few lifts in the car during that time. He wanted to get stuff in town and I swear, Hope, all he talked about was you.'

'He did?'

Adam nods. 'In a sort of indirect way,' he explains. 'Blokes don't do the sort of things girls do, but I got his vibe.'

Adam got his vibe. That's not exactly what I was hoping for. 'Well,' I shrug, 'his vibe has obviously changed. He likes me but not enough to have a long distance relationship.'

'So, move back.' He says it like it's so obvious.

'Move back?'

'Yeah.' Now he's making it sound like I'm a moron. 'I mean you love that place. Anyone can see that. You'll never settle in London again, Hope.'

'Of course I will. London is my home now.'

He shakes his head. 'London was never your home.'

'Yes it was.' I feel like crying. 'Anyway, you're only saying that so I won't be around to cramp your and Julie's style.'

He doesn't reply and I know I've been mean and horrible.

'Sorry,' I mutter meekly. 'You know I didn't mean that.'

His hand finds mine. 'You know Julie and I love you to bits, don't you?'

'Just like I love you two.'

'So, that's why I'm going to say this and you can take it or leave it or think about it. Remember you told me about Tim, your counsellor and the problems he and his wife were having?'

'Yeah.'

'Well, that's you and Logan. One of you has to give way. One of you has to say OK, I will give in and move to where you are.'

'But why me?'

'Because you love those mountains, that's why. Forget about preserving control of your identity and just go for it.'

'It's not as easy as that. He wouldn't do it for me.'

'So do it for yourself.' He pauses. 'Meet him half-way.'

'Oh, so what?' I smile a little. 'I meet him half-way and we live in the middle of the ocean?'

'Oh, don't be so smart.' But he says it affectionately. Standing up, he stretches. 'I'm going for a walk – want to join me?'

'No, I'll stay here.' I watch him leave.

There is no way that I want to see the Irish coastline recede into the grey day.

42

'A ND HE SMILED at me today. He's very intelligent.'
Julie has about a hundred snapshots of her baby nephew and is showing them to me and Adam. Each photo has a ten-minute history and each story has to be 'oohed' and 'ahhed' by both of us.

'You're not listening,' Julie says suddenly.

'We are,' both of us say simultaneously.

'So, what did I just tell you that his first word was, then?'

Adam looks at me and I look at Adam.

'Eh – hello?' Adam says lamely.

Even I know that's a long shot.

'He's two months, he can't talk yet,' Julie says annoyed. 'Now if you're not interested, just tell me. I'd hate to bore you both.'

'I am interested,' Adam lies.

'No you are not!' Julie pouts. 'All you care about is that you've got promotion again.'

Adam laughs. 'My arse!'

'Your arse,' Julie scrunches up her nose. 'Well, if I were you I wouldn't go boasting about it.'

'That's not what you said last night.'

I pretend to puke and stand up from the table. 'Too much information,' I grin. God, I think to myself, I have to get out of here. I've been looking at a few places to move to in London, but so far, nothing has appealed. Even though I have money to buy a place, since compensation for the accident is in the pipeline, I can't see anything I want. 'I'm just going out for a bit. I've another apartment viewing.'

'Oh, by the way,' Julie shouts after me, 'your mother rang.'

'My mother?'

'Yeah, she said to tell you that she's expecting you next week and that your bed is all made up.'

'Oh right. Ta.'

'So, you're flying, are you?' Julie asks.

'Yeah. Nervous about it but I think I have to do it.'

'Good for you.' She gives a little cheer. 'Will you be seeing Logan?' she asks teasingly.

I shrug. I'd been home last month, on the ferry, and I hadn't called in to him. I just hadn't been able to face it. 'I don't know,' I answer. 'If he's around, I might.' Even the mention of his name makes me feel a little sick. I miss him more than I thought I would. I go over and over our kiss every night in bed, bringing it to what should have been its conclusion.

Julie turns to Adam. 'Despite what you thought, Adam, Hope and Logan never got it together.'

'Not yet,' Adam says confidently.

'Still, probably for the best.' Julie picks up a photo and smiles at it. 'Aw, look at that one. He was in his bath there.'

'Why is it for the best?' I can't help sounding cross at her assumption.

'Well, you know, if you didn't love him enough to stay, you mustn't have really liked him all that much.'

'I did so like him.'

'Not enough, though.' Julie dismisses me and turns back to her photos.

The estate agent is a bit pissed off with me. So far, she's shown me at least twenty new homes. So far, I haven't been interested in any of them.

'You again,' she says, and she can hardly contain the weariness in her voice. It's as if she recognises that showing me around this salubrious new penthouse is a waste of her time.

'Yes, me again,' I smile at her. I had been hoping it wouldn't be her, that it would be someone else from the company. 'I hope this one is for me.'

She doesn't reply, her silence saying everything. Instead she walks into the foyer of the newly constructed building. It's all very plush. Wood and chrome, carpeted elevators that hardly make any noise as they whoosh us up to the top floor. The agent click-clacks her way along the polished wooden floor of the corridor, her clip-board in hand. 'Right,' she says, as she unlocks the door of an enormous apartment, 'have a look around.'

Up to this, she'd been doing a hard sell, telling me all the features that this flat or apartment or house had. Now, I think she's given up on me. I'm determined to show interest. Only, as I look about, my heart sinks. It's just not . . . well, it's not cosy, for a start. And it's too new. And expensive. I give everything a quick glance, just to be polite before telling the woman that I'm finished looking around.

'Well?' she asks.

I shrug. 'I'll let you know.'

She sighs. 'Look, Ms Gardner, I've shown you our best properties. There is nothing finer in London. Have you thought that maybe London isn't for you?'

And that's when, as the sun dips its face into the sprawl of the city beyond the huge glass window of the penthouse, it hits me. It's not that London isn't for me, it's that I'm no longer for London. Adam was right and it's taken me two months to realise it, but London was only ever an escape for me. I think, though I don't voice it aloud, Dunport is where I truly belong. And I belong there whether or not Logan wants me. Maybe seeing him and going for what I want is better than not seeing him and saving myself from hurt.

I'll call in to see him this time, I vow. I'll call in to him and ask him if we have a future.

43

THE LETTER AND parcel arrive on my desk in work, the next day. The letter is in a plain white envelope with just my name on the front. The parcel is wrapped in brown paper and tied up with twine. Very classy.

My boss, who I hate, because he's bossy and grumpy and he keeps getting me to make his tea, has thrown it across my desk. 'For you. From reception.'

'Oh right. Thanks.' I finger the envelope. 'Who's it from? Is it a message?'

'Eh, I'm the boss, not ya secretary.'

'Oh, yeah, I forget sometimes.'

He glowers at me and I smile sweetly back at him. He 'harrumphs', rolls his eyes and stalks out of my cubicle. I'll resign next week probably because I'm going home. I'll write a nice letter and hand it to him. I won't storm out and get fired like I used to do. I've sort of grown up now. I'll resign and get another job in Kerry.

I open the envelope, wondering who's sending me letters in work. Inside is a plain white sheet of paper with the most bizarre words.

O. O. Shame! U dope! Miss Lovely gon.

What?

I peer at it again. *O. O. Shame?* Have I a stalker? I stare at the parcel, almost scared to open it now.

Did the boss say he'd got it from reception?

I dial down. 'Hi, is that Carrie?'

'Yes. Who's that?'

'This is Hope in web design. Did you just get an envelope and parcel for me?'

'Yes. I gave it to Gary, your boss, he said he'd give it to you.'

'He did. I don't know what it's about.'

There's silence at the other end.

'Who gave it to you?'

'Some guy, I buzzed him up.'

And then I get the weirdest sensation. I feel I'm being watched. I glance up and what I see makes me drop the phone to the floor. Carrie's tinny voice saying 'Hope, Hope' over and over is soon replaced by the dial tone.

'Hiya.' He's lounging in the doorway, his head against the frame and a sardonic grin on his face.

'Hi yourself.' My voice is a whisper. God, he looks so good.

'Knew all that *Countdown*, I'm such a genius was a load of crap.' He nods to the paper.

'Sorry?'

'It took me ages to do the "O. O. Shame" stuff and you never even copped it.'

'Copped what?' And then I do cop it. I pick the letter up and just by thinking it's an anagram, all the words rearrange themselves in my mind. A small flutter starts up in my stomach.

Unaware of my flutterings, Logan straightens himself up and regards me. 'It took me this long, Hope, to figure out that I missed you.'

406

'I missed you too.' My eyes are drinking him in. I don't even know what I'm saying. I just want to stare at him.

'You couldn't have missed me that much. You visited your mother a few weeks ago and never came to see me.' He sounds hurt.

'I thought it would hurt to see you.'

'Hurts me more when I don't see you.'

His blunt honesty makes me unable to answer.

He nods in the direction of the letter. 'Thick, that's what you are. Will I explain it to you?'

'Do you miss me. Logan loves Hope.'

'Impressive.' But his voice has lost its cockiness. 'Well?' he pauses, 'Do you miss me? I miss you.' He crosses towards me and sits on the edge of my desk. 'I can't work any more.' He indicates the box. 'That's the last thing I was able to finish.'

My hands are shaking as I untie it. It's just a simple bow but it takes me longer than it should. Inside is a white cardboard box. Opening it, I take out a small wood carving. The bust of a woman.

'You,' Logan says, 'that day on the mountain.'

I hardly recognise myself. The lady he has carved is beautiful. Full lipped, slanted eyes and a shaved head. 'Me?' I whisper.

'That's how you look to me,' he says.

'I look gorgeous.'

'Yeah.' He says it matter-of-factly.

'It's . . . it's,' I touch the wood, it's alive and vibrant. 'Thanks.'

'I'll even move over here to be with you,' he says earnestly. 'Honest, Hope, I don't need anything except you.'

Without taking my eyes off him, I pull open my desk

drawer. 'Well,' I say, 'you don't have to. I booked a flight to see you this weekend.'

'A plane?'

'Uh-huh. The quicker the better.' I place the tickets where he can see them. 'I was going to move back home and I thought I'd let you know.'

'Really?'

'Yeah,' I smile, and stand in front of him, where he sits on my desk. He puts his hands lightly on my waist and my heart flip-flops as he pulls me to him. 'If you miss something,' I whisper as his first kiss lands on my lips, 'you always go back.'

SECOND
CHANCES

For Colm with love.

Acknowledgements

Thanks to everyone who helped with the research for this book – especially to Keith Stafford, the editor of The Racing Pigeon website – www.racingpigeon.ie who provided me with lots of brilliant information and contacts.

Thanks also to Tom Fagan of the Celbridge pigeon racing club whose great ideas provided me with all the information I needed to write this book. Any mistakes in the writing of pigeons are mine.

Thanks to the staff in the Department of Transport who helped me out with some queries I had regarding legal issues. Lorraine McGurk and Helen Conway – thanks.

Thanks to the people at Sphere who have made writing such a pleasure for me. Thanks especially to the wonderful Margaret Daly – her talent and her company are two of the things I enjoy most when signing books.

Thanks to everyone who gave me publicity last time around – it means such a lot. And to the booksellers who are always so welcoming.

Prologue

THERE WAS SILENCE as the jury filed in. It had taken them two days to reach a verdict. Lizzie scanned their faces for some sort of a sign. Two days, she thought, when the case was cut and dried. Though not everyone seemed to think so. It was as if the town had been split in two. Her family and their 'supporters' lined one side of the courtroom, whilst Joe Jones and his lined the other. Joe's supporters included his parents, though his dad hadn't turned out to be the best character witness ever.

Lizzie felt a hand in hers and she squeezed her brother Billy's hand back in response. Billy was a shell of the guy he'd once been. His dancing brown eyes and quick grin had been altered for ever when the battered body of his twin sister had been found washed up on Grange Strand. He'd never drive a fast car again or laugh out loud at something ridiculous, Lizzie thought with a pang.

Her mother, once so fussy and bustling, was a hollowed-out shell of a woman, and her dad was broken. That was the only way Lizzie could describe him. He was so utterly sad. The sadness peeled off him like a fog and wrapped itself around anyone who stood too close. He'd given up fishing and sold his boat, swearing never to go on the sea again.

And her, what had happened to her? Besides the devastation, Lizzie had discovered how much she could hate someone. She stared once again across the courtroom at Joe and she wanted to tear his face off with her bare hands for what he'd done to her sister. He was twenty, the same age as Megan would have been. He'd come to their house once or twice and eaten meals with

1

them. Lizzie, at fourteen, had secretly fancied him: he was gorgeous with his tousled dirty blonde hair and brown outdoor-type face. But Joe had never given her a second glance. She hadn't blamed him; Megan had been a bright halogen light to her somewhat dimmer shine. Lizzie's hair was long, brown and uninteresting, her teeth were encased in steel braces and her pudgy face always had a spot or two. Megan's face had been perfect. Well, before she'd been in the sea for two days. Lizzie swallowed back a lump and Billy, sensing it, tightened his grip on her hand.

'Have the jury reached a decision?' the judge asked.

'We have, your honour.'

The foreman crossed to the judge and handed him a slip of paper. The judge glanced at it before asking the accused to stand.

Joe stood up and stared straight ahead.

Lizzie watched as Joe's impossibly glamorous mother clutched her husband. He wrapped an arm round her shoulders.

'How do you find the accused on the charge of murder in the first degree?' the judge asked the foreman.

'We find him guilty, your honour.'

Immediately there was commotion in the courtroom, with one side cheering and the other shouting out their objections. Joe stood, seemingly shell-shocked, staring at the man who had delivered the verdict.

'No!' Joe's mother cried. 'No—no, Joe wouldn't do that.'

She was pulled back, still crying, by her husband.

Lizzie, her mother, father and Billy clung to each other in relief. They were unable to cheer as Aileen, Megan's best friend, was doing. Tears at the decision coursed down their cheeks.

'Thank God,' her father said. 'Thank God.'

Lizzie watched as Joe, looking devastated, was handcuffed. He was shaking his head in disbelief. All through the trial he'd denied the charge, protesting his innocence every step of the way and making it very difficult for her parents as the murder of their daughter was laid out for them in graphic detail.

But, on the last couple of days of the trial, he'd been caught out on two major lies. Those had been the nails in his coffin.

Lizzie watched as Joe was led away, refusing to look at either of his parents. She hoped he rotted in hell.

Though even if he did, she thought numbly, it wouldn't bring Megs back.

1

Fourteen Years Later

THE MAN HANDED her a carved wooden box. It must once have been pretty, but was now dusty and half rotten.

'Found that under the floorboards,' he said jovially. 'Lucky I did or you might have lost it for ever.'

Unaware of how he'd shocked her, he left the house, the smell of freshly varnished floorboards the only clue that he'd been there at all.

Under the floor. This box. She had to sit down. She stared at it for a bit before cautiously opening it. Inside, scattered, were scraps of paper, old photos, a diary with scrawled writing, hand-drawn pictures and, right at the bottom, a dried rose petal. A whole selection of odds and ends.

She paused before touching the diary. Then, her eyes filling with tears, she removed it from the box and began to read.

2

'SORRY I'M LATE.' Lizzie shoved open the door of the small dingy office and a blast of cold air hit Anna, her co-counsellor, in the face. 'Tom and I went out for coffee and we had a row in front of a whole café of people. Mortifying.'

Anna laughed. 'You and Tom had a row? I thought you never rowed.'

'There's a first time for everything.' Lizzie dumped her tasselled bag on the desk beside her phone and strode over to the electric heater to flick it on. It was freezing in the office.

'Not working,' Anna said glumly as Lizzie shook it. 'So, what's the story with Tom? I can't believe either of you'd fight. You're both so easy-going.'

'Oh, it was only a joke.' Lizzie sat down at her desk and pulled her coat around her to stay warm. 'You know the way he's in a play at the moment?'

'Uh-huh.'

'Well, I went to see him last night and he had one line.' To emphasise her point, Lizzie held one finger up. 'One line.'

Anna grinned.

'He was on stage for about . . . ,' Lizzie shrugged, 'two seconds at most. I mean, I sat through the most boring two hours of my life to see him for two seconds. So when he asked me over a ham sambo if I enjoyed the show, I just joked and asked him if he had found it hard to learn his line.'

'Aw, Lizzie, that was a bit insensitive.'

Lizzie squirmed. She knew that now.

'You are a counsellor,' Anna tapped the phone, 'and you go and say that to the love of your life?'

'I know. But honestly, Anna, one line. I was only teasing him. Anyway, he got all huffed and hurt and said that I obviously thought he was a joke. And I don't, Anna, I really don't.'

'I'm sure he'll forgive you. He's mad about you.'

'He's mad at me, more like,' Lizzie said glumly. 'And I'm starving now because I refused to eat the sandwich he bought me. I told him it'd help his ham acting.'

'You didn't!'

'I did.'

'That was mean.'

'I know.'

'Good line, though.'

Lizzie had to agree. She even thought that Tom had smiled before doing his offended act again. Aw well, she'd ring him in the morning when he'd calmed down.

Opening her drawer she took out her notepad – it was important to log all the calls she received. That way if someone rang more than once, the counsellors knew who they were dealing with. Most second-time callers liked to talk to the same person again. Lizzie had quite a few callers who spoke only to her.

She glanced across the office at the heater that wasn't working. 'I'll put an order through for one next week.'

'Aw well, I don't fancy your chances of screwing a new heater out of Mark,' Anna scoffed, referring to their boss. 'He's completely hyper about the fundraiser at the moment. What's the story with it?'

Lizzie was full time at Life, a free counselling service. Besides volunteering on the phones, she earned her living as a paid fundraiser for the charity.

'Well, the story is that it's ages away and he shouldn't be so hyper. But the big fundraiser this year is a parachute jump. We hope to raise enough to get a house for the charity and do face to face counselling.'

7

Anna whistled. 'Impressive if you can pull it off.'

Lizzie shrugged. 'Aw, it'll be fine. Just a question of money, really.' She wished she was like Anna and a genius at counselling, but fundraising did seem to be her forte. She could charm money from a dead man, Mark often said. 'Tea?' she asked Anna.

'Coffee, please.'

Anna's phone rang and she almost fell off the chair in her haste to answer it. 'Hello, Anna here at Life. Can I help you?'

Lizzie made the coffee and a tea for herself. She pulled a packet of biscuits from her bag and offered Anna one. Anna waved her away, she was busy taking notes, nodding and 'uh-huhing'. Lizzie could hear someone sobbing at the other end of the line. She hated when they cried. She remembered her first ever caller, who had cried for at least ten minutes before eventually sobbing out a story of how her husband had left her and wasn't paying any support. The woman was terrified that she'd lose her house. Listening to her, Lizzie had felt so powerless that she'd been tempted to send the woman on some cash. Anna had firmly talked her out of it. Becoming personally involved with a caller was strictly forbidden. And as Anna said, there were so many sad stories floating around the country that, if she helped one, where would she draw the line?

Placing her tea on her desk, Lizzie pulled a biscuit from the packet. Munching slowly on it, she wondered where the woman was now and how she was getting on. As far as Lizzie knew, she'd never rung again. It was something she'd found hard to get used to, but some stories didn't ever have an ending. They just vanished. There one day, gone the next. A bit like Megan.

Lizzie shook her head to clear it. Thinking about Megan was something she rarely indulged in nowadays. It still made her angry. And sad. She knew that her reasons for volunteering at Life in the first place were mainly due to Megan. It was her desire to try to finish other people's stories because her own would never have a satisfactory ending, but it didn't work like that. People had to sort themselves out – she couldn't do it for them. And that had been hard to accept. Was still hard to accept, if she were honest.

Instead she studied Anna, dark hair falling across her face. She'd known Anna for the last three years – they did volunteer counselling together on Thursday nights – but she didn't actually *know* Anna. Anna wore a wedding ring yet never talked of her husband; she had a little girl, Chloe, who was seven and she never mentioned Chloe's father at all. Lizzie often wondered if the man were dead, but if he was she felt sure Anna would talk about him. Instead, there was nothing. But then again, she had never told Anna about Megan. People rarely discussed painful things except to strangers, Lizzie had concluded.

They finished their shift at eleven-thirty. After bidding goodbye to Anna, Lizzie lit herself a cigarette and sauntered along a very quiet Grafton Street, enjoying the walk in the cold air and waiting to hear her favourite late night talk show on her MP3.

'Tanite on Dublen Live,' the DJ cut across an advert, his accent pure Dublin, 'we're talking childbirth.'

'I swear,' a caller said, 'the pain of labour was worse den being at some poncy theatre.'

Lizzie grinned, wondering if Tom was listening, though he was probably in the pub now with the cast of his play.

She turned up the volume and, just as she did so, a passing pedestrian caught her attention. Tall, shaved head, reasonably handsome, the man strode alongside her before passing her out. He was so intent on where he was going that he failed to notice her shocked expression as she stared after him.

No, she thought, it couldn't be.

It couldn't be.

Vaguely aware that people were looking at her because she had stopped walking, Lizzie forced herself to continue up the street. The noise of her programme receded as she stared numbly at the man striding in front of her. Still, most people looked the same from the back, she thought, her heart beginning a slow hammer. If she could just get one more glimpse of him . . . She quickened her pace. He was just ahead of her, bundled up in a big green parka jacket and thick brown boots. His hands were

9

shoved deep into his pockets and his head was bent against the cold. God, it looked so like him, but she was never going to catch up, her long legs no match for his longer ones.

Abruptly he paused and gazed into a shop window. A full-on profile and Lizzie gasped aloud, her mind beginning a slow free fall to the last time she'd seen him. In a suit and tie with the same look of horror she was probably wearing now.

She felt suddenly sick at seeing Joe Jones again.

Joe Jones. The name pounded in her head.

Joe Jones. Joe Jones.

He hadn't crossed her mind in a long time. In fact, she'd done everything in her power to forget about him and what he'd done. Even when her family had been informed that he was up for early release, Lizzie had clamped down her hate and her horror. Being distressed would only make her mother worse, and her mother had been close to a nervous breakdown at that time.

Seeing him now, though, made Lizzie realise that she hadn't forgotten about what he'd done at all. That she was still as affected now as she had been all those years ago.

Bastard! she wanted to shout out. *Murderer!*

She began to shake slightly. Tremble.

And then he began to move off again.

Rage and shock made her clench her hands into fists, before she started to walk as fast as she could after him. It wasn't a conscious decision at first. He was, after all, going in the same direction as she was – up Grafton Street. Little by little she started to gain on him, which wasn't surprising as while she was half running he seemed to have slowed down, stopping every now and then to peer into various shop windows. She didn't want to look at him, but she couldn't help it. It was like he was technicolour in a street of sepia. She noticed the slouching easy walk of him, the skin shaved smooth, the tight, close-cropped haircut, the curve of his jaw, the jut of cheekbones and the length of his legs. And she was furious.

When she had come within two feet of him, she spent minutes observing what she could see of his clothes in the semi-darkness.

He was dressed casually in jeans and a parka, and around his neck he wore a big red and orange scarf. She saw him glance at his watch before suddenly increasing his pace.

Shit!

Lizzie couldn't run and draw attention to herself, but she knew that if he continued to walk as quickly as that, she would lose him. The fact that she was wearing a big heavy oversized coat and thick boots didn't make speed walking exactly easy. Damn it, though, she wasn't going to lose sight of him. She often thought later that maybe it would have been better if she had, if he'd just vanished out of her life as suddenly as he'd reappeared. But that wasn't to be because, just as she'd given up hope of catching him, she saw, with mixed feelings, that he was striding towards the Luas tram – the same one she was catching herself. That was a stroke of luck. Now she could follow him wherever he got off and just hop back on another Luas when she was done. What she was hoping to achieve she hadn't got around to thinking about, but for now it would be enough to know where he lived.

She stood apart from him at the station, not daring to spend too much time looking in his direction in case she would attract attention to herself. In case he might recognise her. She didn't think he would. The last time they'd had contact she had been a chubby fourteen-year-old with mousey brown hair and braces. He had barely registered that she existed. Now she was taller, having spurted up suddenly at sixteen the way they did in her family; her hair, chopped short, was dyed a mishmash of various colours; and her braces had done the job and left her with nice straight teeth. Her skin had even cleared up and now she only got the odd spot.

Joe seemed to be concentrating on something and Lizzie saw that he, too, had an MP3 player.

As the Luas pulled up, Lizzie moved to just behind him in the crowd and followed him on to the third carriage. She sat down and watched as he graciously gave up his seat to a pregnant woman.

Huh, bit late to be nice now, she thought, her hands itching to slap his good-looking face.

He stood the rest of the journey, holding on to the strap as the Luas got going. Little by little, station by station, the tram began to fill. Lizzie kept her gaze firmly on him now as his back was to her. They arrived at Ranelagh and Lizzie groaned as he made to get off. Stupidly she'd thought he might get off at her stop. Still, nothing ventured, nothing gained. She decided to take a chance, she could always follow him and catch the next Luas. If there was one.

He was first off as the Luas came to a shuddering halt. Lizzie let a few people go in front before hopping after him on to the platform.

About ten minutes later, she saw him turn into a street full of old two-storey red-bricked houses. Lizzie watched him from the top of the road. He lived here, she was sure of it, he seemed to be taking keys out of his pocket. It was a nice street – quiet, even though Lizzie had the impression that many of the houses were converted into student flats. She watched as he eventually stopped outside an end-of-terrace house, the last in the street. He bounded up the steps to the front door and let himself in. The slam of the door echoed up to her.

Slowly, Lizzie walked towards his house. As she came abreast of it, she glanced up. Red door, slightly shabby, but the building didn't look rented. Lizzie memorised the number and location of the place.

She shivered suddenly, wondering why she'd followed him.

But it had seemed important. Somehow.

3

JOE LET HIMSELF into his hallway and winced at the cold in the house. Damn! He'd either forgotten to turn on the heating or he was out of oil. He kept his jacket on as he made his way into the small kitchen. Examining the heater switches, he groaned. He hadn't forgotten, so that meant he was out of oil. Great!

Flicking on the kettle, he made himself a cuppa and pulled out a few biscuits from the press.

Carrying his supper outside to his small back garden, he stood for a second inhaling the sharp air and listening to the soft sounds of his pigeons in their loft.

'Hiya, guys,' he half sang and the birds, recognising his voice, fluttered and cooed back.

Crossing to the pigeon coup, Joe smiled. God, he loved those birds. He had a full coup, eighty birds in all: breeders, young birds and old birds, which he raced every Saturday during the racing season, weather permitting. The first race of the new season was this Saturday, all going well. He was quietly optimistic about his chances this year. These birds had saved his life, he reckoned. If he hadn't had them, he'd never have crawled back from the edge – he needed them far more than they needed him.

He drained his coffee before unlocking the loft. The birds, normally quiet when it was dark, fluttered as he entered. Prince, his favourite, the best racer he'd ever had, perched on his shoulder.

Joe stood for another while, enjoying the affection from his birds and showing them the same in return, before locking up the coup for the night and going back inside. He rinsed his cup under the tap before noticing that his answering machine was

13

blinking. Pressing it on, he groaned as he recognised his neighbour's voice:

'Joseph,' she said crossly. 'Joseph?' Then there was an expectant pause. 'Oh, it's not you, it's your answering machine. So you're really not there?' Another pause. 'OK, right. Well, it's Ellen from next door. Your birds did their business on my blouses again today. I can't get the stain out. I'd like if you'd call over tomorrow sometime. Thank you.'

Well, that wasn't true for starters, Joe thought, as the next message whirred and clicked on. He had let his pigeons out in the afternoon before heading to work that day and Ellen had taken all her washing in before then. He'd call and tell her that in the morning.

'Hi, Joe, it's Noel. Just reminding you that the first race of the season is on Saturday. Have your birds down at the club by six tomorrow. Looking forward to beating you.' Joe grinned.

Message three clicked on:

'Hello, Joseph. It's Dad. You might give—'

How had he found the number? Joe reached out and before he was aware of it he pressed 'delete', his heart hammering. His father hadn't contacted him in years. Or, rather, they hadn't contacted each other. And Joe didn't want to contact him ever again. He stood, staring at the machine that had brought his father's voice back into his life and gulped. Unplugging it, he wrapped the cord around it before dumping it in the bin. Some things hurt too much.

4

I T WAS AFTER twelve when Lizzie walked through the Royal
Lawn estate where she lived with her brother and his partner,
Aileen. When they'd bought the house, they'd asked Lizzie if she'd
rent from them to help with the mortgage. Lizzie had agreed as
her flat was costing her a fortune. Still, the estate looked anything
but royal, she always thought: royal places didn't have bits of
paper and tin cans thrown about the streets.

However, number 34 Royal Lawns had a very well tended
garden and was kept clean and cosy, thanks to Aileen who was
very house proud.

Lizzie let herself in and grinned when she saw that Billy, her
brother, was still up. He was making coffee and asked if she
wanted one.

'Yeah, please.'

'You're late,' he remarked as he flicked the kettle on again. 'I
was beginning to get worried about you.'

He was always worrying about her, Lizzie thought. Well, they
worried about each other. But in the last two years since becoming
a home owner, Billy's worrying had got a lot worse. He was stick-
thin now and had developed a nervous habit of scratching behind
his ear whenever something bothered him.

Lizzie threw her bag across a chair and sat down. 'Is Aileen
in bed?'

'Yeah, she's wrecked.' Billy handed Lizzie a coffee and sat down
opposite her. 'She always seems to be tired lately. I told her to
see a doctor but she says she's fine. All she needs is a good night
out, she says.'

They laughed slightly. Aileen, while dying for a house of her own, had found her lack of funds a horrible side effect to having a mortgage.

'So, any mad callers tonight?' Billy asked, changing the subject with a small grin.

'Confidential,' Lizzie grinned back and tapped her nose. 'But nope. It was surprisingly quiet.' She paused, wondering how to broach the subject. She ran her finger around the rim of the coffee cup before venturing, 'But, eh, something a bit mad did happen tonight.'

'Yeah?' Billy looked mildly interested. 'What?'

'I saw a face from the past on the way home.'

'Yeah?'

'Yeah.' Lizzie deliberately got her voice under control before she added, 'Joe Jones.'

Billy's brown eyes widened. He placed his cup carefully on the table and repeated quietly, 'Joe Jones?'

'Uh-huh.' Lizzie nodded. She decided not to tell Billy that she'd followed him. It might sound a bit, well, weird. She could hardly believe she'd done it herself. And Billy would probably kill her. 'He was on the Luas. He got off in Ranelagh.'

'I heard he was in Dublin all right.' Billy whistled softly. 'Jesus. That's a bit of a shocker.'

Lizzie nodded. 'I thought so. He hadn't changed much, you'd know him if you saw him.' Pause. 'Bastard.'

Billy nodded. Now he, too, seemed to be on the verge of saying something.

'What?' Lizzie asked.

'He never admitted it, Lizzie.'

'So?' Her voice rose. 'What does that mean? Even his own dad said that he had argued with—'

'His father didn't have a choice.'

'I can't believe—'

'You can't believe what?' Aileen's six-foot, stripy-pyjama-clad frame swooped into the room, her gaze eager. She plonked into the chair beside Lizzie. 'God, Lizzie, I'm glad you're home. Billy's bad enough when he's only got the mortgage to worry about. You'll set him over the edge altogether.'

Lizzie laughed as Billy made a face at his girlfriend.

'So what's the story? What can't Billy believe?'

'Lizzie saw,' Billy began, then paused, the words seeming to choke on his tongue. 'Well, Lizzie saw Joe Jones tonight.'

Aileen's smile faded. 'Joe?' She thrust her blonde tousled head towards Lizzie's darker one. 'No way!'

'Yep. On the Luas.'

'Did he see you?'

'No. I stayed out of his way.'

'And a good thing, too,' Aileen pronounced. 'Jesus.' She paused before slamming her fist on the table, making Lizzie jump slightly. 'The fecker. I wonder how long he's been up in Dublin.'

Lizzie shrugged.

'You must have got a shock.' She glanced at Lizzie's cup of coffee before saying to Billy, 'Make her something stronger, Bill. Will you have a hot whiskey, Lizzie?'

Lizzie waved her away. 'I'm fine, thanks.' She stood up. 'I'll head up to bed now. I've a busy day tomorrow.'

'You sure?' Aileen peered anxiously at her. 'You're OK?'

'I'm fine, honest,' Lizzie said. 'But I won't be if I don't get some sleep.'

Aileen nodded. 'Me too, I'm completely knackered.'

'We all have work tomorrow.' Billy placed the cups in the dishwasher. 'Let's all get to bed.' He turned back to Lizzie. 'If you see him again, you ring me and I'll collect you, OK?'

'I was hoping you'd say you'd thump him to a pulp.' Lizzie smiled a little.

'I wish I could,' Billy said softly, 'but what good would it do?'

Neither woman answered. Instead, Aileen slipped her hand into Billy's and kissed him softly on the cheek. He smiled a little sadly before nodding, 'Night, Sis.'

'Yeah, night, Bill. Night, Aileen.' Lizzie watched them leave, her thoughts turning back to Joe Jones. How could Billy not want to thump him up? She wished she was a man so she could.

But she knew where he lived now. At that, her heart gave a sudden, small skip. Excitement? Fear? She didn't know. But there had to be some way to make things right. No, she corrected herself, not right – things would never be right. But some way to make things even.

There had to be.

5

My dad has found me a job. I can't believe it.
Despite the fact that I never even said I wanted a
job, my dad got me one. I had planned to have
a really cool summer, hanging out on the beach
with Aileen when she visits and going out with Billy
and maybe then looking for something. But oh no,
Dad has to be the one to tell me that he's found me a
job.

And is it a cool job like working in a clothes shop
and getting loads of discount clothes? Nope, it's in
Geoff Jones' newspaper offices. Selling ads.

I couldn't sell bibles to the Vatican, never mind ads
to complete strangers. Joe Jones, who sometimes works
with my dad on his boat, told him they were looking
for someone and my dad suggested me. Apparently Joe
jumped at it.

Dad said it was just a start until I found
something of my own. I know what he's up to, he's
hoping this job will be so rotten that I will get out there
and look for a proper one. Anyway, I'll give it a go
for a little while. Some money will be handy as I plan
on having a great time this last free summer of my
life.

Dad is determined to ruin my summer. Aside from finding me a job, he brought me, Lizzie and Billy out fishing today. The sea air is terrible for the complexion, I told him, but he laughed and told me to 'go away outta that'.

Billy and Lizzie love fishing and while I deliberately forgot my rod, they brought theirs. Dad was in his element. He loves having the three of us all together, but as I said, why can't he love having the three of us down in the pub together or at the pictures together? Being all together on a smelly old boat is not much fun, I don't think.

'Now,' Dad said, as he put some disgusting worms on the hooks, 'the most important thing is what?' He looked at me.

'The right bait,' I said, rolling my eyes but not able to stop grinning either. It has always been my question. I think he's afraid to ask me anything else in case I get it wrong.

'Exactly,' Dad smiled. 'Good girl.' He cast off. 'Find what they like and they won't be able to resist.'

Billy and Lizzie copied him. Then Dad gave his usual lecture about stillness and patience and silence. 'Easy and gently, no sudden jerks,' he said.

There was silence for ages. I wished I'd brought my *Hello!* with me. Then Lizzie got all red and excited and her line started to pull and Dad was up on his feet, helping her reel the fish in. 'If they don't think they're trapped, it's easy to reel them in,' he said. 'But when they start to struggle, that's the most dangerous part.'

'Dangerous?' Lizzie asked. Though she knew what he meant, she was just humouring him, the way we all do.

'In case he escapes,' Dad said. 'Reel him in rapidly

but with no stops and starts. You're committed to catching him now, you can't turn back.'

And ten minutes later an enormous fish was flopping about on the deck, gasping for breath.

The three of them clapped.

I almost got sick – I'd turn vegetarian only I hate vegetables.

6

LIZZIE RANG TOM first thing the next morning as she ate her breakfast. Billy and Aileen always left before she did. She wondered if Tom was up, he was a bit like her and liked to sleep in late. As she dialled his number her mind flitted back to the first time she'd met him.

It was eight months ago and she was out with Anna in the pub. She'd been queuing to buy a drink at the bar.

'Yo!' the barman nodded at her.

'A v—'

'A Bud and a Carlsberg,' a voice shouted from behind.

The barman ran off to serve the customer and Lizzie turned around to face a tall guy wearing a cool orange hat. 'You skipped the queue,' she said crossly.

Brown eyes glittered down at her. 'Queue?' His voice was nonchalant and mocking. But beautifully resonant. 'I don't see a queue.'

'The barman was talking to me.'

'Yeah, and I was talking to the barman.'

'I was here longer than you!'

The guy feigned a yawn.

When the barman arrived back, the Bud and the Carlsberg held aloft, the guy dug his hands into the pocket of a pair of tattered jeans, pulled out a few notes and took the pints. And then Lizzie did something that she'd normally never do. She banged into him and his drinks sloshed everywhere.

'Oh dear,' she said, wide-eyed, 'what have I done.' Then she turned away and called her order out to the waiting barman.

'Hey, you've ruined my shirt,' the guy said from behind.

'I didn't see you,' Lizzie said, 'just like you didn't see the queue.'

'You banged into me on purpose.' He sounded genuinely hurt.

'You skipped the queue on purpose.'

He looked suddenly shamefaced. 'Technically there wasn't a queue as such.'

'Technically I was in front of you. As such.'

'Technicalities, smechnicalities,' he said in a brilliant Woody Allen. A sudden wicked grin floored her. 'Guess you were the wrong girl to cross.'

Lizzie felt herself blush under the high voltage beam.

'Or maybe the right girl. How about I pay for your drinks to say sorry?'

'Yeah, OK,' Lizzie said. She turned back to the barman and shouted, 'Make them doubles!'

His face had fallen slightly. Then he'd recovered. 'OK. No problem.' And he'd bought them the drinks, bankrupting himself in the process and having to borrow three euro from Lizzie.

But they'd been seeing each other ever since.

Tom had turned out to be the best laugh she'd ever known. He was manic and permanently broke, ditching any job he had once he got a sniff of an acting part. Lizzie admired his attitude.

'Hello?' She was so lost remembering that his voice startled her and it took a second to realise that she was on the phone. His voice always made her heart skip a beat. It was pure sexy. Gravelly and distinct. A real actor's voice. This morning, though, it was groggy with sleep.

'Tom. Hi. It's Lizzie, your number one fan.'

She was rewarded with a semi-laugh. 'OK, number one fan, do you hate me so much that you have to wake me up early?' he kidded.

'No, I just want to say sorry about the awful joke I made yesterday.'

'Well,' Tom pretended to think. 'It did dent my ego but, hey, I guess I can see your point. You're not theatre savvy and you wouldn't know that one line in this play is worth about a hundred in any other.'

'Sort of like the dollar and the euro,' Lizzie said.

'Eh, sort of.' He was smiling, she could tell. 'So, what's the plan for today, gorgeous?'

'Dunno yet. I can meet you for lunch.'

'Aw, no can do. I'm going for a casting for another play. How about Sunday?'

'I'm heading home.'

'Aw, pity. Well, I'll see you when you come back. Take care.'

'Yeah.'

'Kiss your parents for me.'

Her parents hadn't really 'got' Tom when they'd met. 'Will do.' She laughed as he hung up.

Two hours later, still yawning, Lizzie unlocked the door to the Life building and climbed up the stairs.

Life had three small rooms taken at the top of the building. The first room was Mark's office – he was the founder of Life and the boss. Forty years old, he was completely driven by the desire to make Life one of the best help centres in the country. The second office was the counselling office, with two phones and a computer. The volunteer in today was Barbara, a fifty-year-old mother of three, who had spare time on her hands and worked each Friday from eight until two.

'Hi, Barbs,' Lizzie called as she made her way past to her own office. She heard Barbara calling out a greeting in response.

Lizzie's office was cold and she shivered. She pulled her coat around her shoulders and began shifting through the post, which had arrived late the afternoon before. There was a lot of junk mail, which was surprising as she'd definitely told the post office that she didn't want this stuff any more. There was a card from a caller thanking them for some advice. Lizzie tacked it to the wall. Ripping open another envelope, she found a bank draft for five hundred euro with just 'Thanks' scrawled across a white page. Lizzie grinned. Mark would be pleased by that.

As if on cue, Mark came barging through the door. Dressed as if he'd just climbed out of bed, he looked impatient and flustered. One day he'd have a heart attack, Lizzie often thought. He never seemed to have the time to brush his hair or shave properly. Today his hair was tousled and stood out all over his head, while his chin sported more than a day's worth of stubble.

'I got a—' Lizzie attempted to show him the draft.

'What's the update on the parachute jump, Lizzie?' he said, interrupting her. 'Any more developments?'

'I'm fine, thanks for asking, Mark. And how are you?'

Mark rolled his eyes and made a dismissive gesture with his hand. 'When you're saving the world, Lizzie, you don't have time for niceties.'

'Oh, I thought saving the world was nice.'

He laughed. 'You give me any more cheek and I'll fire you.'

'Go ahead.' Lizzie grinned cheekily back at him.

'Oh, fuck off.' He crossed towards her and sat on the edge of her desk. 'Right. Jump. What are we up to?'

'I was going to type it out today and give it—'

'I don't have time to read things.'

'Why do I bother?' Lizzie joked, and then, becoming serious, she said, 'Well, we've about a hundred volunteers so far.'

'Good. So how much? Will we raise enough to buy a house at cost?'

Lizzie shrugged. 'Jim O'Brien of O'Brien's builders has promised to meet with me to see what he can do. If not, I'll scour the phone book. There is bound to be a builder out there who is willing to donate a house for the good publicity it'd give him.'

'Builders don't need publicity, they're making a fortune anyway. Greedy fuckers.'

'I wouldn't say that to Jim,' Lizzie said.

'Eh, I know.' Mark rolled his eyes. 'I'm not stupid. So, you think you can pull it off?'

'Who got the celebs to do the TV ad last year?' Lizzie reminded him.

25

'My genius charmer.' Mark stood up and grinned at her. 'If you pull this off, Lizzie, and we get a house, I'll give you a rise.'

'I'll see how it goes. Now get lost and let me make a few phone calls.'

'Going, boss.' Mark gave her a salute and left.

Lizzie spent the day emailing all her contacts and asking for support. It took ages as she typed up a personalised letter to each one. She also sent out press releases to radio shows looking for some air time. The jump was months and months away but Lizzie liked to concentrate her efforts on one major fundraiser a year. She started canvassing for it a long time in advance.

As she pressed 'send' on the final email of the day, she glanced at the clock. It was only five, an hour before clocking out. She opened up the Google screen on her computer and paused suddenly, her fingers poised over the keyboard. Should she or shouldn't she? It had been at the back of her mind all day. Still, she reasoned, it wasn't as if she was doing anything illegal or dangerous. She could stop when she wanted to. But the truth was, she didn't want to. She wanted to find out about the man who had made her mother half demented with grief, the man who had crushed her father's spark, who had turned Billy into a walking skeleton and had made it unbearable for her to see anyone she'd known from home. She had an urge to find out about the man who had left a hole inside her that nothing could fill. The man who had made her feel such fury last night by just existing.

'To hell with it,' she muttered as she typed 'Joe Jones' into the search engine.

Within seconds a list of eighty-five thousand results came up.

Shit. Joe Jones was obviously a very common name.

Joe Jones, Wexford. Just over one hundred entries. That was manageable. Eagerly she scanned through them, but none seemed to match. The only promising one was an article on a pigeon club site. There was a picture of a pigeon called Prince who had won some major race or other. Its trainer was a Joe Jones from

Ranelagh, originally a Wexford man. She wondered if it was him. And if it was, why on earth had they put a picture of the stupid pigeon instead of Joe on the site? Still, she vaguely recalled something about pigeon racing from years ago. Hadn't his grandfather been heavily involved in it? Lizzie looked at the pigeon for a while, as if the harder she looked the more information she would glean. But all it said was that its trainer was a Joe Jones from Ranelagh.

And then she had an idea.

She rang Billy, just to let him know that she'd be a little late home, and then she left the office.

Thirty minutes later, Lizzie got off the Luas in Ranelagh. What would be the harm in making sure that the Joe Jones she'd seen was the same one whose pigeon she had read about on the internet? And, if it was, maybe she could use it somehow.

It was beginning to drizzle as she made her way towards his house. She stood, a few doors up, and noticed that the house seemed deserted. All the lights were off. Slowly she walked towards it. The street was empty, except for a girl approaching from the opposite direction. They passed each other and, two steps later, Lizzie was going by the house. The curtains were not pulled in the front, she noted. What would be the harm in having a look in the window?

No harm at all.

She was only going to have a look.

Just to see what he had inside.

Trying to compose herself so she looked like a visitor and not some edgy woman spying on a man she barely knew, she climbed the concrete steps to the front door. There was no light at all inside the place so she felt confident ringing the bell, then, if anyone was observing her, they'd think she was a friend. The bell jangled somewhere inside the house and the door remained closed. Good. Lizzie peered inside. Nothing. The frosted glass in the hall door made it hard to see. She crossed to the sitting-room window and pressed her face against the pane. It was hard to judge because of the gloom, but it certainly didn't look like a rented room. It was fairly empty, she could make out a sofa, a TV and a stereo. Wooden floors. A light with no shade hanging from the ceiling. But all in all, fairly neat.

'Hello? Can I help you?'

Lizzie jumped.

'Oh, sorry, I didn't mean to startle you.'

Lizzie turned about, hoping her face wouldn't betray the guilt she felt rushing up through her. A woman was peering at her from the next garden.

'Oh, eh, hi,' she stammered out. 'I was, eh – well, looking for Joe.' It was weird saying his name like that, as if she actually liked the guy.

'He's gone out,' the woman said. She had to be in her seventies, Lizzie guessed. White hair, smiley face and very well dressed. 'He left about an hour ago.'

'Oh.' Lizzie nodded, as if disappointed. 'That's a pity.'

'I'll tell him you called.'

'Oh, there's no need, I'll ring him.'

'No, no,' the woman waved her hand, 'you tell me and I'll pass the message on.' She looked at Lizzie expectantly. 'Now, what's your name?'

'Eh,' Lizzie gulped. 'Just, eh, Mindy.' Mindy? Where had *that* come from?

'Mindy,' the woman nodded. 'And what's it in connection with? Are you a friend? Do you help him with his birds?'

'Birds?' Lizzie's heart leapt.

'Yes, his pigeons.'

'Oh, right. No. No, I don't have anything to do with his birds.' Bingo. She wanted to laugh out loud. It had been so easy.

'I don't blame you, those birds are a nuisance. Oh, I like Joseph, but his birds drive me mad, flapping and circling above the house the way they do. They've ruined about three of my blouses so far.'

'Terrible,' Lizzie nodded, wondering how on earth she could get away without appearing rude.

'Yes, it is. Joseph, well, he always pays me what they're worth. But it's not the same, is it?'

Lizzie shook her head. Maybe she could just say—

'At my age, I find it hard to get into the shops so money is no use. Joseph drives me sometimes, when he's free, he's good like that.'

Lizzie said nothing, reluctant to agree.

'But anyway, Mandy, Mindy,' she clicked her tongue, 'what was it again?'

'Mindy,' Lizzie said weakly.

'Mindy, that's right,' the woman nodded. 'I'll tell him you called and it's not about the birds, is it not?'

'No, not about the birds.'

'Right. Because he took a load of them away in a basket a little while ago.'

'Oh. Did he?'

'Yes, he did. And I hope they get lost on their way home. But of course I don't tell Joseph that. He's a little crazy about those birds. Told me this morning that they hadn't ruined my nicest blouse. Insisted that they hadn't been out at all yesterday morning. I believed him because he's a nice boy and he helps me with my shopping, but I won't the next time.'

'You'd do right not to.' The words were out before Lizzie could stop them and the woman's mouth made an 'oh' of surprise.

'Right,' she said after a little pause. 'Well,' she pulled her blue cardigan about her shoulders, 'that's not a kind thing to say about your friend. I've always found Joseph very nice.'

Lizzie gulped but found she couldn't unsay the words. Instead, she indicated the street. 'I, eh, have to go.'

'OK.' The woman was looking at her oddly and Lizzie, cursing herself for being so stupid, half ran down the steps.

'I'll tell him you called,' the woman shouted after her.

It was when she was clear of the house that Lizzie slowed to a walk. How could she have been so stupid? she thought.

But then again, she'd found out that he did have pigeons. And what's more, that he was a member of the Ranelagh pigeon club. It had all been so simple, almost as if she was meant to find out.

There had to be some way to use the information. But first, she would find out everything she could about this man and his life.

Her heart skipped a beat. She didn't know if it was in fear or excitement. They'd always felt pretty much the same to her anyway.

7

THE TRAFFIC WAS mental. Billy's car crawled along and, two hours later, they still hadn't reached Wexford. Lizzie was dying for a cigarette, but she couldn't ask her brother to stop: Billy hated stopping once he was on the road. And besides, he hated her smoking even more. Every time she lit up, Billy gave her a lecture. That was the problem with living with your older brother: he started to think he was a father figure.

Travelling with Billy and Aileen was not something that Lizzie had ever enjoyed – besides Billy's reluctance to stop, there was Aileen's obsession with Wham. Three hours of George Michael and Andrew Ridgeley was not Lizzie's idea of fun. Aileen insisted on singing along to all the songs in a woefully out of tune way.

'My friend had that song at her wedding,' she turned around to tell Lizzie as 'Wake Me Up Before You Go Go' came on. 'She knew the priest really well and she told him that she wanted this song played. Of course the priest didn't know it and my friend just told him it was about a guy who wanted his girlfriend to go everywhere with him. And when the day came she walked up the aisle to that.'

Lizzie giggled at the image.

'What song would you want played as you walked up the aisle, Lizzie?' Aileen asked then, stealing a glance at Billy, who seemed oblivious.

'Queen,' Lizzie grinned, '"I Want To Break Free".'

Aileen shook her head in disbelief. 'You and Billy,' she said mock sternly, 'you haven't a romantic bone in your bodies. Billy, what song would you like to see me walking up the aisle to?'

Billy flinched. 'I dunno. It's not something I think about too much.'

'So think about it now,' Aileen pressed. 'This is not a marriage proposal; I know we can't afford it.' She made beak shapes with her hands. 'Yadda, yadda, yadda.'

Billy sighed deeply. 'Aileen, you'd pick the music, not me, so it'd be up to you.'

'Oh.' Aileen looked impressed. 'Good answer.' She winked at Lizzie. 'OK, what would I like?' There was a few seconds' silence, punctuated only by George Michael saying he didn't want his freedom. 'I think I'd like something classy,' Aileen said slowly. 'Something that's gonna make everyone cry.' She thought some more. '"In a Country Churchyard", I think.'

'"In a Country Churchyard"?' both Billy and Lizzie said together.

'Yeah. That's what I'd like.'

'Maybe I'd better choose some music, too,' Billy said. 'I am not having my wedding full of Wham and Chris de Burgh.'

'Aw, so you're gonna marry me then?' Aileen teased.

'Only if you're lucky.'

Joe sat in his back garden. The day was gloomy but it wasn't raining, and he even imagined there was a hint of warmth in the air. If so, it was good. Prince liked good weather, he tended to fly better with the sun on his back. Noel, Joe's mate from the club, had rung to say that the birds had been released at nine o'clock. It was now ten-thirty and Joe's heart rattled every time he glanced skywards. No matter what flew overhead, he kept jumping up, hoping it was one of his pigeons.

'Are your birds out today?' Ellen McGrath poked her head accusingly over the wall dividing the two back gardens.

'I'm expecting them back any minute now.'

'I need to hang out my washing.'

Joe grinned. He didn't know how one old lady who lived alone could have so much washing.

'D'you know something,' he said, resting his arm on the wall, 'you're the best woman for washing I've ever met. I'd say if you had the power to wash away sins, you'd give Our Lord a run for his money. Would you agree?'

'You blasphemous man!' Ellen giggled in a surprisingly girlish way and flapped an arm at him. 'That'll end you up in hell, so it will.'

'Aw, I'm going there anyway.'

'Not at all.' She smiled at him. 'You're annoying but nice. Your birds will go to hell, though.'

'Thanks.' Joe looked up at the sky again and flinched. Was that one of his pigeons hovering around up there? He gave a long whistle but the bird didn't react. Disappointed, he figured that it was probably just a seagull or something.

'Oh, by the way,' Ellen shifted her washing basket to her other arm, 'you had a visitor last night. A girl. Young. Pretty. A bit cheeky, though. She was peering in your windows.'

'Yeah?' Joe shrugged. 'Maybe it was someone selling something.' Young, pretty girls never visited him.

'No,' Ellen said, sounding definite. 'She knew you because she asked for you. She said she'd call again. What was her name now?' She screwed up her face as she tried to remember. 'It was an unusual one.'

Joe waited, trying to appear polite but all the time scanning the sky for any little movement. He knew his birds should be in soon.

'It began with an M, that I'm sure of.'

'M?' Joe said, gulping.

'Mandy? No.' Mrs McGrath shook her head. 'Not Mandy.'

The last girl Joe had known whose name began with an M had screwed his life up. He didn't want to go there ever again.

'Maybe you'll remember it later,' he said, wishing she'd leave now. 'You go in and I'll give you a shout when the birds are in.'

'Mindy,' she pronounced triumphantly. 'That's what it was! A Mindy called for you yesterday.'

'I don't know a Mindy,' he said, feeling weirdly relieved. 'Maybe she was at the wrong house.'

33

'No, she knew your name.'

And then he saw it: a flash of white breast against the grey of the sky; a lone bird circling. His heart lifted as it always did to see one of his birds arrive home safely. He forgot about Ellen and instead whistled high and shrill. The bird stopped circling and arrowed down towards him. Joe laughed, but then the smile died on his face as Prince perched on the roof of the loft, his head cocked, observing him.

He whistled again. It was important to get him into the trap so he could remove the race ring from his leg and clock his time. Prince didn't budge.

Joe whistled once more and still the bird remained where he was.

'Eh, Ellen,' Joe said as politely as he could, 'would you please go inside? I think my bird is afraid of you. He won't come to me.'

He was losing precious seconds now. Other birds could be flying into their lofts and his bloody bird was hopping about terrified of this old woman with her washing basket.

'Please will you go in?' he asked again, trying not to sound confrontational.

'Oh, I don't know.' Ellen did not sound at all pleased to be ordered inside but, to his relief, Joe saw her moving towards her house. 'Being told to stay indoors because some birds are flying around? I don't know.'

'I'll let you know when they're all in,' he called after her, before whistling at Prince again. The bird obligingly hopped on to the trap and Joe, as gently as he could, removed the ring from Prince's leg and popped it into the clock. Ninety-four minutes, he reckoned. But it could have been faster if Mrs McGrath hadn't been around.

In the next ten minutes, more and more of his birds returned. He never tired of seeing them come home safely. Blurs in the sky that became more definite as they flew back to him. He loved watching them alight in the boxes or on perches and eat the special mix he always gave them after a race. It was what they flew home for. That and their mating partners.

After twenty minutes, all but one of his birds had arrived. Joe gave it another ten and then reluctantly concluded that it must have met with an accident on the way back. He hated losing birds but it was something that happened at nearly every race or every toss.

He shut up the loft and went to tell Mrs McGrath that she could now hang out her washing.

They arrived in Rossclare about an hour later. As Billy drove along the coast road, Lizzie rolled down her window a tiny bit. She loved the tangy smell of the sea that hit her whenever she came home. Once upon a time she'd have gone swimming, but nowadays she rarely ventured into the water.

'Close that window!' Aileen half shrieked. 'It's freezing.'

Lizzie did as she was told and stared out into the inky blackness as Billy drove up towards their parents' house. The gates were open and Billy pulled into the driveway. Immediately the front door was opened and their parents came out to meet them. They must have been sitting by the door waiting for them, Lizzie thought in amusement.

'Hello!' Polly Walsh half ran across to the car. 'Welcome!' She enfolded her son in a hug, which he returned. Then, turning to Aileen, she did the same.

'Hiya, Mam,' Lizzie said. 'I'm here, too.'

Her mother laughed. 'Yes, Lizzie, I wasn't forgetting about you.'

'And neither was I!' Her dad pulled gently on her hair. 'Come on in and have some dinner, yez must be starving. I believe the traffic is terrible.'

'Awful,' Billy said, joining the two of them. 'It took over three hours to get down.'

After dinner Aileen and Billy went to call on Johnny, an old mate of Billy's, and Lizzie was left to tell her parents all her news. She didn't mention about seeing Joe Jones – that'd put a right dampener on the weekend, she thought. Instead she sat back and answered their questions about Tom. They always asked about Tom. Lizzie reckoned they kept hoping she'd tell them it was over.

'And is he working at the moment?' her mother asked.

'He has a part in a play,' Lizzie said.

'Oh, really?' Her mother sounded impressed. Since Lizzie had started seeing Tom eight months ago, he'd been in two plays. 'Is it a good part?'

Lizzie swallowed. 'Eh, well, he says that being in this play is a big coup. The director is the business, you know.'

Her mother looked at her, a little impressed. 'And what does Tom do in the play?'

'And he has a few auditions lined up,' Lizzie said quickly. She was terrified that if she lied and said he had a great part, they'd want to come and see him. 'He's very hopeful.'

'Lizzie,' her father shook his head, 'that boy will never have any money. Would you not go and get someone who has prospects? I mean, did he even get you a Christmas present?'

'Of course he did.'

'What was it?'

'A CD and a kite.'

'Mmm, you always wanted a kite, did you?' Her parents exchanged meaningful looks.

'No. But flying a kite is good fun. Have you ever done it?'

'No.' Her mother was indignant. 'What on earth would I be doing flying a kite at my age?'

'Your mother's idea of fun is going out in the rain with a placard,' her dad said dryly.

'I don't do that for fun. That's called protecting the community. We're marching tomorrow actually, Lizzie.'

'Oh, Mam,' Lizzie winced, 'not another one.'

'Yes, another one. You can never have too many protests. And this is an important one, isn't it, Kevin?'

Her husband nodded, though Lizzie could detect a hint of resignation in his eyes.

So, obviously, could her mother.

'There's no need for that sort of a nod,' she snapped. 'It affects this area – you'd think you'd be more supportive.'

'I *have* been supportive,' Kevin said indignantly. 'I've made up your banners, haven't I? And I rang the local papers looking for publicity and asking people to turn up. Now what would you call that?'

Mrs Walsh harrumphed and folded her arms. Turning to Lizzie she explained, 'There is a plan in the offing to revamp the harbour – we don't think there'll be enough room for all the boats if it goes ahead. So we're protesting against it.'

Lizzie sighed. Nothing could happen in her mother's part of Wexford without Mrs Walsh expressing an opinion on it.

'Now, it starts at nine, Lizzie, so I'll expect you to be up.'

'Me?' Lizzie couldn't help looking devastated. 'But—but, it's the weekend now.'

'So put it to good use. It's a fine thing when you can sit and help perfect strangers on the phone all night but you won't help your own mother.'

Lizzie said nothing.

'Now, you'll be up the front with me, helping me carry the banner.'

'And what about Billy?'

'What about him?'

'Well, he's home, too.'

'He's down with Aileen. I can hardly expect him to leave her, can I? And she can't come; she couldn't walk half a mile in those high heels she wears.'

Lizzie made a mental note to invest in some stilettos.

'Now,' her mother continued, 'we're marching from the harbour into the planning offices and staging our speeches there.'

Lizzie stayed quiet and her mother, taking that in the affirmative, stood up and brushed some crumbs from her beige skirt. 'Now, I'm going up to print out some copies of the chant. I'll be down in a while.'

She bustled out of the room and Lizzie gave an exasperated sigh, looking over at her dad.

'She's happy once she's got a project to be concentrating on,' her father said mildly.

Lizzie nodded. She supposed it was better than the terrible grief that had engulfed them all that day fourteen years ago, when Megan had gone out the door and never come back.

'And d'you know what else?' her father said, as he poured himself a glass of wine and offered Lizzie the bottle to fill her own glass. 'She's begun clearing out Meg's old room.'

Lizzie froze with the bottle held in mid-air. 'Really?'

'Yeah, she thought that, I dunno, some grandchild or other might like to sleep there when he or she gets older.' He paused. 'Your mam's looking to the future, which is good.'

Lizzie gulped. It was good, but it was heartbreaking too. 'And what'll she do with Meg's stuff?'

'I don't know. Sort it out, I suppose. Give things away, keep things.' He paused. 'There are a lot of things in that room.' Then, smiling, he added, 'Your sister was a terrible hoarder.'

She was, too. Lizzie remembered how Megan had piles of clothes and would invite Lizzie into her room to do makeovers on her. There were masses of half empty perfume bottles standing sentry along the windowsill. And enough hair products scattered across the floor to rival any hair salon. Lizzie had viewed Megan's room much as Aladdin had his treasure trove. 'I wonder will she let me have a root around when she's got it cleared.'

'I'm sure she will.'

Lizzie sat back in the chair and sipped the wine. It was a nice wine, probably bought in honour of Billy and Aileen's visit. 'Well, I'm glad,' Lizzie said.

'Yes.' Her father nodded. 'So am I.'

There was no way she was going to mention Joe Jones now.

That night, as was usual after a race, the club was heaving. Most of the members were over sixty and had been in pigeon racing from their early boyhood. Joe was the youngest member and someone could always be depended upon to give him a slagging over his lack of girlfriends. Joe never minded, they didn't mean it anyway. Most of them agreed that it was easier to keep pigeons if you didn't have a wife.

He stood in line, waiting for the official to check his times on the clock. No one ever knew the results of a race until the times had been checked against the distances flown. He felt confident that Prince had flown well, though of course it was impossible to be sure. The was a great buzz of conversation going on all around him and, though Joe never really got involved with too many people, he savoured the friendliness of it, the banter without the malice or threats that had underlined so much of his time in recent years.

'Hiya, Joe.' Alan, the chairman of the club, greeted him as he reached the top of the queue. He held out his hand for the clock. Joe watched as he opened it to remove the rings. 'Feeling lucky?'

'I don't believe in luck.' Joe sank his hands into the pockets of his denim jeans and grinned. 'I just believe in good birds.'

'Hey, listen, we all believe in good birds,' Alan answered, laughing. 'But then you get married and you realise there ain't no such thing.'

'So cynical,' Cid, another ancient pigeon fancier, croaked from behind Joe. Looking up into Joe's face he asked, 'How did your birds do?' He rubbed his hands together gleefully. 'I fancy my chances big time tonight.'

'They did OK,' Joe said nonchalantly.

Cid was the kind of guy who always fancied his chances and it wasn't just with his pigeons. Tonight his lanky frame sported a cream linen suit and blue open-necked shirt. His thatch of hair was brushed sideways and lacked any sort of a style. 'You coming for a pint after?' he asked.

'Yep.'

'Joe, hiya!' It was Noel. He was the closest thing Joe had to a friend in the club. He'd been the one to introduce him to everyone and get him started off with his loft. A sort of father figure, he kept dispensing advice to him on caring for his pigeons – and on life in general. He was a great laugh for a sixty-five-year-old.

The three moved away to the back wall to make way for other

people who were just coming in. It was a big club and the race had been well attended.

'How'd your birds do?' Noel asked Joe.

'Aw—'

'Brilliant,' Cid interrupted. 'Aw, I think I'm in for a great season. I have one now that seems to have come into form at just the right time. You should see the eyes of her. Nice and bright.'

Joe exchanged a glance with Noel and both of them suppressed a grin.

'I had one that didn't come back,' Joe said then. 'It's a bit of a blow.'

'Good one?'

'Yeah. I was going to breed from him.'

Noel nodded sympathetically while Cid chortled. 'Can't say I'm sorry one of your better birds didn't make it,' he stated. And, at Noel's look of disbelief, he said defensively, 'Well, less competition for us, isn't it?'

'You are bleedin' unbelievable,' Noel said incredulously. Turning to Joe, he asked, 'Isn't he a right friend to have, saying stuff like that?'

Joe just laughed. Compared to the people he'd met, Cid was harmless. 'Aw, he can say what he wants; his crappy pigeons have never beaten mine yet.'

'There's always a first time.' Cid tapped his nose.

'Not for you there hasn't been,' Joe joked and dodged an elbow from him.

John limped over to join them. Apart from Joe, he was the youngest member. At forty-five, he'd taken to pigeon racing quite late, but he was highly competitive and a quick learner. Joe had gifted him a few pigeons when he was starting up and the two had remained good friends.

'OK, EVERYONE!'

Amid much shushing, the chairman of the club stood up. 'I've got the results here. I'm going to post them up but, as usual, I'll announce the top three. Right: in third place was John Daly's Lucy Lou.'

'Yes!' John's fist punched the air. It was his first top three result. 'Yes! Yes! Yes!' He grabbed Joe by the shoulders and said loudly, 'Third place – can you believe it?'

'Eh, no actually,' Cid said sourly, causing people to laugh.

'In second place was Jim Reilly's Autopilot.'

Jim's celebration was a bit more sedate. Ninety years of age and tottering along on a Zimmer frame didn't exactly allow for wild enthusiasm. He accepted the congratulations with a shaky nod of his head.

'And the winner of the first club race of the season is . . . Joe Jones' Prince!'

Joe grinned modestly as Cid gawked at him in disbelief. 'When are you ever gonna strangle that pigeon and give the rest of us a chance?' he said, causing more laughter, though Joe didn't think he'd meant to. 'I bloody mean it!' he shouted out above the noise.

'I'll strangle him when you realise that you haven't a clue about pigeon racing,' Joe answered back and people around the room clapped and jeered.

'Come on up here, Joe,' the chairman said.

Joe made his way to the front of the room, his head low. While he was delighted to win, being the centre of attention in a crowded room freaked him out. It took all his self control to stay calm as he accepted his prize. Then, as was the norm, he waved the cheque about and said, 'Right lads, the first round is on me.'

Lizzie lay staring at the familiar ceiling of her childhood. She'd turned in early and now couldn't sleep. She pulled the quilt her mother had thrown across the bed up to her chin. The quilt was an old one, depicting characters from a show she used to watch as a kid. She'd been thrilled when her mother had bought it for her, and Megan, six years her senior, had pretended to be jealous of her, begging her for it. And Lizzie, always wanting to impress Megan, had given it to her.

She'd adored her elder sister. She'd spent her early girlhood trying her best to imitate her: if Megan liked a band then Lizzie liked it too; if Megan said something was uncool than

41

Lizzie wouldn't have anything to do with it. But really, looking back, she and Billy were more alike than she and Megan could ever have been. Megs was a show stopper. Her dad had called her his princess. Megan would walk into a room and everyone would look at her. She had charm and glamour in spades. She also caused more trouble than anyone else in the house by being way too big for her boots in many ways. But it was impossible to be angry with Megan for long. For one thing—

Her phone suddenly started to ring, playing a loud dance tune Tom had sent to her. Lizzie hopped out of bed, knowing her mother would go spare. Calls late at night frightened her.

Tom had sent a text: *Nite nite. Sleep tite.*

Lizzie smiled and sent one back.

8

LIZZIE, YAWNING WIDELY, had been dragged from bed by her mother to join in the protest.

The start-off point was filled with about a hundred protesters. They were either fishermen or their wives. Some children also darted about, in and out between people's legs, totally hyper. Martha, her mother's best friend, was busy handing out placards and whistles. Lizzie's dad was distributing bundles of leaflets to a number of people who were, Lizzie supposed, meant to hand them to anyone who passed.

There were people on this protest who would turn up to complain about the colour of paint on a litter bin, Lizzie observed. Her mother was one of them and Martha Dowling was another. Her dad generally got involved, too, but it was only to please his wife. He knew his life wouldn't be worth living if he didn't support her. He was coming towards Lizzie now, a few stray leaflets in his hands. 'All set,' he winked.

'As set as a bowl of warm jelly.'

'Ha, ha.'

Lizzie knew she should just walk away. She was twenty-eight, she didn't have to do what her mother wanted any more. But in fairness, she conceded that this at least was a valid protest. It wasn't as if she was marching for the right of flowers to grow on grass verges or the retention of a horribly dangerous historic building. Though she had marched for that in the past. Nope, this was a bona fide protest.

'Elizabeth, here you are.' Her mother handed her a loudspeaker.

'Mam, I'd rather just use my ordinary voice.'

Her mother frowned. 'You could be more supportive, Lizzie,' she said crossly. 'I'll give this to Martha, she'll appreciate it.'

'Good idea,' Lizzie smiled, trying to charm her back to good form.

Her mother tsked a bit and went in search of her friend. She arrived back a couple of minutes later with Martha, who was looking delighted as she examined the loudspeaker.

'One, two, three, four!' Lizzie jumped as Martha's nasal tones were amplified all around the harbour.

'Who on earth do we deplore?' Lizzie's mother shouted out.

'Daniel O'Donnell!' some wise guy yelled.

Lizzie snorted back a laugh as her mother, putting the loud-speaker to her lips, said, 'If that man can't take it seriously, he can leave. Daniel O'Donnell is a fine singer!' The crowd cheered.

'Now, again!' her mother cried. 'Come on, everyone – who on earth do we deplore?' The crowd answered with the rest of the chant.

Despite her embarrassment at marching along, Lizzie had to admire her mother. Nothing put her off. She was a woman on a mission. She strode determinedly forward, loudspeaker planted firmly to her mouth, shouting at the top of her voice. It seemed she was oblivious to the slagging of some less well-informed members of the public.

'Hiya, granny,' someone said. 'I wouldn't mind docking my boat in you!'

Lizzie bristled. 'I reckon you've only got a dinghy,' she shouted back. The man laughed.

'Elizabeth.' Her mother was shocked. 'Have a bit of dignity. Don't give them the satisfaction.'

'Did you hear what he said?'

'No, I was too busy trying to get my point across. Now come on, lift the chin and lift the voice.' Loudspeaker back up, she shouted, 'One Two Three Four!'

'Isn't she marvellous?' someone said in admiration. 'If she doesn't get the council to refuse the planning permission, no one will.'

44

Lizzie wasn't quite sure that she'd use the word marvellous. Her mother was marvellous in the way a tank is marvellous at crushing cars beneath it.

The protest was growing louder as they turned on to the main street. The police were there to guide them along and they'd stopped the traffic to let them through. Motorists beeped their horns as they passed and that only made the protesters more determined. The chant grew in volume.

Lizzie snuck a glance at her watch.

'You go on off now,' her dad said, nudging her. 'We're nearly there. Your mother won't mind.'

'Sure?' She tried to sound as if she didn't mind.

'Don't try and sound as if you don't mind,' her father teased.

She didn't ask again.

9

LIZZIE, WITHOUT CONSCIOUSLY thinking about it, found herself at the gateway to Joe Jones' parents' house. Well, she supposed, she had to get to know about him if she was to – what? Her mind faltered slightly. If she was to know him, of course. If she was to . . . She paused. She'd cross that bridge when she got there. The fact that she felt compelled to find out about him at all scared her a little. It was an out of control thing, like the feeling she had for cigarettes. She knew it wasn't doing her any good, but she couldn't let it go.

Joe Jones had been an only child. His dad, Geoff, owned the newspaper in Rossclare where Megan had worked that last summer. Geoff also had his fingers in quite a lot of other pies and was by all accounts a hard man to please. Joe's mother had been a former model, always wearing the latest fashions, and she had regularly featured in the papers at social events. Since Joe had been imprisoned, they had withdrawn from life in Rossclare.

Joe had grown up, she recalled from the time of the trial, as a doted upon, slightly wild child. Lizzie's dad had known Joe, having let him work on his boat a few times. He was, by all accounts, an exceptional fisherman. Her dad used to say that Joe Jones could smell where the fish were.

The bus she'd caught after leaving the protest dropped her off just opposite the gates to Joe's parents' house. Her biggest fear was that Joe would be there, though if he hadn't noticed her at the Luas station, she felt confident that she wouldn't be recognised. It had been fourteen years, after all, and while his face at twenty was burned into her memory, he hadn't changed

– whereas she had. The only recognisable thing about her now were her eyes, which had been her only asset at fourteen. Now, while not exactly *Vogue* cover material, Lizzie reckoned that she was about a million times better looking than the gawky adolescent she'd once been. At sixteen, she had sprouted suddenly, growing almost overnight to her five-foot-eight. The sudden growth spurt had caused her to be as skinny as the rest of her family.

She stood for a second, observing the opened iron gates and the wide curved driveway beyond. At the top of it, somewhere, was the house. She'd seen pictures of it, a massive two-storey affair with a large garden front and back.

Joe Jones had grown up here, she thought, as she put a foot inside the gates. He'd walked this exact same path, played in that garden. He'd driven the cheap car she remembered up that tarmac driveway. Feck it, she thought suddenly, she was going to walk right up to the house. She'd come all this way and there wouldn't be another bus back for ages. She wondered what she'd do when she reached the front door. Maybe she could pretend she was looking for someone, that she had got lost or something. She just had to see, had to know what life was like for these people now. It shocked her to realise that she hoped they were miserable. The feeling crept over her like night-time and she flinched before shaking it from her head. She didn't hope they were *totally* miserable, just not happy in the way they'd once been.

'Just not happy like before,' she whispered, to push the really horrible thoughts away. Her steps fell into rhythm with the words and her heart beat along with it, too. For one weird moment, she saw herself as if from outside: a lanky figure in an over-large coat striding grimly towards a front door. How ridiculous was that? She paused. It *was* ridiculous. She was being mad. What on earth had she been thinking of? She swallowed hard and had just turned to go when she heard, 'Hello, can I help you?'

Lizzie jumped. A man, he had to be Joe's dad, had spotted her from one of the downstairs rooms and had opened the window to shout after her. 'Can I help you?' he repeated. He didn't sound too friendly.

'Eh, I'm not sure,' Lizzie stammered. She felt her face grow hot. 'Is this the – eh – Connor house?'

'No.' The man, very like Joe to look at, shook his head. 'No Connors here.' He paused. 'There is an O'Connor next door, though – would that be who you're looking for?'

Shit! Of all the names in all the world . . . Lizzie attempted to look blank and shrugged. 'I don't think so.'

'Well, you could try them. It's a bit of a walk, though, if you go back down the drive.' He paused and seemed to consider. 'I can let you across our back garden and into their front garden, if you like?' He didn't seem to think she was going to refuse as he said, 'Just a second, I'll meet you at the front door.'

Lizzie waited with a hammering heart for him to open the door. Thoughts of legging it as fast as she could raced through her mind, but it would only look more suspicious. Nope, she had to brazen it out.

'Now, you can come through.' Mr Jones, front door open, beckoned her inside. Lizzie fell into step behind him. Even though her heart was hammering so much she felt sick, she was strangely elated to be able to gawk at the house. And what a house it was. A light-filled, huge hallway dominated by a sweeping staircase and doors everywhere. She was about to comment on the beauty of the house when he asked, 'Are you a relation of the O'Connors?'

'Eh, no.' A light sweat broke out on her forehead. She hadn't bargained on being asked any questions. 'Just a friend. Though I don't think it's O'Connor I'm looking for.'

'Oh.' He gave a shrug. 'So do you want to try, just in case?'

'Who's that, Geoff?' A tall, slim woman appeared at a doorway straight in front of them.

Lizzie stared at her. This was obviously Joe's mother, Leah. Despite her expensive clothes, she didn't look as haughty as Lizzie remembered from her photos. Instead her face bore an innocent, almost childlike expression, which only emphasised her still beautiful features.

'Hello,' she said to Lizzie. 'We were expecting you?' She looked at her husband in mild confusion. 'Do we know this girl? She looks . . .' Leah frowned. 'Familiar.'

Lizzie felt her stomach heave.

'No,' Geoff's voice became suddenly softer and he crossed over to his wife. He smiled at her. 'This isn't a visitor for us. This girl is looking for a family called Connor. I thought it might be the O'Connors so I offered to let her out the back way.'

'Hi,' Lizzie said. Oh God, what was she *doing*? Her mother would have a fit. 'Sorry to barge in like this.'

'No trouble.' The woman smiled gently. 'It's a long walk back down the drive. But Geoff, I think the O'Connors are gone to Shirley's for the weekend.' She turned to Lizzie. 'That's their daughter.'

'Niece,' Geoff said, nudging her and grinning. 'Shirley is their niece, Leah.'

'Oh, yes, of course.' Leah tinkled out a laugh. 'Anyway, they've gone there until Monday night.'

'OK,' Lizzie said quickly, sensing an opportunity to escape. 'Well, the Connors I know don't have a daughter or a niece.'

Mr Jones grinned sheepishly. 'I suppose I should have asked you that.'

'He was never the brightest.' Mrs Jones smiled softly at him and he smiled back, looking oddly relieved.

'I'll, eh, go.' Lizzie indicated the front door and took a step backwards. 'Sorry to intrude like that.'

'How did you get here?' Mrs Jones asked.

'Bus,' Lizzie said. 'From, eh, New Ross.'

'Oh, but there won't be one for ages to take you back,' Mrs Jones said. 'And where do your friends live?'

Lizzie shrugged. 'I thought they lived here.' She managed a passable laugh. 'I'll have to ring them when I get back to my house. In, eh, New Ross.' Three lies in such short sentences, she thought. It's official, I'm going mad.

'You can use our phone?'

'I don't know their number offhand,' Lizzie gulped.

49

'Well, not to worry,' Geoff said, 'I'm going to New Ross in about twenty minutes. I'll drive you back.'

This was a nightmare. It served her right. 'I couldn't expect you to do that.' Her voice sounded like a terrified squeak. She swallowed hard and with effort brought it under control. 'You don't even know me.' Her jumper was sticking to her, she was sweating so much. And how on earth could she get home from New Ross?

'It's no trouble,' Mr Jones said. 'The buses that go by here are so few, you'd be lucky to get one within the hour.' They both looked expectantly at her.

'But you don't know me,' Lizzie spluttered out, unable to think of anything else to say.

'We're not exactly signing over our worldly goods to you,' Geoff Jones said in amusement, 'it's only a lift. And besides my wife is coming, too, if you feel unsafe.'

'Oh no, it's not that,' Lizzie stammered. God, they were nice enough people, though Mr Jones did have a terrible reputation. 'Right,' she continued, 'that's very nice of you, thanks.'

'I've just to make a few phone calls first,' Mr Jones explained, holding up his mobile. 'Back in a while.'

Lizzie squirmed. Jesus. Shit.

'Have a cuppa while you're waiting,' Mrs Jones said. 'Come on in.'

Now they were offering her tea. It served her right. She'd come full of anger and they were being very nice. She guessed it wasn't their fault they'd had a son like Joe.

'OK, thanks,' she said weakly, following the older woman into the most enormous kitchen she had ever seen.

'So, are you from New Ross?' Mrs Jones asked as she filled the kettle, indicating for Lizzie to sit down at a table that would hold about twenty people comfortably.

'New Ross. Yes.' She couldn't meet the woman's eye. She was too nice to lie to. So to avoid any more fibbing, she said hastily, 'You have a lovely house.'

That at least was true. Light poured into the kitchen, despite the grey skies. It made the Italian marble floor tiles sparkle, throwing light up on to the expensive kitchen presses and gleaming stainless steel kitchen equipment. There was a huge utility room just off the kitchen; it looked at least as big as Billy's house.

'Thanks. It's a bit big for the both of us now, though.'

'Oh. Did you once have loads of children or something?' Lizzie was pleased at her casual tone.

'No.' Mrs Jones smiled, a little sadly, Lizzie thought. 'Just the one.'

'Boy or girl?'

'Boy.' Mrs Jones paused. 'All grown up now.'

'And is he still living around?'

Mrs Jones busied herself with the tea as she answered. 'No, no. He's left here. He's in Dublin. He works up there.' She placed a cup and some milk in front of Lizzie. 'There you are now. I'll get you some tea in a minute.'

'Thanks.' Lizzie poured some milk into her cup. 'Where does he work? I'm in Dublin, too, maybe I'd know him.'

Mrs Jones smiled. 'Big place, Dublin,' she said. Then went on, 'Oh, he works, you know, in lots of places.' She screwed up her eyes and looked up at the ceiling, as if trying to remember the name of where he worked. 'Lots of jobs,' she finished. 'Always busy.'

Lizzie shrugged. 'Oh, right.'

'And he races birds,' Mrs Jones went on. 'Stone mad about pigeons, he is.'

'Really?'

'Always was,' Mrs Jones went on. She began to pour the tea. 'Say when.'

'When,' Lizzie said as the tea reached the mid-way mark.

Mrs Jones poured herself a cup and sat opposite Lizzie at the table.

'And do you see him often?' Lizzie asked.

Leah shrugged. 'Oh, you know. Yes. Lots.' She flushed. 'Would you like sugar?'

She was lying. Lizzie decided not to ask any more. There was a silence then. Lizzie didn't quite know what else to say. She sipped her tea and tried to ignore the urge for a smoke.

'And are you originally from here?' Mrs Jones asked.

'Born and bred.'

'Oh. That's nice.'

'Yes. I love Wexford. Though I suppose Dublin is my home now.'

'Are you long up there?'

'A few years.' She talked then a little bit about the Life agency, though she got the impression that Leah Jones wasn't that interested. Well, who would be interested in a perfect stranger's life? she thought. But she kept talking away, just to fill in the silences.

Just before the clock hit the half hour Mr Jones arrived back, jangling his car keys, and asked her if she was ready to leave.

'You really are very good.' Lizzie stood up. 'But honestly, there is no need.' How the hell was she going to get home from New Ross? It was an hour from Rossclare at least.

'Not at all. I've to buy a few things there, so come on.' Then he looked at his wife. 'Come on, Leah, you too.'

'Me? I don't want to go out.'

'Well,' he smiled slightly and wrapped his arm about her shoulder, 'I want you to come out. I've a surprise for you.'

'Oh, well, in that case,' she laughed, as he helped her put on her coat.

'Come on, so,' Mrs Jones laughed to Lizzie. 'This man,' she indicated her husband, 'he hates to be kept waiting.'

They really were a nice couple, Lizzie thought. Not at all like she'd been expecting.

Mr Jones didn't talk much on the way to New Ross. He stared intently out the window, weaving in and out of traffic as rapidly as he could. The way he drove reminded Lizzie of the way Mark drove.

Leah sat in the front, saying very little, quite content to stare out the window and remark every so often on how cold everywhere looked. Geoff Jones answered her tenderly whenever she commented on anything and Lizzie was struck by how kind he seemed.

She wondered how they'd coped when Joe had gone to prison.

Just as the car reached the outskirts of New Ross, Lizzie said, 'You can let me off here, if you don't mind. This is great.'

Geoff indicated and pulled the car in off the road. 'Bye now,' he said.

'Yeah. Bye.' Lizzie climbed out and watched them drive away. How the hell could she get home now?

She rang her dad on his mobile and, after expressing his surprise that she was in New Ross, he said he'd pick her up in an hour or so, after the protest had ended. Lizzie decided to wander into the town and see if she could find a good bookshop. She knew now what it was she had to do. Her plan was very simple.

It was all about finding the right bait.

10

Well, Dad doesn't know it but he has done me a huge
favour with the job he got me. If he for one minute
suspected just how cool this job is, he'd have me out of
there double quick. Talk about perks!!!! Or pecs!!! Or
whatever you're having yourself . . .

Basically, I decided I might as well make the best of
this job so I dressed up for it. So glad I did now. I wore
my skirt that looks respectable until you cross your
legs. Massive split up the side. And I wore my high
shoes and my gorgeous white blouse that makes the
most of my cleavage. Our family are not blessed with
great busts but this blouse is great.

The first thing that happens is that I meet Geoff
Jones. Geoff owns the paper. He is like the richest man
in Wexford. Or the richest man in Ireland, I don't
know. Anyway, he looks rich. He was wearing a suit
and tie and his face was sort of cross and impatient.
He said hello and buzzed Joe (his son) to come and
collect me. Joe arrives up. Now, Joe is a handsome guy.
Tall, nice bod, cheeky chappie sort of grin. He's a bit
weird though. He likes hanging about with my dad for
starters and on top of that he's big into pigeons. But
as I studied him I thought to myself, yeah, I could
work with him. It must be like when you decide to get
married, you stare at your husband to be and think,

54

yeah, I could wake up to that face every morning. That's what I felt about Joe. He wasn't exactly horrible to look at.

But anyway, Joe brings me down to the office where me, him and another guy are to work and, without beating about the bush, Joe looked like a grey day on Rosslare Strand compared to the guy who was sitting in the office waiting for us. He was like a four star holiday to Ibiza. OH GOD! Beautiful wouldn't even describe him. Turns out his name is Dessie, he's twenty-three, so not too much older than me. He loves selling ads and he has white straight teeth, a gorgeous northern accent that sounds as if he swallowed a tub of cream, dark hair, fabulous dark eyes you could get totally lost in and smooth skin – though I haven't had the pleasure of running my hands over it. I have died and gone to heaven.

Alleluia!!!!

The job involves selling ad space in a newspaper. We ring up companies and try to get them to buy ads. The two lads could sell contraceptives to a priest. Me? I have sold nothing in three days. Joe said he'd give me some of his ads and I could pretend that I'd sold them. When I protested, he just said that his dad could hardly fire him for poor sales, could he?

I guess he had a point.

Then Dessie laughed and told me to take the ads, that there was no point in losing the best looking member of staff! I rang Aileen and told her this and she agreed that things were progressing nicely. I can't wait for her to meet Dessie when she comes down in August.

I really miss Aileen since her and her dad moved to Dublin on another wild goose chase for her mother (her dad is BONKERS!). Aileen told me she reckons that if her dad finds her mother that he will let her come back. AGAIN! Aileen's mother has left her and her dad twice now and her dad has let her come back both times. Aileen says her dad insists that this time will be her last chance but Aileen doesn't believe him. It's awful in her house, she says, as her dad is so upset. That's why Mam has invited her down for a month in the summer.

Anyway, my poor dad can't understand why I like my new job so much. Poor innocent man.

11

W HEN LIZZIE ARRIVED back from lunch on Monday afternoon she saw Tom lounging against the doorway of the Life building. He glanced once or twice at his watch before scanning the street.

Lizzie observed him for a second, wondering not for the first time how it was that a man with none of the classically good-looking features could be so damn attractive. Tom was tall, a bit on the skinny side, his hair and eyes the darkest brown while his face was vampire-pale. His nose was off centre as, according to him, he'd fallen out of his pram when a baby and broken it. But despite this, he had a presence about him that demanded attention; an energy he radiated which lit up those around him; an intensity in his face and movements. The clothes he wore were always a little quirky, too, and Lizzie loved that. People tended to stare after Tom in the street for no obvious reason. They were staring now as they passed. Staring at his faded brown cords and purple and yellow trainers.

'Tom!' Lizzie called out eventually.

'Hey!' He strode towards her, grinning broadly. 'Well, so much for surprising you.'

'What?'

'I turn up here at lunchtime all set to treat you to a five-euro sambo and where are you?' He cocked an eyebrow. 'Gone.'

'Aw, sorry, I left early.' She gave him a gentle shove. 'You should have rung.'

'Eh,' he joked, as if she was thick, 'then it wouldn't have been a surprise, would it?'

Lizzie laughed. 'No, I guess not. So,' she asked, linking her hand in his, 'how'd your weekend go?'

'Good. Missed you.' He tweaked her cheek. 'Yours?'

'Same. And your line? Oops, sorry, play?'

'My line was fabulous, thanks for asking.' He paused and admitted almost shyly, 'I also got a second call back for the other play I went for. Main part.'

'No!'

'Uh-huh.'

'That is brill.' She hugged him and inhaled the gorgeous scent of his aftershave. 'Oh, I'm so proud of you.'

'Well, I have to get it first.' He took Lizzie's hands in his and looked at her, his eyes suddenly becoming serious. 'And I just want to say I'm sorry about last Thursday night. I totally overreacted.'

'It's OK. I was only—'

'Lizzie,' he interrupted, holding his hand up, 'just let me say this, OK?'

He sounded as if he meant business. 'OK,' she said cautiously.

Tom took a deep breath and said determinedly, 'I'm going out with you 'cause I like you. I mean . . .' He paused and, his voice faltering a little, said haltingly, 'I *really* like you.' He stressed the 'really'.

'I know. And I like you.'

'And I know that at the moment I can't bring you to fancy places, but one day I will, you'll see.'

'I don't care about that.' She was appalled that he would think it would matter to her. 'That doesn't matter.'

'It does to me.' He said it firmly, his black eyes holding her gaze and turning her on something rotten. 'You deserve much more than a sandwich in a greasy spoon, I know that, I'm not stupid. And I know that's why your folks hate me, but I swear, if acting doesn't work out, I'll give it up and get a real job.'

'You will not!' Lizzie said. 'I like greasy spoons, I like going to see you in plays. I like pointing you out to my mates and saying, that's my guy up there. I don't care what my parents think.'

'I do.'

His honesty floored her. She swallowed. 'Well, you shouldn't. If I'm happy, they're happy too.'

He tilted up her chin. 'One line is a start, Lizzie. Next time, I'll have more.'

God she loved it when he sounded all passionate and intense. 'I know. And you were great with one line.'

'Thanks.' He smiled bashfully at her. Touched his forehead off hers. 'Was I the best?'

It was a joke they had. It was her job to think up witty responses. 'Were you the best? Is there a massive big hole in the ozone that'll kill us all one day?'

He laughed. 'Eh, not one of your better ones, Liz.'

'Were you the best? Was Thin Lizzy the best band of all time?'

'So I wasn't the best?'

'Oh feck off, there's no pleasing some people.'

She punched him, he caught her hand and, pulling her to him, he kissed her.

'Well, it's a fine thing when I'm looking for my staff and they're out snogging their other halves in the middle of the street,' Mark joked as she walked by him to her desk.

'It's a fine thing when your boss is a peeping Tom,' Lizzie said back. 'I could report you, you know.'

'Yeah, right.' Mark rolled his eyes. 'So how is the famous actor?'

'Not famous enough, but he will be,' Lizzie said cheerily. Mark, like her parents, didn't treat her relationship with Tom as anything other than a fling.

'Yeah, but what will he be famous for?' Mark quirked his eyebrows. 'His ability to be an actor without actually getting any parts?'

'This is my boyfriend,' Lizzie said firmly. 'You are my boss.'

'I am.' Mark nodded contritely. 'Apologies. Sue me if it makes you feel better.'

'What do you want?' She wondered if any other bosses treated their staff the way Mark treated her. She guessed it was because they'd known one another a long time, since the beginning of

Life, so she supposed their exchanges were more frank than other people's working relationships. And while she liked Mark, he did his best to drive her mad sometimes. Still, she was well able for him. He joked that he employed her for her attitude. 'Well?' she demanded.

Mark regarded her for a second with amused eyes. 'OK, I'll stop teasing.' He stood up. 'I only wanted to see if there was any word from O'Brien's builders on the house?'

'I only sent out the email last week. I'll call them first thing next Monday. OK? Happy?'

'I'd be a lot happier if we had a house to buy,' Mark said. 'Still, it's early days I suppose.'

'Very early days.'

'I'd be happy with something concrete to go on,' he said.

'That's what your wife said when she flung you out the window, was it?' Lizzie giggled.

Mark snorted and said, 'My acrimonious relationship with my ex is not your business.'

'My relationship with my boyfriend is not yours,' Lizzie said sweetly back.

'Point taken,' he winked.

12

THE PHONE RANG. Lizzie took a deep breath and picked it up. 'Hello. This is Lizzie at Life. How can I help you?' She forced herself to sound alert, though it had been a very tiring night with non-stop calls since about seven.

Anna, whose phone had temporarily stopped ringing, was taking advantage of the lull to pull on her coat.

'Go,' Lizzie mouthed silently.

Anna made an 'are you sure?' gesture and Lizzie nodded.

'Hello?' she said again into the phone as the door closed gently behind her co-counsellor.

'Hi,' a shaky voice said back. 'I—I, well, I don't know who else to call.'

'That's fine,' Lizzie said gently. 'You take your time. How about just telling me your name for now.'

'My, my real name?' The woman at the other end sounded fearful.

'No, it doesn't have to be. But I'd like to call you something.'

'Sinéad,' the woman said. 'I always liked that name.'

'OK, Sinéad,' Lizzie said as softly as she could, hoping she sounded encouraging. 'Can you tell me what's wrong?'

The woman took a deep breath. 'Well, I don't know if anything is wrong, really,' she said hesitantly. 'I just rang you to find out.'

Lizzie remained silent. It was amazing how many people said that.

'I'm married two years, see,' the woman continued, 'and, well, things seem to have changed.' Her voice shook. 'At least I think they have. Or maybe they haven't. I don't know any more.'

'What kind of things?' Lizzie asked.

'All kinds of things.' Sinéad paused. 'Us. The way he is. Everything.'

The way he is. Lizzie bit her lip. 'Just take your time,' she advised. 'Explain it to me.' What the woman wouldn't realise is that she would be explaining it to herself, too.

'OK.' Another shaky intake of breath. 'Well, when we got married it seemed normal, you know.'

'Your marriage?'

'Yes. We were happy. He made me laugh. He bought me things.'

'Sounds good.'

'Oh, it was.' There was a long pause and Lizzie wondered if Sinéad had hung up but then she went on, sporadically halting after every couple of words as if she couldn't quite catch her breath: 'But now, well, I get on his nerves. I don't know how. I don't mean to. I never know any more what will annoy him. And I'd just like to know.'

'You'd like to know if it's normal to get on someone's nerves?' From experience, Lizzie knew where this was leading and she winced in anticipation at what she might hear.

'Yes.' The woman paused, then stammered out, 'No. I'd just like to know *how* I get on his nerves.'

'What kinds of things annoy him?' Lizzie asked.

'Oh . . .' Sinéad seemed to think. 'Well, yesterday I met a friend of mine, just for half an hour, and he got really upset about it. He said that this friend didn't like him and that I was betraying him by meeting her.'

'And were you?'

'No. Of course not.' Then, 'I mean, my friend doesn't like him but she never says it. We never talk about him. And anyway, I told him that his mother doesn't like me and it doesn't stop him from meeting her.'

Good for you, Lizzie wanted to say, but she couldn't. 'OK,' she said instead, 'and what was his reaction to that?'

'Well, that's why I decided to ring,' Sinéad sniffed. 'Just to see if it's normal.'

'See if what's normal?'

'Well . . .' Sinéad gulped audibly and Lizzie got the impression that she was just about holding it together.

'Take your time,' Lizzie said, 'I'm going nowhere.' Though if she didn't get out in ten minutes she was going to miss the Luas and probably Joe, too.

'He, eh, well, he hit me,' Sinéad blurted out. Then, 'Not hard or anything. Just as if he was sort of exasperated. Not a big hit.'

'He hit you,' Lizzie repeated, as if to emphasise the main words in the sentence. She tried to say it in a non-judgemental way, though she felt like killing the bastard. 'OK. So he hit you but it wasn't hard.'

'That's right.' Sinéad sounded hopeful. 'Not hard at all.'

'Do *you* think that's normal?'

'I don't know,' Sinéad said. 'That's why I rang.'

'Has he ever hit you before?'

Sinéad paused. 'No, and he swore he wouldn't ever again. I mean he begged me not to leave. He got down on his knees and apologised and even said I could meet my friend, even though it hurt him a lot. Like, he must be hurt a lot for him to hit me.'

'Do you hit him when he visits his mother?'

Sinéad laughed a little uneasily. 'Well, no.'

'Why?' Lizzie paused. 'I mean, if it's normal.'

'I just wouldn't.' She paused. Stopped. 'Oh.' Another pause. Then she said, half angrily, 'You think he's wrong, don't you?'

'I didn't say that.' Lizzie strove for a neutral tone. 'I'd just like you to think about why you don't—'

The line went dead.

Lizzie replaced the receiver. 'Damn.' Closing her eyes, she massaged them with the palms of her hands. Sinéad, like others before her, had rung hoping to be told it was normal. That's all she'd wanted. But Lizzie couldn't tell her that and Lizzie knew deep down Sinéad didn't really believe it either.

God, she hoped this woman would ring again. She hated to think of all those people out there who were in trouble.

'That bad, ey?' One of the night counsellors startled her as she came in.

Lizzie opened her eyes and smiled. 'It's been a busy night, all right.' She indicated the book. 'I've a call to write up, but I'll do it tomorrow. I'll just scribble Sinéad in to remind myself.'

Five minutes later she was out on the street, her eyes searching for Joe in the straggly crowd. As before he passed her out, his head bent against the chill April air. He strode along as if he hadn't a care in the world. Well, Lizzie thought, soon he'd have a lot of worries – an awful lot. She would make sure of that.

She shivered slightly and couldn't decide if it was in anticipation or fear of what she was going to do. Was it fair? some part of her wondered. After all he'd served his time, but what was a couple of years in jail compared to being dead? She grit her teeth and remembered how he'd admitted that, yes, he had been the last one to see Megan alive. But instead of saying that he'd been responsible for her death, he had made up some stupid theory that had fallen apart in court. Lizzie remembered his face when things had started to go wrong for him and it was that which had kept her sane until now. Maybe it wouldn't have hurt so acutely if he'd admitted what he'd done, but he hadn't. If he'd apologised or said sorry, but he hadn't. Lizzie blinked back angry tears and put all her concentration into gripping her bag firmly in her hand and walking after him as fast as she dared. If he didn't hurry, they'd both miss the Luas. She thought how funny it was that no one on the street knew that the guy passing them out was a convicted criminal. She wondered what they would do if they knew. Would his neighbours try to get him out of his house? Would that sweet, nosy neighbour still believe that he was a 'good lad'? Would she ignore him? Would she care? Lizzie wondered what secrets the people walking towards her were carrying and if she would care.

The late-night Luas was just pulling up as they arrived. Joe hopped into a half empty carriage and Lizzie hopped in after him, her heart beginning to pound.

* * *

Joe thought it odd that the girl with the oversized bag chose to sit beside him. After all there were a lot of free seats on the tram, but she had plonked herself right beside him, hitting off him in fact and causing him to bang his head against the window.

'Oh, sorry,' the girl said, not sounding that sorry in Joe's opinion, 'I do apologise.'

Something about the tilt of her head made him catch his breath. A tug of something at the edge of his brain, which dissolved as she bestowed on him another apologetic grin. She was cute in a dishevelled sort of way. He liked the way her hair was lots of different colours. It looked cool and sort of funky.

'No worries.' He rubbed his temple. 'I'll send on the medical bill.'

She gave a light laugh, showing him a glimpse of her even white teeth. He smiled back and turned away again. Women as pretty as this one made him uncomfortable.

'I hate the window seat,' she went on in a breathless sort of voice, 'I get sick.'

'Right.' He nodded without looking.

The tram began to move slowly out of the station and the girl beside him started to fidget, her elbow banging off his body in quite an annoying way. Joe attempted to move away but, as he was crammed up against the window, there was nowhere to go. He glanced sideways to see what she was up to. She seemed to be wrestling a rather large book out of a bag. The book looked way too big for the bag and she was pulling at it as if she were trying to wrestle a fish caught in a net. In the end, with a massive wrench, the book came free and fell with a bang on to the floor. People jumped.

The girl looked mortified. 'Sorry,' she called out to the carriage in general.

Joe watched in semi-amusement as she pulled the book on to her lap. To his surprise, it was a pigeon book. A completely crap one, but a book about birds all the same.

'It's probably too heavy a book to be bringing about with me,' she said conversationally to him, for some reason, 'but it just looked so interesting, I had to have it.' She flicked a hand through her mad-coloured hair.

'It's actually not a great book, if you don't mind me saying.' Joe surprised himself by replying but he couldn't help it. It was a combination of the attractive girl and the subject matter. 'It's . . . you know.' He waved his hand about and felt a blush creep over his face as he said shyly, 'Too technical, really. You want to know about birds, you have to work with them.'

'Oh.' She looked surprised. 'Right.' A pause. 'Do you keep pigeons?'

He considered being evasive. The last thing he wanted to talk about was himself, but she looked so interested. And what would be the harm? If it was another guy, he'd have no problem talking. 'Yeah,' he nodded. Then, sensing that more was expected of him he added, 'I started off years ago, my granddad used to keep them, but I've only got back into it in the last few years. I've about eighty birds now.'

'Wow. Cool.'

He smiled shyly, 'You?'

The girl shook her head. 'No. I'd love to but I'm living with my brother and he'd hate it.'

'Why?'

'He's just not into birds. He thinks they're dirty and smelly.'

'Rubbish.'

'Yeah, that's what I say, but it's his place.' The girl paused. 'I'd love to be involved someway without having to keep them myself.' She sighed and passed her palm over the open page of the book. 'This is the nearest I can get.'

Joe felt sorry for her. He knew what it was like not to be able to pursue the hobby. 'You could join a club,' he suggested.

'A club?'

'Yeah.' Joe nodded, warming to the topic. 'That way you could maybe help someone out with their birds or help out on race nights. Every club always needs a hand.'

'Really?'

'For sure.'

The girl paused. 'Are you in a club then?'

'Ranelagh racing club.'

'Would they be interested in me joining, just to help?'

Joe half grinned as he thought of all the members and not a woman among them. He thought of this striking girl walking in on top of them on a Friday night. 'Absolutely,' he nodded. 'Though you could change your mind.'

'No, I wouldn't. I'd do anything just to be near the whole scene.'

'Would Ranelagh be near you?'

'I live in Dundrum, so I could catch the Luas.' The girl paused. 'Would you give me directions?'

'Sure.'

Lizzie watched as Joe drew a map on the cover of her book, his shaved head bent in concentration. She felt sick being so close to him and yet sort of elated, too. Her plan had gone so much better than she'd anticipated, but obviously asking about his birds was the way to this guy's heart. From his closed up demeanour when she'd sat beside him to the animated look on his face now, she knew that if she played her cards right she'd be home and dry. He hadn't changed much since she'd last seen him, she thought. His hair was shaved and his face was more mature, more chiselled. But she'd spent so much of her thirteenth and fourteenth years hoping to catch a glimpse of him with her dad that she'd know him anywhere.

'We meet again tomorrow,' he said, disturbing her thoughts as he handed her back her pen. 'Seven o'clock. I'll introduce you, if you like.'

She widened her eyes in appreciation. 'Would you? Oh, thanks.' Biting her lip, she added, 'You have no idea how much this means to me.'

To her surprise, his eyes darkened a little as he said solemnly, 'Yeah, I do. I was like you once.'

He'd never been like her. Never, Lizzie thought. 'It was such a weird coincidence sitting beside you tonight,' she said as brightly as she could.

'Aw, fate is a weird thing,' Joe said, smiling broadly. Then the smile faltered a little as he stood up abruptly. 'Sorry, my stop. See you tomorrow if you decide to come.'

'Oh,' Lizzie waved her pen about, 'I'll be there.'

'By the way,' he held out his hand, 'I'm Joe.'

Her skin crawled as she took his hand in hers. His grip was firm, his hand warm. 'Lizzie,' she stammered.

'Bye, Lizzie,' he smiled again. 'See you tomorrow.'

That night Lizzie dreamed that someone was coming after her. She knew they had a coat or bag or something to cover her with. Once they covered her, they were going to take her away.

She woke up at five and couldn't go back to sleep.

13

Tom's phone went straight to voicemail. She had deliberately rung him when she knew he'd be at the theatre.

'Hi Tom, it's Lizzie. I might be late meeting you after the play tonight. Don't wait for me, I might be held up. If so talk tomorrow morning. Break a leg. Lots of hugs.' She blew a big smoochy kiss down the receiver, feeling a tiny bit guilty to be standing him up, but she'd make it up to him next time.

Flicking her phone off, she tucked it into her bag and left to catch the Luas to Ranelagh.

'Hi, pigeon girl.' A horn blared beside her. Lizzie looked up from Joe's map, which she had been following, to see Joe in a battered red car, leaning out the window. His good-looking face grinned broadly at her. 'Want a lift the rest of the way?'

'Eh, yeah, thanks.' Lizzie tried to conceal the quiver in her voice. This was it. This was her big chance and she couldn't blow it. Joe leaned over and unlocked the passenger door for her. 'Just give it a huge pull and it should loosen up,' he advised.

Lizzie yanked the door hard and it came away from the frame with a squealing of metal.

'Hasn't been used in a while,' Joe said, looking suddenly shy as she sat in beside him, her long legs almost folded under her in the confined space.

The back seat was down and a number of covered wicker baskets, containing what she assumed must be pigeons, were aligned behind her. 'Are they your birds?' she asked, suddenly interested to see them despite herself.

'Uh-huh.' Joe was concentrating on getting the car back into the flow of traffic. 'They'll be racing tomorrow from Wexford. I bring them down on a Friday to be entered for the race.'

'OK.'

'Eh, look under your seat there,' Joe said. 'If you can bend down.'

Lizzie swallowed hard. Was she completely mad, getting into a car with a convicted murderer? 'Why?' She winced at the fright in her voice.

Joe shot her a quick glance. 'I, eh, well, I found an old book of mine, thought you might like it. It's under the seat.'

'Oh, right.' Lizzie bent down and retrieved an old battered book, a picture of a pigeon on the front. *Pigeon Racing*, it was called. 'Oh,' she gulped, 'thanks.' She didn't know what else to say. If it were anyone other than Joe, she would have been incredibly touched at the thoughtfulness, but all she wanted to do was wallop him with it. 'That's so good of you.'

He flushed. 'Yeah, well, that book you had yesterday, it's not great. It's all technical, there's nothing about, you know, giving the birds affection and stuff. That book,' he nodded in its direction, 'has it all. It was one of my first books.'

Lizzie feigned interest and flicked through some pages. There were pictures of breeders, all old and wrinkled and wearing really odd clothes.

'It's a really old book – the photos are dated, but the stuff in it is sound.'

'Are you sure you trust me with this?' Lizzie asked.

'It's only a book,' Joe said, grinning. 'And anyway, if I don't get it back I'll hunt you down on the Luas.'

'You'll get it back, I promise.' Lizzie tucked it away in her bag. 'God, I can't wait to read it.'

'There's a very good chapter on training the birds,' Joe said, sounding animated. 'You'll love it.'

'I bet I will.'

A silence fell between them.

'Do you work in town?' Lizzie asked eventually, hoping the

question would sound natural after what they'd just been talking about. 'Are you on the Luas every night?'

'Just on my late nights,' Joe answered. 'I'm assistant manager at Fortunes Gym on D'Olier Street. I'm also a swim instructor there. You?'

'I'm in charge of fundraising at Life. I also counsel.'

'Life?'

'You haven't heard of Life?'

'I heard it's something you have to survive,' Joe joked.

Lizzie flinched. Not everyone survives, she felt like snapping at him. 'It's like the Samaritans,' she said, making a huge effort to sound pleasant. 'We help people, or at least we hope we do.'

He looked impressed. Lizzie wondered if she should push the 'I am a good person' angle. 'It's great – but sad at times, too.'

'I'll bet it is,' he nodded. A pause. 'I'd never be able to do it, that's for sure.'

'It's not for everyone.'

'Yeah,' he said, 'I suppose not. Fair play to you. It's a good thing to do.'

In the ensuing silence, Lizzie studied him out of the corner of her eye. Here was a man who looked so perfectly relaxed, so perfectly at home behind the wheel of his battered car. He drove along, his weird greeny hazel eyes scanning the road ahead, the tiniest of smiles on his lips. He smelled of soap and air and fresh clothes. She wanted to banish that complacent look from his handsome face, so she asked casually, 'You're not from Dublin, are you? You sound like a Wexford man.'

It worked. His grin died and he winced. 'Wow,' he said, sounding taken aback but trying not to, 'good guess.'

'That's because I'm from there, too – you still have the twang.' Lizzie smiled disarmingly. Time to cheer him up. 'So, what part?'

'Rossclare,' he said, and she caught the wariness in his voice. 'You?'

She was tempted to say Rossclare, too, and get him worried

in case she might know who he was, but instead she lied: 'New Ross. Do you miss it?'

'Nope.' His answer was final. He gazed with a fierce concentration out the windscreen. It was obvious he wasn't used to talking about his home place.

'Me neither,' she said. 'Dublin is great, isn't it? Do you go out much?'

'Naw.' He shook his head. The smile crept back on to his face. 'The pigeons need a lot of looking after. I have a neighbour, a lovely woman, but for some reason my birds keep shitting all over her clothes.'

It was his bewildered tone that made her laugh, despite herself.

'No shit,' Joe said, then grinned even more. 'Or like maybe lots of shit.'

She laughed again, not able to help it. But perhaps that was a good thing.

He indicated and pulled into a small car park, which was already filling up. Men with baskets identical to Joe's were carrying them carefully into a small red-bricked building. 'So, here we are. You tag along with me if you want and I'll introduce you to everyone.'

'OK. Thanks.' She smiled at him.

'And you can keep that book until you're finished with it. Any questions, just ask.'

'Yeah, great.'

'Come on, so.' He climbed out of his car and slammed the door. Going around, he popped open the boot and pulled the baskets from it. 'You can carry one, if you like.'

'Can I?' She tried to make it sound as if she thought it was a big deal.

'It's not a big deal,' Joe said, sounding amused. 'It's only a basket.'

'Sure, of course.' Lizzie pulled the basket from the back and followed Joe into the building, where they joined a queue.

Lizzie was a bit taken aback to see that the age profile of the members of Ranelagh pigeon club was triple her own. They were old, like her parents. And everyone seemed to be sneaking glances at her. And it was all men. Everywhere. Not a woman in sight. Her unmarried Aunty Betty would love it here.

'Are there no women here?' she asked Joe.

'Nope.' He turned to her and smiled a little. 'And they're all dying to ask who you are only they haven't the nerve.' He winked. 'I'm just waiting to see how long it takes.'

Jesus, Lizzie winced. This was worse than she could have imagined.

'See that skinny guy there with the suit?' Joe said under his breath. 'That's Cid. He'll be the first to crack.'

Lizzie said nothing. Cid looked a little creepy. A weird little grasshopper of a man. The queue shuffled along. At the top a man seemed to be calling out 'Red hen' or 'Blue cock' or words like that. The interest in Lizzie seemed to intensify but Joe didn't introduce her, instead he kept looking forward and ignoring the stares. He was enjoying this, Lizzie realised.

'Hey, Joe.' The skinny little man called Cid scurried over to them, just as Joe had predicted. He was wearing a bright suit that only emphasised his wasted frame. 'Are you going to introduce us to the lady or not?' His eyes roved up and down Lizzie in appreciation.

'Oh, yeah,' Joe said as if it had just occurred to him. 'This is Lizzie, everyone. She'd like to join the club.'

A murmur of approval seemed to sweep through the room.

'No!' Cid gawked at her in surprise. 'Wow!' He nodded to the basket she was holding. 'Are they your birds?'

'No, his,' Lizzie said, indicating Joe.

'Don't you have pigeons?'

'Not yet, but someday I will. I haven't the space at the moment. I'm hoping to learn too.'

'Is he going to show you his loft?' He looked at Joe.

'I dunno,' Lizzie answered as she saw Joe flush.

'You going to show her your set-up, Joe?' Cid asked.

'I dunno,' Joe shrugged and shifted his basket from one hand to the other. 'If she wants. Or she could go somewhere else. It's up to her.'

'Well, if he won't,' Cid said as he stuck out his hand, 'I certainly will. My lofts are the best you'll get. I'm Cid with a C and I'm pleased to meet you.'

'Likewise,' Lizzie smiled.

'Are you going out with Joe?' someone shouted from the back of the queue.

'No, she is not,' Joe said, rolling his eyes. 'I met her on the Luas and we got talking.'

'He has no girlfriend, you know,' the same guy said. 'And you'd be ideal. We're all looking for a woman who doesn't mind her husband loving other birds.'

'Aw lads, will yez feck off,' Joe muttered to a splutter of laughter. 'They're juvenile,' he said to Lizzie. 'Don't mind them.'

'So what is it you want to do, Miss?' An old man on a walking frame was peering at her now. He had bright blue eyes in a faded face. 'Help out, is it?'

Lizzie gulped. She hadn't really decided, preferring a wait and see approach.

'Anything,' she said. 'I'd just like to be involved in some way or other.'

'Well, you leave Joe with his birds and go up to the chairman and ask him what you can do.'

'I was going to introduce her,' Joe said. 'Will yez gimme a chance?'

The old man shook his head. 'You boys have no idea about manners these days,' he said in slight exasperation. 'Letting the girl stand there feeling awkward. Come with me.' He gallantly offered his arm. 'I'll do the honours.'

His offer was met with good-natured cheers and whistles and Lizzie smiled. 'I'd be delighted for you to do that,' she said.

'You'd want to watch him,' Cid said. 'There's a lot more to that walking frame than meets the eye.'

'Have you no respect?' the old man said back sternly. 'Come on, Miss.'

Lizzie took his arm and, feeling as if she were trapped in a bizarre world, allowed him to lead her to the top of the queue.

Ten minutes later she was ensconced behind a desk, writing down details of all the birds entered for the race. Her hand was aching but she found to her surprise that, despite the boring work, the lads were great fun. In fact, she was having so much craic with them that she failed to notice Joe had left.

'Shit,' she muttered at the end of the night. She should have known that he'd go once his pigeons had registered. Now she was stuck writing reams of numbers while the purpose of her visit had vanished.

'Now,' Alan, the chairman, said to her as the last fancier left, 'thanks a lot, Lizzie.' He started to fold the pages of entries away. 'I hope we'll be seeing you in future.'

'Oh, you will for sure,' Lizzie nodded. 'When do you meet next?'

'Tomorrow night for the results.'

Lizzie's heart sank. Tomorrow was out.

'But every Friday and Saturday usually. It's been great to meet you Lizzie and, eh, just a word.' He paused and Lizzie looked at him. 'If you are going to learn from any one, let it be Joe.' He tapped his nose. 'They're all great here, they'll all help out, but Joe is the real deal. Stick with him and you won't go wrong.'

'I'll try,' Lizzie smiled.

'Now, he's a quiet lad but he's helpful. You stick with him.'

'OK.' Lizzie smiled her thanks, her heart pinging. She'd be doing that all right. 'Thanks. See you next week.'

'Bye now.' Alan smiled at her.

Later, in her room, she pulled Joe's book from her bag. Opening it she saw an inscription, written in gorgeous flowing handwriting, the kind they didn't teach any more: *To Joe, my best little grandson. All my love, Granddad Jones.* Beside it, in a big childish scrawl was: *Property of Joe Jones. Aged 10. Wexford. Ireland. Europe. The World.*

Lizzie stared at the writing, a lump in her throat. One so proud, the other so innocent. It wasn't too late to stop, she thought suddenly. She could just vanish from Joe's life as suddenly as he had appeared in hers.

But, then again, he wasn't ten any more. His granddad was long gone. Life had changed them all. Her family had been ruined and all because of him. No, Joe was right. Fate. That's what it was. As she remembered his laughing face from earlier, she grit her teeth and clenched her hand around a page of the book, almost ripping it. How could he laugh when he'd ruined so many lives? How could he move on and grow old while Megan would remain forever young? How could he eat and sleep and love and live while it would never happen again for Megs? How could he laugh?

Well, Lizzie thought, glaring at the book, her eyes filling with tears, he wouldn't be laughing for much longer.

14

I sold my first big ad today. I can't believe it. I rang
up a company from the phone book. Jefferson's, they
were called. When the girl answered, I asked to speak to
their marketing person. (I'm getting better at sounding
confident.) Anyway, the upshot of it was that they are
to take out a full-page ad in the paper for six weeks –
that's six full-page ads!!! They asked for a reduced rate
in return for supplying us with a free gift for every
edition of the newspaper.

A FREE GIFT!!

Dessie was really impressed. Him and Joe even gave
me a clap. I felt as proud as if I'd just performed open
heart surgery.

Thursday, 15th July

The free gift is four thousand packs of tampons.

They arrived today and I swear I nearly got sick.
Dessie and Joe nearly got sick laughing. The boxes are
everywhere. In the office, in the hallway, in the toilets.
Imagine sitting in a small cramped space with two blokes
and about four hundred tampons. It's just not funny.

'I somehow don't think we'll be needing a free gift,'
Dessie laughed to Joe. I said nothing, just tried to ignore
them.

Then Geoff arrives down to the office. 'This paper,' he says, 'does not give out free samples of—' and he couldn't say the word.

'Of what, Dad?' Joe asked innocently and Dessie snorted with laughter.

I tried to hide behind my computer screen.

'Ladies' things,' he spluttered.

Then he says, 'There better be a good explanation.' And he glares at the lads.

They started to laugh again. It was OK for them.

I was about to open my mouth to explain when Joe says, 'Sorry, Dad, my fault. I thought they sold, eh, tam . . . bourines,' he finished weakly.

'Feck off.' Dessie was coiled up laughing.

'Tambourines,' his dad said. 'Are you kidding me?'

I couldn't let Joe take the blame, even though it made sense. His dad couldn't get rid of him. 'It wasn't his fault,' I said. 'It was my fault. I did it. Joe had nothing to do with it.' And then I started to cry. I don't know what was more embarrassing, crying or seeing all those tampons scattered about the place.

'Oh for Jaysus' sake,' Geoff said then. 'Will you stop it?'

Dessie handed me a tissue from a box on his desk.

'I never asked what the free gift was,' I hiccupped.

'Anyone could have made that mistake,' Joe offered feebly. Dessie agreed.

Geoff looked disbelievingly at them. 'Anyone could have ordered thousands of free gifts like that?' he scoffed. 'Really?'

'I'm sorry,' I sniffed. 'I suppose I'm fired.'

'You should be,' Geoff said, 'but you're honest at least.' Then he shot a look at Joe. 'And you,' he said, 'don't take the blame like that again. I need to know how good my workforce is. One more chance,' he said to me. 'But you ring up Jefferson's and you tell them to take their gifts back and you tell them we'll run the ads for free.' With that he turned on his heel and stalked out of the office.

I had just lost the company over eight grand.

15

THE DOORBELL RANG. Lizzie took the stairs two at a time, hopping lightly from one step to the next.

'I'll get it, it's for me!' She opened the door and Tom stood, dripping wet in the porch, holding what was once an impressive bunch of flowers. Lizzie took a look at him and started to laugh.

'Eh – hello?' he grimaced. 'Getting wet here?'

'Oops, sorry.' She cocked her head to the side. 'It's just being wet suits your personality.'

'Bitch!' Tom strode into the hall and hit her playfully with the flowers. Petals flew everywhere. 'They were meant to be for you,' he said as he studied them. 'They cost me a fortune.'

'Prices in the garage gone up then, have they?' Lizzie grinned as she took them off him.

'I got them in a shop, actually.'

'Aw, they're lovely.' She smiled at him. And they would have been, too, if they hadn't been heavily rained on before being decapitated. 'What's the occasion?'

'You.' He pointed at her. 'And me.'

'Aww.' She thumbed to the kitchen and lowered her voice. 'I can't even put them in water just yet. Aileen is giving Billy a big romantic surprise dinner in there.'

'I'll be able to do that soon.' Tom shoved his hands into the pockets of his jeans and grinned. 'Who only went and got cast in the hottest new play to hit the Dublin scene in years?'

'*No.*'

'Uh-huh.' He nodded self-deprecatingly.

'Brilliant!' Lizzie attempted to hug him with the flowers in her hand but it wasn't entirely successful, more blossoms detaching themselves and falling to the floor.

They both laughed a little. 'You want to put them somewhere where they won't die,' Tom advised. He followed her into the TV room, adding, 'The director of this play is massive. If I impress him he'll cast me again, you know what I mean.'

'So you have the main part?' Lizzie found a vase at the back of a press and pulled it out. She began arranging the flowers as Tom sat watching her.

'Not the main part,' Tom shrugged, 'it's another part. About a hundred lines this time.' He smiled at her. 'So you'll even be able to blink and not miss me.'

'So I could fall asleep and maybe still catch you?'

'Technically, yeah.' He hunkered down behind her and wrapped his arms about her waist before dropping a kiss on the top of her head. Sighing contentedly, he added, 'This could be it, Lizzie, my big break. I could actually start making a few bob now.'

'Fantastic. So, what do we do to celebrate?'

Tom grinned. 'What we always do. Have a pint.'

They ended up in the local pub. Both of them were soaked through.

'I'm wrecked,' Tom said, splayed across the seat. He pulled a ragged twenty from his jeans and handed it to her. 'Go and get me a pint, would you?'

'Not able for all that rain,' Lizzie teased him.

He laughed. 'My mammy would kill me,' he nodded. 'No hood. No coat.' Tom's mother doted on him, as Lizzie had found out when she had met her briefly.

Lizzie took his money and ordered two pints. Carrying them back to the table, she noted he did actually look very tired.

'Are you OK?' she asked as she put his drink in front of him. 'You're not about to have a heart attack on me or anything?'

He opened an eye. 'Would it bother you if I did?'

'Eh, yeah,' she said as if he were stupid, 'your pint would go to waste.'

'Ha, ha.' He took a deep swallow of it and sighed. 'I'm grand. It's just going straight from one play into another, it's never happened to me before. I think I'm in shock.'

Lizzie grinned. 'Take more than that to shock you.'

'I wouldn't bet on it.'

'What's the biggest shock you've ever had?'

'Oh, I dunno,' Tom said airily, looking upwards. 'A girl in a pub trying to knock my drink out of my hands 'cause I skipped her imaginary queue.'

She laughed and thumped him affectionately. 'Seriously?'

He didn't answer.

'Can't think of anything?'

'I'm trying to choose,' he said back. 'It was either my first bungee jump or my first parachute jump.'

'A bungee jump?' Lizzie gaped at him. 'You did a bungee jump?'

'Yep. Me and Domo did it.' Domo was his best friend. 'It's a real head rush. I've done a few of them now. But the first one is the scariest.'

'Wow.' Lizzie was impressed. 'I don't think I'd ever do that.'

Tom gawked at her. 'You are organising a parachute jump. That's just as scary, I reckon.'

'Eh, note the use of the word "organising",' Lizzie grinned. 'No way am I doing it myself.'

'You don't know what you're missing. Seeing the ground rushing towards you, it's a blast.'

'I'd have my eyes closed.'

'What would be the point? You're jumping anyway, might as well enjoy the view.'

'I like the view right now,' Lizzie grinned cheekily as Tom's eyes twinkled back at her.

'Am I the nicest view you've ever had?' he asked.

'Is chocolate ice cream with nuts and whipped cream the nicest dessert ever?'

'Is it the chocolate ice cream they serve in Rocco's?' That was their favourite restaurant.

'Yep.'

'Ta.' He kissed the tip of her nose and pulled her tighter towards him.

Lizzie snuggled in beside him, her clothes beginning to steam in the heat. 'You are perfectly mad, d'you know that?'

'Yeah, mad about you,' he said back, his dark eyes appraising her.

'Aww. Cheesy.'

Tom absently began to play with a strand of her hair. Finally he smoothed it down and said, 'I'll be rehearsing a lot for this play and then we'll be performing and touring, so I won't get to see too much of you, d'you mind?'

'Nope,' she grinned. 'I'll come and see you every night.'

'That'd be expensive.'

'Well, I don't intend on paying. Naturally you'll get me complimentary tickets.'

'Cheapskate.'

'Absolutely.'

They smiled at each other and it suddenly dawned on Lizzie how happy she felt. Completely content. Just sitting here, sipping a pint with this guy she'd known for the last eight months, was as good as she reckoned it could get. She didn't feel the need to impress him or entertain him or anything. Maybe it was because he didn't try to impress her either. He had very little cash, a crappy bedsit and no car. He also had a weird way of looking at the world, which charmed her. It was so easy being with him.

'I'm gonna miss you,' he said after a bit. 'But I'll ring you when I can and we'll go out as much as I'm free, will that be OK?'

'Yep.' Lizzie drank some more. 'So, when do rehearsals start?'

'Next week. You'll have to come to the flat and help me learn my lines.'

'Will do.'

There was a slight pause before Tom said, with an attempt at sounding casual, 'You can stay over if you like.'

Lizzie's heart pinged. Tom had never asked her to stay over

and she hadn't pushed it, fearing the rejection. 'Why now?' She tried not to grin too much.

''Cause I know I'm going to make it now,' he said seriously. 'Before this, I wasn't sure and I didn't want you not having stuff from me that maybe some other guy could give you. So I thought I'd play it casual, to let you escape if you wanted.' He laughed, a little embarrassed.

'That is the nicest thing anyone has ever said to me.' Lizzie snuggled into him.

'You sad person.' Tom shook his head.

'So when would you like me to call over?' Lizzie asked.

'Oh, now, I'd better play it hard-to-get.' Tom screwed up his face. 'How about, I dunno, tonight?'

'What are we sitting here for?' Lizzie pulled him to his feet and, laughing, they left the pub.

The rain had stopped. They walked back to Billy's, arms about each other, so that she could pick up some clean clothes for work.

'Hi,' Lizzie called as she pushed open the front door. 'It's only me and Tom. We're heading back out again.'

'In here,' Billy called back.

Lizzie raced upstairs, grabbed her clothes and toothbrush and ran back down. Poking her head into the kitchen she was about to call out a cheery 'goodbye,' but something about the way Billy was sitting alone at the kitchen table, a cold cup of coffee in front of him, stopped her.

'Hey,' she said softly, going in to him. 'Are you OK?'

'Aileen is eight weeks pregnant, Lizzie,' he said flatly.

'Pregnant? No way!' Lizzie shrieked delightedly, making Billy jump. 'Wow! When did you find this out?'

'About two hours ago. She told me over dessert.'

'And where is she now?'

'Gone to tell her dad the great news.'

There was something about the way he said 'great' that made Lizzie flinch. She cast a glance at Tom, who was standing in the hallway. Billy followed her gaze and suddenly noticed her packed bag.

'Hey, hi, Tom,' he said, attempting to sit straighter. 'How's things?'

'Congratulations,' Tom said.

'Huh?' Billy looked at him then nodded. 'Oh yeah, right, yeah, thanks.' He turned to Lizzie. 'Right, well, you'd better be off, so.'

Lizzie shot a look at Tom. 'Eh, see you, Tom,' she said weakly.

Tom cracked a grin. 'Right. Talk again. OK?'

Lizzie's heart sank as Tom turned to go, but there was no way she could leave Billy alone like this. Something must have happened to make him look . . . the only word she could think of was devastated. She ran out after Tom and kissed him briefly. 'Sorry about this,' she whispered.

'No worries. You look after him, ey?'

'Will do.'

She watched glumly as Tom strode up the driveway and round the corner. God, even the set of his shoulders and the length of his stride was a turn on. Still, there'd be more nights, her first priority was Billy.

'So,' she said as she went back in to him, 'spill.'

'I thought you were heading out,' he said.

'Naw. Much prefer to be with my weirdo brother who's going to be a daddy.' She punched his arm playfully. Then, when his only response was a glum shrug of the shoulders, she asked uncertainly, 'It is great news, isn't it?'

Billy said nothing.

'Is it not yours?' she asked then.

Billy laughed unexpectedly. 'Jesus, Lizzie!' he spluttered incredulously. 'Of course it's mine!' He rolled his eyes. 'Thanks.'

'No, I meant—' She pulled back and studied him. 'Well, you don't sound happy about it, that's all.'

Billy's grin died and he sank his head in his hands. 'Oh God, I dunno,' he sighed, before admitting dejectedly, 'I don't know how I'm meant to feel. For one thing, we really can't afford it, Lizzie. We're only scraping by as it is.' He bit his lip. 'Jesus, what a mess.'

'Billy,' Lizzie said firmly, not able to believe he'd just said that, 'Aileen is pregnant with your child and you're acting like this.' She tried to read his face but his eyes were downcast. 'I hope you didn't say that to her.'

He met her gaze. 'I'm not stupid. No, I pretended to be delighted, didn't I?'

Lizzie heaved a sigh of relief. 'Good.'

'She was afraid to tell me, you know.'

'Because of the money issue?'

'Suppose,' he shrugged.

'She would have had to tell you eventually.'

'Yeah.' He didn't sound convinced. 'Still, it explains why she's tired all the time. I was beginning to worry about her.'

'Did you give her a hug and say you were thrilled when she told you?' Lizzie asked.

'Yes!' He sounded defensive. A pause before he added, 'I don't know how convincing I was. I was sort of in shock.'

Lizzie glared at him. 'You don't know how convincing you were?' she snapped. 'Convincing? You're having a little baby, for God's sake! Why would you have to be convincing?'

'Because . . . Because . . .' He shook his head. 'Jesus!' Then, 'It'll be expensive. Everyone says babies are expensive.'

'You will afford it.' Lizzie touched his arm. 'People just do, Bill,' she went on gently. 'For one thing you won't have to pay a babysitter. I'll be here.'

He smiled briefly. 'Thanks.'

'I mean it,' she said. She gave his arm a squeeze. 'You worry too much, that's your problem.' He said nothing. 'Have you told Mam and Dad yet?'

'No.' He shook his head. 'Apparently the first twelve weeks are the risky ones, anything can happen so . . .'

Lizzie barely let him finish. 'But Aileen's telling her dad. Come on, Bill.' Lizzie dashed into the hall.

Billy followed, smiling a little at her excitement. He was glad she was so thrilled, it would boost Aileen up no end. Maybe he should just do as Lizzie advised and wait and see how things panned out, though he really didn't know how to be happy about it. 'OK, you dial then.'

'Me?' Lizzie grinned. 'Really?'

'Really.'

Billy watched his sister dial, her slim finger jabbing buttons with a feverish excitement. He watched her face light up as the phone was answered at the other end. 'Dad, hi? How's things? Is Mammy there?' Lizzie's face dropped. '*What?*'

'What?' Billy asked, his heart turning over in fright.

Lizzie put her hand over the receiver. 'Mam is on an overnight protest.'

'What?'

'What is she doing, Dad? Is she out in that rain?' Lizzie listened then relayed the news to Billy: 'Her and Martha and a few other hard liners are staging an all-night vigil for the harbour. The cops are going to be there, too. Dad says he has to go off now to bring them soup.'

Billy laughed loudly as Lizzie glared at him. 'It's not funny, Bill.' She turned back to the phone. 'No, Dad,' she placated, 'it's not funny . . . you're joking? Wow.' Back to Billy. 'Apparently she's staging it every night from now on. And in a while they're going to chain themselves to the walls permanently.' Lizzie listened patiently as her father continued on with his story and, finally, she said, 'Well, if you need anything, ring here, OK?' He said he'd need a new heart with all the stress, before grumpily asking her why she was ringing.

'Well,' Lizzie tried and failed to keep the delight from her voice, 'we've a bit of news ourselves, Dad. I'll let Bill tell you.'

To her amusement, Billy blushed as he took the phone. 'Hiya, Dad. Yeah, that's mad about Mam . . . No, I'm sure she'll be fine, I'm sure it's not a breakdown. You know Mam.' His face broke into a grin and in a voice that struggled to keep laughter at bay he said, 'No, Dad, I can't see anyone attacking her, she'll be fine. Hasn't she Martha to protect her, ey? And aren't you going down with soup, too?' He paused and shoved his fist into his mouth to stop laughing. 'Eh, my news?' he went on, the smile sliding from his face. 'Well, I suppose it's mine and Aileen's news. She's, eh, well, she's going to have a . . . a baby.' It was hard to say it. Saying it made it real. Pause. 'Well, thanks, Dad. And yes, we're fine for money, we'll manage, I'm sure . . . November, apparently, but she's to get a scan done to make sure . . . Yes, we have enough money. Honestly.' Billy rolled his eyes.

Lizzie half smiled. Her dad was worse than Billy when it came to worrying about money.

'No, Aileen isn't here . . . Yes, Dad,' Billy went on patiently, 'she is happy, she's only gone out to tell her own dad . . . Why didn't I go with her? I dunno, I just didn't think . . . Yes, Dad, I suppose I am happy about it. Can you tell Mam? . . . OK. Good. I'm sure tomato soup is grand . . . Well, just shove it in the saucepan and heat it up and bung it into a flask. I dunno how long for, it'll say on the packet.'

Lizzie started to giggle.

Billy flapped his hand at her to go away in case he'd laugh. 'Bye, Dad. Yeah. Bye.' He clicked down the receiver and turned to Lizzie.

'Poor Dad having to make soup,' Lizzie said, trying to sound sympathetic.

'Poor Mam having to drink it,' Billy chortled. 'He'll probably single-handedly kill off the whole protest himself.'

It was good to see him laughing, Lizzie thought, as it dawned on her that Billy hadn't laughed in months.

16

IT WAS TEN when the phone rang. Joe had just finished checking on his pigeons and bedding them down for the night. Wondering who could be ringing him at that hour he bounded into the kitchen, thinking that it might be one of the lads from the club.

Ellen's number was flashing and Joe hesitated. The last thing he needed was to be shelling out more money for that woman's clothes. Half of the time, he reckoned, he didn't even owe it to her, but he tried to avoid rows with the neighbours if at all possible. Damn it anyhow, he figured as he picked up the receiver, there was no way he was paying her anything this time.

'Hello.' He hoped his voice sounded suitably cold.

'Joe,' Ellen whispered, 'is that you?'

'Eh, yeah.' He paused. 'Is something wrong?'

'I think there's someone downstairs,' she whispered. 'I'm in bed and I can hear something in the kitchen.'

'D'you want me to check for you?' Joe asked.

'Yes, please.' The woman took a shaky breath. 'I didn't call the police because they'd take ages to come so I'll ring them now.'

'Yeah, do that. And don't worry.'

'I'll try not to.'

Joe barely let her finish her sentence. He raced out the door and into his back yard. Taking the dividing wall at a leap, he found himself in Ellen's beautifully manicured garden. It was so long since he'd actually seen a patch of ground so lovingly tended that it stopped him in his tracks. His mother had always been into flowers and plants. Joe swallowed hard, before remembering why he was there.

He crept slowly towards the kitchen window, keeping to the shadows. The kitchen was in darkness. He wasn't quite sure what he should do. Should he hammer on the door and frighten whoever was in there, and hope they made a dash out the front way? But what if they ran upstairs? Would it be better to be quiet and surprise whoever it was?

And then he heard it. The unmistakable sound of someone opening a drawer. And what was worse, they were making no attempt to be discreet. Joe decided that the only thing he could do was to make a run at the back door and break his way in.

Creeping as silently as he could towards it, he saw the door was slightly ajar. A pane of glass, carefully removed, lay against the back step. Joe, not really having a clue what he was at, crept silently into the kitchen. A figure, back to him, was rifling through a kitchen drawer. Joe, careful not to make a sound, leaned toward the countertop and picked up a place mat. Taking a deep breath, he flung it through the kitchen door, where it clattered on to the wooden floor of the hallway. The burglar looked up in a panic and turned to flee out the back. In a flash Joe was on him. He landed a punch to the boy's face and blood spurted out his nose and down his chin.

'Ow!' the lad said, clutching his nose. 'I'll have you for assault!'

'In your dreams,' Joe said. He grabbed the boy's free arm and twisted it up behind his back. 'What the hell do you think you're doing, ey?'

'Nothing.'

'Nothing? You broke in here, you took glass out of the back door, you made a mess of the kitchen. And you're doing nothing?'

'You can't prove it was me.' The boy, who was small and thin with a starved-looking freckly face glared at him. 'I can say it was you.'

'No, you won't,' Ellen, wrapped in a big towelling dressing gown, said from the door. 'You won't say it was Joe. I'll confirm that it was you.'

At those words the boy's face fell. 'I was only looking for money,' he grouched. 'It's not a big deal.'

Joe, without even being aware of it, twisted his arm harder.

'Ow,' the lad winced, 'lemme go! You're hurting me arm and you've broke me nose.'

'Aw, sorry about that,' Joe said in mock concern. 'Have you called the police, Ellen?'

'They're on their way.' Ellen walked slowly to the seat furthest away from the boy. She was pale and had started to shiver.

'Put on the heat, Ellen,' Joe advised gently. 'You've had a shock. This guy is going nowhere.'

Ellen stood up and made her way to the heating box on the wall. She flicked the switch and had to support herself against the counter with both hands before she shuffled her way back to the chair. Joe gave the lad an extra shake in frustration. Ellen needed a cuppa and a rug or something and he couldn't get it without letting go of the boy.

'Take deep breaths,' he said.

The boy inhaled deeply.

'Not you,' Joe said crossly. 'You, Ellen.'

'Me ma is going to kill me,' the boy spoke up. His voice had lowered a notch on the toughness scale. 'She'll murder me, so she will.'

'No, she won't,' Joe said.

The boy looked at him.

''Cause I'm gonna do that for her.'

He was rewarded with a small smile from Ellen before the boy began to struggle again.

Very faintly, just then, there was the sound of a police siren. Despite the fact that he was in the clear, Joe's heart skipped a beat and he unexpectedly felt like vomiting.

After the police had gone, Ellen insisted on making Joe a cuppa. He agreed because he reckoned it was more for herself than him. She was still pale and still shaking. He watched her in concern as she padded about the kitchen in her big pink fluffy slippers. They were the kind of slippers a teenager might have liked.

'Ellen, are you OK?' he asked. 'Maybe I should make the tea.'

'No.' She held up her hand. 'It's the least I can do after what you did.'

'I did nothing,' Joe said firmly. 'He was just a kid. He hadn't a clue. He'd have run if you'd even tackled him.'

She allowed herself a smile. 'I don't think so,' she murmured.

'Well, I'm scared of you.' Joe spread his palms wide. 'Every time my phone rings I think I owe you more money.'

Ellen laughed. 'Oh, you!'

Joe grinned and watched in amusement as she placed biscuits on a plate and cups on saucers. It was all very formal. She poured the milk into a jug and gave him a place mat. Finally she carried a massive pot of tea over to the table.

'Anyone else joining us?' Joe joked.

'Oh, I always make a big pot,' Ellen said. 'My late husband and I used to spend our days drinking tea and I just got used to making it like this.' She carefully poured him a cup, her hand shaking with the weight of the pot. 'Now, there.' She turned to her own cup and poured and, lastly, set the pot on the table between them. 'Sláinte,' she said.

'Yeah,' Joe lifted his cup. 'You, too.'

They sipped in silence, Joe not really knowing what to say to the woman. Their discussions normally cantered around his pigeons and he didn't really want to go there.

'I'll be telling everyone down at my club what you did for me tonight,' Ellen said.

'Club?'

'The old folks,' Ellen went on. 'It's great. I'm one of the youngest there. I'll be telling them all about you. You're a credit to your parents, so you are.'

Joe choked on the hot liquid. Tea spluttered out all over the table. Ellen, after making sure he was OK, went to get a dishcloth to wipe up.

'Sorry about that,' Joe said. Jesus.

'I never had children,' Ellen went on as she wiped up the tea, 'but if I had, I'd have been proud to have a boy like you. Wait until I tell all my friends what you've done.'

Joe squirmed. It was so long since anyone had said anything positive to him that he felt weirdly emotional.

'Yeah,' he murmured instead as he stared hard at his tea, 'thanks for that, Ellen. But really, it was nothing. He was only about fifteen. Hardly a hardened criminal.'

'But he could have been,' Ellen said, and unexpectedly she shivered. She lay back in the chair and closed her eyes. 'Oh, sorry, oh,' she waved her hand about, 'I feel a little faint all of a sudden.'

And she collapsed, hitting her head off the kitchen floor.

17

Joe asked me out for a drink tonight after work. I was knackered. I'd sold one ad, which is a bit pathetic since I'd made about a million phone calls. I don't have the ability to bullshit the way the lads do. Joe jokes that Dessie bullshits so much that he's carved out his own hole in the ozone layer. Well I think it's a joke, I don't really get it.

Anyway, Joe asked me if I wanted to go for a drink and I said that as long as the drink came with free uppers, I'd be OK. He laughed and was about to say something else when Dessie came back. Dessie looked from one to the other of us and said, 'How 'bout ye?'

I love the way he says it with his cute accent and his lovely glittery brown eyes and his quirky smile.

'Joe and I are going for a drink,' I said. 'D'you want to come?'

Dessie rolled his eyes and, sneaking a peek at Joe, said, 'I don't think this fella wants me around.'

'Of course he does,' I said. 'Don't you, Joe?'

'Well, I didn't ask you 'cause I know that you normally head off at the weekends to see Denise,' Joe answered. And the way he said it was kind of pointed.

Who is Denise? I wondered, as my heart sank quicker than a cork in water.

'Well not this weekend,' Dessie said as he grabbed his jacket from the chair and checked his pockets for money. 'She's coming down tonight so I might as well join ye in the meantime.'

And so the three of us went for a drink. I think Joe was a bit pissed off about something.

When he was up at the bar ordering, Dessie asked me what I thought of him. Of Joe. I said that I thought he was OK. Dessie grinned and said airily, 'Well, I reckon that Joe thinks you're more than OK.'

How awful was that? 'I don't fancy Joe,' I blurted out. I stressed the 'Joe' to show that I fancied someone, though.

Dessie quirked an eyebrow and said nothing.

Joe came back with the drinks and I'm sure he was wondering why I barely said a word to him. I just couldn't think of anything to say. I didn't want him to get the wrong impression and have to fend him off. As it happened, he left after one drink. He said he had to look after his granddad's pigeons as his granddad wasn't too well at the moment.

'Joe,' Dessie said with a grin, 'how many times do I have to tell you, you won't get a girl talking about other birds in front of them.'

I giggled, but Joe just seemed to glower at him as he pulled his jacket from the chair and left.

'So,' Dessie said, when Joe had gone, 'have you any plans for the weekend?'

'No.' Then I realised that probably sounded a bit pathetic. Who would be interested in a girl whose life is a social vacuum? 'Not yet,' I added.

Dessie looked at his watch. 'I have to go now and meet Denise from the bus or she'll give Salome a run for her money.'

'Salome?'

'Yeah. And I'll be John the Baptist.' Dessie laughed a little.

I laughed too, but I hadn't a clue what he was on about. Maybe it's a northern thing.

18

ANNA, AS USUAL, was in before her and had put the kettle on for tea. Kneeling on the floor beside Anna's chair, a small girl was bent over an array of half-naked dolls. She looked up as Lizzie came in.

Anna indicated her little girl, 'Lizzie, meet Chloe, my daughter.' Then, apologetically, she added, 'My babysitter is sick. I had to bring her with me.'

'No probs.' Lizzie crouched down beside the small, dark-haired little girl. 'Hi, Chloe. I'm Lizzie. It's nice to meet you at last, your mammy talks about you all the time.'

The child looked solemnly back at her out of large brown eyes.

'Are they Bratz?' Lizzie asked, indicating the dolls.

A nod.

'They're cool.'

'This is Cloe,' Chloe volunteered shyly, holding up a blonde-haired doll. 'Only she spells her name different to me. She's my favourite.'

'Mine too,' Lizzie agreed. 'I'm going to be an aunty soon. My brother is going to have a tiny new baby. It'll be about,' Lizzie put her palms a foot or so apart, 'that size. D'you think it'd like those dollies?'

'A baby would be too small,' Chloe said, looking to Anna for reassurance. 'Maybe if it's a girl and when she's bigger.'

'Oh right, OK,' Lizzie nodded. 'Thanks for that.'

Chloe nodded, smiling slightly.

'She'll probably fall asleep in a bit,' Anna said softly. 'I'll get a taxi to bring us home.'

97

'No worries,' Lizzie said. 'Is your babysitter really sick or what?'

Anna made a face. 'Yeah, a stomach bug, I think. I've had to cancel a night out tomorrow just in case she's not better.'

'I'll babysit for you if you're stuck,' Lizzie said.

'Oh no, I couldn't . . . I wasn't dropping hints or anything . . .'

'Where and when?' Lizzie asked. At Anna's doubtful look she continued, 'I want to get some practice in for when my own little niece or nephew comes, so you're doing me a favour.'

'I somehow doubt that.' Anna grinned a little.

'The offer is there,' Lizzie said. 'It'd be no bother. I'm not going anywhere, I haven't seen Tom since last weekend, he's so busy.' Tom had called her and apologised. When he wasn't rehearsing, he was working in a pub. Lizzie wondered if they'd ever get it together.

Anna winced. 'You sure?'

'Positive.'

'Well, OK.' Anna grinned delightedly. 'Thanks.'

'No bother.' Lizzie gave a cheeky grin. 'So you won't mind answering the phones tonight while I bond with your daughter over a few Bratz?'

'Aw yeah, I knew there had to be a catch . . .'

'Lizzie, for you.' Anna handed Lizzie the phone.

'Hello?'

'Hello, is that Lizzie?'

'Yes,' Lizzie confirmed. 'Who's this?'

'I'm, eh . . .' There was a slight hesitation. 'Eh, Sinéad, I think I said. I rang you a few weeks ago.'

As Lizzie remembered their conversation, she felt a mixture of relief and apprehension. Relief that the woman had rung back and apprehension as to the reason why. 'Of course, Sinéad,' she said. 'You were a bit concerned about your husband's behaviour, weren't you?'

'Well, I don't know if concerned—' Sinéad stopped and said instead, 'I just wanted some advice.'

'OK.' Lizzie picked up a pen. 'And would you like to talk again?'

'Of course I would,' the woman sounded a little annoyed, 'that's why I rang.'

Lizzie ignored her tone. As if she were treading across a minefield she said carefully, 'Great. That's good, Sinéad. I'm glad you rang again. What can I do?'

The question seemed to throw Sinéad. 'Eh, well . . .'

Lizzie waited.

'I just . . . I don't know. I just . . .' Sinéad's voice trailed off.

'Just talk if you want to,' Lizzie said softly. 'I'm not going to tell anyone. You can just say what you like and not worry, OK?'

'Oh,' Sinéad said, just as softly, 'you've no idea how . . . how good that sounds to me. No idea.'

'If it sounds good,' Lizzie said, 'then go for it.'

Sinéad sniffed and seemed to be wiping her nose hard. 'I'm, well, I'm confused,' she said haltingly. 'I just don't know any more.'

'What don't you know?'

'He says I'm being silly, that I'm too emotional.'

'Silly about what?'

'About everything.' A pause. 'For instance, just as an example, I want to do up one of our rooms and no matter what I pick out he says it's horrible. He says I shouldn't be allowed to decorate a doghouse, never mind his home.'

'Well, people do disagree on stuff like that,' Lizzie answered, trying to be fair.

'But—, but, I'm an interior designer by trade,' Sinéad said shakily. 'People pay me a lot of money to do up their houses. I did up ours when we first moved in.'

'And did you tell him this?'

'He says people in general are stupid.'

'He sounds like he doesn't like many people,' Lizzie offered.

'Oh no. He's very popular.' A note of anger crept into Sinéad's voice, which made Lizzie feel better. 'He's Mr Residents' Committee, Mr Tidy Towns, Mr Important In Work. He can charm everyone.' She paused. 'Well, everyone except my friends.'

'So he's different at home to when he's out?'

'Yes, I suppose.' Then, as if afraid she'd revealed too much, Sinéad said hastily, 'But he hasn't slapped me since that one time. He's just, well, it always seems that he's picking on me.'

'Is this a sudden change?' Lizzie probed. 'He wouldn't just be having problems in work, would he?'

'No, he's very successful in work,' Sinéad said almost bitterly. 'And after I talked to you last, well, I began to think and, well, I realised that, in fact, I've changed a lot since I've been with him.'

'In what way?'

'I used to be so confident.' The anger drained out of Sinéad's voice and instead it started to shake, as if she were trying very hard not to cry. 'So sure of myself. So decisive.'

'And you're not any more?'

'Last week I stood in the shopping centre,' Sinéad sniffed, 'and I couldn't even decide what washing powder to buy. I looked at them all and read all the packages, and I was afraid to pick the wrong one so I bought them all.'

Lizzie said nothing.

'All of them. And when he came home I put a wash on and he asked what powder I was using because that was a silk shirt of his I was washing and I opened the press and I took out the powder for silks and he told me I was stupid and that I should have got it dry cleaned.' She took a deep, shaky breath. 'No matter what I do, it turns out wrong.'

He was a bully, that's what he was, Lizzie wanted to tell her. But of course she couldn't. She hated that about her job. She'd have loved to wade in and tell Sinéad to dump him. Instead she asked, 'Do you feel you're being undermined?'

'I don't know what I feel,' Sinéad said, her voice lower but under control again. 'Maybe it's normal after four years of marriage. Maybe he's just bored with me.'

'So why won't he just say that?' Lizzie suggested gently, trying to get the woman to think. 'Surely it's less hurtful than what he's doing now?'

'Maybe he doesn't think so.'

'Maybe you should ask him.'

Sinéad considered this. 'Maybe I will,' she responded. 'Maybe that would be a good idea.'

'Let me know how you get on.'

'OK.' Sinéad paused. 'And thanks. Sorry for snapping at you.'

'Snap away,' Lizzie responded cheerfully, 'it's what I'm here for.'

'No,' Sinéad said with a firmness that surprised Lizzie. 'No one should ever be there for that.' Then she hung up.

Lizzie waited at the corner of the lane until she saw Joe coming along the street, then, as if she had just emerged from the Life office, she breezed out into his path, pretending not to see him.

'Hey,' he said with slight uncertainty, 'Lizzie?'

She turned and he jogged up beside her. 'Thought it was you.' He pointed up the lane. 'Is that where you work, yeah?'

'Yep. A small office, right at the top of the building.'

He fell into step beside her. Then hesitated. 'You don't mind?'

'No, why should I?' she asked archly, trying out a slightly flirty tone. 'You can be my security walking up this street.'

He grinned, 'Sure, yeah. D'you get nervous walking on your own at night in the city?'

'Naw, not really.' Lizzie studied him. Despite the initial hesitation at walking with her he was now quite relaxed, his hands swinging loosely beside him as his stride matched hers effortlessly. 'But it's nice to have company.' She pulled out her cigarettes, she needed one badly.

'Yeah, I guess it is.' He eyed her. 'Especially when that company has a packet of fags in her hand and the other person is gasping for one.'

Lizzie managed a laugh and flicked open the box. 'Want one?'

'Yeah, thanks. I ran out and hadn't time to buy a packet.' He put it to his mouth. Lizzie fished a lighter from her pocket and flicked it on. It spluttered out. She tried again.

'Hey, your hands are shaking,' Joe exclaimed. 'Are you OK?'

'Just cold,' Lizzie lied. Terrified would be more like it. This whole scenario was progressing almost too well. She attempted to flick the lighter again but, instead, Joe gently took it from her and lit his own cigarette, before lighting hers.

'Thanks,' she nodded. Then, 'I'm surprised you smoke, with you running a health centre.'

He grinned. 'Yeah I know, but I can't seem to give them up.'

'Me neither.'

Joe grinned at her and Lizzie was suddenly aware of how attractive he must have seemed to Megan. He was handsome, but it wasn't just that – there was an easy charm about him, his casual way of dressing, his soft way of talking, his semi-bewildered way of asking questions. It was a potent combination. And yet, as far as she was aware, he wasn't seeing anyone.

That was a bit odd, she thought.

They arrived at the Luas and both of them finished their cigarettes almost at the same time. 'Filthy habit,' Joe smirked as he ground his fag out before picking it up and dumping it into the bin.

'Disgusting,' Lizzie agreed lightly. 'One is no good, better off smoking two at a time.'

Joe laughed.

The Luas pulled up and, without discussion, he sat in beside her. Lizzie dragged her bag on to her lap and slid out his book. 'Thanks for this.' She attempted to hand it to him. 'I learned a lot.'

'You can hang on to it if you like,' Joe said, waving her away. 'You might need it when you start up.'

'Oh, thanks very much. I will, so.' She tucked it back into her bag.

'That's some bag,' Joe remarked, eyeing it in amusement. 'I reckon you could fit a pigeon loft in there.'

Lizzie smiled. 'Probably,' she agreed. Then, 'You weren't down at the club last week. I was hoping to ask you something.'

'Naw, I couldn't make it,' Joe said, suddenly looking uncomfortable.

'Oh.'

There was a pause.

'My next door neighbour, she's an old woman, had a bit of a turn. I was doing good Samaritan.'

Lizzie flinched. Good Samaritan, was he joking? She wondered if his neighbour knew what he was really like.

'She was in hospital for a couple of nights and she's out now. She's a little better, but I'm still checking up on her. But I hope to be down tomorrow night with the birds.'

'Well, I'm out tomorrow,' Lizzie said. 'But if you need a hand any other time, I can help.' Then she added, 'With the birds, not your neighbour.'

Joe shrugged. 'Aw—'

'Alan told me to learn from you,' Lizzie gabbled before he turned her down. 'He said you were the best.' Oh God, she couldn't let this pass her by. He had to let her help. It was the only way she could think of to get into his life and earn his trust. At Joe's obvious embarrassment, she touched him lightly on the arm. 'Please?'

He flinched and Lizzie pulled her hand away. Maybe she'd pushed too hard.

'Do you know much?' he asked.

'I'm a quick learner and I really am interested,' she lied. She was surprised at herself. When she was with this guy she could just switch off any conscience she had. But it was the memory of him in court, the lies he told, that made her able to do it. It was like fuel to an engine starved of oil.

He studied her, his head cocked to one side. Eventually a small grin curved the corners of his mouth. 'OK,' he nodded, 'you're on. But I dunno if I'm the best.'

Lizzie's heart hammered suddenly, making her feel sick. This was it. The beginning of the end for Joe. 'Well, Alan said you were,' she said firmly. 'So, when would you like me to start?'

Joe shrugged. 'Next Friday, if you like? You free from around six?'

'Yeah.' Lizzie tried to look thrilled. 'Oh thanks, Joe. You're a life saver.'

'Hardly.' He tipped her a grinning mock salute. With an effort of will she smiled back.

Some fisherman he was, she thought scornfully. She'd fed him the bait and was now reeling him in the way her dad had taught her long ago, very gently, with no sudden jerks.

She hoped her dad would be proud of her.

19

CHLOE WAS ASLEEP at last. She had been great fun but an awful kid to get to bed. Lizzie had played with every single one of her toys and now they all lay scattered about the floor, making the previously immaculate room an untidy mess. As best she could Lizzie tidied up, she didn't want Anna arriving back to this chaos. Each time she'd dragged out something new, Chloe had said innocently, 'It's OK, my mammy doesn't mind. She lets me do anything.' Somehow Lizzie doubted that.

Anna's house was small but brilliantly compact. There was a tiny hall with a small but functional kitchen, a small playroom and a television room. It was the TV room she was in now. Pictures of Chloe adorned the walls. Chloe as a baby, Chloe in her first school uniform. There was also a photograph of Anna with a very striking-looking man. The picture looked as if it had been taken on holiday somewhere, possibly Spain. Both of them wore T-shirts and shorts. Anna looked so much younger, her hair shorter, defining her pixie-like features. The man was stunning, that was the only way Lizzie could describe him. Tall and wearing a white T-shirt that showed off his muscular, tanned arms. His hair was coal-black, as were his eyes. He was smiling but something about the way he smiled struck Lizzie as odd. Whereas Anna looked radiant, the man looked merely tolerant. His arm was wrapped about Anna's shoulder protectively and she was gazing up into his face. There was no doubt in Lizzie's mind that this man was Chloe's dad – the little girl was the image of him. Lizzie wondered what had happened. Anna still wore her wedding ring but it was obvious there was no man in this house.

Lizzie went into the kitchen and flicked on the kettle. Anna had left biscuits out and it touched Lizzie to see that they were her favourite: Ginger Nut. She opened the packet, took four, and, carrying them plus a large mug of coffee, she sat down to watch the late-night Saturday movie.

Anna had offered to let her stay over if she wanted and Lizzie had jumped at it. It would be nice to give Billy and Aileen time to themselves, and Aileen's happiness at finally declaring herself a mother-to-be was a bit wearing. She'd purchased baby books and had enlisted Lizzie in drawing up lists of possible names. Lizzie had discovered that Aileen's taste in baby names was horrendous. One possibility was Linford, seeing as it was a cross between Dublin and Wexford. Rufus and Clementine were two other options, as they were so 'unusual'. Billy had told Lizzie to let her at it and that, when the time came, he'd talk her into calling the child a name that it might actually want to have. Lizzie didn't envy him the task. Aileen had also bought another book chronicling the day-by-day development of the foetus in the womb. Every morning Billy was treated to just how much his child should have grown in the night and whether his new offspring had any teeth or fingernails yet. Billy's attitude reminded Lizzie of the guy in Anna's photo – he was tolerating it. Lizzie wanted to shake him, to tell him to get a grip, but Billy had always found change difficult, so maybe he just had to get his head around it in his own time.

Lizzie had just drained her mug and decided to go upstairs to bed when the front door opened. It was Anna. Lizzie went into the hall to greet her. 'Hi, good night?'

Anna nodded and came quietly towards her, following her back into the sitting room. 'Not bad.' She sank into the sofa. 'It was just dinner with a couple of friends, nothing too major. How was Chloe?'

'Active.'

Anna gave a splutter of laughter. 'She was dying for you to come,' she said. 'The novelty of someone new.'

'How is your babysitter now? Is she better?'

Anna paused and flushed. 'To be honest, Lizzie, she was never sick,' she said, sounding mortified. She shifted uncomfortably on the sofa. 'I, eh, had a row with her.'

'What?' The thought of Anna having a row with anyone was weird.

'Yep,' Anna nodded glumly. 'I'm sorry I lied. It was just easier than explaining everything.'

'You don't have to explain, so long as you don't row with me.'

Anna smiled a little. 'No fear of that.'

'Well then,' Lizzie nodded, 'forget it.'

'It was my mother,' Anna blurted out. 'She is great, taking Chloe from school and everything, but last Wednesday I had to call a halt to it.'

'Oh, well, we all row with our mothers,' Lizzie said, thinking of her own parents.

'Not like this.' Anna sighed.

'D'you want a coffee?' Lizzie asked, unsure if Anna wanted to continue along this subject and deciding to give her the opportunity to change it.

Anna waved her away. 'No thanks, I drank enough coffee tonight to refloat the Titanic.'

There was silence.

'Can I tell you something, Lizzie?' Anna asked, breaking the silence. 'I'd really like your opinion, you're a good counsellor.'

'Not as good as you.'

Anna rolled her eyes. 'I think the beauty of being a counsellor is that you feel good helping others because you're completely unable to help yourself.'

Lizzie giggled. 'Ouch!'

'Seriously, though,' Anna cocked her head to one side, 'I'll bet you decided to do what you do because you wanted to help people.'

'Yep.'

'So something must have happened to make you feel that way.'

Her perception floored Lizzie. She gulped and shrugged and muttered an, 'I suppose'.

'Have I upset you?' Anna was suddenly contrite. 'Oh, sorry. I didn't mean to.'

Lizzie waved her concern away. 'No, it's just, you're so right.' She licked her lips. 'My, well . . .'

'You don't have to tell me,' Anna said softly. 'It's just something that happens. I went into it because my husband killed himself.'

Lizzie's head shot up. 'What?'

Anna nodded. There was no trace of self pity in her eyes or face. Just an acceptance. 'Yep.' She crossed to the fireplace and took down the photo that Lizzie had noticed earlier. 'That was him. Mick.'

Lizzie took the photo. 'He's gorgeous.'

'I know he was,' Anna said. 'I was mad about him. I reckon if we'd lived to be a hundred together, I'd still be mad about him. He was great fun, he could make everyone laugh, he was the clown at every party and yet, look at him there, that's who he really was, I think. The camera caught him just before he painted his grin on.' She replaced the picture. 'That's why I keep that photo up, not the others.'

Lizzie said nothing.

'Christmas Eve, I walked into our old house, I was seven months pregnant with Chloe and I found him hanging from the attic. No note, nothing. And everyone saying that they'd never have guessed.'

'Oh God, Anna . . .' Lizzie voice trailed off.

'It was terrible,' Anna said matter-of-factly. 'And I was grieving and I was so bloody angry too, Lizzie. I hated him for what he'd done. It's weird, you hate yourself for being angry but you can't help it and you've no one to direct it at. My mother was great at that time. She was there when the baby was born, helping out, doing all sorts of stuff for me and I truly appreciated it. Then, about four years ago, I decided that enough was enough and I was going to get some good out of it. Squeeze out the good, you know?'

Lizzie knew.

'So I got counselling, and after I decided to become a counsellor myself.'

'Good for you.'

'And I've moved on, but my mother can't. She won't tolerate me mentioning him. The last straw came this week when Chloe asked her why she didn't like her daddy. I never even knew Chloe noticed. Well, my mother's answer was that Daddy had done a very bad thing and that he wasn't a good daddy at all. I went ballistic. I mean, I flipped. I told my mother she was poisoning the image of him that I'd tried to build up for Chloe.' Anna paused and took a breath. 'I've told Chloe the truth, that her daddy wasn't well, that his mind was so sore that he had to stop it from working. And she accepted that but now she's on about her daddy being bad. Do you think I'm being unreasonable, Lizzie?'

Lizzie bit her lip.

'Sorry, sorry, sorry.' Anna gave an embarrassed laugh. 'I'm putting you on the spot. Sorry. It's just so hard to judge yourself, you know?'

'I don't think you're being unreasonable in trying to explain to Chloe,' Lizzie said carefully, 'but I suppose your mother had to pick you up off the floor when it happened and she hates him for what he did to you. She's still angry.'

Anna blew air out through her lips and nodded. 'I know you're right. But I can't have it affect Chloe, you have to see that.'

'I do.'

'I've told her that unless she starts to talk about him in a nice way, I can't let Chloe visit.'

'Sounds OK, but maybe *you* should still visit.'

'Peacemaker Lizzie,' Anna teased.

'Hardly,' Lizzie said back.

There was a small pause before Anna said, 'I could do with that coffee now, what about you?'

'If you could go back and find out what was on his mind the day he did it, would you?' Lizzie suddenly found herself asking. 'Like, if you had a chance to solve that mystery, would you do it?'

'Nothing I would have said could have prevented him doing it if he'd wanted to,' Anna mused.

'But if you had the chance . . .'

'Then, yeah, like a shot.'

Lizzie nodded, satisfied. Anna wouldn't ever get the chance, but she just might, she thought.

'Why?' Anna asked.

Lizzie shrugged. 'I just wondered when the desire fades, the wanting to know, you know?'

'It never does.' Anna gulped hard and left the room for the kitchen.

And that was what was so hard to live with, Lizzie thought. You could accept death eventually, but you could never accept the not knowing.

20

J OE SAT IN his car in the Luas station car park. He'd agreed
to meet Lizzie there as he reckoned it would be hard for
her to find her way to his house; there were a lot of twists
and turns on the way. It was spitting rain and the night was a
dingy one. She'd have been freezing by the time she found his
place.

He wondered a little at the wisdom of letting the girl help him
out – after all, he didn't really know what she was able to do. But
she appeared so enthusiastic, just like he used to be. Just like he
still was, he supposed. He decided to give her a break. And besides,
he needed the help: he could hardly abandon Ellen, could he?
He guessed he could have asked Noel or John for a hand, but
Joe didn't really like asking for help, so Lizzie's offer had come
at just the right time.

He spotted her suddenly, dressed in a bright red coat, standing
in the car park looking around. He gave a *bip* of the horn and
she ran lightly towards the car.

'Hi.' She climbed in beside him and he got a whiff of straw-
berries. 'Were you waiting long?'

She was so bright and fresh and clean-looking that Joe had to
turn away suddenly. He fired the engine and shook his head.
'Naw.'

'The Luas was delayed,' Lizzie went on, 'some problem with
the line. But still, here I am.'

'Yep.' With an effort he turned to face her and smiled. She
was dressed in a pair of denims and a tight blue top with a
big daisy on the front. 'Do you have a change of clothes?' he

asked. 'You look, eh, a bit dressed up for cleaning out the pigeons.'

Cleaning out the pigeons? Lizzie tried not to shudder. She hoped it didn't mean what she thought it meant. 'These are my old things,' she lied.

They didn't look old, Joe thought.

'It's really great of you,' Lizzie went on, settling her enormous bag at her feet. 'But you'll have to tell me everything and explain it all to me, won't you?'

Joe grinned. A girl after his own heart.

Lizzie's phone rang just as Joe pulled up outside his house. He climbed out of the car as Lizzie fished the mobile from her bag. It was Tom.

'D'you mind?' Lizzie asked.

'Naw, fire ahead, follow me in.'

'Tom, hi,' she said into the phone.

'D'you remember me?' he laughed. 'The guy who is failing miserably to get you into bed?'

Lizzie grinned. 'What's the story?'

'I'm free later tonight, if you are? Sorry about the short notice but I rang the pub and told them I was sick. I've a rehearsal for about two hours and I can meet you after, if you like?'

Well that was bloody typical. 'Eh, I might be able. I'll ring you later – OK?'

In the background, there was a ring on Tom's intercom. 'Yep. OK. Talk then. Love you.'

She turned the phone off.

'Anyone important?' Joe asked as she stepped out to join him.

Did she want Joe to know she had a boyfriend? No, she decided. The less he knew about her the better. 'Nah.'

'Right.' Joe indicated the house. 'Well, here we are.' He pulled his keys from his pocket and strode up the overgrown driveway, a crooked gate squeaking violently as he pushed it open. His driveway was more a narrow little path bordered on each side by some grass. 'Home.'

112

'You own this place?' Lizzie asked, following him. 'Like, you have a house?' For some reason she'd been convinced he'd been renting it, or at least sharing it with others.

'Yep. All mine,' Joe nodded.

It'd be rude to ask how on earth he could afford to own a house, wouldn't it? Instead she went for a fake, 'I'm impressed.'

Joe shrugged. 'Yeah, well, I was lucky. My grandfather left me his pigeon loft when he died and I sold it. With the money I made, I bought this.'

'You sold your grandfather's pigeon loft?' Pigeons could buy you a house – she hadn't known that.

Joe squirmed. 'Yeah, pretty crappy thing to do, but I had no choice.'

'Did you not?' Lizzie reckoned she'd have sold it, too, if it was worth that much.

Joe turned abruptly from her and inserted the key into the lock. 'I wasn't in a position to keep it then,' he said over his shoulder.

'It must have been some loft.'

'The best.' His tone held a note of pride. 'Just like mine will be one day.'

In your dreams, Lizzie thought, and suddenly shivered. But it was typical. There he was, a bloody convict and he had his own house, and poor Billy and Aileen, who had done nothing to anyone, were struggling like mad to pay off their massive mortgage.

She followed Joe into a bare hallway, devoid of any personal effects, and into an equally bland kitchen. The walls were a sunny yellow, but that was about as cheerful as it got. The floor was covered in horrendous brown tiles and the worktops were cheap Formica.

'I haven't exactly got the hang of the whole interior design thing yet,' Joe explained wryly. 'I much prefer getting the latest gadgets for the loft.'

He unlocked the back door and waited as she followed him into the garden. 'You'll love the whole set up,' he promised. His face had changed, Lizzie thought in surprise. He seemed suddenly animated, not at all the careful, cautious guy he'd displayed so far. His step was light and she followed him across the grass.

The lofts dominated the small garden. They were like mini sheds, from inside which came soft cooing noises and the sound of flapping wings.

Joe unlocked the loft and beckoned Lizzie to follow him.

Lizzie took a deep breath before entering. Birds were not her favourite creatures, especially not pigeons. If it had been a loft full of robins or sparrows perhaps it might have been better. She took a hesitant step inside and the scent of pigeon assailed her nostrils. She did her best to keep her face from betraying anything. Oh Jesus, she thought.

Joe seemed oblivious to it. She was aware that he was waiting for her reaction, so she uttered a 'Wow' and hoped it sounded sincere. Her eyes fell on a long, low feeder on the ground. A pigeon fluttered by her towards it and Lizzie flinched.

'That's the hopper,' Joe explained. 'I let them feed themselves from that all day, every day.'

'What's in it?' Lizzie couldn't identify the dry, brown-looking stuff.

'Barley malt,' Joe explained. 'I get it from a brewery. It's great stuff, the birds love it. It has to be watched, though, in case it gets wet or goes off. It causes fungal spores to develop.' He pointed upwards and started on about the ceilings and the wood and paint and stuff. He talked about feeding the birds and what he gave them. Lizzie couldn't make head nor tail of it but she nodded along anyway.

'The important thing to remember when racing birds,' she heard Joe say when she tuned back in, 'is to give them a reason to want to come home. With the cocks, most fanciers will work the widowhood system. Basically they fly home to their mates, whom they haven't seen all week.'

'Oh, that's cruel.' Bit like her and Tom, she thought wryly.

Joe grinned. 'Not really. Cid down the club reckons he'd be quite happy to only see his wife once a week.'

'Ha, ha.'

'Another thing they fly home for is food.' Joe shook the little dish. 'I give them corn and seeds when they come back.'

'So they need a reason to come back.'

'Yeah.' Joe reached in and took out a bird. 'No point in coming home if there's nothing good at the end of it, ey?' His comment had a desolate ring, even though he directed it at the pigeon he was holding. He held the bird tenderly in the palm of his hand, its head against his stomach. His finger ran down the length of the pigeon's body. 'And, of course, you need to love them enough so that they want to fly back to you.'

The words hit Lizzie with such force that she gasped.

Joe looked at her sharply. 'You OK?'

'Fine, yeah.' She swallowed. It was weird to hear him talk that way. Really unsettling.

'Here.' Joe smiled and held out the bird towards her. 'See what you think of him.'

Lizzie gently took the pigeon from his hands. Oh God, this was harder than she'd thought. What if it took a dump all over her brand new T-shirt? She hadn't really thought out the whole 'helping him with his pigeons' issue at all.

'Eh, great,' she tried to say with enthusiasm. She was convinced her finger was sticking up its backside, which was disgusting.

Joe grinned, all white-toothed admiration. For the bird. 'See how well balanced he is.'

'Well balanced?'

'Yeah.' Joe, much to her horror and revulsion, gently took her hands in his and helped her lift the bird up. Lizzie tried not to shiver. 'See how his body follows a line. He's balanced. And look at his wings.' He pulled a wing for her to examine. 'Nice coverage, see?'

'Oh, yeah.' Lizzie hoped she sounded as if she knew what she was talking about.

'Very good coverage. I see that now. That helps him fly well, doesn't it?'

Joe shrugged. 'I think so,' he nodded. 'Other people have different ways of telling. Some use eye-sign. They basically look into the bird's eyes and swear they can tell if it'll be any good.

Some like a low-lying tongue in the mouth. But I reckon you can tell just by holding a bird. See how he just sits so nicely in your hand.'

The bird wasn't sitting too nicely in Lizzie's hand. He was getting a little edgy and his head was moving a little too much for her to feel happy about it. And her finger was definitely in the wrong position. Which might explain why the bird was uneasy, too . . .

'Can I let him go now?' she asked, trying not to sound as if she actually wanted to.

'Yeah.'

They both watched as the bird flew and eventually came to rest in a box.

'His name is Prince,' Joe said. 'My best racer. I'll probably breed off him next year, but for now I just love seeing him take to the skies and fly back home.'

'And he stays in that box all the time?' Lizzie asked.

'Yep, that's his home. See the ring he has on his legs? That tells who he is. Every pigeon has to have one of those.'

'So that's how you know he's Prince?'

'Well, no. I just know it's him from the way he looks.'

Lizzie doubted that. As far as she could see, every bird in the place looked exactly the same.

'And the way he moves,' Joe added.

'I see.' But she didn't.

'So,' Joe looked expectantly at her, 'we'll basket them first.'

'OK,' Lizzie nodded. 'And, eh, how do you do that?'

'I usher them into the corridor and they have no option but to go into the basket. Watch.' He gently went about encouraging the birds to leave their perches and, one by one, they waddled across the loft and into the narrow passageway.

'Now,' Joe said, 'I'll go out and place a basket at that ledge and you get the lads to move towards it. We should get it done in the next few minutes, OK?'

'Sure.' Lizzie didn't feel that confident. She watched Joe leave and, when he was outside, he called to her to usher the pigeons towards the basket.

'Hup,' Lizzie called feebly, feeling stupid. 'Hup.'

The birds continued to peck the ground and wander around.

'Hup,' Lizzie called in a crosser voice. 'Come on!'

Joe was grinning from the other side. 'You're way too polite,' he laughed.

'HUP!' Lizzie shouted and immediately there was a frantic fluttering of wings as birds took off in every direction.

Lizzie screamed as they whirled around her head and Joe raced in, half laughing, half concerned.

'You'll give my birds a heart attack before the race.'

'Sorry,' Lizzie said meekly, kicking herself for screaming. He'd probably feck her out now. 'I guess I need more help than I thought.'

'I guess you do,' Joe agreed, an amused smile dancing on his lips. He tapped the skin next to his eye. 'Watch.' With a clap of his hands and a whistle, the birds stopped their frantic flapping and, like obedient children, started to walk towards the ledge. Lizzie, despite herself, was amazed at the way they obeyed him.

'Respect and trust,' Joe said. 'That's what you have to give them and they give it right back.'

He went outside. Lizzie followed and saw him latching up the basket and setting it on to the ground.

'Now, do you feel like trying again?'

'Do you feel like letting me?'

'Sure.' He observed her. 'You're learning, right? No point in giving up now, ey?'

'Yeah, no point in giving up at all,' Lizzie replied, and the way she said it came out sounding really strange, threatening even. Joe shot her a glance but she managed to disarm him with a smile, turning away quickly in case he saw that she wasn't really smiling. She squared her shoulders and turned towards the loft. 'Now, for the second time.'

'Be firm without being cross,' he advised.

'OK.' God, why couldn't he have a more likeable hobby? she wondered. Like stamp collecting or football? Something she could support without getting her hands dirty or making a fool of herself.

She walked as enthusiastically as she could back into the smelly loft and confronted the pigeons.

'Ready when you are!' Joe called.

Lizzie clapped her hands and there was a small commotion. The birds eyed her warily.

'Come on now,' Lizzie said in her best school teacher's voice, 'come on.'

A couple of birds alighted on the perch.

'In you go.' Lizzie whooshed them with her hands and, to her amazement, they obeyed.

'Yeah!' Joe gave a little cheer and Lizzie smiled, slightly stunned.

The other birds, sensing what was wanted, copied the first two and, to her delight, they were soon all basketed.

'You have the knack,' Joe said as he clipped the other basket shut.

Lizzie couldn't figure out if he was joking or serious.

Joe put the second basket beside the first. 'Now,' he said, 'I'm just going to go next door to see how Ellen, my neighbour, is. D'you want to clean out the boxes?' He made it sound like an honour.

Clean out the boxes? Lizzie looked questioningly at him. 'Clean out the boxes?'

'Yeah, scrape out all the droppings. I'll be back in a bit to help you.'

'Scrape out the droppings?'

'Yeah,' Joe nodded. 'Don't worry, it's easy.'

She wasn't worried. Just horrified.

'I normally do them on a Friday,' Joe went on, 'when the birds are in the baskets. This is what you do, see?' He took a bag from his pocket, pulled out a wooden tray that was resting under a pigeon box and, with a palette knife, scraped the droppings into the bag. 'See. It's easy.'

'Sure is,' Lizzie said as brightly as she could. She wondered if he had gloves anywhere.

'You can use these.' Joe, as if reading her mind, pulled some thick gloves out of his pocket. 'When you finish, you can wash your hands in the kitchen. There's disinfectant under the sink.'

'OK, cool.'

'Brilliant.'

She watched Joe go back into the house, wash his own hands and grab a bag of groceries. He came back out and hopped over the back wall. Lizzie ducked inside the loft in case she was spotted by the old woman who lived next door. She stared around at the empty loft, all its boxes now empty. And it was up to her to clean it. Well, there was no better way to earn trust and respect than doing what she was told. By the time she was finished, she'd have taught Joe a lot about trust and respect.

'Hi, Ellen, how's things today?' Joe called out as he set the bag containing some milk and bread on the kitchen floor. He poked his head into the dining room, where Ellen lay on an old, faded sofa. 'Will I make you a cuppa?'

Ellen nodded. 'Thanks, pet. How much do I owe you for the groceries?'

'Aw, nothing. It's only bread and milk.'

'You didn't get it free, though, did you?' she asked sharply as Joe turned to go and put on the kettle.

'No, but it was only a couple of quid.'

'My purse is over there.' Ellen pointed to her black bag. 'Take the money out of that before you leave, Joe. I mean it.'

Joe said nothing. Instead he boiled the kettle, made Ellen a sandwich and brought it all in to her on a tray. Setting it beside her, he sat in a chair opposite. She still looked a bit shaken, even though it had happened a couple of weeks ago. He supposed that when you got old it became harder to get over something like a burglary and collapsing on to the hard tiles of your kitchen floor – she had given her head a right wallop. It was difficult, though, juggling the pigeons, his job and Ellen. The neighbours on the other side were pretty good, too, at helping out, so between them they were muddling along.

'How you feeling?' he asked her.

'Oh, much better.' Ellen took a bite out of her sandwich and chewed slowly. 'You really don't have to be so attentive, Joe. You've got your own life.'

'Yeah,' he nodded, 'and in my life I've agreed to keep an eye on you, so button it.'

She smiled a little. 'My Sam would have liked you,' she said approvingly. 'In fact, he was a lot like you even to look at.'

Joe knew she thought that already. There were pictures of Ellen's Sam all over this room. They beamed down at him from the mantelpiece and from the walls. A big old photograph of the couple was framed and sat underneath the television. He didn't think he looked too much like Sam, but he never bothered contradicting Ellen.

'He died when he was about your age,' Ellen remarked then. She lifted the mug to her lips with a shaky hand. 'What age would you be, about thirty?'

'Yep.'

'I don't know,' Ellen smiled a little. 'No one gets married any more. Sam and I were married eight years when he died. It was a terrible shock.'

'Yeah, it was pretty young to go all right,' Joe nodded. He wished Ellen would open a window, the air was stifling. 'Will I open a window?'

'No,' she waved him away, 'I like to keep them closed.' A pause. 'He was crossing a road and a man knocked him down. Right in front of me.'

Joe made sympathetic noises. It was awful to see something like that, he was sure, but he prayed like hell that she wouldn't start crying. How would he cope with that?

But Ellen had obviously done her crying a long time ago. 'It took me ages to get over it. I wasn't right for a long time.'

Joe said nothing. He didn't think he was expected to. Ellen seemed to have decided to reveal little bits of her life to him. He supposed they didn't have much in common so it was the easiest thing to talk about. He'd heard about her two dead sisters, her dead parents, a friend who had gone to America and who she'd never heard from again, and the boyfriends.

'They put the man who knocked him down in jail,' Ellen said then, and Joe flinched.

'Did they?' he managed to say, his throat dry, hoping that Ellen wouldn't see the sudden way his own hands had started to tremble ever so slightly.

'Yes. But you know, Joe, I never blamed him. It was a dark night and we were on the road at a corner. It was just bad luck.'

He stared at her.

'So I went to see him and told him that. It was about a year later and the man cried and cried and said he didn't care how long more he was to spend in jail – that hearing those words was his freedom.' She took another sip of tea. 'It's the thing I feel I really did right in my life, you know? Sam would have approved.'

'Eh, yeah.' Joe stood up suddenly, not wanting to hear any more. 'I better go Ellen, I've someone helping me with the birds and—'

'They want me to meet the boy who tried to rob me,' she said then.

'What?' Joe looked at her incredulously.

'It's some kind of thing they do. You can meet with the people who do these things and talk to them and explain how it affected you. They think it does some good.'

'Do they?' Joe rolled his eyes and jammed his hands into his pockets. 'I hope you told them to get lost.'

'No. I said I'd like to meet him. He's only thirteen.' She regarded Joe over the rim of her cup. 'But I'll only feel up to it if you come along. Will you come along?'

Joe bit his lip and didn't quite know how to answer.

What felt like an eternity later, amid much gagging, Lizzie eventually had the boxes cleaned out. It was hard to believe that such small creatures could create so much shit, she thought, as with a final scrape the last of it fell into the bag. Tying a knot in the top, Lizzie dumped the bag outside the loft door and, holding her hands as far away from her body as she could, she marched into the kitchen.

She pulled the gloves gingerly from her hands and plunged her palms under the warm water. The plumbing in the house was almost as bad as at Royal Lawns. The water gurgled alarmingly as it splashed into the sink. Lizzie pulled open the press underneath and found the disinfectant. As she took it out her eye fell on another bottle, tucked into the left-hand corner. Lizzie reached in and cautiously took it out. It was a large bottle, and the label on the side announced that if a few drops of this were regularly added to the pigeons' water supply, it would ward off some disease or other. Lizzie couldn't even begin to pronounce the disease. Her heart skipped a beat. She glanced quickly out the window and, without giving herself time to think it over, twisted the cap on the bottle and shook a few drops into her hand. The liquid inside was the colour of water.

Should she?

She stood for a second with the opened bottle in her hand, the dilapidated clock on the wall tick-ticking the time away. Looking back later that night, it seemed to Lizzie that in this moment she was poised on a cliff edge. If she did nothing and put the bottle back in the press, she'd take a step back from the precipice. But instead she did what she knew she was always going to do and flung herself over the edge, hoping to God that when she eventually landed it would be soft. She turned the bottle upside-down and watched as the liquid flowed out. Oh God, it was slightly darker than water, she noticed then. And it smelled.

Hastily Lizzie turned on the tap to let the stench swirl on down the sink. And, leaving about a quarter of the liquid in the bottle, she put it under the tap and refilled it with water.

Now see how healthy his pigeons stay, she thought, as she gave the top a final vicious screw on.

Joe was preoccupied when he arrived back. He complimented Lizzie on a job well done and said nothing when she told him that she couldn't make it to the club that night as she had other plans.

'Yeah, OK, thanks for your help. If you like you can come over tomorrow and watch the birds come in from the race,' Joe offered, but without his earlier enthusiasm.

'Sure. Maybe.'

Lizzie refused his offer of a lift and insisted that she could walk back to the Luas. It was funny, but the reality of what she'd done had made her feel a little sick and she just had to get away.

21

Tom's flat or 'apartment', as he mockingly called it, was in the city centre. It wasn't exactly situated in the most sought-after area of the city either, Lizzie thought as she neared it. It had the run-down look of Royal Lawns without any potential for charm.

She hadn't known she was on her way here when she'd jumped on the Luas after leaving Joe's. It had been a blur, dumping the stuff down the sink, leaving his house, her thoughts whirling about like mad. Feeling euphoria, feeling guilty, feeling good, feeling like she was the worst person on earth. She hadn't bargained on the guilt at all. She certainly hadn't felt guilty up until now, but then again, she hadn't actually done any harm up until now.

Lizzie stood for a bit, just up the road from Tom's place, looking at his window on the second floor and seeing the dim light through the thin, tatty curtains. She thought she saw Tom move about. She even fancied he looked out and saw her, but it was probably only her imagination. She needed his company tonight, she thought to herself. Tom was calm and reasonable and the norms of society never seemed to bother him. Sure, hadn't she met him after he'd tried to skip the queue in a bar? He wouldn't think anything of what she'd done. Or would he? She didn't know. But, she thought, she'd probably do it again, and the knowledge made her feel worse about herself. After all the pigeons hadn't done anything to her personally. But then again, Megan had done nothing to Joe and look what had happened to her. Once she thought of Megan, her heart squeezed slightly. Hardened. And she found that by focusing on her sister, the pigeons suddenly ceased to matter.

Still, she just needed to see Tom right now. She had planned on going home from Joe's and asking Billy and Aileen all about their baby scan, which had happened earlier today, but she just couldn't talk babies when she'd done what she'd done. No, she had to see Tom. He'd make her feel good again.

She hadn't rung him to say she was on her way. Maybe she should have, but he'd rung her earlier so she knew he was free. She hoped his rehearsal was finished; she didn't want to stand around outside his flat, waiting for him. She just needed him to . . . Lizzie wasn't sure what she needed from him. His easy company, she guessed. Just to be able to sit beside him and feel special. Tom always made her feel like that.

Lizzie started to walk across the large green towards his place, ignoring the stares of the teenagers who had congregated in a large group over at a run-down swing. They watched her from behind a broken-down fence as she passed. She had just got to the door of the apartment block and was about to buzz up when she saw Tom jogging down the stairs.

'Hey,' his grin was crooked, delighted, showing his uneven front teeth, 'I thought it was you. What are you doing here?'

'Just thought I'd surprise you.' She tried to match his grin. 'Surprise!' she sang.

Tom's grin widened. 'I didn't expect you so early, thought you had things to do.' He jammed his hands into his pockets and rocked back on his heels, his over-long hair, just the right side of mussed, falling over an eye so brown it was almost black.

'Yeah, but I'm finished now.'

'Brill.' He winked and ushered her in front of him as they climbed the stairs to his second-floor flat. 'Come on up, I have some beers in the fridge.' He paused. 'Or do you want to head out?'

Lizzie knew he hadn't much spare cash and that he wouldn't like her paying. 'Nope. Here is fine.'

He looked relieved. 'OK.' He pushed open his front door and strode ahead of Lizzie into the apartment.

'You should really lock your door,' she chided gently.

'Yeah?' Tom spread his arms wide, 'And, eh, what exactly would a potential thief actually steal?'

He had a point. His place reflected its owner: broke but optimistic. It was bright; a bit too bright – Lizzie would never have considered yellow and red on opposite walls. He had themed the walls with a green and purple mat that the previous occupant had left behind and had also painted his kitchen presses a purple, to match the mat and to hide the filth of the wood. The whole effect was enough to induce a migraine, but Lizzie was used to it.

The sound of a toilet flushing startled her. 'Have you company?' she asked.

'Just Imogen from the play,' Tom said. 'I told you I had a rehearsal, remember?'

'Here?'

'Uh-huh. We need to work a lot together. So we just met to talk about it.'

Tom turned back to rummage in the fridge and eventually located two cans behind some mouldy cheese. He handed Lizzie one and, taking it from him, she sat down on his sofa, feeling it immediately sink underneath her.

'Hey, Imogen, do you want a can?' Tom called as a very pretty blonde girl emerged from the bathroom. She had blonde bouncy curls and a clichéd good-looking face: peaches and cream skin, rosebud-red lips and long lashes fringing eyes of navy blue.

'No, thanks.' Her gaze fell on Lizzie and she smiled, the dimples on her cheeks adding to the irritating wholesomeness of her. 'Hello,' she said. 'I'm Imogen, the love of your boyfriend's life.'

'In the play,' Tom laughed.

'Hi,' Lizzie said. She couldn't imagine Imogen trying to poison pigeons. The girl looked as if she should be the angel on a Christmas card.

'We're having a laugh, aren't we, Tommy?'

'Yep.' Tom sank on to the sofa beside Lizzie. 'Can we finish up now though? I wasn't expecting Lizzie so early.'

'Sure.' Imogen picked up a colourful coat from the table. 'Nice to meet you, Lizzie.'

'Bye,' Lizzie nodded and watched the girl move her shapely bum out the door.

'Lovely girl,' Tom remarked as he took a slug of beer.

'Is she, *Tommy*?' Lizzie teased, poking him in the chest. She rolled her eyes. 'Tommy, how are ya!' she scoffed.

He grinned. 'I just thought Tommy Lynch sounded a better name than Tom Lynch.'

'Once it's you it sounds good to me.'

Tom laughed and wrapped a companionable arm about her shoulders. 'Cheers.'

'Yeah cheers, you poseur!' They clinked cans and were silent for a bit.

'So, how come you're here early?' Tom asked.

'Are you complaining?'

'Nope.' He leaned in and kissed the tip of her nose.

Lizzie felt tears in her eyes. She didn't deserve that. Right at that moment, she felt like the most horrible person on earth.

'Hey.' Tom, noticing, lowered his gaze to meet hers. 'What's the matter? Have I done something? Are you OK?'

'Yeah.' Lizzie blinked rapidly and put her can down on the floor. 'I'm fine.' She cupped his face in her hands. He was the sexiest guy. He oozed it without even knowing it. The way he walked, his voice, the slow, easy grin. He could make her forget what she'd done. Maybe even make her regret what she'd done. 'Kiss me,' she muttered. 'I mean, *really* kiss me.'

Tom grinned. Gently he covered her two hands with his own and brought his lips to meet hers. Their foreheads touched and he squeezed her hands, letting his lips gently press on hers. Lizzie, he was convinced, was the love of his life. He adored her no nonsense, no bullshit manner. He liked the way she dressed and the way she looked and the way she made him feel. He liked that she needed space and didn't crowd him the way other girls might have done, and he prayed every night that she wouldn't suddenly go off him because he had feck all to give her.

127

'That's not a real kiss,' Lizzie murmured, grinning.

He regarded her with his chocolate-coloured eyes. He landed another soft kiss on her lips. She smelled a little funny, he thought. A sharp smell. But she tasted lovely.

'Yeah,' Lizzie said, 'like that, only longer.'

'OK.' He nodded, untangling his fingers from hers. With one hand in her spiky hair and the other at the back of her head, he kissed her as he'd wanted to for so long. He felt the length of her body as she pressed herself to him. She had her hands up his T-shirt now and was pushing herself so hard against him. There was something desperate in it, though. It wasn't like Lizzie. She normally teased him by pulling away from him and driving him mad until he had no choice but to grab her. Tonight she wasn't doing that. He pulled away.

'Lizzie,' he asked, his breath ragged, 'are you OK?'

'Yeah. What's the matter?'

'Nothing.' He frowned slightly, his body telling him one thing but his mind telling him something else. 'Are you planning on staying?' he asked.

'Are you planning on letting me?' She didn't wait for an answer and leaned back into him. He couldn't help it. He ran his hands over her face, over her body, his face pressed to hers, his mouth not able to get enough of her. 'Oh God,' he groaned.

'Let's keep going and see what happens,' she whispered.

'You know what will happen,' he said back, trying to stop the shake in his voice.

'Good,' was all she said.

She smiled at him impishly and there was no turning back.

Lizzie awoke to the jingle-jangle of her phone. Tom groaned but remained sleeping. Lizzie sat up and immediately the sound of the phone stopped. She glanced across at Tom's alarm clock and saw that it was three in the morning. Jesus, who the hell would be ringing her at that hour? She lay back down and the phone started to ring again.

It was the loudest ring tone ever. It was the loudest phone ever.

She decided that she'd better turn it off and crept out of bed, padding barefoot and semi-naked towards the bedroom door.

'Oh, let me guess,' Tom's sleepy voice arrested her, 'this is the part where you sneak off and leave me a thank you note.'

'No,' Lizzie turned to him, 'this is the part where I switch off my mobile phone and try to get back to sleep.'

'So you're coming back?' Tom said as he chewed his lower lip and regarded her. 'Good. I like the sound of that.'

Lizzie blew him a kiss. She left the bedroom and fished her mobile out of the bag. *You have one missed call: Billy.* Jesus, what the hell was he doing ringing her at three in the morning? Then it dawned on her, maybe it was something to do with the baby. All sorts of horrible scenarios ran through her head, so she hastily dialled him back.

'Lizzie!' Billy's voice shot down the phoneline at her. 'Where are you? What happened to you?'

'Nothing. I'm at Tom's.'

'You never said you were meeting him.'

She laughed slightly. 'Who are you, my secretary?'

'No, I'm your brother and I was worried about you.'

'Jesus, Billy, I'm twenty-eight, give me a break.'

'Are you planning on staying there?'

'I am planning right now on hanging up. You gave me a fright ringing at this time in the morning.'

'You gave me a fright, too, not coming home.'

'I thought something was wrong with the baby,' Lizzie went on, ignoring him.

'Babies,' Billy said.

'And I thought—' Lizzie stopped. 'What did you say?'

'Aileen is expecting twins.' His voice was flat.

'Twins?'

'Yep.'

Lizzie wasn't sure what to say. He hadn't been that enamoured with one baby. 'And how is Aileen? How does she feel?' she asked instead.

'I dunno. She's left me.'

'WHAT?'

From the bedroom she could hear Tom jump up. He appeared at the door and looked questioningly at her. Lizzie waved him away but, yawning, he filled up the kettle and plugged it in.

'She said,' Billy took a deep breath, 'well, she said she saw my face when the nurse announced it. So she left.'

'You mean she left the hospital?' It was too early in the morning to take all this in, Lizzie thought. It must be some sort of a weird dream.

'Yeah,' Billy confirmed, his voice shaking a little. 'She left the hospital and came home and packed a few things and moved over to her dad's.'

'What the hell did you look like?' Lizzie barked crossly. 'For God's sake—'

'I don't know what I looked like,' Billy barked back. 'I was just shocked, you know? Two babies.'

'OK,' Lizzie sighed deeply. 'Let's get this straight—'

'I am not one of your counselling projects,' Billy said curtly. 'I only rang to see if you were safe. You are. So I'll go.' He hung up.

Lizzie stared at the phone. 'The nerve,' she fumed. She dialled his number again but he didn't answer.

'What's up?' A cup of tea appeared over her shoulder.

'Sorry for waking you.' Lizzie, suddenly shy, pulled her T-shirt down as far as it would go. She took the tea from him and her T-shirt moved up again. Tom came round and sat in beside her, a mug of tea in his own hand. 'Aileen has left Billy, apparently.'

'No way!'

'Yes way.'

As she told Tom the story, she found it hard to meet his eyes. Yes, last night had been bloody great, but now, with Tom looking at her as if he truly loved her, she felt . . . she didn't know. Weird would describe it best. Yesterday she could have accepted it. Today she knew that she wasn't as great as he thought she was. What she had done to Joe's birds was horrible. The love in Tom's eyes for her was a lie. She couldn't live like that, but she couldn't let

Tom go either. And she couldn't not find out the truth from Joe or punish him for what he'd done.

'Do you want me to bring you home?' Tom asked, interrupting her thoughts.

Lizzie hugged the mug between her hands and for the first time met his concerned gaze. 'I just want you to hold me,' she said. 'Don't look at me, just hold me.'

Tom didn't ask why, he just got the big duvet and put it around them both and they sat, his arm about her shoulder, watching the sun steal through the window.

22

MARK HAD INSISTED on coming along to Lizzie's meeting with Jim, the builder. Lizzie hoped that Jim would sell a house to Life at cost price. Jim did not get on with Mark.

'He specifically requested that you not be there,' Lizzie eventually admitted. 'You annoy him, Mark.'

'Yeah,' Mark nodded. 'Success annoys people like Jim O'Brien. But I am the director of Life, I know more about it than you, Lizzie, and if he asks detailed questions, what will you say?'

'I'll tell him, as I always do, that I'll find out the information and get back to him,' Lizzie said through gritted teeth, knowing that the battle was lost. If Mark wanted to come, then Mark would come. She supposed it was the reason he had got Life up and running. He didn't listen to reason so, while he annoyed people, he also at times managed the impossible.

'Mark,' she had one more go, 'a house is a big ask. If Jim can give us a house, I think we have to respect his wishes.'

'Rubbish.' Mark made a dismissive gesture with his hand. 'He has houses coming out of his ears. No, he'll be impressed that I took the time out to come.'

'He won't!'

'Calm down,' Mark shook his head. 'Don't go all hormonal on me. Honestly, you haven't been yourself at all these past few days.'

'Don't you dare say I'm hormonal.' Lizzie removed her coat from the hook at the door and pulled it on. 'Well, seeing as you're determined to come and jeopardise our chances of getting this house, you might as well give me a lift in your fancy car.'

'Will do,' Mark nodded imperiously, holding the door open for her as she marched out of the office.

Lizzie didn't say much to him on the way. It was true what he'd said, she wasn't herself. Part of it was stress: Billy was going mental as Aileen wouldn't talk to him and had refused all his calls – she was being a bit over the top, Lizzie had to admit; plus her mother was going mad in Wexford between worrying about Billy and fighting with the local police force. And on top of that, she had Tom totally under her spell and, while she loved him, she felt as if she were deceiving him. But worst of all was that she just didn't think she had the stomach to see Joe any more. Oh, she wanted to. She wanted to make him pay so badly it hurt, but after she'd poured the bird medication down the sink she also realised that living with a revenge agenda was quite difficult, too.

Could she stop seeing him?

She wasn't sure, and the more she thought about it the more confused she became. But maybe, if she stopped seeing Joe, she could get on with her life with Tom.

Or could she?

Could she ever go back to the woman she was before she'd seen Joe? She'd already taken one step away from that person and it wasn't something she could reverse. Did she want to keep going?

'Bloody wanker!' Mark startled her by blasting his horn at a driver in front who had the audacity to indicate and pull into the line of traffic. His horn blasting was followed by a finger gesture which the other motorist replicated enthusiastically.

'Jesus, Mark, will you calm down? We need to be able to concentrate when we get there. Now,' she tried to focus herself, as she really couldn't afford to blow this or they'd be left high and dry, 'let me do the talking and the schmoozing. You sit and listen and don't speak unless you're spoken to, all right?'

He shrugged a little.

'All right?' Lizzie asked a little more sharply.

'Yeah.' He sounded like a sulky adolescent. Then, 'I don't know what your problem is.'

133

Lizzie ignored that. Instead she asked, 'How's Stella?'

Stella was Mark's girlfriend. His first since his wife had left him five years ago. Instantly his face changed. 'Aww,' he said, 'she's fantastic. She's some woman. Brilliant.'

'She must be,' Lizzie joked, 'putting up with you.'

'Cheeky,' Mark pretended to swat her. 'I'll have you know, I could charm the birds outta the trees once upon a time. My wife, before she ended up hating my guts, chased me. She was a very forceful woman.'

'Imagine.' Lizzie rolled her eyes. Mark was oblivious to how forceful he could be.

'You don't want to imagine that!' Mark snorted. 'Still, she got her comeuppance. Ran off with the guy we bought our car off and then he ran off on her. Gave her a nervous breakdown, so it did.'

'Oh, that's terrible.' He'd never told her that bit before.

'What goes around comes around,' Mark said cheerfully. 'I had one when she left, so it was only right that she should have one, too.'

'I see your compassionate side is still missing in action,' Lizzie remarked drily.

'You can only have compassion when someone is at least a bit sorry,' Mark huffed. 'Was my wife sorry that she ran off with our car salesman? Did she say sorry for taking all our money out of the bank before she left? Did she admit she'd been conned? Eheh,' he made a sound like a buzzer and continued in a faux American accent, 'I don't think so.'

And with those words, he answered Lizzie's dilemma about Joe.

23

Joe had a party tonight on his dad's new boat. He
invited me and told me to bring anyone I liked. I just
brought Billy as I wasn't sure how many people I'd be
allowed to bring and anyway, Mammy told me that if
Billy didn't go then I couldn't. Not that I minded.
Billy is great at mixing, just like me.

We went in Billy's new car. Well, it's new to him. In
reality, it's a couple of years old and he imported it
from England. It's black and has sort of flames painted
along the sides and two big exhausts poking out the
back and when it goes it ROARS. All his friends are
dead impressed by it. I don't know what kind of a car
it is but when Mammy saw it, she nearly collapsed. He
got a major lecture on speeding and on all the people
who have died on Wexford roads and Billy being Billy
pretended to take her seriously before asking me and
Dad and Lizzie if we wanted to sit in it.

Dad and I sat in the back because Lizzie is as mad
as Billy and she insisted on sitting in the front. Well,
with Mammy watching anxiously from the driveway,
Billy drove nice and easy away but once we were on the
open road, he put his foot down and I'm not joking
when I say we went from ten to a hundred miles an
hour in about five seconds. Billy had the radio on and
the windows open and Lizzie was whooping from the

135

front seat. I swear that girl would do anything. Dad was shouting for him to slow down and Billy was pretending that he couldn't hear, what with all the noise from the radio. I just pretended to laugh but it was terrifying – like those video games where all you can see is the road whipping by. Billy's car is so low to the ground that it was all I could see from the back seat. Billy and Lizzie are totally fearless – it's like they think they're invincible. Of course, when Billy did eventually slow down, Dad went ballistic and threatened to take the car off him. Billy just laughed and Lizzie turned round and said in this big bored patronising voice, 'Dad, he's got his own job and his own money and you really can't tell him what to do any more.'

'Sad but true, Dad,' Billy chortled.

'Well,' Dad said back, 'if you go and break your mother's heart by dying on the roads or by killing someone else, I'll never forgive you.'

'He won't.' Lizzie is a great one for sticking up for us. Because she's the youngest she gets away with murder. It's handy sometimes. Lizzie has charm. She has Dad wrapped around her finger. She has all men wrapped around her finger. I have the looks, I don't mind admitting, but Lizzie has the wit. Fellas actually try to impress her. Despite me having the better figure and a nicer face they don't hardly look at me. Aileen says that maybe guys feel as if I'm out of their league and that's why they don't approach me and while I'd like to believe this, I don't think it's true. I always find myself being not quite who I am with lads, trying to be funny or trying to be smart (which is a big mistake for me to do, believe me). Lizzie, with her roundy figure and cheeky grin, is just herself and it works. I never had a boyfriend at her age and it wasn't from lack of trying. Lizzie has guys queuing up to go out with her.

Anyway, I'm going off the point. But it's nice to write things sometimes. Just your thoughts, not what exactly happened, because sometimes they can be two very different things, right? But anyway, suffice to say we left a sulky Lizzie behind when we went to the boat party. (I think she has the hots for Joe because she keeps asking me about him in work. He's miles too old for her. Mam would go mad!) Billy drove, accompanied by about a million instructions from Mammy about not drinking and driving. I reckon that he drove so fast we got to the party five minutes before we actually left!

The place was heaving. And everyone was so dressed up. All I had on was a red summer dress, very short, and a pair of high red sandals. I broke out in a bit of a sweat when I saw how everyone else was so glammed up. Billy didn't seem to notice that he was the only one in jeans and a T-shirt and because Billy didn't care, I suddenly didn't either. If it was OK for Bill, it was OK for me.

It's a gorgeous boat, and I hate boats. It was so new it was still a shining white, its name 'Rossclare Rossi' painted in swirling script all along her hull. And it has a kitchen and toilet and everything. There was music playing and a bar all set up. Lights had been strung all across the deck. Joe was somewhere in the middle of a bunch of people. I know because I could hear him laugh.

Billy and I made our way to the bar and Billy got a water while I had a vodka. And then I saw Dessie. And he saw me and he raised his arm and waved. So I took a massive gulp of the vodka.

'Hi.' Dessie, in a brilliant blue T-shirt and a pair of white cotton trousers came over. God, he looked so dazzling, as if he'd been washed in Daz.

'Hi, Dessie,' I said and I knew I sounded breathless as

137

if I was about to have an asthma attack or something. 'This is my brother.'

'Billy.' Billy stuck out his hand. 'I've heard all about you from Megs.'

I wanted to kick him.

Then Billy said in a really untactful way, 'I'll leave you to talk to Dessie then, will I, Meg?'

I shrugged. What are you meant to say to a thing like that? He winked at me then mooched off, and was soon chatting up this blonde model-type girl who was way out of his league.

Dessie smiled at me and I smiled back and took another gulp of vodka.

Next minute, up Joe comes. He was manky drunk. I've never seen Joe drunk and this probably sounds terrible, but it suited him. He was smiling, showing off his lovely white teeth. Normally Joe is really quiet, not in a shy way, just in a sort of self-contained way that makes you think he doesn't need people.

'Hey,' he came between Dessie and me and slung his arms about our shoulders, 'how's my two work buddies?'

'You're drunk,' Dessie laughed. 'Jesus, will you stop breathing in my face?'

'Sorry.' Joe straightened himself up, still keeping his arm around me. 'Great crowd, isn't it?'

'Yep,' Dessie said, scanning the deck. 'Not bad.'

'So,' Joe said into my face and boy, did he reek of beer, 'you got here.'

'Naw, I'm just an apparition,' I said. I'm witty when I don't fancy someone, which is unfortunate 'cause I think guys like funny girls, which is why all the guys I don't fancy fancy me.

'And what an apparition,' Joe said, shaking his head. 'Gorgeous.' Then he asked, 'So where is the real Megan?'

'At a real party,' I said back.

And they laughed. I was actually quite proud of that comment.

'Where's Denise tonight?' Joe asked Dessie. 'I thought you were bringing her.'

Dessie rolled his eyes. 'Massive row,' he confirmed. 'Again. In fact, I think it's definitely over.' He didn't sound that upset over it.

'Yeah, sure!' Joe laughed, unconcerned.

'I was meant to go up to visit her this weekend.' Dessie locked eyes with me. 'So when I asked her down she refused to come, and I said that I wasn't going up as Joe needed me at his party to give it a bit of street cred.'

'Wanker,' Joe said easily, a big lazy grin on his face. 'You'd really want to treat her a bit better, Dessie.'

'Like you would?'

I think there was what would be called a tense silence? Then a very drunk girl wearing what looked like half a dress slithered up to Joe and wrapped an arm in his. She reminded me of a snake shedding its skin.

'Joey, will you show me where I can find the crisps?' She batted her eyes at him.

'Show her there, Dessie,' Joe said, ignoring the girl and keeping his arm around me.

'She asked you,' Dessie said.

They locked eyes.

'Please, Joey?' The girl had her hand on Joe's arm and was running a taloned finger up and down. 'I want you to.' She slipped an arm about him. 'Please.'

Joe sighed. 'Come on, so.' He left us, the girl clinging on to him and barely managing to stagger in her high heels.

'She's mad about him,' Dessie snorted. 'Every time we go out, she throws herself at him. Of course Joe is too honourable to lead her on, but I keep telling him that's what the girl wants.'

'Who is she?' The girl had wrapped her arms about his neck and was attempting to slow dance with him.

'Jessica is her name. She's been after him for years. Joe has quite a fan club, you know. Jessica is at the helm.'

Both of us started to laugh as Joe, reaching behind the bar, managed to grab a six-pack of crisps and thrust it at her, before making his escape.

'A fan club?' I have to say I was surprised. He didn't strike me as the kind of guy girls would go for.

'Oh yeah.' Dessie screwed up his face. 'Even Denise had a thing for him when we met her first.'

How could someone, given the choice, fancy Joe over Dessie? I wondered.

'She said it was because he didn't try to impress her.'

I rolled my eyes. 'What girl wants a guy who doesn't try to impress? If I had a boyfriend he'd have to be impressing me all the time.'

Dessie looked at me in amusement. 'Yeah?'

'Oh yes.' I knocked back the rest of my vodka. 'Or at least he'd have to try.'

'How would he try?' Dessie was regarding me curiously now. 'What impresses a great-looking girl like you?'

'Compliments like that for a start,' I said.

Dessie bit his lower lip and grinned. 'So, compliments. Stuff like being told that you have the sexiest pair of legs on this boat?'

'Uh-huh.' My head was beginning to spin, I don't know if it was Dessie or the vodka, but whatever it was it was cool.

'And that red is your colour and your eyes are gorgeous and that your mouth looks as if it was made to be kissed and . . .'

He went on like this, throwing out compliments as if they were sweets for me to eat. And I thought with each

140

compliment he was moving closer to me. Or maybe it was me moving closer to him, I don't know. If we'd got any closer, I'd probably have had a heart attack. In fact, I'm convinced that Dessie was about to plant a kiss on my lips when the engine of the boat suddenly roared to life, jerking me forward into Dessie's arms. People cheered.

'And off we go!' Joe yelled above the cheering.

'Oh, I am sorry,' I lied as I tried to untangle myself.

'I'm not.' Dessie took his hands from my arms and looked in amusement at me. 'That was quite nice.'

'You have a girlfriend,' I blabbered out. I wanted to appear moral, even if I didn't feel it.

'I do.' Dessie assumed a glum sort of look. Then added, 'For now.'

What did that mean? I wondered. It sounded good though.

The boat sped up and a girl beside us yelped.

'Isn't Joe a bit drunk to be driving this boat?' the girl asked us. I could have killed her for interrupting what was a good line of conversation.

Next thing there was the sound of a speed boat, which actually turned out to be the coastguards. Someone must have rung and reported Joe for taking the boat out whilst drinking. A man with a loudspeaker ordered Joe to bring the boat in.

'Oh-oh,' Dessie sounded slightly amused, 'someone's in trouble.'

The long and the short of it was that the party ended pretty abruptly – Joe was hauled off by the police and Dessie and a couple of others went with him.

Just as Dessie left he turned to me. 'Thanks for keeping me company tonight,' he said. Then he ran to catch up with Joe, who was being treated rather roughly by the coastguards.

I can't wait to see him Monday.

And Billy assures me that Dessie looks as if he's really into me! Though I couldn't say the same about the blonde he'd been chatting up.

24

JOE WAS ALMOST sick as he accompanied Ellen into the police station. For the last five years, since his release, he'd avoided even going past police buildings and now, here he was, in one again. It was still the same as he remembered. The desk, the forms, the noise and bustle. At least this time, though, he was there as a law-abiding citizen. But it still didn't stop him from thinking that he'd be arrested on some misdemeanour he didn't even know he'd committed.

'Hello,' Ellen, full of purpose, marched up to the desk, 'I'm Ellen McGrath and this is my neighbour, Joseph. We're here to meet with,' she unfolded a piece of official-looking headed paper and read out, 'Anthony Carter.'

'Aw, Anthony Carter,' the policeman repeated, in a not-too-promising sort of voice. 'Yes, he's in here. Come on.'

Joe followed Ellen as she went after the policeman. He had to take deep breaths as he was shown to a small interrogation room. Walls bland and white. Bland brown desk. Bland brown chairs. Anthony was sitting in one of the chairs, twisting his stick-thin fingers one about the other. He glanced up nervously as they came in. Then, as he saw Joe, he said loudly, 'That's the fella that broke me nose, Ma.'

Anthony's mother, thinner than her son, was sitting beside him and a woman guard was on his other side.

'Shut up, Anto,' his mother hissed nervously.

'Ellen and Joe,' the guard said, 'welcome.'

Ellen was right, Joe noticed – Anthony was younger than he'd thought the night of the break-in. Sitting here now with his mam, he looked no older than his thirteen years.

143

Ellen slid into a seat opposite the boy whilst Joe remained standing. He couldn't help it. Much as he wanted to sit down, he was afraid that if he did, he'd never be let out of the room. Stupid, he knew.

'Would you like to sit down, Joseph?' the guard asked.

Joe shook his head and gulped audibly. 'No, ta.'

'It helps if we all sit,' the woman said in a slightly firmer voice.

Joe winced, and then nodded. He pulled out a chair and sat, a little away from the table, rubbing his hands nervously up and down his jeans.

'OK,' the guard said. 'Now, I'd like to introduce you both to Anthony's mother, Ann.'

'Hello,' Ann said. Then, in a rush, 'Thank you both for agreeing to this. I know it couldn't have been easy.' Her eyes met Ellen's. 'Especially for you.'

Ellen managed a smile. 'Well, if Joseph hadn't agreed, I'd never have come.'

Anthony's mother swallowed hard. 'OK. Right. Well, thank you, Joseph,' she said. Her voice wobbled.

'It's Joe,' Joe said, without quite knowing why. He guessed he felt sorry for her. A little, anyway.

'Joe,' she repeated.

'Now,' the guard went on, 'Anthony has thought a lot about what he has done, haven't you, Anthony?'

'Uh-huh,' Anthony said. He was staring at his hands.

'What does "uh-huh" mean?' the guard asked.

'It means "yes",' Anthony said defensively. 'Everyone knows that.'

'It would help if you'd say "yes" or "no"' the guard said.

'You answer properly now, Anto,' his mother ordered, poking him in his arm.

'Sorry,' Anthony muttered. Then, lifting his head slightly from the desk, he said, 'I'm sorry for what I done.'

There was a silence.

'Would you like to say anything, Ellen?' the guard asked.

Ellen swallowed and opened her mouth but nothing came out.

144

'Ellen?' the guard pressed gently.

'She collapsed,' Joe said suddenly, startling everyone. 'She collapsed after you were taken away, Anthony, d'you know that?'

Anthony was like a rabbit caught in headlights.

'Joe—' Ellen began, but Joe held up his hand to silence her.

'No, Ellen, let me tell him. She collapsed, Anthony, and she had to be brought to hospital. If I hadn't been there, she could have died, d'you know that?'

Anthony shook his head.

'Yeah,' Joe nodded as he moved nearer to the table. 'Would you like a death on your conscience, Anthony? Would you?'

Anthony shook his head.

'Is that a "no"?' the policewoman asked.

'Because I'm telling ya, Anthony, living with a death on your conscience is no joke. Even if you hadn't meant it to happen, it's no bloody joke. Even if you didn't even know it happened and you found out, it's no joke. So think hard before you decide to rob anyone the next time, ey?'

There was a silence. Joe scanned the room. Ellen was staring at him, looking almost as shocked as Anthony and his mother. The guard was trying to smile to normalise the situation – this outburst was not part of the rehabilitation plan.

Joe stood up and made his way to the door.

'I'm going out to get some air,' he said as he pushed the door open. 'You carry on.'

Lizzie had asked Billy if she could borrow his car to go into town.

Billy, who was still shell-shocked by Aileen leaving him, had barely registered the request, so Lizzie had taken advantage of that before he could change his mind. She grabbed the keys and, hopping in, fired the ignition. The car chugged a little before finally getting going.

Billy's car was a wreck, she thought as she pulled out into traffic. A one-litre ten-year-old shuddering piece of metal. Still, it did manage, after a fashion, to get from A to B. Driving it was an experience, as everyone on the road seemed to want to pass it out. If the car was a person it would be the class nerd, shaking and shivering in a corner as it watched all its super buddies glide along through life.

Lizzie hoped she knew where she was going. She'd consulted the internet for directions and found a Dublin street map online. She was looking for Duke's Road in Dun Laoghaire. She knew roughly how to get to Dun Laoghaire but, beyond that, she was lost.

Twenty minutes later she pulled up by the side of the road to ask someone.

'Oh yes,' the man said, grinning, and, sounding almost delighted, announced, 'it's *miles* away.'

Lizzie's heart sank.

'You're way out of your way,' he went on. Then, pointing, he said, 'Now, go down to the crossroads down here, then turn left. Right? Then take a right and another left. Right? Then after that you'll come to a roundabout, don't take the first right, take the second one and you'll be on the right road. It's straight on from there. You can't go wrong.'

But she did. Lizzie cursed in frustration. Jesus, she should have asked Tom to go with her, he could have read the map. But Tom was very busy at the moment, so she hadn't really been able to meet up with him. They'd gone for a drink once or twice, but Lizzie had feigned tiredness and come home early. She knew he was wondering what was up and why they hadn't spent the night together since, and she knew she'd have to confront it sooner or later. Make a decision. But for now, all she wanted was for Tom to still be in her life, to be her normality, even if it was on the fringes. The thought of losing him hurt her, but so had the thought of not knowing what had happened to Meg.

And then she saw it, like a little miracle: Duke's Road, printed on a signpost at the beginning of a lovely leafy avenue. Wow, Lizzie thought as she drove up Aileen's dad's street, she had no idea that Aileen came from such a fancy area. Big detached houses with large front gardens. Nice.

She pulled up outside number 13 and saw that there was a

car in the driveway, so someone must be home. Taking a deep breath, she hopped out of Billy's car.

'What just happened in there?' Ellen startled Joe as she came up behind him. He was having a smoke outside the door of the police station.

'Nothing.' He blew the smoke out in a long, thin stream and watched it being carried away on the calm air. 'Just, I dunno, lost it for a second, that's all.'

'Really,' Ellen said, not sounding as if she believed him. 'OK. Are you ready to come back in?'

Joe met her gaze. 'Can you carry on without me? I'll wait here for you and bring you home, but that bloody place,' he indicated the station behind him, 'gives me the creeps.'

Ellen stood beside him and touched him gently on the arm. 'I'm just going to say this once, Joseph,' she said calmly. 'You helped me, and if you ever want me to return the favour, I will.' A squeeze. 'OK?' Then she turned on her heel and left him staring after her. It wasn't until he turned to take another drag of his fag that he realised he had a huge lump in his throat.

Aileen's dad was the biggest man Lizzie had ever seen. In fact he was even bigger than the last time she had seen him. His huge shoulders seemed to fill up the whole door frame. A giant fist was curled about the front door, holding it open.

'Lizzie,' he said, his eyes widening. 'Nice to see you.'

Well, at least he wasn't going to give her an ear-bashing about her brother, Lizzie thought in relief.

'Thanks, eh . . .' She tried to think of his name and couldn't.

'Abe,' he supplied with a small smile. Then, indicating the hallway behind him, he lowered his voice and said, 'Have you come to talk some sense into herself?'

'Well,' Lizzie shrugged, 'I don't know if sense is the word, but I know Billy misses her and is trying to ring her.'

Abe nodded. 'She won't talk to him. I keep trying to make her, but she won't.'

That didn't seem too promising. 'Can I see her?' Lizzie asked.

'Oh, be my guest.' Abe stood out of the way to let her by. 'She's still in bed, though. She spends her time in bed when she's not at work. When I try to talk to her, all I get is hysterics.' He winced. 'There are some things fathers just aren't good at.'

'There are some things none of us are good at,' Lizzie joked feebly.

'Well, when you've finished, you're welcome to join me for a cuppa,' Abe said. 'I could do with someone to talk to who's not going to blame men for all the wrongs in the world.'

Oh God, it sounded as if Aileen was really furious, Lizzie thought. She gave Abe a weak smile and slowly ascended the stairs.

The landing was wide, with doors leading off it in all directions. Luckily there were signs saying Bathroom, Dad's Room, Spare Room, and then one that said Aileen's Room. It had a picture of ballet shoes on it and a teddy. It had obviously hung there for years and years as it was faded and dusty.

Lizzie knocked gently on the door.

'Go away, Dad, I already told you I feel sick.'

'It's, eh, me, Aileen,' Lizzie said timidly. 'Lizzie.'

'And what do you want?' The sound of pounding footsteps followed by an opening wrench of the bedroom door. 'Huh,' Aileen turned on her heel and flounced back towards the bed, 'have you come to plead for him?'

'He doesn't even know I'm here.' Lizzie took a hesitant step inside.

'Yeah. Sure.' Aileen had her face buried in the pillow again. 'Well, you can tell him from me that he's wasting his time calling me. I am never going back to a man who does not want his own children.'

'Aileen,' Lizzie tried to keep her voice nice and calm, 'of course he wants his own children. And he wants you.'

Aileen's body stiffened. Then relaxed. Then she turned over on the bed and slowly sat up. 'You didn't see his face, Lizzie. You weren't there.' Her voice sounded teary. 'Oh God, it was so humiliating.'

A big tear trickled down her cheek and she furiously scrubbed it away. 'I don't even know why I'm crying,' she said half savagely. 'I hate him. I hate him.'

She sounded as if she did too, Lizzie thought despairingly. 'What did he look like?' she asked instead.

'Has he not told you what happened?' Aileen asked.

'Nope.' Lizzie took the chance of moving in beside her on the bed. 'You know Billy, he doesn't talk about stuff like that.'

'Oh, I know him all right,' Aileen's tone was bitter, 'and I wish I didn't.' Her hand touched her tummy briefly. 'My poor little babies.'

Lizzie waited, saying nothing.

Eventually Aileen spoke again. 'We were getting a scan done,' she said. 'The first one. And you know how excited I was, Lizzie. I just couldn't wait to see our little baby on the monitor. Billy said he couldn't wait either. And in we went and the nurse rubbed the gel on my stomach and got the little roundy thing so that she could see the baby and next thing, she turns to us and says, "Oh my God, there are two little ones in here." And I laughed and turned to Billy and, oh, Lizzie, you should have seen him.' She sniffed and shook her head. 'The nurse didn't know where to look. He was like a statue and his mouth was wide open and his face was white and he says, "Two" as if he'd never heard the bloody number before and the nurse nods, that's right, she says, two. Twins. You're having twins, congratulations. And he tried to smile but he couldn't, Lizzie. He physically couldn't. I saw it, Lizzie. And so did the nurse. And when I walked out of there I told him I was leaving. And he asked why and I just said, because I saw the way you looked. And he didn't say anything because he knew what I meant. He knew.' More tears.

Lizzie patted her on the back in a lame gesture of support. 'He's awful sorry, Aileen,' she said softly. 'I suppose at the time he couldn't help it. It was a shock to him. But he's sorry now.'

'It's too late to be sorry,' Aileen said in a vicious sort of a whisper. 'The damage is done. Some things you just can't take back.'

Lizzie's hand froze mid-pat. Naw, she thought, she couldn't mean it. Aileen and Billy were like her Mecca of relationships. They were mad about each other. Weren't they?

'I know he's your brother and everything,' Aileen said, 'but he's not the Billy I used to know.' She looked at Lizzie. 'D'you remember the way he used to be, Lizzie?'

Lizzie shrugged. Of course she remembered.

'He used to be mad,' Aileen said softly. 'Totally mad. Sometimes a little too reckless maybe, but Jesus, Lizzie, he lived. He was fun. He drank, he made me laugh.' A pause. 'Now he only makes me miserable.'

'He just worries.' Lizzie tried to stick up for Billy. He'd be heartbroken if he could hear Aileen, she was sure of it. 'You've got the house and a mortgage and he worries.'

'He never used to.'

'No,' Lizzie said softly, 'I know that. But ever since Megan—' She didn't finish.

'Ever since Megan,' Aileen repeated, then shook her head. 'Well, Lizzie, Megan was my friend too and I miss her and I loved her, but you have to keep going.'

Lizzie said nothing.

'You loved her too,' Aileen said, 'and you've kept going.'

Lizzie gulped. Megan's death had changed everything. The way things like that do, she supposed. She had moved on, but she'd changed, just like Billy had.

'Billy has moved on too,' she said eventually.

Aileen said nothing.

'He loves you, Aileen, he's so miserable and so sorry and you won't even talk to him.'

'He humiliated me. He humiliated his own children.'

'He never meant to.'

'And how would you know? He never even told you what happened.'

'Because I know my own brother.' Lizzie's voice rose despite herself. 'I know Billy.'

'Yeah, well,' Aileen shook her head, 'I just need to be away

150

from him now because I feel like I could kill him.' She sniffed and turned back to her pillow. Lizzie sat like a spare not knowing what to do.

'You can go now,' Aileen said. A pause. 'Thanks for coming over.'

'It was his first robbery,' Ellen filled Joe in on the way home. 'He's only thirteen, the poor pet.'

'The poor pet?' Joe almost laughed.

'Oh, don't take that tone,' Ellen said, a little annoyed. 'You didn't stay to hear why he'd done it.'

'Ellen, he broke into your house, he tried to take your money. You collapsed. And he's the victim?' Joe looked at her in disbelief.

'Keep your eyes on the road,' Ellen said primly as she fluffed up her hair and adjusted her skirt. 'His father died, if you must know. There is no income going into that house and the poor child needed money for next year's school books and his mother didn't have it.'

'Are there not grants for that sort of thing?'

'What little boy is going to know about grants?' Ellen looked at him in surprise. 'Honestly, Joseph, I'd never have had you down for a cynic. I'd have thought you'd have compassion.'

'I have compassion for you,' Joe said patiently.

'Well, I have compassion for Anthony,' Ellen replied. 'And I have asked him to help me with little jobs after school to earn some money for his books.'

'You *what?*' Joe almost crashed into the car in front of him, he was so shocked.

'Yes, I did. And his mother said he was a great lad really and the lady guard who was there, the, whatever you call her – facilitator – thought it was tremendous.'

'Tremendously stupid,' Joe replied. 'I mean, how do they know it was his first robbery? He took the glass out of your door pretty good. I'd say he was a pro.'

'Are you trying to frighten me?' Ellen turned from him. 'Because I won't be put off, Joseph. There are some things that you just

151

feel are right to do. That's all there is to it. And anyway, everyone deserves a second chance.'

Joe said nothing. Maybe she was right, who knew. She was obviously feeling a lot better anyway, now that she was back to arguing with him.

'What are you smiling at?' she asked archly.

'You. You're back to yourself again, having a go at me.'

Ellen laughed. 'Joseph, if I was fifty years younger, I'd have a go at you.'

'Christ!' Joe spluttered. 'You dirty old woman!'

25

LIZZIE HADN'T COME on a Saturday night to the pigeon club before and the place was buzzing. Who would have thought that a few birds flying about the place could cause such excitement? She stood for a second in the door, unsure of what she should do, when, to her relief, Cid called across to her. 'Oy! Gorgeous! Over here.'

A few lads laughed. Lizzie wasn't sure if it was at the 'gorgeous' reference. That would be a bit insulting.

'You watch that lecher,' some guy laughed as she passed him.

'Watch him?' Lizzie raised her eyebrows. 'I can hardly bear to look at him.'

There were whoops and cheers at that and even Cid smirked.

Joe was standing beside Cid and two other men. He grinned at her as she approached.

'Hey, how's it going?' he asked. He indicated the two men she hadn't met before. 'This is Noel and this is John.'

'Hi.' Lizzie shook their hands. Noel was around sixty-five, with a big smiley face, whilst John was younger, maybe in his forties. He seemed to have a bad hip or leg as his body was slightly lopsided.

'Haven't seen you in a few weeks,' Joe remarked. 'I thought I'd frightened you off.'

'Nope,' she made herself grin back, 'just really busy these last couple of weeks, that's all.'

'Yeah. I never even spotted you on the Luas or anything.'

She'd been leaving later to avoid bumping into him, but now that her mind was finally made up, she wasn't going to shy away any more. Step two of her plan was riskier, but focusing on Megan dispensed with any qualms of conscience she'd experienced. And her conscience was like a bold child, rearing up when she least expected it. Thinking of Megan was how she'd learned to tame it.

'So how're the birds?' she asked.

Before Joe could answer, Alan held up his hands for hush.

'Right everyone, we've the results here.'

Immediately people began sussing each other.

When there was relative silence, Alan said, 'I'll read out the top three, as usual, and post the rest on the board. OK, it was a close call today. The times are all within seconds of each other. Here we go. In third place was Jim's Autopilot.'

'Again?' Cid bit his lip in frustration as Jim smiled amicably around.

'In second was Peter Doyle's Judas.'

'No way!' That was Peter. He'd never been placed before. 'Brilliant!'

'And first place . . .' Alan rolled his eyes and joked, 'This is getting boring now, it's Joe's bloody Prince. Yet again.'

There was laughter and congratulations. Lizzie expected Joe to be jumping around the place but he just smiled in a half embarrassed way as he went up to accept the cheque.

'It's getting boring for me, too,' he said to the room at large, 'having to finance the drinks every week.'

Someone clapped.

'That bloody bird can't be normal,' Cid grumbled. 'Jaysus, it won almost everything last year and now it's at it again.'

'Be happy for your friend,' Noel said back, patronisingly. 'You know, smile a little.'

Joe arrived back. 'You coming to the pub with us?' he asked Lizzie. 'I'll get you a drink. My way of saying thanks for cleaning out the birds the other week.' He turned to the others. 'I swear, the boxes were never as clean as when she did them.'

'You can do my box if you like,' Cid scoffed, poking her.

'I can give you a box if you like,' Lizzie said back, causing the lads to laugh.

'You've a very sharp tongue on you for such a pretty girl,' Cid muttered.

'You'll never know anything about her tongue,' Noel spluttered. 'You dirty auld fella!'

'Awful,' Joe rolled his eyes as he held the door open for Lizzie. 'You can't bring them anywhere.'

The pub wasn't too crowded and the five of them found seats around a small table. Joe handed the barman his cheque and asked to have the change out of it once he'd ordered for everyone.

'You won again?' the barman asked in amusement.

'Yep.'

'OK. No worries. Now what's everyone having?'

Joe carried five drinks down to the table. He was glad Lizzie had come back, he was afraid he'd put her off or scared her away or something. That would have been a shame as all he'd wanted to do was show her how wonderful the birds were. She was chatting easily to John and he marvelled at her ability to fit in. It had taken him weeks to build up the courage to even assume that he could sit with a particular group at a table, but, he guessed, he hadn't always been like that.

'Now,' he said, putting down the drinks. Everyone helped themselves.

'To Prince,' John said, stealing a sly glance in Cid's direction. 'A prince among birds.'

'Yeah,' Cid raised his own glass, 'let's hope he gets some disease and dies.'

Lizzie flinched as the others threw beer mats at him and told him to shut up.

'You OK?' Joe asked in an undertone. 'Don't mind Cid, no one takes him seriously. He's not a bad guy half the time.'

'Telling you what,' John said as he put his pint down, 'it'd be the worst thing to happen though, wouldn't it? It happened to a friend of mine. All the pigeons died on him and he had to knock the lofts down and rebuild.'

'It would have been the best thing for my marriage, though,'

John said dryly as they all laughed. He turned to Lizzie. 'My wife hated the pigeons. She kept saying I loved them more than her.'

'She was right, though, wasn't she?' Noel smirked.

'Yeah well, birds don't nag, do they? They don't tell you to put the top back on the toothpaste or to put the lid down on the jax. Nope, me and my birds, a match made in heaven.'

'Yeah, you've so much in common,' Cid nodded, 'all yez do is eat, shit and drink.'

'Exactly.'

'If my birds died, I might as well be dead,' Noel went on. 'I'm years building up that loft.' He looked at Lizzie, 'D'you think we're all mad?'

'No,' she said. 'I'd feel the same, I suppose.'

'Joe,' Cid said seriously, 'you make that girl fall in love with you.' He turned to Lizzie, 'Jesus, where were you when I was looking for love all those years ago? I had to settle for the wife, I couldn't find a decent woman to put up with me at all.'

'Eh, newsflash,' Noel said. 'Not entirely your pigeons' fault, I wouldn't say.'

Cid stood up abruptly and glared at Noel. 'I dunno why I always sit with yez,' he snapped. 'All I get is insults. I'm going over to another table.'

'You sit with us because,' John began to sing: 'We are the winners. You are the losers.'

'May your pigeons turn around and cripple your other bloody leg,' Cid said crossly as he pushed his way out, his pint held aloft.

'Ouch!' John said mildly, rubbing his bad leg. 'That hurts, Cid.'

'Aw, fuck off!'

Noel looked at his watch. 'Twenty minutes tonight,' he chortled. Then, at Lizzie's questioning look, he said, 'The time it takes for Cid to get insulted and leave.'

She grinned. 'That's not nice.'

'Neither is he,' John said.

Lizzie didn't know whether to agree or not.

*   *   *

156

The night ended around twelve-fifteen. Lizzie had no idea that she'd spent that long in the pub. She'd meant to leave in time to catch a Luas home but there was no hope of that now. Despite herself, she'd found the lads very entertaining. And Joe continued to surprise her. He was far quieter than she'd anticipated. He never got involved in the arguments or slagged anyone too harshly. He laughed a lot, though, and it transformed him. It gave him the look of someone who could be great craic. If she hadn't known better, she'd have assumed that he was really quite gentle. But people who were gentle didn't hit women, did they?

'How are you getting home?' Joe asked as he saw her preparing to leave. He glanced at his watch. 'The Luas has stopped, hasn't it?'

'I'll walk,' Lizzie said more cheerily than she felt. It was about three miles in the dark. She supposed she could ask Billy to pick her up but he was so bloody moody at the moment, she didn't want to risk it. Plus he was drinking a lot more since Aileen left, and she didn't want him arrested for drunk driving.

'You will not,' the three men said together, looking appalled.

'Where do you live?' Noel was putting on his coat.

'Dundrum.'

'Aw, that's only about five minutes from my place. I'll drive you.' He jangled his keys. 'I've only had one pint, promise.'

'You sure it's not a problem?'

'Yep.'

'OK. Thanks.' They really were a nice, if odd, bunch of men, Lizzie thought as she made to follow Noel.

'Oh,' Joe called after her as he jumped up from his seat. To her surprise he looked a little awkward. 'I'm, eh, going on a training toss early Tuesday morning if you like.'

No matter how early it was, she'd be there. 'How early?'

'Well, probably six o'clock. I'm driving about thirty miles out of the city, letting them go, and then driving to work. Should make it into the city for nine. Does that suit you?'

'Yeah. I'll be at your place for six.'

'Naw, I'll pick you up from yours,' Joe said. 'Sure, you'd never make it over to me. What's the address?'

So she told him to meet her on the main road – there was no way she could risk Billy seeing him.

'OK, see you then.'

'Hey Joe!' Cid yelled loudly from a nearby table. 'You play your cards right with that young wan and you might be able to poker!'

Lizzie laughed as Joe flushed. 'I apologise for that,' he said, rolling his eyes.

'No worries. See you Tuesday.' She ran to catch up with Noel.

'Joe must like you,' Noel remarked as they emerged into the dark night. He pressed his keys and immediately the lights flashed on his car. A big sturdy Volkswagen.

Lizzie said nothing, just sat into the passenger seat.

'He doesn't normally bother with new members.' Noel started the car and pulled out of the car park on to the road. 'If you want your own loft, you're in with the right guy there.'

'That's what Alan said.'

Noel smiled. 'That's what anyone will tell you. Listen and learn, Lizzie.'

'How is he so good, d'you reckon?' Lizzie asked, wondering what story Joe had spun for the club.

Noel shrugged. 'Some people just are,' he nodded. 'Joe says he learned a lot from his granddad, though I can't say I ever heard of the man. Joe just has that something. You don't see it often but, when you do, you recognise it. Staf Van Reet has it. You ever heard of Staf Van Reet?'

Lizzie shook her head.

'You've never heard of Staf Van Reet?' Noel looked at her in amazement. 'Van Reet?' he repeated.

Lizzie flushed. 'Eh, oh yeah,' she gulped. 'Van Reet. Sorry, I thought you said Venret.'

Noel smiled. 'Jesus, I got a shock there. Van Reet pigeons are only world famous. I met Staf once,' he said then. 'Bought an egg from him. One of the best pigeons I ever had.' He then went into a very boring monologue about the Van Reet line of birds, and how exactly his bird was related to some big fancy pigeon.

It was going to be a long drive home, Lizzie reckoned. And then, very uncharitably for her, she thought: no wonder hardly any of these men had wives who stuck around. Before feeling ashamed of herself.

Noel dropped her off at a house that wasn't hers and, bipping his horn, he drove off. Lizzie, making sure he was out of sight, immediately ran down towards Billy's place. Even though the night had been stressful, she'd learned one thing – Joe was definitely the golden boy of the club. So that was something else she'd have to change.

26

TUESDAY MORNING SHE was standing at a bus stop, waiting for Joe to show up. It was early and the sun was peeping above the houses opposite. Lizzie yawned. She hadn't been sleeping too well. Despite her resolve of the other night, she had been tempted, yet again, to walk away from today, to walk away from Joe.

Her determination seemed to crumble whenever she was with Tom. It was as if she had to learn to function on two levels. The girl she was when she was with Tom was the real Lizzie: funny, affectionate and happier than she'd been in a long time. Being in his company eased the conflict in her head, his love was like heat on ice, making the hardness inside her dissolve and grow warm again. Then, when she was apart from him, her thoughts inevitably turned to the next meeting with Joe and her overpowering desire to build up a trust with him, only to abuse it as brutally as she could. These thoughts hardened her resolve once again. She felt as if she was see-sawing between two mind sets, trying hard to keep her balance. On Sunday night, as Tom had kissed her, she wondered if he would still love her as much if he found out what a vindictive person she could be. As his lips teased hers, as his black eyes burned into hers, she'd seen her vendetta as something crazy – but then she was steadied by the sudden thought of Joe's pigeons flying disastrously in their next race because they hadn't been getting their medication. Then, as Tom murmured in her ear how much he loved her, she thought about how great she'd feel if she could just wipe that bewildered grin from Joe's face; as Tom ran his thumb down her jawbone and caressed her chin, she wondered how Joe would cope if she played a few mind games on him. So this morning she had got up and dressed and headed out of the house to meet Joe, almost as if she was being pulled along by some sort of magnetic force.

A *bip* and she turned to see Joe waving at her from the front seat of his car. He looked incredibly awake, bright-eyed and sunny, so much so that she felt a stab of pure malice.

'Hey,' he greeted her as she sat in beside him, 'you look tired.'

'Yeah, I am.' She found it hard to look at him.

Joe pulled out into traffic. 'I love the early mornings,' he said, and there was a smile in his voice. 'No one around to hassle you, not much traffic, it's cool.'

'So where do you take the pigeons?'

'Well, I take John's and Noel's birds, too. We do it every third week for each other. I generally drive to Kildare and let them go. There's a field that I pull into, the guy who owns it doesn't mind. It's flippin' magical when you see them take to the air. You'll see.'

Lizzie didn't bother to reply. God, why did he enjoy life so much? She wished so hard for him to be miserable. To calm herself she concentrated on looking out the window, as the city gave way to the open fields of the countryside.

'You're very quiet,' Joe remarked after a bit. He sounded a little uneasy.

'I'm just tired,' she said. Then, on impulse, she decided to tell him about Billy. She knew from experience that sometimes if you shared information with people they were more open to sharing with you. And who knew what she might find out then? So, despite her misgivings, she blurted out, 'I'm worried about my brother. He's split up with his girlfriend. And she won't talk to him at all.'

It was the wrong thing to say. Joe seemed to tense up and his hands gripped the steering wheel tighter.

'Sorry,' Lizzie managed a small laugh, 'you don't need to hear that. Sorry.'

With what seemed to her a huge effort of will, Joe's face relaxed into a smile. 'Naw, it's terrible to break up with someone.

I have to say, I wouldn't be the best relationship counsellor in the world.'

'No? Why?'

He shrugged. 'Well, relationships aren't exactly top of my agenda at the moment. It's kinda hard to meet women when you've your head stuck in the sky looking at pigeons.'

Lizzie laughed. 'Yeah, I guess so. Have you no girlfriend, then?'

'Nope.' He didn't sound as if he wanted one either.

There was silence then. It began to spit rain and Joe turned on the wipers. The steady swish of them lulled her and she felt her eyes closing, before realising where she was and jerking awake.

Joe laughed. 'You can sleep if you like.'

'And miss the pigeons? No chance.'

He seemed to like that answer because his grin broadened.

They arrived at the field and Joe jumped out and pulled open the gate. Driving his car through, he stopped just at the entrance. 'OK, Lizzie, hop out and pull out the baskets for me, will you?'

Lizzie did as she was told, taking a basket in each hand and handing them to Joe. He carried them into the centre of the field and Lizzie followed up with two more.

'Now, you ready?' His eyes were gleaming. 'This is just like the coolest part. Lift open the baskets and just let them out.'

Lizzie copied what he did and watched as the birds hopped out on to the baskets, looking around before taking to the air, where they circled before heading for home.

'See the way they circle,' Joe said, pointing. 'That's so they can get their bearings. See that guy?' He pointed to a white pigeon that was still going around and around, 'He's going to get lost if he doesn't move soon.'

They watched the bird for a bit, until finally he seemed to make up his mind and head back in the direction they had come.

Lizzie studied Joe as he watched the last bird fly out of sight. 'It's brilliant, isn't it?' he said, finally taking his eyes from the sky. 'If I were to drive home now, some of those birds would be back before me. It's amazing.'

162

'Yeah, isn't it?' She supposed it was, not that she'd ever thought about it.

'Come round to my place next Saturday, if you like, and you can wait with me.'

'I might be going home next week,' she said. 'I haven't been home in ages so I'll let you know.'

'No worries, sure there are lots of other Saturdays.'

'Do you not go home at the weekends at all?' Lizzie kept her voice deliberately casual as they walked back with the empty baskets to the car.

'Nope.' His answer was abrupt as he placed his baskets in the boot and took hers from her.

'D'you go home during the week then?' She relished his discomfort.

'Nope.' He walked round the side of the car and hopped in.

Lizzie joined him. 'Oh.' She watched him start up the car, his face flushed, his hand trembling slightly as he inserted the key into the ignition. Then she said, 'Sorry if I said something I shouldn't.'

It worked. He turned to face her, the car juddering slightly. 'No, you didn't say anything you shouldn't. I just don't visit my parents, that's all.'

'Oh.' Pause. 'Right, well, moving swiftly on . . .'

Joe smiled a little. God, he was so predictable. 'They don't like me, I don't like them.'

'Oh.'

'Yeah.' He shrugged a little. 'Oh.'

He said nothing more as he got the car out of the field and on to the main road. Instead he flicked on the radio and began tapping his fingers to the beat of the music.

He bought her breakfast in a small cafe on O'Connell Street. He had the full fry-up while she settled for a cup of coffee. She wanted nothing from him, not his coffee nor anything else. She watched him as he ate his food with relish, putting tomato sauce on his sausages.

163

'That is disgusting,' she teased. 'You really are the worst person to be working in a health centre.'

He laughed loudly and nodded. 'I know. I'm such a hypocrite.'

He got that much right at least.

'How come swimming?' she asked then. 'Are you really good at it?' God, it was great, she knew just how to make him uncomfortable. Everyone in Wexford knew that Joe was a class swimmer. He could have saved Meg but instead he had chosen not to . . .

Joe swallowed a mouthful of sausage and shrugged. 'I'm OK,' he said modestly. 'I teach it because it's important for everyone to learn.' He looked down at his half empty plate and shoved it away from him. 'Right, are we ready to go?'

'But you haven't finished.'

'Yeah, I have.'

There was a message to ring Jim O'Brien when she got into work. Lizzie's heart lurched as she saw his name on the pad along with his mobile number. Without taking time to shrug off her coat, she picked up the receiver and dialled him. Oh God, she prayed, please let him donate the house. Please. Please. Please.

The phone started to ring at the other end and Lizzie held her breath.

'Hello?'

'Jim, it's Lizzie.'

'Hi, Lizzie, just give me a second to go somewhere quieter.' She was cut off into the limbo land of on-hold before Jim's voice came back to her a few seconds later. 'Hello, darling!'

'Jim, hi yourself.' He'd called her 'darling', that couldn't be too bad.

'I'm calling you about the house, Lizzie.'

'Yeah, sorry I wasn't here. I'm a bit late in this morning. I was out with a friend early. I—' She was babbling. She sounded nervous. She stopped. 'Anyway,' she breathed.

'Anyway,' Jim said back. Another pause. 'I was thinking about your proposal, Lizzie, and, well, I'm afraid—'

'Oh, Jim.'

'I know, darling. But things are tight here. You've no idea. I've had to let lads go all over the place as the houses aren't selling. I am sorry that you're going to have to take one off my hands.'

'I almost had—' She paused. 'Sorry, what did you say?'

'A five-bed, middle of Kildare. It's two hundred thousand cost.'

'You beauty!' she yelled. 'Jim O'Brien, I love you!'

'Yeah I know, but I'm married.'

'Mark will be thrilled!'

'Don't make me feel bad about this, Lizzie, for Christ's sake.' She laughed out loud.

Now all she needed was to raise the cash. Four hundred people had to parachute jump. Lizzie began to make some phone calls.

She gave herself the rest of the day off to celebrate. Mark wouldn't dare to give out to her. She had lined up a prime slot on the Declan Darcy radio show to promote the jump, but unfortunately the researchers wanted Mark to speak as he was the founder. Lizzie had a feeling that the interest in the jump would be minimal once Mark started to rant on about people not caring about each other. She'd have to brief him on what to say.

She was busily working out in her mind the most tactful way of doing that when she passed a pet shop. There were pigeon baskets displayed in the window and Lizzie, sensing the ideal opportunity to smuggle one home while Billy was out at work, went in and bought one. Ten minutes later, she was on the Luas on her way home to store the basket in Billy's garden shed. She also had a handy supply of unsalted peanuts and corn, which the pet shop owner assured her every pigeon would love. She knew what she was going to spend the rest of her day doing now. And little did Joe know just how helpful his book was.

She spread the peanuts and corn on the tiny little bird table out in Billy's back garden. Then she sat in the kitchen and waited.

Finally, after fifty minutes or so, the pigeons landed. Three of them.

Lizzie grinned.

Life was only going to get better.

27

THERE WAS A clattering noise coming from Ellen's back garden. Joe, sitting out in the weak sunshine waiting for his birds to return from the race, heard it. It sounded like metal on metal. A bird distracted him as it flew overhead, but it wasn't a pigeon.

Joe groaned. Where were they? Noel had rung over an hour ago to say that the birds had been released, and Joe was expecting to see his first bird any time now. He hoped Lizzie would make it; she had agreed to come over, telling him that her plans to visit home were on hold as her brother didn't want to go home now. She'd been a bit evasive and he'd been glad. He didn't know what he'd do if she told him any personal stuff, he'd been a long time out of that loop. And yet . . . it'd be . . . he tried to think . . . normal. And healthy. Joe sighed. Lizzie was great company, she made him smile and if he were a regular bloke he would like that, but the fact of it was that he wasn't totally normal and getting friendly with a girl would mean telling her all sorts of stuff and he didn't think he was ready for that. Still, he thought wistfully, it must be nice for her, able to go home when she felt like it. His birds had been released from Wexford this morning and it gave him a weird feeling inside.

His thoughts returned to the noise in Ellen's garden. He decided to risk looking over the wall. It was Anthony. The boy was inexpertly digging a flowerbed. His shovel had just struck a rock or something and he was cursing under his breath.

'Anthony,' Joe said loudly, and tried not to grin as the lad jumped.

Anthony's eyes narrowed. His face assumed a sulky teenage look that Joe remembered from his own childhood.

'It's Anto,' he barked out, leaning on the spade and glowering. 'Digging the garden, ey?'

'No,' Anto snapped, 'I'm having it off with me girlfriend.'

Joe laughed loudly and Anto gave a reluctant half smile.

'I asked for that,' Joe said.

Anto said nothing.

'You do a good job for Ellen, do you hear?' Joe assumed a stern voice. 'She's not in the best of health and I'm telling you don't give her any trouble.'

Anto glowered some more and started to dig again.

Joe, satisfied that he'd said his piece, turned his gaze back to the sky.

Lizzie pulled up in the back lane a few doors down from Joe's house. The basket, containing some pigeons, lay at her feet. They were stupid birds really, she thought. She'd baited them with good food all week and crept closer to them each time until they weren't too bothered by her presence. Then yesterday, before Billy had come back from work, she'd walked up behind them and thrown a towel over their heads, just like Joe's book had advised. It had been a bit messy trying to lift them up and put them into the basket and she was afraid she might hurt them, but she hadn't. The birds didn't seem too distressed either, she thought – they were cooing away to each other and no fights had broken out.

And now, stage two of her master plan: she didn't know if it would work, it was all a bit of hit and miss but it would definitely have some sort of an effect. And if it didn't, she'd just have to try something else. She left the car engine running because if it did work, she reckoned she'd have to make a quick getaway.

Joe had told her that the first birds should arrive in about an hour. So here she was, watching and waiting.

* * *

Joe looked at his watch. Lizzie was late. She'd sent him a text to say she was on her way and hoping that she wouldn't miss the action. He'd sent her one back to say that she'd want to hurry.

He prowled around his garden, unable to relax, when suddenly he saw a flash of grey against the sky. He knew instinctively that it was one of his. He knew by the way it flew, perfectly balanced, beautiful to look at, by the way it hovered and by the way it started to dive. It was coming in. It was coming in.

And then suddenly, from nowhere, three birds took to the sky. Three birds right in the path of his bloody pigeon. Joe groaned. Who the fuck was releasing pigeons now? Jesus. He watched in despair as his bird mingled with the others, circled with the others. Precious seconds ticked off his time. Joe whistled frantically. His pigeon heard but was caught up in the circle of flight with the others. More seconds lost. Jesus Christ! He whistled again and, to his relief, his bird dived. Joe's heart dived with it.

Damn it anyway!

Lizzie parked her car and made her way along the street to Joe's house. She had to be careful not to grin too much. It had been great! Her three birds were now just grey blurs in the distance. She hoped they knew where they were going. She hoped they'd make their way back to Billy's back garden, where there was a huge supply of peanuts waiting for them. She hoped like mad that the lone pigeon she'd seen had been Joe's. She reckoned it was as it had been making straight for the house when she'd done what she'd done. And nope, she didn't feel guilty at all, which was a relief. Well, there was nothing to really feel guilty for, was there? No one had been hurt. Nothing had suffered, except, hopefully, Joe's race results.

She walked up to Joe's and noticed that the back gate was open.

'Hiya,' she said as she pushed it inwards.

There was no answer.

She walked further into the garden and was there just in time to see Joe shoving the pigeon's race ring into the clock.

'Aw, don't tell me I missed it,' she said, creasing her brow up in disappointment.

'You did.' He was grumpy.

'Oh, sorry about that.'

'No,' he waved his hand, 'I'm not mad at you. I'm mad at whatever idiot released some birds just as my fella was coming home.'

'What?'

'Yeah,' he half laughed in disbelief, 'Prince came in and three bloody birds from I dunno where just launched themselves at him. They flew off that way.' He indicated the south. 'I swear to God, if I find out who it was I'll kill them.'

Lizzie flinched. Her stomach lurched suddenly as the realisation crashed in that she was playing a very dangerous game here.

'Hey, are you OK?' Joe looked at her in concern. 'You've gone very pale. D'you want a drink or something?'

'No, I'm—'

'Hey!' She was immediately forgotten about as he spotted another bird. 'Look, up there, d'you see it?'

Lizzie glanced up and, sure enough, there was another grey spot against the brilliant blue of the sky, closely followed by two more.

'Get ready,' Joe grinned widely at her, his disappointment forgotten, 'it's going to be mad now.'

And, despite herself, as bird upon bird came into the loft, responding to Joe's whistle, Lizzie was weirdly moved. Just to see them all returning home safely after their journey across the country was miraculous. Joe was kept busy taking the tags from their legs. As Lizzie watched, she became aware of a thin, hungry-looking lad peering over the wall. The boy was cautious at first, before abandoning all semblance of shyness and sitting up on the wall, gaping in wonder as birds flew around and alighted on perches.

'Wow!' he said.

Joe glanced up at him but said nothing, so Lizzie didn't either. After about twenty minutes Joe reckoned that all the birds were in, and he turned to Lizzie and smiled.

'Well?' he asked. 'What did you think of that?'

'Savage,' the young lad answered. 'It was brilliant. Do you own all them?'

Joe paused and studied Anto. 'Yep. Why? Do you like birds?'

Anto reddened and shrugged. He jumped back down off the wall and disappeared.

'Was that a "yes"?' Lizzie laughed.

Joe laughed, too, and asked her if she wanted a cuppa.

Later that night Lizzie called round to Anna, who had invited her over for a drink and a sleepover. Feeling like a kid going to a slumber party, Lizzie had packed her overnight bag.

She felt better leaving Billy on his own now. Whilst he still continued to call Aileen on a daily basis in the hope she'd crack, his drinking had eased off after she'd told him she was worried about him. But he was still miserable. She wished Aileen would just give him a chance. She was being very harsh, Lizzie thought, and Aileen wasn't normally like that.

'Hiya.' Anna met Lizzie at the front door, her fingers on her lips. 'Shush, I've just got her to bed.'

'At nine-thirty on a Saturday? A seven-year-old?' Lizzie feigned mock horror. 'She should have been in bed hours ago.'

'I like her company,' Anna confessed. 'It's lonely here at the weekends.'

Of course it must be, Lizzie thought suddenly. How awful to sit night after night on your own, looking at pictures of what was and what might have been. She touched Anna briefly on the arm and dumped her overnight case on the floor.

'You're in Chloe's room,' Anna continued to whisper as she led Lizzie into the television room. 'She's in with me tonight. She's so excited.'

Lizzie laughed.

'Now,' Anna held up two bottles of wine as Lizzie sat on the sofa, 'red or white?'

'Red.'

Anna uncorked the bottle and poured them both a generous

171

glass. Then she produced a big bag of sour cream crisps and some dips.

'Yum,' Lizzie pulled a handful of crisps from the bag. 'Do you know, this is the most sophisticated thing I've done in weeks. I never realised before how Aileen ran the house. Dinner and tea and all sorts of food. Now there's only some mouldy cheese and a rotten tomato in the fridge.'

Anna laughed. 'Well maybe, sweet thing, you should invest in some grub.'

'I know, but I've had a lot on.'

Anna cocked her head to one side and smiled, 'Tom wearing you out, is he?'

'I wish. I haven't seen him, to be honest. Nope, I'm busy soft soaping Mark for his radio interview next week.'

'Soft soaping Mark?' Anna grinned. 'You'd normally eat him for breakfast.'

'Well, I'm not in the humour for breakfast.' Lizzie said back. 'Oh Anna, if he goes on air and alienates half of Ireland, I'll never forgive him.'

'He won't. He's changed a bit since he's been seeing Stella. He'll be grand and anyway, if he does, it's not your fault.'

'Suppose.' She heaved a sigh and looked at Anna. 'So, how about you? Any news?'

Anna crunched on a couple of crisps and regarded Lizzie. 'Well, not much really. A Sinéad rang the helpline when I was filling in on Friday, looking for you. She refused to talk to me.'

Lizzie frowned. 'Sinéad?'

'I looked her up on the database. Husband seems to be a bit of a bully.'

'Oh yes,' Lizzie nodded, remembering. Sinéad hadn't rung in a while. 'And how did she sound?'

Anna shrugged. 'She wasn't on long enough for me to gauge that but, at a guess, I'd say a little upset.'

Lizzie sipped her wine. God, it was gorgeous. She wondered idly how it was that when she chose wine, it never tasted as nice. She could spend up to twenty quid on a bottle and it was still awful.

'I hope she rings back,' she said.

'She will, I think,' Anna nodded.

'Mammy?' A cute face with a head of curls peered round the door. 'Mammy, I can't sleep.' Chloe, however, was looking directly at Lizzie. 'Hi,' she said with a beaming smile. 'I met you before.'

'You did, that's right.'

'Chloe, I think it's bed time,' Anna said gently.

'But I can't sleep.' Chloe was still gawking at Lizzie. 'Is your brother's baby born yet?'

'No,' Lizzie felt a pang as she answered. 'And you know one thing? It's two babies now.'

'Two? No way? How?'

'Like twins.'

'Two ladies are having babies.'

'No. One lady is having two babies.'

'Two babies in her tummy?' Chloe was wide-eyed.

'Yes.'

'How did two babies get in there?'

'Eh . . .' Lizzie looked desperately at Anna. 'Well, eh—'

'Yes, Lizzie, how *did* two babies get in there?' Anna grinned.

'So, Chloe,' Lizzie said, 'how have you been? I hear you're making your first holy communion this year.'

Anna chortled, but it worked. Chloe nodded vigorously. 'Yes, and I went to my first confession.'

'Yeah?' Lizzie grinned. 'And what would a little girl like you have to tell? You don't have any sins, I bet.'

'I do. I did something Mammy told me not to. And I told a lie.'

'Did you?' Anna grinned. 'Well, there's a surprise.'

'And the priest said it was OK, that it wasn't really a sin and that if I wanted to tell you, I should.'

'Good for him.' Anna leaned against the table and looked fondly at her daughter. 'So are you going to tell me?'

Chloe looked from one to the other of them.

'OK,' she said, sounding quite excited. 'Well, it was that Nana rang the other day and I told her I would try and get you to call her. But it was lie because I know you're angry at her.'

173

'Oops,' Lizzie made a face, 'maybe I shouldn't have heard that.'

'Nana rang the other day?' Anna said, her voice slightly cross. 'The sneaky thing, trying to get you to do her dirty work.'

Chloe frowned. 'No, it wasn't dirty. She just said—'

'You don't talk to her again, do you hear?' Anna said.

Chloe gulped hard and Lizzie thought she was about to cry. 'But I like my nana. She's nice.'

'I know you do,' Anna glanced at Lizzie ruefully, 'but it's me she should talk to, not you. So tell her that next time, OK?'

'You said I can't talk to her.'

'Well, you can. Only not about me. Tell her to ring me if she wants to talk, OK?'

Chloe nodded.

Anna tousled her daughter's long dark hair. 'Sorry for getting cross. You were good to tell me.'

'That's what the priest said: it's good to tell your mother things.'

'Does he want a job working the phones at Life?' Lizzie giggled.

Prince had clocked fourth. Joe grinned and clapped as the winner waved his cheque in the air and said that the drinks were on him.

'Hey, what happened to Prince today?' Cid asked, barely able to conceal his delight.

Joe shrugged. He was tempted to tell the others about the three pigeons being released just as Prince came in, but it just sounded like an excuse. He didn't want them to think he was a bad loser. He knew the truth and that's what mattered. He grinned to himself. Sometimes that wasn't what mattered at all, actually. It was what people believed that counted. Still, he'd gone beyond caring what people believed.

'Just an off day,' he murmured as he made his way up to the list that Alan had pinned on to the wall. Glancing down it, he almost groaned in frustration. The top three were within a second of each other. Prince was two seconds behind them. He'd lost at least thirty seconds with what had happened. Maybe more. Prince had won that race, of that Joe was certain.

'An off day, would you listen to him?' Cid scoffed. 'Face it, Joe, Prince is worn out. He's suffering burn out.'

'He was only two seconds behind the winner, Cid. Where were your lads?'

'Good point,' Noel said. Then, feigning surprise, he jabbed the list of times. 'Oh look! Your first is three minutes behind. But they're not suffering burn out though, are they?'

'Nope,' Cid said defiantly.

'Incineration, I'd call it,' Noel went on.

As Joe, John and Noel started to laugh, Cid announced that he wouldn't sit with them that night.

'Ten seconds,' Noel grinned as he glanced at his watch, 'now that's a record.'

Anna was talking about her husband. She'd got on to the subject when Lizzie asked her if she ever stopped thinking about what could have been.

'You never quite stop,' she said. 'In the beginning it was harder, though, especially when Chloe started to do all the cute baby stuff. I just felt so angry that he was missing out.'

'I feel like that about my sister,' Lizzie said. 'Angry that she's missing out.' She paused as Anna looked at her with interest. Lizzie never talked about Megan. Well, not to anyone besides her family and Tom. And the fact that she'd told Tom made her know he was special.

'My sister was, you know, killed.' She took a breath. 'Murdered,' she clarified.

'Oh, Lizzie.'

'Yeah, and I can't stop thinking about her. Like not all the time any more, but in flashes. When I moved to Dublin I thought, oh wow, she'd love this, and every time I go out, it's like she's with me. I reckon she would have lived in the pubs.' Lizzie smiled a little. 'She hated school and Mammy used to worry so much about her but Dad always used to say that with her looks she'd marry "a really rich fella who'd keep her in the style to which she was unaccustomed".'

Anna smiled. 'What age was she?'

'Nineteen,' Lizzie said softly. It seemed so young now, looking back.

Anna shook her head.

'You should have seen her, Anna,' Lizzie said wistfully. 'She dressed like she belonged in Hollywood. Well, I always thought so. I was fourteen and a big frump; she was like this rainbow in the house. Mammy used to always say her skirts were too short and her make-up was too thick. And she'd say back it wasn't her make-up that was thick, it was Mammy.'

Anna laughed and Lizzie did, too.

'Her and Mammy were always fighting. But when she . . . she died, the house was just way too quiet. I couldn't wait to leave.'

'Did they get someone for it?'

'Yeah. A neighbour. My dad was very fond of him, it broke his heart. The town was divided though, some said he was guilty and others said no way. He was, though. He told lie after lie on the stand and got caught out on them all. He said she'd been drunk for a start, and yet there was no alcohol found in her system. Big bloody liar, trying to make out she'd been drinking. And he also said she was meant to meet another guy that night, but the other fella denied texting her and no text was ever traced from him. Such a liar.'

Anna said nothing.

'Every time I think of him, I just,' Lizzie paused and unclenched her fists, 'well, I hate him, Anna.'

'I'll bet you do.'

'He was freed after only twelve years. Twelve years. I don't know why.' Lizzie took another gulp of wine. It was partly to calm her and partly to stop the huge rage inside her breaking out. 'He killed my sister and he's free to walk about now. My mother was devastated all over again.' She paused. 'I saw him,' she bit her lip and went on, 'a few weeks ago.'

'Oh, God. Did he see you?'

Lizzie shook her head. She'd probably said too much. It was the wine. She put down her glass and decided not to drink any more. 'I just saw him and wanted to kill him, Anna. It's like he's brought it all back.'

Anna opened her mouth to say something but stopped.

'What?' Lizzie asked.

'You have to let it go,' Anna said quietly. 'You know that, don't you?'

Of course she knew that. But she also knew that she couldn't. Maybe when she'd destroyed him she might just manage to do it. 'It's hard. I mean, I really hate him,' she said again.

'I hated Mick too, at times, for a different reason obviously, but I hated him for what he'd done to us,' Anna nodded as Lizzie looked at her. 'He'd devastated our world just as that man devastated yours. But, in the end, it was a choice I had to make. I had to get on with my life. I decided that I wanted a good life for me and Chloe. And do you know what I realized, Lizzie?'

'What?'

'I realised that love and hate aren't the opposites of each other at all.'

'Are they not?' Her feelings for Joe and Tom were certainly polar opposites.

'No, they're not,' Anna said. 'Hate is much more powerful than love. It eats into your soul far more than love. I hated Mick with more intensity than I'd ever loved him. Isn't that scary?'

Lizzie nodded. She knew Anna was right. She spent way more time thinking about Joe than Tom these days.

And it *was* scary, but she couldn't help it.

28

Sunday, 8th August

Fab!!!

   Fab!!!

   Fab!!!

   Wonderful news. Dessie kissed me. And not just in my steamy imagination. It started like this . . .

We had the office to ourselves all week because Joe is out apparently being fined and cautioned and in shit with his dad. It was awful actually because Joe's dad, in the interests of public information, had to run a piece in the paper on Joe driving the boat whilst being drunk. It was only a column on page four, which wasn't too bad because Dessie said any other paper would have run it at least on page two if not front page.   .

I took full advantage of the week alone with Dessie and wore my shortest skirts and tightest tops into work. Mam, of course, had to get her dig in and asked me if I was selling myself as well as the ads. So I told her that I would if the price was right, which made her go mad. Anyway, Dessie complimented me every single day on what I wore.

Then on Friday I wore a glittery skirt, just over my knee, a little glittery top and a white fake-fur jacket. I also put on my highest heels, which I can barely walk in. And anyway, I tripped over the phone cord which runs along the floor and crunch, I was right over on

178

my ankle. That cord is a total danger. Oh, the pain. Dessie jumped up. I think he was in the middle of a big sell, but he abandoned it and rushed over to me and lifted me up and I clung on to him and I have to say, he wears this delicious aftershave. He carried me to the chair and took off my shoe. My toes looked all cute as I'd painted them in gold. He put his hands around my ankle and the pain was awful but, to be honest, he could have broken it and I wouldn't have told him to stop. Then he asked me if I could walk and I said yes, if he supported me, so he lifted me up and we stood there, body to body and I didn't move for a second and neither did he. His eyes looked into mine and then there was this sort of swelling romantic music but it was only my mobile phone, which we both ignored.

'You OK?' he asked and his voice was all husky.

'I am now,' I said and I smiled at him.

'Me too,' he said and he cocked his gorgeous head to one side and asked if I was trying to lead him astray, what with me pressing myself into him and that.

'I have hurt my ankle,' I played it really cool, 'it's you taking advantage of me.'

'You are gorgeous,' he said.

'I try my best,' I said back and he laughed.

Then he said, 'Joe is mad about you, you know.'

'And you?' I asked. (My mother would have freaked.)

'I just lust after you,' he grinned.

It wasn't exactly a great answer but, to be fair, I think he was joking. 'Lust away,' I said back.

Then he kissed me, but it was very brief because my ankle was really sore so he had to stop.

I haven't heard from him all weekend but anyway, I can't go out because my ankle is all strapped up.

Dad drove me into work as I couldn't get the bus – my ankle is still strapped up. Mammy was all self-righteous and only just stopped short of saying I told you so.

Anyway, I actually got in early and when I walked into the office, there was Joe, already at his desk. He gave me a really embarrassed grin as I stood in the doorway with no idea what to say to him.

'Welcome back, sailor boy,' I stammered out eventually.

He sort of laughed and shrugged and said that he felt about as welcome as an STD, which made me laugh. His dad is really coming down heavy on him, he said then. He told me that no matter how much he apologises his dad keeps going on about it, so he's moved in with his granddad. He says he would have moved in anyway as his granddad isn't well and his mother asked him to keep an eye on him. So he figures in the short term, until his dad calms down, that it's the best place to be. Then he asked me what happened to my ankle and I told him, leaving out the part where Dessie kissed me. I only told Aileen that. And she says she can't wait to see the two lads when she comes down. Anyway, then Dessie arrived in and started singing a song about a drunken sailor and Joe laughed and threw a pen at him which unfortunately hit his dad, who had just come in.

'Sorry,' Joe said. But he was trying not to laugh.

'Get to work!' Geoff flung a list of names on Dessie's desk and told him to ring them all by the end of the day. 'I'm not paying you to mess,' he shouted.

Then he turned on me. 'What are you looking at?' Stupidly, I could feel tears forming in my eyes so I looked down at the desk. It's not that I was scared, it was just his shouting was so unexpected.

'Hey,' Joe said, standing up. For the first time I noticed how scruffy he looked. Obviously no one was doing his washing for him. His T-shirt was an old one – I know this because it said 'The Eight Legged Groove Machine' on it in black writing. His jeans were creased and looked as if he'd slept in them. 'Don't take it out on her. It's my fault. Shout at me.'

Geoff strode over to Joe, who, to give him credit, didn't flinch. He poked him hard in the chest. 'Oh, don't worry,' he said in a really menacing voice, 'I'll be shouting a lot at you. You look a disgrace. Be cleaner tomorrow.'

Then he marched out, slamming the door after him.

Joe heaved a sigh and sat back down, without looking at either of us. He flicked on his computer and stared hard at the screen. Dessie and I didn't know what to say and none of us could look at each other.

'Bastard,' Joe muttered after a bit.

There was an awkward silence until Dessie said casually, 'How much would you bet on your dad spontaneously combusting before the day is done?'

We laughed.

'If I thought he would I'd help him along,' Joe answered, grinning. He pointed at Dessie's sheet of numbers, 'Anyway, give us some of your numbers, Dessie, and we'll make a start on ringing these people.'

We all took some numbers and began to work.

And then, about an hour later, just as I was actually making some progress and selling some space to a toilet paper company that had recently moved premises, the door was flung open. The handle of the door smashed itself off the opposite wall and we jumped.

'You piece of shit!'

'Pardon?' the person at the other end of my line said.

'Sorry, it's just—'

'Slimy little toerag.'

'Can I ring you back?' I asked and then, without waiting for an answer, hung up.

The girl in the doorway, there was no doubt about it, was Dessie's northern girlfriend. Or ex-girlfriend. At least, I hoped she was his ex. I knew it was her though, because despite the fact that she was dressed like some throwback to the eighties, she was gorgeous. And totally furious. She was wearing skin-tight black jeans and biker boots. This was teamed with a shocking pink string vest top over a black long-sleeved T-shirt. Her spiky hair complemented her spiky attitude.

'You snake in the grass!' she said, still not moving but pinning a very guilty-looking Dessie with her enormous hazel eyes. In fact her eyes looked like they didn't belong with the rest of her.

I shot a glance at Joe, who was watching the unfolding drama with interest.

'Hi, Denise,' he said.

That threw Denise a little. 'Hi,' she said, before turning back to Dessie. 'Snake in the grass,' she repeated slowly, glaring at him.

'And, eh,' Dessie attempted a bit of a grin, 'what sort of a snake would that be then, Dee?'

Joe spluttered on a laugh, then tried to make it sound like a cough.

'What sort of a snake?' Denise swaggered into the room. 'Why, the sort that strangles its victims, that sort! The sort that slithers around and sneaks up on its prey and looks and acts ugly. That sort.'

'Are you insulting my good looks?'

I laughed then and she whirled on me. 'What are you laughing at?' She looked me up and down. 'I suppose he's chasing you now, is he?'

I went bright red.

'Dessie,' Denise shook her head, 'what is it you see in her?' She swaggered towards me. 'I suppose it's the lack

182

of an outfit, the display of white flesh, the big red guilty-looking face.'

'Hang on a second,' I said, not wanting to be outdone, 'you can't talk to me—'

'Denise, can we take it outside?' Dessie said.

'Would you like to go out with a guy who tells you he's coming to visit and then doesn't turn up? Two weekends on the trot?' She was still focused on me. 'Is this the reason, Dessie?'

Well, I thought, he hadn't been with me this weekend just gone.

'You could have come to the party. It was a great one.' Dessie ignored the question. 'Joe even got arrested.'

'Thanks, Des,' Joe nodded, 'glad you enjoyed that part of it.'

'If I had my way, I'd have you arrested,' Denise spat at Dessie as she swaggered across the room, her head jutting out like a rooster on the attack. 'You asshole. You think you're so smart, don't you?'

How could he go out with such a person? I could hear my mother now going, 'Where is her dignity?' and she'd have a point.

'Have you come all the way down here just to shout at me?' Dessie asked calmly.

'Yes.'

Joe made motions for us to leave. He stood up from his chair and beckoned to me. I didn't want to go, but it was none of my business and that girl was scary.

'Megan and I will go on an early lunch, so,' Joe said, attempting to keep his tone light. 'One hour, Dessie.'

I pulled my jacket from the back of my chair and followed Joe from the room.

'Is that the, eh, girlfriend?' I asked Joe when we were sitting down in the pub with some coffee in front of us. I hated calling her Dessie's girlfriend. It gave me a chill. And made me feel like a heel for kissing him. I mean, I

183

wasn't so desperate that I had to become a boyfriend stealer.

'Uh-huh,' Joe nodded, then took a gulp of coffee and began to splutter. 'God, that's hot!'

I half laughed. What had he expected? 'That's coffee for you.'

'Smart arse,' he grinned.

'She seems,' I tried to be tactful, 'kinda bossy.'

'Nah, Denise is sound,' Joe nodded. 'She wouldn't be as bad if Dessie treated her right.' He paused and regarded me with speculative eyes. 'Dessie likes to mess her around. He likes to show her who's boss. So then she messes him around. It's the way they work.'

'Has he broken up with her?'

'Oh yeah,' Joe laughed, 'loads of times.'

That wasn't what I meant. I wanted to know if it was all off NOW. Only I couldn't ask because Joe was giving me a strange look, up and down as if he was considering what to say next. 'Whenever Dessie has other fish to fry,' he said, 'Denise gets the boot. He calls it being honest with her.'

'Dessie goes on fishing trips?' That was news to me. All I bloody needed was another fisherman in my life.

Joe spluttered out some more coffee. I think he was laughing before he suddenly went all serious again. He said quietly, almost as if he didn't want to, 'I think he's after you now.'

'Me?' I gave a huge smile that, I hoped, conveyed surprise. 'Me? Why?'

Joe didn't smile back. He didn't even sound as if he particularly wanted to tell me this.

'Why?' he repeated, looking intently at me. 'Because he can.'

I opened my mouth to say something but nothing came out. That was a bit insulting.

'Sorry,' he winced, 'that sounded awful.' He put his

184

coffee on the table and leaned in towards me. His eyes are a bit weird, I noticed then: one is hazel; one is a deeper shade, nearer brown. He shifted about on the seat, 'Look Megan, I'll be honest with you, OK?'

I wasn't sure I wanted to hear this.

'I liked you a lot. I got you the job in the newspaper by lying to my dad and telling him you could sell wool to sheep farmers. I wanted to get to know you. Like when I go fishing with Kev (that's my dad and it was weird to hear him say Kev), I don't only go because I like your dad, you know. I used to keep hoping I'd see you.'

I gawked at him.

'I take it that's a look of horror,' he joked half-heartedly. Without waiting for me to reply, he went on, 'Anyway, once Dessie saw I fancied you, he started going after you, too.'

This was mad. 'Why would he do that?'

'To hurt me. To hurt Denise.'

Joe was mad. Paranoid. 'You've lost me,' I said.

'About a year ago, Dessie and I had a falling out over Denise. She fancied me, he fancied her. He accused me of trying to move in on her, which was crap, but anyway, he eventually got Denise and she's mad about him, but I dunno, he doesn't quite trust it. So he treats her like shit to pretend to her that he isn't as mad about her as he is. Right now he's trying to piss her off by chasing you, and into the bargain piss me off too.' He paused, then asked, 'You like him, don't you?'

I didn't answer. Instead I said, 'I thought you two were mates.'

'It's just the way Dessie is,' Joe explained. 'He hates that she fancied me first. He hates when I sell more ads than him. He hates when I get more bonuses than him. Everything is competition. You just happen to be the prize this time.'

I was speechless. The prize?

'Now, I'm pretty sure I haven't a hope in hell with you.' Joe gave this rueful grin. I think that's the right word. 'But trust me, leave Dessie well alone. Dessie is out for Dessie.'

I have to say he sounded sincere.

'I'm just letting you know, Megan,' Joe said after a bit. 'I know you like him but he'll use you.'

'Well, eh, thanks for that, Joe,' I said. 'And I do like you, you know – just not—'

He waved me away. 'Don't even finish that sentence,' he half grinned. 'I'll live with the disappointment. I was playing out of my league anyway.'

Why do men always talk about sport? I decided not to mention the kiss with Dessie. I would tell Dessie not to mention it either. I was not going to be used, that was for sure.

'Dessie is a good mate,' Joe went on then, as if he was sorry to have said anything bad. 'I just don't want to see you get hurt, Megan, that's all.' To my surprise, he blushed, as if saying something so personal was embarrassing for him.

So I told him that I appreciated his thoughtfulness and that I would definitely think about what he'd said. Then I gave him a quick peck on the cheek.

Then, 'What is this?' from Geoff Jones, who had just walked into the pub. He was fuming. 'Didn't I tell you to stay in work?' He glared pointedly at Joe. 'I go into the office and Dessie is there having a slanging match with some girl who doesn't even work in the place and the two of you are—' He narrowed his eyes. 'Are what?' He glared at me.

'Having a discussion,' Joe answered for me, standing up and pulling on his jacket. 'We're going back now, Dad.'

'Well your office discussions must be interesting affairs,' Geoff growled.

186

Dessie was busy making calls when we got back as if nothing had happened.

'So?' Joe asked him. 'What's the story?'

The story was that Denise had gone, but not before having dumped a cup of coffee all over him. And then Dessie says, 'So we can take up where we left off on Friday, Megan, ey?' And he winked at me.

And yes, I felt bad for Joe, who I hadn't been honest with. He tossed me a hurt look before leaving work early, but the minute he was gone Dessie certainly did take up with enthusiasm where we'd finished. And Joe is wrong and Cher is right: it's in his kiss. Dessie likes me.

29

L IZZIE STEPPED INTO Joe's kitchen. It looked different. Cleaner. Or something.

'Did you do something to this place?' she asked, looking around.

Joe grinned sheepishly. 'Eh, just washed the floor. Wiped down the counters. The place was in a bit of a state.'

'Good job.'

Joe watched as she glanced around the room, glad suddenly that he had made an effort. He didn't want her to think he lived like a pig, though apparently pigs were very clean. Lizzie looked good, he thought. Cute. The more he was with her, the more he liked her. It scared him a bit. She chatted about home a lot, which in the beginning had made him uncomfortable, but now he liked to hear her talk on.

'So, d'you want a cuppa before we start?'

'Sure, great.'

Lizzie carefully laid her paper down on the table where he could see it. Just before she'd come, she'd managed to pop into a shop and buy the *Rossclare Read*. She was sure it would give him a jolt. She watched as Joe flicked on the kettle and took some milk from the fridge. He really had made an effort, she thought. Even his fridge looked cleaner than the last time.

'So how have my favourite birds been?' she asked.

He turned around and his grin was so sunny that she had to catch her breath. 'Good, though I didn't enter them in any races this weekend. They all seem a little tired or something. I can't quite put my finger on it. Hopefully, it's just a little bit of burn out.'

'Oh.' She quashed her momentary guilt. 'That's weird.'

He shrugged, not appearing too concerned. 'I've checked them for funguses and stuff, so they're clean. I don't think it's much to worry about. He carried her cup to the table and put it down. And then, just as she'd hoped, his eye caught the paper. His cup jerked a little, slopping coffee over the sides.

'That your paper?' he asked, sounding as if he was trying to be cool about it.

'Yeah. I just got it when I saw that piece about the harbour in Rossclare. D'you want to read it?'

'Eh, no, no, it's cool.' His hands trembled slightly as he laid his cup down. Well, Lizzie fancied that they trembled. If she hadn't known who he was maybe she wouldn't have noticed.

'Do you know anything about the harbour?' Lizzie asked innocently. 'Aren't you from Rossclare?'

'I'm out of the place too long now.' Joe didn't look at her. He carefully poured milk into his tea. 'I dunno what's happening down there at all. I—' he stopped. Drank some tea.

'You what?' Lizzie asked.

His eyes met hers. 'I used to fish out of there. Before,' he indicated the room, 'well, before I came to Dublin.'

'You were a fisherman?'

'Uh-huh.' He nodded. 'Loved it. Would have stayed but came up here instead.'

'Why?' Lizzie could barely contain her excitement. Maybe he'd confess. Maybe he'd tell her everything. Maybe then she could—

'Just did.' He stood up, his back to her. 'Now, I definitely have some biscuits. Hang on until I find them.'

'But if you loved fishing . . . ?'

He ignored that. Instead he pulled a packet of Ginger Nut from the press and tore open the wrapper. 'Hope you like these. They're my favourite.'

They were Lizzie's favourite until right at that moment, when she found she couldn't eat a single one.

*　　*　　*

Twenty minutes later, after not getting any more information from him, Lizzie stood in Joe's back garden, prepared to clean out the boxes. She hated this job. It was smelly and dirty and she really wasn't in the humour for doing it. But for her next plan to work she needed to get access to his coup. She watched with hungry eyes as he unlocked the loft and left the keys dangling from it. Before she had a chance to take them, he had handed her a bucket and palette knife. Soon she was scraping away, trying not to look too revolted.

Joe was humming tunelessly, relishing the whole experience. All she needed was for him to leave her alone for a few moments, that was all. But he didn't. He seemed determined to stay as if to make up for the first time when he'd left her on her own. Oh, how she wished she'd had the foresight to take action then, but she'd been teetering on the brink a few weeks ago – now, she was finding it easier to slip into her role as interested pigeon-girl. The more she played her part, the more she believed in it. She knew she had to find out what happened that night just to have some peace. Either that or ruin his pathetic life . . .

Finally they'd finished cleaning and Joe began clearing up, taking her bucket from her and mooching about as he washed it out. Lizzie watched him and when she was sure he wasn't looking, she gently reached over and removed the bunch of keys from the lock. Now all she had to do was to get out as quickly as she could before he noticed that they were gone. With a bit of luck, she could drop them in his garden later on and he'd think they had fallen from his pocket. She excused herself and went inside to wash her hands. As she reached for the disinfectant, she noticed that the bottle she'd filled with water was now mostly empty. Those pigeons were not getting their medication and she grinned.

'Hey, Lizzie!'

She jumped as Joe came in behind her.

He took a step back, looking as startled as she felt. 'Sorry, I didn't mean to frighten you like that.'

'No, it's fine.' Had he sneaked up behind Megan before he killed her? she wondered, as a sudden wave of nausea hit her.

'Hey, are you OK?' Joe scanned her face. She had gone very pale. 'D'you want to sit down?'

This was her chance to leave. 'No, no, I think I'll go home. I don't feel well at all.' And she didn't.

'Do you want me to drive you?'

'No! No, it's fine.' Lizzie shakily made her way to the door.

'Right, if you're sure.' Joe accompanied her into the hall and held the door open for her.

'Thanks.'

'Oh, just before you go, you haven't seen my keys, have you? I can't think where I put them.'

'No,' Lizzie shook her head. 'I remember you leaving them down all right.'

'Leaving them down? Are you sure? I thought I left them in the lock.'

'Naw, I'm sure you opened the lock and took them out.' Lizzie felt her stomach heave a little more with the lie and she knew that she had to get away. 'Listen, I better go and get back home. Talk to you during the week, OK?'

And then she came face to face with the old woman who lived next door to Joe, who was just coming up the steps with a young lad in tow. Lizzie tried to avoid looking at her but the old woman was sharper than she appeared.

'Mindy,' she said. 'Hello.'

Joe let out a splutter of a laugh. 'That's Lizzie, Ellen. Her name isn't Mindy.'

Ellen frowned. 'No, I met her a few weeks ago and she told me her name was Mindy. Isn't that right, love?'

'Sorry, excuse me,' Lizzie pushed past her and ran down the garden path, not knowing what else she could do.

'She's not well,' she heard Joe say to the woman.

Joe stared at Ellen, who was staring after Lizzie.

'She definitely said her name was Mindy,' Ellen said. Then added, 'And she said she wasn't interested in your birds.'

'Yes, well, Lizzie *is* interested in the birds,' Joe replied,

191

wondering if Ellen was going a bit funny and mixing people up. 'So it couldn't be her.'

Ellen didn't seem convinced but instead of pursuing it, she pulled Anto towards her. 'Well,' she said as she shoved him forwards, 'here's another person who is interested in your pigeons.'

Joe looked blankly at her. Then looked at Anto. 'So?'

'See?' Anto glowered at Ellen. 'I told you he wouldn't let me near them.'

'You want me to let you near my pigeons?' Joe looked at him. 'You bloody well tried to rob a house and you want me to let *you* near my birds?'

'No. No, I don't. You and your birds can rot for all I care.' Anto shoved his hands into his pockets and, pushing past Ellen, he stomped off.

'Oh, Anto, come back, come back!' Ellen called after him. She whirled on Joe. 'It took him all his courage to come here today,' she snapped, 'and now look, you've ruined it!'

'I've ruined nothing,' Joe said, stunned. 'For God's sake—'

'He loves birds. His dad used to keep them before he died. Anto helped him out.' Ellen raised her eyes to heaven. 'He is a child, Joe. You are an adult. You should give him a chance.' Then she, too, stomped off.

Joe looked after the two of them in amazement. The whole scene had been totally unexpected. Maybe if he'd been prepared for it, it might have made a difference. He might have had time to think about it, but Jesus, to let a wild kid like that near the most precious things he had? That would be stupid.

Wouldn't it?

Four o'clock. Two hours since the light had gone off in Joe's bedroom window. Lizzie, too nervous and keyed up to feel tired, walked up the road towards his house, looking very carefully to her left and right. All was still, there was no one around, no one looking out on the street. Very carefully, keeping to the deepest shadows, Lizzie slunk into Joe's front garden and was soon engulfed by the gloom to the side of his house. She gently unlatched the side gate and let herself into his back garden.

Silence.

Carefully she unlocked the door to the racing loft. The birds wouldn't react until first light. Lizzie crept into the loft and, taking a tiny bottle of water from her pocket, she poured it on to the malt in the hopper.

She felt detached suddenly. An onlooker. She was fully aware of what she was doing but there was no emotion behind it: no elation, no guilt. There was just the instinct to strike out. She wondered, still in a detached way, when it would hit her. Or was she beyond feeling bad for what she was doing? 'I am making his birds sick,' she told herself. Nothing. It was a relief but it was a little scary, too. Revenge, she thought, must be a little like taking exercise. The more you did, the more you were capable of doing and the less it hurt. Finally, she thought, she was wrestling control back from the man who had ruined her past.

She left the loft door unlocked and then dropped Joe's keys on to the grass. And tucked her new spares into her pocket.

Joe found his keys in the grass in his garden the next morning. He couldn't understand why they were over next to his side gate. He didn't remember being near it – all he'd done was go between the loft and the kitchen. And what was even weirder was that one of his lofts was unlocked. Not open, which was good or all the birds would have flown.

Still, Joe vowed, he'd just have to be more careful next time.

The guilt hit her the next day as she showered. She wasn't thinking about anything when the reality of what she had done leapt out. She had stolen into a garden in the early hours of the morning and . . . Lizzie pushed it out of her head, not wanting to confront it, afraid that if she did she might lose her nerve. She squirrelled the guilt away in a small corner of her mind and squashed it down.

30

'WHAT IS THE situation with you and Aileen?' was the first thing Mrs Walsh demanded of Billy when he and Lizzie arrived home to visit at the weekend. They hadn't been down in a while, and Polly Walsh had rung wondering idly if her children were abandoning her.

Billy glared at his mother. 'I am sorting it out.'

'Oh, are you indeed,' Mrs Walsh ignored Lizzie as she struggled to pull all the bags out of the car, preferring instead to follow behind her son as he stomped into the house, 'and how are you doing that exactly?'

'Mammy, it really isn't your business,' Billy said in exasperation as he strode into the kitchen and flicked on the kettle. 'It's my life.' He nodded at his dad, who was at the table reading the paper.

'When a woman is carrying two,' Mrs Walsh took a deep breath and said again, in a louder voice, '*two* of my grandchildren, I think it is my business if my son is not with her.'

'She is not with me,' Billy corrected.

Lizzie sat at the table alongside her father. He glanced at her over the pages of his paper and she shrugged.

'Well, you get her back.' Mrs Walsh began banging cups as she took them from the press. 'You tell her you want her back. I will not lose my grandchildren!'

'I'm only in the door, will you leave it?!'

'It's bad enough setting up house with a girl you didn't marry, but when you get her pregnant and then decide you want to opt out of fatherhood, that beats all.'

'I didn't decide to opt out!' Billy's voice rose in exasperation. 'Mam, I am thirty-four, I don't need this shit from you!' He stormed on by her and out of the kitchen door, slamming it hard.

'Charming!' she shouted after him.

There was a silence.

'I told you to wait until after dinner before mentioning it,' Mr Walsh said calmly. 'What did you hope to achieve by having a go at the chap the minute he walks in the door?'

'I hoped to bang some sense into that stubborn head of his, that's what I hoped,' Mrs Walsh snapped.

'He has tried to talk to Aileen,' Lizzie offered meekly, 'but she won't listen to him.'

'Oh, that's it, stick up for your brother, go on. That's all you ever did.' Mrs Walsh laid both her hands on the table. 'Well, I'm telling you both,' her voice trembled a little, 'I lost a daughter once and I will not lose my grandchildren.'

'Oh, Polly,' Mr Walsh put his paper down and stood up. 'It's not going to be like that. Come on.' He held his arms out to his wife. 'Come here, come on.'

Lizzie left the two of them and went in search of Billy.

He was round the back, his hands sunk into his pockets.

'Hiya,' she said.

He didn't answer.

She pulled a packet of cigarettes from her pocket and offered him one. He shook his head. 'Naw, ta.'

She put one between her lips and struck a match.

'If Mam sees you smoking she'll kill you.' Billy managed a small grin.

'She won't care. She's only interested in you at the moment.' Lizzie took a long drag and blew out smoke circles as Billy watched.

'You've always been a really cool-looking smoker,' he said, half admiringly. 'It suits you.'

She grinned. 'Tom hates me doing it.'

'Tom loves everything you do,' Billy scoffed.

'Just like you did with Aileen.'

He shrugged. 'Aw, I dunno.'

'You did.'

There was a small silence before he said quietly, 'Lately I'm thinking that we only got together because Megan died. We both needed comfort. And then it was too hard to break free, you know.'

Lizzie gawked at him, shocked. 'You don't mean that!'

He shook his head despairingly. 'I don't know what I mean. I just wish she'd talk to me.' He looked at her. 'I can't go on like this, Lizzie, being ignored.'

'You have to convince her that you want the whole of family life, that's what you have to do,' Lizzie said as she took another drag of her fag. 'You just have to keep at it.' Then, because he seemed in a relatively mild mood, she added, 'And you have to get your life back on track, Billy, and start buying food for the house and looking after yourself again. I mean, look at that shirt, it's manky.'

Billy plonked down on the grass and said nothing for a bit. Lizzie sat down beside him, knowing he'd talk eventually. This was the first real conversation they'd had since Aileen had left, mainly because, unless drunk, Billy never talked about things that upset him and tended to leave the room every time difficult stuff got broached.

'I just can't care about stuff like that,' Billy admitted quietly as he looked down at his shirt. 'Like, if Aileen hadn't left, I'd never have thought the stuff I'm thinking now. And the stuff I'm thinking about now just, I dunno, paralyses me.'

'What stuff?'

'Me being a father,' Billy murmured. 'It's not something I wanted, Lizzie. I mean, Aileen is right, I didn't exactly cheer when I was told there were twins on the way.'

'And now?' A feeling of dread was spreading through Lizzie. She hadn't expected Billy to be like this.

'I don't know.' He gave her an anguished look. 'I can't sort my head out, Lizzie. I mean, I was happy in our flat with Aileen, but oh no, she wanted a house we could barely afford and I went along with it. Then, just as I was getting used to having all our money swallowed up by a mortgage, she's pregnant. I feel like she's hijacked my life. She's trying to make me into something I never wanted to be.' He pulled up a fistful of grass and observed it as it blew off on the breeze. 'It's not something I'm sure I *can* be.'

'It's something you are now, though,' Lizzie said quietly, 'whether you want it or not.'

His answer was to get up and leave.

Just like always.

Later that evening Martha called in. Billy had gone to bed early after refusing to talk to anyone about Aileen, and Lizzie and her parents were watching the Lottery show on the TV. Someone had just won a car and Mrs Walsh was remarking on how awful the woman looked: 'If I was going on television, I'd definitely dress up a little bit more. I mean, where did that woman get her shoes from?'

'Hello? Hello? Anyone home?' Martha had let herself in the back door. 'Polly? I've got the banners and handcuffs for the march tomorrow.'

A march? Tomorrow? Lizzie's heart sank.

'Oh, good,' Mrs Walsh called. 'Come in here, Martha. Let's have a look.'

Martha appeared round the door with two enormous signs and four pairs of silver handcuffs.

'We're chaining ourselves to the harbour railings,' her mother announced proudly. 'They'll have to forcibly remove us. They've ignored our night-time protest so it's time for tougher measures.' She turned to her friend, 'Now, Martha, put that stuff down and have a coffee.'

'Oh, lovely.' Martha put her placard on the floor and rested her handcuffs on top. As she received a cup, she said, 'Oh, I've another bit of news for you.'

'Yes?'

Lizzie could tell that her mother didn't really want to hear Martha's bit of news. Her eyes had swivelled back to the screen

197

where the contestants for the following week's show were being drawn out.

Martha sensed this too and said dramatically, 'Leah Jones has Alzheimer's disease.' Then, once she'd got their attention, added, 'Apparently.'

Her mother and father were all ears now.

Martha nodded, delighted that her titbit had got such a reaction. 'Yes. I heard that she got lost yesterday in town and didn't know who she was or anything. Geoff had to collect her from Dunnes stores and he told a girl there that she was having tests for it. But I mean, you don't go getting lost if there's nothing wrong with you, do you?'

'Oh, poor woman,' Polly Walsh said.

'Yes, and she isn't even that old,' Martha nodded vigorously. 'And,' she went on, lowering her voice for maximum impact, 'apparently, now I heard this from Julia who's a good friend of Angela who knows the wife of a friend of Geoff's, and she said that Joe Jones will not even come down to see his poor mother before she forgets him altogether.'

'No!' the two of them gasped.

'Now.' Martha looked around, then sat back in the chair. 'Isn't. That. Awful?'

'Yes,' Mrs Walsh said. Then added, 'But I'm not surprised. Any fella that can—' Her voice faltered and she bit her lip and stopped.

'Exactly,' Martha agreed. 'Exactly.'

'Poor Leah, though,' Mrs Walsh said then. 'She's had it tough and now that.'

'Huh, I don't think that's tough,' Lizzie surprised herself and the others by saying. 'Makes it easier for her to forget what her horrible son did, doesn't it? Wouldn't you like to be able to forget, Mammy? Wouldn't you?'

'Oh, now, Lizzie,' her father said softly, 'there's no use being like that. Only makes you hard.'

'Being hard is OK,' she said. 'Means you don't get hurt.'

'Means you don't feel,' her dad said. 'There is a difference.'

'Not from where I'm standing.' The bitterness in her voice surprised her. 'I feel all right. I feel glad, so I do. Serves them right. They have their son. We don't have Megan. That woman can forget, we can't. Where's the justice in that?'

There was a silence.

'Come on,' Mrs Walsh said gently, 'don't go upsetting yourself, Lizzie. I know I wouldn't ever want to forget little Megan.'

'Trouble and all as she was,' Mr Walsh smiled.

That made them chuckle.

31

LIZZIE DIDN'T THINK she would ever forget the sight of her mother being hauled off in the back of a police van. She stood with Billy on the fringes of the protest, holding a placard which read NEW HARBOUR PLANS HARBOUR DISASTER, as she watched her mother screaming at the crowd not to give in. Not to give way. Everything she said was met by cheers and whoops.

A youngish looking policeman was laboriously cutting through the handcuffs that bound her to the harbour wall. Each time she moved he winced, afraid that he'd cut her. Finally he dispensed with the saw, pulled apart the broken cuffs and hauled Polly Walsh to her feet. Some guy up front was busy snapping pictures.

'Where is my husband?' Polly demanded, scanning the crowd.

Mr Walsh sheepishly put up his hand. He had, under pressure, extricated himself from his own set of handcuffs and so had Dolly. Martha however, like her mother, had remained staunch until the end.

'You're supposed to be in chains!' Polly yelled at him.

'Someone has to feed the chickens,' Mr Walsh said. 'I'll follow behind, love. OK?'

'I wouldn't like to be in Dad's shoes when Mam gets hold of him,' Billy said wryly.

Lizzie laughed slightly but stopped as she saw her mother being manhandled into the back of a van along with Martha. Her dad suddenly looked concerned.

'Do you want me to come with you to the police station, Dad?' Lizzie asked, worried at his troubled expression.

He waved her away. 'No, no, the two of you go back. I don't

know how long this will all take.' He shook his head. 'I just hope she knows what she's doing.' Handing his placard to Dolly, he began to walk towards his car, Billy and Lizzie following.

'Now,' he said when he reached it, 'feed the hens and lock up the coup. I'll be back as soon as I can.'

They watched as he drove away, then they, too, drove towards home.

Later that night, when their dad still hadn't returned, Lizzie went to pack in preparation for leaving the next day. As she climbed the stairs she saw that the door to Megan's old room was ajar. Since Megan had gone, Lizzie hadn't wanted to venture past the threshold of the room, finding all Megan's old stuff hard to look at without getting upset. It was as if time stopped in that room the day Megan had died. All her old bottles and perfumes and clothes waiting for their owner to come back. Like a dog that refuses to accept its master is dead.

She tentatively approached the door to close it when she noticed a figure sitting on Meg's old bed.

'Bill?'

He looked up and Lizzie wasn't sure if he'd been crying or not. 'You OK?'

He nodded, swallowing hard. 'I just came in to talk to her,' he said.

'Did you?' Lizzie pushed open the door a little and ventured in herself. The room was much barer than it ever had been. Her mother had been busy, stripping all the posters from the walls and taking the bed linen off the bed. Bits and pieces of Megan's make-up and hair products were all tidied away in a box. Her fireplace had been cleaned and the brass sparkled. The floor-boards had been varnished.

'It's not like her room any more,' Billy said as Lizzie sat in beside him.

'No, Mam is clearing it out. Or at least she was.'

'It's good, I suppose, that she can do that.'

'Yeah,' Lizzie nodded. 'She's trying to move on, I guess.'

Though, even as she said the words, Lizzie wasn't sure if they were true.

'I miss her, Lizzie,' Billy said. 'I thought it would get easier but sometimes it just hits me.'

Lizzie rubbed his arm and blinked hard. She knew what he meant.

'She was the noise in the house, wasn't she? It all went when she went. Mam used to say that Megan was like a cat, always landing on her feet. She never worried about her, did she?'

Lizzie shook her head. 'She only worried about her catching cold in the short skirts she used to wear. D'you remember Mam told her the breeze going up her legs would give her kidney disease?'

Billy snorted back a laugh. 'And she told Mam that was impossible as your kidneys are in your chest.'

'She meant lungs.'

'She was awful thick, wasn't she?'

They laughed quietly.

'I miss her, you know.'

'Yeah.'

The curtains had been washed, too. There was no sense of Megan in the room now. Whatever smell of her that had been there had disappeared.

'Since she died, I just think my life has gone all wrong.' Billy's voice broke slightly.

'Aw, Billy,' Lizzie pulled her brother into a hug. He clung to her, not crying but holding her as if he were drowning. 'It's just this stuff with Aileen, it'll work out, you'll see.'

He said nothing, just let her hold him, which was scarier than any words would have been.

32

'NOW REMEMBER, MARK, it's important not to preach.'

Lizzie yawned. All her late nights were catching up on her, but it was worth it. Each time she saw Joe, he looked, she fancied, slightly more bewildered than the last. Finding his lofts open most mornings would do that to a fella, she reckoned. Now it was time to really start putting the heat on, but for right now, her priority was to tutor Mark before they went on air.

Mark looked at her in exasperation. 'Who are you? My PR woman?'

'You could do with one.'

He ignored that. 'Look, the radio station asked for me. They didn't ask for you and they didn't ask for me to parrot your words on air. They asked for me and me is who I will give them.'

'If I asked for an alligator to come into my radio studio, do you think it'd be reasonable to expect it to be in a cage so it couldn't bite me?' Lizzie asked.

Mark frowned. 'I'm not sure where this is going,' he said. 'Are you saying I'm an alligator?'

'Yep.'

He rolled his eyes and smirked. 'Stella calls me a tiger. Her big, furry tiger.'

'Please,' Lizzie said, revolted.

'Ah, jealous, are you?' Mark nudged her. 'Is your poncy actor boyfriend not being all he should?'

'*Tom*,' Lizzie stressed the name, 'is very busy doing his play. He rehearses during the day and he works in a bar at night. He is not poncy, the same way your girlfriend is not sane. Now can we get back to the task at hand? You are going to give an overview of—'

'Oops.' Mark looked at his watch. 'Time to go. And try not to be jealous that Declan Darcy doesn't want to talk to you, it's OK. You'll get over it.' He patted her patronisingly on the shoulder as she came around the car to join him.

'Mark, take this in the spirit that it's meant: go fuck yourself.'

'Nope, I've got Stella, remember?' He winked at her and Lizzie had to smile, though inwardly she was praying hard for the man not to make a national joke of himself.

They were ushered into the studio and given headphones to put on. Declan nodded a greeting and explained that he would talk to them after his newspaper spiel at the beginning.

'We just take a quick gander through the papers and I make a few witty comments and the like,' he said.

Mark nodded confidently. 'No problem, Declan,' he replied, sounding really official. 'We've all the time in the world.'

What a lick-arse, Lizzie wanted to hiss, though she probably would have said the same herself.

The countdown to the programme began. The music banged out a fanfare and suddenly Declan was transformed from a weird-looking middle-aged schoolboy to super smooth DJ.

'Hi, folks,' he began in his Dublin accent, 'welcome to the best radio show in the land: mine. Declan Darcy. Now, let's have a look at the papers today.' He picked up the bundle from his desk and immediately snorted with laughter. 'Well, folks, no matter what paper you pick up this morning, variations of this photo will feature in them all. I'm looking at the *Indo* – and what a picture! What an amazing sight! Godzilla is only in the ha'penny place compared to these two ladies. Martha Dowling and Polly Walsh were arrested in Rossclare after they tied themselves to the harbour wall and refused to move. They're protesting against the development of Rossclare harbour. Well, I have to say, Polly, you've a face to ground a thousand ships.'

He gave a cackle of laughter as Lizzie sat frozen in her seat.

She took a quick glance as Declan casually threw the paper across his desk. Oh God, her mother looked pure evil. She wouldn't be pleased with that photo. Her hair was sticking up in all directions and her teeth were bared in a grimace. Lines criss-crossed her face, making it look like some bizarre road map.

'That's one scary-looking bird,' Mark whispered.

Lizzie ignored him. She barely heard the rest of Declan's opening speech. It had been a terrible weekend. Her mother and Martha had remained in custody and were due up in court in the next few days. It was all very stressful, especially on her dad, whom her mother was refusing to speak to since he'd unchained himself from the railings.

'An' now,' Declan said with a flourish, his hoarse voice crashing through Lizzie's mournful recollections, 'I've a special guest in the studio today, accompanied by his secretary.'

Under the table Mark kicked her and Lizzie made a face at him.

'This man is probably a stranger to most of you but by the end of our slot, let's hope you'll all know him a bit better. He's the founder of the Life counselling service. Mark Delaney, welcome to the studio.'

'Thanks, Declan, and can I just say that the woman beside me is not my secretary, she's actually the fundraiser for the charity. I know she looks like a secretary, but she's not.'

Declan gave a huge guffaw of a laugh and Mark smiled politely, unaware he'd just insulted every secretary in the land.

'So now, Mark, first tell us a bit about Life.'

She'd tutored him on this one, Lizzie thought in satisfaction.

'Basically Life is an over-the-phone counselling service. Every call only costs ten cents, no matter how long the duration. We counsel on everything from bereavement to relationship break-up. I've a team of volunteers who work twenty-four seven to bring this service to the public. Some of them are professionals who want to give something back and others, like Lizzie here, are amateurs. Well, that's the wrong word, she's had training but she doesn't do it for a living.'

Lizzie squirmed. Oh God.

'Who trained you, Lizzie?' Declan asked, pouncing on her.

'A professional is employed to train each new batch of coun-sellors,' Lizzie said, making her voice sound as efficient as possible. 'Then each new person is monitored for a few months and their performance is assessed. We have a very high stan-dard of care.'

'Nice one,' Declan said before turning, to Lizzie's dismay, back to Mark. 'And what made you set it up, Mark? You were,' he rummaged about in his pile of papers, 'the owner of a stationery company, were you not?'

'Stationary being right,' Mark scoffed, 'in that the company wasn't going anywhere.'

Declan laughed, as did his researchers behind the screen.

All he had to do was follow what Lizzie had told him, but oh no, he was determined to go his own way. Lizzie sat back, folded her arms and waited for him to blow it, like he'd blown so many meetings before.

'Yeah,' Mark said when the laughter stopped, 'I owned the company with my wife, we set it up together. Then of course she decided that she was going to wreck our marriage by having an affair and we had to divide up everything, including the company. Well, I don't mind telling you, Declan, it was a hard time. I had a fistful of cash and nothing to spend it on and I had to look at my wife all shacked up with her new man.'

'Terrible.'

Lizzie winced. She hoped Mark wasn't going to tell of the time—

'And I knew I reached a low when I started ringing all the weird chatlines. I mean, those women have great voices but . . . *ugh*.' Mark shuddered. So did Lizzie, for a different reason.

'I just wanted to feel connected to someone, you see,' Mark went on. 'Anyone would have done me, even that woman at the front of today's paper.' More laughter. Lizzie bristled. 'But the end came when I tried to talk back to these women, to tell them how I was feeling, and they hung up on me. One of them even called me weirdo. *Me*?' Mark's voice rose in indignation. 'There she was, a bloody granny in a house in Russia or some-where, doing all her heavy breathing while she was, I dunno, minding her grandchildren or something, and she tells *me* that *I'm* weird.'

'Mad,' Declan said. 'So you decided to set up your own helpline?'

'Yep. After having the biggest breakdown of my life. You might not think it, Declan, looking at me. I mean I seem so together, but in those days I was really fraying around the edges, d'you get me? After it happened, I decided to set up a helpline for break-ups and then it just evolved. People ring us for everything now. Even if they just feel lonely, like I did.' He paused. 'Loneliness is the root of a lot of our problems, you know. Even my horrible wife was lonely, I understand that now.'

There was a pause when he'd finished and, to Lizzie's surprise, someone in the studio started to clap.

Declan beamed. 'Great story, Mark. Well told. So tell us, why are you here now? What is Life's next project?'

'Oh,' Mark said magnanimously, 'I'll let Lizzie explain that. She's the brains behind the fundraising.'

Lizzie jumped. Shit! He hadn't told her was going to let her speak. She looked at him and he smiled cockily at her.

She gave him a grin back.

His loft was open again. That was three times this week. Joe took his keys from his pocket and inserted the key into the lock.

Click.

It was working perfectly. It didn't make sense. He had defin-itely locked up last night, he had even written a note when he had done it and stickered it on the wall inside the loft. He opened the loft again, stepped inside and nothing . . . the note was gone. Had he even done it in the first place?

His head swam and he had to sit down. And it was then he noticed the malt.

It was wet.

How on earth . . . ?

He looked wildly around for a leak, for a reason for the dampness.

None.

He'd have to ring in sick. He needed to check his birds for spores.

His boss would go mental.

The show ended, and Declan wished them all the best, before saying, 'And Mark, we've had an amazing response to you from our female audience.'

'Yeah?'

'It seems a lot of women out there want to know if you're available.'

To Lizzie's amusement Mark blushed. 'I'm not, as it happens, but if they'd like to meet me they can sign up for the parachute jump.'

Wow, that was slick, Lizzie thought, pleased.

'There now, girls, you heard it here. CKY Radio and Declan Darcy.'

As Declan played 'Parachute' by Something Happens, Mark turned to Lizzie. 'There now, see, I wasn't so bad, was I?'

'No, actually,' Lizzie nodded, 'you were pretty great.' There would be no stopping him now, she thought, half amused – he'd be unbearable.

Later that night, to distract himself from the fact that he seemed to be losing his mind, Joe attempted to do a bit more on the clean-up of his house – it really was a state. He hadn't much noticed before Lizzie arrived on the scene, as no one ever visited him at home, but when she'd stepped into his kitchen he'd suddenly seen it through her eyes.

He was now tackling the dining-room floor. He couldn't actually remember ever cleaning it. The pigeons lived in a tidier environment than he did. To his relief he hadn't found any traces of spores among them, but he'd have to keep a check on it. And they really didn't seem as active as they had been. Maybe the older ones were just a little tired from all the racing.

He had just managed to spray some disinfectant on to the floor when his phone rang. Wiping his hands along his old jeans, he went into the hall and, without looking at the caller ID, he picked it up.

'Hello?'

'Joseph, it's Dad.'

Joe froze, his hand seemed to be stuck to the receiver.

'Joe?' his dad said again. 'Are you there? I need to talk to you.'

'I've nothing to say to you, Dad. I'm out of your life now. Don't ring me again.'

He vaguely heard his dad shouting out something to him as he replaced the phone on the hook. He stood for a second looking at the phone before it began to ring again. Joe walked away from it. He just couldn't go back, not after all that had happened. Not after what his dad had done to him. He had a new life now – OK, it was a little lonely and not the sort of life he'd ever wanted, but it was working out all right. He was happier than he'd ever thought he could be. He had no desire to see his parents ever again.

The phone continued to ring for the next hour, but he ignored it.

Her mobile phone rang at nine that night. Picking it up, she was surprised to see Aileen's number displayed. With fumbling fingers she pressed the accept button. 'Hello, Aileen?' This was a surprise.

'Oh, so you're still talking to me then?' Aileen said shyly.

'Of course I am,' Lizzie said warmly. 'How's things?'

'Not too bad,' Aileen answered. 'I'm not as sick as I was in the beginning.'

'Great. Good.'

There was an awkward pause.

'Anyway—'

'Can I—'

'You first,' Lizzie said.

'I was just going say that, well, I saw your mother on the front of the newspaper today.'

'You and about a million other people,' Lizzie answered glumly.

Aileen gave a weak laugh. 'Well, I just rang to say I hope she's OK and that you're OK and . . .' Her voice trailed off a little. 'And that . . . that Billy's OK with it.' She had difficulty saying his name.

'I can put you on to Billy,' Lizzie suggested gently. 'He'd be glad to hear from you. You're the only one he ever talks to about stuff anyway.'

'Oh no, no, I don't think so.' Aileen sounded suddenly scared. 'No, I just thought, you know . . .'

There was a silence.

'I don't want to be sweet-talked into going back,' Aileen admitted after a bit. 'I can't be like my dad, Lizzie.'

'Your dad?'

'Yeah. He . . .' Aileen swallowed. 'You know, kept taking my mother back. And she kept leaving him. I can't be like that.'

'Oh, Aileen,' Lizzie felt a rush of sympathy for her, 'Billy wouldn't leave you. He loves you, he's just—' She paused. After what Billy had said at the weekend, she didn't know any more. She would have bet her life on him loving Aileen, but now . . . She gulped. 'Anyway,' she said, 'it's great to hear from you.'

'Yeah, and I rang also to apologise for the way I behaved the day you called by. I was horrible.'

'You were, but you were upset.'

'I was.'

Her voice dipped. 'My dad is driving me mad.' She sounded like Aileen all of a sudden, girly and giggly. 'I'm going to have to look for somewhere to live. He keeps reminding me of how hard it is to be a single parent.'

'You won't be a single parent,' Lizzie said, 'Billy will be there. He's not running off.'

There was a pause.

'And I'm going to be here all the way,' Lizzie offered. 'Like being an aunty is a responsible job, too.'

210

'Would you like to come in for the scan?' Aileen said suddenly. 'I'm going on Thursday and my dad can't come, so will you go instead?'

She'd take Thursday afternoon off. 'I would totally love to,' she declared.

33

AILEEN WAS WAITING for her at the entrance to the maternity hospital. She smiled uneasily as Lizzie walked up toward her. Lizzie beamed back.

'Come here!' Lizzie enfolded her in a hug before holding her at arms' length and scrutinising her. 'You look fab,' she announced emphatically. 'Being pregnant suits you.'

Aileen laughed a little. 'I'm getting so fat, I can't fit into anything any more.'

'You're not fat!' Lizzie waved her away. 'And your skin looks so great.'

'Thanks.' Aileen nudged her. 'I'm glad you're here. My dad would never think of saying anything like that.'

Lizzie grinned and linked her arm. 'Come on, Mammy, let's get you inside.'

They walked down the corridors, following signs for the antenatal clinic. There was a large queue of pregnant women in front of them. Some women had partners with them, while others were on their own. Aileen and Lizzie sat down and waited. A few people looked curiously at them. Lizzie's phone started to ring. She smiled apologetically and flicked it open.

'Hello?'

'Hey, gorgeous!'

'Hi, Tom.'

'You free Saturday? I've got the night off.'

Lizzie winced. Of all the nights – there was no way. It had been too carefully planned. 'Eh, I'm going out with Billy, Tom.'

'Can't you cancel? I've got a surprise for you.'

'No way. Sorry.' She felt awful lying to him. Since she'd started her campaign, as she called it, the guilt she was experiencing wasn't so much at what she was doing to Joe, but rather at the way she was deceiving Tom. He loved someone who was beginning to disappear. Each time she'd stolen into Joe's back garden at four in the morning, part of the girl she'd been and who he loved seemed to steal away, too. She knew she didn't deserve him or, worse, that he certainly didn't deserve her. It was becoming an effort to pretend that she was the same as she used to be.

'OK,' he sounded disappointed, 'you're coming to see the play next week though, ey?'

'I wouldn't miss it for the world.'

'Well, I'll catch you after, so.'

'Yeah.'

She hung up and found Aileen staring at her with her mouth open. 'You're cancelling Tom in favour of Billy?'

Lizzie shrugged. 'He's a bit down.'

Aileen flushed and the two sat in silence until a nurse called: 'Adrienne Lowry?'

A very pregnant woman stood up and waddled towards the doctor's office. The queue moved up a seat.

Eventually, after about an hour, Aileen was called in. Lizzie watched in fascination as Aileen's stomach was spread with gel and a scanning device was pressed to her belly. Immediately the *whoosh whoosh* of the heartbeats sounded.

'Oh my God!' Lizzie put her hands to her mouth as sudden tears sprang to her eyes. 'Is that their little hearts?'

The doctor smiled. 'Yes. And see here: there they are on the monitor.'

Lizzie gawked at the monitor, where she made out some kind of moving blurs. They didn't look much like anything.

'Hello, babies,' she waved. 'Hello.'

Aileen laughed and the doctor smiled, then she began clicking buttons on a computer and taking measurements. Lizzie turned to Aileen. 'This is brilliant, thanks for inviting me. Isn't it amazing?'

'Yeah,' Aileen nodded. 'That's what I think, too.'

Lizzie was about to say that Billy would love it, when she stopped herself. There was no point in getting involved. She just had to take what she was given and be grateful for it. It was up to Billy and Aileen to sort themselves out.

'Would you like a print-out?' the doctor asked.

'Oh yes, please,' Lizzie said.

'I meant for Mum?' the doctor said, amused.

Aileen laughed. 'That'd be lovely.'

'Can you do two?' Lizzie said impulsively as Aileen shot her a dark look. 'I'll pay for it if I have to.'

The doctor smiled slightly. 'Well, don't tell anyone else, will you?'

'Cross my heart.'

'Why did you ask for another scan picture?' Aileen said as they sat over two cups of coffee.

'To show Billy.' Lizzie stirred some milk into her cup. 'He'd like a picture, I'd say.' She knew Aileen was annoyed but was trying to ignore it.

'I was wondering when Billy would be mentioned,' Aileen said crossly. 'I was wondering when you'd sneak him in.'

'I wasn't trying to sneak him in,' Lizzie said honestly. 'He's already involved and no matter what you think, Aileen, he is their daddy.'

Aileen ran her finger around the rim of her cup. 'We need to sort out what to do with the house.'

'What?' Lizzie felt sick. That sounded so bloody final. So awful. Watching Billy and Aileen split up was like watching her own parents do it, she thought. They were her family when she was in Dublin.

'Aileen, don't be hasty,' she said. 'Please think about it. You're throwing something great away – for what? For a look that was a spur of the moment thing? It's, it's . . .' she sought for the right words, 'ridiculous.'

Aileen glared at her before gathering up her belongings and standing up. 'I'm going now. Tell Billy that my dad will be in contact to sort the house out.'

'Tell him yourself,' Lizzie fired back.

Aileen nodded, as if it was all she expected from her, and said, 'I'll make my own way home.'

'Aw, Aileen—' Lizzie pleaded after her. Aileen flapped her away.

Even a smoke wouldn't be any use now, Lizzie thought glumly, as she faced down the stares of the other customers.

Another night off work. His boss was not going to be pleased, but John and Noel had both said they were available to come over that evening and Joe needed their opinion. It was the first time, aside from when he'd started up, that he'd asked for help.

'Thanks for coming tonight, guys,' he said as he let the two men into his house.

Noel whistled softly as he looked around. 'Oh, someone has discovered the duster!' He grinned slyly. 'I wonder why.' He marched ahead of Joe into the kitchen and laughed loudly as he remarked, 'Wow, much nicer than when we were here last.'

'That was ages ago,' Joe flushed.

Noel ignored him. 'The floor all cleaned up and everything. It wouldn't have anything to do with a pretty young wan who's just joined the club, would it?'

'Feck off,' Joe answered without looking at him. 'I just never had time to clean up before.'

'Course you didn't,' John joked. 'And it was driving you mad, wasn't it?'

'Like I said, feck off,' Joe answered pleasantly as he pushed open the back door to let the lads into the garden. His pigeons were up, flying around. As he crossed to the loft a number of them came swooping down, landing on his shoulders and head. Joe affectionately flapped them off.

'I can't quite put my finger on it,' he explained. 'They're in good form, just not as good as before.'

John scanned the birds. 'They look good to me,' he remarked.

'They're lethargic,' Joe said. 'It's not something anyone else might notice.'

'You giving them their antibiotics?' Noel asked.

'Yep.'

'What sort?'

'The bottle is in the kitchen.'

Noel turned and followed Joe back into the house. Joe took the bottle from his press and shook it. 'Not much left.'

Noel examined the bottle before unscrewing it. He swirled it about, then sniffed. 'Not much of a smell from the stuff,' he remarked.

'It's nearly gone,' Joe said.

'No, come here. Smell.' Noel thrust the bottle under Joe's nose and Joe sniffed. Then sniffed again. Then he tipped the bottle towards his lips and tasted a liquid drop.

'Jesus,' he winced, 'it's water. Or as good as. Taste, Noel.'

Noel took a sample taste. 'There's your problem, Joe. The stuff is too weak.'

'Yeah, but how?' Joe sniffed again.

Noel shrugged. 'Happened to me once. Well, not that exactly, but I had to go away for work one time and the wife told me she would give them their treatments and she didn't. The birds were in bits when I got back.'

Joe barely heard him. His mind was reeling. How could that have happened?

'Stuff must be faulty,' Noel said, taking it from him and dumping it down the sink. 'Surprised you didn't notice. You think you'd notice that it didn't smell.'

'Yeah well, I normally don't go shoving my nose into it.' He watched as Noel rinsed out the bottle. 'You got any more?' Noel asked.

'Yeah. Yeah I have. I'll do it now.' From the back of the press he pulled another bottle, opened it, and assured himself that it was all right before diluting it for the birds.

'Who's the kid?' Noel pointed at a skinny boy perched on the wall, who seemed to be having an animated discussion with John.

Joe glanced up. 'He's a lad who works for Ellen, my neighbour. He does odd jobs for her. Hey, what the hell is John doing?'

John had handed Anto one of Joe's pigeons to hold.

Joe was about to race into the garden when he noted the reverent way Anto took the bird and held it close to his chest. He watched as Anto ran his index finger along the length of the bird's body with a gentleness that belied the rough look on his face. John was nodding and encouraging him.

'Boy knows how to hold a bird,' Noel said admiringly.

'Yeah,' Joe answered, not at all sure what to do. He had to go outside, though – that was Prince Anto was holding. As he stepped into the garden, Anto flinched and hastily handed the bird back to John. John was left startled as Anto hopped down from the wall and ran off.

'Nice kid,' he remarked. 'Loves the pigeons.'

Joe didn't answer. Instead he held up the medicine. 'We found the culprit. Or at least we think we did.'

'No way!' John let Prince go and whistled softly. 'Gone off, was it?'

'I guess,' Joe nodded. He started to dole out the fresh anti-biotics. 'We'll find out Saturday week when I fly them again.'

'Cid will hate that. He came third last week.'

'No!' Joe grinned. 'I wish I'd been there.'

'No, you don't.' John shook his head. 'He was unbearable. I left early.'

The other two laughed before starting to look for the source of Joe's damp.

'Hello, is that Lizzie?'

She recognised the caller's voice. 'Sinéad.'

'Yes, that's right.' Sinéad sounded relieved.

'I haven't heard from you in a while, how have things been?'

'Not good,' Sinéad answered bluntly. 'I tried to ring you before but you weren't there and then things calmed down again and now, well, he hit me. Again. Last week.'

Lizzie remained silent.

'And I ended up with a bruise the size of a fist on my face and I couldn't go outside the door for days.' Now the woman's voice wobbled.

'And what happened?' Lizzie asked gently.

'I told him that he couldn't do that,' Sinéad said, sniffing. 'I told him that I was not going to let him hit me. Like since I talked to you, I was thinking back. And I've changed so much. I used to have loads of friends. I used to see my family. Now there just seems to be the two of us. And I'm nervy all the time. All the time.'

'What did he say when you stood up to him?'

'He said sorry,' Sinéad said. 'And, well, he sounded as if he meant it. So I said it was fine so long as he didn't do it again. And he said that I just made him so angry and I said I'd try not to make him angry and then tonight, well, I let a cup drop because he raised his voice and then he made me clean it up and then he told me he could see a piece under the chair and would I get to it and so I did, and then I'm under the chair thinking, why am I doing this? Why doesn't he do it if he saw it? And I pick up the cup and he says I better buy a replacement one and I said that they were willow pattern and couldn't be replaced so he took them all out of the press and smashed them up one by one. Just picked them up and smashed them. One by one. And I jumped each time he did it, I couldn't help myself. Then he told me to clean them all up.'

Lizzie gritted her teeth. It took all her will power to keep quiet. 'Did you clean them up?'

'No,' Sinéad said. 'They're still there and he's gone out and said he hopes it'll be clean when he gets back and I just want to run away.'

'You want to run away,' Lizzie deliberately raised her voice in the hope of catching Anna's attention.

Anna glanced up and Lizzie beckoned her over.

'Yes, I'm so scared but I'm not cleaning up, I'm not.'

'Well then, get out right now and tomorrow go and see if you can get a barring order against him. It'll stop him coming near you.'

'Just leave now? Where will I go?'

Lizzie gave her the address of a women's refuge and told her she would ring in advance to say Sinéad was on her way.

'It's Lori,' Sinéad said tearfully. 'That's my real name.'

'Well, Lori, you'll be safe. I promise.'

'Will you come and see me?' Lori asked.

'Come and see you?'

Anna shook her head.

'Eh, Lori, I can't. I'm not allowed.' Lizzie hated having to say that to her. 'But there is a lovely woman in the shelter who'll take care of you. Her name is Julie, all right?'

'Oh.' Lori sounded devastated. 'Right, thanks.'

The phone went dead.

Lizzie heaved a sigh and flopped back on her chair.

'Well done.' Anna gave her a brief hug. 'Good girl.'

Lizzie didn't feel as if she'd done any good at all. 'I wish I could just go and meet her,' she said.

'Yeah, and the next time someone calls you'll want to meet her. You know you can't, Lizzie.'

She didn't answer.

Despite the fact that they didn't find any source of damp, it was a good night. It had been so long since he'd had people over for a chat and a few cans that he'd forgotten how much fun it could be. They talked all night about birds and races and form.

It was Joe's kind of night.

34

'HE'S WELCOME TO help me with the birds if he likes,' Joe said to Ellen as he took a chair in her fussy sitting room. From the look of the place it didn't seem as if Anto was doing much cleaning at all. Dust lay on everything.

Ellen smiled and her face suddenly appeared younger. 'Oh, I knew you'd come around.' She stood up and pinched Joe on the cheek. 'You're a good boy really, aren't you?'

'I'm stupid is what I am,' Joe said, half in jest. He shrugged a little. 'He seems to know how to handle a bird and that's good enough for me for the moment.'

'So now you'll have two helpers: that pretty Mindy and a very happy Anto. Aren't you Mr Popular all of a sudden?'

'Lizzie, Ellen, her name is Lizzie.'

'Does she have a sister?'

Joe shrugged. It occurred to him suddenly that he knew nothing much about Lizzie. Maybe he should ask her. Girls liked when you showed an interest in them. And despite not wanting to get involved with anyone, Joe suddenly realised how involved with people he was becoming. Ellen, Noel, John and now Anto. He wasn't too sure if he liked it. Though he knew that he liked Lizzie – there was something about her. He wouldn't mind being involved with her. He shifted about uncomfortably on the seat.

'Anyway, I'll be getting back. You can let Anto know that the next time he's here, if he does a good job cleaning out this room, he can have half an hour with the birds.'

'This room is fine.' Ellen sounded indignant. She looked about. 'I don't let him in here. These are my important things that only I touch.'

'Oh, right,' Joe shrugged. 'Well, get him to do something for you and I'll inspect it.'

'You are so self-righteous,' Ellen said crossly. 'He does his best. He's only a small boy. He can't clean really well. He doesn't need to be judged, just accepted.'

'You'd better look out or you'll collapse,' Joe said, amused at her cross voice.

'Collapse?'

'Due to your bleeding heart.'

'Get out,' she pushed him towards the door, 'you dreadful man. Get out.'

Joe laughed. It occurred to him that he was laughing a lot more than he used to.

Two in the morning. Lizzie was psyching herself to get out of the car when her phone bleeped. *Can we meet 2morrow? Tom.*

She winced. She'd planned on calling to Joe tomorrow. So she texted back: *Morning only.*

OK. R u having a good night with Bill?

Yep. Great. C U tomorrow.

She wondered what he wanted, but it would be good to see him all the same.

Putting her phone in the glove compartment, she stepped out of her car. Then, opening the boot, she pulled her pigeon basket from it. Carrying the basket, she pulled her black jacket around her and, making sure she wasn't being observed, slipped quietly up Joe's driveway and into his side entrance. She slowly pushed open the gate. It squeaked a little and she winced. A little oil the next time.

Closing it after her, she crept across the silent garden. She knew where it all was now and she hurried as quietly as she could across the grass. Then, very gently, she inserted the key and pulled open the door.

Nothing stirred.

Slowly, with that sense of detachment growing stronger each time she came here, Lizzie opened the lid of the basket.

35

LIZZIE AWOKE TO the sound of the phone the next morning. Groggily, she glanced at her watch. Her head felt muzzy, as if her mind was caught in a thick fog. Eight-thirty. Who would ring on a Sunday at eight-thirty? Oh God. Her stomach heaved as she remembered what she had done the night before. Maybe it was the police. Or Joe. She felt suddenly sick.

She wouldn't answer it. She lay in bed, the duvet pulled up to her chin, and let the phone ring out. It was a relief when the noise stopped, but it started again a minute later. Joe hadn't got her home number, she remembered, so it couldn't be him. She felt sick again with relief.

A sudden vision of the panic she would feel if she were caught out unnerved her. But she wasn't going to be caught. There was no way. Joe was becoming friendlier as time went on. Why, one day last week, after she'd yet again cleaned out his pigeon coup, he'd told her about his day at work in a sort of halting way, which, under other circumstances, would have been charming.

Downstairs the phone continued to ring.

Lizzie listened for a second wondering if Billy was going to get it, but when she heard nothing from his room, she stumbled from her own bed. She'd barely slept the night before, high on adrenalin.

'Hello?' she said sleepily, hoping to convey to the caller that early on a Sunday was not a time to ring anyone. She yawned widely.

'It's me.'

'Dad, hey.' He sounded cross or worried, she couldn't decide.

'I'm worried, Lizzie.'

'Why?'

'It's your mother. She's refusing to apologise for what she's done. She was up in court Friday.'

Her mind had to play catch-up. She yawned again. 'Court?'

'Yes, I didn't want to worry you or Billy. It was on the news last night. Did you see the news last night?'

'No.'

'Well, I thought she'd apologise, see, but she didn't. Told them she'd fight all the way.'

'Did she?' Well, that was no surprise.

'So the judge asked her how she'd like to fight from behind bars and, Lizzie,' he sighed, 'she's in a cell here awaiting a trip to Mountjoy.'

That woke her up. 'You are joking!'

'Six months until she apologises.'

'Oh my God.'

Her dad said nothing.

'But—but, sure she's not a danger to anyone.'

'No. Only herself. It's like she's on self-destruct. I have been up all night worrying about her. I can't sleep, I can't eat. Oh, this has been coming a long time.'

'Are you OK?' Lizzie asked.

'No, I'm not. Haven't you been listening? I can't sleep, I can't—'

'OK, calm down. Look at this rationally. I—'

'You're my daughter, Lizzie, not my counsellor. There is no rational explanation for your mother's behaviour. Even Martha says it.'

'Martha apologised?'

'She did. On Friday, and she thought your mother would too, but oh no, that'd be way too normal for your mother.'

Lizzie didn't know what to say. Her dad sounded very agitated and it wasn't good for him to be like that.

'Anyway,' he went on, 'I need to visit her when she's up there, so I'm going to have to come and stay. Will Billy be OK with that?'

224

'Of course he will. Look, Dad, we'll all go and visit her.'

'She's going to be in today's papers,' he said glumly. 'Front page again. And the funny thing was she used to have no interest in the harbour.'

'Dad, get some sleep, and eat something, for God's sake. We'll sort it out.'

'If you saw the way she was carrying on, you wouldn't be able to sleep either.' He muttered a 'goodbye' and hung up. Lizzie vowed to ring Martha to get her to keep an eye on him.

Joe sauntered to the shops at the end of his road to get the Sunday papers. He loved Sundays: drinking coffee in the local coffee shop, having a read of the newspapers and then going back to his lofts and setting up the bird baths.

The woman behind the counter had his order ready before he'd asked for it. A large black coffee and a fry-up.

'For someone who eats that every week, you're still the best looking thing in the place,' she chortled as she handed his breakfast over to him.

She said that every week, too.

'For someone who makes such great food, I'm surprised you're still single,' Joe said back.

'I'm waiting on a proposal from the right man, so get your skates on, young fella.'

'I'm not great on skates,' he shrugged, grinning.

'Good, you can fall down. I can fall on top. We can see what happens.'

Joe laughed and carried his breakfast to the table. Sitting down, he wondered a little glumly why it was that all the women over fifty liked to flirt with him. Did he look so safe and boring that all he could manage were a few suggestive comments from older women? Aw well, he thought as he cut into a massive sausage, he had to take what he could get.

He opened up the paper and, with a clatter, dropped his knife on to the floor, making the people at the table beside him jump. There she was again: Mrs Polly Walsh. This time she had her head held high and the headline was NO BACKING DOWN. Joe stared and stared at her. He'd spent so long trying to forget this woman who had stared empty-eyed at him all through his trial that now, seeing her again, it made his head reel. Truth was, prison had been a cakewalk compared to the trial. All those people he'd been friendly with staring at him with horror. And he hadn't deserved it – that was the worst thing. At least he didn't think he deserved it. Not fully. Only no one understood that.

Joe shoved the paper away from him and stared for a second at his breakfast, before standing up and walking out.

'Lizzie,' Billy called, knocking on her door.

Lizzie groaned and rolled over. She hadn't been able to go back to sleep after the bombshell news about her mother. She was wrecked.

'I'm awake,' she yelled back.

Billy came in looking worried, about to say something, before he suddenly froze. Too late Lizzie realised what he had spotted on the floor beside her bed.

'Is that,' he sounded hoarse, 'is that . . . where did you get that?'

Lizzie said nothing as he bent down and picked up the scan of the babies. After visiting Joe's last night she'd suddenly wanted to look at something that made her feel good, she hadn't felt much of anything in such a while now, so she'd taken the scan out and studied the two innocent little shapes curled up around one another. Two pure little lives about to begin. She'd fallen asleep with it in her hand. She watched as Billy stared at the flimsy piece of film paper. If Aileen could see his expression now, she'd never have walked out, Lizzie thought. Billy brought his eyes to meet hers.

'Are they my babies?' he said eventually.

Lizzie nodded.

'How?' His forehead crinkled up. 'How did you—'

'Aileen invited me to go for a scan with her.'

She watched as Billy took that in. His expression flinched in momentary hurt.

'You never said,' he muttered.

'I thought I should go, see how she was and then tell you.'

'Then why didn't you?' There was no mistaking the hurt in his voice now.

'Because,' Lizzie took a deep breath, 'we had a bit of a row.' She tried to think of a way to airbrush it. 'I, eh, told her she was being unreasonable and she stormed out. I was afraid to let you know.'

Billy didn't seem to care. Instead he continued to study the picture, before running his finger over it.

'Did you see them move?' he asked quietly.

'Yeah.' Lizzie climbed out of bed and came to stand beside him. She, too, looked at the picture. 'They're just perfect, aren't they?'

He nodded. 'Can I keep it?'

'I got it for you.'

'Thanks.' He looked at it again before suddenly remembering what he'd come in for. 'Tom rang looking for you last night. He seemed under the impression you and I were going out together, so I told him you'd just left to go to his place.'

Oh shit.

When Joe got back, Anto was in the back garden, peering into the racing loft.

'Oy!' he shouted out at him. 'What are you doing here?'

Anto jumped and turned to face him. 'Ellen said that you said that I could help,' he shouted back, a little belligerently.

'Yeah. I didn't say you could creep into my garden and spy on my birds.' Even as he said it Joe knew he sounded childish. It was the shock of seeing Megan's mother in the paper. And his edginess about the lofts being mysteriously open now and again.

'I'm not spying on your birds,' Anto spat back. Then, 'But you're a bit stupid all the same.'

Joe gawped at him. 'Pardon?'

'Feral pigeon in your loft. How did you let her in?'

227

'There isn't a feral pigeon in my loft!' Joe sputtered at the boy's cheek. 'I'd know a wild pigeon if I saw one.'

Anto said nothing, just pointed smugly at a grey, tatty-looking bird that was pecking away at the food in the hopper. Joe did a double take. A wild bird? In his loft? How the hell . . . ?

'Jesus.' He scrabbled in his jacket pocket for his keys. Hastily he unlocked the loft and, with Anto's help, shooed the pigeon out. These wild ones were riddled with disease. Joe felt a little sick. If his birds had caught anything . . . Grudgingly he turned to Anto. 'Thanks.'

Anto shrugged cockily. 'You should be more careful.'

'I am careful,' Joe said through gritted teeth. 'I don't know how it got in there.'

He took the hopper from the floor and, with Anto following, he rinsed it out, dried it and put more food into it for the birds.

'I definitely didn't see it last night,' he said, half to himself, as he deposited the hopper back on the loft floor.

'Maybe it got in through a trap or something,' Anto suggested.

Joe barely heard him. His heart suddenly skipped a beat as his eyes scanned the loft. Oh shit. Oh no. But he couldn't have.

'It could have squeezed through that trap there,' Anto inserted his hand into the trap and frowned, 'but nah, no bird would—'

'Prince is gone,' Joe said, staring wildly about. 'He's gone.'

'Is that the bird I held the other day?' Anto asked. 'The really good-looking one with the tiny dent in his wing?'

Joe nodded. He was pacing wildly now, picking up birds and discarding them, alarming some who hopped hastily out of his way.

'Oh God!' He felt sick. 'He's gone.'

'Did he come in yesterday?' Anto asked.

Joe nodded. He was sure he had. Definitely he had. Or had he? Maybe he was thinking of the day before. But if Prince hadn't come back, he'd have noticed last night. His best bird. Of course he'd have noticed. But then again, sometimes important things went by your notice. Like Megan that time. Or the way he kept forgetting to lock up. He shook his head. There had to be a

228

mistake. He was upset because of the paper. He took deep breaths. Prince *couldn't* be gone. He turned to Anto, who was starting at him in apprehension.

'We are going to go through every bird here,' he said, suddenly firm. 'We'll pick them up, look at the ring and put them in a basket. Prince is bound to be hiding somewhere.'

An hour later, having double-checked, Joe was forced to admit that Prince was nowhere. He whistled and Prince didn't come. He held up food and Prince didn't come. In the end, he let Anto bathe the birds and he went inside and tried his best not to vomit.

Tom looked wrecked, as if he hadn't slept. He came into the house, hands buried deep in the pockets of his pin-stripe suit jacket, which he wore with a bright red shirt and a loosened skinny black tie. His jeans had holes in the knees and a pair of bright red trainers completed his unconventional look. He looked effortlessly cool, Lizzie thought with a pang.

'Hey.' She attempted a grin.

He shifted from foot to foot. 'You didn't go out with Bill last night then, ey?' was all he said.

'No.' Lizzie flushed.

'And you didn't go out with me.'

'No.'

'So,' Tom was deliberately casual, 'where did you go, ey? And why did you tell me that you were going out with Billy?'

Lizzie walked into the kitchen and he followed. She'd thought in vain all morning, trying to come up with a plausible excuse. But she knew she couldn't lie to his face. She couldn't tell the truth either. For one thing he'd despise her for what she'd already done, and for another, he'd try and talk her out of it and there was no way she was going to stop. Not now. And then he might tell Billy and all hell would break loose.

'Well?' Tom asked again.

'I just had somewhere else to go,' she tried to say with confidence. 'Nobody's business but mine.'

'Fair enough,' Tom said, nodding. An edge of steel crept into his voice as he asked, 'So why lie to me? And why pretend that you were out with Billy when I texted you at two o'clock?'

'Were you trying to set me up?' She felt a flash of anger. 'Trying to make me incriminate myself?'

'I was trying to see what the hell was going on.' His voice rose. With an effort of will he lowered it. 'So, what *is* going on? Are you going to tell me?'

'One little white lie,' Lizzie said. 'For God's sake.'

'And if it had been me telling you that one little white lie?'

She flushed. 'What exactly do you want me to do, Tom? I'm not going to tell you where I was. I can't tell you where I was, where I might be again if you ring. I'm sorry, but I can't.'

He looked stunned. 'So where does that leave us?' he asked, dazed.

'You have to trust me.' She knew she was clutching at straws.

'You lied to me, Lizzie.'

'I said I'm sorry!'

'You didn't, actually.' Then slowly he muttered, 'Have you met someone else?'

Not in the way you mean, she wanted to say.

'No. Are you saying you don't trust me?'

There was a silence. 'I love you, Lizzie. I don't want to lose you.'

'Then let me go out with who I want, when I want.' Even as she said it she knew it was unfair.

'I do. You never normally lie about it. How would you feel if I did that?'

She glared at him. 'I wouldn't send you texts hoping to catch you out.'

'That is not the issue here,' he snapped, asserting himself suddenly, 'and you know it. You lied, Lizzie, and yeah, it is kinda hard to trust someone who tells you lies. How many other times have you done it, ey?'

'Everyone lies!' she shouted at him. 'Are you so brilliant you never told a lie in your life? For God's sake!'

There was a pause. 'I never told a lie to you,' he said simply.

It brought her up short. She swallowed hard. 'I'm sorry.'

'So?' He looked hopefully at her.

'I can't tell you, though.' She winced as his face fell. 'You . . . you, well, you don't want to know.'

His shoulders slumped and he stared down at the foot of one red trainer. 'D'you remember when we met first and I had to work nights and you'd come and sit at the bar keeping me company as I served the customers?' At her nod he said quietly, 'Well, you don't do that any more.'

'I didn't know you missed me that much.'

'Yeah, well, I do.' His eyes met hers. 'You're lying to me and I can't go out with someone who does that, Lizzie. I just can't.'

What was he saying? 'What do you mean?' she whispered, dreading his answer.

'You know what I mean.'

The words seemed to drop into the ocean of silence that followed, sending out ripples. Lizzie shook her head.

'Don't, Tom. Don't say that.' Her voice broke a little.

'What else *can* I say?' He looked hopelessly at her. 'You won't tell me where you've been. I will accept anything, Lizzie. Anything. If you're seeing someone else and regret it, maybe we can work it out. Just tell me.'

It was those words that made her realise Tom was way too good for her. He didn't deserve a manipulating woman like her, a woman who kidnapped prize birds and was cruel to animals. Even if he did understand, which he wouldn't as he'd never do what she was doing, she couldn't let him believe she was something she wasn't. The time had come to choose, she realised. Tom or Joe. She couldn't live with both now. And it would be better for everyone if she chose Joe. Holding on to Tom would suffocate them both. Her with guilt and regret for allowing Joe to escape, and Tom with despair at her unhappiness.

'I can't tell you,' she said, trying to keep her voice level. 'I just can't. You deserve better than me, Tom. You're right.'

He blinked. One. Twice. 'Is it drugs or something?'

'No.'

'Just tell me.'

For a second she was so tempted. For a split second, as she took in his brown eyes and the cute little scar just above his lip. For one second she wanted to blurt it all out, to cry in his arms for as long as it took to feel clean again, to have him hold her and tell her that she wasn't going mad, that it was OK to hate so much that you shook in the morning and felt your heart grow smaller with every passing thought of revenge. That it was OK to do bizarre acts and feel nothing. Maybe she could live with just letting it go. The thought glimmered for a second, shining like a beacon.

Just for a second, though, and then the feeling passed and she was swamped once again with steely resolve. She wanted to go mad if it meant wiping that grin from Joe Jones' face. If she could drive Joe mad, her own sanity would be worth it.

'Just go, Tom, will you?'

He stood for a second or two, then gulped out, 'You really want this?'

Of course she didn't, he was the most precious person in her life. But it would be for the best. She wasn't sure she even had enough space in her to love him any more. 'Yes. I think so.'

'Fine. Fine, so.' He sounded hurt and pissed off in equal measure. 'See you, so.'

'Bye.' She didn't look at him as he left.

She waited until the front door slammed before bursting into tears.

And she didn't think she was just crying for Tom.

She cried for about twenty minutes. Then, as she wiped her eyes with some kitchen paper, she consoled herself with the thought that everything would be easier now. She wouldn't have to lie to Tom and she could pursue Joe with a clear conscience. And yet she felt sick, like someone who had won the lotto but lost the ticket.

But then she remembered Prince sitting in his basket in the garden shed, waiting to be released, and thought of Joe, who surely must be searching frantically for him by now, and the sick feeling hardened into something more concrete, something she could use. Doing what she was doing would ease the pain of losing Tom and hopefully banish the pain of losing Megan.

She had made her choice and now she'd have to get on with it.

From under her bed she retrieved the new heavy-duty secateurs she'd purchased at the local hardware shop and went down to the shed in the back garden. She had to be quick, Billy had told her he'd be back in an hour – he'd left to give her time to talk to Tom.

The cat from the house next door was busy pacing up and down outside the shed and Lizzie hastily shooed it away. A big black tom, it was lethal where birds were concerned. Lizzie closed the door of the shed behind her and took a second to get used to the gloom. Very gently, she took the basket from behind some old sheets where she had hidden it. Thank God Aileen was gone, as she'd never have got away with it otherwise. Billy never came in here now and, as a result, the garden was as wild as the rest of the greens on the estate. Inside the basket, the bird cooed expectantly.

God, she'd love to see Joe's face this morning with his wonderful bird gone AWOL. She was going to ring him later and she knew exactly what to say, too.

Joe had rung the club to get them to put out the word that his bird was missing, just in case Prince showed up in someone else's loft, which, if he had, meant that he wasn't really fit for racing any more. He found it hard to believe that Prince would do that, though. He was such a good bird. Lizzie had rung, offering to come over and help with the birds, and had been shocked when she heard that Prince had disappeared. She was sitting here now in his kitchen, her hair braided in two quirky tiny plaits, having made him a cup of tea and brought along a packet of Ginger Nut, which was very thoughtful of her. She looked a little rough, though.

'Are you OK?' he asked Lizzie hesitantly. 'You're very quiet.'

Lizzie flinched. 'Fine,' she said.

Joe recoiled. Maybe he'd overstepped the mark. He wasn't good with this stuff, having spent all of his twenties in jail.

'It's just, you know, your eyes look all swollen and sort of red and—' He shuddered to a stop. 'I'll shut up now.' He managed a small grin.

Lizzie shrugged. She knew she looked awful, that's what happened when you cried. She'd wondered how long it would take for Joe to ask, though. For a while she'd been afraid he'd ignore her huge swollen eyes and blotchy complexion.

'It's all over with my boyfriend.' Her voice wobbled and she sniffed. A tear plopped into her coffee. She wasn't acting in front of him, for a change.

Joe winced. 'Oh, right.'

'Bet you wish you hadn't asked,' Lizzie said wryly. 'The last thing you need right now is an upset female in your kitchen.'

'You in my kitchen I can handle.' He smiled a little awkwardly. 'Your boyfriend must be mad.'

'Thanks,' she said softly.

'No worries.'

She smiled back but her eyes filled up again. Hurriedly she blinked the tears away, but not before Joe noticed and turned away too, staring out the window, his eyes automatically drifting skywards.

Lizzie observed him, her tears vanishing as she took in his devastated profile. This was better than she'd hoped. He was devastated. Of course he could never be as devastated as she had been fourteen years ago, but still, there was more to come. A lot more.

He turned back to her and gave a half-hearted grin.

'Thanks for coming,' he said, crossing over and touching one of her braids. It took every ounce of her will power not to shudder. And he didn't let it go. Instead he was staring into her face with a weird sort of look.

'Stops me thinking.' She said it as breezily as she could.

'Yeah.' Joe pulled away abruptly, looking confused. 'Thanks again,' he said, 'and sorry about you losing your boyfriend.'

'Sorry about you losing your pigeon.'

They sort of smiled at each other, before he turned back to the window.

36

BILLY LEFT FOR work the next day at seven. For once Lizzie was awake. Not that she'd been able to sleep. Her mind seemed to be constantly buzzing. When she heard Billy's car leave, she ran downstairs and out into the back garden. The neighbour's cat was pacing up and down outside the shed again and Lizzie had to shoo it off.

She took the pigeon basket out and opened it. Prince blinked in the light and hopped up to the rim of the basket. Lizzie had to admit that he really was a beautiful bird.

She looked at the cut on the bird's leg and winced – she hadn't meant for that to happen. She'd tried to treat the bleeding yesterday and it did look better today.

'Sorry,' she whispered.

Then she wondered why she felt sorry. She had stolen this bird's medication, watered its food and now all of a sudden she was feeling guilty? She rubbed her face with her hands. Most days it was easy and she could switch off, but actually seeing the damage on Prince's leg and knowing that she had directly caused it was a reminder of what she was at. A brutal reminder that she didn't want to face. She had never hurt anything before. Ever. She cried when her dad's chickens died, for God's sake, and now she had cut this bird's leg. Still, it should heal – she'd read that birds, especially pigeons, healed quickly.

'Off you go,' she said gently and Prince took flight in one fluid movement. He circled above the garden awhile before getting his bearings, then, like an arrow, zoomed back towards his loft.

* * *

Joe was pulling on his jacket when he noticed the bird outside, perched on top of the racing loft. He glanced out the window and did a double take.

He was back!

Wherever he'd been, he was back!

Joe wrenched open the back door and whistled. Prince immediately flew to him and it was then that Joe noticed the cut on his leg. And with horror he noticed that someone had removed the bird's ID tag.

It took a second for it to register as his mind tumbled with every possible scenario. Prince could never race again. His ID was gone. He'd never race again. He was only good for breeding now. Jesus. And on top of that, someone had deliberately removed the tag. Someone had taken Prince, somehow, and removed his ID. Who the hell would do that?

His relief at Prince coming back was suddenly tempered with anger.

There was only one person he could think of.

'So how did the meeting go?' Mark demanded as Lizzie hurried in to work, two hours late.

Lizzie flushed. She didn't like lying to Mark. She'd never lied to him before.

'Not too good,' she said. 'Not even a donation.'

'So why did he want to meet you?'

Lizzie forced herself to look at her boss. 'I have no idea.'

'Who was it?' Mark laid his hands flat on her desk and poked his head in towards her. 'I'll ring them up, give them a piece of my mind. I'll tell them not to waste my valued employee's time.'

'Eh, no,' Lizzie shook her head, her back turned, 'not a good idea. Who knows, maybe in the future . . . ?' She let her voice trail off. 'Now, I've a few things to do, so if you wouldn't mind.'

'Well, I suppose you're still talking to me so I should be grateful for that,' Mark said jovially.

'Sorry?'

'Well, dating an acting superstar has probably gone to your head.'

'What?' Was the man finally cracking?

'You. Dating a superstar.' He spoke as if she were stupid. He looked at her encouragingly. 'Has he not called you?'

'Who?'

'Your fella, the hotshot actor.'

Lizzie swallowed hard. She didn't want to have to tell Mark, but—

'He's in the paper today with some blondy wan hanging off him. Is he in a play or something?'

'Yeah, it's opening tonight.' Of course, she couldn't go to that now.

'Hang on there now, I'll just get the paper.'

'No, don't, it's—'

But he was gone. She could hear him rummaging about in his office, throwing files and pens everywhere as he searched for that morning's paper.

'Here we go.' He sauntered into the room. 'Now, what do you think of that?'

She thought Tom looked bloody gorgeous, that's what she thought. He was staring out of the page with a wistful, lost look in his eyes and Imogen, all blonde bouncy curls, was staring up at him with such a look of devotion that it made Lizzie catch her breath. If she wasn't careful, Imogen would nab him. Then she realised that it didn't matter. He wasn't hers any more. The real-isation was a physical pain in her chest.

'I'd watch that girl.' Mark jabbed the page. 'Still, your fella doesn't look too interested. But then again, blonde is what most fellas go for, except for me of course. Now, I'm more a—'

'He's not my boyfriend any more,' Lizzie said, surprised at how calm she sounded. 'It doesn't matter.'

'Not your boyfriend?' Mark gawked at her. 'Did he break up with you because he got famous? Were you not glamorous enough for him? Jesus, if that's the case I'd punch him for you, Lizzie.'

'There's no need. It was a mutual thing.'

'Mutual, my arse. You certainly don't look like it was mutual. You look horrendous. You have for ages now.'

'Thanks.' She handed him back his paper. 'Now can this vision of horrendousness get back to work?'

'Just say the word.' Mark tapped his nose. 'He wouldn't know what hit him.'

'Yes, well the debate is currently on as to what exactly you are,' Lizzie quipped with a small grin.

Mark grinned back. 'You need any time off you just tell me, OK?'

'Ta.'

'No worries.' He patted her on the shoulder and left.

Eight o'clock. There was a sharp rapping on his front door. Joe yawned widely and stretched. He hadn't slept that well the night before, worrying about Prince and where he could be. The knocking came again. Furious hammering. Through the glass, he thought he made out Ellen's silhouette, though why she should seem angry at him he couldn't fathom.

He opened the door and grinned, 'Yes?'

'Joseph, you did it again, didn't you?'

'Sorry, I'm not with you.'

'You let your birds out in the morning. Here.' A blouse, covered in bird droppings was thrust in front of him. 'Look at what they did.'

She was back to herself anyway, he thought in amusement.

'Ellen, I don't let the birds out early on your washing days, you know that. It wasn't me.'

'Oh.' She looked at him in abject disappointment. 'I never had you figured for a liar, Joseph. Never.'

'I'm not lying.' He attempted to smile at her but she wasn't having it.

'Anto had to whistle your birds in,' she said, as if talking to a very slow child. 'They were out all day, flying about, in and out of the loft. Anto said it was very bad management, if you don't mind me saying so.'

'Naw, I never—' Joe shook his head. 'The loft was locked.'

'Are you calling *me* a liar now?' Ellen tut-tutted. 'Joe, I'm very fond of you, even if you are a little odd. But your birds were out. Anto said it looked like you forgot to lock the loft or something.'

He *had* locked the loft. He always locked the loft. But then again, he'd forgotten a couple of nights these past few months, too. 'Anto called them in?'

'Yes. He's a very nice boy, despite everything. It took him a while, though – he tried to mimic your whistle or something. He had to lock your loft up with some string. You should check it. He also said to tell you that he thinks your stray bird has come back, but that she's got nothing on her leg.'

'His leg,' Joe corrected automatically. He swallowed hard. 'Ellen, sorry if they were out. I'll double check the loft next time.' He glanced at her blouse. 'How much—'

'Oh, nothing,' she flapped him away, 'I wouldn't expect you to pay, it was a mistake. But those birds scare me, Joe. Just try and keep them in next time.'

'Yeah. Right.' He *had* bloody locked it. He had.

'Anto wants to know if he can help tomorrow.'

'Sure.'

'Thanks.' Ellen reached out and unexpectedly caught his arm. 'Anto is happy being with the birds, his mother told me so.'

Joe nodded. He had to get away. He needed to think.

'Why do you think I offered him the job?' Ellen smiled slyly.

He should have known, Joe thought as he managed a smile back.

Though Lizzie knew she wasn't going to go to Tom's opening night, she rang up the theatre to get tickets for the play during its run. She'd get a seat right at the back, so Tom wouldn't see her but at least she could sit and look at him. She could stare at his face and listen to his voice, see him walk and smile and pretend that he was hers again.

Just for one night.

* * *

Joe didn't get much time to think because, ten minutes later, another person hammered on his door. What now? he wondered irritably. He was still trying to figure out how the birds had got out. The lock seemed secure, so it looked as if—

As Joe approached the front door, he froze. It wasn't Ellen this time. Or his neighbour from the other side. The silhouette in the frosted window was a tall person, a man. Grey coat. Grey hair. It couldn't be. Joe swallowed hard and wondered if he should pretend to be out. But his car was in the drive, an upstairs window was open.

Maybe he just wouldn't answer.

The doorbell rang. Once. Twice. Three times. And then, to his dismay, his dad's voice yelled, 'I know you're in there. Open up or I'll say what I have to right here in the street.'

Joe wrenched the door open and stood in front of the man he hadn't seen in fourteen years. His breath caught in his throat as he took in the fact that his dad had aged. The face was lined, the back no longer as erect. The clothes not as slick as they used to be.

Geoff's hand dropped limply from the bell as he, too, looked at the son he hadn't seen.

'Well?' Joe said, trying to keep his voice steady, trying not to betray the weird emotions flooding through him. His hand held the door frame, barring the way in.

His dad coughed. 'Can I come in?'

'No.'

Geoff flinched, pursed his lips and sighed a little. 'OK. Fine. I didn't want to have to tell you like this, but if that's the way you want it—'

'What do you want me to do?' Joe asked, bewildered. 'You let me down. You were prepared to believe that I—that I—' He couldn't say it. The words stuck in his throat.

'I wasn't prepared to believe anything,' his dad said. 'But I had to say what I'd seen.'

'It wasn't what it looked like.' Joe raised his eyes upwards to stop the stupid tears that had sprung into them unexpectedly.

'Anyway,' he swallowed hard, 'I'm sure you haven't come to talk about that again, have you?'

Geoff shook his head. Then asked, 'Please can I come in?'

His dad in his house? 'No.'

His father bowed his head, his shoulders slumped. 'OK,' he nodded, 'fair enough. I, eh, just came to let you know . . .' He gulped. 'Well, I just came to tell you that your mother, well, she isn't too well.'

'What?'

'She—' His dad wiped a hand over his face. 'She's got early onset Alzheimer's. She's forgetting things. I thought you might like to see her before . . .' His voice faltered. 'Well, before she forgets you, Joe.'

Joe's hand dropped from the door. His mind whirled. His mother? She'd written to him every week when he was inside and he hadn't replied. Short letters. Funny letters. Sad letters. He'd read them all but he'd never written back. Not once. But she'd remembered him. Every single week.

After a pause, he said dully, 'Maybe better for her if she does forget me. Why would she want to remember, ey?'

His dad met his eyes. 'She loves you, Joe. We never believed you did anything, never. And her, most of all.'

Well, that was crap for a start. His father had twisted all the nice stuff he'd done into evidence against him.

'Please think about it,' Geoff said. 'You might regret it one day.'

'I can add it to the pile, so,' Joe made his voice hard. He nodded to his dad. 'See you.'

He closed the door on him, watching as his father turned and slowly made his way down the drive.

Joe stayed standing in the hall for twenty minutes before realising that tears were dripping off the end of his chin.

37

Thursday, 12th August

Aileen arrived two days ago. She's staying for a
month. Unfortunately I have to work for the next
week, but then I have holidays. Billy and Lizzie have
promised to look after her in the meantime. Billy
especially seems to be taken with her in a massive
way – I have never seen Billy offer to let any girl
drive his car, but when Aileen said she'd love to drive
it, Billy said OK. Lizzie and I gaped at each other,
then Lizzie said that Billy must have found it
tough.

'Found what tough?' Billy asked.

'Your personality transplant.'

We all cracked up and Billy went bright red –
another first. Then Aileen patted him on the head and
told him he was great and he said, 'See, see? Someone
appreciates me.' Then, to my horror, Dad offered to
bring her out on the boat and before I could warn her
she'd agreed to it. That made Dad think she was
great, too. Aileen is great, she sort of fits in with
everything in our house, just blends in as if she's
always been there. She says I'm so lucky to have
such a nice family and I suppose I am – though they
can be right pains sometimes.

Friday, 13th August

At the moment in work it's just me and Dessie, as Joe's granddad is sick and Joe is minding him and looking after his birds, too. I think he's deliberately not coming in to avoid being with me and Dessie. There's nothing to avoid really. Nothing has happened in work since, though Dessie did say he'd meet me in Dancesplash tomorrow night. I told him I'd text him when I got there if he gave me his mobile number and he said he'd give it to me but he forgot. He has mine, though. I gave it to him but he hasn't texted me yet.

Joe came to dinner in our house tonight. Even though he's not at work, he still managed to go fishing with my dad. And Dad invited him in for tea and in he came and, right through the meal, he totally ignored me. It was a bit hurtful so I told him I was sorry if I hurt his feelings but he didn't have to ignore me.

And he says, 'I'm not ignoring you. I just have nothing to say to you.'

I said, 'You ARE ignoring me.'

He said, 'Get over yourself, will you?'

And I said, and this was a good one, 'Well, there's no fear of me getting over you.'

So he upped and left and, of course, I had to try and explain why to Mammy and Dad. I said some rubbish about him being worried about his granddad and they muttered about how kind he was. But I told Aileen and Billy the real story. Aileen said he must be more hurt than he was letting on and Billy said that I was a bitch to say what I did. I feel a bit mean now.

Sunday, 15th August

Last night was great. Talk about dreams coming true.

We all went out clubbing. Aileen sat in the front seat

of Billy's car and shrieked obligingly as he drove like mad. It actually looks more dangerous than it is – Billy knows the roads we travelled so well. He knows when they widen so there really is no possibility of crashing. Lizzie, me and Billy's mate Johnny sat in the back and laughed at Aileen. She kept turning round and telling us to shut up. We arrived at the club and tumbled out of the car. Aileen told Billy that her legs were shaking so much she could barely walk. Billy gallantly offered to support her and she obligingly hung off him, all high heels and short skirt. Then she turned round and gave me a great big wink. I think she's quite into him, too.

Johnny looked a little glum. 'You're taken,' he said to me. 'Your friend seems to be taken. Who is left?' He glanced at Lizzie.

'I will call you,' Lizzie said, 'when I've exhausted all my other options.'

'Oh, I'd say you'd exhaust your other options all right,' Johnny chortled.

Lizzie belted him with her, quite frankly, horrendous red handbag.

The club we go to is over-eighteens and Mammy lets Lizzie go with us on condition that she won't drink. But of course Lizzie does. She can lash them back and it doesn't seem to take an effect on her. I think she shows off just to be in with Billy and me. I sometimes worry about her but Billy laughs and says there's no point, it's her parents' fault if she's out drinking at fourteen years of age. Anyway, loads of her friends get in too and she normally spends her night yabbering away to them and shrieking with laughter over silly things. I don't know how they're even let in, they don't even look eighteen.

Inside the place was heaving, but we grabbed a few seats in a little quiet corner that no one else wanted to sit in. And then I saw Dessie and I was so relieved as I hadn't heard from him since Friday and I had no way of contacting him. He waved and I walked over to talk to him, Billy whistling after me like the headcase he is.

'So, how you been since I last saw you at work?' Dessie asked. He was lounging against the wall and his eyes were all sparkly and his teeth all white and my heart flip-flopped like a pancake being tossed in the air.

'I've been good.' My voice shook a little. I was mad for him to touch me.

'I've been terrible.' He made an anguished face.

'Yeah. How?'

'Missed you.'

'That's the cheesiest line ever.'

'Aw,' he said, as the tip of his finger brushed the tip of my nose, 'but did your mother never tell you that cheese is good for you?' His brown eyes held mine like a hypnotist's. He moved in closer. His hand briefly touched mine.

I grinned. 'She did tell me that but I find cheese disgusting.'

'What do you like, then?' His voice was smooth as that shiny material that's impossible to sew.

'You,' I said. My mother would have had a fit. According to her, you should never tell a fella you like him. Well, I said, are men mind-readers? Are they psychic? She said, 'Well, I never told your father that I liked him. Men like a challenge.' I said back that Dad certainly found her a challenge and she had freaked. As usual.

'You like me?' Dessie feigned surprise.

'I certainly do.'

'How much?'

So I snogged the face off him.

Then we went outside to his car. Suffice to say that it wasn't just for driving.

Mam would have double freaked!

Monday, 16th August

Today in work was a bit mad. Seeing him respectably dressed. All nice and neat. I grinned at him as I came in and he grinned back.

'Thanks for Saturday,' he said.

'Thank you,' I said back. 'You've got a nice car.'

He laughed at that.

And that was it. That was all he said about it. I thought we'd be sneaking little kisses and little touches, but nothing. Instead, he indicated his desk. 'Got piles of work to do.'

My heart sank quicker than my sponge cakes had in home ec.

Then he said, 'Joe's granddad died Saturday night, did you hear?'

'No. Poor Joe.'

'Yeah, he found his granddad dead in an armchair when he got in from feeding his birds.'

'Oh God.'

'So he won't be in for ages now. You and me will have to sell a lot of ads to make up for him. Plus the funeral is tomorrow so I have to go.'

'I'll go, too.'

He didn't offer me a lift. I thought he would.

As it turned out Mammy, Dad, Lizzie, Billy and Aileen went to the funeral as well. The whole crowd from the paper were there and some of them had blagged lifts from Dessie, so maybe he couldn't have offered me a lift anyway.

Joe was up the front looking totally gutted, as were

his parents. His mother is a beautiful woman. Joe kind of looks like her. He's got her blonde brown hair and nice skin. I sat with my family and apologised to Aileen for bringing her to a funeral.

'Oh, it's cool. Billy has taken a half-day from work, so he's bringing me on a drive. We're getting lunch out. Your mother says she might come too but Billy hopes she won't as he'll have to drive really slowly to stop her nagging.'

I laughed.

My mother grimaced and pointed up the church at the coffin.

Friday, 20th August

I called over to Joe today. In his granddad's house. I felt I had to as I'm on holidays now. And by the time I get back to work the funeral will have been forgotten about and I might never get the chance to say sorry to him. And I don't want to be fighting with him now that he's so upset over his granddad.

It was a very weird experience. Joe is weird. Weirder than I thought.

He was out the back, sitting on his own on a kitchen chair, a can of lager beside him. He was looking at the birds. There seemed to be birds everywhere, some flying about, others locked up in these little sheds and making cooing noises. The grass was all squelchy and my heels sunk right into it. A bird shat on my shoulder.

'Shit!' I said, startling Joe.

'Literally,' he said wryly and we both kind of smiled at each other.

'Here, let me get a cloth.' He went into the house and I followed him. He located a smelly cloth under the sink and handed it to me. He watched as I wiped the stuff off my shoulder. It was disgusting.

'So,' he said, 'what brings you here?'

I put the cloth down, my hand STUNK! God, the hygiene in this house was not hygienic, to say the least.

'An apology to you,' I said, 'plus I want to say that I'm sorry about your granddad.'

He smiled, sort of wearily. Or warily – anyway, as if he wasn't quite trusting me.

'Well, apology accepted. Life's too short and all that, ey?'

'Yep.'

There was a pause then.

'D'you want a cuppa?' Without waiting for an answer, he shoved on the kettle. Out of the blue, he said, 'It was sudden in the end. Better for him. Better for me.'

'You must have got a shock.' I assumed it was the right thing to say. I've never had a friend who had someone who died on them before.

'Uh-huh. But he looked happy. Peaceful even.'

'God, he couldn't have been that happy.'

Joe laughed and shook his head and told me I was great.

'And how are you?' I asked then. He looked pretty rotten to me.

There was a slight hesitation before he admitted, without looking at me, 'Crap. But I just have to get on with it.' He passed me a cuppa and asked, 'How you getting on with Dessie?'

The subject change wrong-footed me. I didn't want anyone to ask that. Billy, Lizzie and Aileen kept teasing me and I had to pretend that we were having great fun in work. I embroidered the small positive things and tried to believe them myself. But work was just work. More work than before, in fact.

'Well?' Joe asked.

'Well, we're working loads. Dessie takes his work seriously as you know—'

'He's gone all cold on you, hasn't he?' Joe said. I don't think he was being mean.

'No!' I laughed a little and waved my hand in the air and hit it off the table which hurt like hell.

'That looked sore,' Joe remarked.

'It's fine. We're fine. Work is great.'

He said nothing to this.

'Anyway.' I went on, making things worse for myself now that I think about it. 'Dessie and I have a working relationship when we, eh, work and anyway, what we have is like nothing to do with you. So butt out.'

'I said nothing,' Joe answered. I think he was a little bewildered.

'And,' I said, 'if you for one moment think he used me – well, you're wrong.'

'I never said that either,' he said.

'Oh shut up!' I said. I actually think I shouted it.

'Hey, Meg—' Joe grabbed my arm, which was not a good idea.

'Let me go!' I shouted. 'You pontificating know-it-all!'

He actually laughed which made me furious and I slapped him.

And in walked his dad.

To my absolute shame, I burst into tears and ran out.

I don't know what happened after that.

38

Anto was enthusiastic, that was for sure, Joe thought. Even though the boy didn't talk much, his eagerness was evident in the way he did whatever was asked of him. Joe laughed to himself at how Anto talked to the birds as he deposited them in their basket. He knew all their names and could mimic Joe's whistle so that the birds flew to him sometimes.

'That's great,' Joe said as he closed the lid of the basket on the final pigeon.

'Can I come with you tonight to register them?' Anto asked, following him to the shed. 'I used to go with me da all the time.'

Joe said nothing, reluctant to commit himself. He might end up having to bring the kid all the time then.

Anto turned away. 'Forget it.'

'I didn't say no,' Joe muttered.

'You didn't say yes.'

'You're a cheeky little brat, aren't you?'

'Feck off.'

Joe laughed and Anto turned and glared at him.

'OK,' Joe relented, feeling sorry for him, 'you can come if your mother says it's OK. But you better behave.'

Anto didn't smile. 'Are you only messing with me?'

'Nope.'

'Right. Thanks.' He didn't say it in a delighted way. Joe admired that. It was like a, 'Hey, don't put yourself out, I don't care'.

'So,' Joe attempted some ordinary conversation, 'how many pigeons did your dad have?'

Anto shrugged. 'Not as many as you. And none as good-looking as Prince. But one of his birds came second in a race once.'

'Yeah?'

'He won money and we went to the pub and he bought drinks for everyone and Mam went mad and Dad said,' Anto assumed what Joe supposed was his dad's stance, '"That's the way it's done".'

'It sure is.' Joe put the basket of birds on the ground. 'You have to share your winnings. Bet you miss him, huh?'

Anto nodded. 'We had to sell his birds. I was really angry about it.'

Joe remembered selling off his granddad's birds. It had been horrible, too. 'I bet you were,' he nodded.

'You would have liked my da,' Anto said, following behind Joe like an over-eager puppy. 'And he might have liked you. A little bit anyway.'

'Gee, thanks,' Joe deadpanned.

Anto sniggered.

Getting in to see their mother was like getting into Fort Knox. They had to produce their visitors' passes, they had to flash ID and finally they were led into the visiting room with the strict instruction that it was non-smoking.

'This just gets better and better,' Lizzie grumbled.

'I thought you'd be glad there was no smoking,' her father said.

Lizzie sighed. 'This might be a good time to tell you, actually—' she began.

'Here's Mam,' Billy announced loudly, poking Lizzie in the ribs.

She didn't know what had come over her. Trying to upset her father by admitting she smoked, just as his prisoner wife was being escorted in to see him? But surely her smoking would be the least of his problems now. And besides, she was twenty-eight and entitled to ruin her health if she wanted. Not that she did, but she liked a smoke.

'—you?'

Lizzie suddenly realised that her dad, Billy and her mother were all looking at her.

'Sorry? What?'

'She hasn't been herself since you went to prison,' her father said reprovingly to his wife.

'Oh, don't blame me because she's got thin,' her mother snapped back. 'I was asking how you were, Lizzie.'

'Fine,' Lizzie said.

'Well, you don't look fine.' Her mother looked her up and down. 'Big black circles under your eyes, white face. Are you working too hard?'

'It's off with Tom,' Billy said for her. 'She's been a bit upset.'

Even the mention of his name made Lizzie weepy.

'And him about to make it big!' Her mother threw her eyes skyward. 'I saw him in the paper. What happened?'

'Just broke up,' Lizzie said. 'It doesn't really matter.'

'*He* doesn't really matter.' Mrs Walsh patted her daughter's hand. 'You don't pine after him, now. I always said there's something wrong with a man who pretends to be somebody else for a living just to be clapped by a bunch of strangers in a silly room with curtains.'

Lizzie smiled. 'Nice to see you haven't lost your practical side in here, Mam.'

'Not at all. Here isn't so bad.'

Billy was looking around. His eyes came to rest on a small, slim, blonde girl across the way. 'Is she a prisoner, too?' he asked.

'Yes. She's in because . . . Oh now, what did she tell me?' Mrs Walsh screwed up her eyes. 'Oh yes, she's a teacher and she had an affair with a sixteen-year-old boy. It was in the papers, apparently.'

'Lucky boy,' Billy grinned as his mother slapped his arm.

'Disgusting, it is,' she snapped. 'But I must say, she's a very nice girl. She's helping some of the others to read in here. And the boy she slept with comes to visit her, which is nice I suppose. No hard feelings.'

'No, it's not his feelings that'd be hard,' Billy snorted.

Lizzie giggled too.

'It's no wonder Aileen left with that sort of filth for a brain. Have you heard from —'

'So, when are you going to apologise?' Kevin Walsh demanded, cutting short the exchange. 'Or am I going to have to get used to living on my own for the foreseeable future?'

Polly Walsh looked aghast. 'Apologise? Me? I'm not going to apologise. They'll have to let me out sooner or later. They can't keep me in here with all these people who've broken the law.'

'*You've* broken the law,' her husband said.

'I have not!' His wife glared at him and some people visiting the blonde woman glanced across, before quickly averting their eyes. 'I have only stood up for my rights as a free Irish citizen.'

'By breaking the law.'

'Well, I won't be apologising,' Mrs Walsh folded her arms.

'Wonderful.'

A silence descended on the four of them.

'They've all sorts of weirdos in here,' Polly Walsh said after a bit, when she realised her husband was no longer going to talk. 'The woman in the cell with me, she's in because she burned her ex-boyfriend's house down.'

'Christ!' Billy exclaimed.

'She said he had it coming. He was having this big affair with a work colleague and he kept telling her he was on business trips and stuff and then she found out.'

'How?' Lizzie asked. Her mother had a great way of telling a story. Normally by embroidering the details, though Lizzie had a feeling that the stories behind the people here wouldn't need improving.

Mrs Walsh lowered her voice. 'Well, she decided to go away for a weekend with a few friends and then had a huge row with one of them and decided to come home. And what does she find?'

'What?' Billy and Lizzie asked together.

Their dad had crossed his arms and was feigning disinterest.

'Her boyfriend in bed *with another man*. He was gay on top of it all! He said he was just experimenting. She said, "Experiment with this", and she lit his curtains on fire and the place went up like a house of straw. Apparently.'

'God.'

'Yes. She's sorry about it now, of course. And her ex-boyfriend has forgiven her, as well he might, but she's in for another few months. I told her that she should have just got on with her life and not let her ex ruin it for her. She said that's what she's going to do.'

'And what did she tell you?' Mr Walsh asked in a very superior tone of voice.

'Nothing. I'm right and that's it. I'm not for turning.'

'So you're saying that we'll have to trudge up here week after week to see you?'

'No. Only if you want to.'

Mr Walsh sighed.

'Of course we want to,' Lizzie intervened, 'but it's just we'd like to see you out, Mammy.'

'I'd like to be out,' Mrs Walsh said. 'You've no idea of the awful people in this place. But at the same time I can't give up on my principles. We are what we do, you know.'

Lizzie winced.

'Oh, well that's it then, isn't it?' Mr Walsh rose to his feet. 'You're obviously a woman who puts a harbour plan before the good of her family.'

'Before *your* good, you mean,' his wife scoffed. 'Just because you have to make your own dinner now and clean up after it, that's all you're worried about.'

'Don't be ridiculous.' Mr Walsh leaned his hands on the table and glared at his wife. 'I'm well capable of cooking a meal. I just don't like you being in this place, that's all.'

'I don't like being here either, but I will stay as long as I have to.'

'A simple sorry and you can continue with the protest. Martha is organising something for this weekend.'

'Well she might,' Mrs Walsh sniffed. 'She abandoned ship pretty quickly.'

'Look, Polly—'

'No, I'm not discussing it. I'd rather talk about how you all are. Billy, I believe, before your father interrupted—' she shot her husband a withering look, 'that we were discussing Aileen. How is she?'

Billy flinched. He hated talking about Aileen just as much as Lizzie hated talking about Tom.

'She refuses to take my calls,' Billy said, 'so I don't know how she is.'

'Wonderful!'

'Yes, well maybe if you weren't behind bars you'd have a better chance of sorting your kids out,' Mr Walsh said with a hint of triumph.

'You're their father, you sort it out.'

'Eh, newsflash,' Billy said, 'I can sort myself out, thanks.'

'And how are you managing the mortgage?' Mrs Walsh asked.

'Aileen's still paying her share,' Billy said. 'She has to if she wants to keep it going.'

'Well, aren't we a wonderful bunch?' Mr Walsh said wearily. 'Mother in jail, son separated from his pregnant girlfriend, daughter split from boyfriend and father at home trying to stay sane.'

'Oh, don't be so negative.' Mrs Walsh dismissed him with a wave of her hand. 'We're going to have two grandchildren; Lizzie has split from a man who bought her a kite; and you have a wife who sticks to her principles. You always were one for looking on the gloomy side, Kevin.'

'No, I've always been a realist,' Mr Walsh said. 'You, on the other hand, have lived all your life with your head stuck firmly in the sand.'

'Here.' Billy, to stop the argument in its tracks, shoved forward the picture of the baby scan. 'It's the twins.'

They watched as Polly slowly reached out and picked up the scan. She brought her face close to it as she wasn't wearing her glasses. Her features softened and her mouth opened in an expression of wonder. Her eyes caught Billy's.

'Beautiful,' she whispered. 'I can actually see the two of them.'

'Yeah.'

'Oh, Billy, you have to get that girl back. She was good for you.'

Billy winced once more but didn't deny it.

'I think this one is the image of you,' his mother said then, pointing at the baby on the left. 'He has your nose.'

'That's his foot, Mammy. You're holding it upside-down.'

It made them laugh.

It was no use – he had to talk to someone. After Anto left he tried to distract himself by doing all sorts of stupid things. Making his bed. Cleaning the windows of the house. He even swept the kitchen floor. But all the time thoughts of his mother kept flitting in and out of his head. She was ill. She'd forget him. Maybe it was for the best. How could it be for the best?

There was only one person he felt he could ask, but he wasn't sure how he could explain it right. He didn't want Ellen to judge him. But she'd forgiven the man who had killed her husband and was presently trying to rehabilitate the boy who'd broken into her house, so surely she could listen to him.

He made it to her front door and had his hand up to press the doorbell, when he suddenly felt violently ill. There was no way . . .

'Joseph?' Ellen had obviously seen him. She had the door open and was peering at him in surprise. 'What do you want?'

He stood like a thick, with his mouth open and his hand half in the air. 'Aw, nothing. It's fine.'

'Are you OK? You've gone a little pale. How's Anto? Is this about Anto? His mother says he's like new since you've let him help you. I must say it's a very good thing you're doing Joseph and I—'

'It isn't about Anto.'

'Oh.'

'Can I come in?'

Without saying anything she stood aside and let him into her hall.

257

'Would you like a cup of tea?'

He needed more than a cup of tea but he nodded anyway. In silence he followed Ellen into her kitchen and sat at her table as she bustled about getting biscuits and milk and putting them in front of him. Finally she handed him a huge mug of tea and sat opposite him as he poured some milk into it.

'What's the matter?' Her voice was suddenly gentle. 'You look upset.'

This could be the last time he might ever sit at this table, Joe thought in a detached way. He'd come to like Ellen and her spiky ways. Even though she was old, he liked her company.

'My dad called to see me the other night,' he said haltingly.

Ellen's mouth dropped open. 'I thought you had no parents,' she said.

Joe shrugged and looked into his cup. The tea was still and he could almost see the reflection of his face.

'I haven't talked to them in a long time,' he muttered. 'They let me down.'

'Oh.'

He wrapped his hands about the mug. 'Anyway, my dad, he told me that my mother is ill. Alzheimer's. He wants me to visit her before she forgets.'

Ellen said nothing.

Joe brought his eyes to meet hers. 'I don't know what to do.'

There was the longest pause. Ellen seemed to be thinking.

'You do,' she said simply.

'No, I don't.'

'Can you forgive them for how they let you down?'

'He says he didn't mean to. That he had to.'

She said nothing.

'I think it's crap.'

'Joe, do you want to tell me the whole story?'

He shook his head.

'Look,' Ellen said, 'I can't tell you what to do. You have to decide. I can't even advise you because I don't know what they did to you. If they hit you or abused you, then I wouldn't worry

258

about going to see them. But sometimes . . .' She paused. 'Sometimes we think people have let us down and they haven't.'

'They let me down.'

'Anto was angry at his dad for a long time because he died. That's the way kids think, you know?'

'I wasn't a kid.'

'Oh.'

'I was twenty.'

'I see.'

Only she didn't. She couldn't possibly see. This wasn't at all what he'd hoped for. He needed someone to tell him what he should do. He couldn't decide. He hated what they'd done, but he loved them too.

'My dad,' he began, swallowing hard, wondering how he could explain without shocking her. 'Well, I was up in court a few years ago. My dad testified against me.'

'Should he have?'

'I didn't do it, if that's what you mean.'

'Do what, Joe?' Ellen's voice had gone quiet. She touched his arm. 'What did you not do?'

He flinched. No one had touched him in so long. Not in a caring way, anyway. He swallowed hard and closed his eyes.

'They—they accused me of . . .' He couldn't say it, he could never say it.

'Go on.'

'A girl was found on the beach, washed up and the last person she'd been with was me. On my dad's boat.' He met Ellen's eyes. 'She was dead. Apparently someone had hit her across the head. It wasn't me, Ellen. I swear.' He dashed his hand across his face. He hadn't talked about this in years. He'd never talked about it, actually.

Ellen looked shocked, he'd known she would.

'My dad testified that I'd had a row with the girl a few days previously. He testified that I liked her and that I'd been a little aggressive towards her during the row. I'd only grabbed her arm, Ellen.'

259

There. It was out.

'Joe,' Ellen said softly. 'Anyone who knows you knows you'd never do that.'

'The jury didn't. I got life.'

'Oh, you poor lad.'

'I didn't do it, Ellen. I don't know how she ended up on that beach. I kept thinking I was in a nightmare and I'd wake up, only it got worse. My dad put the nail in my coffin.'

'What could he do, Joe? If he lied, I'd imagine it would be because he didn't believe you. He probably thought he had no choice. He probably thought telling the truth was the best thing.'

Joe said nothing. He hadn't looked at it like that. If his dad had lied, maybe that would have been because he believed the evidence damning. Instead, he'd told the truth and been devastated when Joe was convicted. He'd written but Joe had ignored his letters, refusing to have any visitors.

'You sometimes have to look at things from a different angle,' Ellen said, 'in order to fully understand.'

'Thanks for believing me,' Joe said quietly.

'Of course I believe you!' Ellen looked at him as if he were bonkers. Then added, 'Can I give you some advice?'

He shrugged.

'I often wondered why you never went out. Why you never had a girlfriend. Why all the people who call to your house are older then you. Now I know.'

'Yeah, I'm a complete saddo.' He said it with a small grin.

'No,' Ellen shook her head. 'You're still living as if you're in prison. You have to get back out there, Joe. Start to live again.'

He supposed she was right. But it was harder than anyone knew to step back out into the world again. Even getting a job was a huge task. His parole officer had arranged it for him. Another person who'd thought he was innocent. Walls, though, became safe after a bit.

'Do you think I should go home?' He asked the question he'd come to ask.

'Joe, you are obsessed with birds that fly home to you. You

260

spend your Saturdays looking into the sky to see them arrive. Why is that?'

He swallowed. This woman knew more about him than he knew himself.

'It's just brilliant to see.'

'Yes,' she said.

He knew that was the end of the conversation.

39

'LIZZIE, IT'S LORI.'

'Oh, hi,' Lizzie grinned, delighted the woman had rung. She had been dying to find out what had happened her. 'You sound happy.'

'I am,' Lori said. 'Thanks to you.'

'Oh now, you did it yourself. I just listened.'

It was so good to have a happy ending, Lizzie thought. Things like this rarely happened. Callers, once they had their lives sorted out, forgot about ringing again, which Lizzie supposed was a success of sorts. But it was good to know. To be told. To have a definite end to a problem.

'And so did Larry. That's my husband. He is so apologetic, you wouldn't believe.'

'Pardon?' Her heart gave a quick flip over. 'Your husband?'

'Yes. He came over last week and begged, I mean *begged* me to lift the barring order and I said "no way".'

'Good for you.' Her heart slowed down a bit.

'And yesterday he came again, with flowers and tickets to Barcelona. I've always wanted to go there and he remembered that. And he said he would do anything, *anything* to see us back together again.' She paused before adding, 'He can't live without me.'

'And you said?' Lizzie desperately hoped her instinct was wrong.

'I said . . . well, I sort of made him sweat, like I had a right to do, but in the end, we got back together.'

'Why?' Lizzie's voice came out sounding quite sharp. Across the office, Anna glanced at her. 'Why did you do that? Are you so cheap you can be bought off with a tacky bunch of flowers and some tickets?'

'They were not tacky flowers!'

'This man bullied you. Is he going for anger management?'

'Well,' Lori swallowed, 'well, yes. If you think he should.'

'Lori, what do *you* think? For God's sake—'

Anna firmly disconnected the call.

'What did you do that for?' Lizzie whirled on her. 'The woman is insane. Do you know what she did? She—'

'Lizzie, you are there to listen. From what I heard, this woman just wanted you to do that. You can't go abusing people.'

'Yes I can, especially when some woman is about to make a huge mistake.'

'No, you can't.' Anna gently shook her head. 'You know you can't.' She paused, and then asked, 'What is wrong with you, huh?'

'What is wrong with you, more like?'

Anna said nothing.

'Sorry,' Lizzie mumbled, bowing her head. 'I'm sorry. I know I shouldn't have done that, but when someone is doing something stupid, and you can't warn them, what can you do?'

'In my experience, Lizzie,' Anna said, 'people will always pretty much do what they want to do. You can talk to them all you want but in the end they'll do what suits.'

'I don't believe that.'

'I begged my husband not to take his life.'

Lizzie swallowed hard.

'I knew he was depressed, I knew he wanted to die and I begged him, Lizzie.' Anna sat on the desk. 'I pointed out all the good things to him, but it made no difference. He wanted . . .' She paused. 'No, I think he felt he needed to die.'

'He wasn't well.'

'Neither is Lori. She's in love. It's another type of insanity. Only she can get rid of that man and you have helped her do it once. She'll ring again. You'll see.' Anna looked at her sympathetically. 'Come on, Lizzie, cheer up.'

Lizzie swallowed hard. Anna was right, she knew that. 'I'm sorry. I'm a bit all over the place recently.'

'I noticed. Is it Tom?'

'Partly.'

Anna squeezed her arm. 'Want a coffee?'

'Yep.'

'Sit tight.'

They smiled at each other.

Graham, the owner of the health centre, called him in just as he had pulled on his parka jacket. A few of the women from his late class called out a 'goodbye' to him as they left and Joe waved.

Since the chat with Ellen, he'd made more of an attempt to try to connect with people, to be the way he was before. But he knew, of course, that that would never happen. But then again, no one was ever the same as they were when they were younger. And, if he were honest, he preferred some aspects of himself now. He had always been quiet, and now he accepted he was quiet instead of having to fight against it by drinking too much and doing stupid things. He accepted the fact that he didn't have a magnetic personality like Dessie and that was OK, too. He realised he had finally accepted himself. And he was kind of proud that he had survived twelve years in prison.

'Joe,' Graham beckoned him into his office, 'come here a second, would you?'

'Yeah?' Joe stood just inside the door, his hands sunk deep into his jacket pockets, trying to give the impression that he really would like to go home.

'It's just a warning to you not to ring in sick at short notice again, OK?'

'Yeah,' Joe dipped his head, 'sorry about that. I couldn't help it.'

'Joe, I know you've been in prison,' Graham went on. 'I know what for. You told me at your interview. You also told me you were innocent and you also told me you would work hard. I wasn't sure whether to believe you but my brother, the do-gooder in the family,' he raised his eyes and Joe tried not to grin, 'told me to give you a chance. He said I wouldn't regret it. Now so far I haven't regretted it. Don't make me. OK?'

Joe swallowed hard and nodded. He loved this job. He couldn't lose it. It was important to him to teach people how to swim. So that they wouldn't drown and be washed up on a beach somewhere.

'Go on, then.' Graham paused. 'You're the best teacher here, Joe. Just so you know.'

'Ta.'

'And the best assistant manager we've had.'

'Good.'

'Hop it, right.'

He met Lizzie at the Luas stop. She seemed to be in glum form.

'What's up?' he asked.

'Nothing.' She wouldn't look at him. Then she asked, 'How did your birds do on Saturday? Sorry I couldn't be there.'

'I had a second and a fifth.'

'Second?' She seemed surprised. 'I thought Prince was out of action.'

'He is, but Hero came good for me. And if he hadn't spent so much time hopping around the place when he got back, I might have got a first.'

'Great.' She knew she didn't even sound convincing. But honestly, what was she to do now? Kidnap Hero? She was running out of options. No matter what she did, Joe just seemed to bounce back. Tougher measures were called for.

'You're in a bad mood,' Joe remarked, sounding amused, as the Luas came to a stop. 'Bad day?'

'You could say that.' She wished he'd get lost. It was all his fault she felt so lousy. Joe followed her on to the train and sat in beside her. To her annoyance, he actually seemed happy.

'You must have had a good day,' she said.

He shrugged. 'No, I didn't. My boss gave me an earful just before I left.'

'Oh.'

'Listen, Lizzie, are you up for doing me a favour?' He nudged her with his elbow and smiled at her.

Unbearably upbeat. Lizzie wanted to slap the handsomeness from his face. She wanted to tear his eyes out. She wanted to cry. But she couldn't.

'A favour?' she asked.

'Yeah. It's a bit of a biggie. I just thought you might like to do it. If not, I'll ask one of the lads in the club.'

'What is it?'

'I'm heading away for a night next week. Would you feed the birds for me? Anto will probably be around, too, so you'll have help. I can leave you instructions and stuff.'

Lizzie nodded. 'Sure. No worries.' She attempted a smile. 'Thanks for thinking of me.'

'Thanks.' Another grin. 'Glad that cheered you up.'

Oh, she thought, it certainly had.

40

THE FOYER OF the theatre was crowded, which was a relief. At least, thought Lizzie, I can blend. She unwound her bright orange scarf from her neck in an effort to do just that. Pushing her way through the throng, she ordered a glass of wine at the bar before finding a corner in which to drink it.

The place was buzzing, which was good sign. Tom had told her once that when a theatre foyer buzzed, it signalled that the play was a success. Lizzie hoped it was true. Up on the walls there were pictures of the production. Small groups of people were gathered around some of them, chatting and making remarks about the actors. A black-and-white of Imogen and Tom locked in an embrace caught her eye and she told herself firmly that it was only acting.

'Hey.'

Lizzie's wine slopped out of her glass. She hadn't noticed Domo, Tom's best friend, at all.

'Hi,' she said faintly.

'How's things?'

'OK.' Lizzie wondered if she should she ask about Tom. About the play.

The silence dragged a little until Domo broke it by muttering, 'Good to see you, you know.'

Lizzie lifted her gaze from the contents of her wine glass and smiled. 'Good to see you, too.'

'I suppose I shouldn't say this,' Domo said awkwardly, 'but he misses you like hell. Like he doesn't say it, but we all know because he's back to the way he was before.'

'Before?'

'Yeah, before you came along. Jesus, he could be a miserable bastard.'

Lizzie couldn't imagine Tom being grumpy – well, not unless he got teased about having one line in a play. The memory was bittersweet.

'He's probably just stressed,' she offered.

'Oh, he's stressed all right.' Domo rolled his eyes as he finished his drink. Placing the empty glass on the sill behind he said, 'Anyway, he'll be glad you came, I'd say.'

'Have to support him, see what all the fuss is about.'

Domo grinned. 'It's a good play, I saw it the opening night. Are you going to come for a drink afterwards?'

'No, no, I don't think so.' She smiled. 'I don't think Tom would appreciate it.'

'I think he would.'

Lizzie shook her head and was saved from answering by the announcement that the play was about to start.

Domo bent over and kissed her cheek and asked her to think about it.

She said she would, but knew she wouldn't.

In the pub things were a bit strained. Try as he might, Joe could not shake the feeling that Cid had something to do with Prince's tag being removed. Of course he couldn't just blurt it out or say anything, Cid would have him up for slander or something. But the guy was doing his head in. Ever since it had happened, Cid had been making jokey comments about Prince retiring early from competitive sport.

'I've heard of women retiring from their career to start families, but this is ridiculous,' he chortled.

'Shut up,' Joe said quietly.

'Aw, will you relax, I'm only having a laugh,' Cid said.

'My bird is out of action because *someone*,' Joe stressed the 'someone', 'took his tag off and in the process hurt his leg. I don't think that's particularly funny. Do you, John?'

John held up his hands. 'Look, maybe we'll change the subject.'

'I'm only having a laugh. Can you not take a joke, Joe?'

'I've taken a lot of shit from you,' Joe said firmly, 'but I'm not taking any more.'

'Shit from me?' Cid looked genuinely bewildered. 'What shit have you taken from me? I helped you build your lofts. I gave up my Saturday once to help you build them.'

'Yeah, once I wasn't winning you'd do anything to help, ey? I wonder now if you have a spare key to my loft, seeing as you fit the locks.'

'Aw, Joe,' Noel made placating motions with his hands, 'you can't—'

'And what is that supposed to mean?' Cid pushed back his chair and, standing up, poked Joe hard in the arm. 'Go on, what are you saying?'

'He's saying nothing, sure you're not, Joe?' Noel glared at him.

'I'm just saying,' Joe stood up, too, 'that it's very funny that now I'm winning, my bird suddenly goes missing. That you somehow think it's a laugh.'

Cid's eyes narrowed. 'Come again?'

'You heard me.' Joe gave him a shove. 'And you know what else? The only other time you got placed was when my birds didn't race. And another time Prince didn't win, it was because someone let a fecking load of pigeons up when he was flying in.'

'Joe!' Noel stood now. 'Will you stop!'

'Now that,' Cid rolled his eyes and appealed to the table, 'is mental. You're some liar, d'you know that?'

Liar. If there was one thing he hated being called it was a liar. He lunged out and caught Cid by the scruff of his jumper.

'Don't you ever call me a liar, you little toerag!' He shoved Cid from him and Cid was about to lunge towards him when he was caught by Noel and held back.

'Let me at him. How dare he! That is – is – slander, so it is!'

John put a restraining hand on Joe's arm. The barman came hurrying over.

'That is enough,' Noel said firmly to Joe. He turned to Cid, 'And you, you stop annoying him, right?'

'I'll sue you!' Cid shouted, his face red and furious.

'Yeah, right!' Joe shouted back.

'Out!' The barman said. 'NOW!'

Lizzie didn't want the lights to go on at the end of the play. She had sat in the dark, watching, her heart sore as Tom wowed the audience. His beautiful resonant voice was clear as sunlight in a blue sky as it flowed out over the auditorium. It was like listening to a brilliant musician as he played his instrument. And he dominated every scene: Tom was the actor everyone looked at, even when he wasn't doing anything. Imogen, who played the love of his life, was not so brilliant, Lizzie thought with something approaching delight. And no way was she being bitchy. The people sitting beside her, right at the back, thought so, too. She overheard them wondering how Imogen had got cast.

'Probably sleeping with the director,' the man scoffed. 'Oh no,' the girl with him said, 'I read in some column or other that she's dating Tommy Lynch.'

Lizzie flinched. But Domo would have told her if Tom was seeing someone. Or would he? Well, he certainly wouldn't have asked her for a drink afterwards if that were the case.

As the second half got under way, she tried to imagine how she would feel if she was still seeing Tom. How proud and happy she'd be watching him. She'd probably go most nights and, by the end of the run, she'd know all his lines by heart. She'd definitely have dragged her parents along and he'd have impressed them big time.

But it was stupid speculating like that, she chided herself midway through the second half. Watching Tom perform was akin to looking at a train she'd narrowly missed. Waving from the platform as the life she could have had trundled on by. She wasn't with Tom any more – she was just a member of the audience. She didn't realise that tears were trickling down her face until just before the end.

As the house lights went up, the audience began to rise, applauding all the while.

Lizzie dashed a hand over her face and rose, too. The cast stood onstage, holding hands and bowing. One. Two. Three times.

Then the male lead stood out from the centre and bowed. People cheered. She saw Tom, who was holding hands with Imogen, say something to her and Imogen's face lit up and Lizzie saw, as if magnified, the extra squeeze she gave his hand.

Tom was happy, Lizzie knew it by looking at him. Domo had probably been trying to make her feel better by saying he was miserable. In all her time with him, Lizzie could never remember Tom looking so alive as he did at that moment, holding hands with the pretty girl who played opposite him. It was funny how she felt so detached about it. And yet, she thought in amazement, she was crying.

Without thinking, she started to push her way out. Luckily she was only three seats from the edge and at the very back. She excused herself and was soon out in the foyer, taking deep, calming breaths.

She had lost him, she realised, and not because he had let her go but because she had wandered so far away that she wasn't sure she could ever go back.

'You idiot,' John scolded as he drove Joe home. 'What on earth did you let him get to you for?'

Joe shrugged.

'You've walked into it now, you know. He's just the kind of man who'd have you for assault.'

'I've been accused of worse,' Joe muttered.

John obviously didn't believe him as he took no notice. 'I think you're barking up the wrong tree anyway. Cid would never do that.'

Joe rubbed his hands over his face. 'I can't think of anyone else who would.'

'Cid is a pain, I'll admit. But he loves the birds. You're way out of line, Joe.'

'So how do *you* think Prince lost his tag?'

John shrugged. 'I dunno. It's a mystery. Maybe some kids . . . I dunno.' His voice trailed off before he asked, 'And what's the story with the pigeons getting in Prince's way?'

Joe told him the story and finished to find John staring at him incredulously.

'It's true, I swear.'

John said nothing. Joe got the uneasy feeling that John thought he was imagining things.

Billy was at home when Lizzie arrived back. His mobile phone sat on the table beside him.

'Aileen's dad rang. She's coming to collect all her things next week,' he said glumly. 'And then she wants to discuss what to do with the house.'

Lizzie's heart sank even further. 'How does that make you feel?' She sat beside him and tried to peer into his face.

'If I could take back that look, I would,' Billy said. 'But I can't. And apparently she can't forget it.'

'But sure,' Lizzie spluttered, 'when she comes, just say that to her.'

He shrugged. 'Sometimes no reason is good enough for how much you hurt someone.'

A small chill wrapped itself around her. 'She'll come round, you'll see.'

Billy didn't reply.

41

ALONE. IN JOE'S house. He'd gone off about an hour earlier, apparently heading home.

'I thought you didn't like home,' Lizzie said, enjoying his discomfort.

Joe had dumped his coffee down the sink and stared out at the back garden. 'My mother is sick,' he'd said, 'so I figured . . .' He let the sentence hang.

She had feigned concern but he'd brushed it off. Instead he'd handed her the keys to the house and the lofts, accompanied by a list of instructions.

'You can get Anto to help you,' he said. 'He's not a bad little guy. And John and Noel are around if you run into problems. Noel will call to bring the birds on a training toss tomorrow.'

Lizzie had just fed the birds. Well, overfed the birds, and now here she was, standing in the centre of Joe's living room.

She gazed around and contempt for everything in it rose within her. It seeped right through her so she wasn't even aware that she was grinding her teeth and clenching her hands. She detested his crappy pale cream walls and scuffed floorboards. His CD collection and his DVDs. He seemed to like thrillers and comedies and his CDs were mostly singer-songwriters. She was so tempted to take them all out and grind them under her feet. But, knowing him, he'd have insurance and get the whole lot replaced with new stuff.

There were no photographs, no cards, nothing personal in the room. It was as if Joe was a blank canvas. A nowhere man.

She left the front room, giving the door a bit of a kick on the way out, and turned to climb the stairs, her hand gripping the banister. She knew what she was doing was wrong, but that only made it better. She was beyond caring what she did to Joe now, so long as she didn't get found out.

It wasn't a huge house. A narrow landing with three bedrooms and a bathroom leading off it. The first room she went into was small and totally empty, the floorboards dusty and neglected. Nothing in the built-in wardrobe.

She left and entered Joe's bedroom. She knew it was his because bits of him were all over the place. A pigeon racing magazine was thrown casually across his bed, which had been pushed up alongside the window. It sported a surprisingly clean blue and white duvet. The walls were painted a disgusting green and more books on pigeons were piled higgledy-piggledy on the floor at the end of the bed. A mirror and some aftershave took up space on a battered bedside locker. A small TV stood on a table in the corner. No lampshade covered the bulb. The room was functional, a place to sleep. Lizzie peered inside his wardrobe. Jeans and tracksuits. Nothing. She rifled along the shelves. Again, nothing.

Finally, after a fruitless search, she made her way to the bathroom. It, too, was clean. There was lino on the floor that was vaguely ugly and white tiles on the wall. Shampoos and a bottle of cleaning fluid were lined along the bath. Boring.

At length she entered the third bedroom. Small, like the first, there were a couple of sealed cardboard boxes on the floor. One of the boxes had split and books poked out through the tear. Lizzie very gently made the hole larger. More books spilled on to the floor. Bird books and fishing books. Nothing else.

Lizzie wasn't exactly sure what she'd hoped to achieve by poking around. Maybe just knowing that she'd invaded his privacy would be enough – just to hug the knowledge to herself while she broke his life. The thought made her jump. *Broke his life*. Lizzie winced. But what else was she doing? This man had murdered

274

her sister. Taken her on to a boat, hit her and then thrown her overboard. And now he was out. Free. Living his life. There was no way around it, no way she could see over it. She would only be happy when she'd broken his life.

So she hunkered down and pulled the sealing tape off the second box, knowing she could retape it. Inside, more books. Jesus, did this guy ever stop? There was surely only so much you could know about birds. There were a few videotapes, too, all about pigeons and pigeon breeders. It was no wonder he was still single, she thought. And then, right at the bottom of the box, she found some envelopes bound with elastic. Letters from Rossclare. It suddenly dawned on Lizzie that this was the stuff Joe had taken from prison with him. He'd boxed it and never looked at it since.

With shaking hands she pulled the first letter from its envelope.

Joseph, darling,

We miss you terribly and cry every night. You know we don't blame you for what happened, but we can't understand it either. Think, Joseph, please think. Try and remember the phone number of the text. Anything. Try, please, to give us some explanation for what happened that night. Is it possible you blanked out and don't recall? That can happen, you know. She was on your boat. With you. You have to know.

Your father is devastated. He blames himself for your conviction. I'm only trying to help both of you. Please read this and reply.

Please say you'll let us visit.

Your mother, who loves you.

Dear Mr Jones,

Your application for appeal has been lodged.

Yours sincerely,

Messrs Frank O'Toole & Associates.

Dearest Joseph,

I know you do not wish us to contact you, but I feel you must be reading our letters as they are not being returned. I am sorry to hear that your appeal will not go ahead. It is not fair. I know how upset you must be and I wish I could visit you.

I also want to tell you what happened yesterday. I hope it will give you hope. I was in church, on my own, lighting a candle for you and praying for a miracle when, just as I turned to leave, in walked Megan Walsh's father. I forget his name. I got a terrible shock, Joseph, not because I believe you are guilty but because this man does. I didn't know what he would say or do.

Anyway, we looked at each other for a bit and then he held out his hand.

And I started to cry.

He patted me on the arm and said that he didn't blame me or your dad for any of this. I wanted to say to him that he shouldn't blame you either, Joseph, but I didn't. I wish I had but this man had lost his daughter and we still have you and so I just told him that I was sorry for his loss.

He thanked me and said we should always be able to pass each other and nod. That meant a lot because some people are not talking to us any more.

I know you are innocent, Joe. You are my child. I know what you're capable of. Anyone who knows you knows this. I will hold out for the miracle.

Lots of love,
Mammy.

Lizzie swallowed hard at the thought of her dad doing something like that. Part of her wanted to hug him for his gesture, and part of her hated him for being nice to these people who had sided with his daughter's murderer.

She opened another letter.

Lizzie felt her hand curling involuntarily around these letters from Leah Jones. She must have written every week for years, Lizzie thought. Silly deluded woman. The letters in her hand made a sort of scrunching noise before she realised that she was twisting them. Jesus, she couldn't rip them up, Joe might notice. Instead, she flattened them back out.

There was another envelope, smaller than the rest, that she hadn't noticed. Unfolding the page inside, Lizzie realised that it was a newspaper clipping.

It was headlined GUILTY.

Joseph Jones, son of newspaper man Geoff Jones, was yesterday found guilty of murdering 19-year-old Megan Walsh in a case that has divided Co. Wexford. Joseph Jones now faces life in prison. The body of Ms Walsh was found washed up on a beach ten miles from her home town a year ago last August. She had been missing for two days and the finger of suspicion fell on local man Joseph Jones when it was established that he was the last person to see her alive. Ms Walsh was wearing Joseph Jones' jumper when she was found on the beach. Coronary reports confirmed that she suffered a severe blow to the head in the hours before her death. A witness told how she had seen Megan Walsh climb on to Jones' father's boat and—

Lizzie felt her stomach heave and just made it to the bathroom before she vomited.

42

IT TOOK HIM exactly two and a half hours to get home as, mid-week, the traffic was light. He couldn't help the sweat that coated his hands and forehead as the roads became ever more familiar. And, finally, he was two hundred yards from home. As he neared the gateway his stomach heaved and he drove past, before pulling into a layby some distance away.

It was no use, he couldn't do it. He couldn't face them and pretend what they had done was all right. His parents had thrown him to the lions and watched as they savaged him. But his mother was sick. And his dad didn't look much better.

Joe closed his eyes and lay his head back on the headrest. What was he to do? He couldn't ever go back to the way he used to be with them – charming his mum and annoying the hell out of his dad with his passion for nature and birds instead of words and news. But he couldn't move on, either. He wasn't sure if he could build a relationship out of the ruins of the old one. And yet at the same time, seeing the familiar stone wall that surrounded the house had made his heart twist with something he thought he'd forgotten long ago. The comfort that only home can give.

To hell with it, he thought as he started his car up. Maybe he'd never move on, maybe they wouldn't, but surely he could just go this once and have a look and see how bad those ruins were.

He pulled his car on to the opposite side of the road, earning him a screech of brakes and two fingers from a driver he hadn't seen. Joe raised his hand in apology but it didn't stop the man rolling down his window and yelling something totally unintelligible at him.

Joe didn't care. Things like that never bothered him any more. He rarely overtook on roads or got annoyed waiting in queues. To him the whole idea of just being outside was wonderful. He drove as slowly as he could get away with and then, finally, with a huge intake of breath, he turned and drove up the driveway to his parents' house.

There was no car there.

A sense of anticlimax washed over him. He hadn't rung to say he was coming, just in case he did chicken out, and now he was on his own. He pulled the car up in front of the house and knew by the way all the windows were shut that it was empty. He'd hang around for a while, he decided. It'd be nice to wander around the back and walk through the garden. He'd loved the garden when he was a kid – it was big and open and green.

He pulled on his jacket and stepped out of the car. The freshness of the air hit him and on it came the scent of the sea. Slightly salty. Joe closed his eyes and took a deep breath and began to walk.

The back garden was just like he remembered. He stood looking at it for a second before becoming aware of birdsong and the flutter of wings in the trees. He shoved his hands into his pockets and began to walk.

'Oy!'

Joe jumped and turned. A man was peering at him from the garden of the house next door.

'Who are you?'

Joe recognised his old neighbour. Mr O'Connor. He couldn't remember the man's first name. They'd been really friendly with his mother and father.

'It's, eh, Joe,' he said, feeling ashamed having to admit it.

Mr O'Connor's face registered shock, then wariness. There was no welcome.

'Oh,' he said. He started to back away. 'Right. Well, your parents should be back soon. I think they've just gone into town for a bit.'

'Thanks,' Joe said despondently as the man hurried off, no doubt to inform his wife that the murderer was back.

He moved further along towards the back of the garden, where the trees and bushes were thickly planted. At least he could walk between them and not be observed. He didn't want to run into anyone else, even if it was highly unlikely.

It was about half an hour later that he heard a car pulling up. It sounded as if it was coming from the front of the house. He knew that his dad would recognise his son's car and be looking for him, so he left the protection of the trees and walked some way back towards the house. He didn't want to go right up to the door. He wasn't even sure if he wanted to go in. Instead, he stood almost in the centre of the garden as his parents came around the side of the house, obviously searching for him.

His father led his mother by the arm. Joe watched him talk to her as her eyes eagerly scanned the garden. And then she saw him. And he saw her. And they all stood looking at each other for what seemed like ages.

Joe couldn't move, even if he'd wanted to. His mother looked so frail: still beautiful, with her dark hair streaked very liberally with a brilliant white, but unsteady and unsure. His dad looked old, too. He didn't know what to say. He just remained standing, his legs apart and his hands shoved ever deeper into the pockets of his jacket. He met their steady gaze with a defiant gaze of his own.

'It's Joseph,' his dad said to his mother, breaking the silence. 'He's back.'

'Joseph?' She mouthed the name, framing it, saying it, tasting it like unfamiliar chocolate. 'My Joseph?'

'Our Joseph,' his dad nodded, his gaze going between his wife and his son. 'He must have come to visit.'

Joe watched as his mother walked swiftly towards him, her hands to her mouth. She came to a stop about two feet in front of him.

'Joe?' she said.

'Hi, Mum,' he said back. He wanted it to come out sounding normal. As if it hadn't been fourteen years since he'd seen her. Instead his voice shook a little and caught in his throat.

281

'You came back?'

He wasn't sure what this meant. 'I came for a . . .' He paused. 'A short visit. To say hi.'

His dad jangled his keys. 'Will you come in for a cuppa?'

His mother looked hopefully up at him.

'Yeah. Sure.'

'Good,' his mother nodded. She touched him briefly on the sleeve of his jacket. 'Great.'

Joe allowed himself a tiny smile.

The house looked fantastic. He had taken it for granted when he was a kid but now, having lived in a tiny cell and then in his bare house in Ranelagh, it was great to be sitting in a bright airy kitchen with a gleaming kettle bubbling away.

But he didn't slouch in the chair. He sat stiffly upright, uncomfortable in front of these two strangers who were looking at him with so much love. It made him feel claustrophobic.

'What made you come back now?' his mother asked as she got the tea ready.

His father shot him a sharp look.

'Eh, I dunno.' Joe looked at his hands. 'I just felt, well, that . . .' He paused, unable to frame a proper answer. He never would have come back if his mother hadn't been sick. At least he didn't think so. Why would he? He couldn't forget, no matter how hard he tried.

'Well, whatever the reason,' his mother said, 'I'm glad to see you.'

Joe nodded.

Silently his father put cups in front of them all and poured the tea. He placed a packet of biscuits on the table and sat down beside his wife. Joe put milk in his tea, then stared into it.

'So, how have things been?' his mother asked. 'You know, since,' she swallowed hard, 'since they let you out.'

'OK.' He fiddled with his teaspoon. 'My parole officer got me a job working with his brother in a sports centre. I teach swimming.'

'Oh.'

He nodded. 'And I have a loft of pigeons that I do well with.'

'So you're still into the pigeons,' his mother said. 'I'm glad about that.'

There was more silence.

'And do you go out and have a social life?' his mother asked. 'Are you happy?'

He shot her a look. 'I'm OK. I don't bother with going out.'

'Why?'

All this concern made him flinch. 'Got my fingers burned once. I won't be doing it again.'

'Oh, Joe.' She said it with sadness.

'Yeah well, I'd rather be at home on my own than stuck in a bloody prison cell.'

'You won't go to prison for going out and having a life,' she said.

'That's what I thought before.' He knew he sounded bitter, but damn it, he still felt angry and cheated and betrayed. He bit his lip and tried to get a grip on himself.

'So, how have you both been?'

A look passed between them and Joe saw his father nod.

'I'm not well, Joseph, I might as well tell you,' his mother said. She spoke firmly, without any emotion. 'I've been diagnosed with Alzheimer's.' She smiled a little. 'You picked a good day to come. Another day and I'd have been all over the place.'

His father laid a hand on her shoulder. 'She's being very good about it. She knows I'm always here, don't you, Leah?'

His mother nodded and caught her husband's hand. 'I'm so afraid I'll forget everyone,' she said. 'Not know who anyone is.'

'It'd take some disease to forget that I was in prison.' Joe managed a smile. 'That might be a good thing for you.'

'Never.' She shook her head. 'You never say that. You have made me proud, Joseph. I know with every part of me that you were innocent and I'm only sorry that I can't fight for you any more. But,' she took a breath, 'you don't stop fighting for yourself. You owe yourself a good life. You have fun. Do you hear me?'

283

He said nothing.

'We can't say anything but sorry,' his dad said. 'I didn't intentionally set out to be the star witness for the prosecution, Joe. They twisted everything.'

'You didn't have to say anything about the row.'

'I didn't think it meant much. They asked how well you had known the girl, that's all.'

'And what did you say? Well enough to have a row with?'

'I told the truth because I honestly believed you had nothing to fear. If I didn't believe in your innocence, would I have even let slip about the row?'

Joe gulped. He knew his dad was telling the truth and he wanted to let them in, but he knew that would involve pulling down a lot of his defences. He trusted very few people now. Forgetting and forgiving would leave him wide open all over again.

'I have to go now.' He stood up. 'Thanks for the tea.'

'Will you not stay a little longer?' His mother looked at him beseechingly. 'Please?'

'I can't.' He stared at them. 'Sorry.'

They didn't move as he stumbled towards the front door.

Some hours later he checked into the B&B he'd booked.

As he dumped his bag on the floor, he found it hard to remember what he'd done since leaving his parents' house. He'd driven around the county, revisiting old haunts and remembering. He'd walked the beach where Meg's body had been washed up, he'd walked along the harbour and seen big signs asking for Polly Walsh to be set free. Other signs telling people to protest about the harbour plan. His dad's boat was still there, the one he'd taken out all those years ago. It was more battered now, the name had peeled from the side. Joe knew that no one used it any more, probably hadn't in fourteen years. He'd walked by the newspaper offices, wondering if he'd catch a glimpse of Dessie, but he hadn't. Dessie hadn't contacted him since Joe had said that Meg was there to meet him that night. He'd been convinced that Joe was trying to frame him, but Joe hadn't been – that was what Meg had said. She had received a text . . .

Joe shook his head to clear it. There was no point in thinking about the past. He had to move on.

But he wished he knew where he was going.

43

Tomorrow, I am going to confront Dessie. I have made up my mind.

I have been a week on holidays and the slimy toad hasn't even rung me. I hope it's because he's really busy. I mean, he's bound to be, isn't he, being in the office all on his own without me or Joe. But at the same time, I have rung him about forty-two times – once an hour. It just occurred to me when I went to ring him again that he has never given me his mobile number. I've asked for it and he keeps saying he can't remember it offhand and that he'd get it to me, but he never has. Maybe it was a hint all along, but if it was I'll find out tomorrow and, if he was using me, I'll have it out with him. I might not be the cleverest person on the planet but there is no way I'm going to be some easy woman for him to tell all his mates about and for Joe Jones to look smug and say that he told me so. No way. Dessie will learn that I am like that woman in England who they called the Iron Lady – I think it's the queen or someone. Anyway, he'll learn that he cannot mess me about like that.

Friday, 27th August

I told everyone in the house that I was meeting Dessie for lunch. Billy gave a bit of a cheer and said that

286

maybe now I'd finally stop moping about the place and I said that I haven't been moping and Mammy, of course, had to get her oar in and say that if going around with a face like a dead cat wasn't moping she didn't know what was. I said that if she didn't know what a mopey face looked like, maybe she should look in a mirror.

Now she's not talking to me.

Anyway, I'm in my room, having cried my eyes out and made my headache worse by doing so. It did not go well. Not at all. Joe Jones was right. Dessie is just out for Dessie.

I dressed up to go see him. I wore a short green skirt, even though it was lashing rain and I was going to be freezing waiting for the bus. On top I wore my cute little white T-shirt with a picture of a Christmas tree saying, 'Christmas is for life not just December'. And I had a red short jacket and my red high heels. I looked great, I thought. And so did the bus driver because he let me on for free and gave me a wink.

Then I hopped off the bus in Rossclare town and stood outside the paper building for ages. I didn't really want to meet anyone and yet I had to go inside. So I went into the foyer, which was empty – the receptionist is hopeless actually. Then I scurried as fast as I could down to the ad office. Inside I could hear a phone ringing and I pushed open the door.

Things get a bit hazy here. It's weird, I can't quite remember what happened. I only know that Dessie's old girlfriend was perched on the desk and he was talking away to her. And she was messing his hair up. They looked happy. I said something like 'very cosy', and they both looked at me.

Then he went pale and asked really crossly what did I want and she looked from me to him in a sort of shocked way. Well, I thought to myself, no way is he going to treat me like just some ordinary person. So I said that last week I wanted him and that I was pretty sure that he'd wanted me as we'd done it in his car. Only I didn't say 'done it', I said 'fucked', which sounded a bit sluttish now I think about it. Anyway I probably didn't come across very well actually because I think I was shouting. Then Dessie's girlfriend hopped off the desk and demanded to know what the hell was happening. So I asked Dessie to explain and he turned to her and told her I was mad.

Me?

He said I'd been chasing him or some rubbish like that and I remember denying it and saying he chased me.

Then his girlfriend got cross and Dessie got cross and he called me a tart and told his girlfriend to look at the state of me. And he said, and this hurt, he said, 'Look, Megan, I sell ads. I bullshit. That's what happened with you and like all my customers you fell for it.'

Anger like I have never known before flooded right through me and, OK, I was going to cry too, so I knew I had to leave or I would throw something at him, which is what I should have done, or maybe I did I can't remember. Next thing I'm on the floor with the two of them bending over me, looking all shocked.

I'd fallen over the telephone cord as I'd made to run. Fallen over the cord and banged my head off the filing cabinet and the floor. How embarrassing. My head was full of stars and fireworks and my brain was muzzy. I had to get away, but I felt really sick so I had to put my head between my legs – how humiliating. Then it's a bit of a blur, they made me sit down and gave me water and I wouldn't drink it. It was all confused. I told them I was fine. I hardly remember what happened after only that I somehow left and got the bus back and have been here since.

I hate him for what he's done and I hate Joe for being right.

OK, all that last bit can be scrapped because . . .

44

I T WAS AFTER eight and Lizzie had just locked up the lofts
when Joe arrived back.

Anto had ruined her plans to stuff the birds with food. He'd
been horrified to see corn and seeds in the bird feeders and had
immediately emptied them out, looking at her accusingly and
shaking his head and muttering stuff about Joe being a complete
dickhead leaving her in charge.

As she pulled the side gate behind her, mentally cursing Anto,
she almost banged into Joe, who didn't look particularly happy.
When he saw her, however, his face broke into a grin.

'Hey, how's things? Those birds behaving themselves?'

She decided that she'd better come clean about the overfeeding
or Anto would surely rat on her.

'I made a bit of a mistake with their food,' she said ruefully.
'Luckily Anto was on hand to put me right. I think I was overfeeding them.'

He looked a bit taken aback for a second but, with a wave of
his hand, said, 'Aw, don't worry about it. Did Noel take them for
the toss?'

'Yep. They were back within twenty minutes.'

'Not bad.'

She handed him his keys and he unlocked the front door.

'See you.' She turned to go.

'Hey!'

His shout stopped her. She turned back, heart hammering.
Had he somehow noticed that she'd been poking around? She

was certain there was nothing out of place. Well, there was nothing in his house to *be* out of place.

Joe was looking at her in a half embarrassed way, tossing his keys from hand to hand. 'Would you like to, eh, you know, go for a drink? My treat? To say thanks for minding the birds.'

'Go for a drink?' she stammered.

'Yeah.' He suddenly looked mortified. 'Well, only if you want. It's not a date or anything.'

Joe Jones drinking. He might let his guard down. She shrugged, trying to sound casual.

'Sure? When?'

'Tomorrow? I can meet you after work and we could grab a bite to eat? My shout?'

'OK. Great. Meet you at six-thirty outside Bewleys in Grafton Street.'

His mouth curved upward in the biggest smile Lizzie had seen in a long time. He was a bloody good-looking guy, she thought suddenly, hating him for it.

'See you then,' she called.

Lizzie was a few doors from home when Aileen's dad drove by her and pulled up outside the house. She watched, without going any closer, as he strode around to the passenger side of the car and opened the door for Aileen. Lizzie tried not to grin as he hauled his enormously pregnant daughter out of the car and held her as she swayed slightly. My God, Aileen was huge, she thought. She wondered why they were calling before realising that Aileen was probably coming to collect the remainder of her stuff. Obviously she'd brought her dad along for moral support. Poor Billy would be gutted, but if Aileen had her dad along, then Lizzie would be there for her brother.

'Hi,' Lizzie called, not sure if they'd spotted her.

They both turned and watched her approach. 'Hello, Lizzie,' Aileen's dad said pleasantly. 'How are you?'

'Good. You?'

'I'm very well, thank you.'

'You look, eh, great,' she said to Aileen, who managed a small smile.

'Yeah, great as in enormous. I'm as big as a house.' She giggled a little and Lizzie saw a touch of the old Aileen underneath the prickly mother-to-be.

'Only a duplex one, though,' Lizzie said and they smiled.

'Aileen has just, eh, you know, come to pick up some things,' her dad said, shuffling uncomfortably and unable to meet Lizzie's eye.

'There is no need to sound apologetic about it.' Aileen turned to her father, her smile vanishing. 'They are my things and this is half my house and Billy and I have to sort things out before the babies come.'

'I know, I was just saying—'

'Well don't just say!'

'Hormones,' Abe mouthed at Lizzie as they both followed Aileen up the path.

She strode with a speed that belied her size. At the door she fumbled with her house keys, but before she could insert her key into the lock, the door was wrenched open.

Billy stood glowering at them. He opened his mouth to speak but gulped audibly as he took in Aileen's changed shape. He had never seen her swollen belly, Lizzie realised, and she wanted to hug him as his scowl turned to wonder. He seemed incapable of saying anything and, without uttering a word, he opened the door wider to let them through.

'Billy,' Aileen said curtly as she passed him.

'Hi.' Billy attempted a small grin. 'You look . . .' He paused. 'Wow.'

Aileen glared at him. 'Pity you couldn't have said "wow" a few months ago.'

'Yeah, I know,' Billy agreed.

There was an edgy silence.

'Well, let's hope there's no confusion about who owns what,' Aileen said, recovering first.

'I'll need some space to sort through the things and I've some boxes in the car to pack stuff away in. Dad,' she looked at her father, 'would you get the boxes, please?' She spoke as if she was a matron in charge of a hospital.

'I've been thinking,' Billy blurted out, as Aileen's dad made a move, 'and, eh, Aileen, I'd really like you to hear what I've thought.'

'I don't think so, Billy,' Aileen said.

'Aw, come on, you haven't spoken to me since you left. That's not fair.'

'You didn't need any words to say what you meant that day in the hospital.'

'Jesus!' Billy threw his hands up in the air in exasperation. 'Do you want me to beg? Is that it?'

'No, I just want my stuff. It's the classy stuff.'

'Oh, yeah, I'm the Palestine.'

'It's philistine, actually.'

'Oh, get lost!' Billy rubbed a hand over his face and turned away from her. Lizzie went to comfort him but he shoved her off. He was near tears, she realised with a shock.

Aileen's dad must have realised it, too, because he said, 'Oh, Aileen will you give the lad a chance.' As Aileen tossed her head in a dismissive gesture, he continued softly, 'It's not like you to be so . . . so hard.'

'I'm hard because I have to be.'

'No one has to be hard.'

'Well, there is no way I'm going to be like you, Dad, that's for sure.'

'Pardon?'

'Taking Mam back every time she apologised. That's not for me, thanks.'

Her dad looked as if she'd struck him. Then, with a quiet fury, he said, 'Don't you talk to me like that. Don't you dare. I took your mother back for you. For you, every time. Because you loved her.'

'And so did you.'

'Yes,' Abe nodded. 'And I gave her a second chance. And a

third. I gave us every chance and, if you love Billy at all, you'll give him a chance to explain. I think, Aileen, it's time you faced facts. Now,' he started to count the facts on his fingers, 'you are pregnant with twins, you have left the house you bought with your boyfriend, you have left your boyfriend, and you will not give him a chance to explain or apologise. That is ridiculous. The lad has rung you night and day begging for a chance and you have blanked him. Well, I will not help you until you listen to what he has to say.'

'Eh, thanks, Abe,' Billy muttered, his voice suspiciously wobbly.

'Oh, I'm not doing it for you,' Abe said wearily. 'I'm doing it for my own sanity. She spends all her time giving out about you even though she says,' he made quote signs with his fingers, 'oh, I'm so over him.' He glared at his daughter, 'Now, you listen to him and then make up your mind.'

Aileen looked suddenly terrified. 'Dad!'

'And if you don't, I'm driving home right now and leaving you stranded here.'

'You can't do that!'

'Watch me!'

The two glared at each other.

Lizzie desperately wanted to leave, but if Abe was staying then so was she. The silence stretched on as father and daughter stared stonily at each other.

'Fine,' Aileen spat eventually, breaking the silence like scissors on a taut elastic band. She turned to Billy. 'Say what it is you have to say and then we can move on.'

Billy swallowed hard.

'Any chance of a cuppa, Lizzie?' Abe asked.

Thank God. It meant she wouldn't have to listen to what Billy had to say. 'Every chance, Abe.'

'No!' Billy's shout stopped them. 'I want everyone to hear this. I need you to back me up, Lizzie.' He indicated the sitting room. 'So can we go in here.'

Back him up? What was he on about? She watched as Billy led the way, with Aileen stomping in behind him. Abe shrugged and Lizzie rolled her eyes as they both followed Aileen, who had come to a standstill in the centre of the room, a look of horror on her face.

'Do you and Lizzie ever clean anything? Look at the dust on that fireplace.' She ran her finger along the ledge and Lizzie cringed. It had never occurred to her to dust that.

Aileen's eyes scanned the room. 'And you have stains on the table. I bought this table with my own money. Who put a hot mug on the table like that? Where are the coasters?'

'Aileen, can you give me a second here?' Billy said. He was rubbing his hand through his hair and making it stick up in spikes. It occurred to Lizzie that the sitting room wasn't the only thing that needed cleaning.

'Oh, believe me, that's all you're getting.' Aileen said. 'I can't believe you did this to my table.'

Billy looked desperately at Lizzie, who shrugged.

'Listen!' Abe snapped.

Everyone jumped.

'Will you sit down and listen?' Abe implored his daughter. He took her hand in his. 'Stop trying to distract yourself. Stop being so horrible. Stop being so scared of what Billy has to say.'

'I'm not scared,' Aileen said, a little too quickly.

'You are,' her dad said. 'You're scared you'll be like me. You're scared to listen to him in case he sweet-talks you like your mother did to me. But, Aileen, Billy isn't like your mother. He didn't leave you. You left him.'

Aileen paled. 'Whose side are you on?' she sniffed.

'Yours. Totally and firmly.' He wrapped an arm about her shoulder and led her gently to the sofa.

There was silence for a second. Billy coughed a little. 'Ready now?'

Aileen's dad nodded in her stead.

'It's, eh, hard to start,' Billy gulped out. 'Like, I had it all planned – what to say – and now . . .' He looked up at the ceiling and shoved his hands into the pockets of his trousers.

'Now, I want to find the right words to make it better and I'm scared I won't.' He swallowed hard. 'I don't want to blow it.'

'You've already blown it, Billy,' Aileen said, though she didn't sound angry, just sad. 'I don't trust you to stay with me now.'

'Billy would never leave you,' Lizzie said, indignant on Billy's behalf. 'Look at him, he's not like that!'

'Lizzie!' Billy snapped and then, more quietly, 'Just, just let me explain to her, OK?'

'Yeah, but she thinks—' Lizzie stopped at her brother's warning look. 'Sorry,' she muttered.

Billy turned back to his girlfriend. 'I was scared, Aileen,' he said, 'and I know it sounds crap but, well,' he winced, 'this is coming out all wrong. Look, you know the way you and I got together after, after . . . Well, after Megan died?'

Aileen didn't react, but Billy continued earnestly. 'I liked being with you because you were fun and all, but I liked it too because you were her best friend. And I felt close to her when you were with me and I know it was the same for you.'

Aileen's eyes glistened.

'She was my twin, closer to me than my own shadow, and when she died it wrecked our family.' He turned and asked Lizzie quietly, 'Didn't it, Liz?'

'Yep.' Lizzie wished he wouldn't talk about that. She studied the mark on the coffee table instead.

'We'd been happy before that,' she heard Billy say, 'only we never realised how happy, I guess. We were just a normal family. But when Megan died, it ripped the heart out of each of us. My dad refused to go out on the boat any more, he ended up selling it and farming instead. It doesn't make him happy. Mam got really cross and bitter and started fighting the whole world with protest after protest and Lizzie, well, she upped and left and refused to see anyone who reminded her of Meg, while I clung on to anything that reminded me of her like a life raft.' He paused and took a deep, shaky breath.

'So what has that to do with us?' Aileen asked quietly.

'Everything,' Billy answered earnestly. 'I was with you because

296

you reminded me of the good times. I never wanted it to change. But things did change. We moved to Dublin, got the flat, took out the mortgage and God, Aileen, though I was happy, I was scared all the time, too. And then you got pregnant.'

'And?' Aileen's voice shook.

Billy crossed the room and sat down beside her. He held her gaze for a second before saying haltingly, 'Megan's death taught my family that life could change in a second and that nothing was guaranteed. And the closer you get to real happiness, the closer you are to complete devastation, too, Aileen. And I didn't want what happened to my folks to ever be us.'

Lizzie swallowed hard. She'd felt like that, too. That mark on the table wasn't so bad. Polish would remove it.

'I didn't want a family, I found it too scary. I didn't think I'd cope if anything happened. But I'm not coping now, Aileen, and I'd rather be scarily happy with you than like this.' He tried to catch her hand but she pulled away. 'Please give me another chance.'

Aileen didn't seem to know what to say.

'I just got scared, Aileen. People don't always know what they really want.'

'I did.' She suddenly looked small, despite her size. 'I wanted you and our little house and especially the babies.'

'I know,' he said back.

'I never had a proper family before, Billy. It's all I ever wanted. I loved your family. I loved you. You never said you were scared. If you had only said instead of humiliating me . . .' Her voice broke.

'How could I? I wanted you to be happy.'

'Oh, yeah,' she sniffed, a big tear running down her face and on to her chin, 'look at me, I'm sooo happy!'

'So come back and I swear I'll make you happy.'

'You used to be fun,' Aileen said through her tears.

'I know,' Billy said back. Then, on a half smile, 'You used to be thin.'

'Don't make me laugh,' Aileen said, sniffing as she laced a hand on her stomach.

'Why not? I love you and you look lovely.' He touched her face gently.

'I just can't forget that look you had that day.'

'If I could take back that look I would,' Billy said. 'Only I can't. And I know you're scared of taking a chance on me and I know I'm not perfect but I'll be the best I can be for you.'

'What if you get so scared that you do run off? Or what if something awful does happen?'

'Then I'll do what I'm doing now and try to fix it. I'm not going anywhere, Aileen.'

'I just wanted it to be perfect.'

'Oh, for God's sake,' Aileen's dad said, sounding as if he'd heard enough and he just wanted to be out of there. 'There is no such thing as perfection. We make our own perfection. People who think everything will be perfect all the time find it really hard when things go wrong. Like your mother. Like you, Aileen.'

'Pardon?'

'You ran off when Billy didn't give you perfection – that's what your mother did to me. You have to be scared to want to work at it, Aileen.'

'I thought you said you were on my side.'

'I am. Being on your side does not involve letting you throw your happiness out the window. Now, if you'll excuse me, Lizzie offered me some tea a while ago and I'm going to take it.' He looked at Lizzie. 'All right?'

Lizzie nodded.

She followed Abe out the door and was surprised when he hugged her.

'You poor girl. Here,' he handed her a handkerchief, 'they'd no right to make you cry like that.'

She was crying. Much the same way she'd been crying at Tom's play. Silently. Hardly aware she was doing it. It occurred to her that she was barely aware of anything she was doing these days. She sniffed hard and dashed a hand across her face and dabbed her eyes with the hankie. The only emotion she really seemed to truly feel any more was anger, and that was in Joe's presence.

298

'Sorry,' she sniffed as she followed him into the kitchen, where he put on the kettle and hunted for the coffee. 'I don't know why—'

'Because you had to listen to crap from the two of them, that's why!' Abe smiled at her.

Lizzie smiled shakily back though she knew, and he knew, that that wasn't the reason.

Then he gave her another hug and told her she could keep his hankie.

45

I T WAS A beautiful evening in the city. Lizzie left work slightly later than normal so that Joe would be at Bewleys before her. She didn't want to be first there and have him think she was actually eager to meet him.

She saw him as she approached, lounging against the wall of the café, one foot planted firmly against the brick of the wall. He checked his watch before pulling a cigarette pack from his jacket and lighting up. He inhaled and blew a long stream of smoke into the air.

'I'll have one of those,' Lizzie said from behind him.

'Hey,' he grinned in greeting as he held the packet out to her, 'take whatever you like, I'm trying to cut down.'

'Hate that.' She let him light the cigarette for her and the two of them stood, side by side, smoking contentedly.

'Yeah, my boss offered me a job managing a new sports centre in Meath today, so I reckon it's probably better if I don't smoke.'

'A promotion?' Lizzie couldn't believe it. How on earth could someone give an ex-con a job like that? Huh, he was probably going to be earning way more than her. Life really was not fair.

'Don't they know—' She stopped abruptly, horrified at what she had been about to say.

'Don't they know what?' Joe asked.

'That you're, eh, totally addicted to nicotine?' she gulped.

'Totally addicted might be pushing it a bit,' he said, his eyes sparkling. 'Mildly addicted.'

'You can't be mildly addicted to anything.' Lizzie couldn't help grinning, she felt so weak at the mess she'd narrowly avoided making. 'Chancer.'

He shrugged. 'Aw well, I've only smoked five so far today, so that's good. Now, where to? There's a great little place at the top of O'Connell Street, if you like.'

'Rocco's?'

He nodded. 'Yeah, that's the name I think.'

Lizzie was a bit stunned. That was her favourite restaurant in the whole of Dublin: gorgeous food, good wine list, reasonable prices and, even better than all that, a lovely warm smokers' lounge out the back.

'Good choice,' she nodded.

Joe looked relieved and pushed himself from the wall.

'Righto, let's head, so.' He looked at her footwear. 'Flat shoes. I like your style.'

She fell into step beside him. As they walked she couldn't fail to notice the admiring glances women tossed in his direction. Joe, however, seemed oblivious.

'So, how come you got a promotion?' Lizzie asked. 'Are you a real lick-arse?'

'Yeah. Basically.'

His answer made her laugh, despite herself.

Joe grinned. 'I just work hard and keep the head down,' he said. 'I was in trouble a few weeks ago for not turning up, but I did the humble worker thing and this is my reward.'

'And will you have to move to Meath?'

He shrugged. 'I dunno. I'll see what the commute is like. And to be honest, I'm not sure about moving the birds. I might stay for them.'

'I've heard of staying for kids and schools, but for birds?'

He looked a little surprised. 'Well, I'm responsible for my birds and I love them, so how could I upset them?'

Lizzie wanted to kick herself. Of course she should know that, her being a pretend pigeon-lover and all. Talk about stupid, it was her that seemed to be letting her guard down. 'Yeah, of course,' she said as she waved her cigarette about. 'Right.'

'And I'd miss the lads in the club. Well, most of them. I had a row with Cid the other night.'

'Did you? I can't imagine you rowing with anyone.' And, funnily enough, it was true. He just didn't seem the type. But he must be. Obviously.

Joe nodded ruefully and told her what had happened. She was horrified that he had started to blame Cid for her actions. That hadn't been in the plan at all. He was supposed to think he was going a bit nuts. Or that he had Alzheimer's, like his poor mother. Not start alienating his friends in the club. Though maybe that would be good, too – to leave him friendless. But still, bad as she was, she had to defend poor Cid. Hurting the pigeons and Joe was one thing, but someone being blamed unfairly for what she'd done was something even she couldn't live with.

'I can't see Cid doing something like that,' she stammered out. 'Like, he's a pain, but I doubt he'd ever hurt a bird.'

Joe just shrugged and flicked some ash on the ground.

'Are you sure Prince didn't just get his leg caught somewhere, and in order to help him someone cut the tag off?'

'I dunno. Maybe.' He blew out a long stream of smoke. 'I'm just uneasy about it, that's all.' Then he said softly, 'The lofts keep opening, too.'

'You forget to lock them, more like,' she teased, hoping to plant the thought in his head.

'Naw,' he shook his head, 'I always . . .' He paused. Took another drag of his cigarette before stamping it out.

Lizzie decided to change the subject. It was making her pretty uneasy talking about it now.

'So,' she said as they crossed over O'Connell Bridge, 'how'd the reunion go with your parents?'

He rolled his eyes. 'Don't ask.'

'That good, huh?'

'Do you get on with your folks?' he asked by way of reply.

Lizzie shrugged. 'Yeah, most of the time. Why?'

'No reason, just prefer to talk about you than me.'

'What do you want to know?'

Joe faced her and smiled. 'Everything.'

There was something in the way he said it, as if he really wanted to know every little thing about her. Did he fancy her or something? Would it help her if he did? Could she feign interest in him? The questions bounced about one after the other, alarming her. What if he wanted to kiss her? What then?

'Like?' she gulped.

'Anything you want to tell me.'

So she told him about her family. Omitted Megan and changed Billy's name to Alan. Told him about Aileen being pregnant and how Alan had begged her to come back.

'So now there's a sort of a truce. She's moving back in and they're having a trial period. It's all a bit stressful. I wish I could move out but I can't because he wants me to think up romantic things he can do for her. Tonight he's buying her all the Wham stuff he can get his hands on.'

Joe laughed. 'Must be nice to have a brother or sister,' he mused. 'I'm an only kid. I always hated it, all that pressure to be perfect.'

'Oh, I'm sure you were perfect.'

'No. No, I wasn't,' he said. 'Or at least not in their eyes.'

'How come?'

Joe didn't answer. He pushed open the door of the restaurant for her, where they were shown to a table and handed a menu each. When they had chosen what they wanted, Lizzie returned to the subject of Joe's parents.

'So, how come?'

'How come what?' He looked puzzled.

'How come you disappointed your folks?' She was gratified to see him wince.

Joe took a gulp of wine and looked across the table at her. 'I want you to like me,' he smiled lightly, 'so let's not go there.'

'I do like you,' Lizzie forced the words out and took a gulp of wine herself, 'but you play everything very close to your chest. You're hard to know.'

Joe flicked an uneasy glance at her. He rubbed his hand hard

303

over his face, fiddled with the cutlery, unfolded the napkin and drank some more wine. Finally he took a deep breath and said haltingly, 'I haven't dared to get too close to anyone in the last couple of years because of stuff that happened to me.'

'What stuff?' Her heart began a slow hammering. Was he going to tell her or not? How would he explain it?

'I like you, Lizzie,' Joe went on, with a sincerity that unnerved her. 'I've cleaned my house more times in the past few months than in the last few years put together.'

'Charming,' she offered, trying to break the mood.

He didn't return the smile. 'And I don't want to hurt you so . . .' He paused. 'Well, what I'm trying to figure out is, is it worth telling you stuff about me?' He poured some more wine into his glass. Jesus, he was going to be pissed. Which was good.

'Do you feel we could . . .' He gulped. 'You know, ever be . . .' He looked at her, her big gorgeous eyes and shiny multi-coloured cap of hair and asked himself if he was bonkers. 'Naw, forget it. Forget it.'

'Hey.' With a huge effort of will, Lizzie took his hand gently off the wine glass and squeezed it in hers. Her stomach rolled. 'I like you, Joe, we have fun with the birds and stuff, don't we?'

'Yep.' He smiled bleakly. Not what he was looking for.

'So, if you want to tell me something, that's fine. It'll go no further.'

Oh God, she hoped he wouldn't want to kiss her. The thought made her feel queasy. But if she said she liked him, she might get behind the barriers he'd created and find out the truth.

'I like you.' She swallowed hard. 'A lot.'

Joe's heart trembled. She liked him. A lot. He liked the feel of her hand in his. He liked her, full stop. But would she want to know him when he told her? Could he face the scorn in her eyes if she didn't? Would it be a sign of things to come? Was it worth the risk?

'Please tell me,' she said.

Oh shit. Oh shit. 'Promise you'll listen until I'm finished explaining and you won't get scared?'

'Sounds bad.'

Joe dipped his head. 'It is.'

'I promise.' Once again she squeezed his hand. His fingers were entwined with hers. He had good hands. Fisherman's hands.

Just then the waiter came and placed their main courses on the table with a big flourish, expecting a smile at least. Neither of them took any notice.

'Thanks,' he sniffed, stalking off.

Joe waited a second before saying softly, 'Can we eat up and then I'll tell you everything?'

'Sure.' She hoped he wouldn't lose his nerve. 'But you'd better let go of my hand, so.'

'Oh yeah, sorry.' He laughed a little and slowly let go of her fingers.

He watched as she took up her fork and began spooning pasta into her mouth. He didn't think he'd be able to eat a bloody thing. Damn, why did he have to say he'd tell her? Could he not have asked her out like any normal bloke and then maybe when things were going well, tell her then? Why now? He supposed he was trying in a stupid way to be honourable. Letting Lizzie know what she might be in for if she went out with him. He hoped she would consider a relationship, but he doubted it. She wouldn't go out with a convicted murderer. He liked Lizzie a lot. In fact, he couldn't stop thinking about her. She was the first girl he'd let himself be interested in since coming out of prison. Everything he'd ever wanted in a girl, she had. It was almost as if she'd known him in another life. He wondered where he could tell her. Here or at home? But before he broached it, a gang of people coming in the door caught her attention and she suddenly paled.

'Shit!'

Joe looked around and noticed that a guy in the group was staring at Lizzie the way she was staring at him. Then the guy came over to the table. He was handsome in an odd way. Lots of unattractive features that somehow made him attractive. Very weird clothes.

'Hiya,' the man said and Joe knew by his tone of voice that there was some sort of history there.

'Hi, Tom,' Lizzie said in a clipped voice. 'I see you're out with your friends.'

'Yeah.' Tom turned to Joe. 'And I see you're out with your *friend*.' He stressed the 'friend'. He sounded slightly aggressive.

'Joe, this is Tom. Tom, Joe.'

Joe nodded at Tom, who ignored him.

'So, there was no one else, was there not?' Tom said, as he lounged by the table. He flicked hurt, angry brown eyes at Lizzie. 'You didn't waste any time, though, did you?'

'It's not like that,' Lizzie said. 'We're only having dinner.'

'Hey, Tommy! Tommy, get over here!' Imogen called. Then she saw Lizzie and her eyes widened. 'Oh, hi, Lizzie. How are you?'

'Good.'

Imogen tottered over and came to stand beside Tom. She linked his arm possessively in hers.

'We're just celebrating getting an extended run, aren't we, Tommy?'

'Yeah.' His voice sounded curiously flat. 'Did you like it?' he asked Lizzie. 'The play? I heard you came one night.'

'Yeah,' she nodded, trying to keep her voice from wobbling, 'it was great. You were both great in it.'

Tom nodded his thanks then said, 'I thought you'd join us for a drink after but maybe you had other stuff on.' A quick glance at Joe.

'Come on, Tommy, let's order.' Imogen gently pulled him away. 'Good to see you, Lizzie,' she said pleasantly.

'You too,' Lizzie called after them. She watched as they both took their seats across the other side of the restaurant. A couple of people, obviously from the cast, threw curious glances in her direction as Imogen no doubt filled them in on who they'd been talking to.

'Friend of yours?' Joe asked.

'Ex,' Lizzie said, and despite her best efforts she sounded upset.

'He's the guy who you broke up with just a while ago?'

'What?'

'You know, you told me—'

'Yeah,' Lizzie suddenly remembered, 'that's him. It's the first time we've seen each other since.' She paused. 'He's a very good actor, you know. He's the best in his play.' As she said it, she felt a huge tug of sadness inside.

'You still like him, don't you?' As he asked, Joe felt like a thick for thinking that he even stood half a chance with Lizzie.

To his relief, she shrugged. 'I'm over it.'

Her smile was a little too bright, he thought. A little too quick. But she heaped her fork with pasta and said teasingly, 'Come on, eat up, I want to hear your deep dark secret.'

His heart lurched.

He brought her into his living room. It was the nicest room in the house and the tidiest. He asked her if she wanted tea and she shook her head. He asked if she wanted a beer and she said no. He said that he needed a beer and pulled one from the fridge, snapped the tab and cursed as it fizzed all over his jeans.

After wiping himself down he rejoined Lizzie in the front room and was startled to see her flicking through his DVDs.

'My favourite films,' he remarked.

'I guessed,' she nodded, putting them back and turning to him. 'So?'

'So,' he said back lamely.

'Are you going to tell me?'

'Do you want to sit down first?'

'That bad, ey?'

'Worse.' He couldn't look at her.

'Well?'

She was sitting down, looking expectantly up at him. She didn't seem too worried and that worried him. A lot.

'Well, you won't like it and please don't be frightened. The door is open,' he gestured to the living room door, 'you can leave any time you like.'

Lizzie wasn't about to go anywhere, not until he told the whole story. Not until the truth came out. It seemed too good to be true, the whole thing within her grasp like this. She felt terrified and excited in a way she couldn't even begin to explain. She didn't want to hear the story and yet she needed it like she needed to breathe. The pasta sat like lead in her stomach.

'I'm not going anywhere,' she said, her voice barely a whisper.

Joe clenched his can as tight as he could in his hand. This was it. He was launching himself into the unknown.

'Well, the reason my parents don't talk to me and stuff is that I was in . . .' He paused, knowing that what he would say next would change everything. 'Prison,' he finished up.

'Prison,' she repeated, and he was encouraged by the fact that she remained sitting.

'For twelve years. Originally it was life but there was an early release thing and stuff . . .' His voice trailed off.

'Life?'

'Uh-huh.' Would she realise the sort of people who got life? She didn't, obviously. Still she remained sitting. There was an eagerness and a fear on her face that he couldn't get his head around. And then she asked it. Like he knew she would.

'What did you do?'

He stared up at the ceiling, down at the floor, trying to think of a good way to put it. But of course there was no other way of saying it except just saying it straight out. It was as if he was in free fall and could do nothing about it.

'I got sent away for . . .' He winced, screwing up his eyes. 'For murder.'

Lizzie still didn't move. Just stared at him. Her face paled a tiny bit.

'I swear, Lizzie, on my life, that I didn't do it.'

'You didn't do it?' she said slowly. 'So why—'

'Wrong place, wrong time. I dunno.'

'What happened?'

She sounded suddenly hard, for some reason. Maybe it was finally hitting her just who she was in the room with. He bit his lip.

308

'You're not running off, that's good,' he said despondently, trying for lightness.

She didn't smile back so he said haltingly, 'A girl I knew was found washed up on a beach, wearing my jumper. She had a head injury and the last person she'd been with was me.'

That much was true, she knew that. Lizzie considered the best way to frame her next question but before she had, Joe continued, 'I liked this girl. A lot, actually.' He stopped and took a drink. 'She was involved with a friend of mine who had treated her badly and this night, the night she died, I met her. She was waiting on the pier just right where my dad's boat was berthed. I was there, attempting to drink myself stupid as my granddad had died and, well, I guess I missed him. A week or so before I'd rowed with this girl and made an eejet of myself. Anyway, I went to talk to her to see if she'd speak to me again and we get talking and she tells me that she's waiting for my friend to show up. He sent her a text and told her to wait there for him. So we talked but he never showed up. That got her all upset. She was in a terrible state over it. She was this madcap girl so, like, seeing her cry was kinda, well,' he shrugged, 'scary, I guess. Especially when you're only nineteen and haven't a clue about making people stop crying.'

Lizzie gulped hard to quell the tears that threatened. She didn't want to think of Meg crying.

Joe kept going with his story, unable to stop now he'd started. 'Anyway, I gave her a can and we had a drink but she didn't drink hers because she was really pissed. Anyway—'

'She was—' Lizzie stopped herself. Megan had not been pissed. That was a bloody lie. 'She was what?' she asked, trying to make out she hadn't heard properly.

'Pissed. Drunk,' Joe said. 'She asked me to bring her out on the boat. And I said no 'cause I'd been drinking, but she kept asking me and, well, I liked her and so . . .' He shrugged. 'And we went out and I wasn't so drunk that I couldn't drive the boat, Lizzie. She didn't fall overboard or anything. We went out and the night was calm and she was laughing a little and had stopped crying, then she said she felt a little sick and she got sick over the side of the boat. I joked a bit about her being sorry in the morning. Then she started to cry again and she kept asking me where she was and stuff, and I told her to lie down and she said that was a good idea as she had a headache. So I decide to bring the boat in and get her home. I was worried she'd pass out. But she went mad, saying she didn't want to go home. But I brought the boat in anyway and I get off and tell her that I'll walk her back. And she shouts at me to get lost and I tell her that I'm bringing her home. And I grab her hand and she walloped me across the face.'

Lizzie watched as he touched his cheekbone, rubbing the skin that had been bruised in the days after Megan went missing.

'So I grabbed her hand and pulled her,' Joe swallowed hard, his voice shaking slightly, 'I pulled her on to the pier to try to get her to walk with me. She's staggering all over the place and she starts hitting me. So I have to let her go.'

Megan's wrist had been bruised. He hadn't just pulled her. Lizzie could feel her hands tremble so she sat on them.

'I think I hurt her wrist,' Joe said then. 'I didn't mean to but I wanted to bring her home. She was really bad, Lizzie. Anything could have happened to her.'

Anything did happen to her. She had died. 'And?'

Lizzie's voice was oddly cold. Joe flinched. She sounded like the judge the day he'd been sentenced.

'And she went missing that night. She never got home. I last saw her walking away from me up the pier.' He sank into a chair opposite Lizzie. Talking about this made him feel sick. 'Next thing is she's missing and they want to trace her steps that night, so I go to tell them she was on my boat only someone else has already told them that and before I can get to the station, they're knocking on my door. My granddad's door, as I was living there at the time. Of course they see my face with the big bruise on it and it didn't look good. I tell them my story. It turns out no one comes forward to say that she was seen getting off my boat. No one. So I'm the chief suspect but without a body they can't prove anything.'

Joe swallowed hard and shot a glance across at Lizzie. She was staring at him intensely, her eyes wide.

'You OK?' he asked.

She nodded. 'Go on.' She couldn't keep the anger from her voice. It came out hard and flat. This was the same crap he'd told in court. She wanted to shout at him to confess but she knew she couldn't.

Joe didn't seem to notice. Haltingly, he continued, 'Well, she was found a couple of days later, washed up on a beach, wearing my jumper, with bruises on her wrist where I must have pulled her. Everything crashed for me then. My story didn't stand up. Tests showed she hadn't been drunk and that she'd been killed by a blow to the head. I'm suddenly up on a charge for something I never did.'

'Who do you think did it then, if you didn't?'

Joe flinched at the tone of Lizzie's voice. Shock probably made her sound harsh.

'I dunno. I just know it wasn't me. She was drunk, I don't care what anyone else says. She was sick and staggering and drunk. And worse than that, the guy she said she was there to meet swore that he never sent her a text. No text is found on his phone. And her phone is in the sea somewhere, so they think I'm trying to frame my friend. We'd argued about this girl before. My dad then told the court that he'd walked in on a fight between me and this girl a week or so before she was . . . was killed. So there I am, living the ultimate nightmare, with no way of proving I'm telling the truth.' He blinked back tears. He'd never get used to talking about it. Never. 'No one saw her after she got on my boat. No one. And I'd already been in trouble with the police for skippering a boat when drunk so, all in all, I wasn't exactly a dazzling example of a good citizen.' He shook his can. All gone. 'I would have convicted me,' he said hopelessly. Then he added, 'But I'm not a murderer, Lizzie.'

To his surprise, she stood up. 'Is that the truth?' she asked, and he thought that she seemed about to cry.

'Hey.' He stood up but she took a step back from him. He flinched.

'There is no point in telling me all this stuff if it's not the truth.'

311

'Yeah, it's the truth.' He didn't even sound convincing, but he was beyond that. No one had believed him in court so why should she? 'I don't go about beating women up, Lizzie.'

'Well then how would you explain it?'

The question was fired at him, half in anger, half tearfully.

'I can't,' he said without looking at her. 'I wish I could.'

'You said she said there was a text. Did you see the text?'

'No.'

'Did you see her drinking?'

'No, she never even finished the can I gave her. But she was well on.'

'So why did they find out she wasn't drunk?' God, Lizzie thought in anguish, would he just not admit it? She just needed to know and she was so close to finding out and he was still lying. If he only admitted it then maybe she could start to get over it. To release the huge anger inside her that was slowly eating her away.

'I don't know.' Joe looked up at her. 'Do you not think I ask myself a million times why that was? I do, Lizzie. Please believe me.'

But she didn't. He could see it in her eyes. Why had he told her anything?

'You must know more,' she said. 'How could she be drunk when she wasn't?'

He shrugged. 'You don't believe me, do you?'

There was a silence.

Lizzie stared up into his face and knew that was it. He wasn't going to admit it. She was wasting her time. Disappointment and frustration washed through her. She stood, wondering if there was anything she could say. Just a word to get a confession. The silence went on.

Joe hardly dared to move. Lizzie was shaking and staring up at him. He desperately wanted her to believe him. It would give him hope that he could maybe live again. Then, as he watched, she turned from him and picked her coat from the sofa.

'Lizzie—'

But she was gone.

The hurt he felt was like being stabbed.

Lizzie walked up the road in a fury, hoping he wouldn't come after her. She didn't know what she'd do if he did. Hit him, probably. Or scream at him. She had spent months being nice to this guy, only to be told the same crap he'd said in court. She remembered sitting in court the day he was found guilty and seeing the look in his eyes and wanting to kill him. She felt like that now. This whole getting to know him was suddenly pointless. Everything she'd done to date had achieved nothing. All the guilt she'd quashed had been for this? She wanted to cry. She was crying, she realised. She wanted to lash out. Her mind was disorientated and confused and not a place she recognised. A black hole that was pulling her in with more force the closer she got to it.

He needed to be hurt the way they had been hurt.

46

JOE WONDERED IF he should try to contact Lizzie, but it suddenly occurred to him that he had no phone number or address for her. For someone who'd been so free with information about herself, he suddenly realised he had no way of finding her again. Unless he met her on the Luas or at the club, of course.

He was finding it hard to concentrate on his work today, thoughts of what had happened the night before filled his head. Had he frightened her off? There was nothing he could do if he had. That was his story and he couldn't change it. He wondered if she'd tell anyone else. He didn't want everyone in the club knowing, that would be a nightmare. But Lizzie didn't seem the sort to do that.

'Hey, Joe,' a girl called Sharon called, 'look!'

She swam a couple of strokes before stopping.

His face broke into a delighted smile. 'Brilliant. That's great. That's how you do it.'

'It's not that hard.'

'Nope.'

Joe watched her again. Wading cautiously out from the bar and ducking her head under. Then she started to swim and move away from the safety of the side. It was always a bittersweet moment when they learned to swim, as you knew that they didn't need you any more.

She ditched work that afternoon, telling Mark that she had a pain. She didn't wait for the inquisition – instead she caught the tram back to Billy's.

Both him and Aileen were at work. Things between them seemed to be slowly improving. The Wham stuff had gone down well, with George and Andrew singing about being 'Bad Boys' well into the night. Billy was quiet, though, almost afraid to say anything that would make Aileen take off again. The easy relationship they'd shared would take a lot of rebuilding.

Lizzie let herself into the house and sat for a few minutes, thinking about what she was going to do. She wished she could be a fly on the wall when she saw Joe's face but, damn it, he'd had the chance to confess to her and he hadn't – and despite all her sabotage, his pigeons continued to thrive. His life continued to improve.

A part of her mind that she had ignored this past while sneaked through and whispered that it wasn't his birds' fault he had done what he'd done. Lizzie winced but managed to push the thought away and it dissolved instantly.

Taking deep breaths, she reflected that Billy had been so accurate in pinpointing the damage Joe had caused to them all. None of them had been left the same. Her relationship with Tom had always been terrifying because of its very happiness – that was Joe's doing and hated him for it. Twelve years in jail only to have a great life afterwards was *not* a punishment, she thought in despair. He deserved to really be taught a lesson. He had taken away their precious thing. She would take away his. An eye for an eye and all that.

'Here,' Anto handed Joe a present. 'Dat's for you.'

Joe took it in surprise. 'This? Why?'

Anto shrugged. 'Me ma thought you might like it. I think it's to say thanks for letting me help out. She bought something for Ellen, too, only Ellen's box is bigger.'

Joe suppressed a grin. 'Right. Thanks.'

'Open it,' Anto said. 'I actually picked it. She wanted to get you a poncy box of chocolates but I didn't think that was a good idea.' He hopped from foot to foot as Joe unwrapped the book on pigeons. 'My dad swore by that book,' he said finally, as Joe flicked through the pages. 'He said there wasn't a thing about birds that wasn't in there.'

Joe swallowed. No one had given him a present in ages. He looked at Anto.

'That's brilliant,' he grinned. 'Thanks.'

'No worries,' Anto nodded. Then, awkwardly, he muttered, 'And doing this with you . . . it's stopped me being, you know, sad and shit.'

Joe nodded. The pigeons had saved him, too, he reckoned. 'Know what you mean,' he said. He handed Anto a bucket. 'Now for the fun part, let's clean them out.'

And though he had meant it as a joke, he knew that Anto did find it fun.

The following Thursday was the night she had decided to do it.

It's what she should have done at the start, only in the beginning part of her had been repelled by the idea of revenge. Looking back, it was probably why she had tried to get friendly with him, in the hope that he'd hang himself by confessing. But that hadn't worked. Doing things bit by bit, though, had made her decision easier. Like wading into cold water and getting used to the temperature. She'd numbed herself to the implications now and could stride all the way in.

She had decided that she would skip counselling that night – Anna would manage on her own, she was sure of that. Now that she had made her decision, the hard part was over. Succumbing to the temptation had been a relief. She was finally stepping into the abyss and she knew it was as far as she could go. That there was nothing else she could do or, a part of her mind whispered, no lower she could fall. His failure to confess would cost him.

At the thought of what she was about to do, she wasn't scared. Or happy. Or sad. There was just an overriding instinct to even things out.

47

'I'M GOING FOR a hospital appointment today.' Aileen tossed the comment at Billy as he was heading to work.

Billy froze in the act of opening the door. He half turned. 'Yeah?'

'Yeah.' Aileen spooned some flakes into her mouth.

Lizzie, who had just arrived down, prayed that he would say the right thing. Billy seemed to be trying to second guess Aileen all the time these days.

'Well, eh,' he smiled a little too brightly, 'what time?'

'One.' She wasn't looking at him any more and had turned her attention to a magazine.

'Eh,' Billy made a production of zipping up his jacket, 'd'you need any company, like?'

'Company?' She shot him a look.

'As in, can I go in with you?'

Aileen shrugged. 'I suppose. If you want.'

'I'd love to, actually.'

There was a pause. Aileen slowly brought her face up from her magazine.

'Good.' She smiled a little hesitantly.

'Will they do a scan, d'you think?' Billy asked shyly.

'I'd imagine so.'

'Great. Good.' He nodded a 'good morning' at Lizzie. 'See you at one, so.'

'Bye.'

Lizzie, who had been watching the exchange with some trepidation, felt that finally they were going to make it. She vowed to ring Billy up later to tell him to bring Aileen out somewhere nice afterwards.

She only felt a little guilty that it would suit her, too.

Joe hadn't slept since he'd told Lizzie. His dreams consisted of his mother crying and Megan calling for help and no matter how he tried, he couldn't help either of them and because he couldn't, Lizzie walked away and, by trying to catch hold of her, the other two women started to drown. He awoke at the point where Lizzie walked out of his house, slamming the door behind her.

He dragged himself from bed and, as he showered, he pondered whether to wait for Lizzie that night, as he'd recently started to do, or whether he should just avoid her. She hadn't contacted him at all, which could be a good sign or a bad sign. On one hand she didn't say that she wanted nothing to do with him, but on the other, by not contacting him, maybe it meant she wanted him out of her life completely. He wished he'd never met her, but it was too late now. She'd shown him normality for the first time in years, given him hope for a future.

To hell with it, he decided, he'd wait for her. And if she didn't want to talk to him, well, fine. At least he'd know.

Lizzie rang Anna at around five.

'Hey, could you manage without me tonight? I'm feeling sick.'

Anna's sympathetic reaction made her feel like a heel.

'Of course I can, what's the matter?'

'Just some kind of a bug,' Lizzie mumbled. 'I haven't been well all day so I'm going home early. Do you want me to see if I can get a stand-in?'

'No. You go home and get to bed, I'll manage.'

'Thanks, Anna, I owe you.'

She put the phone down and knew that she couldn't turn back now.

Eleven-ten. Joe left work early. Paperwork could wait, he decided. He was determined to see Lizzie, to have another go at explaining it to her. So, rather than waiting in Grafton Street as he normally did, he took up a position outside the Life offices. He would beg her to listen if necessary and, if that didn't work, he'd concede defeat. At least he'd have tried.

He glanced at his watch. Eleven-fifteen. She'd be out in quarter of an hour.

There was an older woman waiting by the building, too. She seemed as edgy as he was. Then she seemed edgy because it was just her and him. Joe smiled a little at her.

'It's OK,' he tried to reassure her, 'I'm harmless.'

The irony of him saying it almost made him laugh.

'I'm just waiting on my daughter,' the woman confided, sounding relieved. She thumbed to the LIFE sign. 'She works the night shift here on a Thursday.'

Joe winced. 'It's not Lizzie, is it?'

'No, her name is Anna. I've heard her speak of a Lizzie, though. They seem to be good friends.'

Joe shrugged, he didn't know. It struck him as slightly odd that Lizzie had never mentioned any friends.

'Are you waiting on Lizzie? Is she your girlfriend?' the woman asked. Now that she'd established that he wasn't out to mug her, she seemed eager to talk. Though it was in a nervy, babbling way.

'She's not my girlfriend,' Joe said, 'just a mate. I think she's angry at me so don't be surprised if she ignores me when she comes out.' He felt he had to say that, it'd save embarrassment if that's what happened.

To his surprise the woman laughed. 'Oh, a right pair they'll be, counselling tonight. I haven't talked to Anna in about eight weeks. I'm here to grovel and make peace. Kids, they don't know all you're doing is your best, even though you make a right mess of things sometimes.'

Joe smiled weakly.

Lizzie parked Billy's car two doors down from Joe's house. She would rather have waited until later but, with Aileen back home, there was no chance she could sneak out in the early hours without being heard.

Aileen was finding it hard to sleep with two babies growing inside her and Lizzie had been given a blow by blow on the various sleeping positions that hadn't worked for her. She'd also been given a blow-by-blow account by a newly-infatuated father on the state of Aileen's rapidly expanding uterus. The scan had been a roaring success and the two were now out having a meal before coming home. The newfound harmony only pointed up the frozen iciness in her own head.

Very gently she took her basket from the back seat of the car. This basket had come in handy, she thought objectively. She lifted it out and closed the car door as quietly as she could. A few people walked by but they didn't even glance in her direction. Joe's house was in darkness, as was his nosy neighbour's. Lizzie walked as confidently as she could up the street and stood opposite the two houses.

No one.

She swiftly crossed the street and, still scanning left and right, she walked into Joe's garden.

Nothing.

She slunk into the shadow at the side of his house, took some oil from her pocket and hastily lubricated the hinges on his side gate. Very gently she unlatched it and stepped into the darkness of the back garden.

A tall girl came out of Lizzie's building and she stopped dead at the sight of the woman Joe had been talking to. Joe watched a little awkwardly as they stared at each other.

'Hi, love.'

'Mammy.'

'I decided to come tonight in person to say that I've been wrong, but it was only because I loved you, darling. And because he hurt you so much.'

Joe shifted uncomfortably and moved a step away, scanning the door behind Anna as someone else slipped in. No one seemed to be exiting, though.

Anna was now hugging her mother and her mother was hugging her back. It all seemed terribly emotional and Joe had to turn away. Then he coughed slightly to remind them he was there so that they wouldn't say any more.

'Oh,' the woman said to Anna, 'this man here is looking for Lizzie.'

'Hi,' Joe said in as friendly a voice as he could, 'is she ready yet?'

Anna frowned. 'She's not on tonight.'

Joe felt his heart plummet. 'Is she not? I thought she always worked Thursdays.'

'Yeah, but she called in sick.'

He didn't even have the stomach to reply. Well, that was it then, he thought. His answer.

'Can I say who was looking for her?'

'Naw, it's OK. Thanks.'

'You sure?' Anna smiled at him, her arm still about her mother's waist.

'Yep.' His smile wasn't convincing so he turned away as quickly as he could.

He wished he'd never met Lizzie.

Again, like the first time she'd stolen into the loft, Lizzie waited to feel something. If guilt had hit her, she might have backed down. But there was nothing. As usual. Not even triumph that she was about to destroy Joe. There was just a hardness that was impossible for any emotion to break through.

She wondered if that's the way Joe had felt when he'd done what he'd done.

48

H<small>E WAS HAVING</small> the same dream again, only this time there was more noise than just the slamming of a door. Someone was screeching and wailing and then, suddenly, the screeching became his pigeons. And his pigeons were flying around and Joe was trying to catch them. Prince's leg had come right off.

'NO!' Joe shouted, waking himself up.

Outside, the noise of his dream continued. It was early morning; dawn light was splashed across his bed. He very rarely drew the curtains at night, preferring to look out at the sky. He rubbed his eyes, sleep ebbing away, fragments of his nightmare scattering until it registered in his still half dazed mind that the sounds he was hearing were coming from his garden. His loft.

Jesus.

He flung off his covers, his feet getting tangled up in the sheet. He fell out of bed, banging his head on the wooden floor. The pain didn't even register. Taking the stairs two at a time, he raced into the kitchen and, with clumsy hands, unlocked his back door before running barefoot across the lawn to his loft.

Oh, Christ.

He froze for half a second before unlocking the loft door and wrenching it open. He grabbed the shrieking cat by the scruff of the neck and flung it out into his garden. It arched its back and hissed before taking off over the wall.

Joe stood inside the door of his loft and swayed slightly before grabbing on to the door frame. He couldn't take in how many of his racers lay blood-soaked on the floor. How many of his birds lay unharmed but shocked and shivering around the loft.

How many were dead already. The place was awash with blood and feathers.

Joe blinked. Once. Twice. He pinched himself, dazed, convinced he was dreaming. He turned around and vomited into the garden.

He blanked his mind to how it could have happened – he'd deal with that later. Instead he called the vet and, as he waited for him to arrive, he placed the injured birds gently into a basket and brought them indoors to keep them warm. He did the same with the birds he considered to be shell-shocked, talking softly to them all the time, letting them pick bits of grain and corn from his hands. Birds that were all right he placed into their boxes and left them there. And then he turned to survey the real carnage. Hero was dead. His one hope to replace Prince as a good racer. His body lay right at the front of the loft. His head had been torn from his little body. Nine other birds were dead, too. Some from shock, some from the cat. Over half his loft. Gone.

Joe dumped their bodies into a black sack that he'd got from the kitchen. As each corpse went in, he felt his heart twist. He'd spent years building up his loft and now the ground had been ripped from under his feet. How the hell had it happened? He was sure he'd locked up last night. And how had the cat got in? There was no way for a cat to sneak in. He felt numb inside, it was too big for him to take in just now. He had to concentrate on getting it back to normal.

The vet arrived within half an hour and Joe brought him into the house.

He groaned at the damage. 'When did the cat get in?' he asked, peering around at the shivering birds.

'Dunno,' Joe said dully. He watched the vet handle one of the birds. He gently pulled out a ragged wing.

'Broken.' He looked at Joe.

Joe winced.

'A cat wouldn't attack unless there was some movement, so it must have only begun once the birds started fluttering about.'

'Once there is light at all, they'll start to stir,' Joe said.

'Well, you've been lucky. It could have been worse. It was so early when you caught him.'

Lucky. Joe didn't feel lucky.

Another bird. Another broken wing. Joe could have told the vet that, only he hadn't the heart to go examining them himself.

'How did the cat get in?'

'Dunno. The loft was locked when I got to it.'

The vet raised his eyebrows. 'D'you think someone put it there?'

'I can't think of anything else,' Joe said.

'You should report it to the police.'

Joe flinched. He never wanted to get involved with the cops again. 'I might,' he said.

The vet handed Joe some sedatives for the birds. 'It'll calm them down.'

'Thanks.'

'Bloody brutal thing to do,' the vet said sympathetically.

Joe nodded and watched him leave.

Lizzie got up and showered. She knew she was going to be late for work, but she didn't want to run into Billy and Aileen. She couldn't relate to them. To the fact that while their lives were going on, hers seemed to have stopped. Their budding happiness was pulling them further and further away from her. What she had done last night, if she thought about it, was completely inhuman. Cruel. Disgusting. It marked her as different from everyone else, put her in a different place from everyone else. She wasn't going to think about it. It was easier to cope that way. In fact, in the past few months, Lizzie realised with a little jolt, she had stopped thinking about anything she had done – good and bad. If she was off guard and happy, she found that the horrible stuff seeped in like a bad smell under a door, poisoning the air. It was easier not to think, just to keep going. But it was hard trying to get through the day when inside she felt like a stranger to herself. Today, she knew it would be harder still. She let the water cascade over her for ages and scrubbed herself hard, hurting herself a little in the process, making her arms and legs bright red.

She was about an hour late for work.

She found she didn't really care that much.

John came round after Joe had rung him. He took one look at Joe's devastated face and made him sit down.

'You stay there, right? I'm going to clean the place up for you.'

'Naw, let me help, OK?'

John eyed him. 'If you're up to it. I know I'd never be able to face it if it was my loft.'

Joe didn't say anything else, but he watched John searching around for cleaning agents and straw and then, when he'd got everything, Joe stood up and walked outside with him. Together they stared on the horrible job of washing down the loft.

John took up the hopper. 'Hey, your malt is wet,' he exclaimed. 'You'd want to watch that, Joe.'

'Wet?' Joe examined it. Then shrugged hopelessly. 'The lofts are as dry as a bone, John.' He gulped. 'That always seems to be happening. I dunno, I think I'm going mad.'

'Either that or someone is out to get you.'

Joe shivered.

John looked at him questioningly. 'Have you done anything to anyone? You know, made any enemies?'

'Cid?'

John waved him away. 'Come on, Joe, you don't really believe that.'

'I don't know what to believe.'

He watched as John began to scrape feathers from the floor. Hero's feathers. Joe crouched down and picked one up and held it to his face. John leaned on the brush, watching him.

'You sure you haven't annoyed someone?'

Even in prison he hadn't offended anyone, Joe thought. He'd kept his head down, served his sentence and left. He looked at John, wondering if he should tell him. John was watching him, willing him to remember some little detail. Joe swallowed hard. Taking his silence as a negative, John started his sweeping again.

'I was in prison, John,' Joe blurted out.

John turned to face him. His expression was more curious than shocked. That'd soon change, Joe thought dismally. He barely cared. Right at that moment he felt as if everything had been taken away from him and it was only a matter of time before the rest was, too.

He stood up and faced his friend. 'I got convicted of murder.'

Now John's expression turned to incredulity.

'You?' he said.

Joe nodded.

'Self-defence?'

'Nope.' Joe shoved his hands in his pockets and sighed. 'I don't suppose you'll believe me, but I was innocent. They said I killed a girl.'

'You?' John said again. His face was unreadable.

'Me.'

The silence went on for ages. Joe wondered if John would walk out, the way Lizzie had done. He winced, trying not to think of her.

'You couldn't kill anyone,' John pronounced. 'Look at you now – your birds die and you're in bits.'

Joe couldn't speak for a second. There was a big lump in his throat.

'Thanks for saying that,' he gulped out.

'What happened, Joe?'

So Joe told him. Standing in his blood-soaked loft, he told him everything. When he finished, John stood staring at him.

'You poor fucker,' he said slowly. 'If I was you, I'd go and find out who did it. I'd make it my mission in life.'

Joe smiled glumly. 'I thought of that, too, once,' he said, 'but then, well, I figure that I'd only be wasting the rest of my life letting it dominate everything. I just wanted peace. The pigeons make me happy, so that's what I did.'

John nodded.

'And now—' Joe indicated the loft, his voice catching.

'We'll sort it out,' John promised. 'Honest.'

Joe swallowed hard. His best bird. Gone.

'Is it someone from prison, d'you think?'

'I dunno.'

'Who has been in here lately?'

'Just Anto and Lizzie.' He winced saying her name. 'Anto did say he'd check the loft for me last night, so I'll talk to him later.'

'And Lizzie?'

'Haven't seen her in a few days.'

'Oh.'

'I told her about – well, what I just told you.'

'And she didn't like it?'

Joe shrugged. 'I don't think she believed me. She hasn't rung or anything.'

John said nothing, just slapped him on the shoulder and got back to work.

'You're late,' Mark said as she arrived in. 'I'll have to dock your pay.'

Lizzie wasn't in the humour for him.

'Lizzie, I'd like to think we're mates—'

'Well, we're not.'

It was the first time Mark recoiled from her. Then, as usual, he regained his composure. 'Well, regardless of what you think, I want you to know that coming to work late and leaving early is not acceptable.'

Lizzie kept her head down, pretending to examine her desk. She knew that it wasn't on. And she knew he was only saying it to her because he was annoyed.

'Now, I can accept it if you tell me why you're so damned weird these days.'

Lizzie glanced up at him. 'Takes one to know one.'

There was a silence.

'Is it Tom?'

'I am not going out with Tom any more.'

'Good. At least you're not in denial. I was in denial after my wife left me and—'

'Mark, I don't need to hear about you and your wife. Now,

there are three hundred and fifty people signed on for the parachute jump. We need fifty more, which we will probably get, and—'

'I don't give a damn about the bloody jump,' Mark said edgily. 'What is wrong with you, Lizzie?'

'Nothing.' She knew she had snapped but she didn't apologise.

'Well,' Mark said, in a voice mixed with hurt and anger, 'if there is nothing wrong, then please be on time for work. Right?'

'Right.'

Mark seemed to wait for her to say more and when she didn't he left the office, banging the door behind him.

Lizzie flicked on her computer and her eye fell on a note in her inbox.

Lizzie – fab guy waiting outside for you last night!!! Who is he? Guys like that should NEVER be stood up! Also, Lori rang again. Wouldn't talk to me, says she wants you to talk to her. Wouldn't give me her number so I guess you'll be hearing from her soon.

And my mother turned up outside last night, too. She said she reckoned she had to do something totally unexpected to show me how much she cares and standing about in that lane at eleven at night was a bit of madness. She thought your hunk was out to rob her at some stage! Anyway, all good again.

Hope you're feeling better. Love, Anna.

Lizzie typed in a *Gld u will soon hve ur bbysttr back* and pressed 'send.' She didn't bother telling her who the guy was.

John stayed with Joe all day, sending out for lunch in the midst of cleaning up. Anto arrived after school and, jumping over the wall, he stopped dead at the sight of John.

'Cat got into the loft last night,' John said, carefully observing Anto's face for a reaction.

'No way!' Anto said in disbelief, striding toward the loft, 'Was there much damage?'

'Twelve birds so far,' Joe muttered.

'Twelve!' Anto looked as devastated as Joe. 'Dead?' At Joe's nod, he asked, 'How'd that happen?'

'Dunno,' Joe said. 'What time did you check them last night?'

'Nine-thirty, just before me ma collected me.'

'And did you notice anything? Was the loft open?'

'No, the loft was not open,' Anto said, as if Joe was a moron. 'D'ya think I'm stupid?'

'No,' Joe tried to reassure him, 'but, I dunno, maybe a cat sneaked in and you didn't see.'

'There was no cat in there when I checked.' He sounded hurt. 'D'you think it was me?'

'No, but just say—'

'You do,' Anto said. 'You do think it was me. Maybe it was you, maybe the cat sneaked in when you checked them after you came home from work.'

'I didn't check them,' Joe said dully. Normally he would have but last night he hadn't. The non appearance of Lizzie had upset him. And anyway, if a cat was quiet he mightn't have spotted it. 'So you were the last person to be in the loft.'

'I didn't let a cat in!' Anto shouted, his face red.

'I'm not saying you did—' Joe tried to say.

'The malt was wet, too,' John volunteered.

Anto looked from one to the other. His eyes rested on Joe.

'I thought you trusted me,' he said. 'You can keep your stupid birds.' Then he hopped back over the wall.

'Aw, Anto—'

But Anto was gone, back over the wall and into Ellen's. Joe groaned, he knew it was only a matter of time before she appeared to question him.

'You believe him?' John asked.

Joe nodded. 'Yeah. I'll talk to him later. If he said he checked . . .'

'Come on,' John said then, 'let's keep going.'

329

They worked on in silence for another while, before John asked quietly, 'How did you cope in prison, Joe?'

'Huh?' The question came out of the blue.

'In prison. How did you cope?'

Joe shrugged as he checked the walls for draughts. 'Just did. Told myself it'd be over one day and that when I got out I could do anything I wanted.'

'Fair play.'

Joe, despite himself, laughed. 'Eh – lots of people wouldn't agree with you.'

'Your life flipped and you dealt with it. That's great.'

'I had no choice.'

'You did, you could have cracked up.' John indicated his leg. 'See this?'

Joe nodded.

'I got that in a car crash when I was eighteen. Before that, I'd had dreams of playing professional football. In two seconds flat that disappeared. I had a new life without sport and a wife who kindly married me out of pity, then she realised her mistake and fecked off with my best friend.'

'No way. I thought she left because of the pigeons.'

'Nope. And I still hate her.' He grinned and rolled his eyes. 'I also had no job and a lot of time to drink. I was a mess. It took me ten years to figure out what you learned in prison. And even then, it was hard. You,' he nodded, 'did well, Joe.'

'I hang around with a bunch of old men – no offence, John – I steer clear of relationships, I have no contact with my folks . . .' He grinned a little. 'I'm doing great.'

'And you can smile about it,' John said firmly. 'You're doing better than great.'

Joe had never looked at it like that before.

49

'I'M SORRY. I thought I could but I can't.'

Mr Walsh shook his head firmly and crossed his arms as Lizzie looked at him in alarm.

'But Dad, Billy can't come as Aileen's dad has invited them over and you – you just decide not to come.'

'I didn't just decide,' her dad said, eyeballing her, 'I have been thinking of nothing else all week.'

'But why did you come up here if you'd already decided not to visit her?'

'First,' her father sighed, 'I'm finding it lonely without her at home. And second, I thought I could go through with it and I can't.' He sat back down at the kitchen table and looked up at Lizzie. 'I am sorry, Lizzie, but it's just seeing her in that place, surrounded by all those people, I just can't seem to handle it.'

'Yeah, I know it's horrible, Dad, but she really needs to see you, to keep her spirits up.'

'I don't want to keep her spirits up,' her father retorted. 'I want her home with me and if the only way to do that is to stay away, then I will. Keep her spirits up,' he snorted. 'That woman is breaking my heart.'

'Dad, please?'

'I can't, Lizzie. It's not good for either of us.'

'Please, Dad, I can't go on my own.' And she couldn't, she realised. Her mother being in jail was worse than she thought it would be. 'Please? Just today?'

Mr Walsh flinched. He didn't like to see Lizzie upset like this. He wondered what else was bothering her, she didn't seem to be as bubbly as usual. It was probably that actor fella she'd broken up with, he'd never liked him. Though at the time he couldn't help thinking how well suited he and Lizzie were, both of them with their weird dress sense, both of them loving that ridiculous film *Amelie* which he couldn't make head nor tail of. Both of them cheating at cards the only time Tom had come to visit. Really, the man was a bad influence on his daughter.

'Please, Dad? For me?'

He sighed deeply and, placing his hands on his knees, he hauled himself from the chair.

'Just today,' he warned. 'And I'll tell her that, too.'

Great, Lizzie thought glumly.

Her mother was sitting just inside the door, in the same place she'd been in the last couple of times they visited.

'Hi, Mammy.' Lizzie sat down. Her dad prowled behind her.

'Why don't you sit?' Mrs Walsh said to her husband, with a slight edge of irritation in her voice. 'There is a chair over there.' She pointed to the opposite wall.

'I'd prefer to stand, thanks.'

'Suit yourself.' She sniffed.

'Like you do, you mean.'

'And what is that supposed to mean?'

Mr Walsh leaned across the table to his wife and said in a cross voice, 'Will you ever go and apologise? You're making a holy show of yourself.'

'I am not! How dare you!'

'You are. What do you hope to achieve, ey? All this,' he waved expansively about the room, 'all this anger, what is it going to achieve?'

'It'll highlight the harbour plan.'

'Bollocks!'

Whether it was the fact that her dad shouted or the fact that for the first time in his life he cursed, Lizzie wasn't sure, but it shocked her.

'That is total rubbish,' he said.

'Everything OK?' a prison guard called over.

'OK, aside from the fact that my husband seems to be having some sort of a mental breakdown,' Polly said sarcastically.

'Well, we'll be company for each other then, won't we?'

The guard issued a gentle warning for them to keep it down.

'When did you become so angry?' Mr Walsh asked, his voice a mixture of sadness and defeat. 'I hardly know you any more, Polly.'

With that he straightened himself up and walked out of the room.

'Oh, that's charming.' Mrs Walsh shook her head as he left. 'Charming.' She turned to Lizzie. 'Well, I hope you'll do better than that.'

When *had* her mother got so angry? Lizzie wondered. It had been a sort of gradual thing. She'd been a worrier, a fretter, a comforter. But she never used to have that slash between her eyebrows and that permanent downturn to her mouth. The council could have built the Empire State building in her back garden and she probably wouldn't have gone to jail for it. But now it was like she was fighting the whole world.

'It's since Meg, isn't it?' Lizzie said, her voice catching at the mention of her sister's name.

'What?'

'You've been angry since Meg.'

'What are you talking about?'

'Mam,' Lizzie lowered her voice, tried to sound soothing the way you would counselling someone, 'Dad said he wasn't coming to see you any more. It upsets him to see you in here. Does that bother you?'

'Spineless. It bothers him because he hadn't the guts to join me.'

Her mother was completely delusional. 'No,' Lizzie shook her head, 'it bothers him because he sees his wife ruining her life. He sees his wife sitting in jail because she's angry at the whole world.'

Her mother had opened her mouth to protest but shut it again and glared balefully at her daughter.

'You can't change the fact that Megan isn't coming back by being angry,' Lizzie said gently.

'I can change the world that let her die,' Mrs Walsh said bitterly. 'I can make it better. I can—'

'You can't. You can't, Mam. You have to take what's left for you. Make the best of it. You've got Dad and me and Billy and we love you and want you home.'

Her mother said nothing, just curved her face away slightly.

'Please say sorry, Mammy.'

'I want to ask you to do something for me,' Mrs Walsh said instead, startling her.

'Mammy, are you listening?'

'Yes. But I need a favour.'

Lizzie sighed. 'What?'

'I want you to trace this mobile phone number.' She recited a number.

Lizzie looked blankly at her.

'Will you put it in your phone?' she snapped as Lizzie looked puzzled. 'They won't let me hand you anything.'

Lizzie took out her phone and keyed the number in.

'Is this to do with the harbour?'

'Just trace it, I'll tell you why later. I'll ring you during the week, OK?'

'Do you know how mad you sound?'

'Are you going to do this or not?'

'I will if you apologise.'

Her mother glared at her.

'Just say sorry, Mammy. That's all you have to do.' Lizzie leaned in towards her, 'You can't change anything by getting angry. It won't bring her back, you know.' And then her own words hit her. She paused with her mouth open and sank back down on to the seat, staring at her mother. She felt suddenly sick.

'Lizzie, do you know how mad you look?' her mother asked, quirking an eyebrow.

The rest of the visit went by in a blur.

When it ended and her mother had called after her again to

334

trace that number, Lizzie bolted right past her dad's car and told him that she didn't need a lift, that she needed a smoke. That she needed to think.

'A smoke? As in a cigarette?'

'Yes, Dad. I smoke. It's not the worst thing in the world.'

'Can I have one?'

Without saying a word, she handed him one. He stood beside her, smoking. Inhaling and exhaling with her until she'd calmed down.

'What happened?' he asked eventually.

She didn't answer and he didn't ask again. She wasn't even sure she knew herself.

Instead he wrapped an arm about her shoulder and led her back to the car.

It was true what she'd said to her mother: nothing could be changed by anger. Megan could never come back no matter how many roads or planning permissions her mother blocked. She'd never come back if Lizzie killed a million pigeons. She'd never come back if her mother never said sorry. She'd never come back if Lizzie never said sorry. Megan could never be avenged because there was nothing to replace her. Dead birds and altered roads were no substitute. They only fed the anger inside. Made it worse.

And her rage had grown the longer she'd been with Joe. And it hadn't changed anything except the way she felt about herself. Which wasn't good. What she had done was—. Lizzie couldn't even put a name on it. It danced before her, let out of the box in which she'd carefully stowed it away. 'Horrible' wasn't the right word. 'Justified' didn't seem to fit. What she had done was wrong, she realised. Wrong for her. Wrong because she'd managed to alter who she was. And wrong because it would never be right.

Her head was flooded with it. With the wrongness of it. By looking at the futility of her mother's battle, she had suddenly seen the senselessness of her own.

Lizzie pulled her duvet up around her shoulders and tried to get warm. It was as if in the past few months, she'd been on a drug. A drug that at first had made her feel sick but that eventually she'd become immune to. A drug that made her feel a false happiness and importance. A drug that had numbed her. But now she was cold turkey and she could see what it had done to her and she was sick. Too sick to cry. Too sick to think properly.

She picked up her mobile phone and dialled a number.

50

Anna had hugged her and listened to her and made her cups of coffee. She'd told her that what she had done was understandable, horrible but totally understandable, which had given her a huge sense of release. But still, Lizzie knew what she had to do if she was to feel any better about herself. It didn't mean it was going to be easy – in fact, it was probably going to be the hardest thing she'd ever done. Well, the hardest apart from that first step she'd taken months ago, on to the road she was now determined to get off.

She had to apologise, or at least own up to what she'd done. In person.

To a guy she detested.

He'd never apologised to her family, so at least in doing this she'd know she wasn't like him.

Joe normally spent Sundays at home so she hoped he'd be there when she arrived. Lizzie told Billy that she was going shopping and instead caught the Luas to Ranelagh. As it pulled into the station her legs were shaking so much she could hardly get off. She made herself take deep breaths before she began the ten-minute walk to Joe's home. It passed in a blur. She paused, two doors up from his house, and saw that his battered car was parked alongside the kerb. He was in.

Maybe if she just stopped, if she just disappeared and didn't bother him again, would that do? The thought flitted through her head and she quashed it. How would she live with herself? She'd be just like him then, not owning up to her misdeeds. Refusing to apologise for what she'd done. No, she was better than that, she decided. She was going to start over once the apology was done. Push it all away and start over.

With a thudding heart and clammy hands, her heavy black boots clunked up his driveway. She pressed the bell on the door and suddenly an odd calmness overcame her. She took more deep breaths. This was it. This. Was. It.

Her calm began to fray slightly when she heard noise from inside the house and saw Joe's tall silhouette through the glass. He pulled open the door and the smile he gave her made her feel worse than she already felt, if that was possible. It also made her resent him more, which she knew was impossible.

'Hey,' he said hesitantly, his large hazel eyes looking her up and down, 'thought I'd never see you again.'

She shrugged, her mouth suddenly dry.

His face fell when she didn't return his grin. He pulled the door wider and asked softly, 'D'you want to come in?'

Lizzie shook her head. She wondered if she'd be able to actually talk when the time came.

'Oh,' Joe nodded glumly, 'it's like that, ey?' He paused, his hand still on the door. It took a second before he spoke and then it was in a resigned sort of voice: 'Don't feel bad about it, I know I wouldn't be anyone's idea of a perfect partner.' He managed a rueful smile. 'But I didn't kill anyone, I swear.'

'That's not why I'm here,' she croaked out.

Joe looked startled. 'Have you had a cold?'

She shook her head. Her heart had started to pump so fast she was beginning to feel that she couldn't breathe. 'It's, it's about the . . . the birds.'

His eyes clouded. 'You heard, then,' he said flatly.

'Heard?'

'About the cat in the loft?'

'Eh—'

'Bastard got fourteen of my birds in the end.' He swallowed and looked away.

'Fourteen?' Lizzie winced. But surely—. 'I thought you checked the loft before you went to bed?'

'Not that night.' He pinned her with his gaze. 'I waited for you outside work and when you didn't show,' he shrugged, 'I forgot about the birds.'

Lizzie felt her stomach heave. Oh God. He'd go mad with her.

'Hey, are you OK? Come in.' Joe reached to touch her and she sprang back.

'No!'

He pulled his hand away as if he'd been burned. 'Sorry.'

She thought about running then. Just legging it up the road and out of his life. But she forced herself to stay still. She was here and she had to do this. Had to be better than him.

'It was me,' she blurted out.

'Huh?' he looked at her, uncomprehending.

'I— I put the cat in the loft.'

Joe looked as if he didn't understand. 'What?'

'I did it.' Lizzie gained courage from the admission. 'I did it.' As she watched the disbelief etch itself across his face, she went on, 'And I did everything else, too. I diluted their medicine, I put in the wild pigeon, and I took Prince.'

'What?' His brow was wrinkled. He seemed stunned, as if he'd been hit on the head or something.

'It was all me,' Lizzie said, not able to help the slight edge of malice that crept into her voice.

Joe looked at the pretty girl in front of him. Her vibrant scarf wrapped snugly about her neck even though it was heading into summer. Her long coat that he thought was cool on her. Her flyaway hair that he longed to run his hands through, if only she'd let him. He blinked, dazed. 'I don't understand,' he said. And he didn't. It was as if he'd been plunged into a surreal conversation.

'It was me.' She said the words slowly as if he was stupid. 'I did it. And, well, I just came to say that I won't be doing it any more.' She shrugged, her voice dipped. 'I'm sorry.'

She didn't sound that sorry, Joe thought. It just didn't make sense. Her? Lizzie? 'You took Prince?'

A nod.

'And, and, the cat—'

'Me.'

He knew he should be angry. He should shout, but he couldn't understand. Instead he just said, 'Why? Why would you do that?'

Lizzie seemed to take her time answering. Instead she searched his face as if she couldn't believe he wouldn't know. In the end she half whispered, 'Can't you guess?'

Guess? He shook his head.

How could it not dominate his every waking thought, the way it did hers? Lizzie thought angrily. How could he not guess?

'My name is Elizabeth Walsh.' Pause. 'I come from Rossclare.' Her voice rang clear and she stared him in the eye.

All the colour drained from his face. 'Walsh,' he repeated. And he suddenly knew. He'd known when he'd seen her first, only she'd disarmed him, so that he hadn't let the thought register.

'Megan's sister.' She felt her heart constrict again with the hate. And it was hate. 'That's why I did it.'

'Christ,' was all he could say. He flinched back from the look she gave him.

'How *dare* you have a good life?' she went on, her voice rising. 'How dare you! And she's dead.' Her voice broke and he did nothing, just looked at her. She swallowed hard. 'But what I did, well, I shouldn't have done it. It wasn't—' She hesitated. 'Right. And I don't know how I did it. It's, it's not me. Or it didn't used to be. You can report me to the police if you like.'

Joe didn't move. He seemed to look at her for a long time. When he spoke, his voice was soft.

'I already told you,' he said, 'I never laid a hand on Megan.'

'That is a lie!'

'No,' Joe shook his head. His voice rose now, too, only not as loud as hers. 'It's not. It's bloody well not!' He sounded angry. 'You can kill the rest of my birds if it makes you feel better.' He jammed his hands into the pocket of his jeans and pulled out his keys. 'Here.'

Lizzie took a step back.

'Take them,' he said, thrusting them towards her. Then he

paused. 'Oh, I guess you have your own.' He indicated the side gate. 'Go on in, kill them all if you want. But I am sick of being judged for stuff I did not do.'

'Look, I just came to say sorry.' She swallowed. 'It's more than you ever did.'

'I did twelve years for something I didn't do. I owe you *nothing*.'

Lizzie pulled her coat around her. 'Well, I felt I owed you an apology.'

'Did you? To make yourself feel better? Or because you felt bad?'

'Both.'

'Well, apology accepted,' Joe said. 'I wouldn't want you having a burden like that on your conscience.'

For some reason, she felt small. She turned to go.

Joe's eyes scanned the street. 'Did you not bring back-up with you?'

'Huh?' She turned back.

'In case I murdered you in a fit of rage.'

'Stop!'

He felt ashamed as her eyes filled up. But he didn't apologise. Instead, he closed the door in her face.

Why hadn't she thought to bring someone with her? Lizzie wondered. OK, she was deeply ashamed of what she'd done and didn't want people to know, but Billy would have come after first giving her an earful. It occurred to her suddenly that she hadn't felt the need for protection. She hadn't thought for one second Joe would do anything to her. And that made her head reel. Either she was very stupid or she didn't believe he would have hurt her.

And that made things worse.

Joe leaned his back against the front door and stayed there for a long time, letting the complete and utter devastation work its way through him like a slowly rising tide. His head still couldn't get around it. Lizzie was a cool sort of girl. The kind he liked. Lizzie was Megan's sister. Lizzie had done all that stuff to him. He supposed that he should be relieved that he wasn't going mad or

341

losing his touch. But he wasn't. The only girl he'd actually liked in a long time had hated him. Maybe he'd got so used to being despised that he didn't notice when people didn't like him the way he would if he was normal.

Damn it – he *was* normal. Well, as normal as anyone would be if they'd just spent twelve years in jail for a murder they didn't commit.

He smiled ruefully. Bloody hell.

But there was something he'd said to Lizzie that he suddenly realised was true. He was sick of being blamed and silently judged for something he knew was not his fault. He was sick of hiding his past and hiding who he was and being afraid to go home. To hell with it, he was going, from right now, to throw off his victim role. He didn't care who knew what had happened him. He had nothing, nothing to be ashamed of. From right now . . .

Without giving himself time to think, he dialled John.

'Yo!'

'It's Joe.'

'How's things?'

'That stuff I told you the other day—'

'Won't go any further.'

'No, I'd appreciate it if you told a few guys. Billy and Alan and that. If you don't mind.'

There was a pause. 'Oh. OK. If that's what you want.'

'Yep. It is.' Joe didn't prolong the conversation. He put the phone down and decided that what he had to do now was to locate one very annoyed teenager.

Ellen had been very abrupt with him. No, Anto was not there. No, she wasn't sure where he was. Joe should know better than to falsely accuse someone. Really, she said, if anyone should know about doing that, it had to be Joseph. He'd been contrite, told Ellen that he knew Anto hadn't done anything and that the boy had taken him up wrong. Where was he now, please?

She had grudgingly supplied him with an address after telling him he should have gone and sorted it out with Anto the other night instead of leaving it until now, but Joe had left in the middle of her rant and was now at the top of Anto's road, thanking his lucky stars that all he drove was a crappy car. A decent car wouldn't have stood a chance in a place like this. The only thing close to Anto's estate was a war zone in the Middle East. The kerbs were ripped from the sides of the roads, litter was everywhere and gangs of teenagers were congregated on a green.

Joe hopped out of his car and studied the address he had written down.

The teenagers turned to look at he passed. A roar of laughter followed him up the street. Joe didn't turn. After what he'd been through, walking past a gang like that was child's play.

Anto's house was a lovely oasis on a street of bedlam. There were no flowers in the garden but the grass was neatly trimmed and the windows of the house looked all shiny and clean. It looked a lot better than his own place, Joe thought ruefully.

He rang the bell, wondering what sort of reception he'd get.

A woman who he recognised as Anto's mother answered the door. Her eyes widened in recognition as she took him in. Then they narrowed. 'What?' she barked out.

Joe flinched. 'Eh, I just came to, eh, thank you for the present you got me.'

She inclined her head. Then muttered, 'You didn't deserve it.'

Joe ignored that. 'And mainly I'm here to talk to Anto.'

'You going to accuse him of doing something else he didn't do now?'

God, he was sick of women hating him. Though at least she wasn't disguising her feelings. Joe sighed. 'I never accused him of anything, he just assumed that I had. I was just wondering why he hasn't been around the last couple of days.'

'That's not the version I got.'

He met her steely gaze, but she outstared him. 'Can I talk to him, please?'

Anto's mother was a lot tougher than she had appeared in the police station that day, Joe thought in grudging admiration. 'Look,' she said, 'you either trust Anto or you don't. Make up your mind. I'm not having him getting upset any more.'

'I trust him. He's great with the birds.'

'I didn't see a cat in the loft.' Anto surprised Joe as he spoke from behind his mother. He must have crept into the hall unnoticed.

His mother stood aside but didn't leave them alone.

'Yeah, I know.' Joe attempted a grin. 'I am sorry if you thought I didn't trust you.' He shrugged. 'Nine of the birds had been killed at that stage, Anto. I was in shock, you know.'

'When my dad died, I never said it was anyone's fault,' Anto said.

'I never said it was your fault.'

'You didn't have to.'

Joe wondered if he should say that he knew it was Lizzie, but decided not to. It might sound worse. 'Look,' he crouched down a bit to be on Anto's level, 'I know you're great. I know you'd see a cat a mile off. I know it wasn't your fault.'

'Good.' Anto folded his arms.

'Good.' His mother folded her arms.

Joe looked from one to the other. 'Will you be coming back to help me?' he asked.

Anto looked unsure. He glanced at his mother.

She gave a bark of a laugh. 'Help you? He'd rather cut his ears off, wouldn't you, Anto?'

'Eh—'

'I can pay you,' Joe said. 'For your help.'

'He doesn't need the money. Do you, Anto?'

'Eh—'

'Sure, have a think about it,' Joe said, looking at Anto's mother and trying not to grin at the desperate look on Anto's face. 'If he likes, I can even give him a pigeon of his own.' He paused then went on quietly, 'I am sorry, Anto. I know what it's like to have someone think you did something when you didn't and it's a horrible feeling. And I know I was hard on you at first because you broke into Ellen's, but you're not a bad lad.'

'He's a great lad!' his mother said.

'He is,' Joe nodded. 'And a great help and I need him, so if he'd like to come back minus his ears, I'll have him.'

The three stood looking at each other.

'Mam?' Anto said hesitantly.

His mother looked at him. Then looked at Joe. 'How much?'

'Sorry?'

'How much will you pay him?'

'Oh. A tenner an hour?'

'Wo—'

'Fifteen.' His mother elbowed her son to shut up.

'Twelve.'

'OK.'

Joe indicated his car up the road. 'D'you want to start now, Anto?'

Anto's smile almost made his day.

51

W HEN SHE GOT back, she had planned to go straight to her room. She knew people on the tram had been looking at her strangely. It was probably because she had been shaking violently all the way home. They probably thought she was on drugs or something.

It was the relief that made her tremble. The final letting go. The obsessive fixation that she'd had for the past few months was draining from her body and it was strange, but it was as if she could feel it loosening its hold on her heart and mind. She wondered how she would feel when it was gone. Would she feel again? Would she lose the anger inside that made her feel like snapping at everything, the way she'd snapped at Lori for taking her husband back? The way she'd snapped at Mark for caring enough to ask what was wrong?

Tears sprang into her eyes. She would focus on the parachute jump; focus on raising money for Life. Her life suddenly seemed simpler. Yes, the hole where Megan's loss was felt was still there, would be there for ever, but it was natural to feel like that. What she had been doing the past few months was not abnormal exactly, but it was unhealthy. Her shivering was helping her to detox, she thought wryly. And no matter how bad she'd feel for what she'd done, at least she'd be feeling something other than hate.

As she walked through the door, her father was talking urgently into the phone. He turned to face her and took a step back.

'What has happened to you?' he exclaimed.

Lizzie waved him away. 'I'll be fine.' Her voice broke a little. 'Can you excuse me a moment?' he said to the person at the other end of the phone. Placing it down on the hall table he stared at his daughter. 'Lizzie?'

'Oh, Dad,' she suddenly needed him to hug her, to pat her on the back and smooth her hair with his fingers the way he used to do when she was a kid.

'I have to go,' he said into the phone as he slammed it back on to the cradle. Then he opened his arms and held his daughter while she cried.

After a bit, after she'd wiped her face, he continued to pat her on the back, eventually asking her what was wrong.

'It's just a bad day,' she sniffed. There was no point, it was over now, and he'd go ballistic with her and worry about her and he had enough to worry about. 'I'll be OK in a bit.'

He looked at her in concern. 'A bad day?' he asked sceptically. 'You look awful.'

Something suddenly dawned on him and he flushed a deep shade of red.

'What's wrong, Dad?'

He coughed a bit and didn't meet her eye. 'Eh, just wondering if there's something you'd like to tell me,' he stammered out.

'What?' She sounded alarmed. Did he know?

He nodded encouragingly. 'You can tell me, I know it's more a women's chat sort of thing but your mother isn't here so . . .' He flushed a deeper shade and his voice trailed off.

Lizzie was lost.

'Are you,' he nodded in the direction of her stomach, 'pregnant?' He could barely get the word out.

Lizzie found herself giggling. At him. At the very idea. 'No. No, no, no,' she shook her head, laughing. 'God, Dad!'

He looked relieved, though whether it was because she was laughing or because she wasn't pregnant, Lizzie didn't know. She hugged him impulsively.

He hugged her back.

'It's probably just hormones, though,' she said, smiling impishly.

'Will you go away outta that and don't be embarrassing me even more.' He flapped a hand at her.

Then he chucked her under the chin as he let her out of the circle of his arms. 'You OK now?'

'I'll be fine,' she said.

And she knew she would.

Eventually.

Joe handed Anto the keys to the loft and told him that he was going to make him responsible for the pigeons for that day and tomorrow.

'There is somewhere I have to go,' he said.

Anto looked thrilled. 'At twelve euro an hour, how much will I earn?' he asked.

Joe hadn't thought of that. It would be expensive. 'Eh – well, let's see, two hours today and maybe four on Monday. That's seventy-two. How does that sound?'

'Sweet!' Anto tossed the keys into the air and laughed.

His mother was right, Joe thought. He was a great kid.

'I think,' Mr Walsh said later at dinner as Billy dished up, 'that your mother is on the verge of apologising.'

Billy dropped a potato on the floor and, picking it up, placed it on Lizzie's plate.

'Oy! I don't want that.'

'Did you hear me?' Mr Walsh said crossly. 'Your mother is going to apologise.'

Billy looked at Lizzie. Aileen kept her head down.

'Eh, I wouldn't get your hopes up, Dad,' Billy tried to say tactfully. He took the spud from Lizzie's plate and reluctantly gave it to himself. 'You know Mammy.'

Mr Walsh nodded. 'I do. But I was on the phone today,' he said, 'and apparently she has asked to go before the court again. I was talking to her solicitor when Lizzie arrived home all upset.'

'You were upset?' Aileen asked. 'Why?'

'Eh, I'm trying to speak,' Mr Walsh said. He picked up a forkful of very overdone carrot and glanced at it suspiciously. 'Billy, how often does Aileen let you cook?'

'I thought you were trying to speak,' Billy prompted, evading the question.

'Oh yes, well, your mother is very upset. Probably because I walked out on her at the last visit and I think she's going to give in.'

Nobody said anything.

Lizzie shuddered. Her mother would not be happy having to give in. But maybe, behind it all, she knew it was the right thing to do. It was good to let go, she knew that.

'So,' Mr Walsh looked around at them all, 'I would appreciate it if, or rather when, she comes out, you would all ignore the fact that she has given way.'

'That might be a bit difficult, Dad,' Billy spluttered out.

'Take this seriously,' Mr Walsh snapped. He sighed then went on in a more composed voice, 'She'll be upset. And she'll feel she's let down—' he swallowed, 'well, herself and, and—' He couldn't say it.

'Megan,' Lizzie prompted softly.

Her dad nodded and caught her hand. 'Yes, Megan,' he said. 'But we know she hasn't, so let's make sure she knows that, ey?'

Billy and Aileen nodded.

Mr Walsh put his head down and scraped his carrots over to the side of his plate.

Joe arrived outside his parents' house after two solid hours of speeding. It was a wonder he hadn't been stopped. But he knew if he took his time he might turn back, and he desperately didn't want to.

He pulled up on the gravel outside his parents' front door with a screech. Then switched off the engine. The sudden silence unnerved him for the first time since his impulsive decision.

It had been a weird sort of day. He'd lost Lizzie – but he'd never had her in the first place, he knew that now. It hurt and he wanted to cry for the way she'd dashed his dreams into ashes. He wanted to yell at her for what she'd done, and yet, in a funny sort of way, he could understand it. And it would take more than losing Lizzie to ruin his life, he realised. You didn't spent twelve years in prison without appreciating every day of freedom. Lizzie was gone but his parents weren't. And he wasn't sure if he wanted to lose them. Despite everything, he had to try. Thrash it out with them. Try to see things from their perspective. He had all the stuff he needed to say in his head. Swallowing hard, he stood out of the car and slammed the door.

He hadn't even made it to the front door before it was opened. His mother and father stood there, a hesitant look of hope on both their faces.

All Joe's words disappeared. Everything he meant to say just seemed to dissolve. His eyes watered. He took a step towards them and then stopped.

They made to move, but didn't.

An eternity seemed to pass before Joe blurted out, 'Maybe I was wrong about stuff.'

And suddenly his dad was dragging him into the house. His mother had her hands up to her mouth.

He knew then that there'd be no need for any more words.

He had come home.

52

LIZZIE WALKED INTO Mark's office without knocking. He looked up from his desk and quirked his eyebrows.

'I am sorry for being late the other morning,' she mumbled.

Mark made a face and held his hand to his ear. 'Pardon? I didn't quite get that? Could you repeat it?'

'I said,' Lizzie smirked, 'that I am sorry for being late the other morning. I can assure you, as your humble employee, that it won't happen again.'

In response, Mark jumped from his seat and started to rotate his fists in a circular motion whilst chanting, 'Oh ye-ah, oh ye-ah!'

'I take it my apology has been accepted.'

He stopped and grinned. 'Oh ye-ah!'

Lizzie grinned back and, just as she was leaving, he called out, 'I take it that whatever was bothering you is over?'

Lizzie froze for a second before nodding, 'I guess. In a way. Anyway, I'm totally focused on the parachute jump now.'

'Good to have you back, only—'

'What?'

'Don't apologise in future, it freaks me out a little. It's not like you.'

'No problem, asshole.'

'That's my girl!'

Lizzie had landed him in it, and not just with Anto, Joe thought as he pulled up outside a ramshackle house in the middle of north county Dublin.

Fields lay in every direction, which was just as well as any sane person wouldn't want to live within five miles of the tumbledown heap. Joe could never understand why Cid came all the way to Ranelagh to race his birds when there was a club right beside him. Knowing Cid, however, he'd probably fallen out with everyone in that club and had been forced to go further afield. He hadn't even come back to the Ranelagh since the fight with Joe, which had made Joe even more suspicious of him and led the rest of the lads to believe he didn't do it and that he was mortally offended.

Joe resigned himself to being made to feel terrible as drove his car up the pot-holed driveway. Cid's front door was bright yellow and the paint peeling. Joe located a bell under some overgrown ivy and pressed it.

Cid opened the door within seconds. He stood back to look at Joe and smiled a little expectantly.

'Yes?' Then, before Joe could say anything, he asked, 'Where's the lunch box?'

'Lunch box?'

'Well, I presume you bought a big hunk of humble pie with you.'

'I ate it before I came,' Joe said back.

'Good. Tasty, was it?'

'Nope.'

Cid grinned and laughed softly.

Joe plunged, like a swimmer into cold water. 'I'm sorry I accused you over Prince, I should have known better.'

'Yeah,' Cid was serious now, 'you should have. I'd never do that. I heard from Noel that it was Lizzie. It's always the pretty ones you have to watch. You should report her.'

Joe shrugged.

'So,' Cid opened the door wider, 'you gonna stand here all day or you gonna come in and see my birds?' He paused and said, 'I've, eh, thought about gifting you an egg if you want, for your loft. It's from one of my best racers.'

Joe swallowed. 'Really?'

'Yeah.' Cid looked at him. 'Of course, if it does well, I'll want credit for it being my egg, you know.'

Joe nodded, touched. 'Thanks.'

'Well come on, so, don't be shy.' Cid pushed a bag full of rubbish out of the way and invited Joe inside.

Lizzie only remembered her mother's request to trace the mobile phone number later that day. And it only sprang to mind because she'd been enrolling for the Life parachute jump in an effort to atone for her sins. It would be the second most terrifying thing she'd ever done. As she keyed her own phone number into the online application form, she suddenly recalled that her mother was ringing her that evening to find out if she had managed to trace another mobile number. Shit!

Hastily, she flipped open her mobile and scrolled through the names until she found the one she had titled 'Find out'. Dialling it, she wondered what on earth she'd say to the person at the other end. It would have been handy if her mother had given her some clue as to why she needed the number traced.

'Hello,' a bright northern voice said.

'Eh, hi,' Lizzie stammered. 'Is that Laura?'

'No, wrong number, I'm afraid.'

'Oh.' Lizzie tried to sound as if she was puzzled. She'd grown good at lying over the last while, she realised uncomfortably. 'I've been told to ring this by my boss. I wonder if I've got your name wrong. I can't remember the name she told me. Sorry, what's your name?'

There was a tinkling laugh. 'Denise.'

'Denise Duggan,' Lizzie pronounced, as if she'd just unearthed the Golden Fleece.

'No, sorry. Denise McCabe.'

'OK, sorry about that. I must have the wrong number.'

'No bother. Hope you find who you're looking for.'

Lizzie hung up.

Joe left Cid's two hours later, having eaten the most revolting sandwich of his life. Cid had bustled about, examining the contents of his fridge to see what was still edible before putting it between two inedible slices of bread.

'All that crap about you being a murderer,' Cid pronounced as Joe bit into the bread, 'I don't believe it for a second.'

'Thanks,' Joe said.

'Anyone who understands birds like you do wouldn't murder one.'

And then he laughed.

It wasn't the only thing that could be described as bad taste, Joe thought in semi-amusement.

'Did you trace that number for me?' was the first question her mother asked that night.

Lizzie was a little put out. 'I'm fine, Mammy, thanks. How are you?'

'Did you trace the number, Lizzie?'

'Well, I know whose phone it is.'

'Is it Dessie O'Sullivan's?'

The name startled her. 'Dessie?' she whispered, shocked. Then she asked, 'Mammy, what is this? What are you doing?'

Her mother took a deep breath. 'Is it Dessie's number?'

'No. It was a Denise McCabe.'

There was a pause from her mother's end of the line. 'Would that be Denise Owens, by any chance? Is she northern?'

'Yes. I think so.'

'His girlfriend,' Mrs Walsh said. 'We have to talk to her. You have to ring her again. Or I'll get the police to talk to her. Yes, that's it. I'm in the right place anyway, loads of police here.'

'Mammy, will you tell me what is going on?'

'Lizzie, I have something I want you to read. I'm going to post it to you. Read it as soon as you get it. Promise me.'

Her mother was going mad. She had to be. 'Mammy, are you—'

'Promise me.'

'OK, I promise.'

'And don't tell your father, not yet. Or Billy.'

This was ridiculous. What was wrong with her mother?

'Dad said you were going to apologise, is that true?' she asked sharply. She had to get her mother out of there.

There was a pause. Then Mrs Walsh said softly, 'Yes, it's true.'

Thank God. She heaved a silent sigh of relief. 'It's the right thing, Mammy.'

'I know that now, Lizzie. You were right what you said.'

Lizzie didn't reply.

Her mother went on gently, 'I'll bet you're a great counsellor.'

'I tend to be a lot better when it's someone I care about.'

Her mother swallowed hard. 'I never got on with her, you know,' she said shakily. 'We fought all the time. The day she disappeared, we weren't talking. But—but I loved her, Lizzie.' Her voice cracked.

'We all did, Mammy.'

'Hurry up, would ya? It's not *Oprah* yer on.' Someone at her mother's end of the phoneline said.

'I have to go, Lizzie. Look out for that package, OK?'

'I will.'

'And when you've read it, bring it to the police.'

The line went dead.

53

T HE PACKAGE ARRIVED two days later. It was delivered to Lizzie at work and, as she tore it open, assuming it was work related, she unthinkingly pulled out the contents.

MEGAN'S DIARY: SUMMER was emblazoned across the front.

Lizzie dropped it with a clatter on to the desk. Was this a sick joke? Who could possibly know? An envelope fluttered to the ground. Opening it, her hands shaking, Lizzie recognised her mother's writing.

> *Lizzie, thought I'd send this to you in work so Billy won't be curious. Please read it as soon as you can and if you think it should be passed to the police, do so. I will be out within the month – all red tape, total rubbish – and I don't want to waste time. I found it under the floor-boards in Megan's room when I was cleaning it this year. I read it just to feel close to her, not realising what it was.*
>
> *Love you. xx*

It took a second before Lizzie could open the diary of her older sister, who would for ever be nineteen years of age. It was bright and colourful, just like her. She'd written along the margins, drawn love hearts all through the text. *Megan loves Dessie. Aileen fancies Billy.*

It made her smile to see it.

Hoping Mark wouldn't notice, Lizzie took the phone off the hook and began to read.

Joe knocked on his boss's door and was beckoned into the office.

'About that job you offered me,' he said. 'Is it OK if I refuse it?'

'Refuse it?' his boss looked at him incredulously. 'Can I ask why?'

Joe shrugged. 'I teach people to swim, that's what I do. I was behind a desk once and I hated it.' He offered an apologetic smile. 'Life's too short to do what you hate. I've wasted too much of it already.'

Graham looked ever so slightly pissed off. 'So you're not interested?'

''Fraid not. You've made me like it too much here.'

'You might regret it.'

'Maybe.'

But he knew he wouldn't.

OK, all that last bit can be scrapped because I just got a text. It's him. Well, I guess it is.

It said: R U OK? D.

I texted back: Am I OK? Wot a stupid question. No.

He texted: Do U feel rele bad?

I texted yes.

He texted: Can we talk. D.

So I have arranged to meet him at the harbour at five. Enough time to get my red puffy eyes down. The others won't be back until at least ten.

I'll wear my really short skirt and do my hair. I've been sick twice since coming home, I knew I shouldn't have eaten that fish Dad caught yesterday. Mam cooked it and it was practically raw. She said, in front of Aileen, that I was so ungrateful. There are lots of people who would like fresh fish. I told her I'd prefer a fresh man, only I don't think she knew what I meant. Billy and Aileen did, though. Anyway, the fish has made me sick.

I also have the most massive headache. Probably from crying.

I am not going to tell anyone I'm meeting him just in case he makes a fool of me again. No one will know until I have him back again. And I will.

I will unleash the full power of the Megan Walsh charm.

Lizzie put the diary down, dazed, wondering what it all meant. It proved one thing though: Joe had been telling the truth about the texts. And the number, where had her mother got the number she'd asked Lizzie to dial? She scanned the diary and then she saw it, scrawled in the margin – *number for love – Dessie 045789326*. It was surrounded by a huge love heart.

Only it hadn't been Dessie who texted her at all, had it?

Lizzie felt suddenly sick with the realisation that since Joe had told the truth about the texts, he might have told the truth about everything else, too. Oh God, what if Joe hadn't done it? What if he was actually innocent? What if everything he'd said was true and he had only tried to help Megan? What if – and here her mind froze – what if he'd actually spent twelve years in jail for a death he hadn't been responsible for? *The poor guy.* Lizzie's stomach heaved. However bad she felt at what she'd done to him, she'd coped by telling herself that he was a murderer. And now . . . little flashes of Joe with his birds popped into her head. His gentleness, his soothing way of talking to them, his affectionate way of dealing with them. His thoughtfulness when he'd given her his granddad's book to read. She still had that book, she suddenly remembered.

If she hadn't been so filled with hate, maybe she might have seen what other people saw in him. What his neighbour saw, what his boss saw, what the lads in the pigeon club saw. But she'd been blinded.

And now, too late, her eyes had opened and what she saw was horrifying in its implications.

She picked up the phone and dialled the police.

54

T HE TWO FAMILIES sat on opposite sides of the room. Joe, handsome in a grey suit and white shirt, kept his eyes pinned on the man who was about to speak. His face betrayed no emotion. On either side of him sat his parents. His dad looked slightly more apprehensive, his shoulders rigid, his lips set in a straight line. He wore an expensive suit and stared ahead of him, too, not acknowledging the family across from him. Joe's mother, slightly bewildered-looking, sat on his right. Her eyes darted here and there and finally came to rest on a tall, gangly girl, who sat alongside the family opposite. Leah Jones thought she recognised the girl, but then again, she knew that her memory wasn't as accurate as it used to be, so she turned away and studied her beautiful son. She'd always known that this day would come and tears sprang into her eyes as she slipped her hand into his. He wrapped it in his two hands and she marvelled at the strength of him. She would remember this moment, no matter what.

Mr and Mrs Walsh, too, looked anxious, but she in particular looked relieved. As if she'd finally found what she'd been looking for. Her face was softer, her eyes not as flat as they had been. Beside her sat Billy, his hand held firmly by Aileen, who was by far the most enormous person in the room. She wore a bright green long flowing blouse and black trousers. Her face was flushed and she looked uncomfortable. She hoped that the judge or whatever he was would get a move on. Lizzie sat, head bowed, unable to look up lest she catch Joe's eye or that of his parents.

The case had come up in court a lot quicker than anyone had anticipated. Lizzie had done well so far to avoid Joe and his parents – she wished she had never met him that time, never seen him on the street. Bad as she had felt when she thought he was guilty, she now felt worse. There had been no pretence about him, she realised. He was a good guy. A really nice fella. She couldn't, just couldn't, look at him.

She kept her head down as the man started to speak. As the photographers snapped and the journalists took notes. This would be front-page news tomorrow. As the man talked, she felt tears drip from her eyes, slide down her nose and on to her hands.

Joe's solicitor made a statement outside the court as the cameras snapped. Then the Walsh family's solicitor did the same. Then the two families unexpectedly came face to face. Lizzie hid behind Aileen. She couldn't bear for them to recognise her. The crowd quietened down.

Mr Walsh found himself in front of Joe. He opened his mouth to speak but realised that there was nothing he could say. Swallowing hard, he slowly extended his hand towards the boy he had been so fond of.

Joe gazed at it for a second before clasping it tightly in his. There was a moment of emotional silence when everything stopped. When even the cameras ceased clicking. Finally Joe said softly, 'I'm sorry you lost your daughter, Kev.'

'Thank you,' Mr Walsh gulped out, his voice barely audible as Polly wrapped her arms around him.

It was a 'sorry', but not the sorry Lizzie had imagined Joe would ever utter. This sorry meant more. Meant a lot to her dad, who had squeezed his eyes shut and was massaging them with his thumbs.

Lizzie watched in a daze as the two families exchanged handshakes. She stepped back, afraid Joe's parents would recognise her. Even though she'd had a haircut and coloured it red, she thought it would be unlikely they'd forget the girl who had come calling only a few months ago.

And yet she needed to see Joe. Had to.

She waited until he was slightly apart from his parents before crossing towards him. He saw her coming and waited. It was as if nothing else existed for him in that moment except seeing Lizzie again. It had to happen, but he was dreading it.

She looked up and her face flushed with shame.

'Hi, Lizzie,' he said quietly.

'There's nothing I can say to you that would excuse what I did.' Oh God, she was going to burst into tears.

'No,' he said softly, 'there probably isn't.'

Lizzie flinched and her voice wobbled. 'I am truly sorry, Joe. I'm sorry for believing you could do such a thing. I should have known.' She sniffed and said on a half sob, 'When I saw you with your birds, I should have known you weren't capable of it. I'm so sorry.'

There was a silence. When she looked up, she saw that Joe was studying her with solemn eyes.

'I'm not gonna lie, Lizzie, and say it was easy.' He spoke quietly. 'Twelve years for something I didn't do was . . . I dunno.' His eyes grew shiny and he blinked hard and didn't finish. Instead he added, 'But being in there and having nothing and coming out and having what I have, well, it has made me love my life now. I love life more than I ever would have otherwise.'

'Still—'

'Apology accepted, OK?' he interrupted, reaching out and touching her lightly on the sleeve. 'Don't beat yourself up over it. Let it go, ey?'

'Thank you.'

'No worries.' There was a pause, before he uttered, 'See you around.'

'Yeah,' she nodded. Then, as he turned to go, she said tentatively, 'Maybe I might see you walking up Grafton Street some evening after work?'

He hesitated for what seemed like the longest time. Then nodded. 'Yeah, maybe.' He gave an uncertain smile and quirked an eyebrow. 'You could give me my book back.'

'I will.' She felt tears brimming and one slipped out and down her cheek.

'Don't cry, ey? Life is good.'

With that he turned away and Lizzie knew that whatever it took, she'd make it up to him.

He'd dreaded meeting Lizzie more than anything else and it had hurt a lot when he'd seen her, but it was over now. He couldn't be angry at her, she'd set him free in a way. Thanks to her, he'd told the lads in the club about his past and, with one or two exceptions, they'd all declared that they didn't believe a word of it. It was good to know and now their faith in him had been proved right. Thanks to Lizzie, he'd decided to reclaim his life and not be blamed any more for something he was innocent of. Thanks to Lizzie, Cid had unexpectedly gifted him an egg that was looking incredibly promising. Thanks to—

'What on earth is that?' His dad broke into his thoughts as he pointed to a huge banner that was flapping in the breeze outside Joe's house.

'Christ,' Joe laughed loudly as he stared out the car window, 'where did that come from?'

CONGRATULATIONS ON YOUR INNOCENCE it said in three-foot-high writing.

Ellen bustled to meet him, her face red. Joe rolled down the window of the car.

'I couldn't stop them,' she said, casting her eyes heavenwards. 'I knew you'd hate it.'

In the doorway his friends from the club cheered and held aloft a bottle of champagne. Anto and his mother stood shyly to the side. His mates from work were there, too. Ellen made a hopeless gesture.

'Sorry,' she muttered.

A huge cheer went up as Joe emerged from the car.

His dad poked him in the back. 'You told us you hadn't got many friends,' he said, amused.

Joe didn't have time to answer because Cid had already legged it down the driveway. 'Hurry up, you're on telly, come on!'

And the party began.

55

HER MOTHER AND father were spending the night with Aileen's dad and Billy and Aileen had gone to bed, so Lizzie stretched out on the sofa and savoured the first bit of quiet she'd had all day.

It had been an unexpectedly good day, too, despite the sadness of finally finding out how her sister had died. After all these years and in light of Joe's original testimony, the pieces had slotted together and suddenly made sense. She felt sick when she thought of Joe spending twelve years in prison when he hadn't been to blame, felt sick when she thought of him and his family being gossiped about by their neighbours when all along he'd only tried to help. And then she had come into his life and done what she'd done and now he'd told her it was OK. His forgiveness was the greatest gift she'd ever received, which sounded a bit corny but which was absolutely true. She would make it up to him, she knew she would. She'd repay him for every pigeon he'd lost because of her. She would rebuild what she'd torn apart as best she could. She'd start by focusing on the parachute jump, which was taking place in two days' time. She'd try her best to help all the people who called her on a Thursday night. She'd keep her fingers crossed that Lori would ring again. She'd try to finish all those other stories for people she might never meet. No, she corrected herself, not finish. Begin. Help them to begin again, just like she was going to.

Just then the doorbell rang.

Standing up, Lizzie wondered if it was a neighbour coming by to give them their best. People had been calling all day, neighbours they didn't even know, to congratulate them and say how great it was for them to have closure. Lizzie thought Royal Lawns might be a good place to live, after all.

She opened the door and was shocked to see Tom standing there. He looked pretty good, dressed in a purple shirt and green jeans. Only Tom could wear something so horrendous and still have street cred.

'Tom, hi,' she said, her heart beginning to thump sickeningly. What was he doing here?

'Hi.' He smiled his devastating crooked-toothed smile and her heart went into free fall. 'You're probably wondering what I'm doing here.'

She could only nod.

'I'm here because I'm a bit annoyed with you, actually.' He was all casual nonchalance but she knew he was as nervous as she was.

'You are?' She tried to match his tone and failed.

'I always wanted to be the one on telly and you got there before me.'

She drank him in, not even able to smile at his feeble introductory joke. His eyes, his boxer's nose, his beautiful gorgeous sexy smile. It was months since she'd seen him that awful night in the restaurant, yet he still had the ability to make her want him.

'You looked sensational.'

She smiled a little. Not as sensational as him.

'The hair is great.'

She absently touched her violently red tresses. 'Thanks.'

His eyes became serious. 'I'm glad you finally got the truth.'

'Thanks.' Her voice wobbled.

He dug into his jeans and pulled out two tickets. 'So, in celebration, I got these for you. Freebies for a show next week. D'you want them? You can bring anyone you like.'

Oh, God.

'I'm free.' He smiled a little crookedly.

She couldn't pretend to be the person he thought she was. She was starting over and though it was tempting to forget what had gone on before, she wouldn't be able to live with herself. Or him. 'I don't know, Tom.'

'In case you haven't noticed, I'm willing to humiliate myself here.'

'There are things you don't know about me, Tom. You'd hate me if I told you.'

He paused and nodded before saying softly, 'I saw him on the telly, too, Liz, that guy in the restaurant. It doesn't matter.'

'It does.' Her heart flipped and she bowed her head. 'He was the reason I lied to you that night. I—I, well, I did awful things to him.'

Tom reached out and clasped her arm, squeezing it slightly. 'Well, good,' he declared. 'He was way better-looking than me. I don't mind telling you, he had me worried.'

She spluttered out a laugh but she still had to tell him. Let him know how horrible she'd been. If he still wanted her afterwards, well, that would be brilliant. If not . . . well, it was her own fault.

'D'you want to come in?' she asked. 'So I can explain?'

'You don't have to.'

'I do.' She held the door open wider and he stepped into the hall and looked around. 'Billy and Aileen are in bed. They don't know anything. Come in here.' She led the way into the front room, which was now really tidy since Aileen had moved back in. Tom stood in the centre of the room before sitting down. Lizzie suddenly understood how Joe must have felt when he was telling her about being in prison. How had he done it?

'I saw him on Grafton Street one night when I was coming out of Life,' she began. 'I recognised him and something inside me flipped, Tom. Just to see him living his life when Megan was dead, I couldn't take it.'

'Here,' Tom stood up and gently led her to the sofa, 'don't cry, for fuck's sake. It's only me.'

'Yeah, and I've treated you so badly. But Tom, I only got friendly with Joe to hurt him. Nothing ever happened. I wanted to get at him the way he'd got at us. So I set out to sabotage his pigeons. That's what I did at the weekends. I stole his keys and messed about with his lofts.'

Tom said nothing.

'And when that didn't seem to work, I—I got a cat and I killed his birds.'

Tom flinched but he kept hold of her hand.

'I even went and stole his best bird.' Tears dripped off her chin and plopped on to Tom's hand as she relived how horrible she'd been.

'Yeah, well,' Tom placed his two hands around her face and with his thumbs he wiped her tears away, 'he stole mine.'

She sniffed.

'He did,' Tom said more seriously.

'I never fancied him.'

He grinned softly at her before asking solemnly, 'Why didn't you tell me?'

'You would have tried to stop me.'

'Maybe.'

'Plus I didn't want you to see how horrible I could be.' She said it quietly, her voice fading away at the end.

'Everyone can be horrible. I used to be horrible before I met you.'

'Did you?' He made it sound almost enticing.

'Well, I admit I wasn't a pigeon killer, but I lost a lot of mates.'

'You did?'

'Yep.' Now he looked ashamed. 'I was jealous and bitter. I hated that other people could get cast in a play and I couldn't. No one would work with me, I was such a temperamental bastard. The night I met you I'd been passed over for an ideal part and I was in shit form. Then you hauled me up over skipping that queue and in between feeling really annoyed I somehow copped on that you were the best thing ever to happen in my life. Bingo. The parts start flooding in. Why? Because I'm bloody happy.' He took her two hands in his. 'You bring out the best in me.'

'Do I?'

'Yeah. Do you not know that?'

She shook her head.

'I was nearly fired from *Angels Down* after we split. Poor Imogen had the job of keeping me on the straight and narrow. The night you came to see me in it, Imogen was hoping you'd come for a drink and get back with me. Only you didn't. I think she was more devastated than I was.'

'I saw you holding Imogen's hand onstage and looking really happy, that's why I didn't go.'

'I looked happy 'cause I thought I'd see you. I thought maybe we could patch things up.'

'Oh.'

'You fool,' he said tenderly as he brought his forehead to meet hers.

'I get scared,' she said, 'when I'm really happy. I sometimes wonder if Joe's pigeons weren't the only thing I sabotaged.'

He pushed her hair back from her face. She could taste his breath. Feel his lips move.

'Life is like a bungee jump,' he said.

'What?'

'You can either be scared and close your eyes, or just let go and enjoy the ride.'

'Are you offering me a ride?'

He laughed loudly, then his brown eyes suddenly grew serious. 'I have missed you so much.'

'AAAAGGGGHHHHHHHHHHH!'

The yell came from upstairs and Tom and Lizzie jumped away from each other as if scalded.

'The babies are coming!' Billy shouted. 'Lizzie, are you awake?'

'Down here!' She raced into the hall, Tom in her wake.

Billy appeared at the top of the stairs. 'Get her case, would you? Ring Mam and Dad. I'm driving her in.' He was about to go back and get Aileen when he spied Tom. 'Hi, Tom. You back on the scene?'

'AAAAGGGGHHHHHHHHH!'

'Jesus!' He ran back into the bedroom as Lizzie searched

368

frantically for Aileen's case. She'd packed it over a month ago and Lizzie finally located it under the hall table. Lizzie and Tom watched as Billy led Aileen carefully down the stairs. She was dressed in a stripy nightdress and looked to Tom like a marquee.

'Are you sure the babies are on their way?' Billy asked her as he got her down the final step.

'Sure? Am I sure! AAAGGGHHHHHH!' Aileen clenched her stomach and glared at Billy. 'Does that answer your question?' She suddenly spied Tom. 'Oh, Tom, are you talking to Lizzie again? Oh, great. I think it's so important to talk out any troubles you have.'

'My arse, you do,' Billy snorted. 'It took you ages to talk to me. Don't mind her, Tom, she's full of shit.'

'I'm ringing Mam and Dad and your dad now,' Lizzie said as she gave Aileen a brief hug. 'Good luck.'

'Thanks.' Aileen hugged her back. 'Oh, this is so scary.'

'It'll be great,' Billy kissed her cheek, 'and I'm going to be with you all the way.'

'You better mean that,' Aileen said, smiling at him.

Lizzie's niece and nephew were born in record time and, despite being all scrunched up and wrinkly, were the most beautiful people she had ever seen. So pure and innocent and they smelled all cuddly. OK, bits of dried blood clung to their scalps, but everyone ignored that as they passed them around for a look.

'It's like a new start,' Mrs Walsh said, her face glowing as she kissed her little granddaughter.

Lizzie thought how calm her mother suddenly looked now. New life, new hope.

Mr Walsh put his arm about his wife. 'It's been some day, ey?'

She put her arm about him, too. 'It has. A good day.' Then she glanced at Lizzie. 'Are you back with . . .' she indicated Tom with a nod of her head, 'him?'

Lizzie smiled across the ward at Tom, who was hanging back now that her parents had arrived. 'I think I am.'

'Did he get dressed in the dark?'

'No, they're his normal clothes.' She blew him a kiss, he bowed extravagantly and blew her one back.

Her mother snorted but said, 'It's great to see you smile like that.'

One of the babies started to cry suddenly.

'Oh, I think it needs to be fed,' Billy announced as he took his new son and passed him to Aileen. She unbuttoned her pyjama top and latched the baby to her breast. He was soon feeding away.

'Look at that,' Billy said in admiration.

'Right.' Mr Walsh, totally mortified but trying not to show it, clapped his hands together. 'I think we'd better get out of your way.'

'I think so, too,' Abe said. He laid his new granddaughter into the bed beside Aileen. 'Take care, love.'

One by one they said their goodbyes and Billy walked them to the hospital exit.

'So,' Lizzie hugged her brother as she left, 'how does it feel, Daddy? Are you still scared?'

'Terrified,' he admitted. 'And d'you know what?'

'What?'

'When Aileen held them, she told me she knew what I meant now. She said she doesn't know how Mammy and Daddy coped.'

Lizzie looked at her parents as they argued about where her dad had parked his car and shrugged. 'I don't know how any of us coped,' she said. 'I think we all went a little crazy.'

Billy nodded.

'You take care of your little family, OK?' she said.

'I will.'

She turned away and left him talking to Aileen's father, who was congratulating him.

Tom slung an arm about her shoulder before glancing uneasily at her. 'May I?'

She pulled Tom to her. 'Can we go back to your place and finish what we started a few months ago?'

'That's a question you don't have to ask,' Tom replied, his voice husky. He stopped walking and enfolded her in his arms. She inhaled the scent of him and it was like coming home.

'Oh, by the way,' Tom said nonchalantly, 'I'm doing your parachute jump.'

'Me too,' Lizzie said back, just as nonchalantly. 'I mean, I can't expect people to jump when I won't do it myself.'

He grinned delightedly at her. 'Yeah?'

'Yeah. I said to myself,' she attempted to mimic Tom's gorgeous voice, "great, a new experience".'

He laughed loudly. 'You gonna keep your eyes open?'

'What's the point otherwise?' she smiled.

And then she closed her eyes as he kissed her.

Epilogue

CONVICTION OVERTURNED IN DRAMATIC NEW TWIST

Joseph Jones (34), who was convicted of the murder of Megan Walsh fourteen years ago and who subsequently served twelve years in prison, yesterday had his conviction overturned as dramatic new evidence came to light.

Megan Walsh went missing from her home in Rossclare, Co. Wexford, and two days later her body was washed up on Grange Strand. She had bruising to the wrist and had suffered a severe head injury before her death. The last person to see her alive was Joseph Jones. It emerged during the trial that Ms Walsh spent the last night of her life on Mr Jones' boat. Joseph Jones denied that the girl had fallen overboard or that he had pushed her. He maintained throughout his trial that he had attempted to bring Ms Walsh home because she was drunk, an argument had broken out and that the last sighting he had of her was as she walked away from him.

Mr Jones was convicted on two key pieces of evidence: no alcohol was found in the young woman's bloodstream despite Mr Jones' assertion that she was drunk; and no text message was ever traced back to her boyfriend's mobile phone asking Ms Walsh to meet him at the pier. It was stated by the prosecution at the time that Joe Jones was annoyed with Ms Walsh as she had rejected his advances in favour of his friend, Mr Dessie O'Sullivan. Joe Jones' father stated that he had witnessed Ms Walsh slapping his son during a row at his father-in-law's house.

It has since emerged, through a diary kept by the victim, that Megan Walsh suffered a head injury at her place of work earlier that day. An altercation had broken out when she had found her boyfriend and co-worker, Mr O'Sullivan, in the office with his ex girlfriend Denise Owens, now Denise McCabe. According to both witnesses, and the diary, when Ms Walsh attempted to leave, she tripped over a phone cable and hit her head. She was unconscious, according to Mrs McCabe, for 'about ten minutes'. When she recovered consciousness, 'she seemed fine, if a bit confused' and left without wanting to see a doctor. Mrs McCabe had later acquired Ms Walsh's mobile number from her boyfriend's phone and text messaged her to see if she was all right. Mrs McCabe never told her then boyfriend that she had sent a text to Ms Walsh as she feared he'd 'go mad'. Mrs McCabe did not meet Ms Walsh on the night in question as she had seen her chatting to Mr Jones at the pier and assumed that she was fine. She was 'horrified' to find out that her texts had been confused by Megan Walsh as coming from her former boyfriend. 'At the time, I thought Joe was just lying to stitch Dessie up. He had liked Megan too and was angry at Dessie for stealing her.'

It was also established that Ms Walsh's apparently drunken behaviour on Mr Jones' boat could be directly attributed to the head injury she sustained in the office. The court judged it most likely that Megan Walsh simply fell into the water of Rossclare harbour while slipping into unconsciousness as the injury to her head was severe. Mr O'Sullivan and Mrs McCabe are being charged with withholding evidence that might have helped Mr Jones at his former trial. They maintain that at the time they didn't believe Ms Walsh's fall was relevant to the murder and that, if they had mentioned it, it might have cast unnecessary suspicion on Mr O'Sullivan, whom Mr Jones seemed to want to implicate.

Mr O'Sullivan and his former girlfriend spent the night of the murder in a nightclub and had been ruled out of the inquiry at an early stage.

Outside the court, the two families shook hands and Joseph Jones said that while he regrets the time he spent in prison, he is now looking forward to getting on with his life.

'I've been given a chance to start again,' he said, 'and I'm going to grab it with both hands.'

Author's note

While I realise that fourteen years ago mobile phones and texting were not in common use, I have included them as part of the plot. This, I think, ensures that the book will not date as quickly.